W.I.T.C.H.

Will Irma Taranee Cornelia Hay Lin

Part IV.
Trial of the Oracle
Volume 2

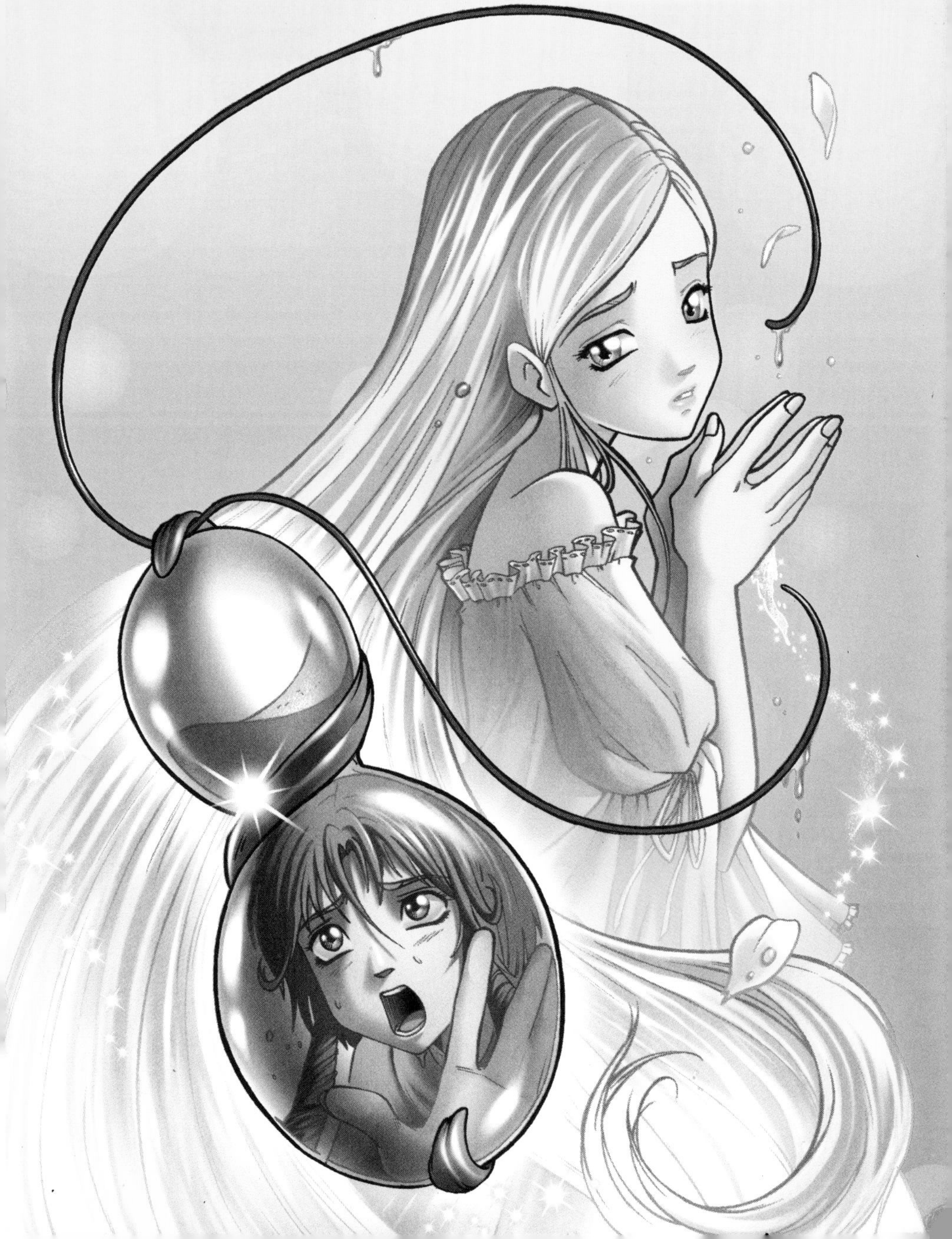

W.i.t.c.h.

Will   Irma   Taranee   Cornelia   Hay Lin

Part IV.
Trial of the Oracle
Volume 2

CONTENTS

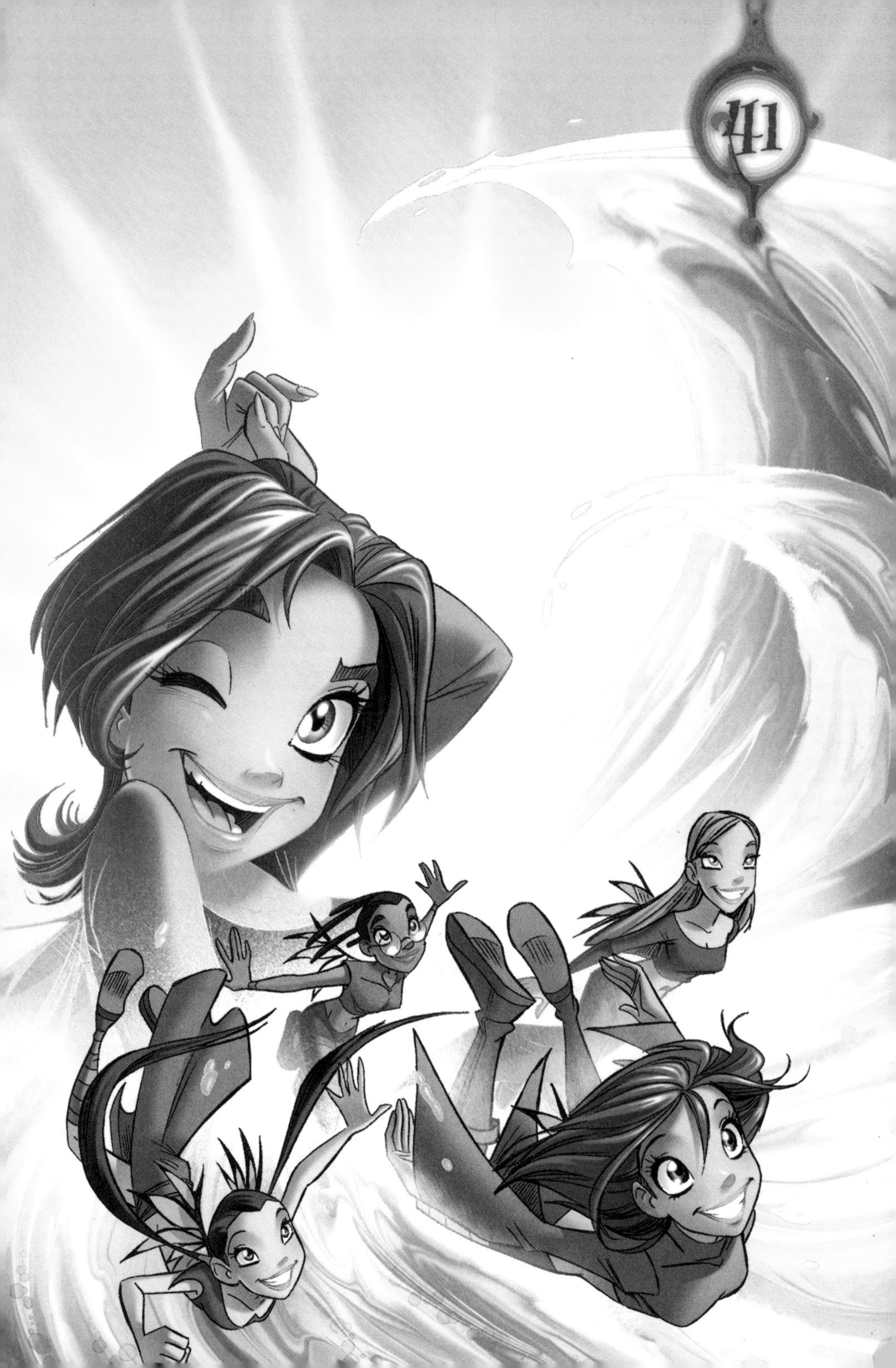
41

The Whole Truth

"I'm the Custodian of the Heart, and I was found out!"

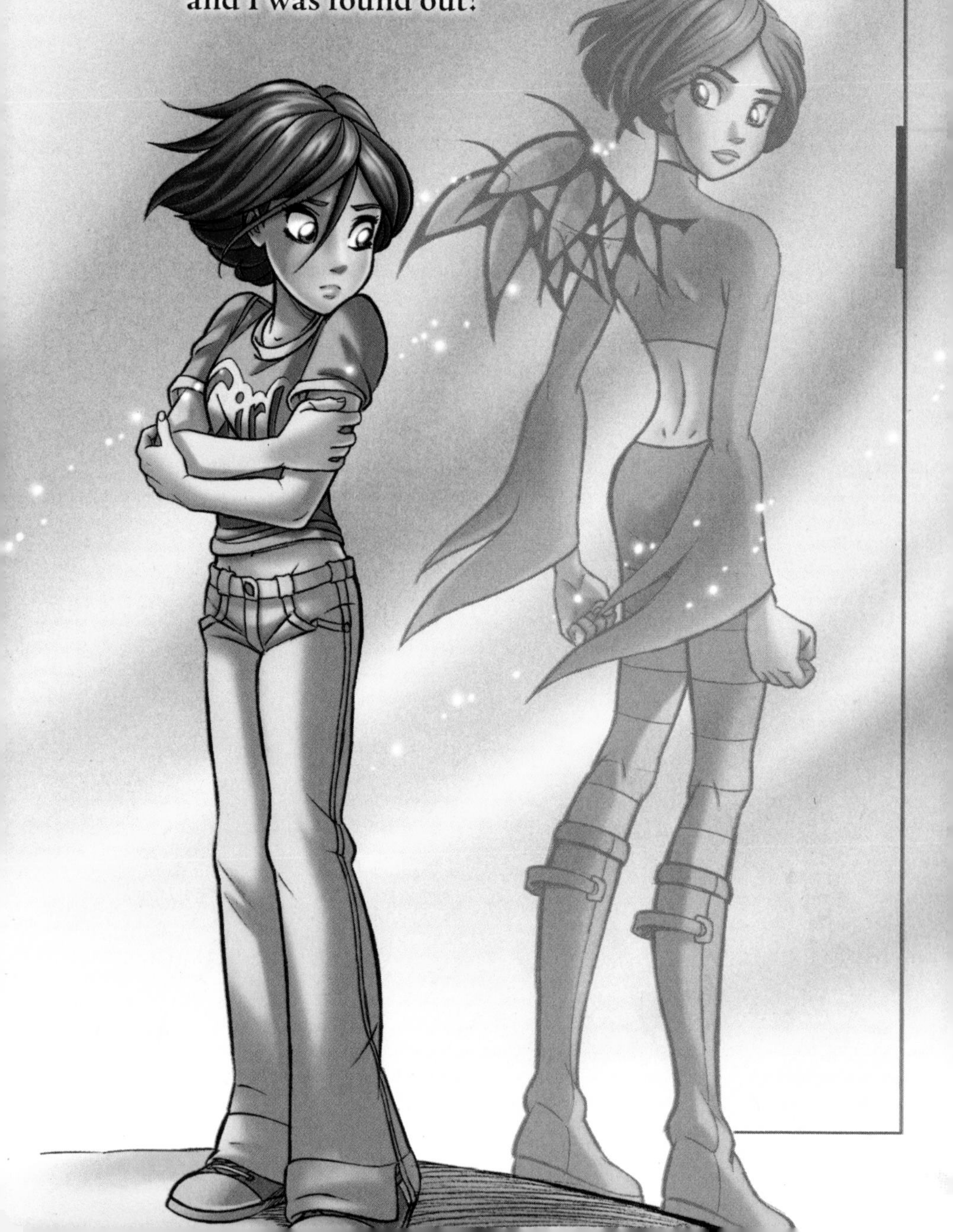

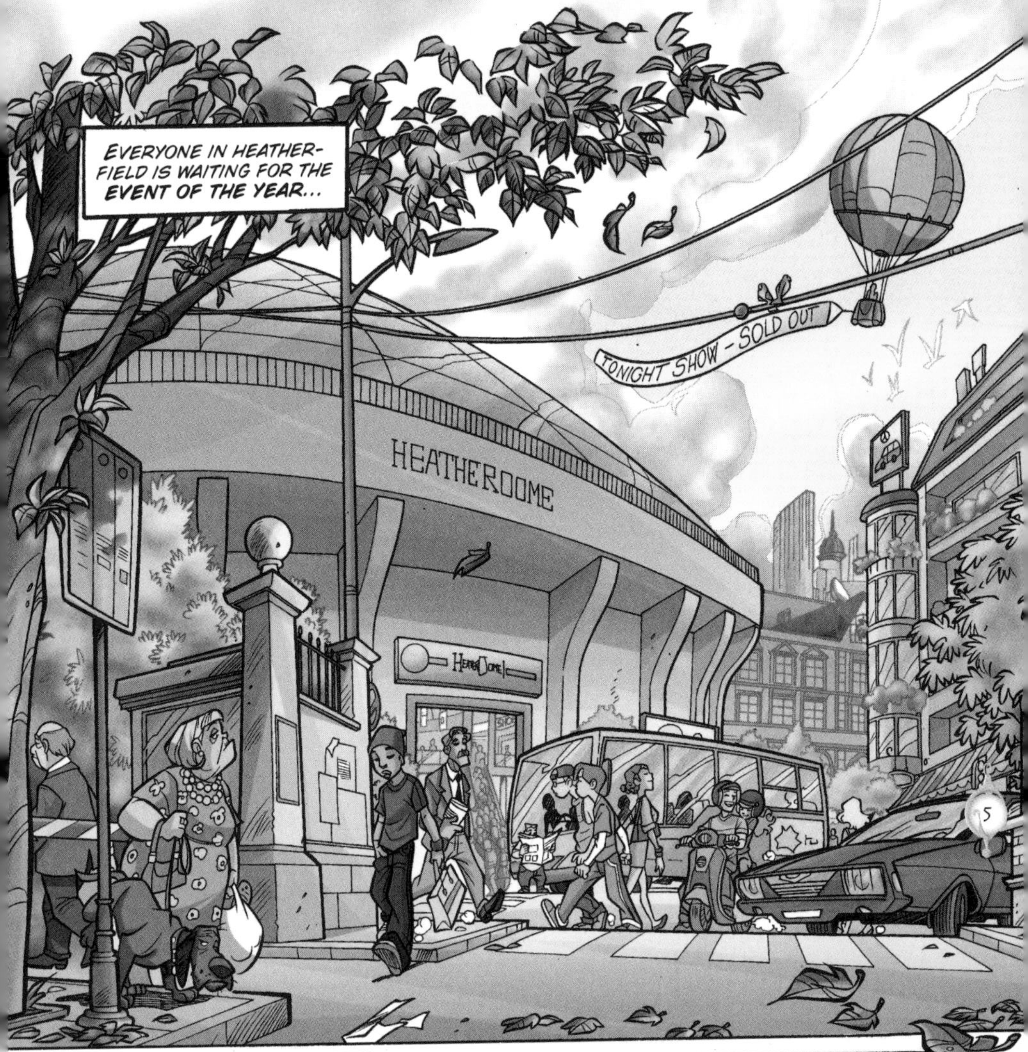
EVERYONE IN HEATHER-FIELD IS WAITING FOR THE EVENT OF THE YEAR...
TONIGHT SHOW - SOLD OUT
HEATHEROOME

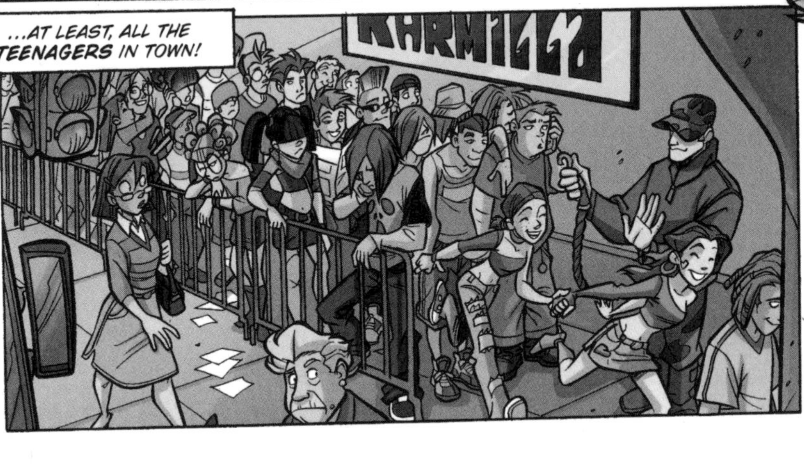
...AT LEAST, ALL THE TEENAGERS IN TOWN!

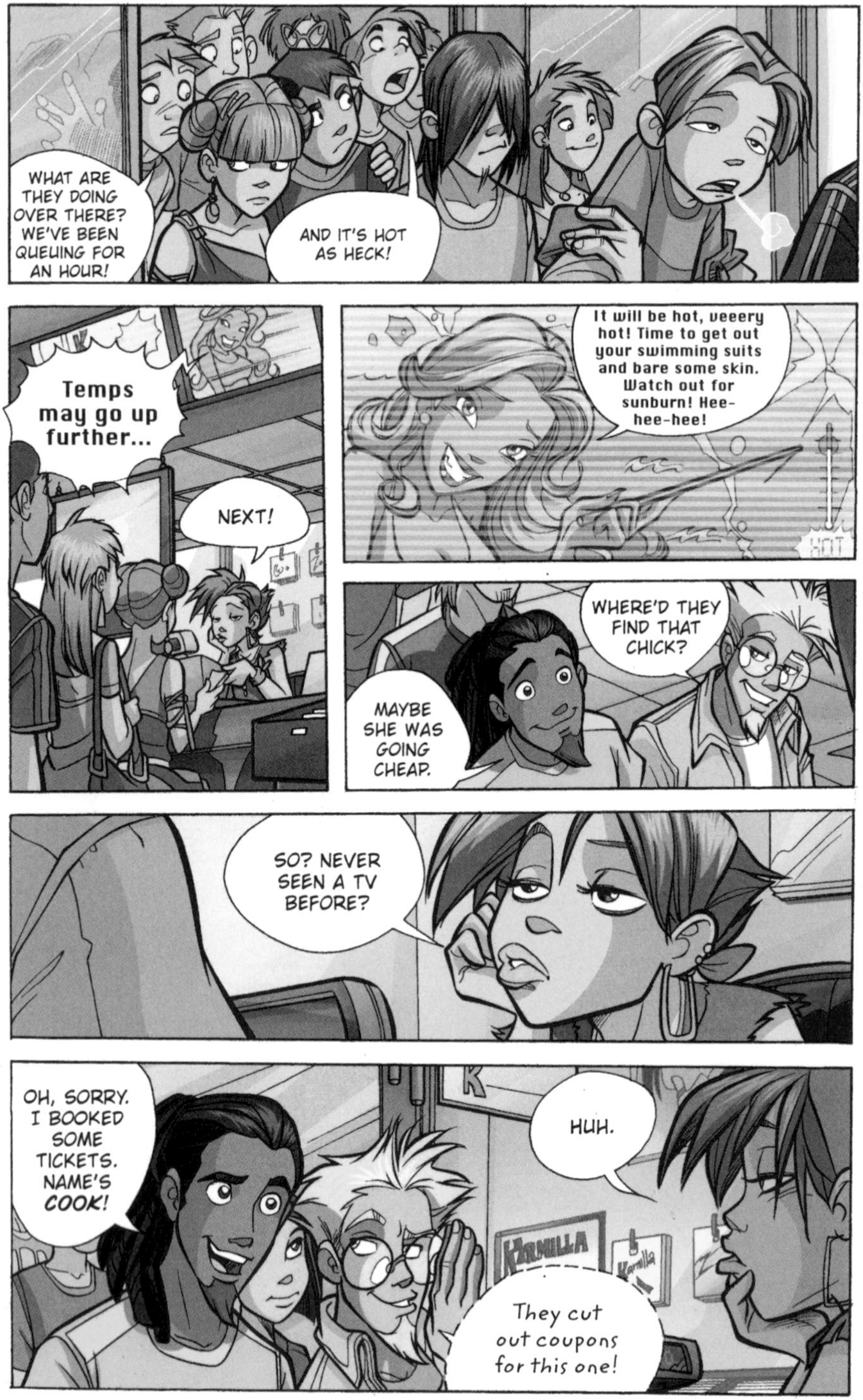
WHAT ARE THEY DOING OVER THERE? WE'VE BEEN QUEUING FOR AN HOUR!
AND IT'S HOT AS HECK!
Temps may go up further...
NEXT!
It will be hot, veeery hot! Time to get out your swimming suits and bare some skin. Watch out for sunburn! Hee-hee-hee!
HOT
WHERE'D THEY FIND THAT CHICK?
MAYBE SHE WAS GOING CHEAP.
SO? NEVER SEEN A TV BEFORE?
OH, SORRY. I BOOKED SOME TICKETS. NAME'S COOK!
HUH.
They cut out coupons for this one!

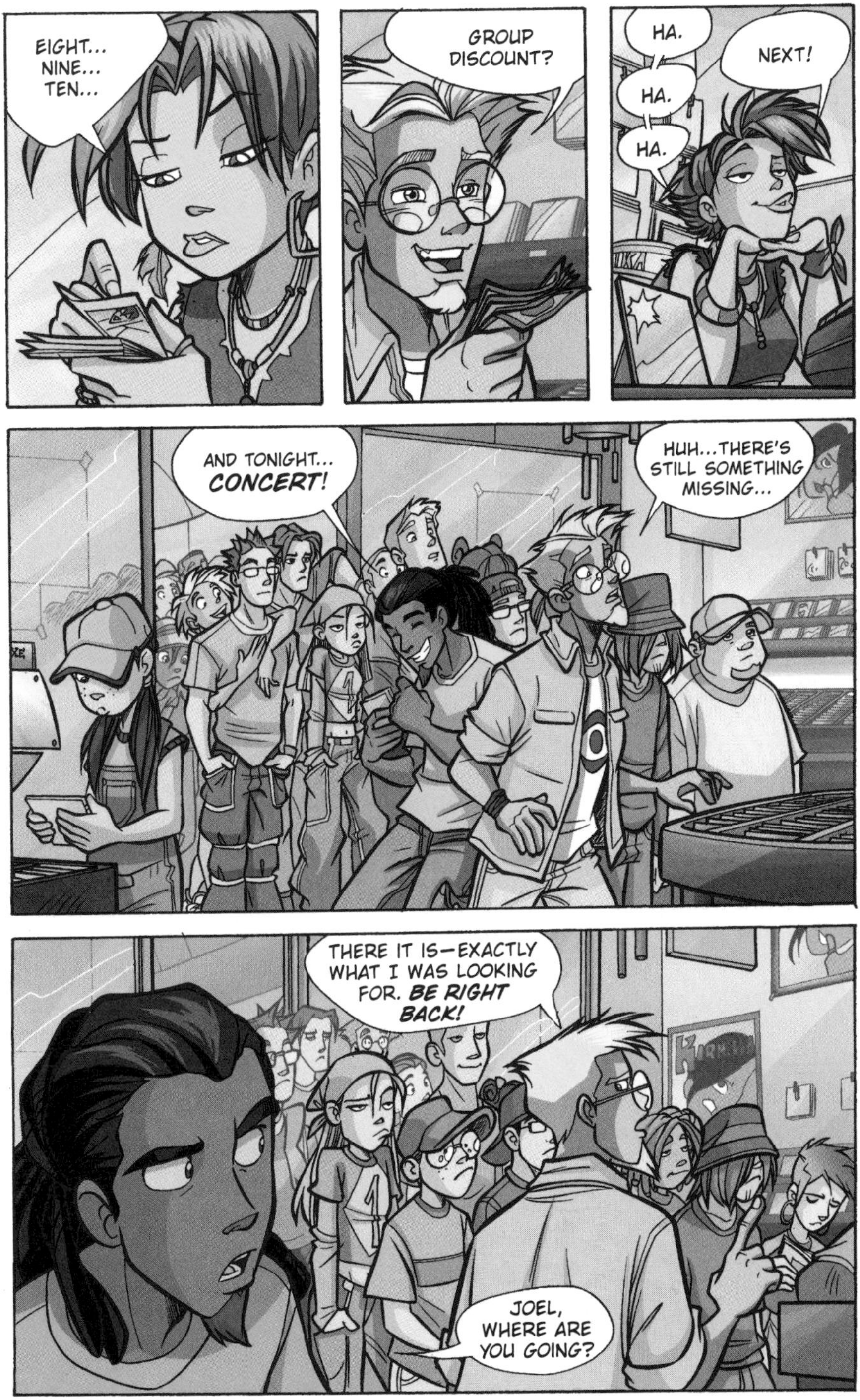
EIGHT... NINE... TEN...
GROUP DISCOUNT?
HA.
HA.
HA.
NEXT!
AND TONIGHT... CONCERT!
HUH...THERE'S STILL SOMETHING MISSING...
THERE IT IS—EXACTLY WHAT I WAS LOOKING FOR. BE RIGHT BACK!
JOEL, WHERE ARE YOU GOING?

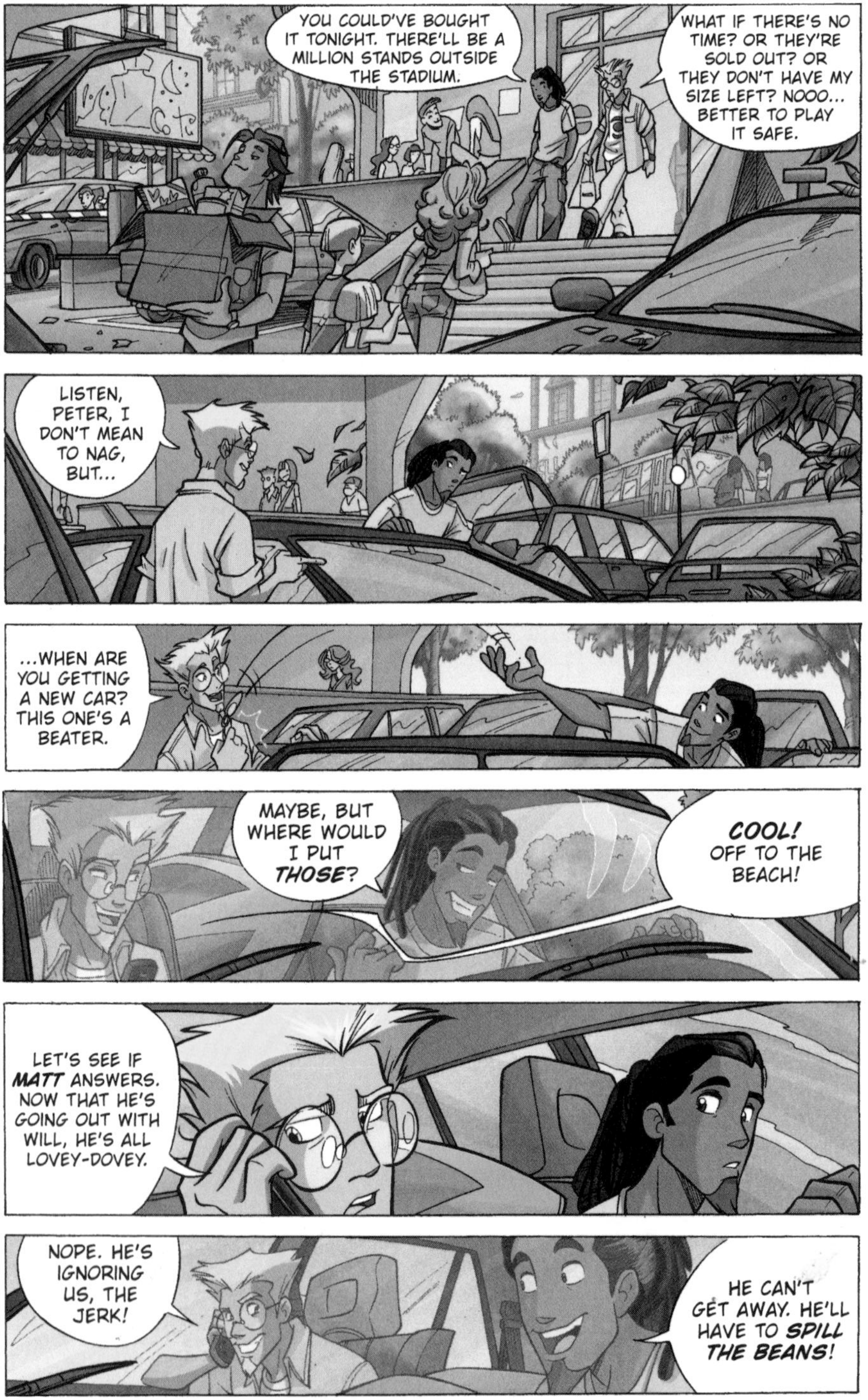
YOU COULD'VE BOUGHT IT TONIGHT. THERE'LL BE A MILLION STANDS OUTSIDE THE STADIUM.
WHAT IF THERE'S NO TIME? OR THEY'RE SOLD OUT? OR THEY DON'T HAVE MY SIZE LEFT? NOOO... BETTER TO PLAY IT SAFE.
LISTEN, PETER, I DON'T MEAN TO NAG, BUT...
...WHEN ARE YOU GETTING A NEW CAR? THIS ONE'S A BEATER.
MAYBE, BUT WHERE WOULD I PUT ***THOSE***?
COOL! OFF TO THE BEACH!
LET'S SEE IF ***MATT*** ANSWERS. NOW THAT HE'S GOING OUT WITH WILL, HE'S ALL LOVEY-DOVEY.
NOPE. HE'S IGNORING US, THE JERK!
HE CAN'T GET AWAY. HE'LL HAVE TO ***SPILL THE BEANS***!

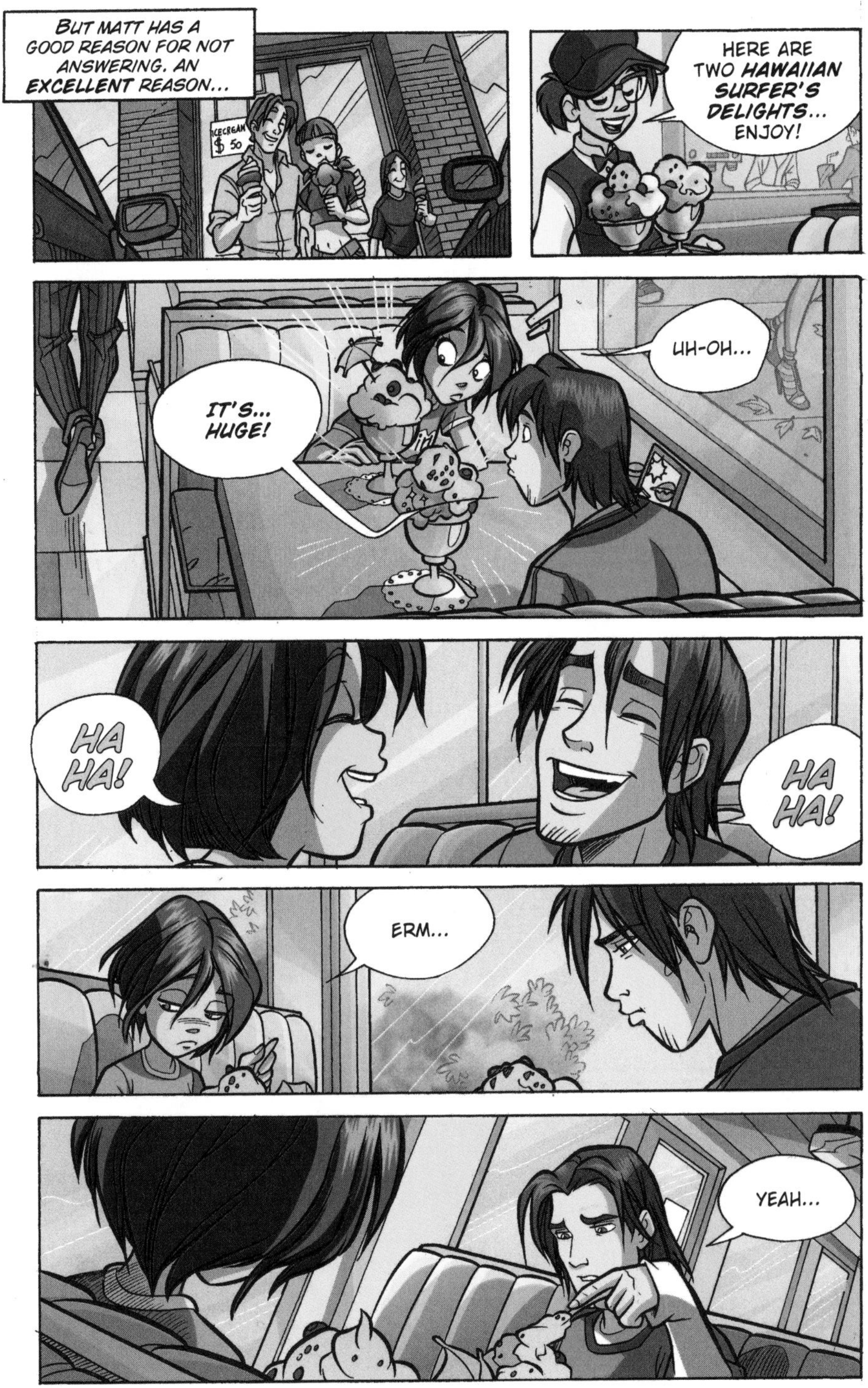
BUT MATT HAS A GOOD REASON FOR NOT ANSWERING. AN EXCELLENT REASON...
ICECREAM $ 50
HERE ARE TWO HAWAIIAN SURFER'S DELIGHTS... ENJOY!
UH-OH...
IT'S... HUGE!
HA HA!
HA HA!
ERM...
YEAH...

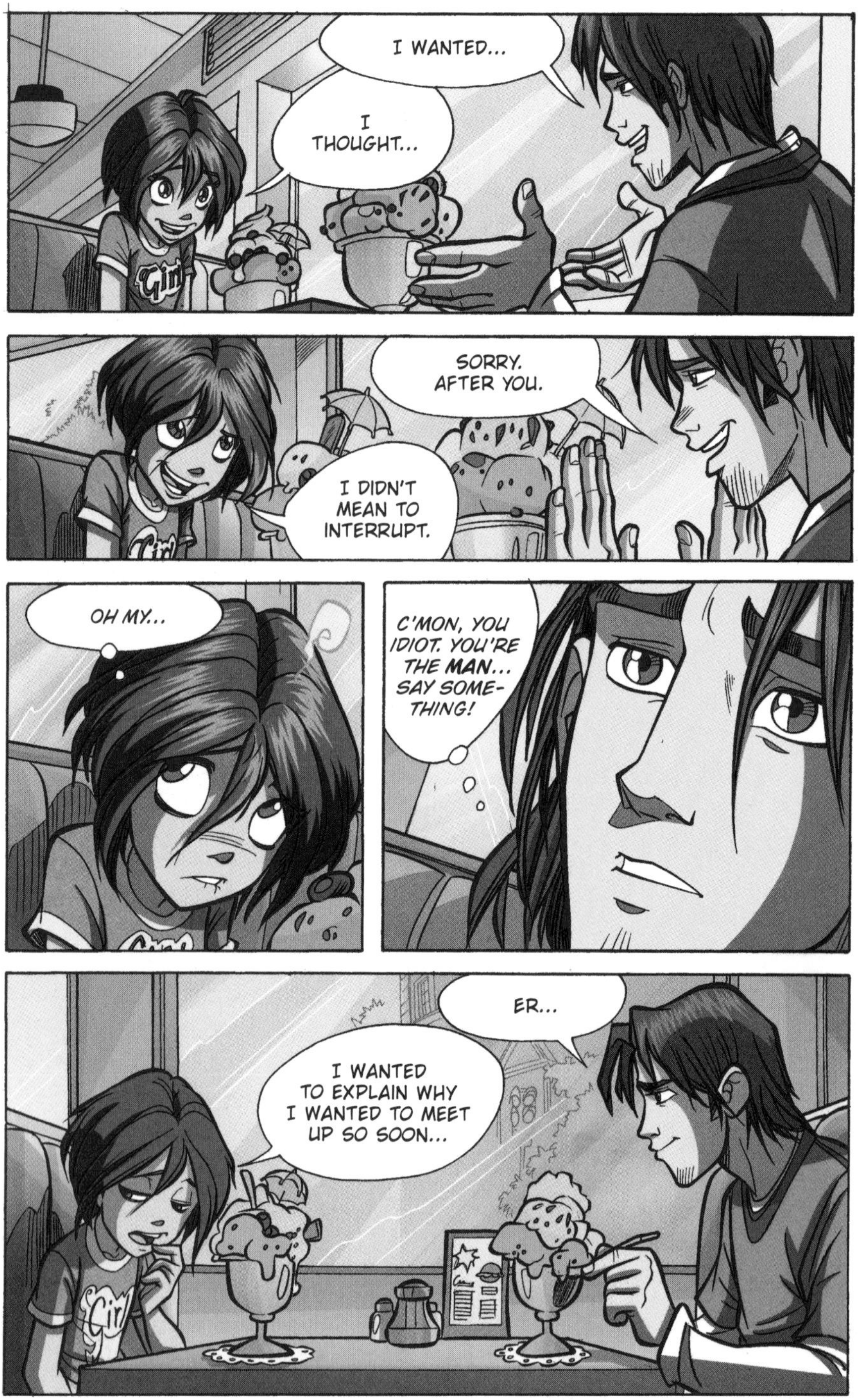
I WANTED...
I THOUGHT...
SORRY. AFTER YOU.
I DIDN'T MEAN TO INTERRUPT.
OH MY...
C'MON, YOU IDIOT. YOU'RE THE **MAN**... SAY SOME-THING!
ER...
I WANTED TO EXPLAIN WHY I WANTED TO MEET UP SO SOON...

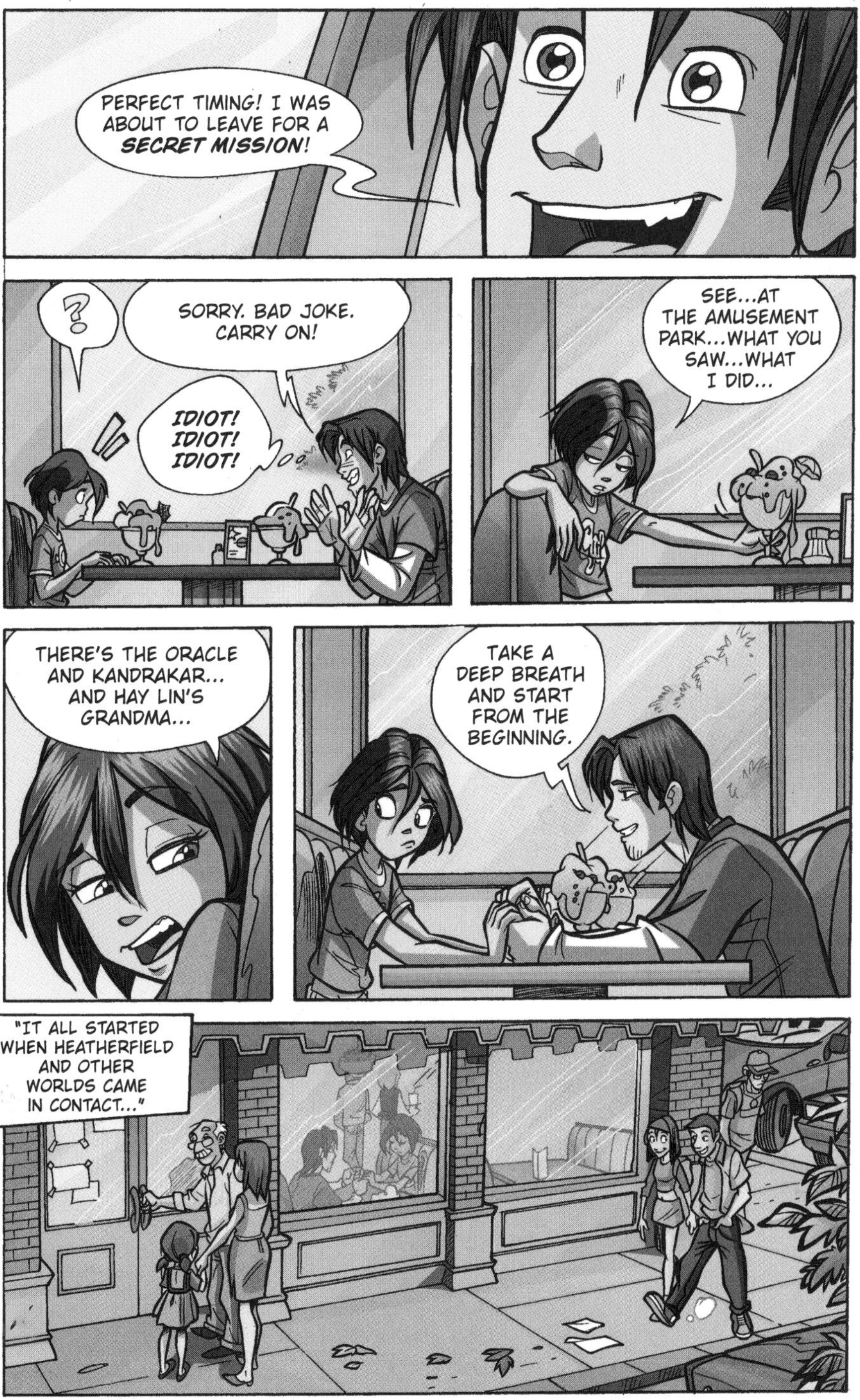
PERFECT TIMING! I WAS ABOUT TO LEAVE FOR A **SECRET MISSION**!
?
SORRY. BAD JOKE. CARRY ON!
IDIOT! IDIOT! IDIOT!
SEE...AT THE AMUSEMENT PARK...WHAT YOU SAW...WHAT I DID...
THERE'S THE ORACLE AND KANDRAKAR... AND HAY LIN'S GRANDMA...
TAKE A DEEP BREATH AND START FROM THE BEGINNING.
"IT ALL STARTED WHEN HEATHERFIELD AND OTHER WORLDS CAME IN CONTACT..."

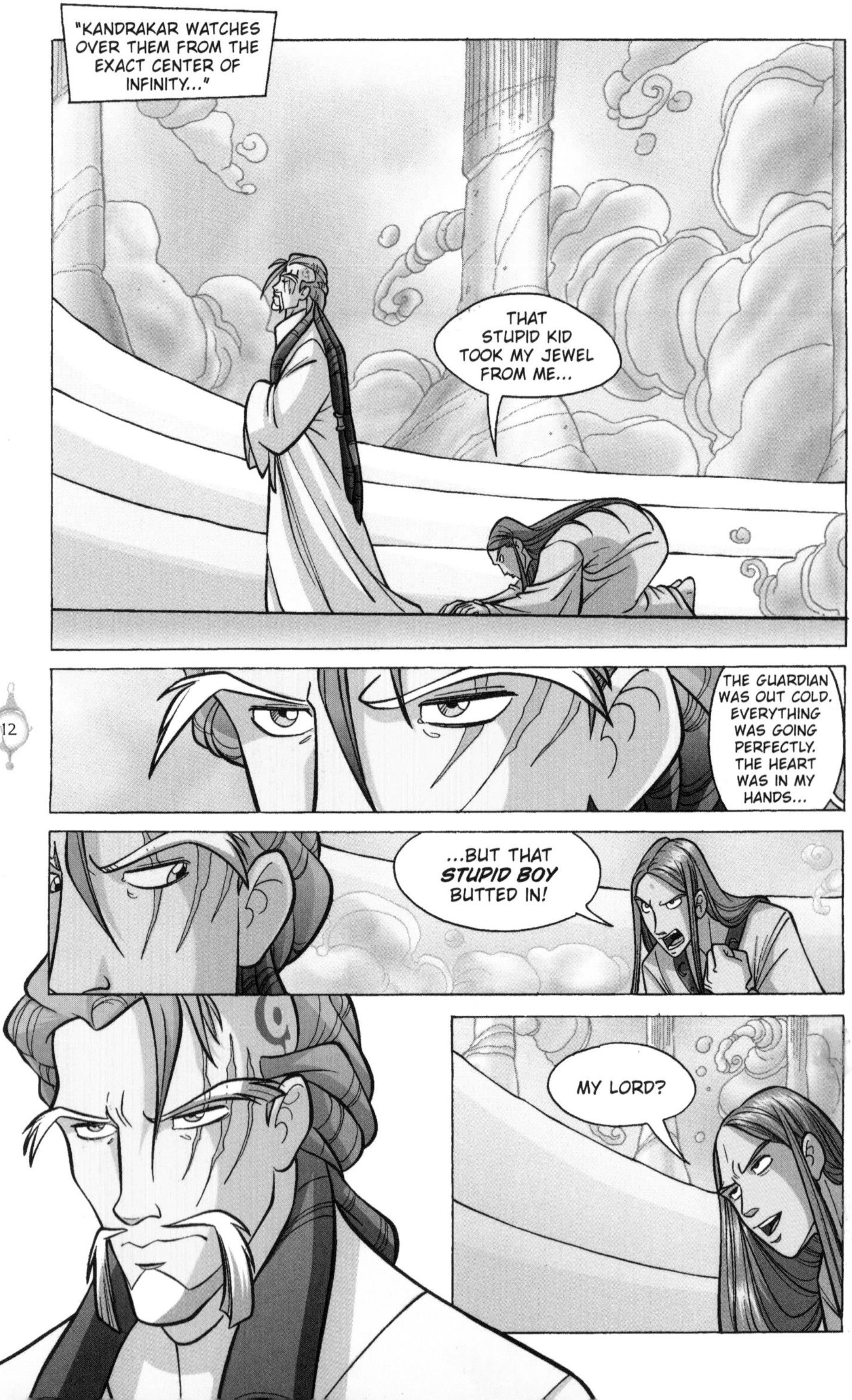
"KANDRAKAR WATCHES OVER THEM FROM THE EXACT CENTER OF INFINITY..."
THAT STUPID KID TOOK MY JEWEL FROM ME...
THE GUARDIAN WAS OUT COLD. EVERYTHING WAS GOING PERFECTLY. THE HEART WAS IN MY HANDS...
...BUT THAT ***STUPID BOY*** BUTTED IN!
MY LORD?

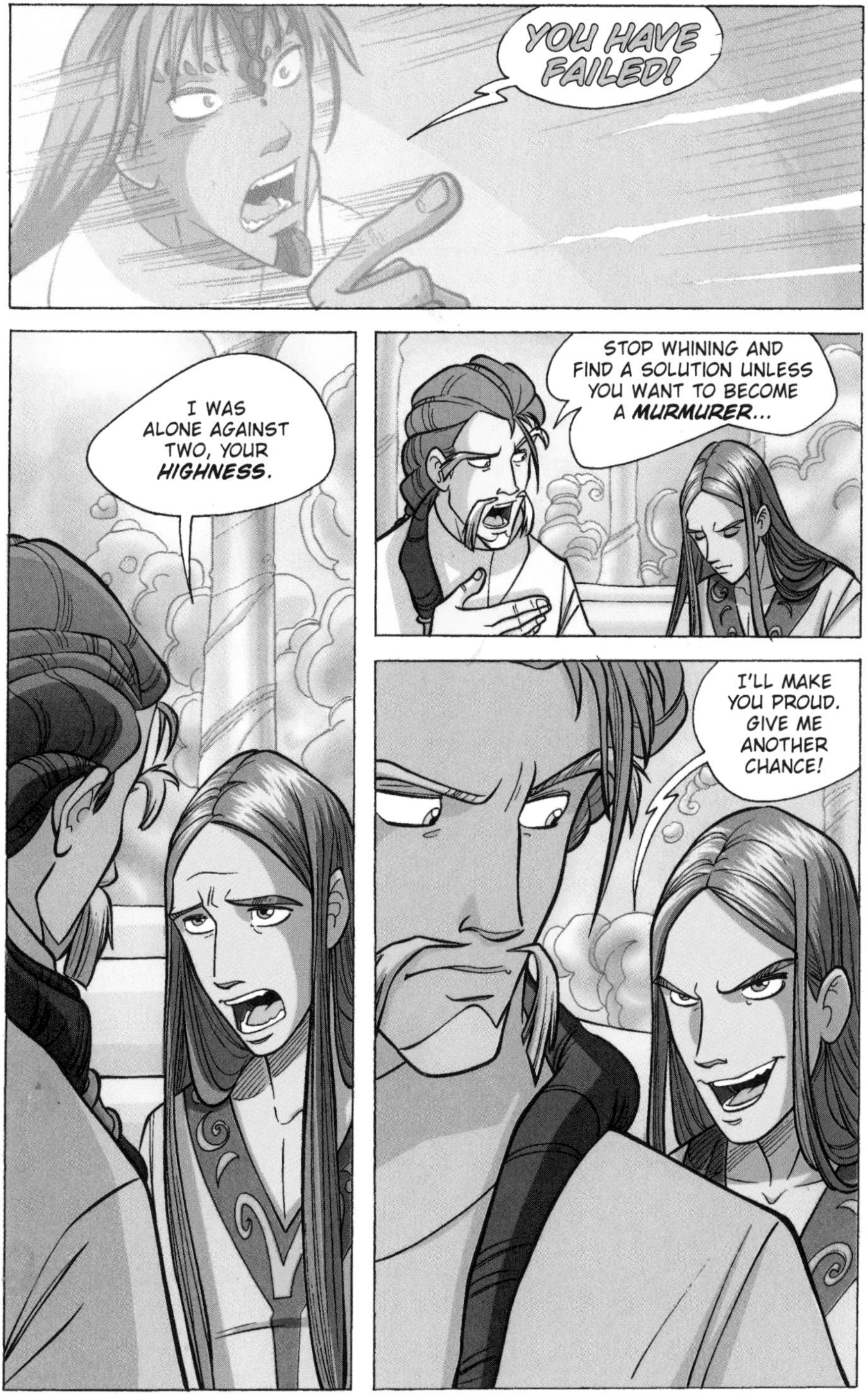
YOU HAVE FAILED!
I WAS ALONE AGAINST TWO, YOUR HIGHNESS.
STOP WHINING AND FIND A SOLUTION UNLESS YOU WANT TO BECOME A MURMURER...
I'LL MAKE YOU PROUD. GIVE ME ANOTHER CHANCE!

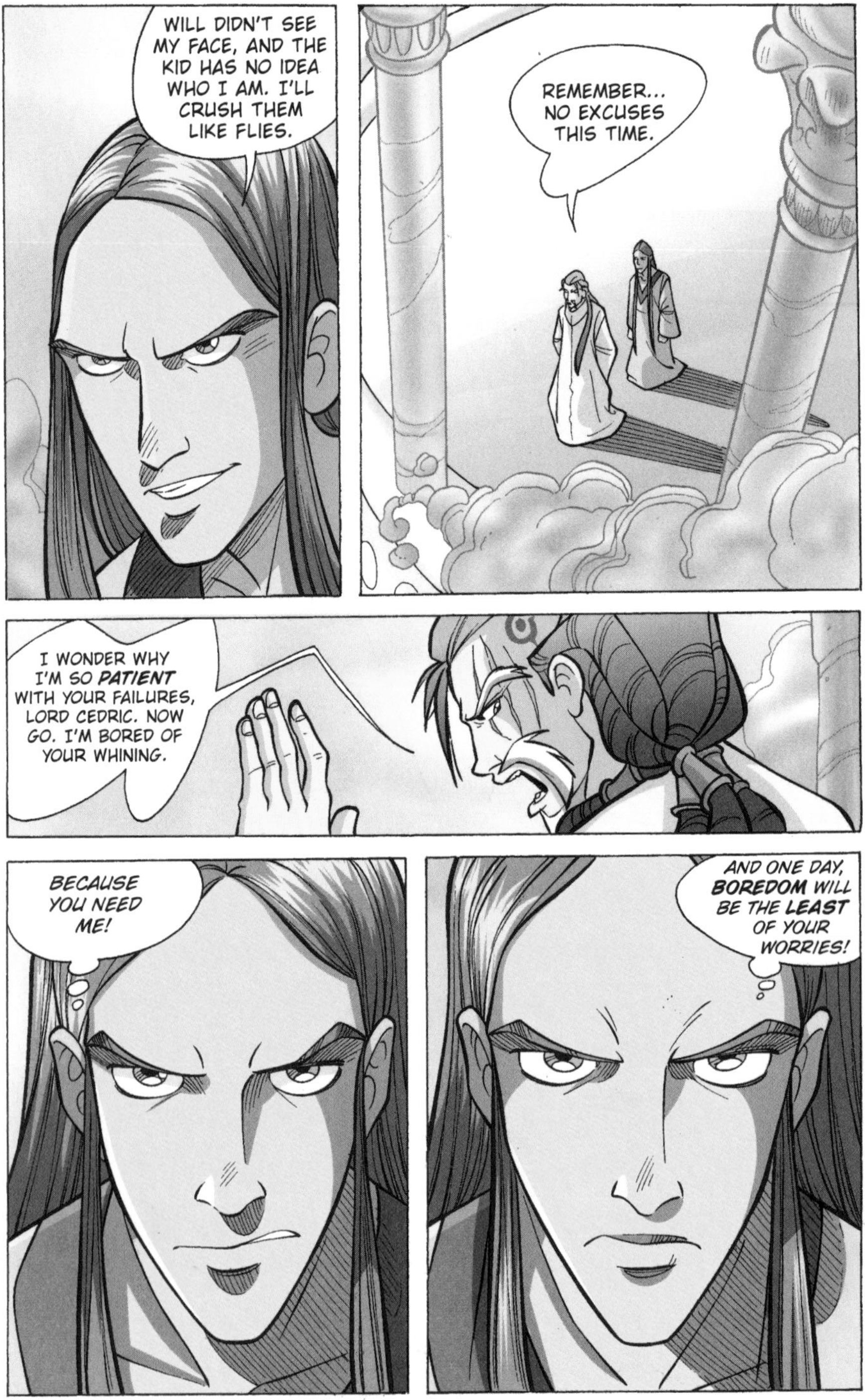
WILL DIDN'T SEE MY FACE, AND THE KID HAS NO IDEA WHO I AM. I'LL CRUSH THEM LIKE FLIES.
REMEMBER... NO EXCUSES THIS TIME.
I WONDER WHY I'M SO PATIENT WITH YOUR FAILURES, LORD CEDRIC. NOW GO. I'M BORED OF YOUR WHINING.
BECAUSE YOU NEED ME!
AND ONE DAY, BOREDOM WILL BE THE LEAST OF YOUR WORRIES!

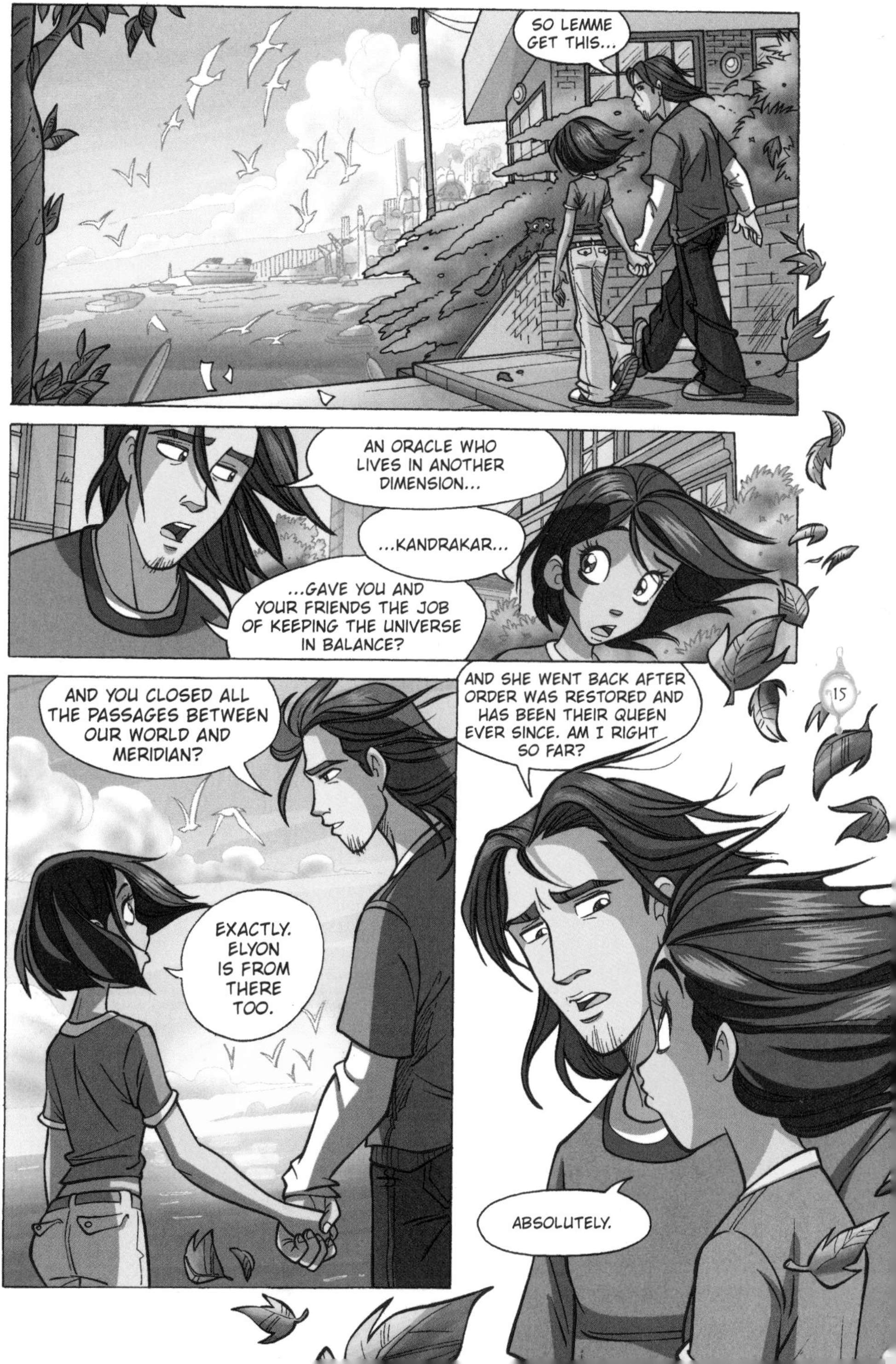

SO LEMME GET THIS...
AN ORACLE WHO LIVES IN ANOTHER DIMENSION...
...KANDRAKAR...
...GAVE YOU AND YOUR FRIENDS THE JOB OF KEEPING THE UNIVERSE IN BALANCE?
AND YOU CLOSED ALL THE PASSAGES BETWEEN OUR WORLD AND MERIDIAN?
EXACTLY. ELYON IS FROM THERE TOO.
AND SHE WENT BACK AFTER ORDER WAS RESTORED AND HAS BEEN THEIR QUEEN EVER SINCE. AM I RIGHT SO FAR?
ABSOLUTELY.

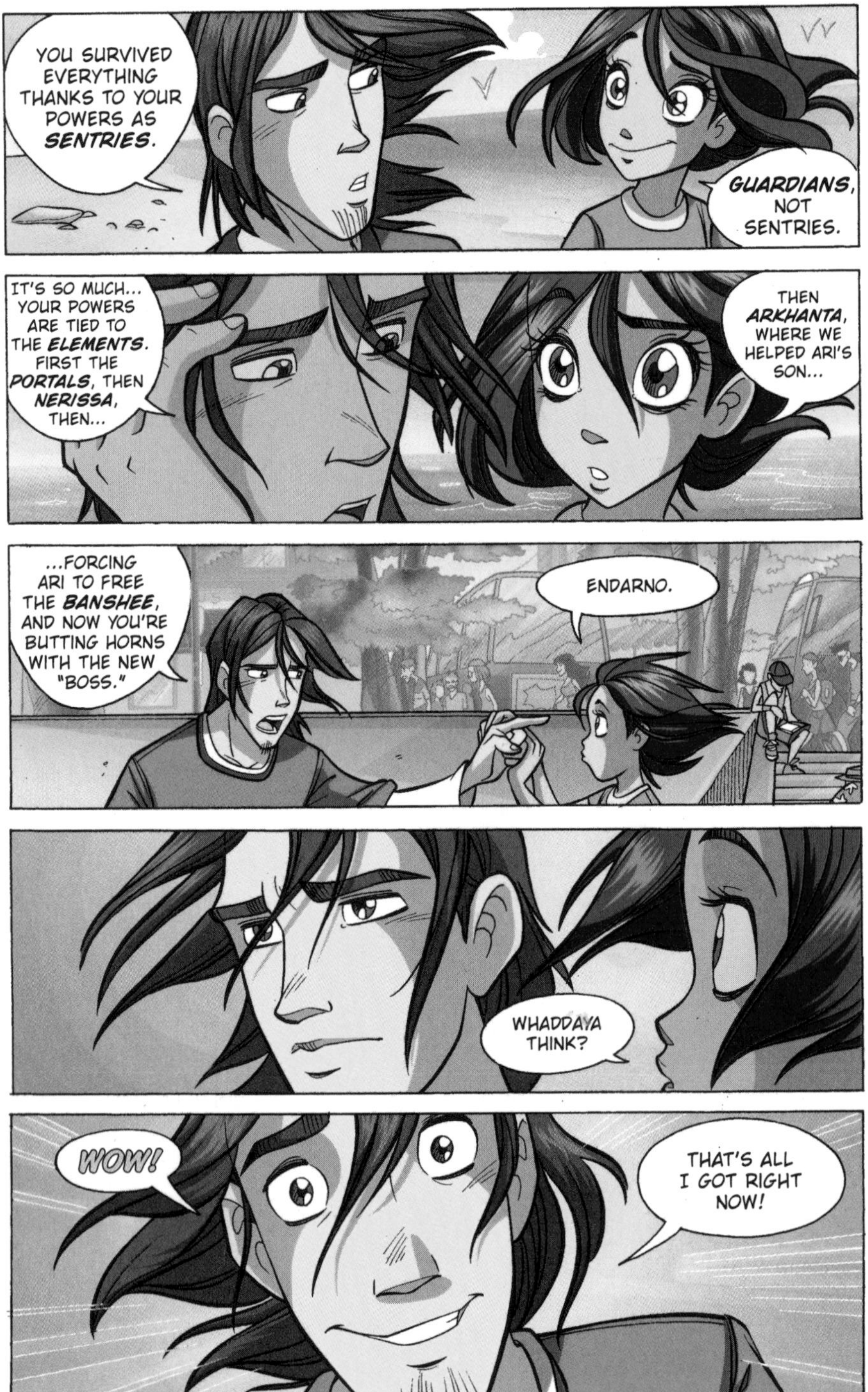
YOU SURVIVED EVERYTHING THANKS TO YOUR POWERS AS SENTRIES.
GUARDIANS, NOT SENTRIES.
IT'S SO MUCH... YOUR POWERS ARE TIED TO THE ELEMENTS. FIRST THE PORTALS, THEN NERISSA, THEN...
THEN ARKHANTA, WHERE WE HELPED ARI'S SON...
...FORCING ARI TO FREE THE BANSHEE, AND NOW YOU'RE BUTTING HORNS WITH THE NEW "BOSS."
ENDARNO.
WHADDAYA THINK?
WOW!
THAT'S ALL I GOT RIGHT NOW!

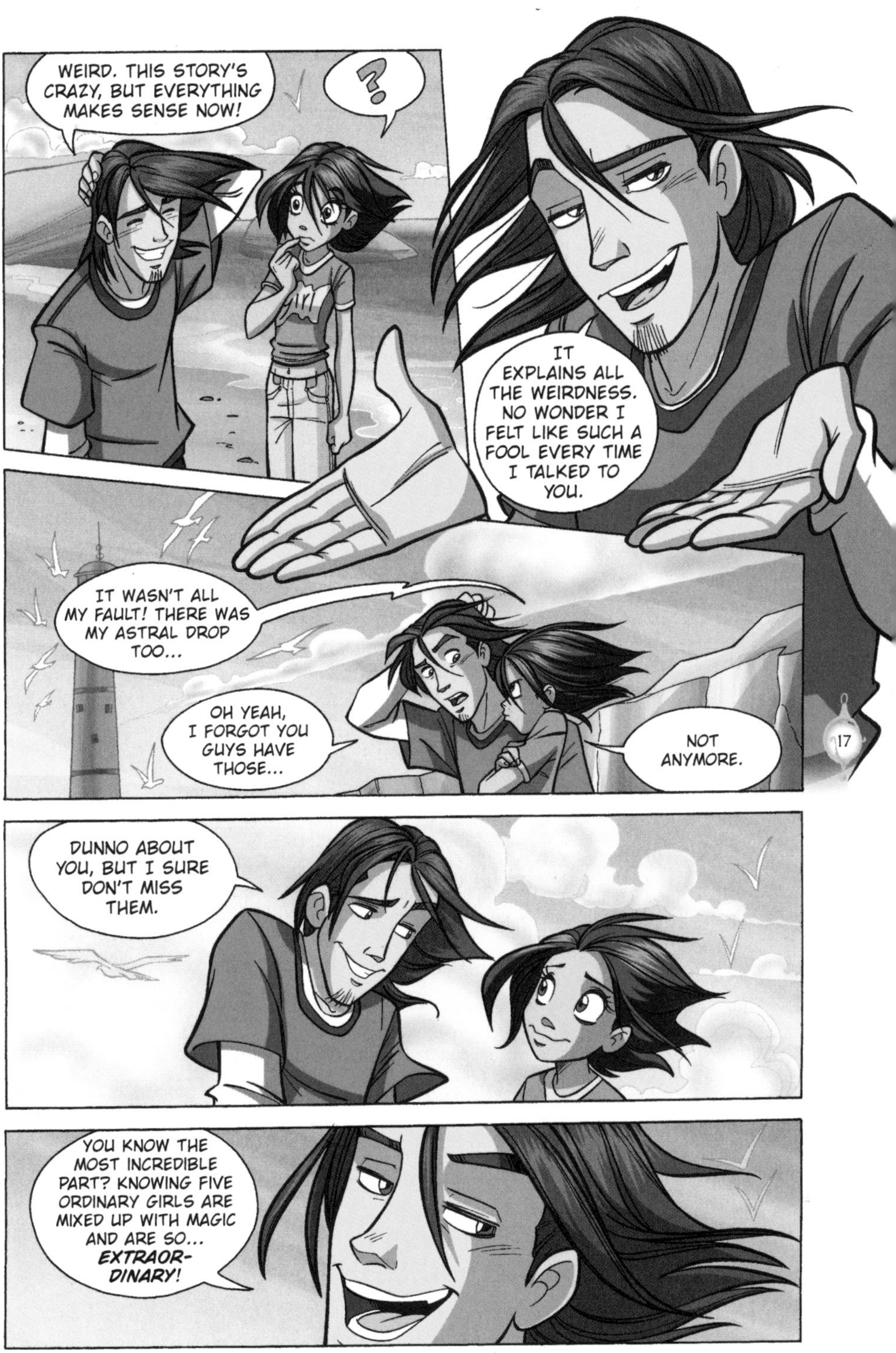
WEIRD. THIS STORY'S CRAZY, BUT EVERYTHING MAKES SENSE NOW!
?
IT EXPLAINS ALL THE WEIRDNESS. NO WONDER I FELT LIKE SUCH A FOOL EVERY TIME I TALKED TO YOU.
IT WASN'T ALL MY FAULT! THERE WAS MY ASTRAL DROP TOO...
OH YEAH, I FORGOT YOU GUYS HAVE THOSE...
NOT ANYMORE.
DUNNO ABOUT YOU, BUT I SURE DON'T MISS THEM.
YOU KNOW THE MOST INCREDIBLE PART? KNOWING FIVE ORDINARY GIRLS ARE MIXED UP WITH MAGIC AND ARE SO... ***EXTRAOR-DINARY***!

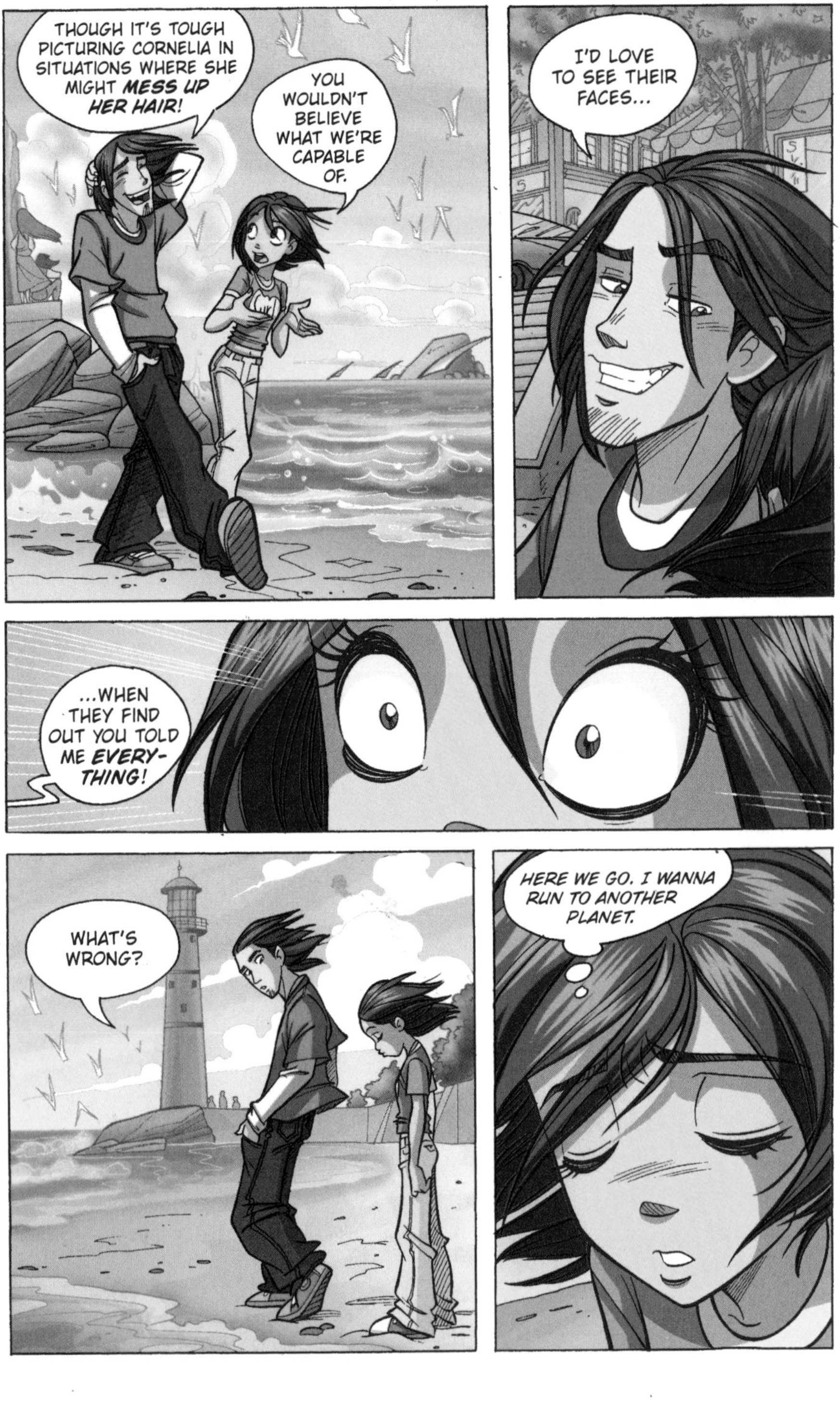
THOUGH IT'S TOUGH PICTURING CORNELIA IN SITUATIONS WHERE SHE MIGHT **MESS UP HER HAIR**!
YOU WOULDN'T BELIEVE WHAT WE'RE CAPABLE OF.
I'D LOVE TO SEE THEIR FACES...
...WHEN THEY FIND OUT YOU TOLD ME **EVERY-THING**!
WHAT'S WRONG?
HERE WE GO. I WANNA RUN TO ANOTHER PLANET.

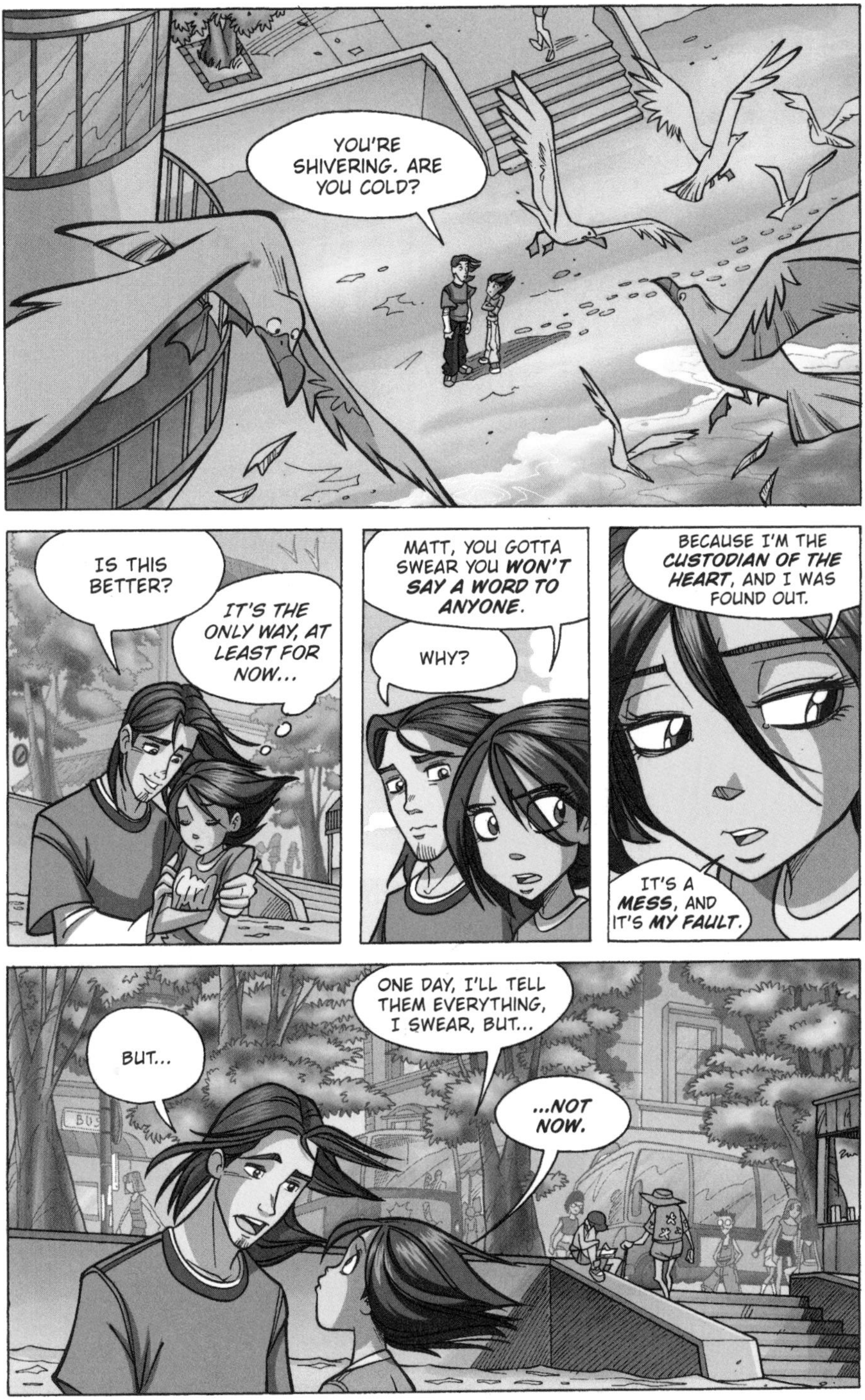
YOU'RE SHIVERING. ARE YOU COLD?
IS THIS BETTER?
IT'S THE ONLY WAY, AT LEAST FOR NOW...
MATT, YOU GOTTA SWEAR YOU WON'T SAY A WORD TO ANYONE.
WHY?
BECAUSE I'M THE CUSTODIAN OF THE HEART, AND I WAS FOUND OUT.
IT'S A MESS, AND IT'S MY FAULT.
BUT...
ONE DAY, I'LL TELL THEM EVERYTHING, I SWEAR, BUT...
...NOT NOW.
BUS

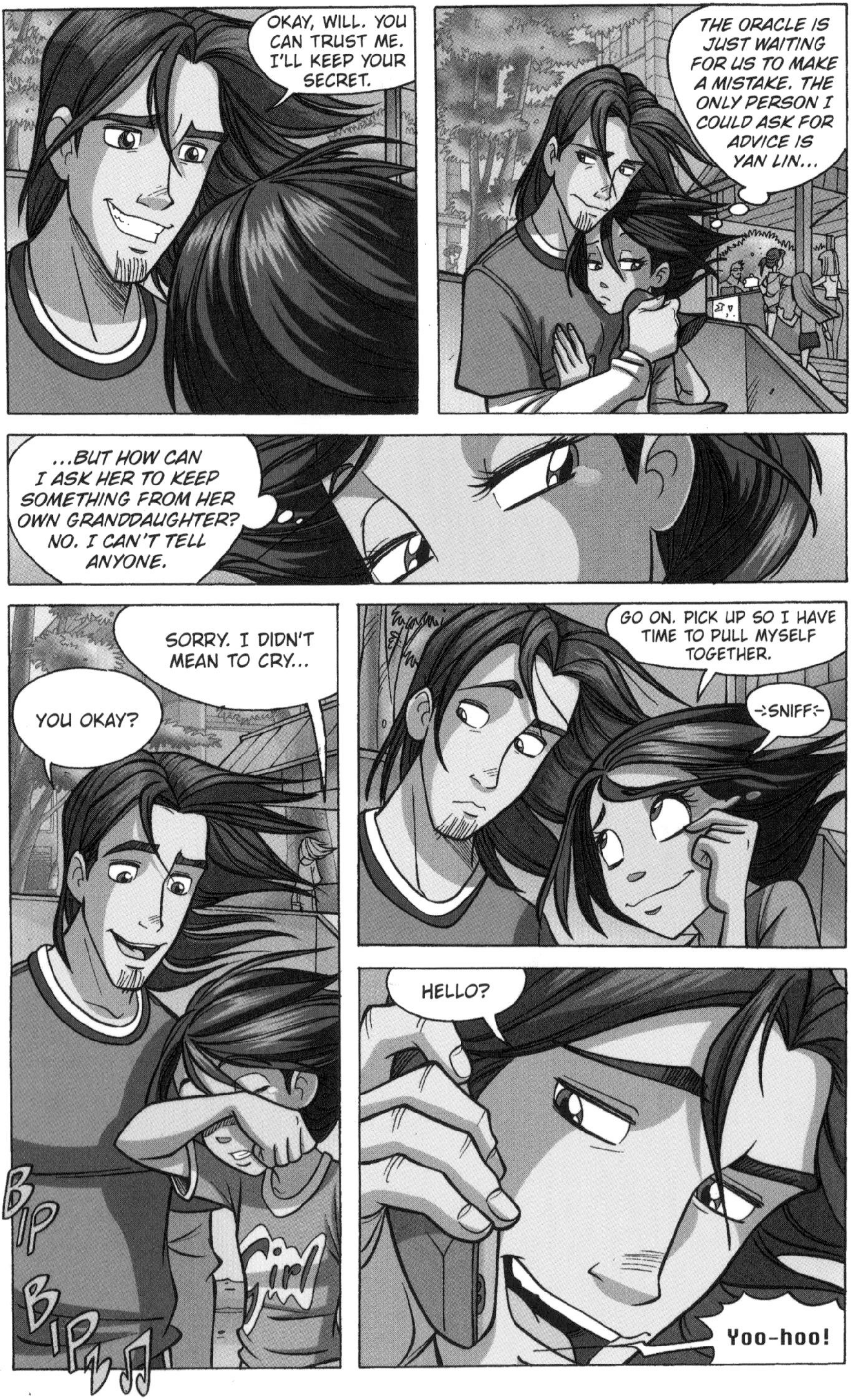
OKAY, WILL. YOU CAN TRUST ME. I'LL KEEP YOUR SECRET.
THE ORACLE IS JUST WAITING FOR US TO MAKE A MISTAKE. THE ONLY PERSON I COULD ASK FOR ADVICE IS YAN LIN...
...BUT HOW CAN I ASK HER TO KEEP SOMETHING FROM HER OWN GRANDDAUGHTER? NO. I CAN'T TELL ANYONE.
SORRY. I DIDN'T MEAN TO CRY...
YOU OKAY?
BIP
BIP
Girl
GO ON. PICK UP SO I HAVE TIME TO PULL MYSELF TOGETHER.
SNIFF
HELLO?
Yoo-hoo!

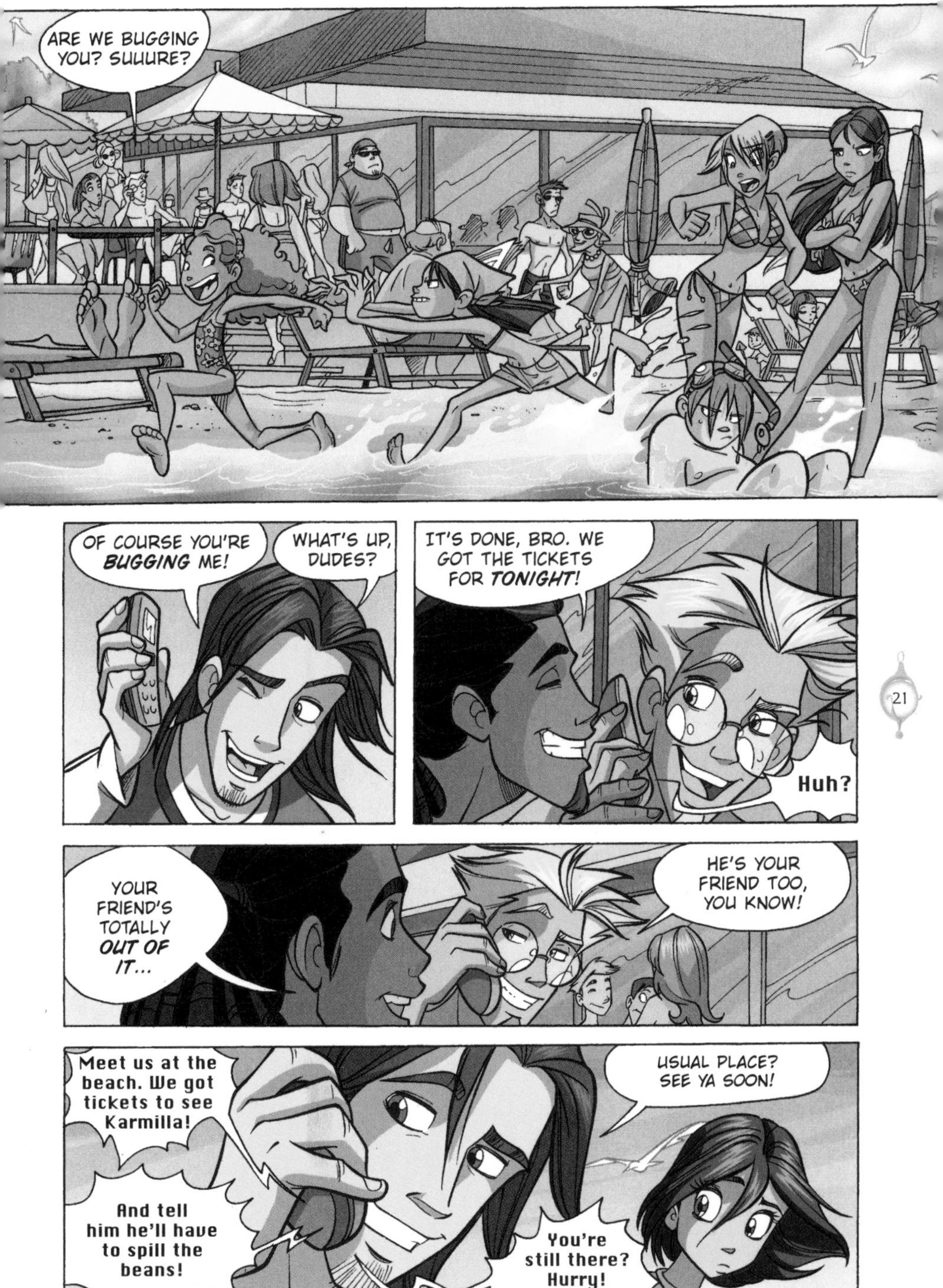
ARE WE BUGGING YOU? SUUURE?
OF COURSE YOU'RE BUGGING ME!
WHAT'S UP, DUDES?
IT'S DONE, BRO. WE GOT THE TICKETS FOR TONIGHT!
Huh?
YOUR FRIEND'S TOTALLY OUT OF IT...
HE'S YOUR FRIEND TOO, YOU KNOW!
Meet us at the beach. We got tickets to see Karmilla!
And tell him he'll have to spill the beans!
USUAL PLACE? SEE YA SOON!
You're still there? Hurry!

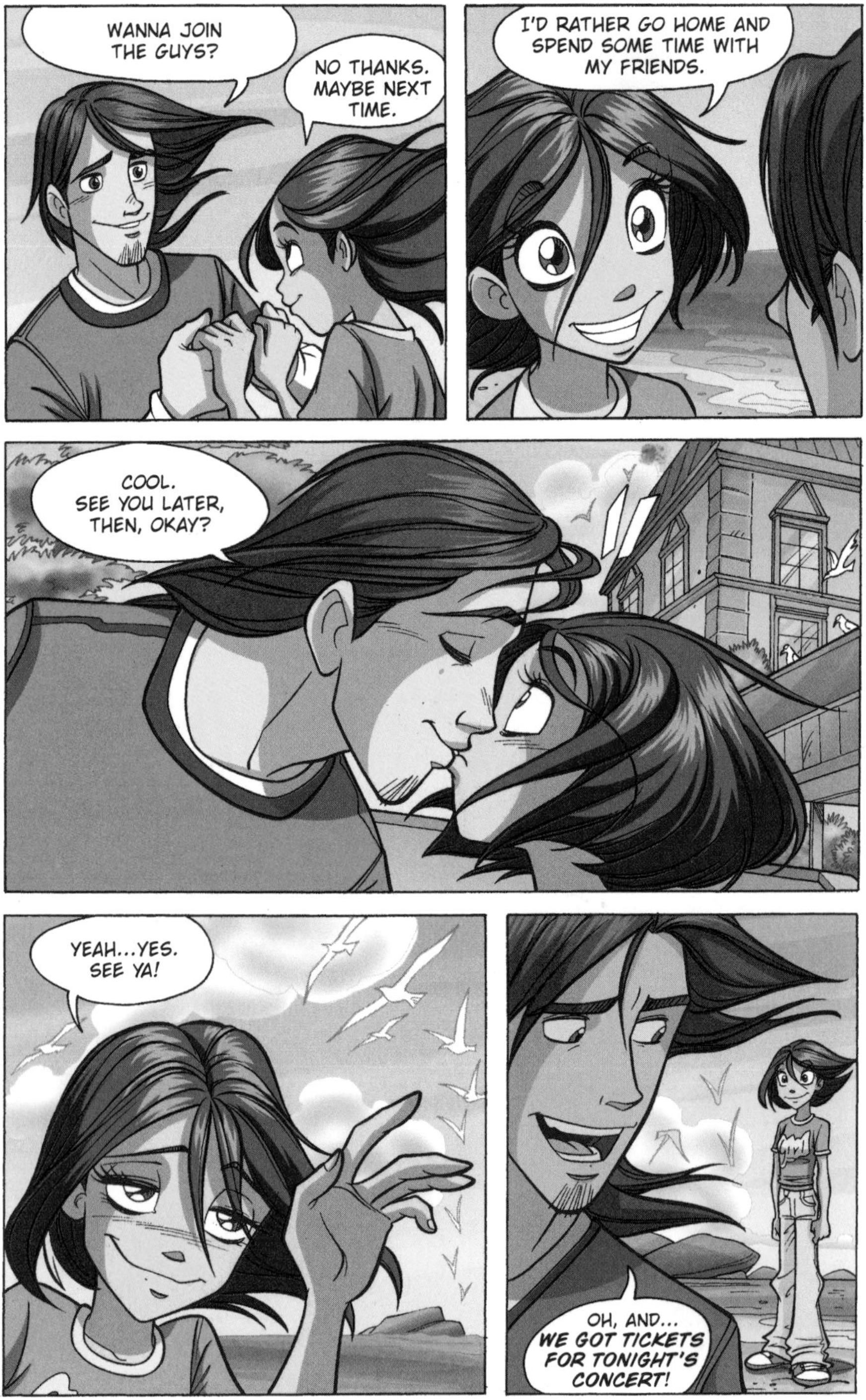
WANNA JOIN THE GUYS?
NO THANKS. MAYBE NEXT TIME.
I'D RATHER GO HOME AND SPEND SOME TIME WITH MY FRIENDS.
COOL. SEE YOU LATER, THEN, OKAY?
YEAH...YES. SEE YA!
OH, AND... WE GOT TICKETS FOR TONIGHT'S CONCERT!

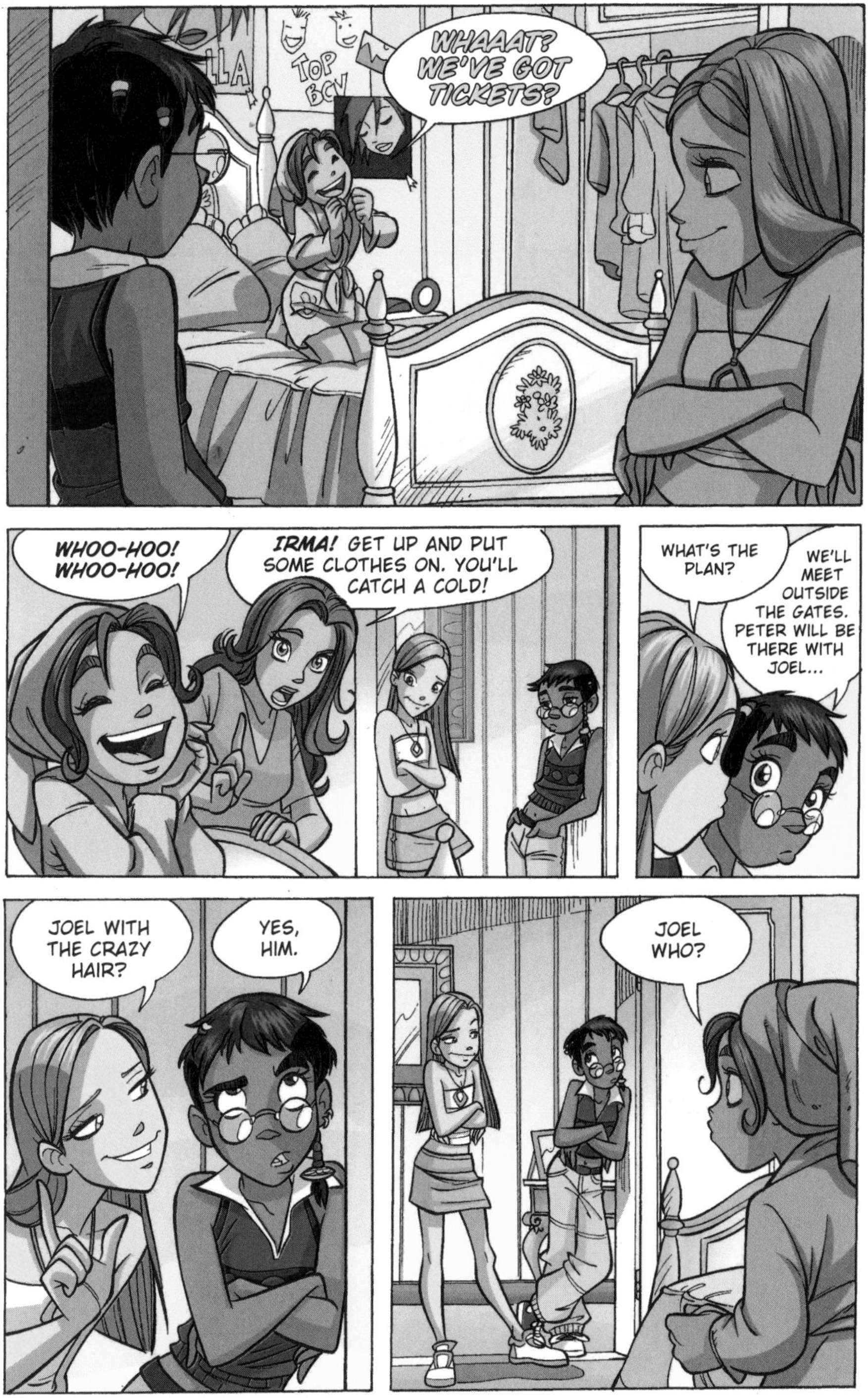
WHAAAT? WE'VE GOT TICKETS?
WHOO-HOO! WHOO-HOO!
IRMA! GET UP AND PUT SOME CLOTHES ON. YOU'LL CATCH A COLD!
WHAT'S THE PLAN?
WE'LL MEET OUTSIDE THE GATES. PETER WILL BE THERE WITH JOEL...
JOEL WITH THE CRAZY HAIR?
YES, HIM.
JOEL WHO?

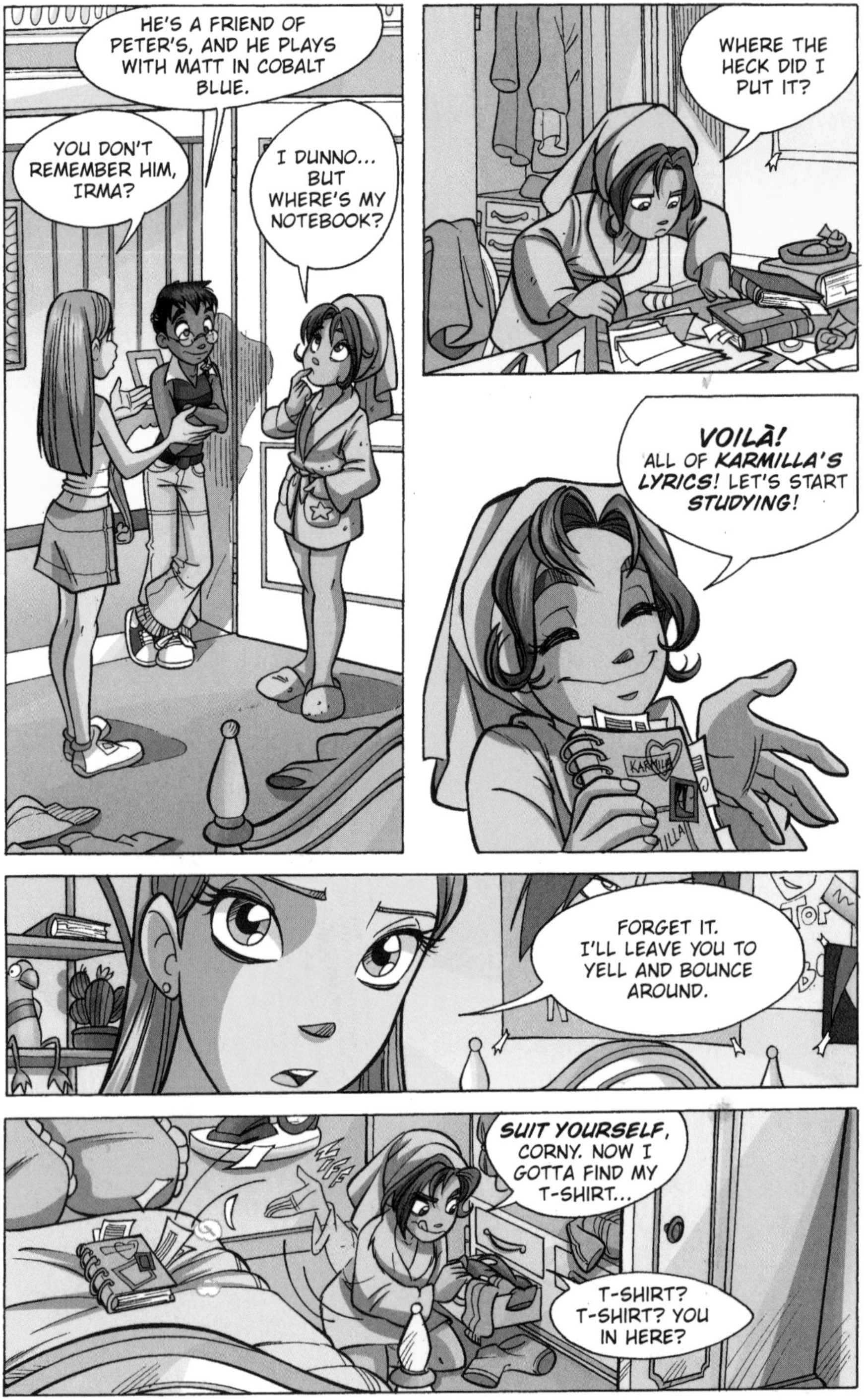
HE'S A FRIEND OF PETER'S, AND HE PLAYS WITH MATT IN COBALT BLUE.
YOU DON'T REMEMBER HIM, IRMA?
I DUNNO... BUT WHERE'S MY NOTEBOOK?
WHERE THE HECK DID I PUT IT?
VOILÀ! ALL OF KARMILLA'S LYRICS! LET'S START STUDYING!
KARMILLA
FORGET IT. I'LL LEAVE YOU TO YELL AND BOUNCE AROUND.
SUIT YOURSELF, CORNY. NOW I GOTTA FIND MY T-SHIRT...
T-SHIRT? T-SHIRT? YOU IN HERE?

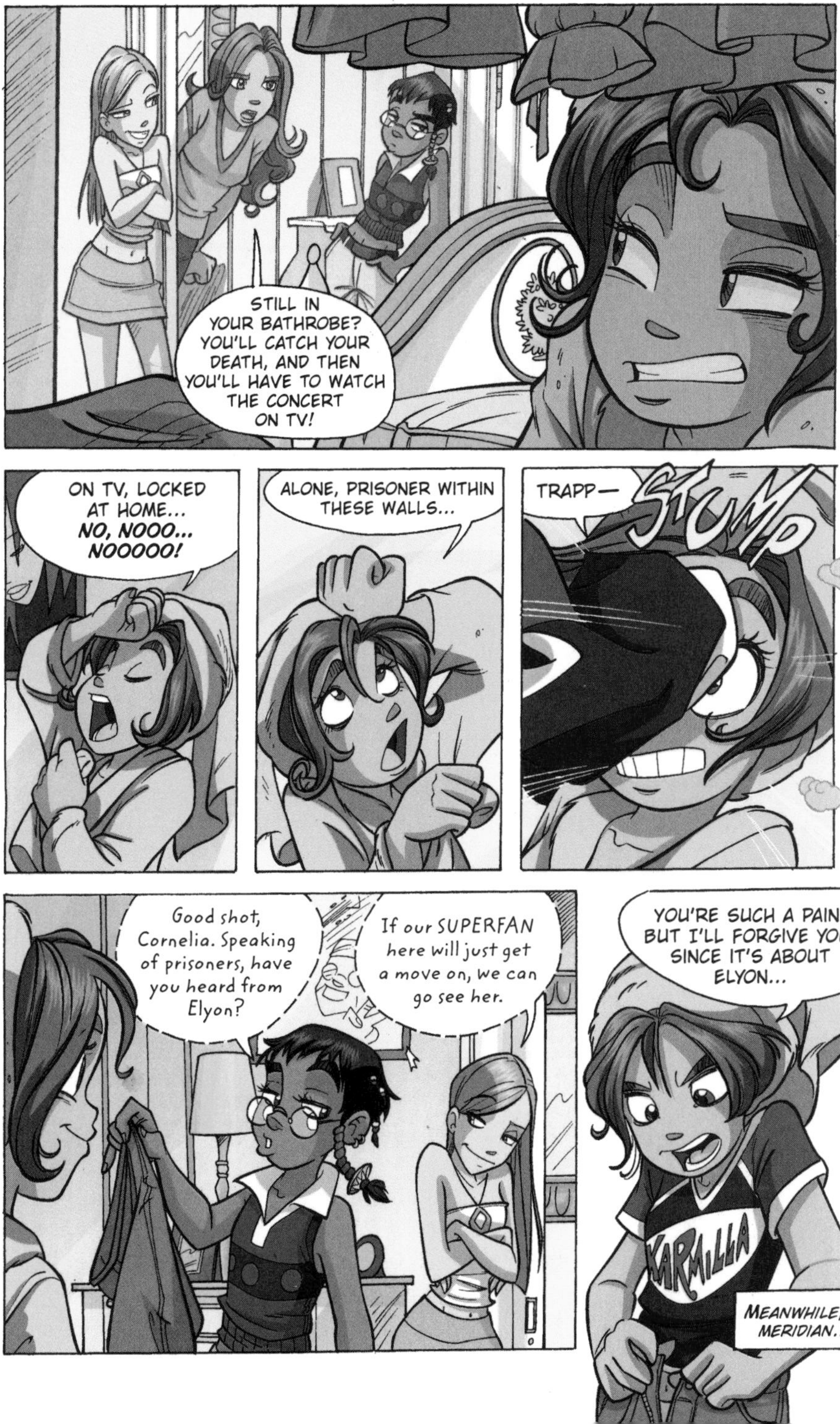

STILL IN YOUR BATHROBE? YOU'LL CATCH YOUR DEATH, AND THEN YOU'LL HAVE TO WATCH THE CONCERT ON TV!
ON TV, LOCKED AT HOME... NO, NOOO... NOOOOO!
ALONE, PRISONER WITHIN THESE WALLS...
TRAPP—
STUMP
Good shot, Cornelia. Speaking of prisoners, have you heard from Elyon?
If our SUPERFAN here will just get a move on, we can go see her.
YOU'RE SUCH A PAIN. BUT I'LL FORGIVE YOU, SINCE IT'S ABOUT ELYON...
KARMILLA
MEANWHILE, IN MERIDIAN...

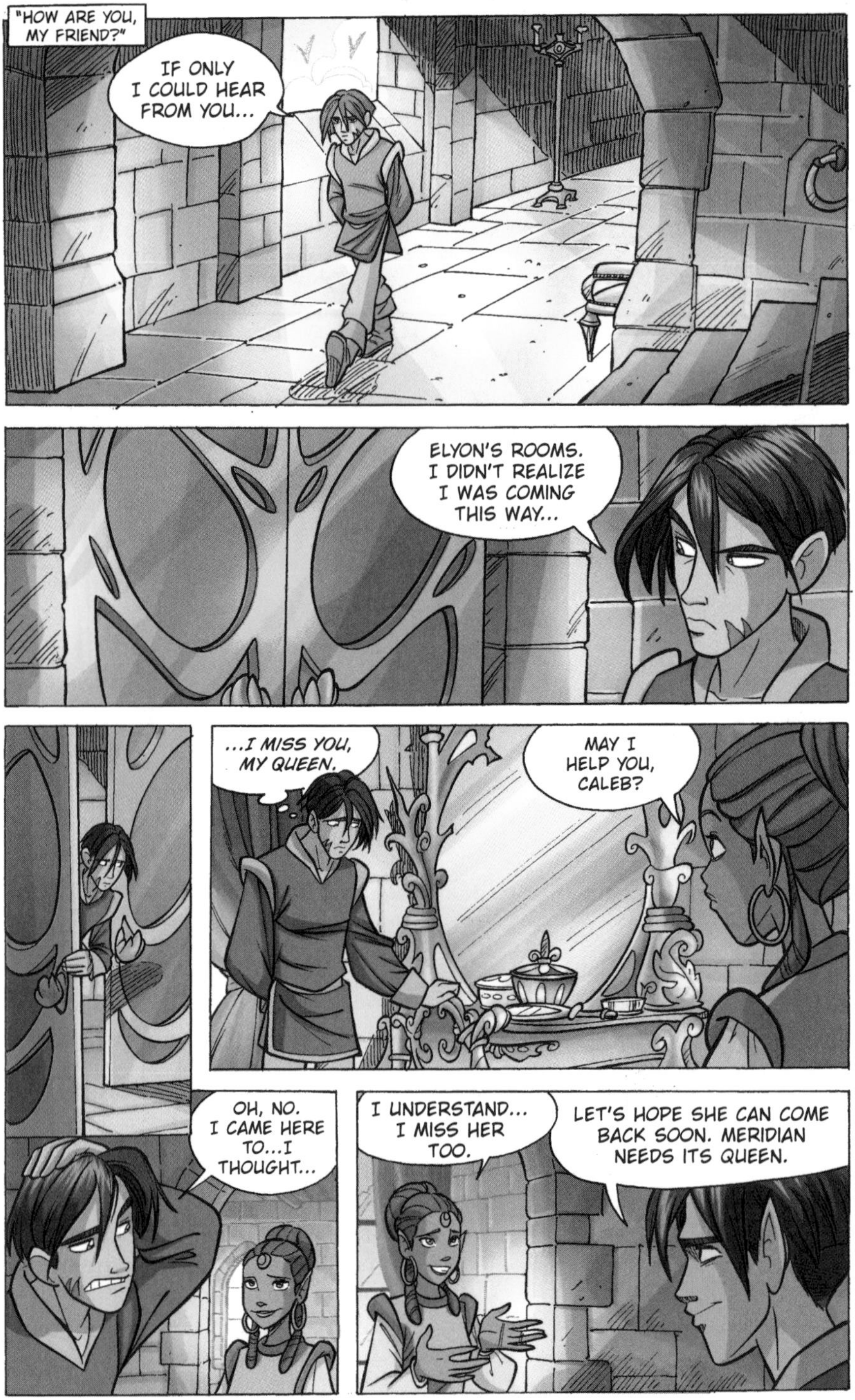
"HOW ARE YOU, MY FRIEND?"
IF ONLY I COULD HEAR FROM YOU...
ELYON'S ROOMS. I DIDN'T REALIZE I WAS COMING THIS WAY...
...I MISS YOU, MY QUEEN.
MAY I HELP YOU, CALEB?
OH, NO. I CAME HERE TO...I THOUGHT...
I UNDERSTAND... I MISS HER TOO.
LET'S HOPE SHE CAN COME BACK SOON. MERIDIAN NEEDS ITS QUEEN.

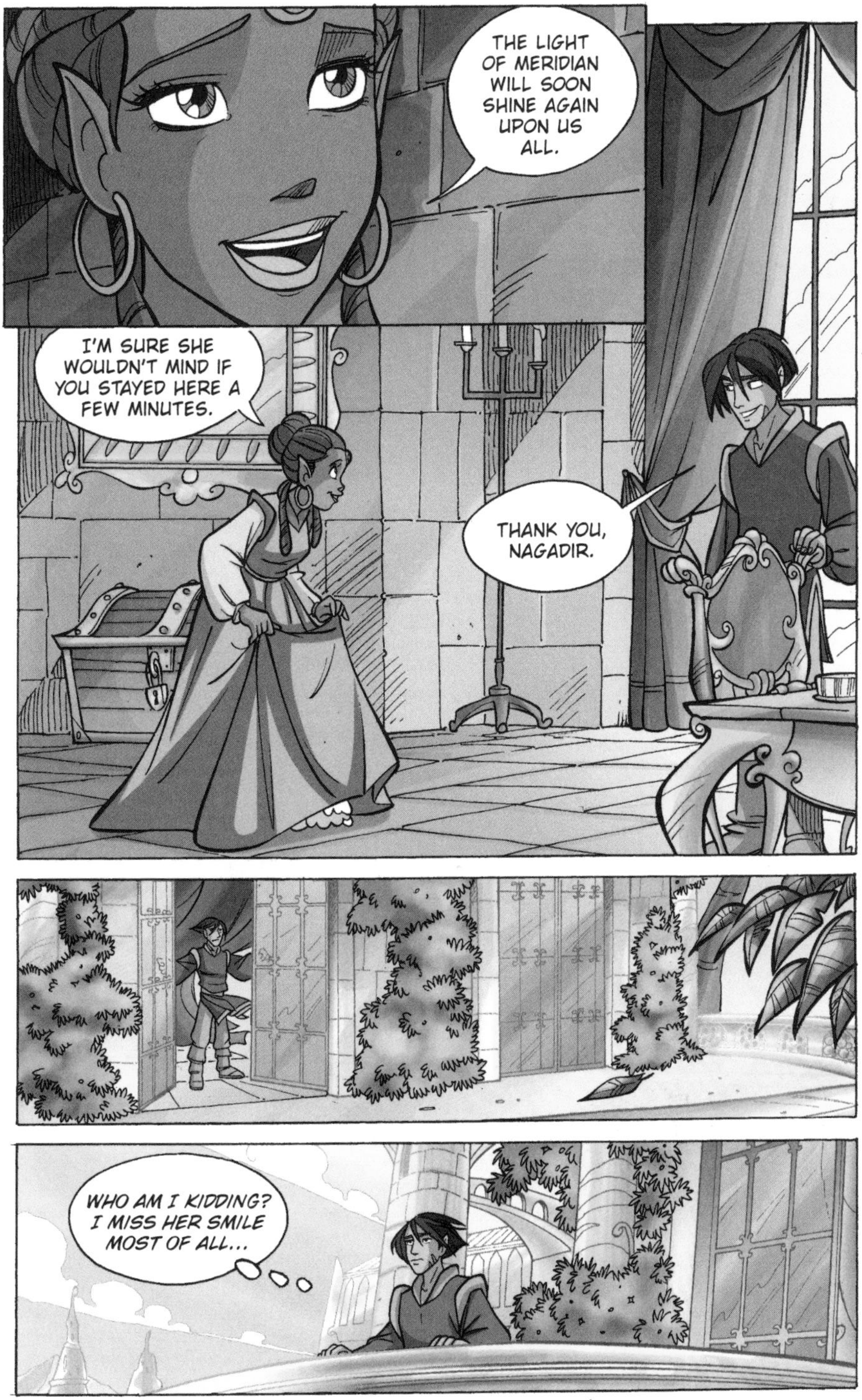
THE LIGHT OF MERIDIAN WILL SOON SHINE AGAIN UPON US ALL.
I'M SURE SHE WOULDN'T MIND IF YOU STAYED HERE A FEW MINUTES.
THANK YOU, NAGADIR.
WHO AM I KIDDING? I MISS HER SMILE MOST OF ALL...

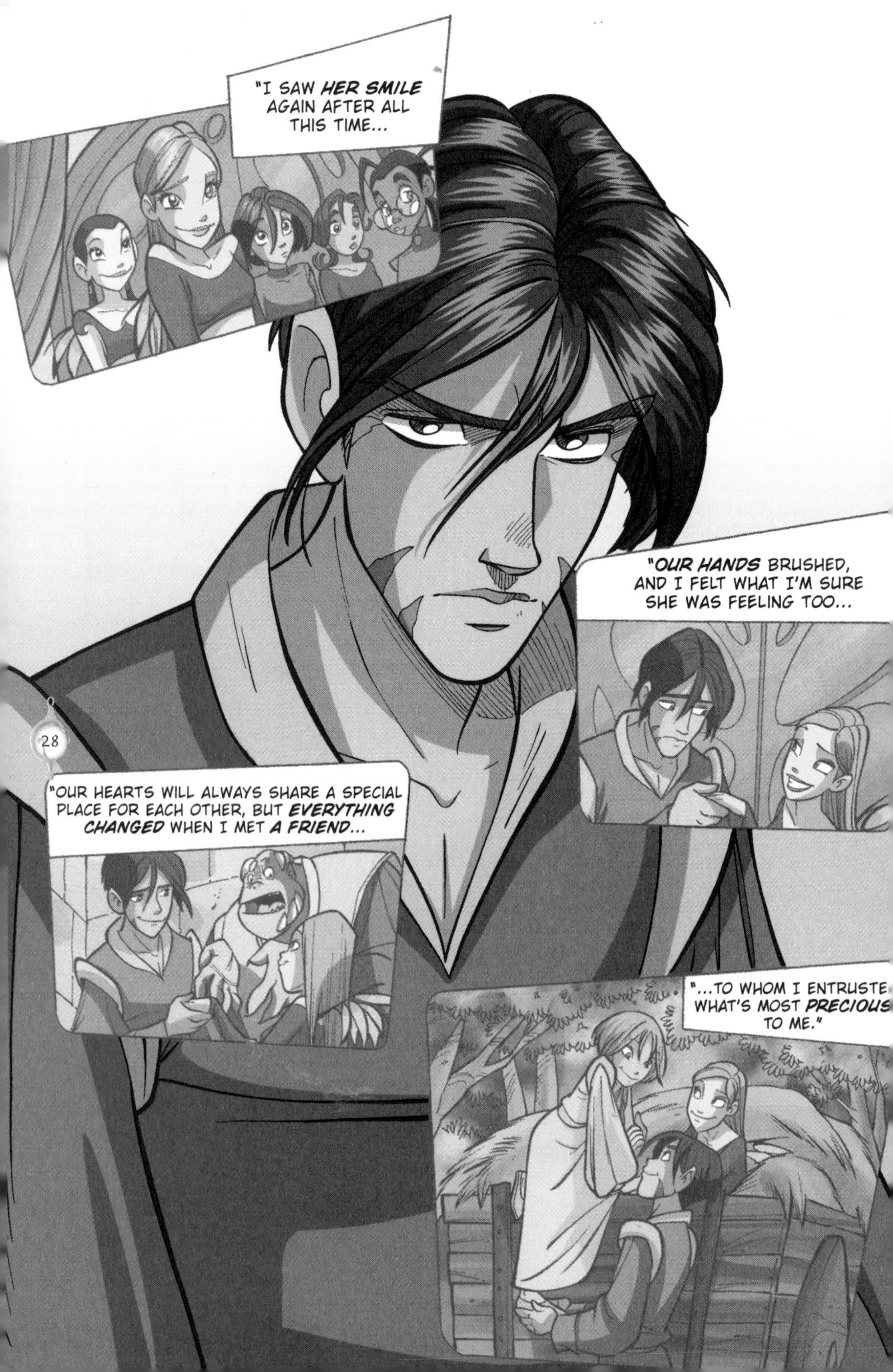

"I SAW HER SMILE AGAIN AFTER ALL THIS TIME...
"OUR HANDS BRUSHED, AND I FELT WHAT I'M SURE SHE WAS FEELING TOO...
"OUR HEARTS WILL ALWAYS SHARE A SPECIAL PLACE FOR EACH OTHER, BUT EVERYTHING CHANGED WHEN I MET A FRIEND...
"...TO WHOM I ENTRUSTE WHAT'S MOST PRECIOUS TO ME."

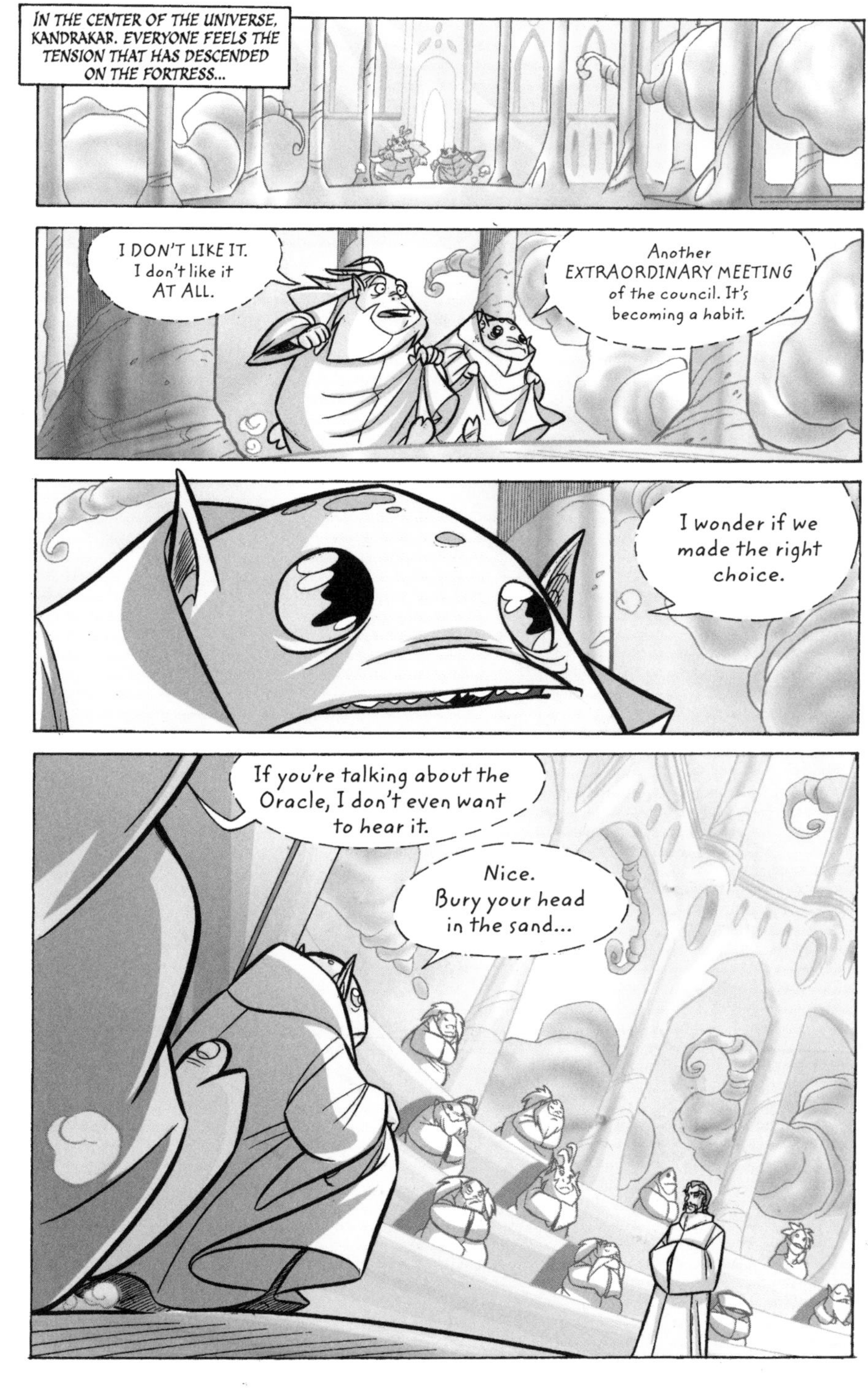
IN THE CENTER OF THE UNIVERSE, KANDRAKAR. EVERYONE FEELS THE TENSION THAT HAS DESCENDED ON THE FORTRESS...
I DON'T LIKE IT. I don't like it AT ALL.
Another EXTRAORDINARY MEETING of the council. It's becoming a habit.
I wonder if we made the right choice.
If you're talking about the Oracle, I don't even want to hear it.
Nice. Bury your head in the sand...

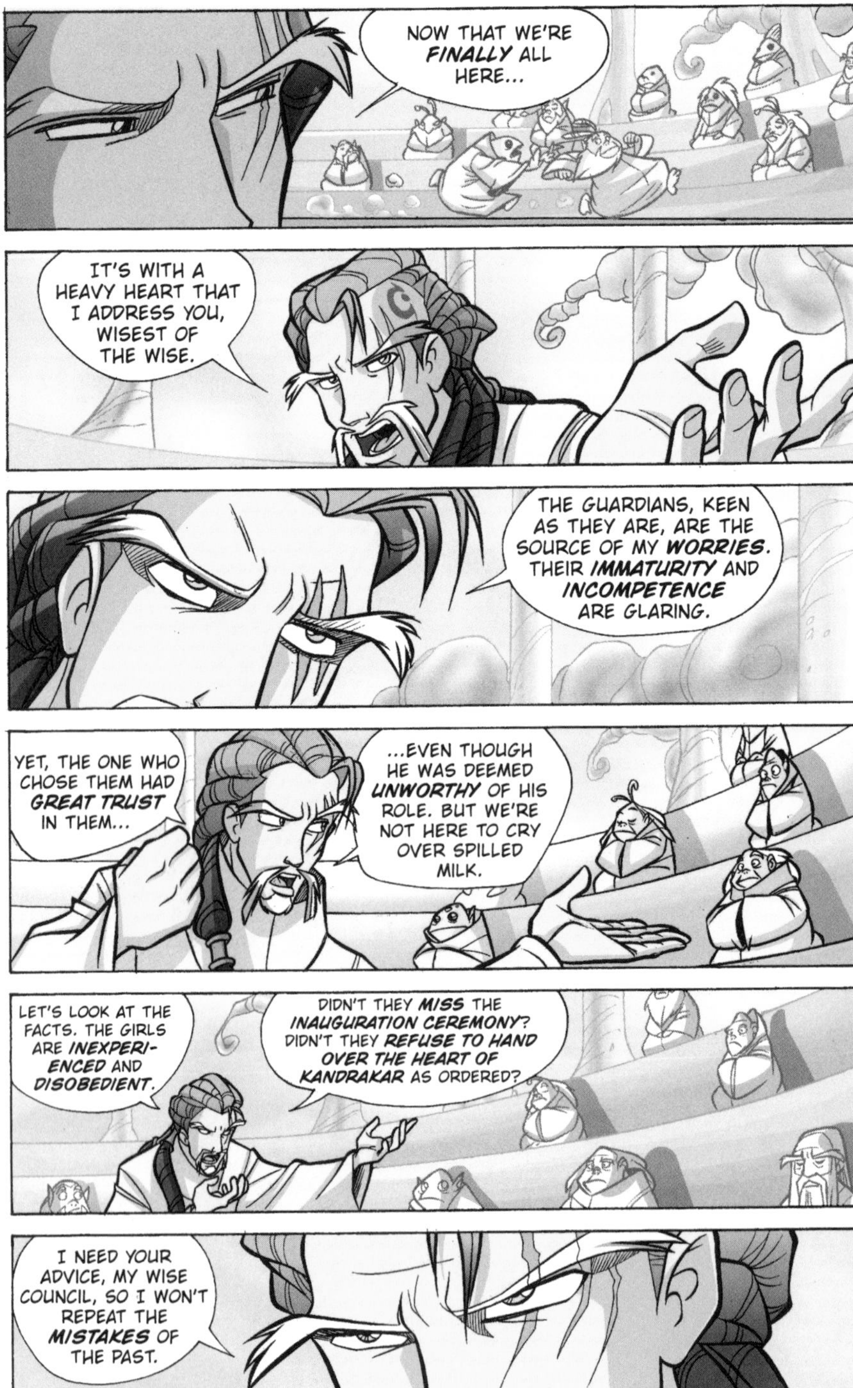
NOW THAT WE'RE FINALLY ALL HERE...
IT'S WITH A HEAVY HEART THAT I ADDRESS YOU, WISEST OF THE WISE.
THE GUARDIANS, KEEN AS THEY ARE, ARE THE SOURCE OF MY WORRIES. THEIR IMMATURITY AND INCOMPETENCE ARE GLARING.
YET, THE ONE WHO CHOSE THEM HAD GREAT TRUST IN THEM...
...EVEN THOUGH HE WAS DEEMED UNWORTHY OF HIS ROLE. BUT WE'RE NOT HERE TO CRY OVER SPILLED MILK.
LET'S LOOK AT THE FACTS. THE GIRLS ARE INEXPERI-ENCED AND DISOBEDIENT.
DIDN'T THEY MISS THE INAUGURATION CEREMONY? DIDN'T THEY REFUSE TO HAND OVER THE HEART OF KANDRAKAR AS ORDERED?
I NEED YOUR ADVICE, MY WISE COUNCIL, SO I WON'T REPEAT THE MISTAKES OF THE PAST.

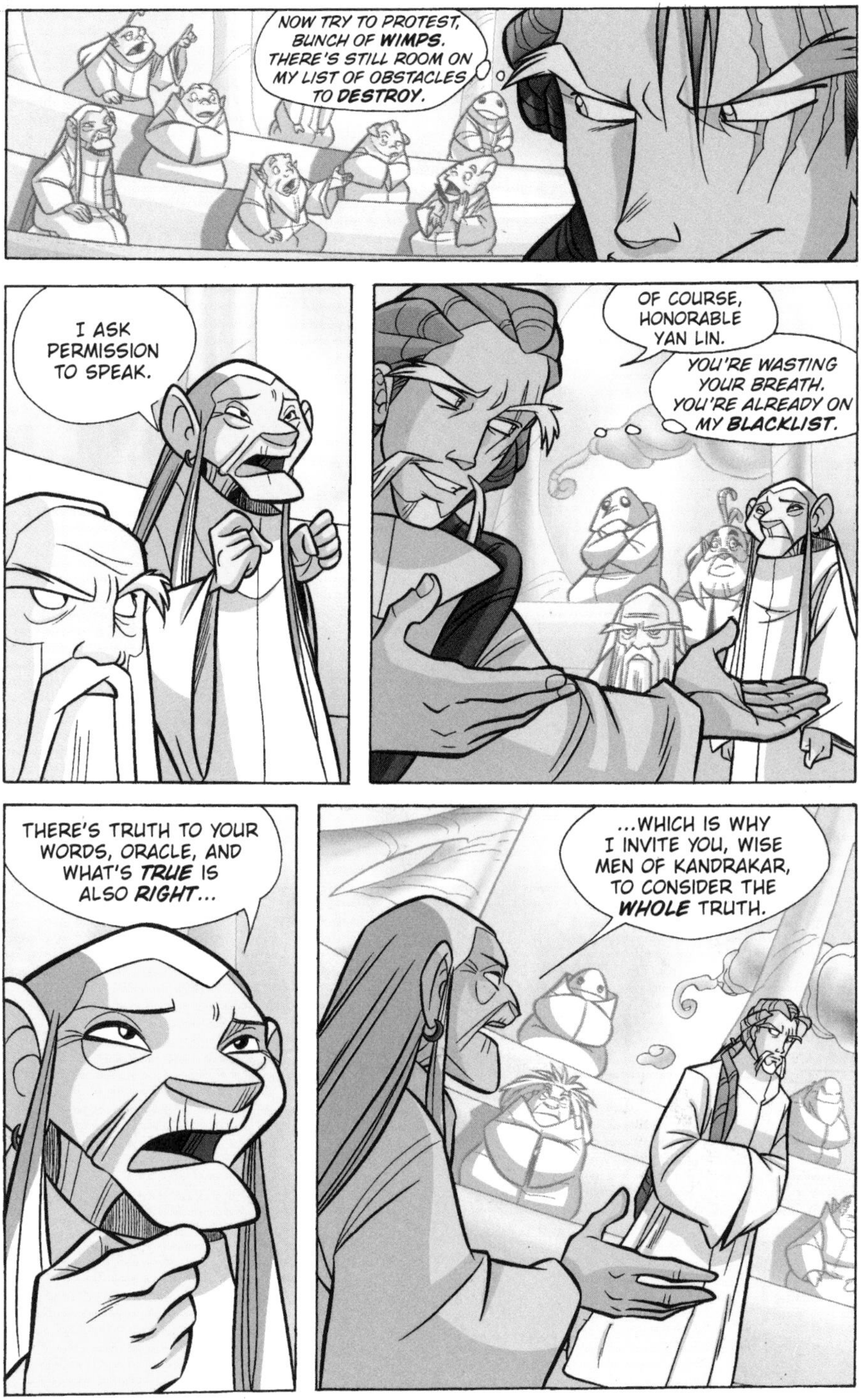
NOW TRY TO PROTEST, BUNCH OF WIMPS. THERE'S STILL ROOM ON MY LIST OF OBSTACLES TO DESTROY.
I ASK PERMISSION TO SPEAK.
OF COURSE, HONORABLE YAN LIN.
YOU'RE WASTING YOUR BREATH. YOU'RE ALREADY ON MY BLACKLIST.
THERE'S TRUTH TO YOUR WORDS, ORACLE, AND WHAT'S TRUE IS ALSO RIGHT...
...WHICH IS WHY I INVITE YOU, WISE MEN OF KANDRAKAR, TO CONSIDER THE WHOLE TRUTH.

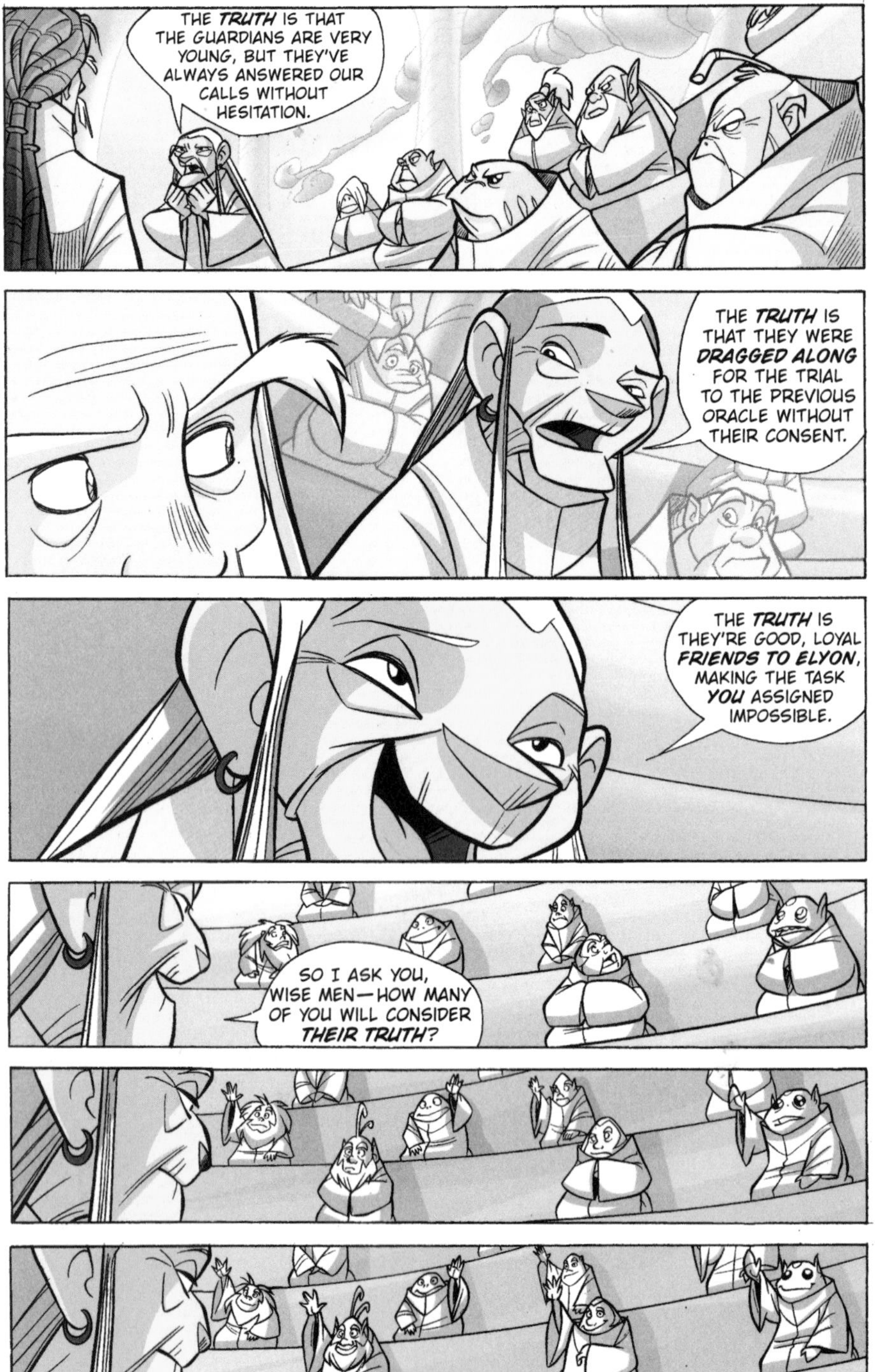
THE TRUTH IS THAT THE GUARDIANS ARE VERY YOUNG, BUT THEY'VE ALWAYS ANSWERED OUR CALLS WITHOUT HESITATION.
THE TRUTH IS THAT THEY WERE DRAGGED ALONG FOR THE TRIAL TO THE PREVIOUS ORACLE WITHOUT THEIR CONSENT.
THE TRUTH IS THEY'RE GOOD, LOYAL FRIENDS TO ELYON, MAKING THE TASK YOU ASSIGNED IMPOSSIBLE.
SO I ASK YOU, WISE MEN—HOW MANY OF YOU WILL CONSIDER THEIR TRUTH?

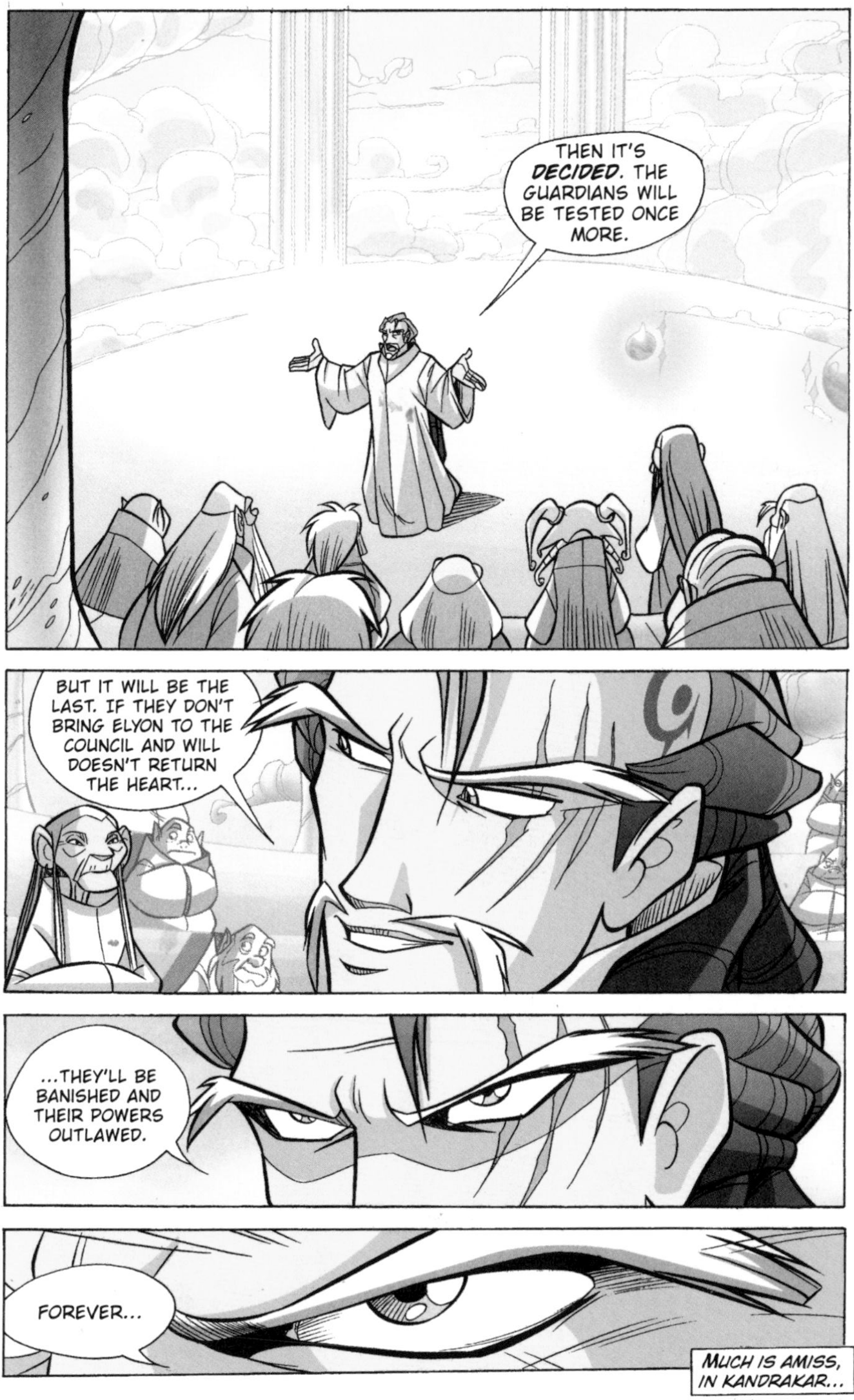
THEN IT'S *DECIDED*. THE GUARDIANS WILL BE TESTED ONCE MORE.
BUT IT WILL BE THE LAST. IF THEY DON'T BRING ELYON TO THE COUNCIL AND WILL DOESN'T RETURN THE HEART...
...THEY'LL BE BANISHED AND THEIR POWERS OUTLAWED.
FOREVER...
MUCH IS AMISS, IN KANDRAKAR...

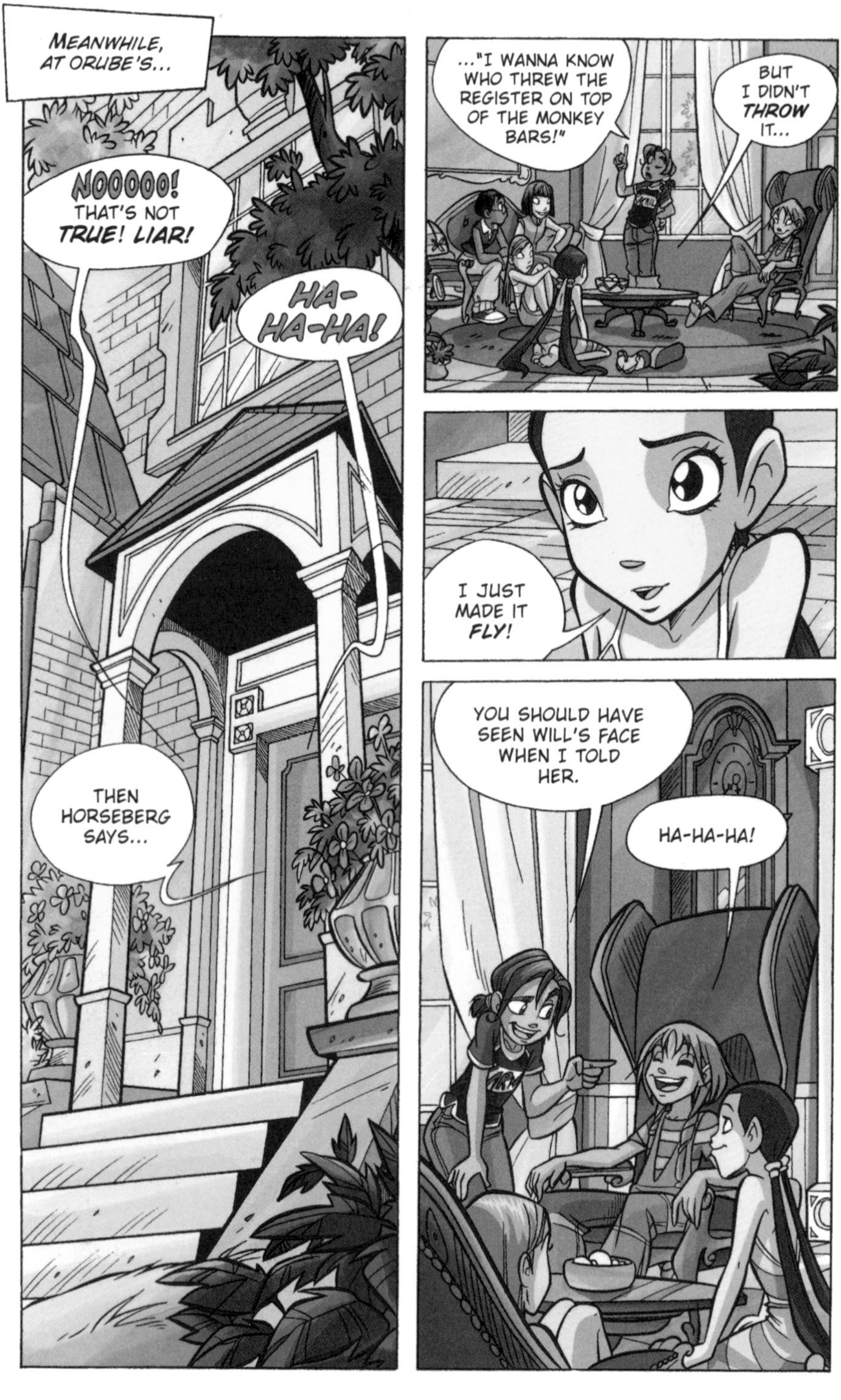
MEANWHILE, AT ORUBE'S...
NOOOOO! THAT'S NOT TRUE! LIAR!
HA-HA-HA!
THEN HORSEBERG SAYS...
..."I WANNA KNOW WHO THREW THE REGISTER ON TOP OF THE MONKEY BARS!"
BUT I DIDN'T THROW IT...
I JUST MADE IT FLY!
YOU SHOULD HAVE SEEN WILL'S FACE WHEN I TOLD HER.
HA-HA-HA!

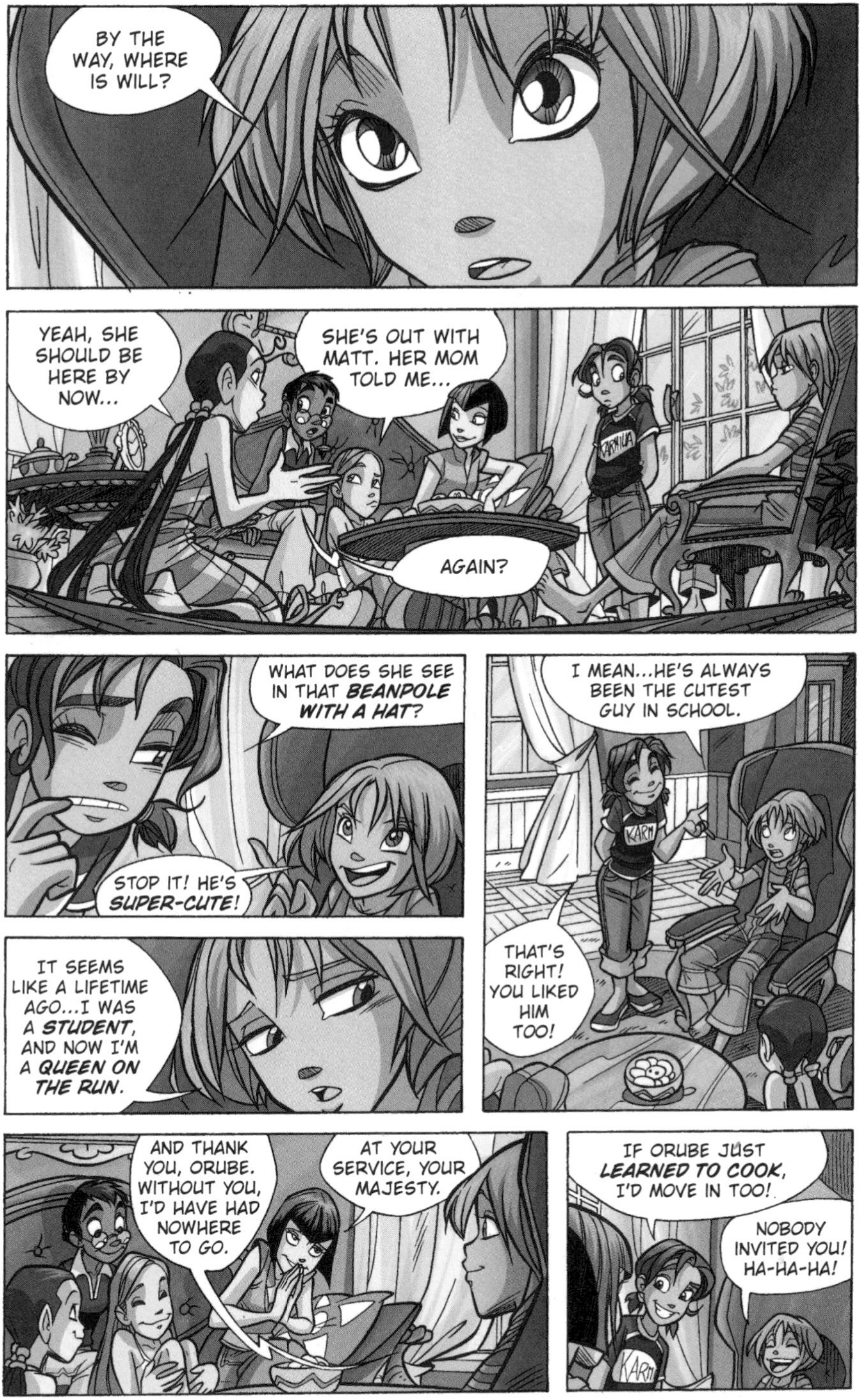
BY THE WAY, WHERE IS WILL?
YEAH, SHE SHOULD BE HERE BY NOW...
SHE'S OUT WITH MATT. HER MOM TOLD ME...
AGAIN?
KARMILLA
WHAT DOES SHE SEE IN THAT **BEANPOLE WITH A HAT**?
STOP IT! HE'S **SUPER-CUTE**!
I MEAN...HE'S ALWAYS BEEN THE CUTEST GUY IN SCHOOL.
KARM
THAT'S RIGHT! YOU LIKED HIM TOO!
IT SEEMS LIKE A LIFETIME AGO...I WAS A **STUDENT**, AND NOW I'M A **QUEEN ON THE RUN**.
AND THANK YOU, ORUBE. WITHOUT YOU, I'D HAVE HAD NOWHERE TO GO.
AT YOUR SERVICE, YOUR MAJESTY.
IF ORUBE JUST **LEARNED TO COOK**, I'D MOVE IN TOO!
NOBODY INVITED YOU! HA-HA-HA!
KARM

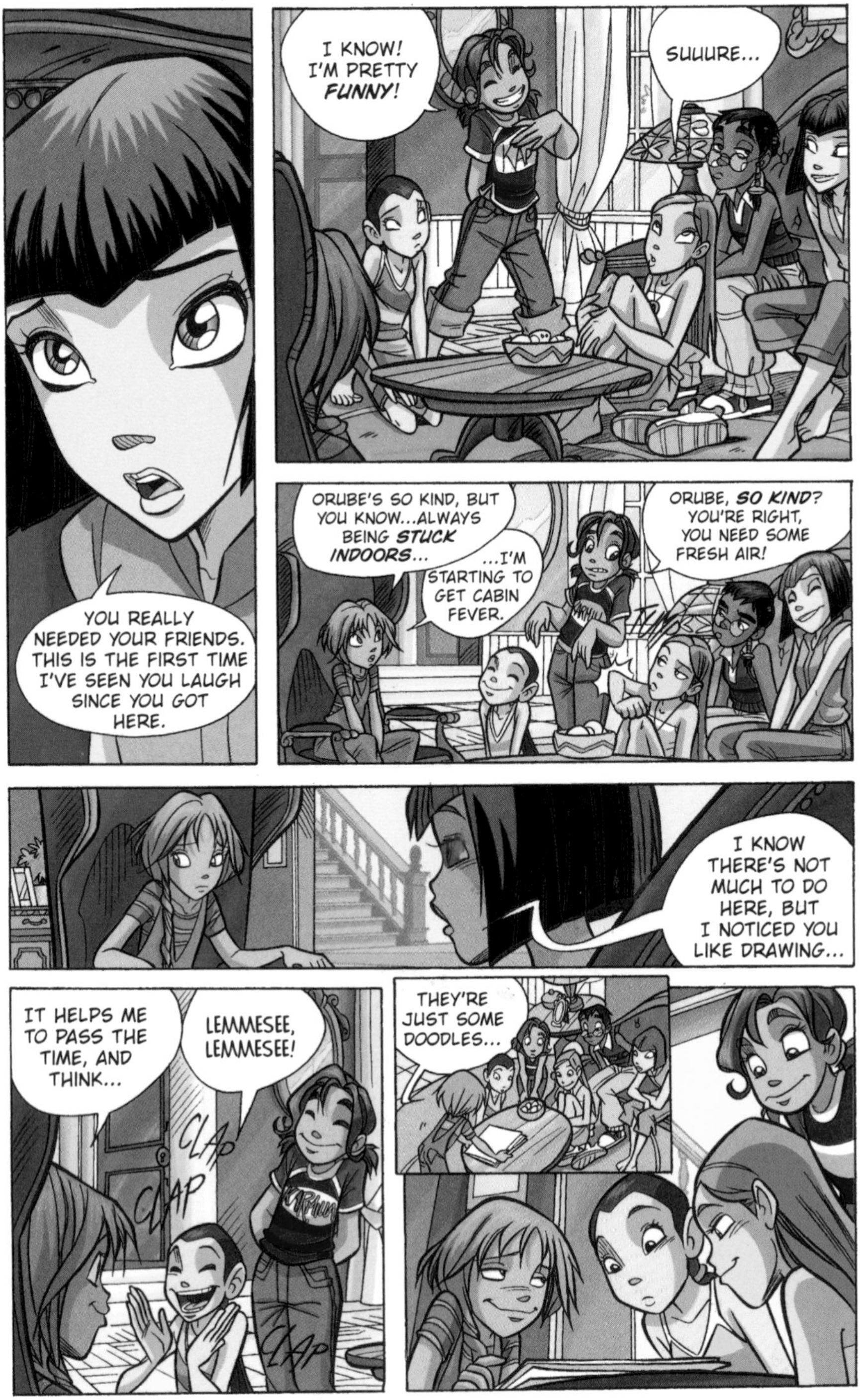
I KNOW! I'M PRETTY FUNNY!
SUUURE...
YOU REALLY NEEDED YOUR FRIENDS. THIS IS THE FIRST TIME I'VE SEEN YOU LAUGH SINCE YOU GOT HERE.
ORUBE'S SO KIND, BUT YOU KNOW...ALWAYS BEING STUCK INDOORS...
...I'M STARTING TO GET CABIN FEVER.
ORUBE, SO KIND? YOU'RE RIGHT, YOU NEED SOME FRESH AIR!
I KNOW THERE'S NOT MUCH TO DO HERE, BUT I NOTICED YOU LIKE DRAWING...
IT HELPS ME TO PASS THE TIME, AND THINK...
LEMMESEE, LEMMESEE!
CLAP
CLAP
CLAP
THEY'RE JUST SOME DOODLES...

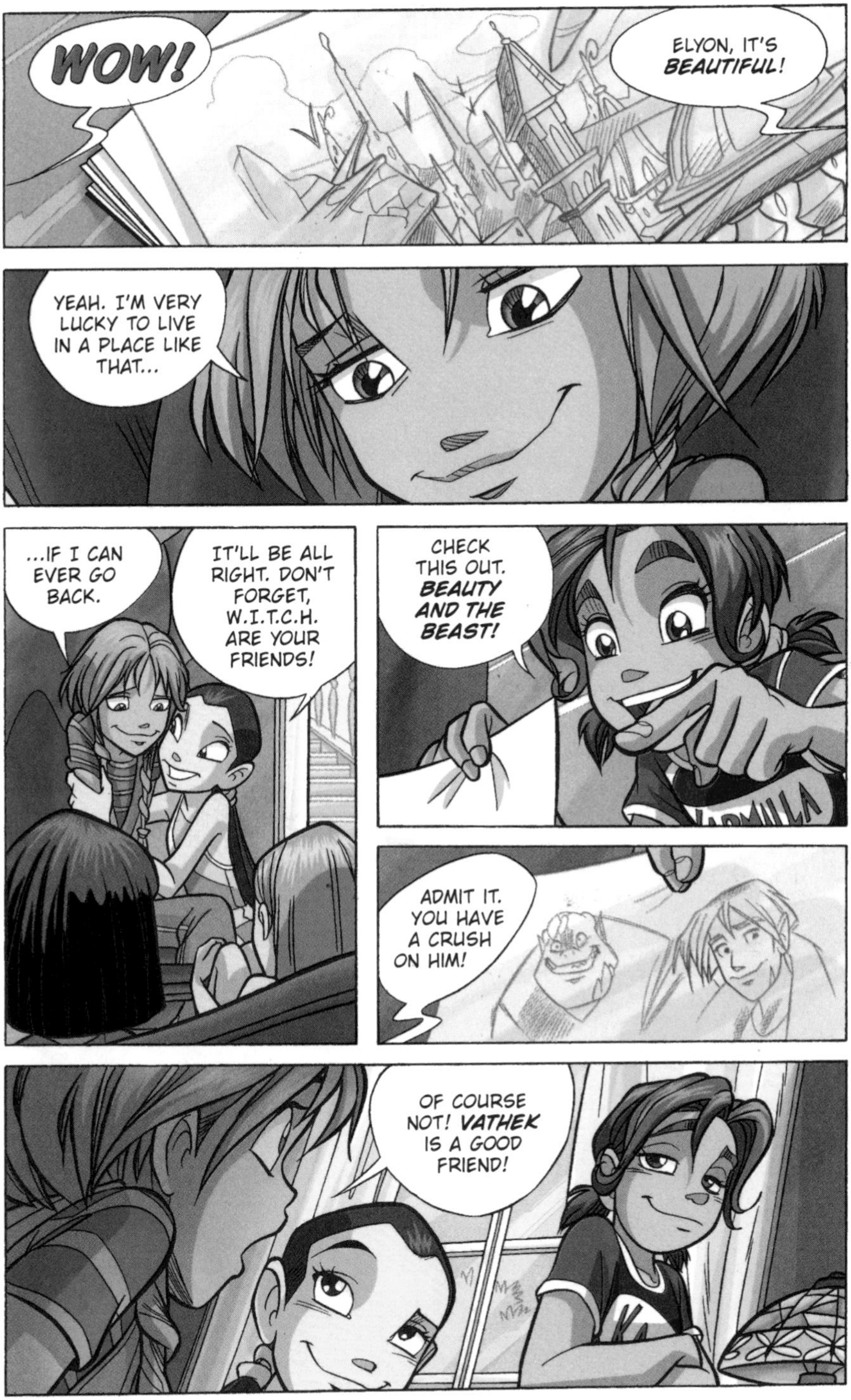
WOW!
ELYON, IT'S **BEAUTIFUL!**
YEAH. I'M VERY LUCKY TO LIVE IN A PLACE LIKE THAT...
...IF I CAN EVER GO BACK.
IT'LL BE ALL RIGHT. DON'T FORGET, W.I.T.C.H. ARE YOUR FRIENDS!
CHECK THIS OUT. ***BEAUTY AND THE BEAST!***
ADMIT IT. YOU HAVE A CRUSH ON HIM!
OF COURSE NOT! ***VATHEK*** IS A GOOD FRIEND!

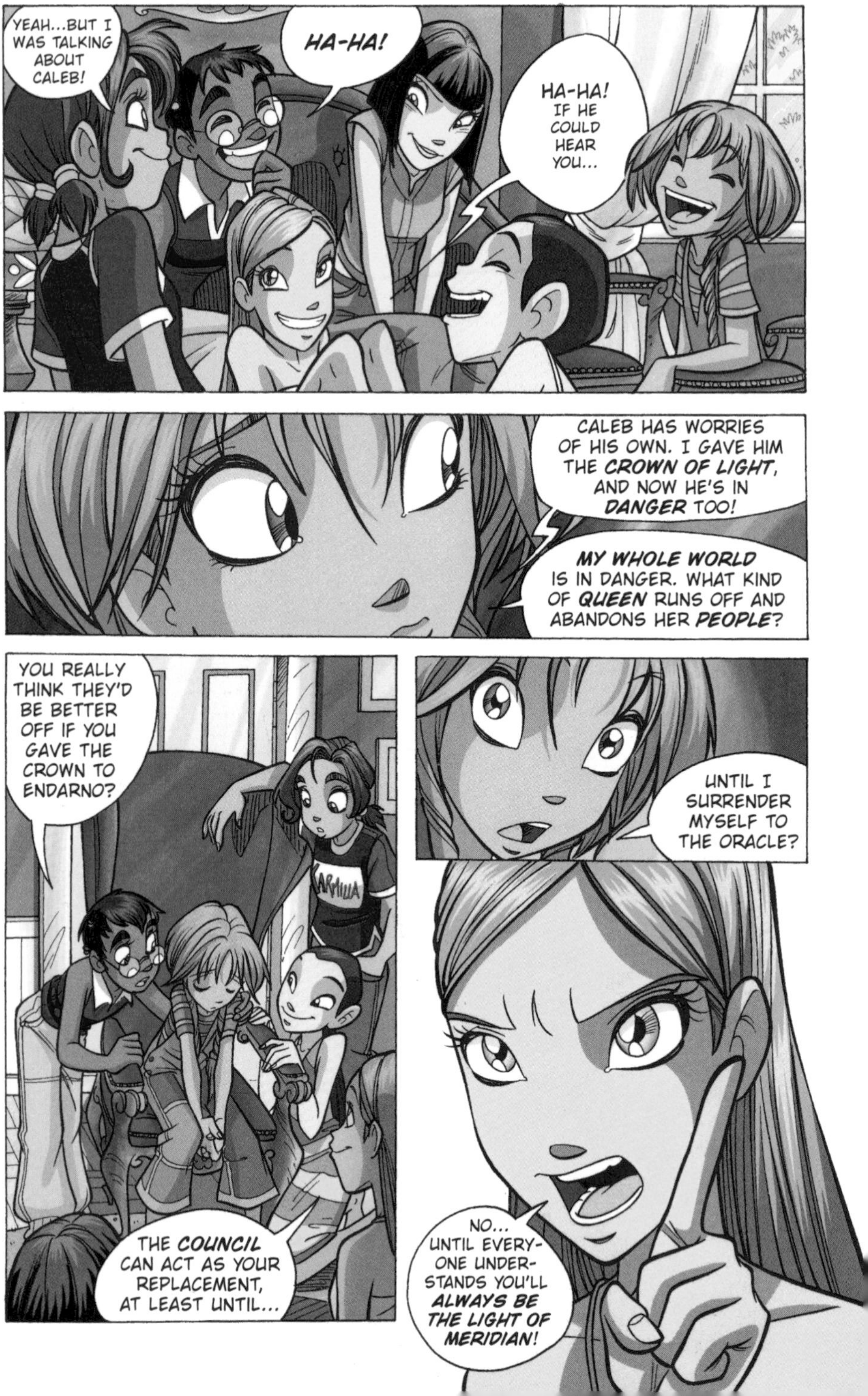
YEAH...BUT I WAS TALKING ABOUT CALEB!
HA-HA!
HA-HA! IF HE COULD HEAR YOU...
CALEB HAS WORRIES OF HIS OWN. I GAVE HIM THE CROWN OF LIGHT, AND NOW HE'S IN DANGER TOO!
MY WHOLE WORLD IS IN DANGER. WHAT KIND OF QUEEN RUNS OFF AND ABANDONS HER PEOPLE?
YOU REALLY THINK THEY'D BE BETTER OFF IF YOU GAVE THE CROWN TO ENDARNO?
KARMILLA
THE COUNCIL CAN ACT AS YOUR REPLACEMENT, AT LEAST UNTIL...
UNTIL I SURRENDER MYSELF TO THE ORACLE?
NO... UNTIL EVERYONE UNDERSTANDS YOU'LL ALWAYS BE THE LIGHT OF MERIDIAN!

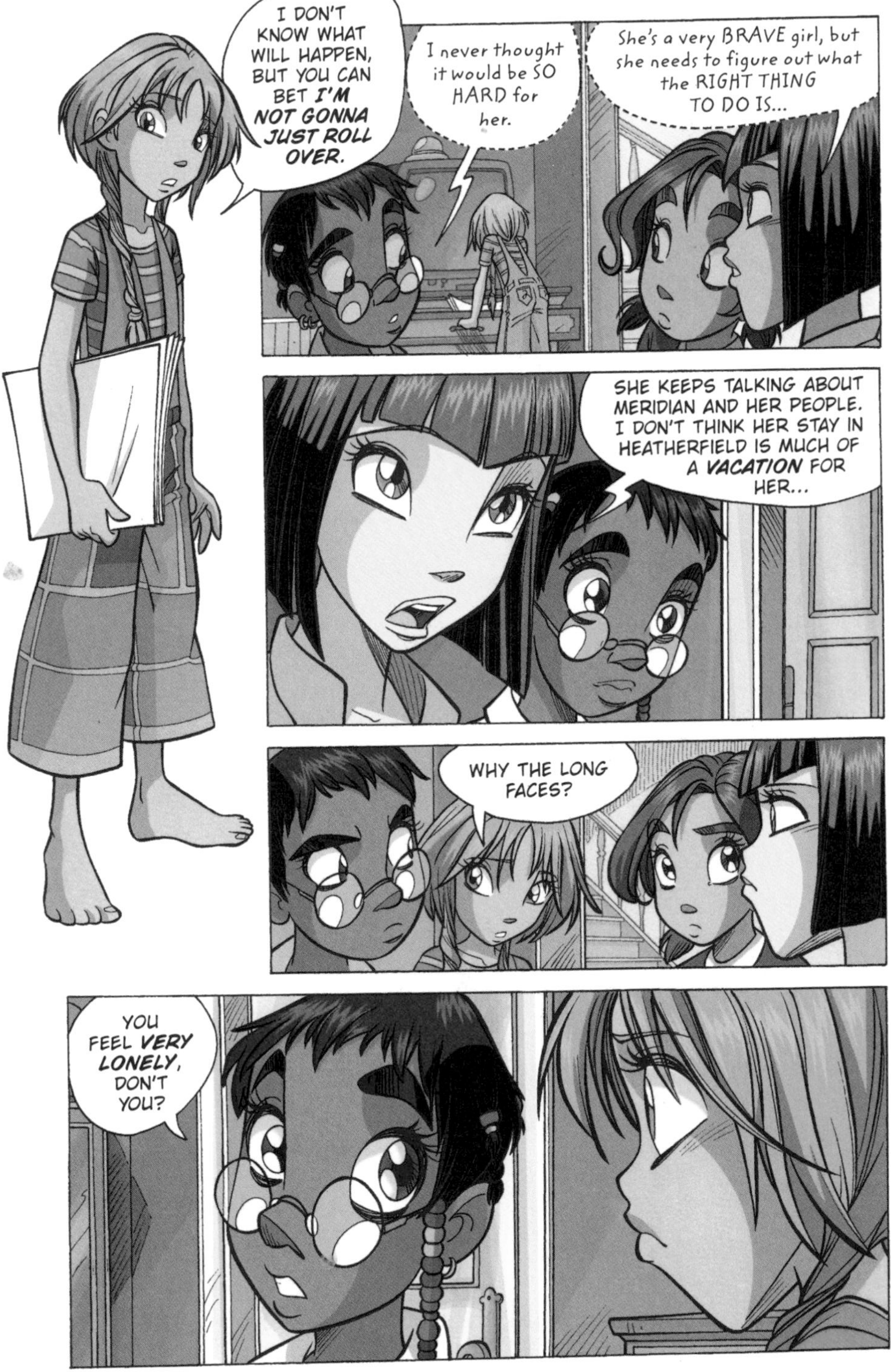
I DON'T KNOW WHAT WILL HAPPEN, BUT YOU CAN BET *I'M NOT GONNA JUST ROLL OVER.*
I never thought it would be SO HARD for her.
She's a very BRAVE girl, but she needs to figure out what the RIGHT THING TO DO IS...
SHE KEEPS TALKING ABOUT MERIDIAN AND HER PEOPLE. I DON'T THINK HER STAY IN HEATHERFIELD IS MUCH OF A *VACATION* FOR HER...
WHY THE LONG FACES?
YOU FEEL *VERY LONELY*, DON'T YOU?

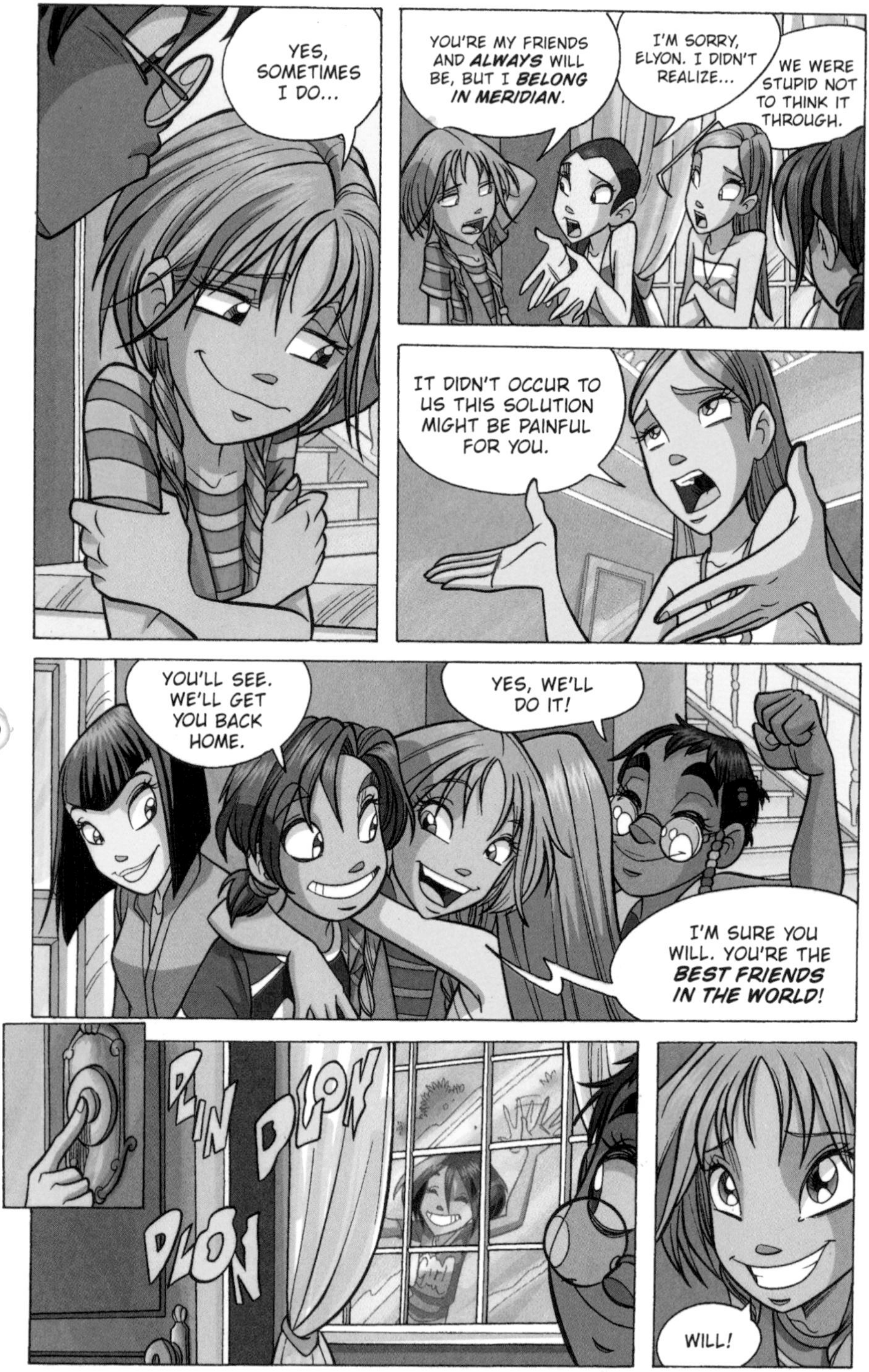
YES, SOMETIMES I DO...
YOU'RE MY FRIENDS AND ALWAYS WILL BE, BUT I BELONG IN MERIDIAN.
I'M SORRY, ELYON. I DIDN'T REALIZE...
WE WERE STUPID NOT TO THINK IT THROUGH.
IT DIDN'T OCCUR TO US THIS SOLUTION MIGHT BE PAINFUL FOR YOU.
YOU'LL SEE. WE'LL GET YOU BACK HOME.
YES, WE'LL DO IT!
I'M SURE YOU WILL. YOU'RE THE BEST FRIENDS IN THE WORLD!
DLIN DLON
DLON
WILL!

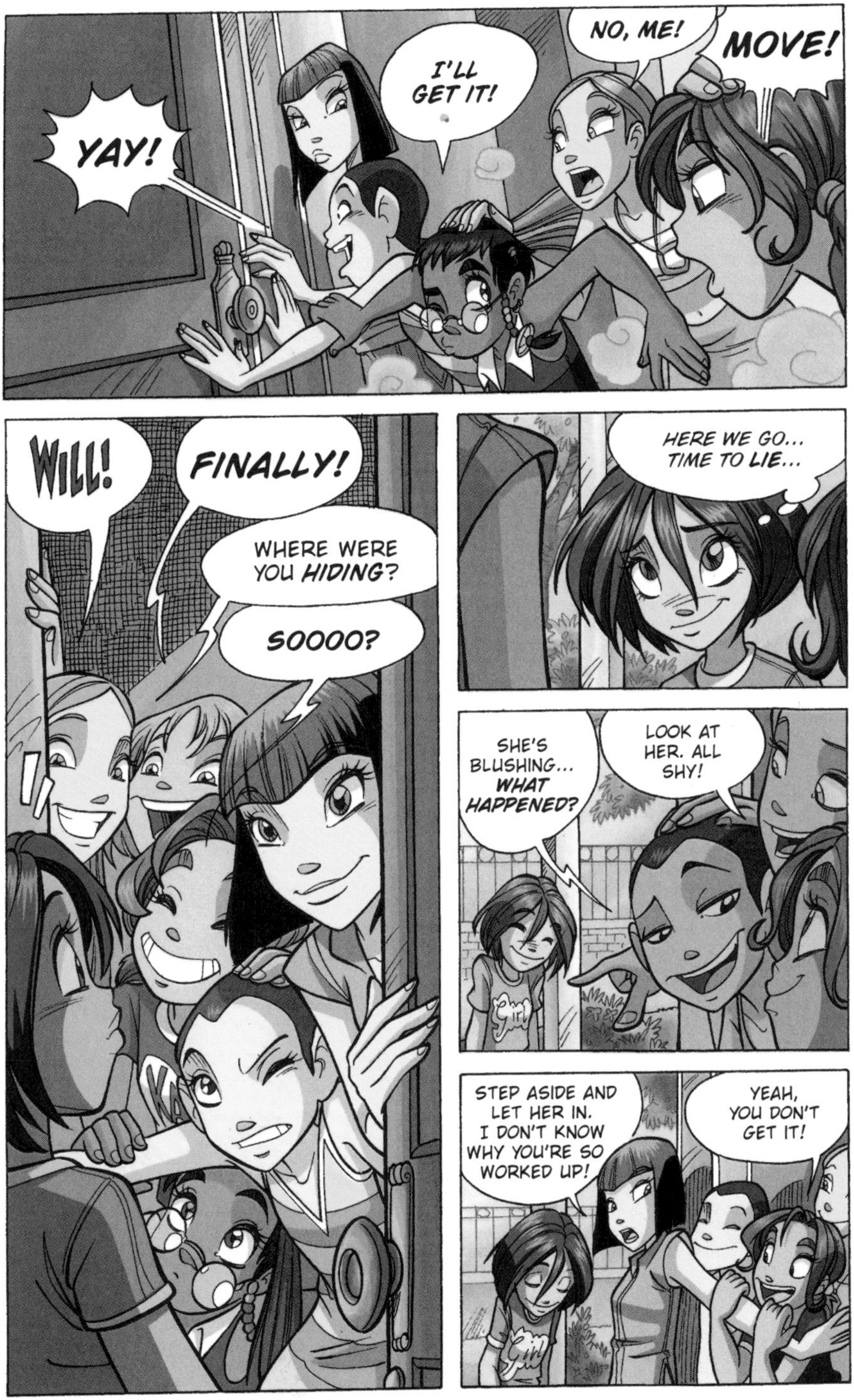
YAY!
I'LL GET IT!
NO, ME!
MOVE!
WILL!
FINALLY!
WHERE WERE YOU HIDING?
SOOOO?
HERE WE GO... TIME TO LIE...
SHE'S BLUSHING... WHAT HAPPENED?
LOOK AT HER. ALL SHY!
STEP ASIDE AND LET HER IN. I DON'T KNOW WHY YOU'RE SO WORKED UP!
YEAH, YOU DON'T GET IT!

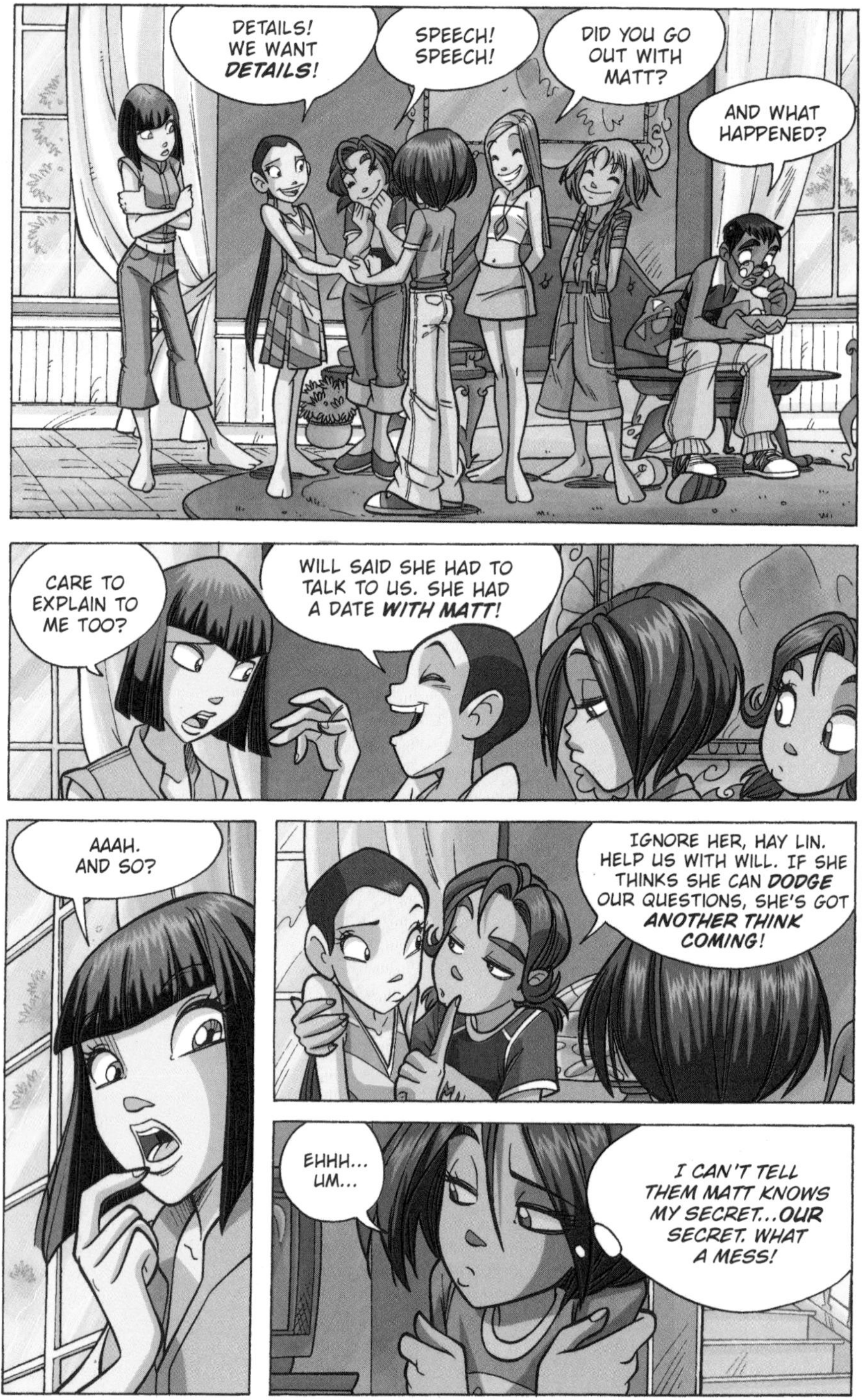
DETAILS! WE WANT DETAILS!
SPEECH! SPEECH!
DID YOU GO OUT WITH MATT?
AND WHAT HAPPENED?
CARE TO EXPLAIN TO ME TOO?
WILL SAID SHE HAD TO TALK TO US. SHE HAD A DATE WITH MATT!
AAAH. AND SO?
IGNORE HER, HAY LIN. HELP US WITH WILL. IF SHE THINKS SHE CAN DODGE OUR QUESTIONS, SHE'S GOT ANOTHER THINK COMING!
EHHH... UM...
I CAN'T TELL THEM MATT KNOWS MY SECRET...OUR SECRET. WHAT A MESS!

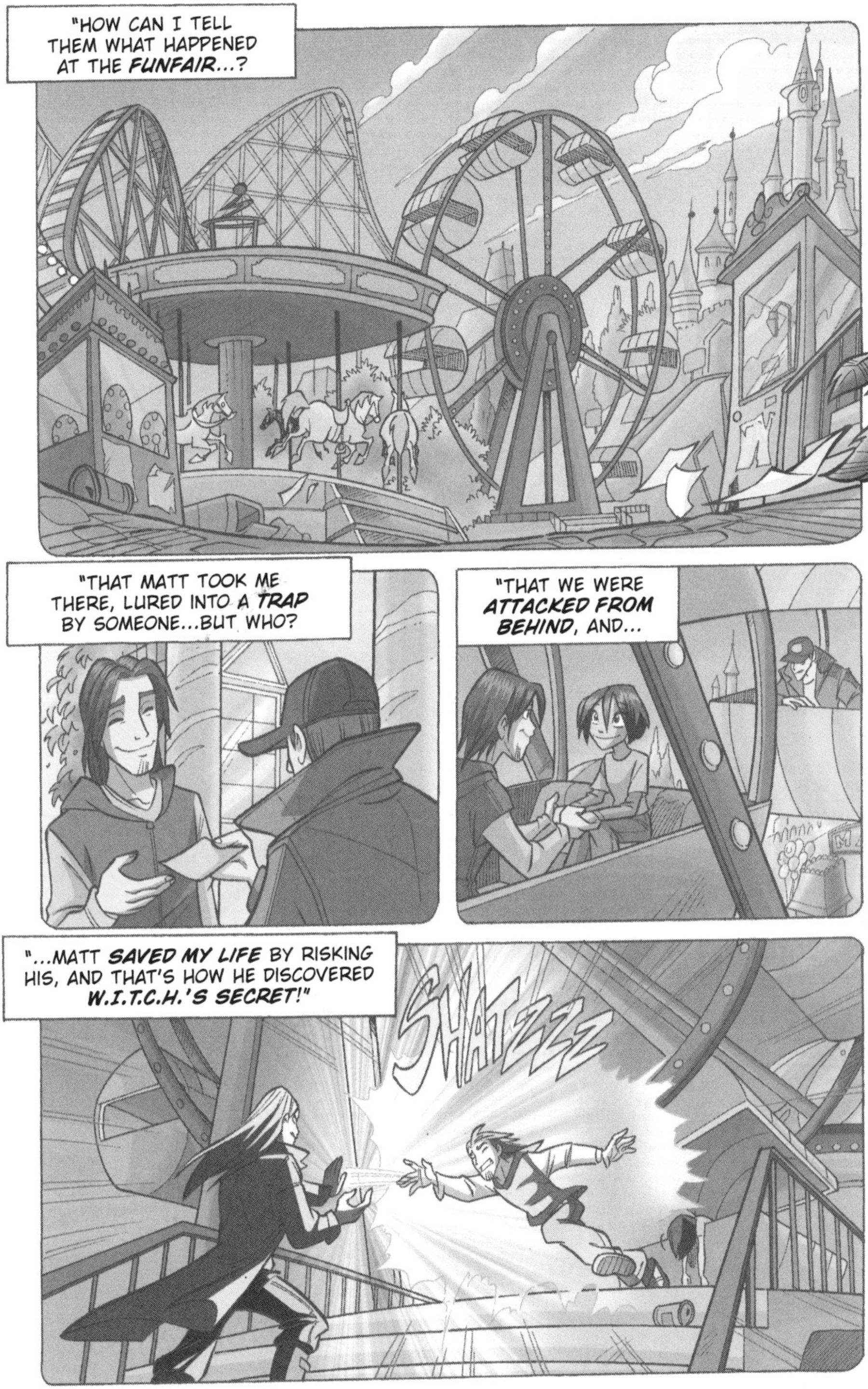
"HOW CAN I TELL THEM WHAT HAPPENED AT THE FUNFAIR...?
"THAT MATT TOOK ME THERE, LURED INTO A TRAP BY SOMEONE...BUT WHO?
"THAT WE WERE ATTACKED FROM BEHIND, AND...
"...MATT SAVED MY LIFE BY RISKING HIS, AND THAT'S HOW HE DISCOVERED W.I.T.C.H.'S SECRET!"
SHATZZZ

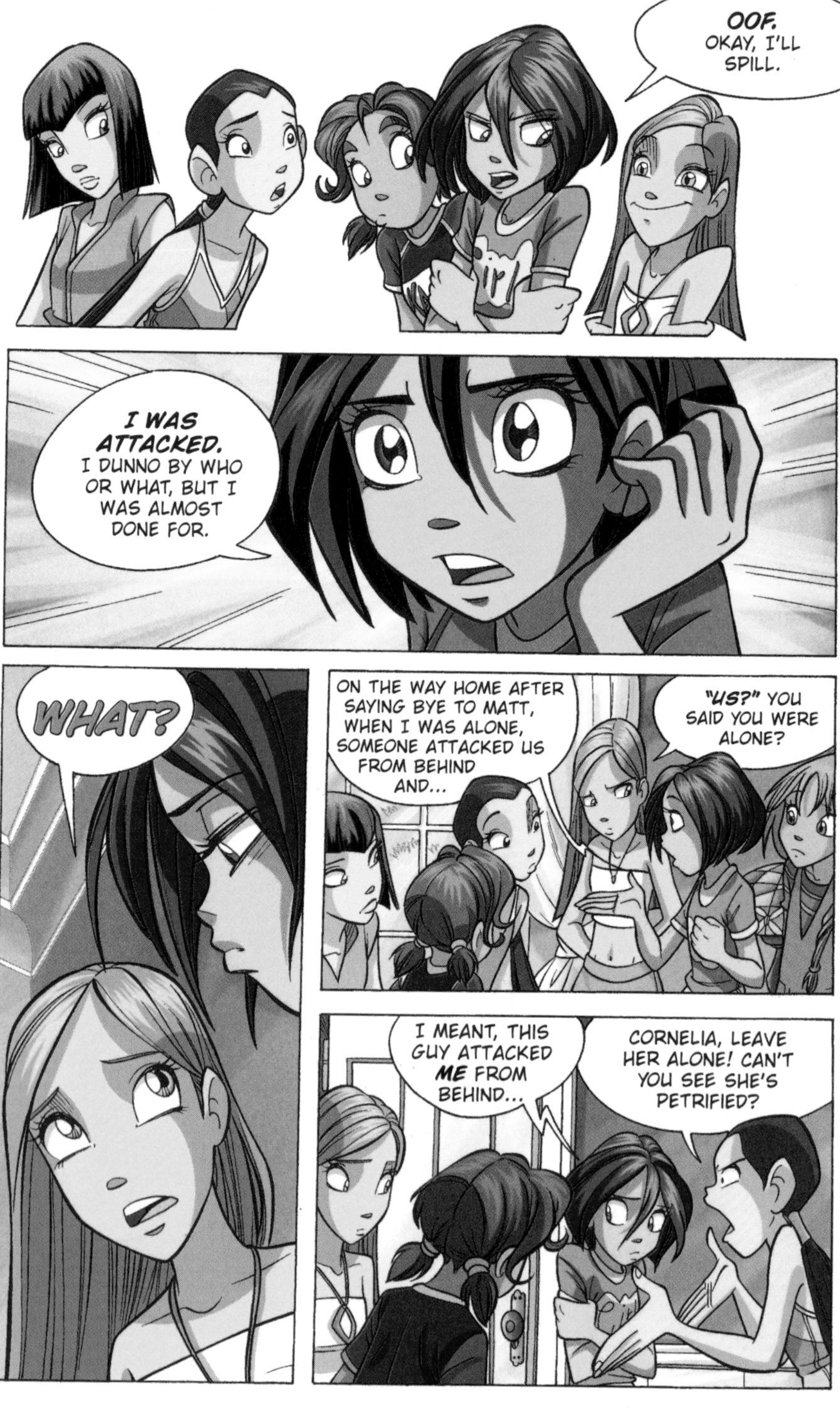
OOF. OKAY, I'LL SPILL.
I WAS ATTACKED. I DUNNO BY WHO OR WHAT, BUT I WAS ALMOST DONE FOR.
WHAT?
ON THE WAY HOME AFTER SAYING BYE TO MATT, WHEN I WAS ALONE, SOMEONE ATTACKED US FROM BEHIND AND...
"US?" YOU SAID YOU WERE ALONE?
I MEANT, THIS GUY ATTACKED ME FROM BEHIND...
CORNELIA, LEAVE HER ALONE! CAN'T YOU SEE SHE'S PETRIFIED?

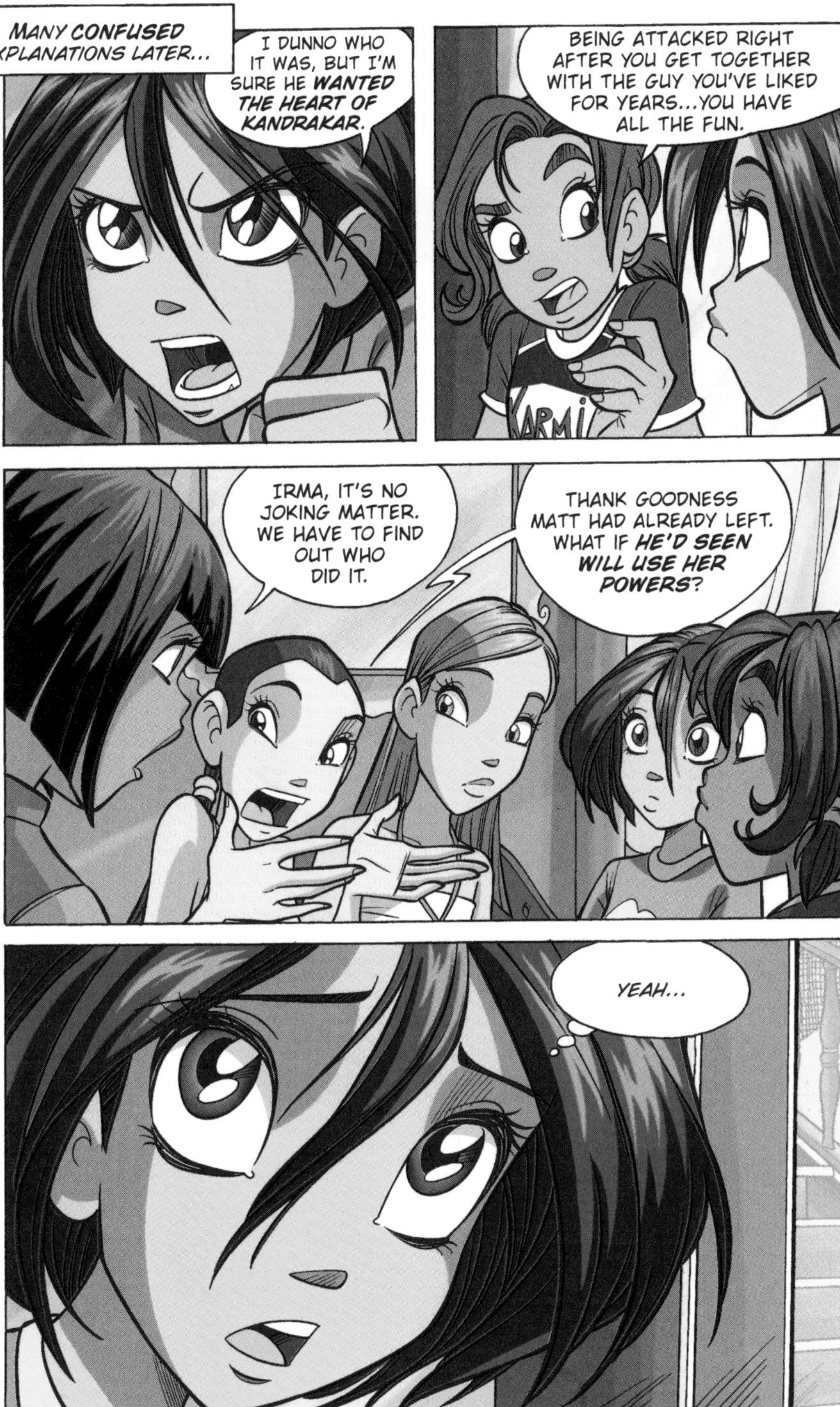
MANY **CONFUSED** EXPLANATIONS LATER...
I DUNNO WHO IT WAS, BUT I'M SURE HE ***WANTED THE HEART OF KANDRAKAR***.
BEING ATTACKED RIGHT AFTER YOU GET TOGETHER WITH THE GUY YOU'VE LIKED FOR YEARS...YOU HAVE ALL THE FUN.
IRMA, IT'S NO JOKING MATTER. WE HAVE TO FIND OUT WHO DID IT.
THANK GOODNESS MATT HAD ALREADY LEFT. WHAT IF ***HE'D SEEN WILL USE HER POWERS***?
YEAH...

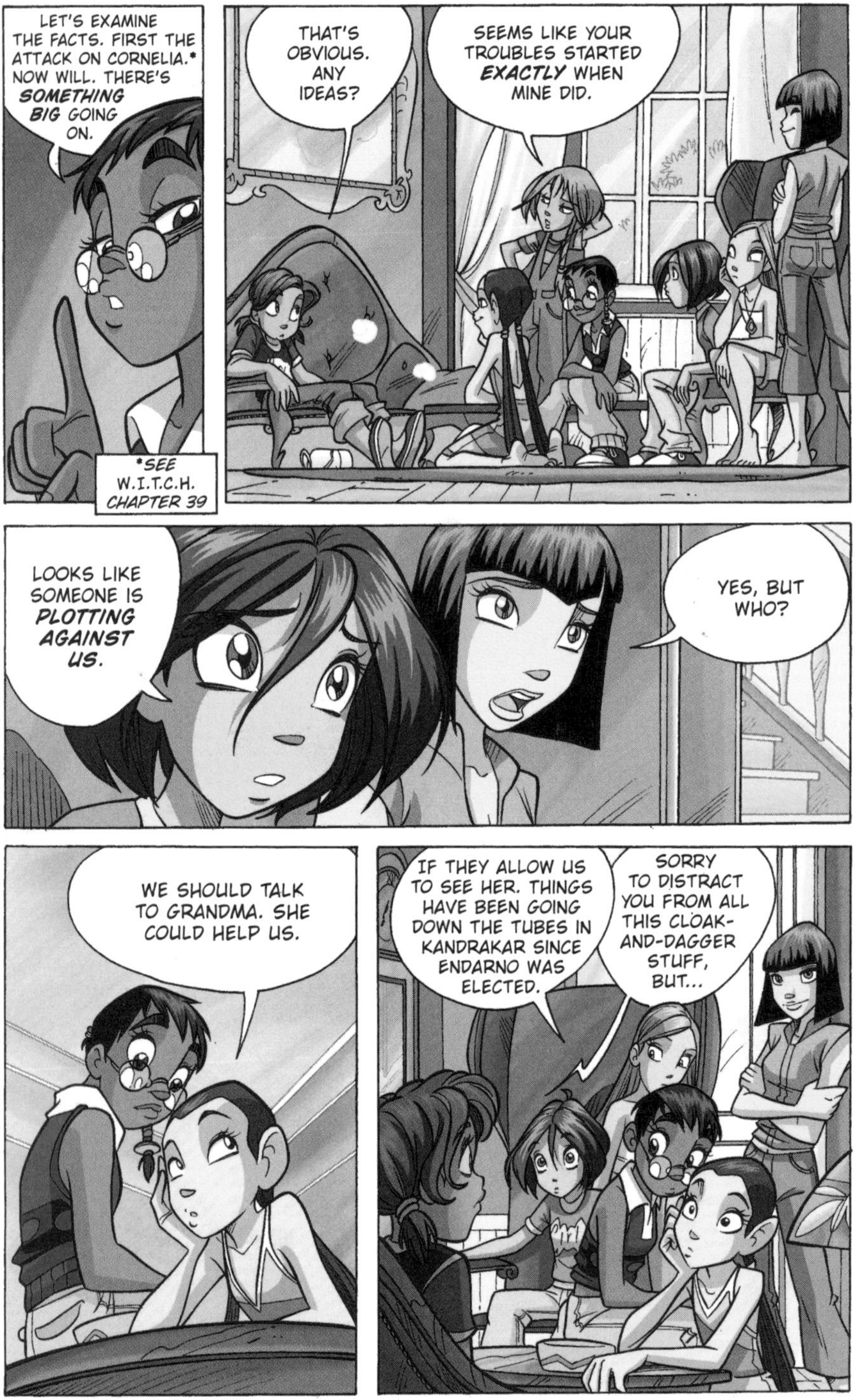

LET'S EXAMINE THE FACTS. FIRST THE ATTACK ON CORNELIA.* NOW WILL. THERE'S SOMETHING BIG GOING ON.
*SEE W.I.T.C.H. CHAPTER 39
THAT'S OBVIOUS. ANY IDEAS?
SEEMS LIKE YOUR TROUBLES STARTED EXACTLY WHEN MINE DID.
LOOKS LIKE SOMEONE IS PLOTTING AGAINST US.
YES, BUT WHO?
WE SHOULD TALK TO GRANDMA. SHE COULD HELP US.
IF THEY ALLOW US TO SEE HER. THINGS HAVE BEEN GOING DOWN THE TUBES IN KANDRAKAR SINCE ENDARNO WAS ELECTED.
SORRY TO DISTRACT YOU FROM ALL THIS CLOAK-AND-DAGGER STUFF, BUT...

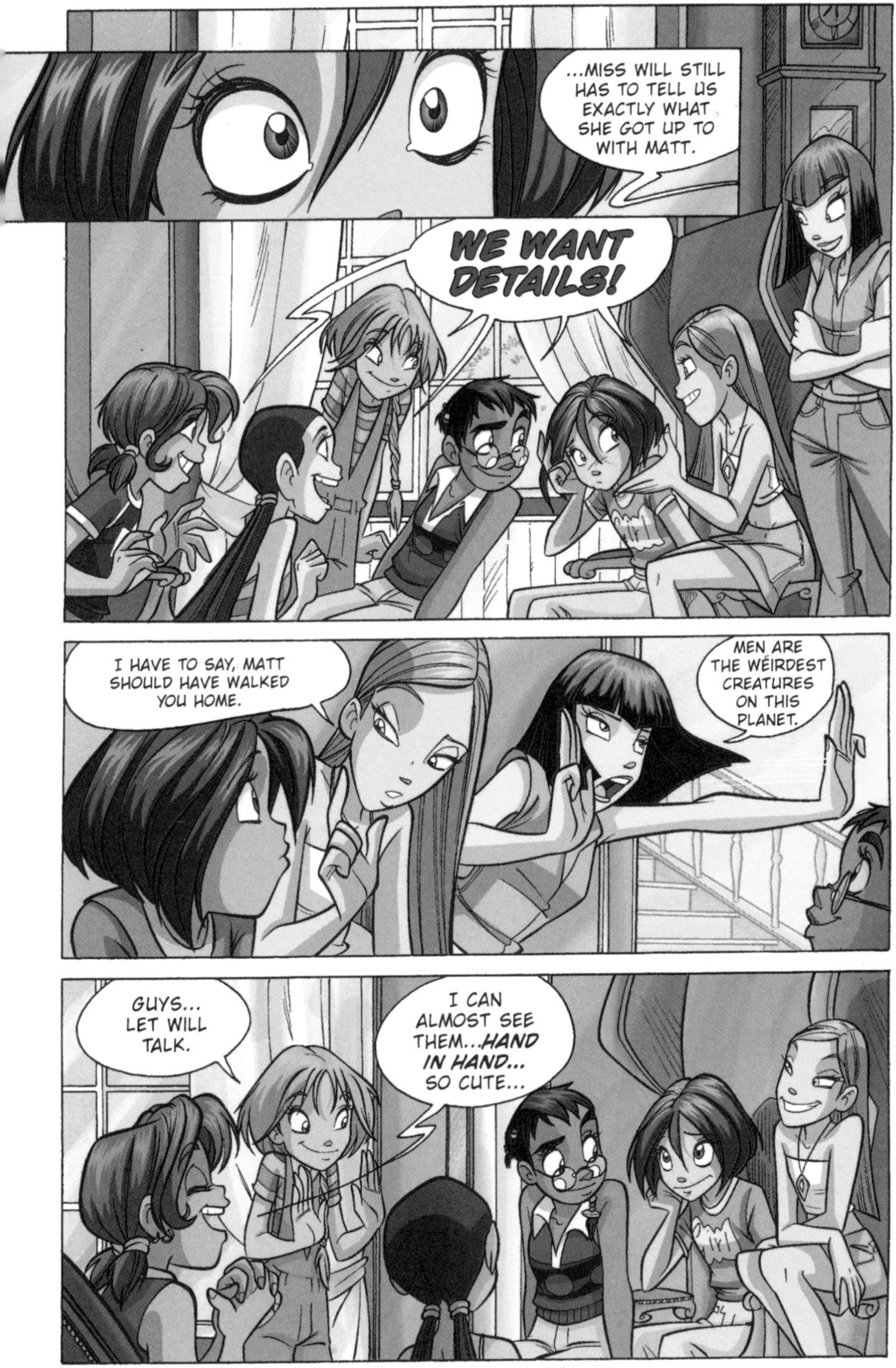
...MISS WILL STILL HAS TO TELL US EXACTLY WHAT SHE GOT UP TO WITH MATT.
WE WANT DETAILS!
I HAVE TO SAY, MATT SHOULD HAVE WALKED YOU HOME.
MEN ARE THE WEIRDEST CREATURES ON THIS PLANET.
GUYS... LET WILL TALK.
I CAN ALMOST SEE THEM... *HAND IN HAND...* SO CUTE...

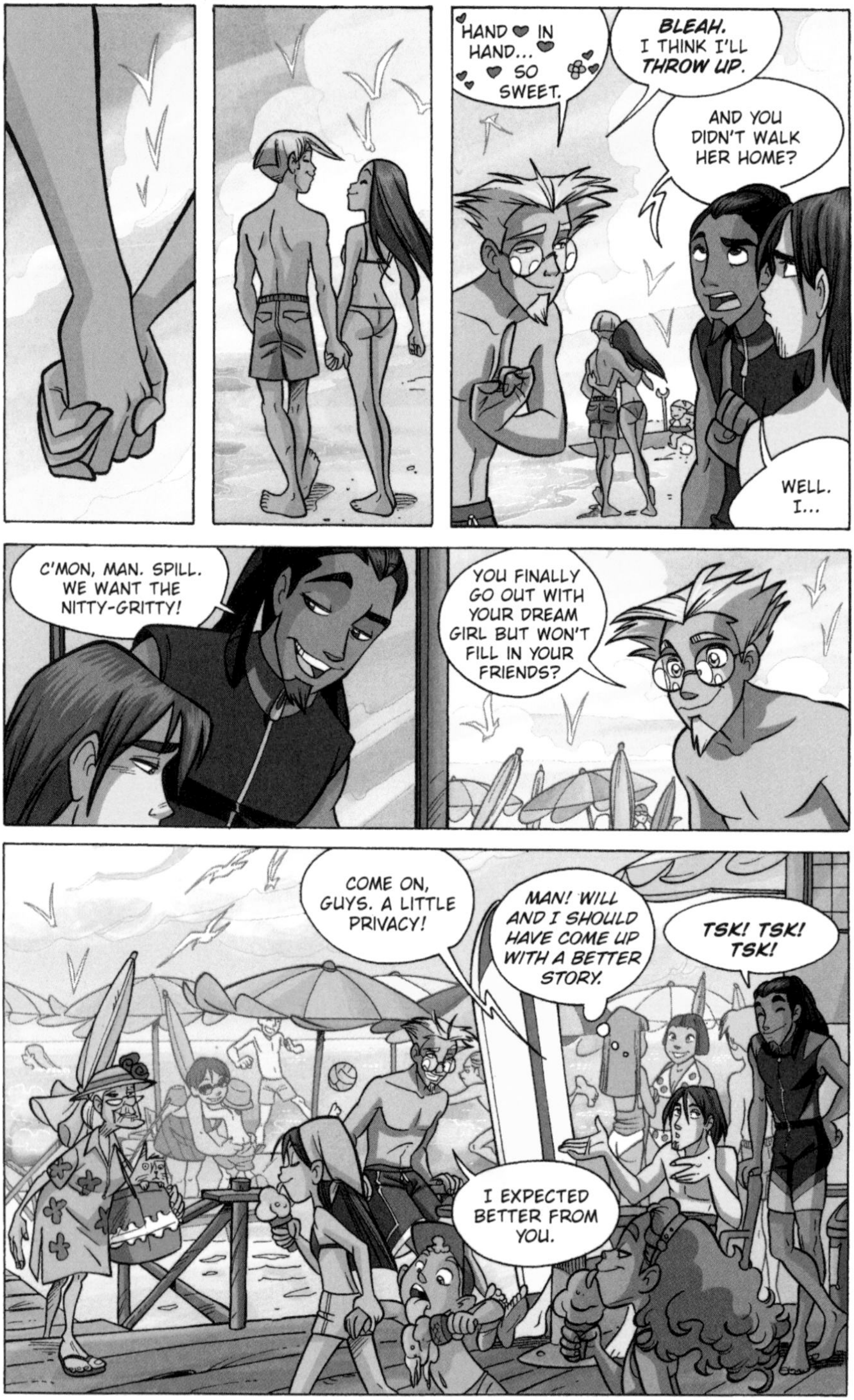
HAND IN HAND... SO SWEET.
BLEAH. I THINK I'LL THROW UP.
AND YOU DIDN'T WALK HER HOME?
WELL. I...
C'MON, MAN. SPILL. WE WANT THE NITTY-GRITTY!
YOU FINALLY GO OUT WITH YOUR DREAM GIRL BUT WON'T FILL IN YOUR FRIENDS?
COME ON, GUYS. A LITTLE PRIVACY!
MAN! WILL AND I SHOULD HAVE COME UP WITH A BETTER STORY.
TSK! TSK! TSK!
I EXPECTED BETTER FROM YOU.

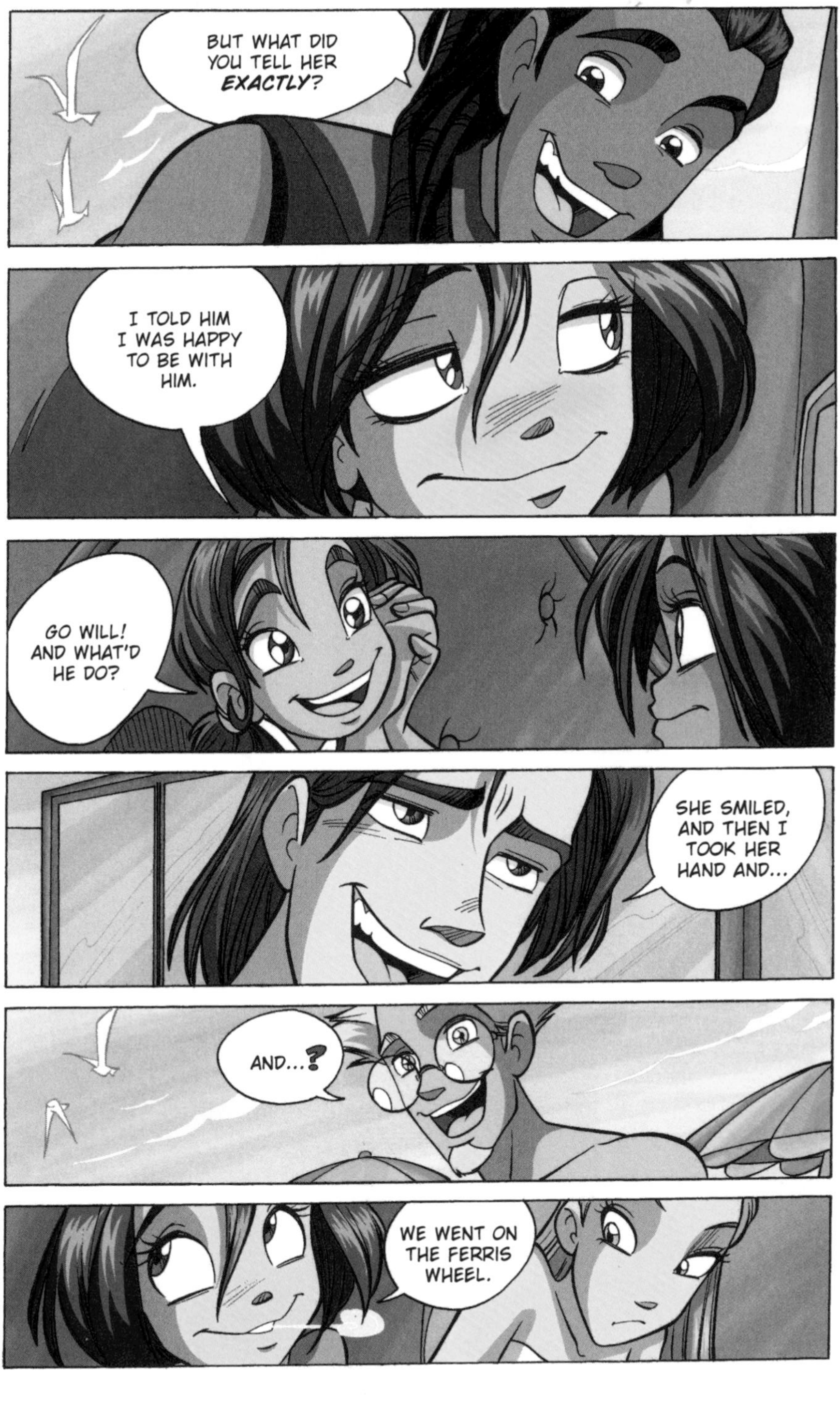

BUT WHAT DID YOU TELL HER *EXACTLY*?
I TOLD HIM I WAS HAPPY TO BE WITH HIM.
GO WILL! AND WHAT'D HE DO?
SHE SMILED, AND THEN I TOOK HER HAND AND...
AND...?
WE WENT ON THE FERRIS WHEEL.

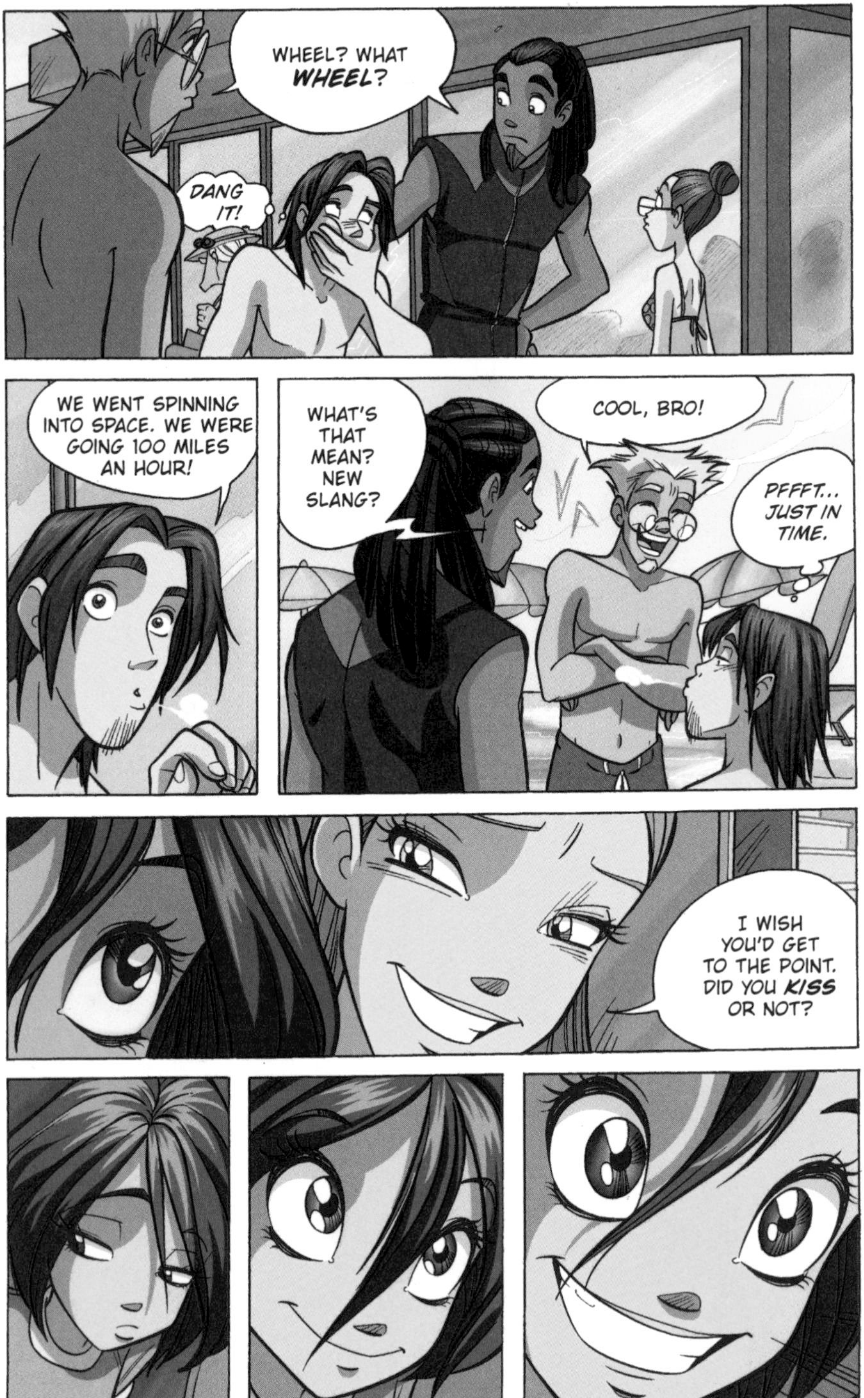
WHEEL? WHAT **WHEEL**?
DANG IT!
WE WENT SPINNING INTO SPACE. WE WERE GOING 100 MILES AN HOUR!
WHAT'S THAT MEAN? NEW SLANG?
COOL, BRO!
PFFFT... JUST IN TIME.
I WISH YOU'D GET TO THE POINT. DID YOU **KISS** OR NOT?

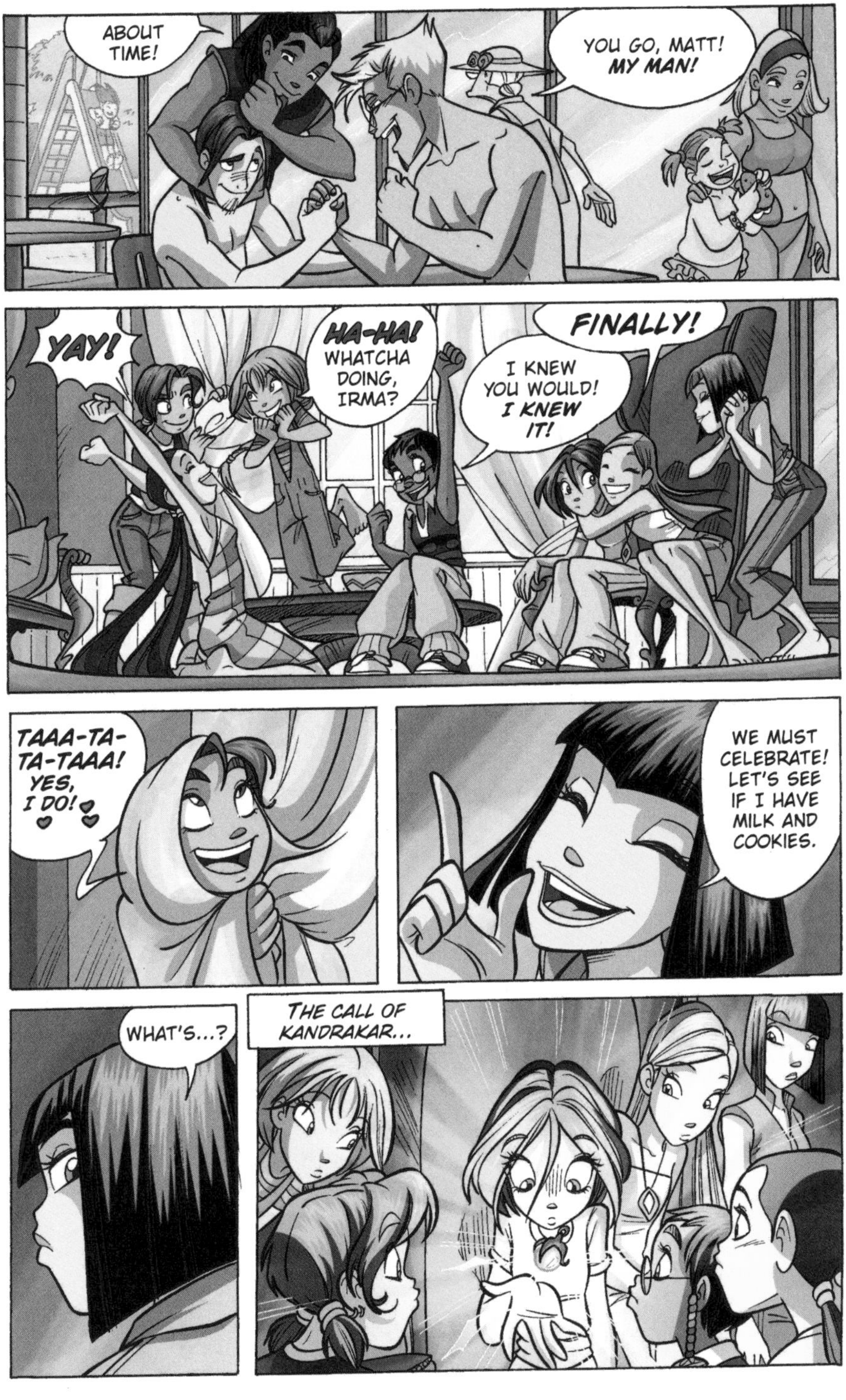

ABOUT TIME!
YOU GO, MATT! MY MAN!
YAY!
HA-HA! WHATCHA DOING, IRMA?
FINALLY!
I KNEW YOU WOULD! I KNEW IT!
TAAA-TA-TA-TAAA! YES, I DO!
WE MUST CELEBRATE! LET'S SEE IF I HAVE MILK AND COOKIES.
WHAT'S...?
THE CALL OF KANDRAKAR...

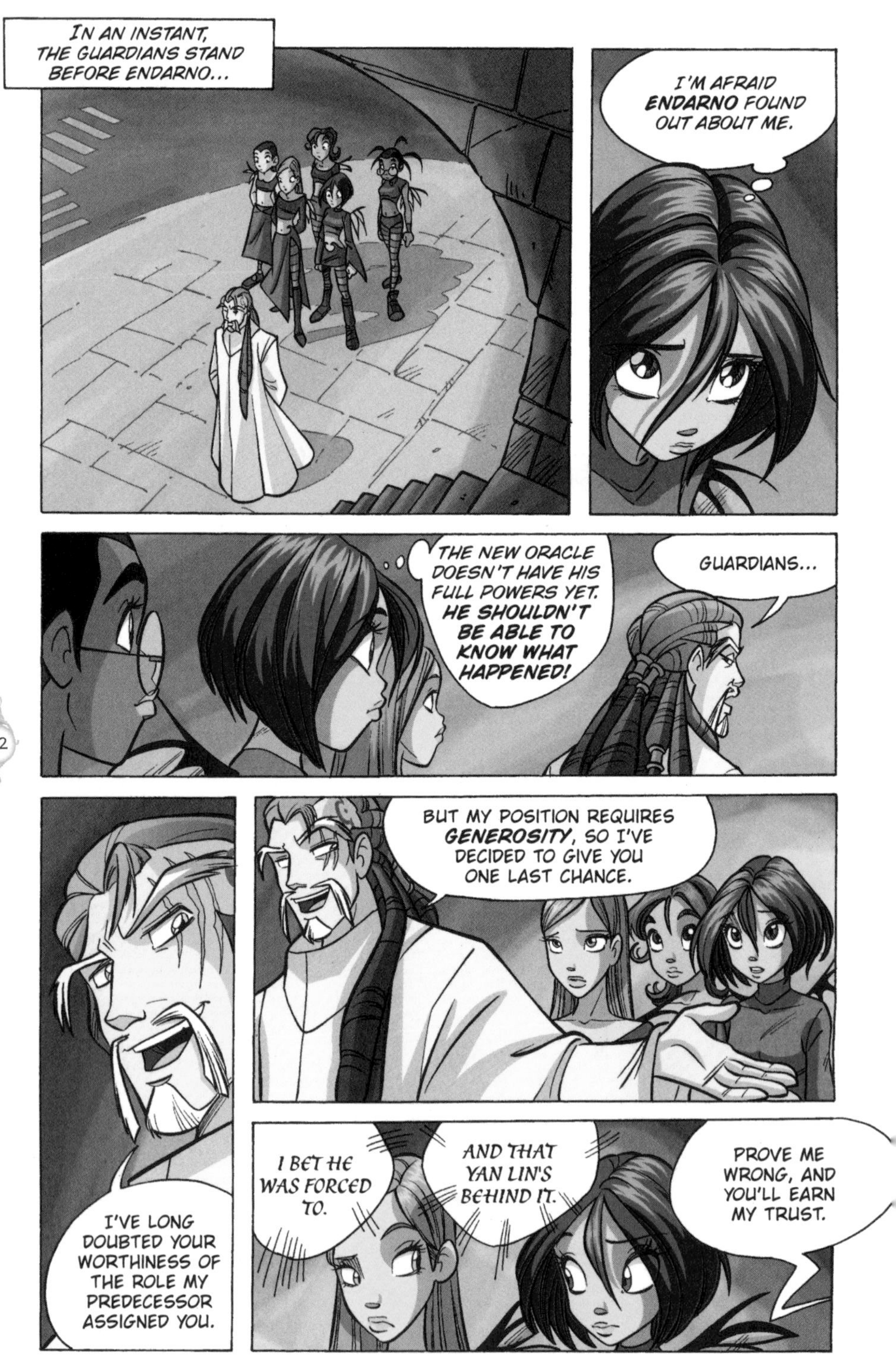
IN AN INSTANT, THE GUARDIANS STAND BEFORE ENDARNO...
I'M AFRAID ENDARNO FOUND OUT ABOUT ME.
THE NEW ORACLE DOESN'T HAVE HIS FULL POWERS YET. HE SHOULDN'T BE ABLE TO KNOW WHAT HAPPENED!
GUARDIANS...
I'VE LONG DOUBTED YOUR WORTHINESS OF THE ROLE MY PREDECESSOR ASSIGNED YOU.
BUT MY POSITION REQUIRES GENEROSITY, SO I'VE DECIDED TO GIVE YOU ONE LAST CHANCE.
I BET HE WAS FORCED TO.
AND THAT YAN LIN'S BEHIND IT.
PROVE ME WRONG, AND YOU'LL EARN MY TRUST.

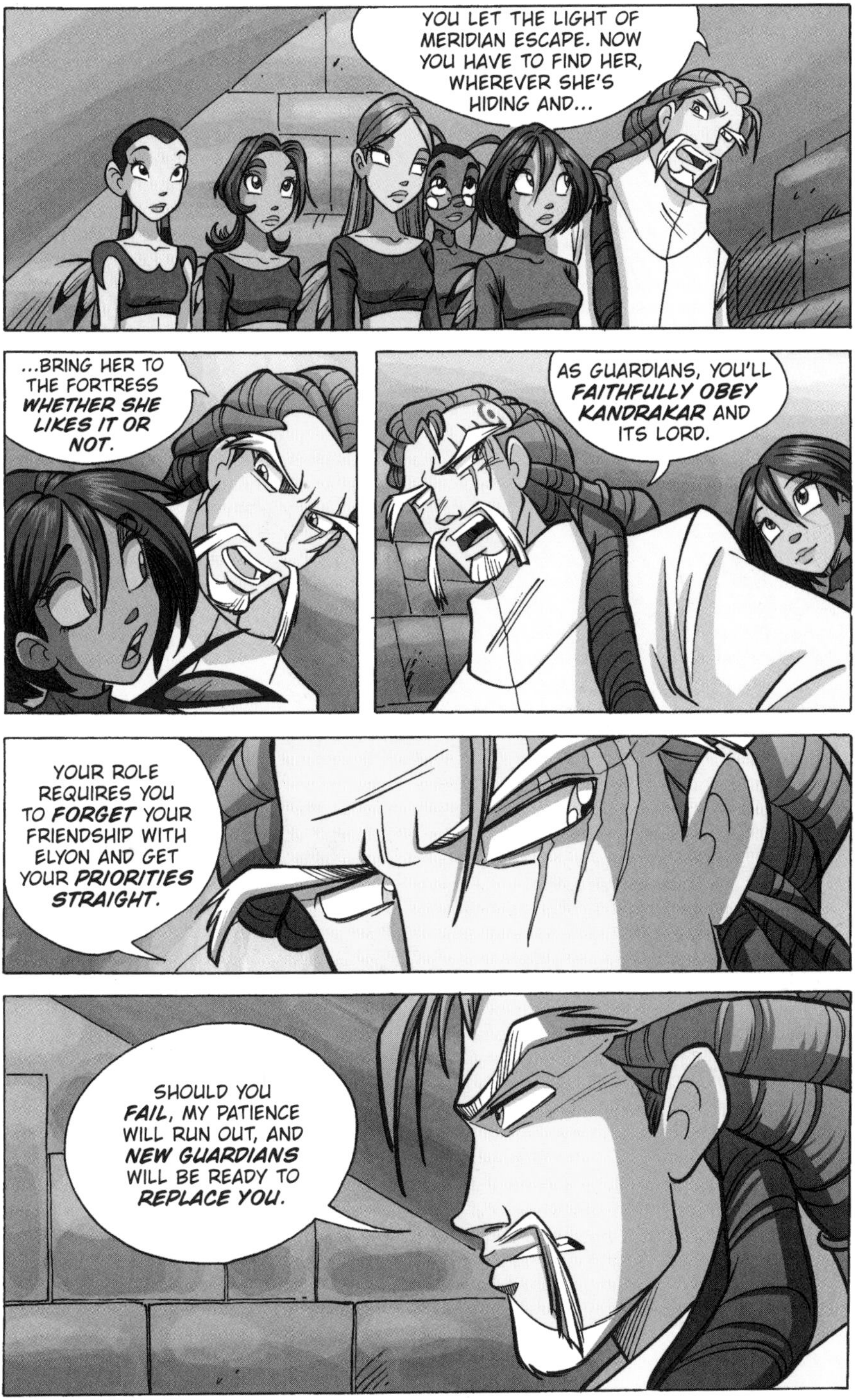
YOU LET THE LIGHT OF MERIDIAN ESCAPE. NOW YOU HAVE TO FIND HER, WHEREVER SHE'S HIDING AND...
...BRING HER TO THE FORTRESS ***WHETHER SHE LIKES IT OR NOT***.
AS GUARDIANS, YOU'LL ***FAITHFULLY OBEY KANDRAKAR*** AND ITS LORD.
YOUR ROLE REQUIRES YOU TO ***FORGET*** YOUR FRIENDSHIP WITH ELYON AND GET YOUR ***PRIORITIES STRAIGHT***.
SHOULD YOU ***FAIL***, MY PATIENCE WILL RUN OUT, AND ***NEW GUARDIANS*** WILL BE READY TO ***REPLACE YOU***.

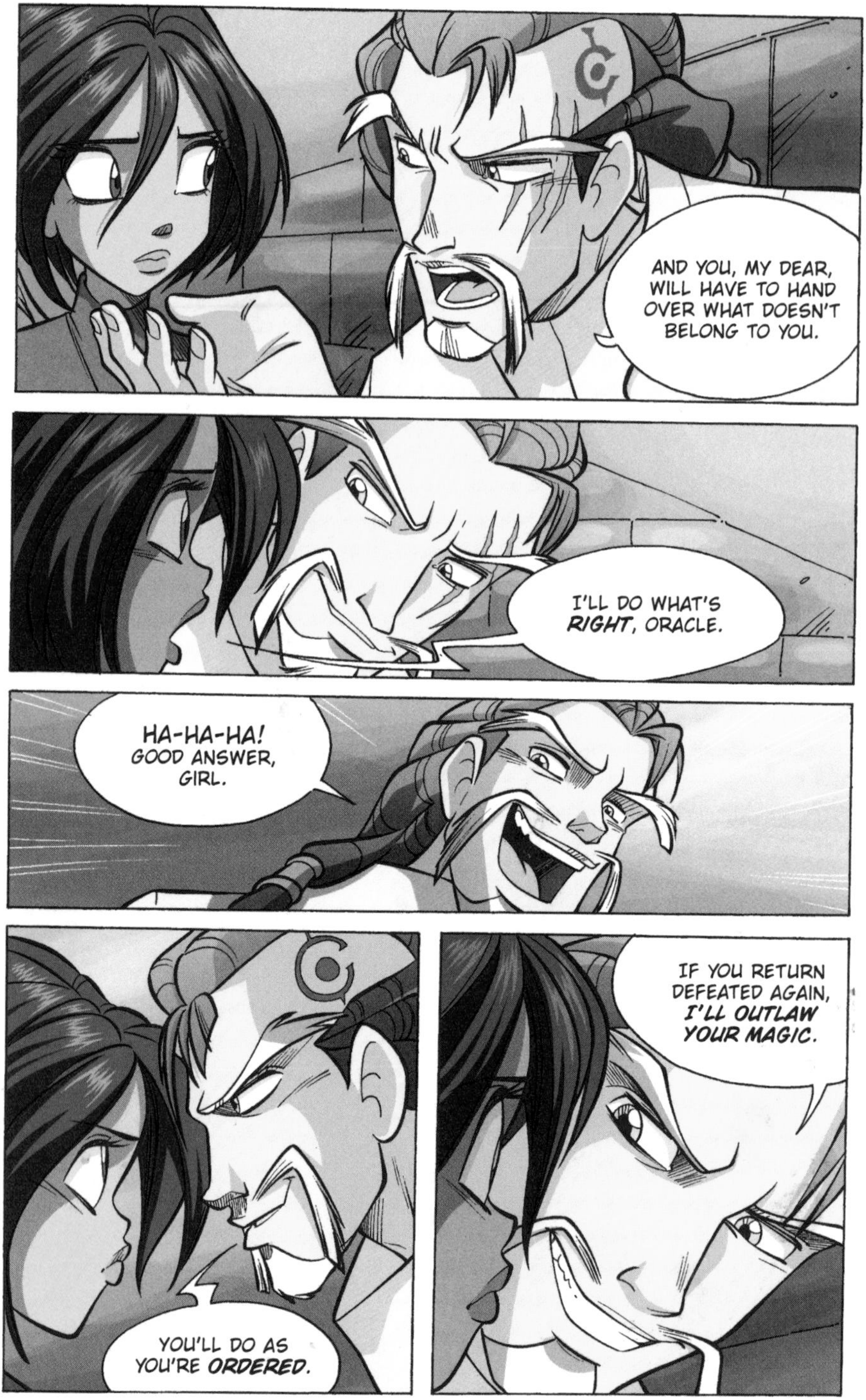
AND YOU, MY DEAR, WILL HAVE TO HAND OVER WHAT DOESN'T BELONG TO YOU.
I'LL DO WHAT'S *RIGHT*, ORACLE.
HA-HA-HA! GOOD ANSWER, GIRL.
YOU'LL DO AS YOU'RE *ORDERED*.
IF YOU RETURN DEFEATED AGAIN, *I'LL OUTLAW YOUR MAGIC*.

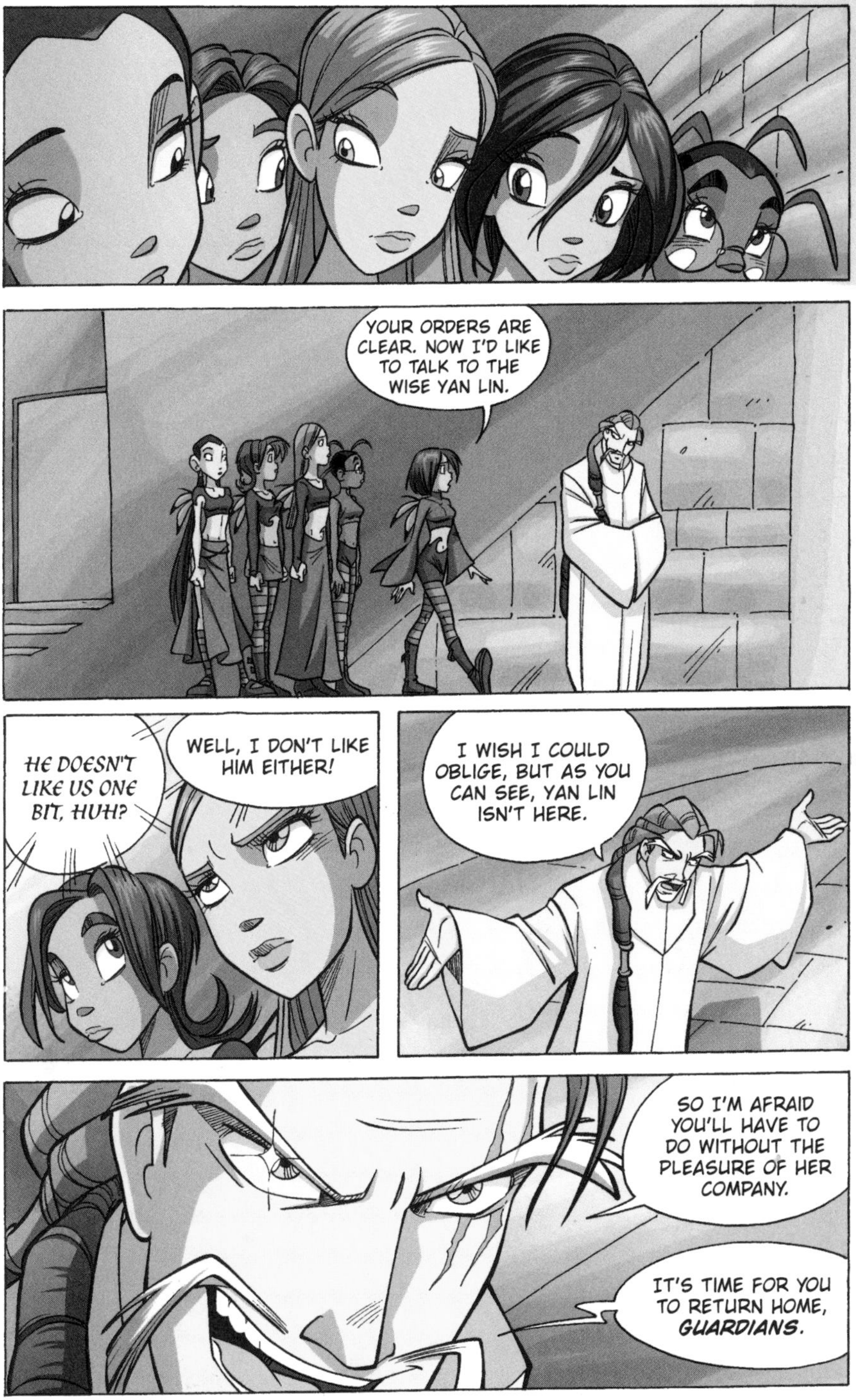
YOUR ORDERS ARE CLEAR. NOW I'D LIKE TO TALK TO THE WISE YAN LIN.
HE DOESN'T LIKE US ONE BIT, HUH?
WELL, I DON'T LIKE HIM EITHER!
I WISH I COULD OBLIGE, BUT AS YOU CAN SEE, YAN LIN ISN'T HERE.
SO I'M AFRAID YOU'LL HAVE TO DO WITHOUT THE PLEASURE OF HER COMPANY.
IT'S TIME FOR YOU TO RETURN HOME, ***GUARDIANS***.

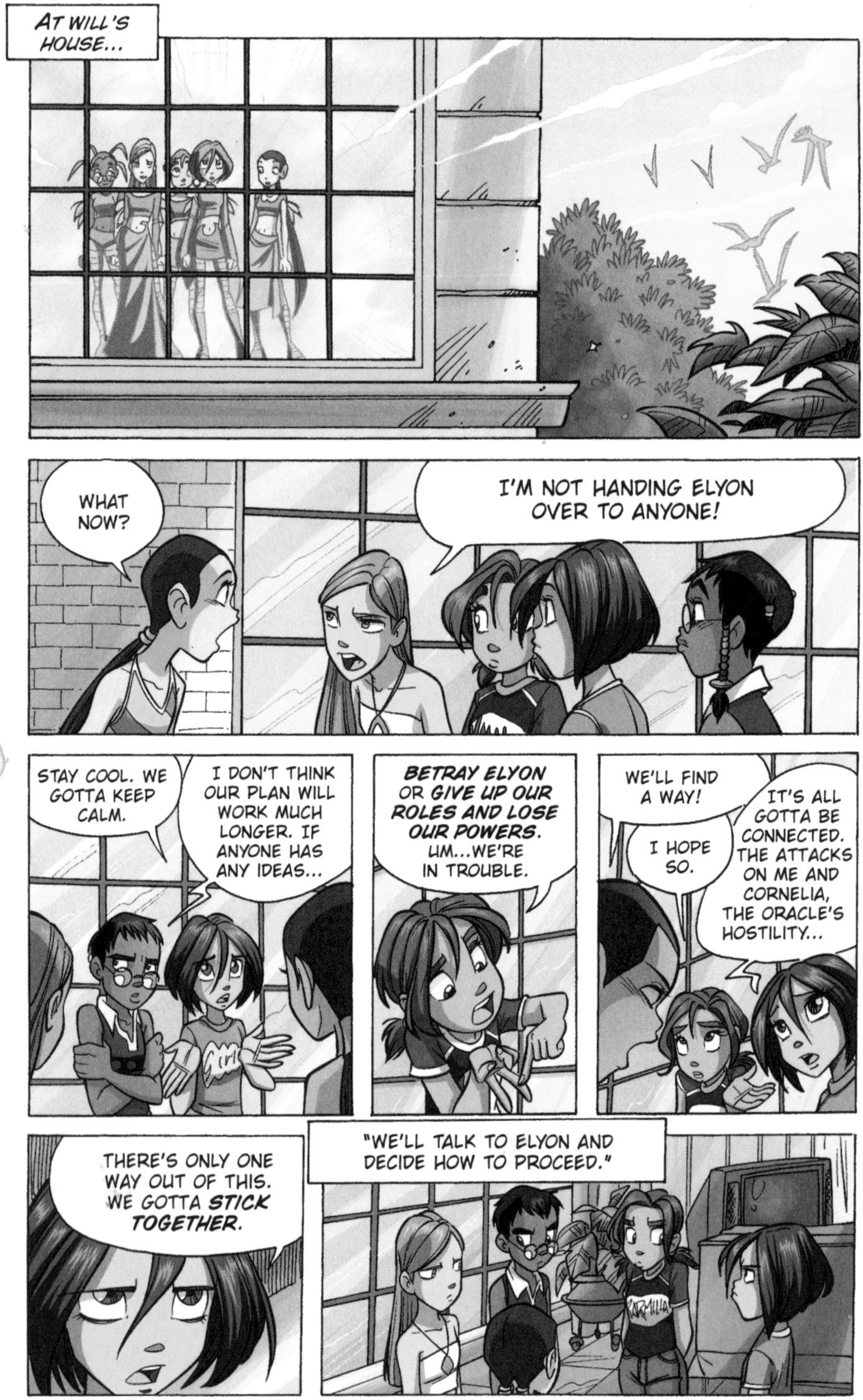
AT WILL'S HOUSE...
WHAT NOW?
I'M NOT HANDING ELYON OVER TO ANYONE!
STAY COOL. WE GOTTA KEEP CALM.
I DON'T THINK OUR PLAN WILL WORK MUCH LONGER. IF ANYONE HAS ANY IDEAS...
BETRAY ELYON OR GIVE UP OUR ROLES AND LOSE OUR POWERS. UM...WE'RE IN TROUBLE.
WE'LL FIND A WAY!
I HOPE SO.
IT'S ALL GOTTA BE CONNECTED. THE ATTACKS ON ME AND CORNELIA, THE ORACLE'S HOSTILITY...
THERE'S ONLY ONE WAY OUT OF THIS. WE GOTTA STICK TOGETHER.
"WE'LL TALK TO ELYON AND DECIDE HOW TO PROCEED."

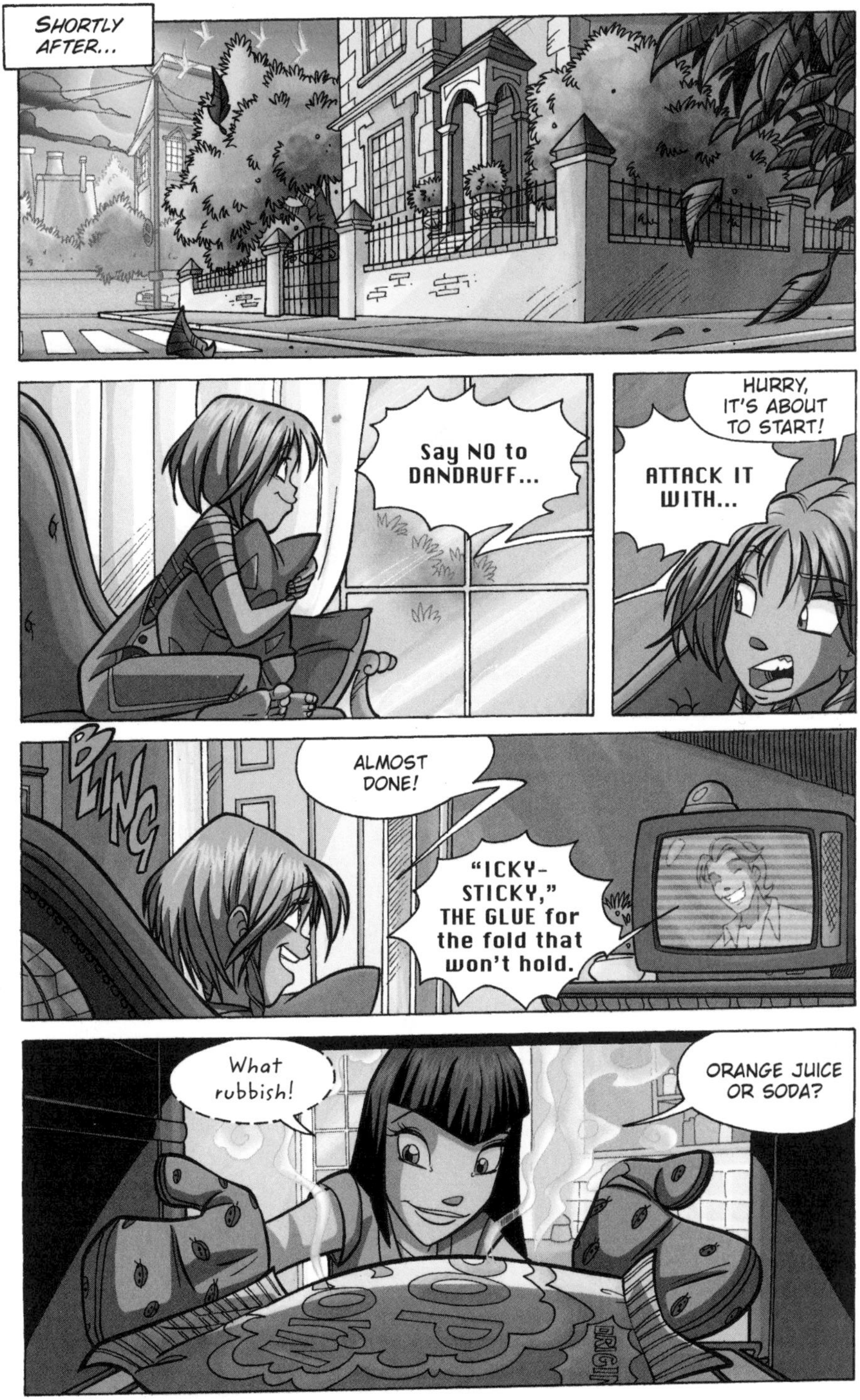
SHORTLY AFTER...
Say NO to DANDRUFF...
HURRY, IT'S ABOUT TO START!
ATTACK IT WITH...
BLING
ALMOST DONE!
"ICKY-STICKY," THE GLUE for the fold that won't hold.
What rubbish!
ORANGE JUICE OR SODA?

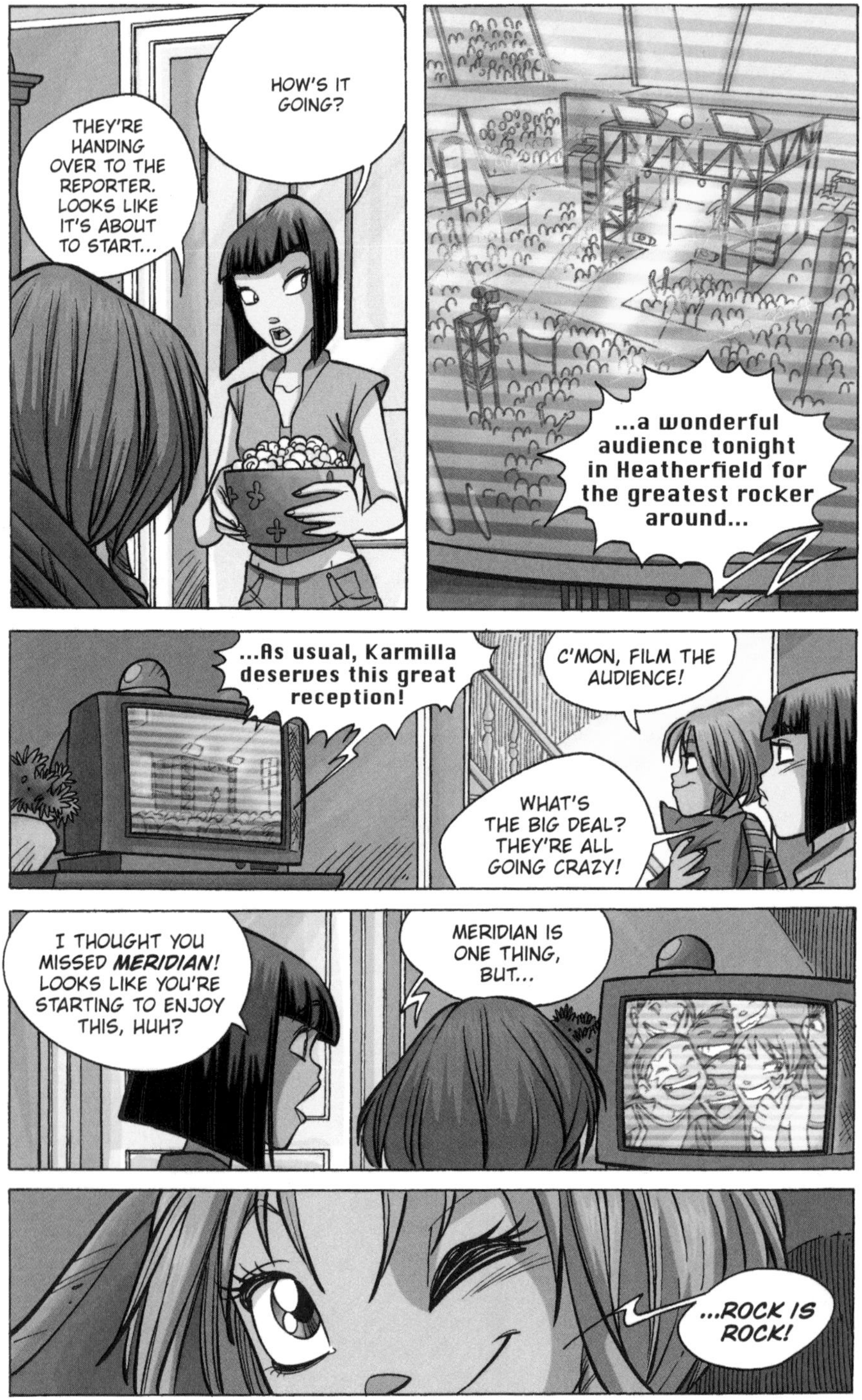
HOW'S IT GOING?
THEY'RE HANDING OVER TO THE REPORTER. LOOKS LIKE IT'S ABOUT TO START...
...a wonderful audience tonight in Heatherfield for the greatest rocker around...
...As usual, Karmilla deserves this great reception!
C'MON, FILM THE AUDIENCE!
WHAT'S THE BIG DEAL? THEY'RE ALL GOING CRAZY!
I THOUGHT YOU MISSED MERIDIAN! LOOKS LIKE YOU'RE STARTING TO ENJOY THIS, HUH?
MERIDIAN IS ONE THING, BUT...
...ROCK IS ROCK!

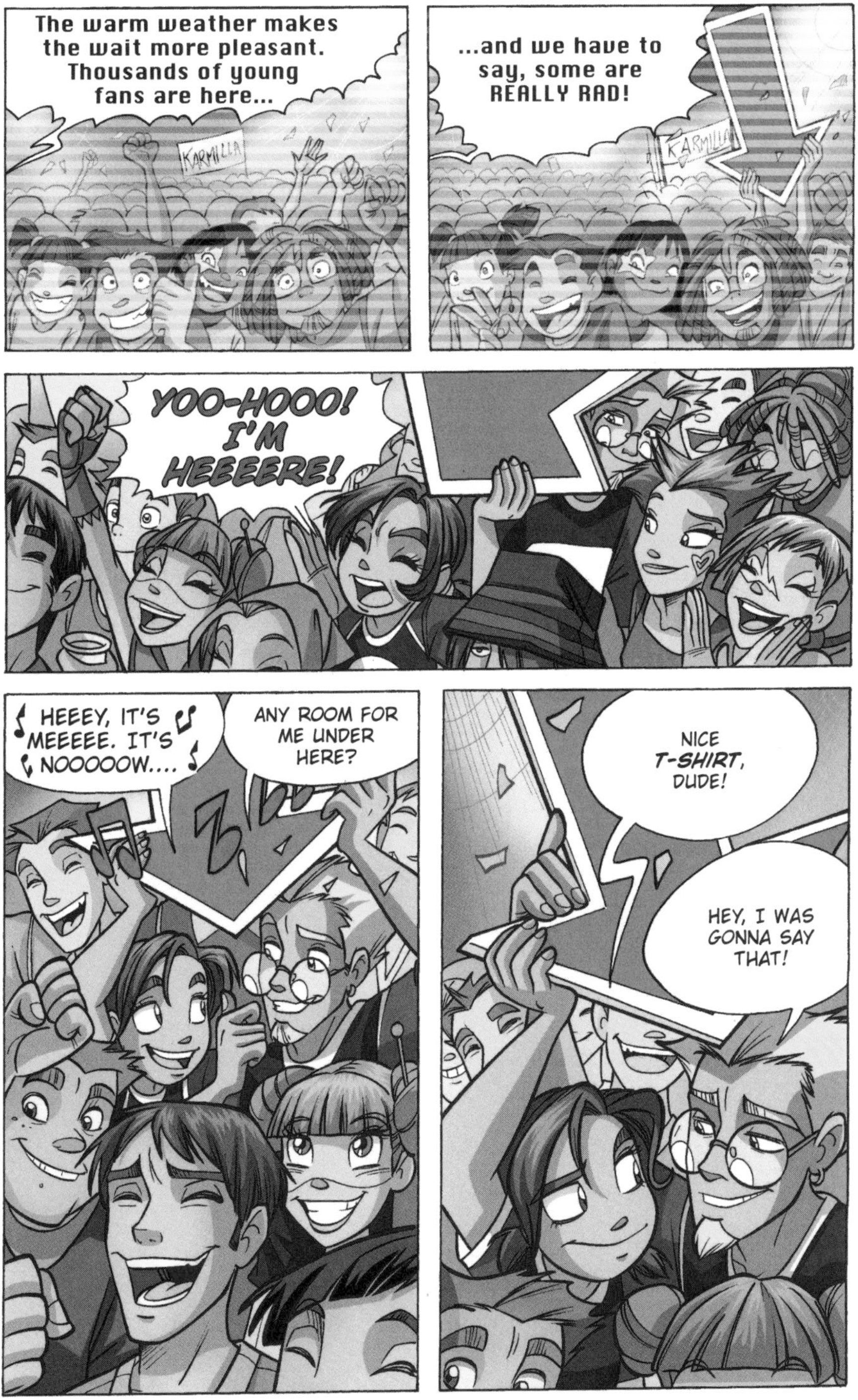
The warm weather makes the wait more pleasant. Thousands of young fans are here...
KARMILLA
...and we have to say, some are REALLY RAD!
KARMILLA
YOO-HOOO! I'M HEEEERE!
HEEEY, IT'S MEEEEE. IT'S NOOOOOW....
ANY ROOM FOR ME UNDER HERE?
NICE T-SHIRT, DUDE!
HEY, I WAS GONNA SAY THAT!

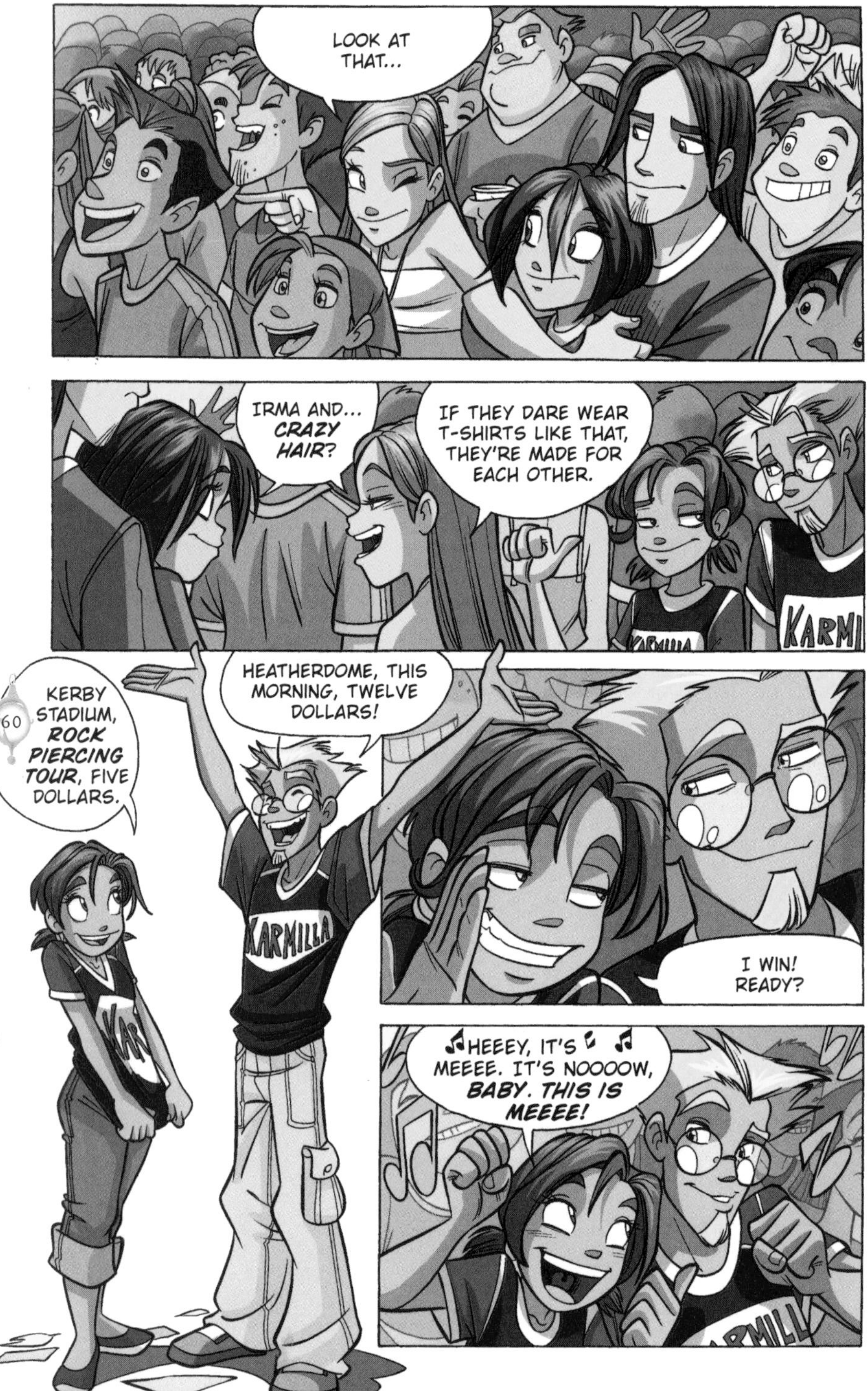
LOOK AT THAT...
IRMA AND... CRAZY HAIR?
IF THEY DARE WEAR T-SHIRTS LIKE THAT, THEY'RE MADE FOR EACH OTHER.
KARMILLA
KARMI
KERBY STADIUM, ROCK PIERCING TOUR, FIVE DOLLARS.
HEATHERDOME, THIS MORNING, TWELVE DOLLARS!
KARMILLA
I WIN! READY?
HEEEY, IT'S MEEEE. IT'S NOOOOW, BABY. THIS IS MEEEE!

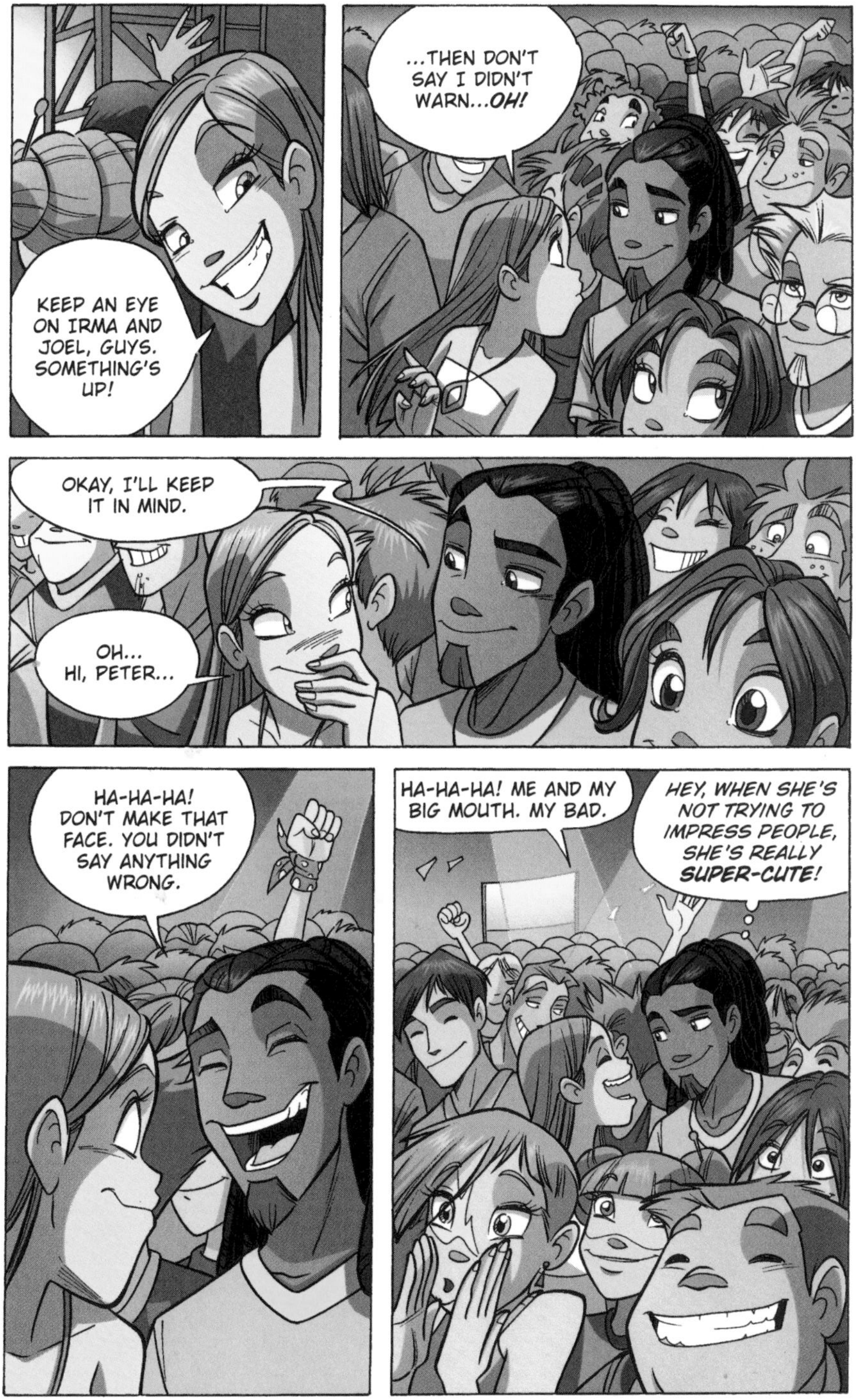
KEEP AN EYE ON IRMA AND JOEL, GUYS. SOMETHING'S UP!
...THEN DON'T SAY I DIDN'T WARN...OH!
OKAY, I'LL KEEP IT IN MIND.
OH... HI, PETER...
HA-HA-HA! DON'T MAKE THAT FACE. YOU DIDN'T SAY ANYTHING WRONG.
HA-HA-HA! ME AND MY BIG MOUTH. MY BAD.
HEY, WHEN SHE'S NOT TRYING TO IMPRESS PEOPLE, SHE'S REALLY SUPER-CUTE!

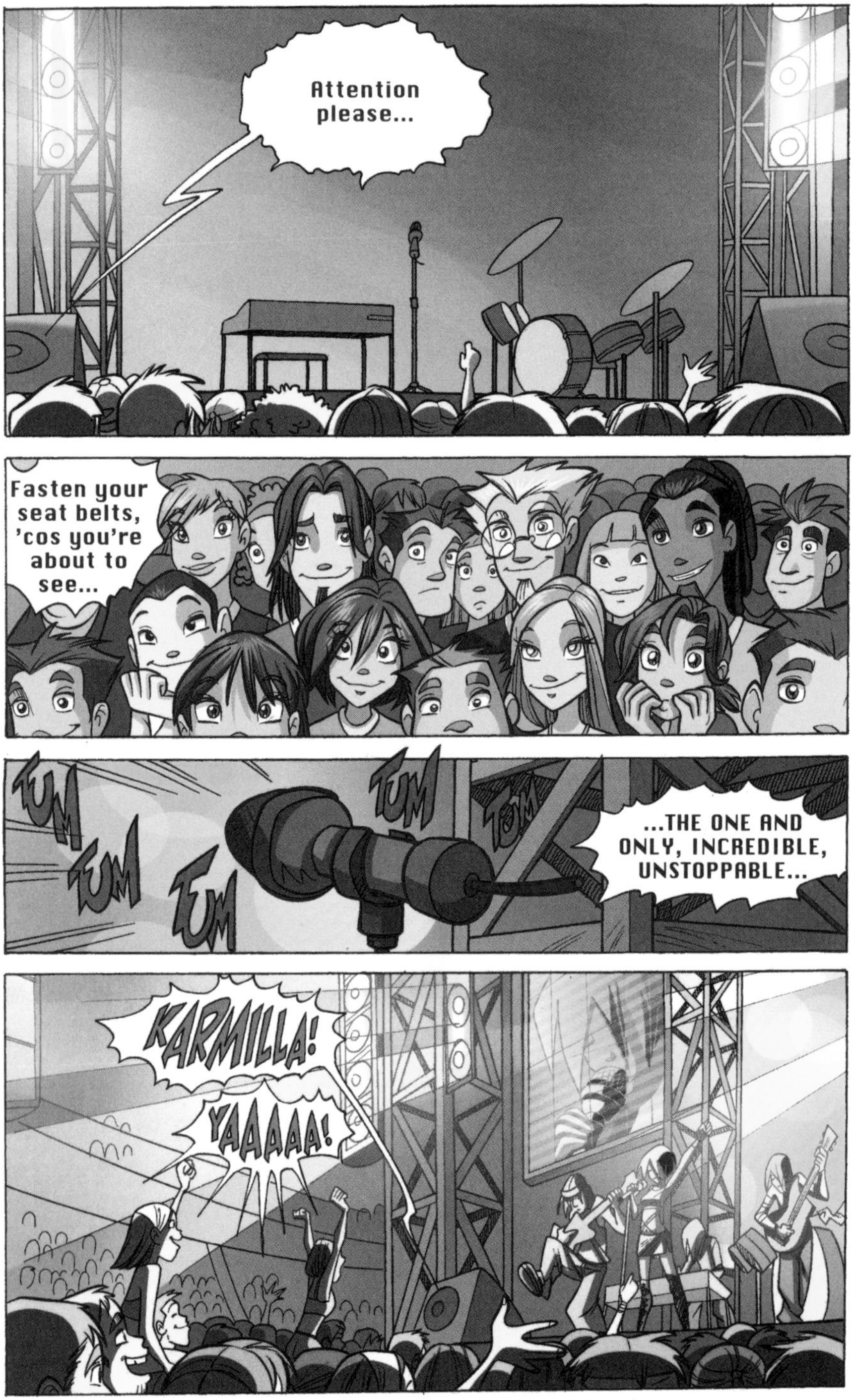
Attention please...
Fasten your seat belts, 'cos you're about to see...
TUM
TUM
TUM
TUM
TOM
...THE ONE AND ONLY, INCREDIBLE, UNSTOPPABLE...
KARMILLA!
YAAAAA!

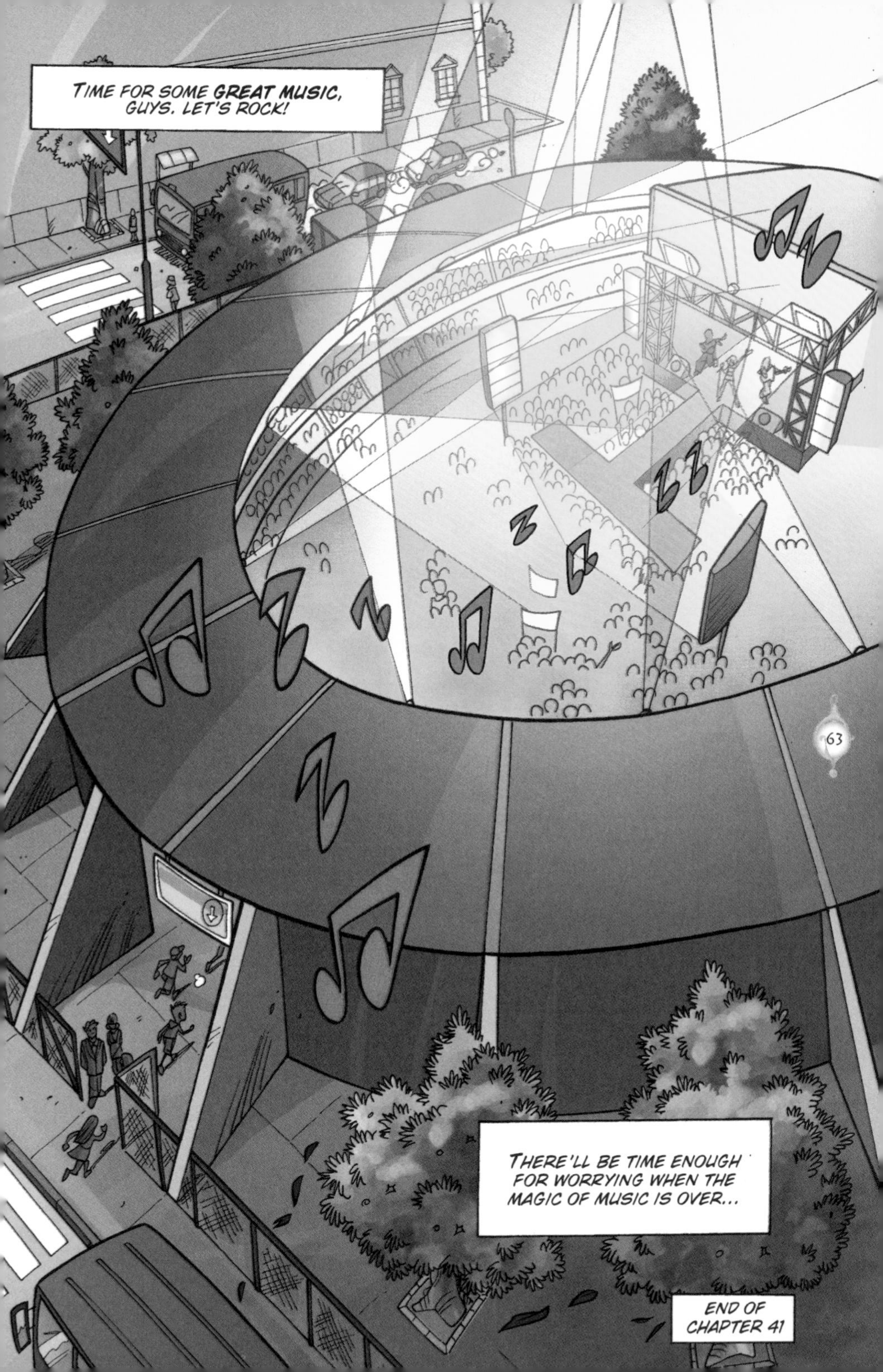
TIME FOR SOME GREAT MUSIC, GUYS. LET'S ROCK!
THERE'LL BE TIME ENOUGH FOR WORRYING WHEN THE MAGIC OF MUSIC IS OVER...
END OF CHAPTER 41

W.i.t.c.h.

Will Irma Taranee Cornelia Hay Lin

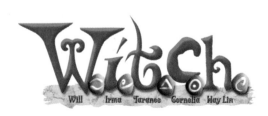

42

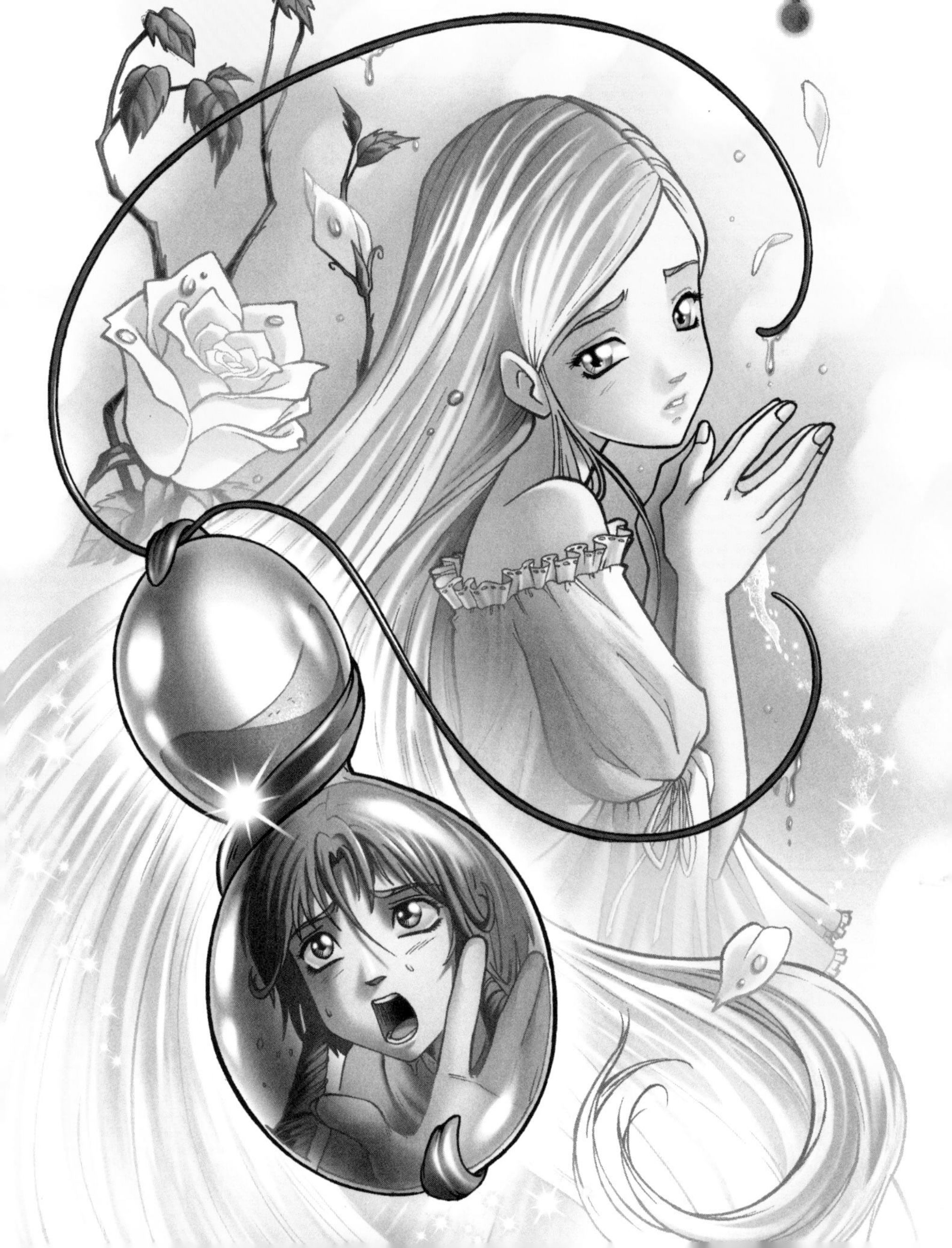

No Hope

**"We've got nothing left—
no weapons, no hope…"**

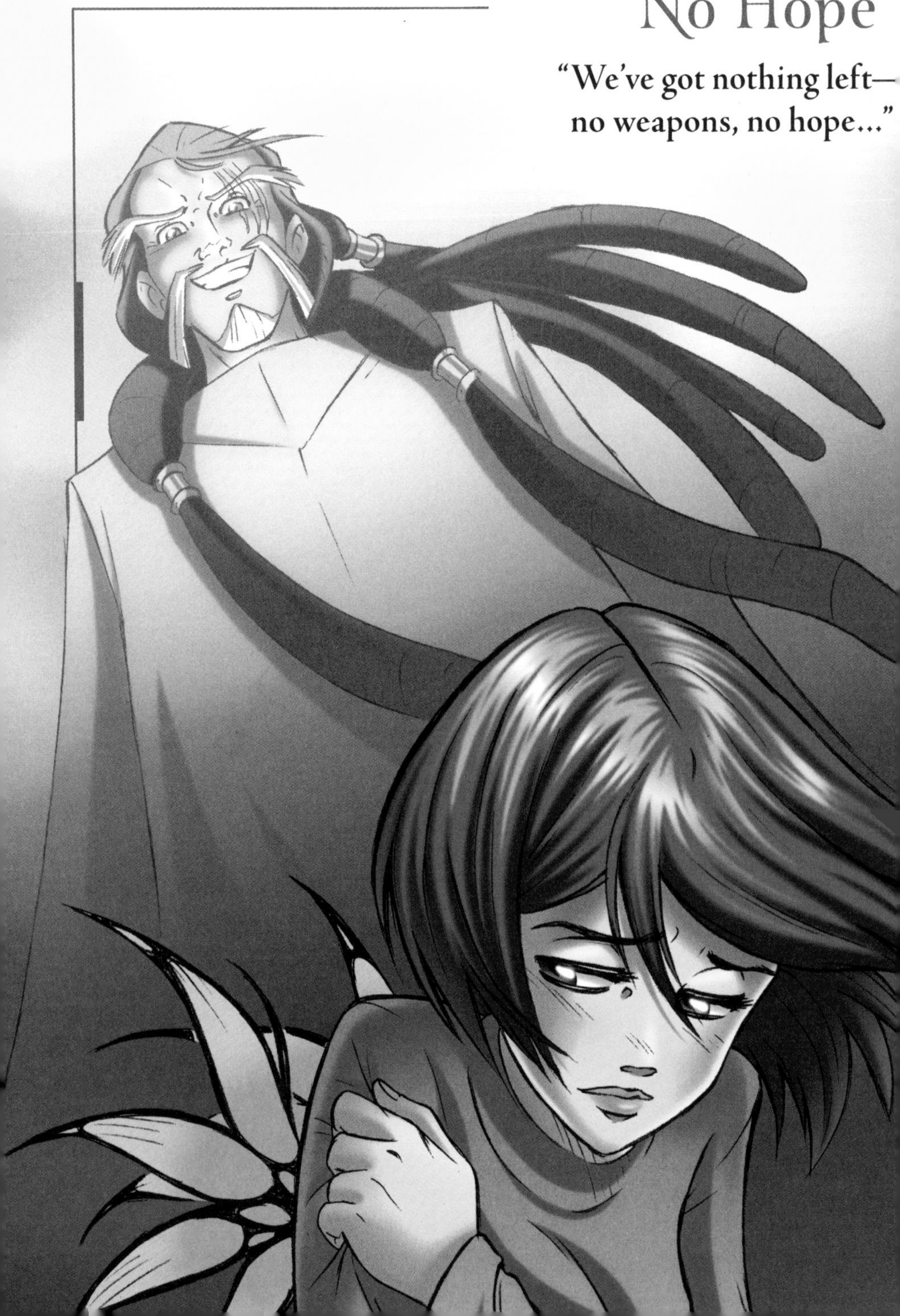

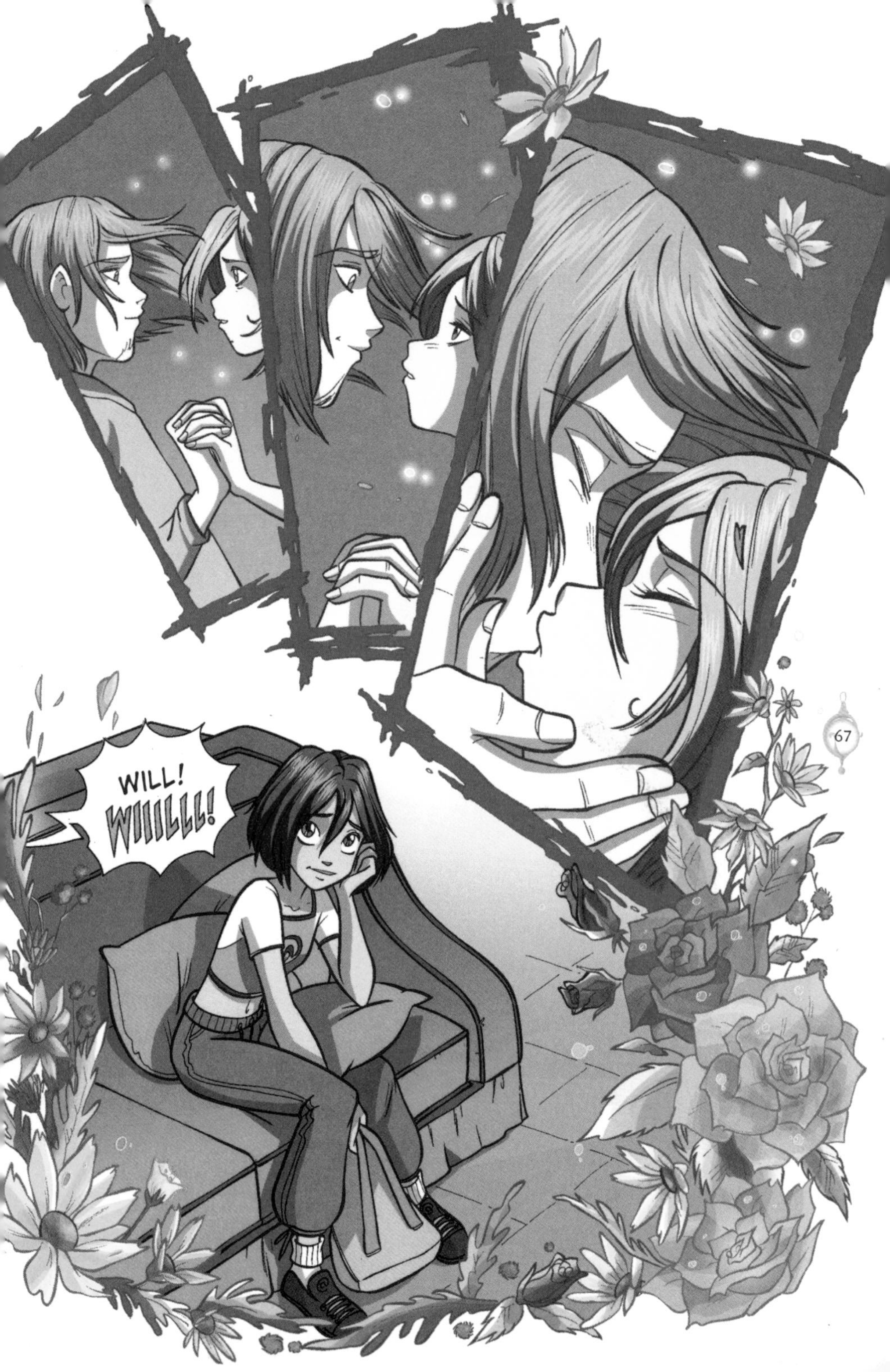
WILL! WIIILLL!

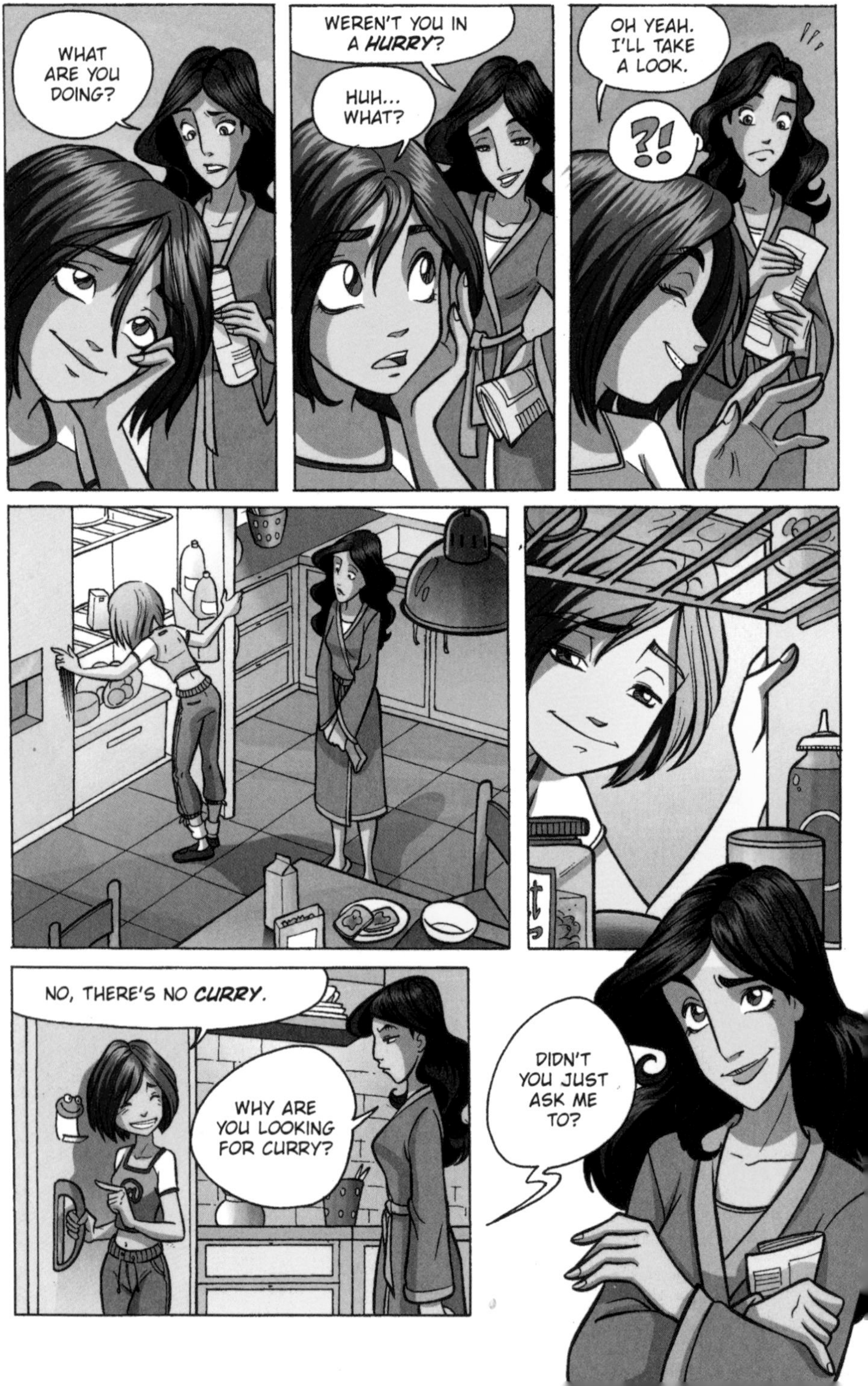
WHAT ARE YOU DOING?
WEREN'T YOU IN A HURRY?
HUH... WHAT?
OH YEAH. I'LL TAKE A LOOK.
?!
NO, THERE'S NO CURRY.
WHY ARE YOU LOOKING FOR CURRY?
DIDN'T YOU JUST ASK ME TO?

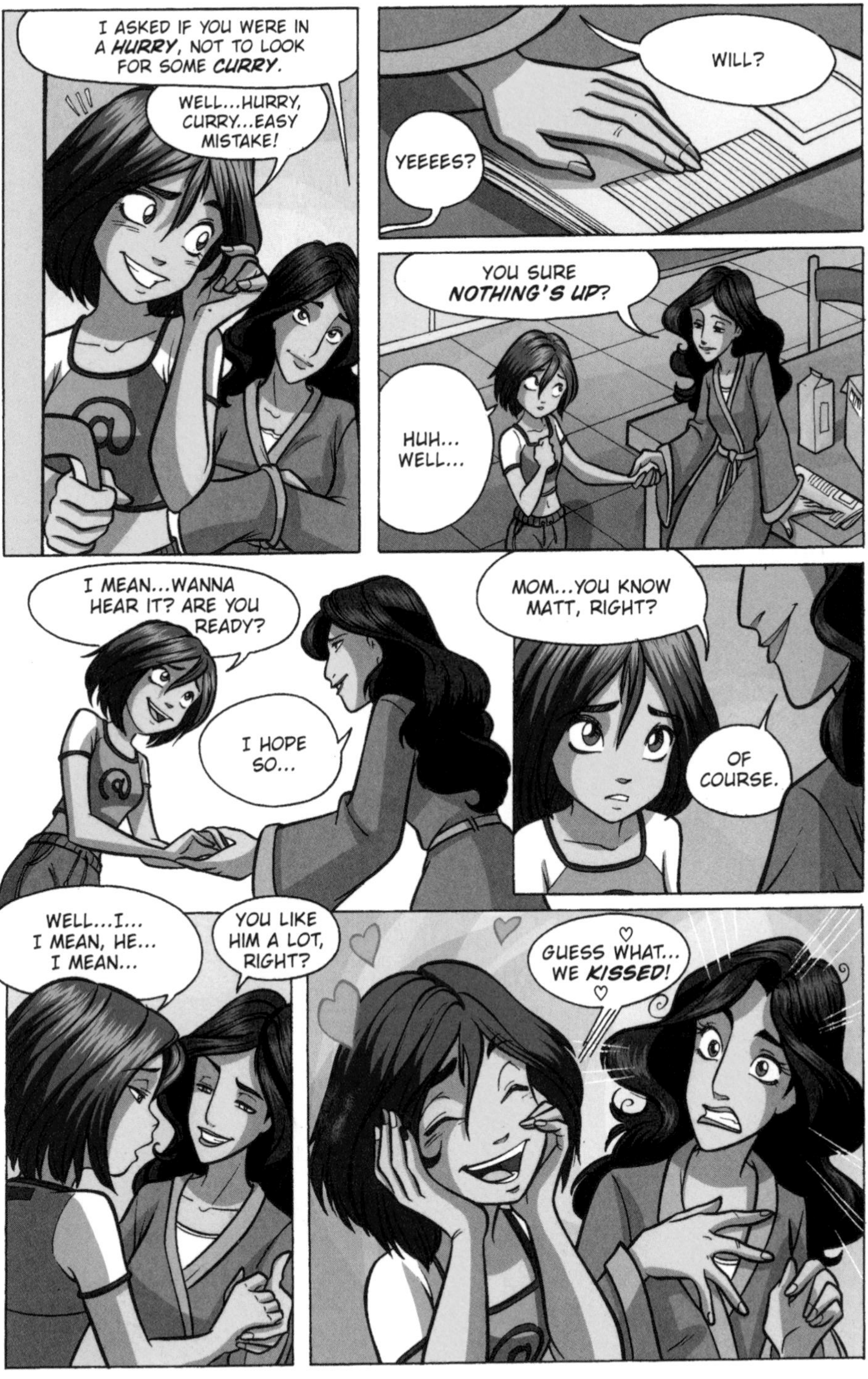

I ASKED IF YOU WERE IN A HURRY, NOT TO LOOK FOR SOME CURRY.
WELL...HURRY, CURRY...EASY MISTAKE!
WILL?
YEEEES?
YOU SURE NOTHING'S UP?
HUH... WELL...
I MEAN...WANNA HEAR IT? ARE YOU READY?
I HOPE SO...
MOM...YOU KNOW MATT, RIGHT?
OF COURSE.
WELL...I... I MEAN, HE... I MEAN...
YOU LIKE HIM A LOT, RIGHT?
GUESS WHAT... WE KISSED!

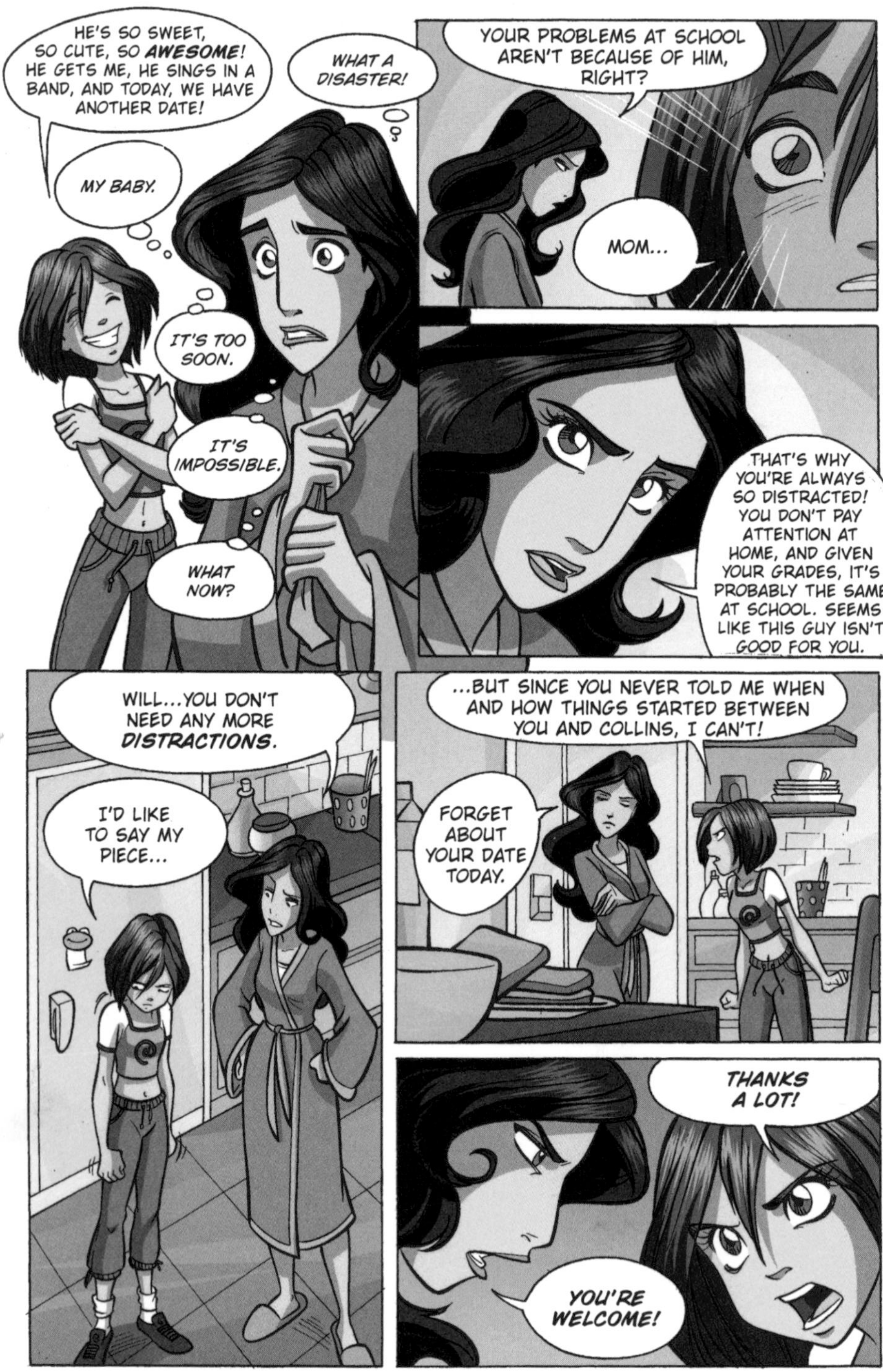
HE'S SO SWEET, SO CUTE, SO **AWESOME**! HE GETS ME, HE SINGS IN A BAND, AND TODAY, WE HAVE ANOTHER DATE!
MY BABY.
WHAT A DISASTER!
IT'S TOO SOON.
IT'S IMPOSSIBLE.
WHAT NOW?
YOUR PROBLEMS AT SCHOOL AREN'T BECAUSE OF HIM, RIGHT?
MOM...
THAT'S WHY YOU'RE ALWAYS SO DISTRACTED! YOU DON'T PAY ATTENTION AT HOME, AND GIVEN YOUR GRADES, IT'S PROBABLY THE SAME AT SCHOOL. SEEMS LIKE THIS GUY ISN'T GOOD FOR YOU.
WILL...YOU DON'T NEED ANY MORE **DISTRACTIONS**.
I'D LIKE TO SAY MY PIECE...
...BUT SINCE YOU NEVER TOLD ME WHEN AND HOW THINGS STARTED BETWEEN YOU AND COLLINS, I CAN'T!
FORGET ABOUT YOUR DATE TODAY.
THANKS A LOT!
YOU'RE WELCOME!

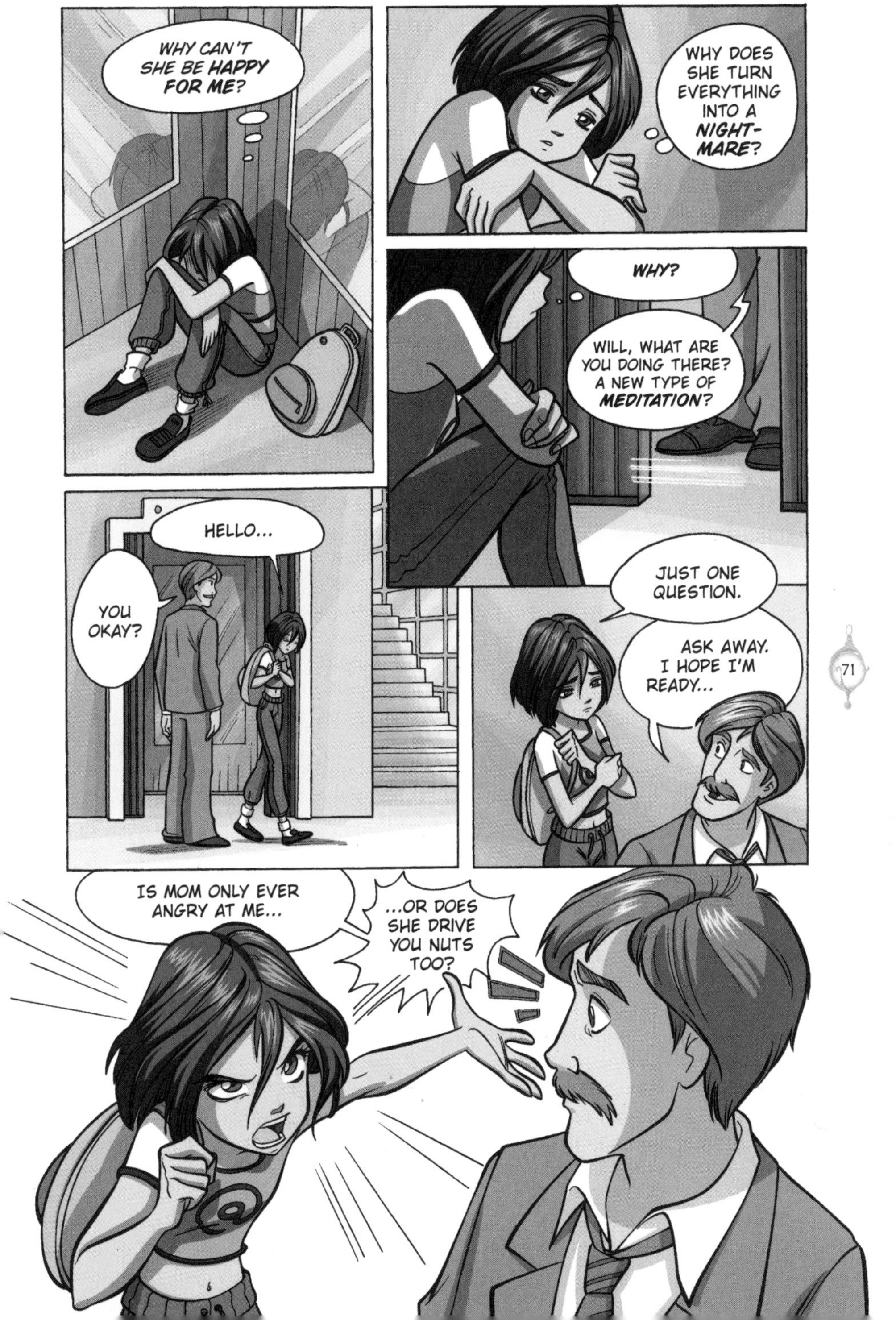

WHY CAN'T SHE BE HAPPY FOR ME?
WHY DOES SHE TURN EVERYTHING INTO A NIGHT-MARE?
WHY?
WILL, WHAT ARE YOU DOING THERE? A NEW TYPE OF MEDITATION?
HELLO...
YOU OKAY?
JUST ONE QUESTION.
ASK AWAY. I HOPE I'M READY...
IS MOM ONLY EVER ANGRY AT ME...
...OR DOES SHE DRIVE YOU NUTS TOO?

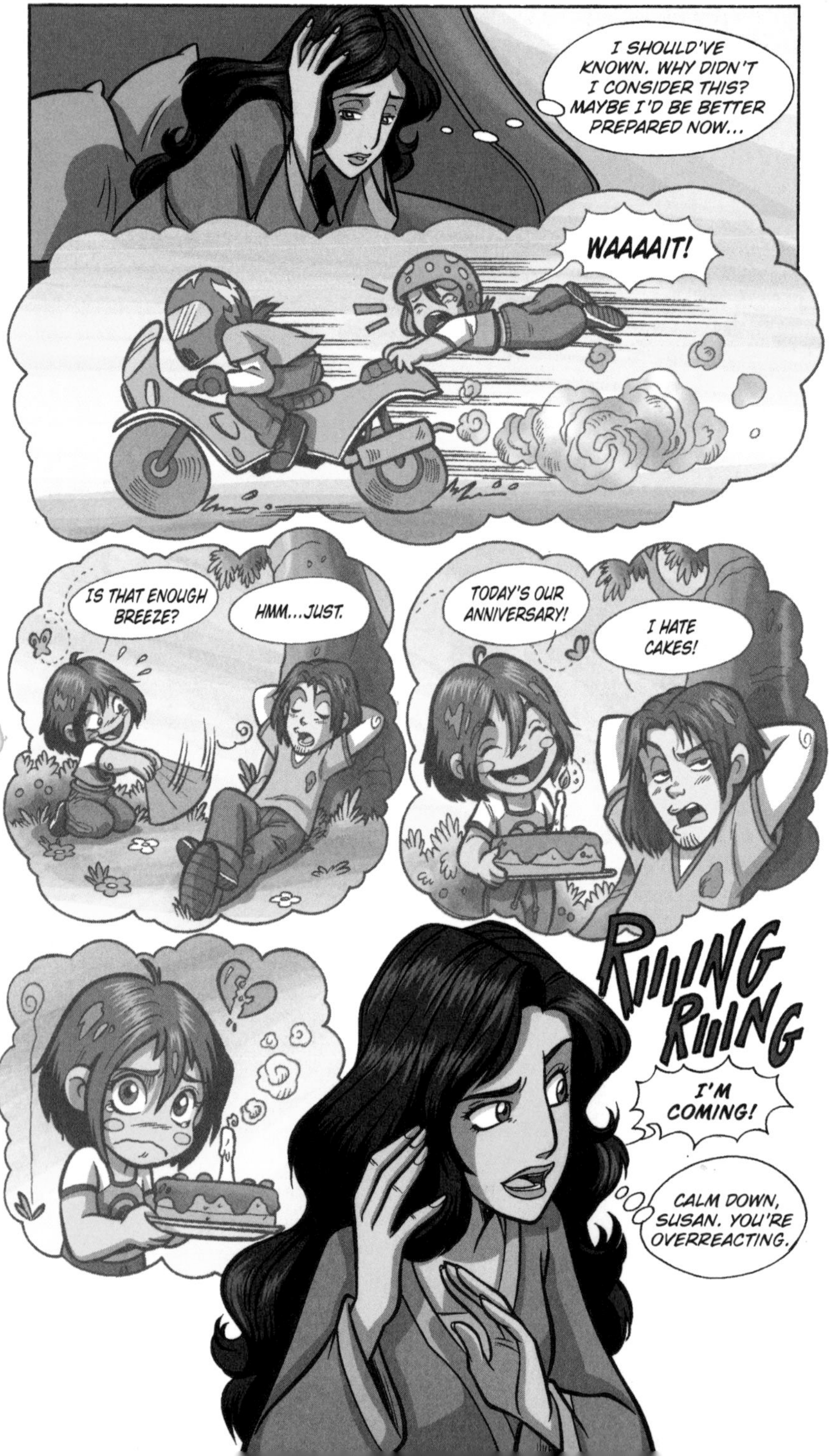

I SHOULD'VE KNOWN. WHY DIDN'T I CONSIDER THIS? MAYBE I'D BE BETTER PREPARED NOW...
WAAAAIT!
IS THAT ENOUGH BREEZE?
HMM...JUST.
TODAY'S OUR ANNIVERSARY!
I HATE CAKES!
RIIIING RIIING
I'M COMING!
CALM DOWN, SUSAN. YOU'RE OVERREACTING.

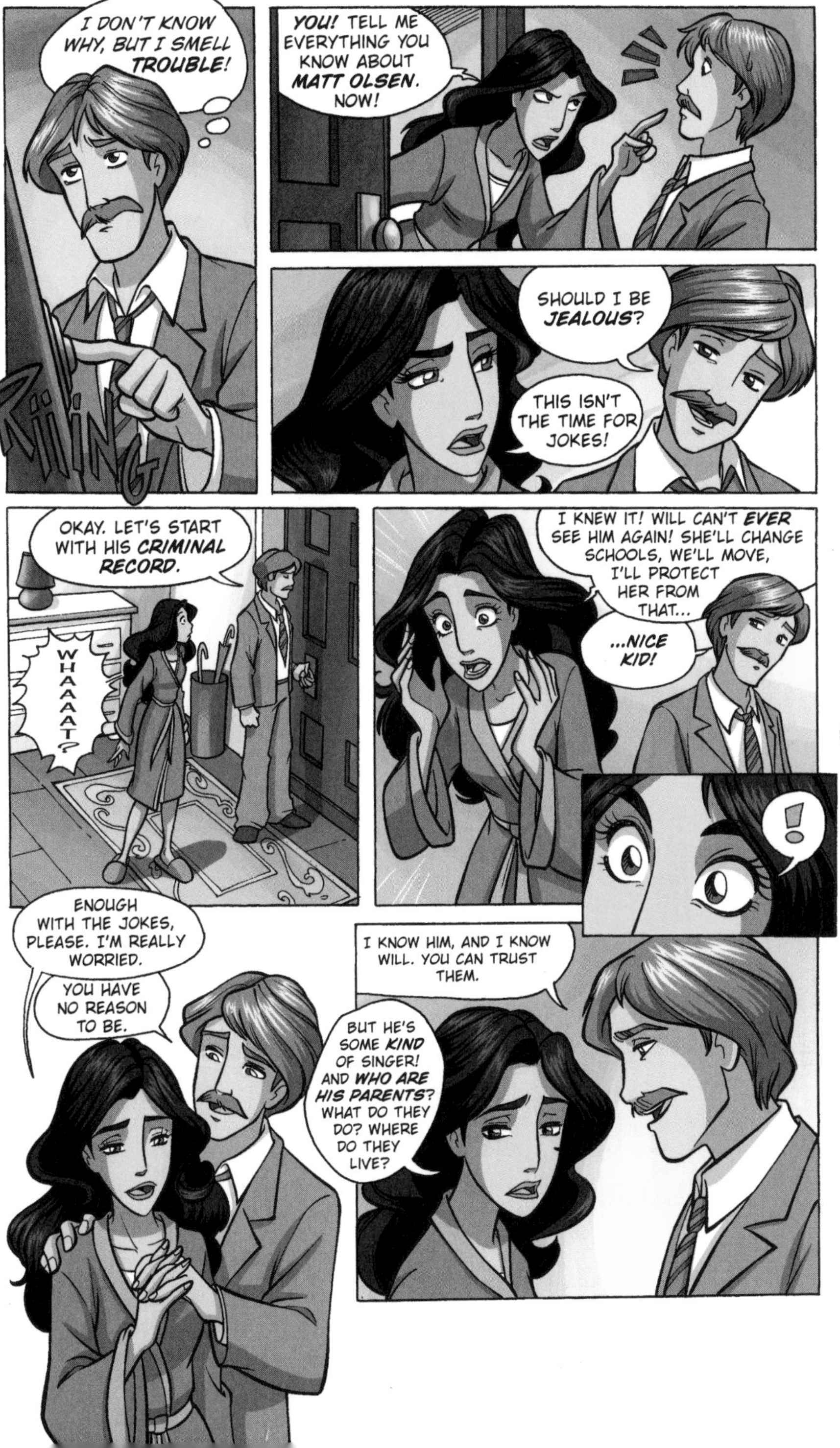
I DON'T KNOW WHY, BUT I SMELL TROUBLE!
RIIING
YOU! TELL ME EVERYTHING YOU KNOW ABOUT MATT OLSEN. NOW!
SHOULD I BE JEALOUS?
THIS ISN'T THE TIME FOR JOKES!
OKAY. LET'S START WITH HIS CRIMINAL RECORD.
WHAAAAAT?
I KNEW IT! WILL CAN'T EVER SEE HIM AGAIN! SHE'LL CHANGE SCHOOLS, WE'LL MOVE, I'LL PROTECT HER FROM THAT...
...NICE KID!
!
ENOUGH WITH THE JOKES, PLEASE. I'M REALLY WORRIED.
YOU HAVE NO REASON TO BE.
I KNOW HIM, AND I KNOW WILL. YOU CAN TRUST THEM.
BUT HE'S SOME KIND OF SINGER! AND WHO ARE HIS PARENTS? WHAT DO THEY DO? WHERE DO THEY LIVE?

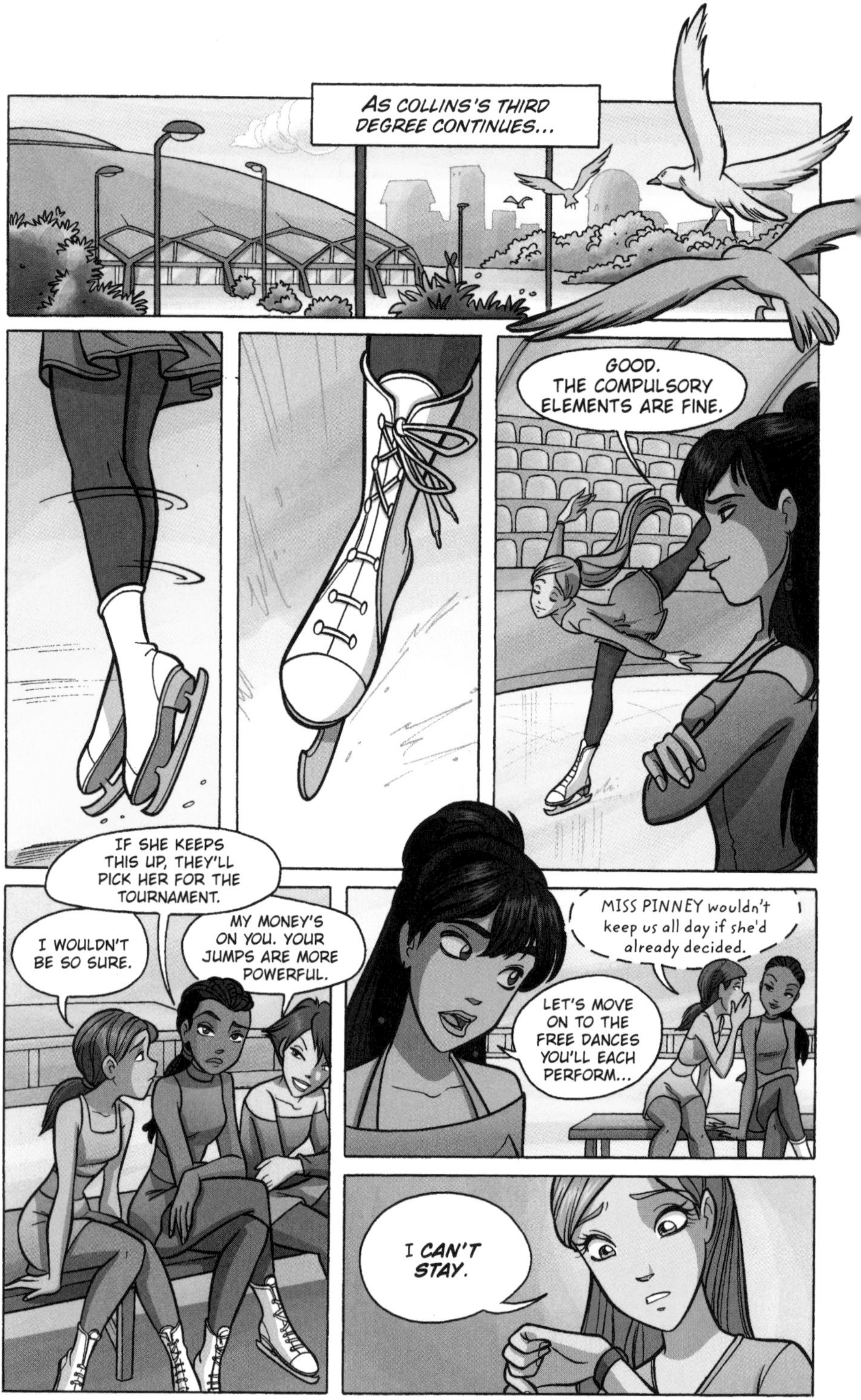
AS COLLINS'S THIRD DEGREE CONTINUES...
GOOD. THE COMPULSORY ELEMENTS ARE FINE.
IF SHE KEEPS THIS UP, THEY'LL PICK HER FOR THE TOURNAMENT.
I WOULDN'T BE SO SURE.
MY MONEY'S ON YOU. YOUR JUMPS ARE MORE POWERFUL.
MISS PINNEY wouldn't keep us all day if she'd already decided.
LET'S MOVE ON TO THE FREE DANCES YOU'LL EACH PERFORM...
I CAN'T STAY.

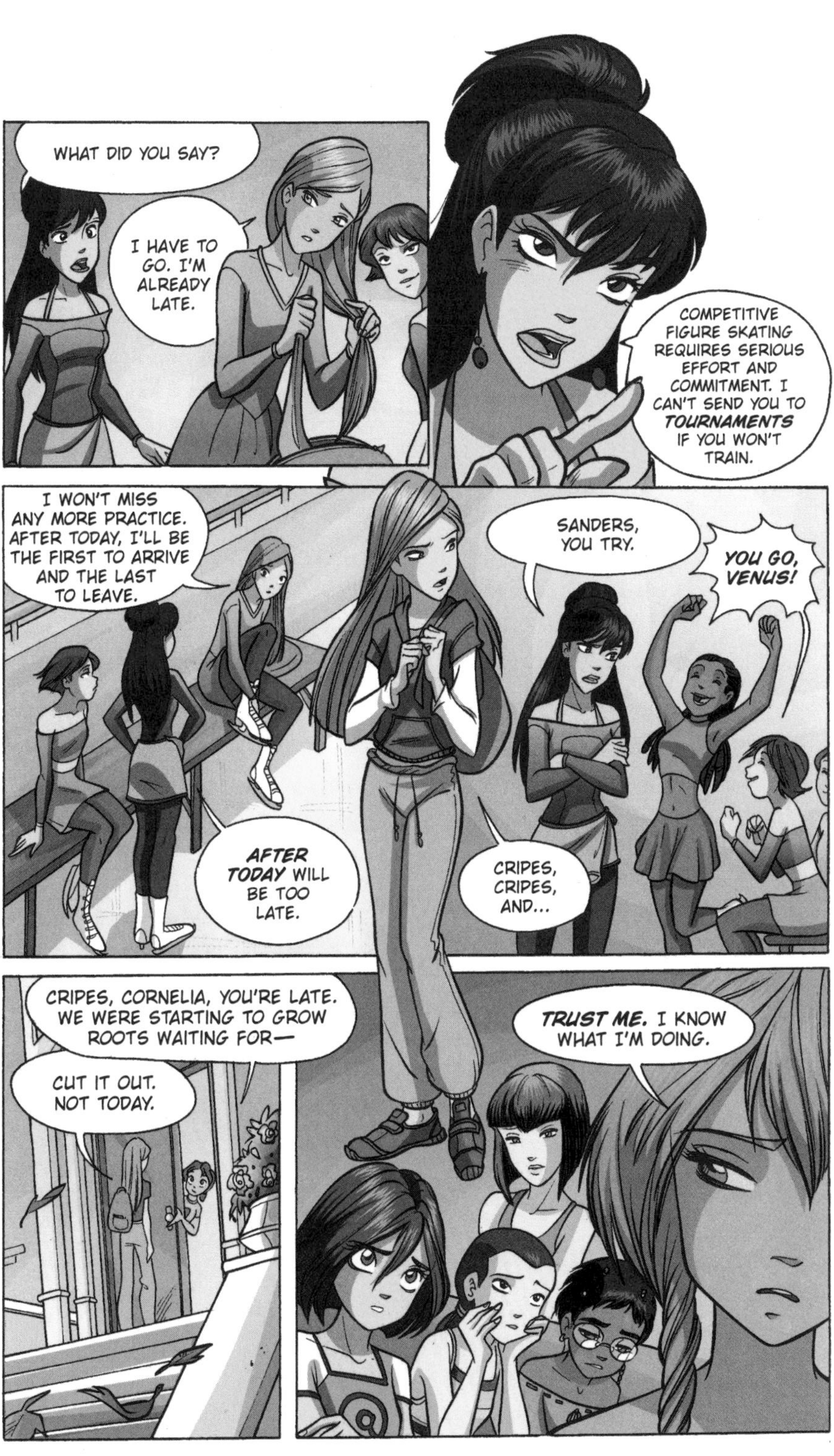
WHAT DID YOU SAY?
I HAVE TO GO. I'M ALREADY LATE.
COMPETITIVE FIGURE SKATING REQUIRES SERIOUS EFFORT AND COMMITMENT. I CAN'T SEND YOU TO TOURNAMENTS IF YOU WON'T TRAIN.
I WON'T MISS ANY MORE PRACTICE. AFTER TODAY, I'LL BE THE FIRST TO ARRIVE AND THE LAST TO LEAVE.
AFTER TODAY WILL BE TOO LATE.
SANDERS, YOU TRY.
CRIPES, CRIPES, AND...
YOU GO, VENUS!
CRIPES, CORNELIA, YOU'RE LATE. WE WERE STARTING TO GROW ROOTS WAITING FOR—
CUT IT OUT. NOT TODAY.
TRUST ME. I KNOW WHAT I'M DOING.

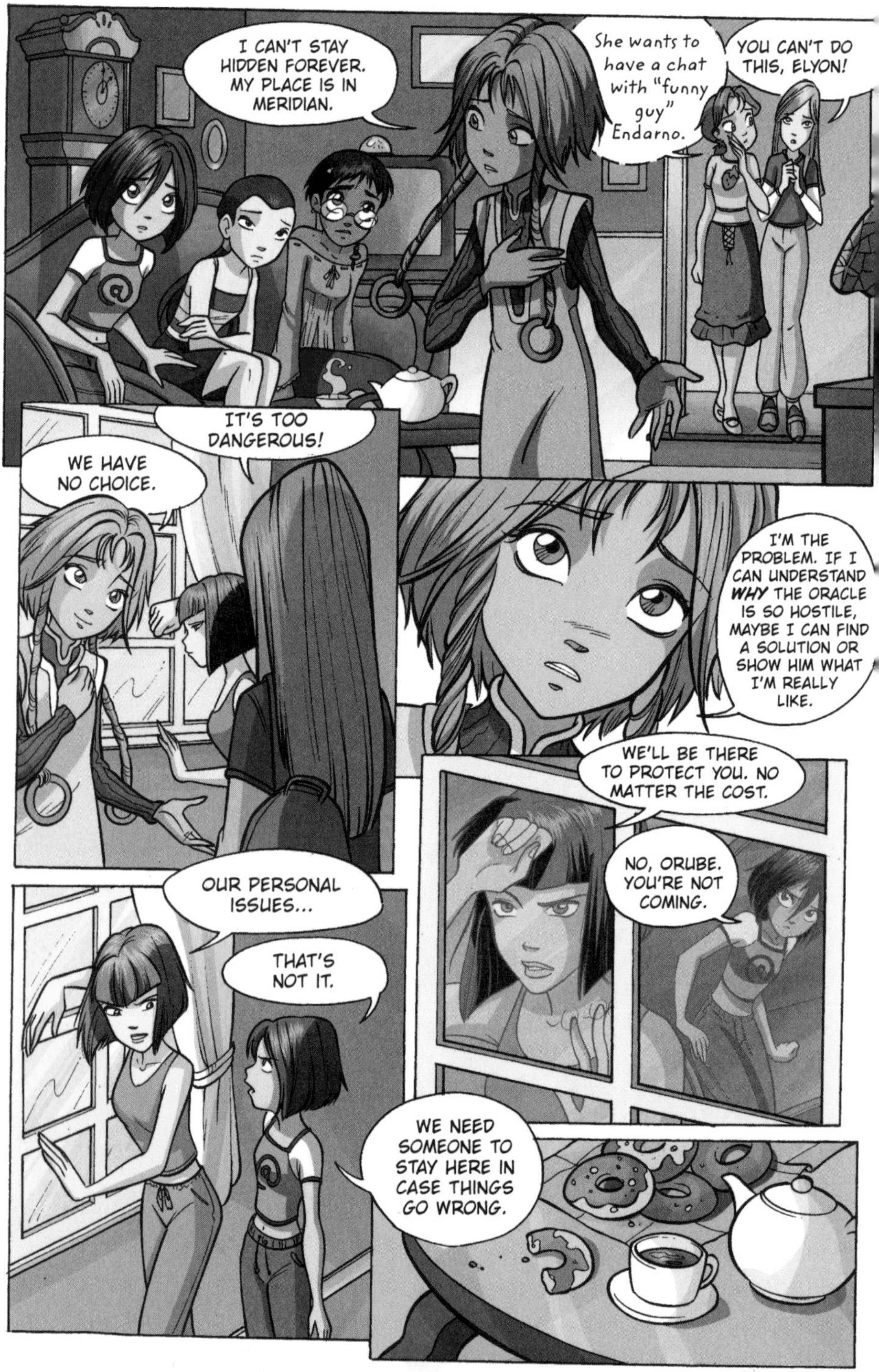
I CAN'T STAY HIDDEN FOREVER. MY PLACE IS IN MERIDIAN.
She wants to have a chat with "funny guy" Endarno.
YOU CAN'T DO THIS, ELYON!
IT'S TOO DANGEROUS!
WE HAVE NO CHOICE.
I'M THE PROBLEM. IF I CAN UNDERSTAND *WHY* THE ORACLE IS SO HOSTILE, MAYBE I CAN FIND A SOLUTION OR SHOW HIM WHAT I'M REALLY LIKE.
WE'LL BE THERE TO PROTECT YOU. NO MATTER THE COST.
NO, ORUBE. YOU'RE NOT COMING.
OUR PERSONAL ISSUES...
THAT'S NOT IT.
WE NEED SOMEONE TO STAY HERE IN CASE THINGS GO WRONG.

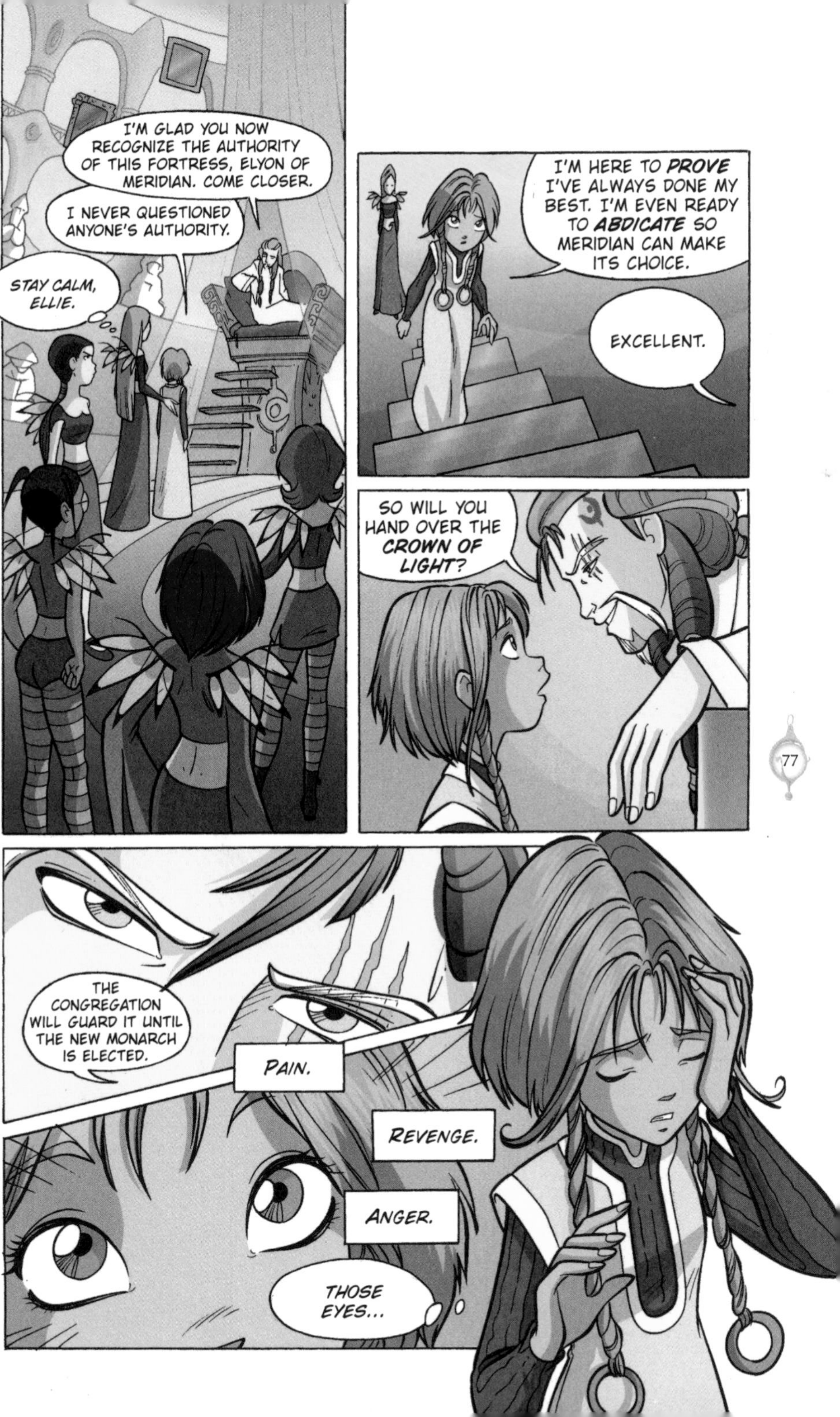

I'M GLAD YOU NOW RECOGNIZE THE AUTHORITY OF THIS FORTRESS, ELYON OF MERIDIAN. COME CLOSER.
I NEVER QUESTIONED ANYONE'S AUTHORITY.
STAY CALM, ELLIE.
I'M HERE TO PROVE I'VE ALWAYS DONE MY BEST. I'M EVEN READY TO ABDICATE SO MERIDIAN CAN MAKE ITS CHOICE.
EXCELLENT.
SO WILL YOU HAND OVER THE CROWN OF LIGHT?
THE CONGREGATION WILL GUARD IT UNTIL THE NEW MONARCH IS ELECTED.
PAIN.
REVENGE.
ANGER.
THOSE EYES...

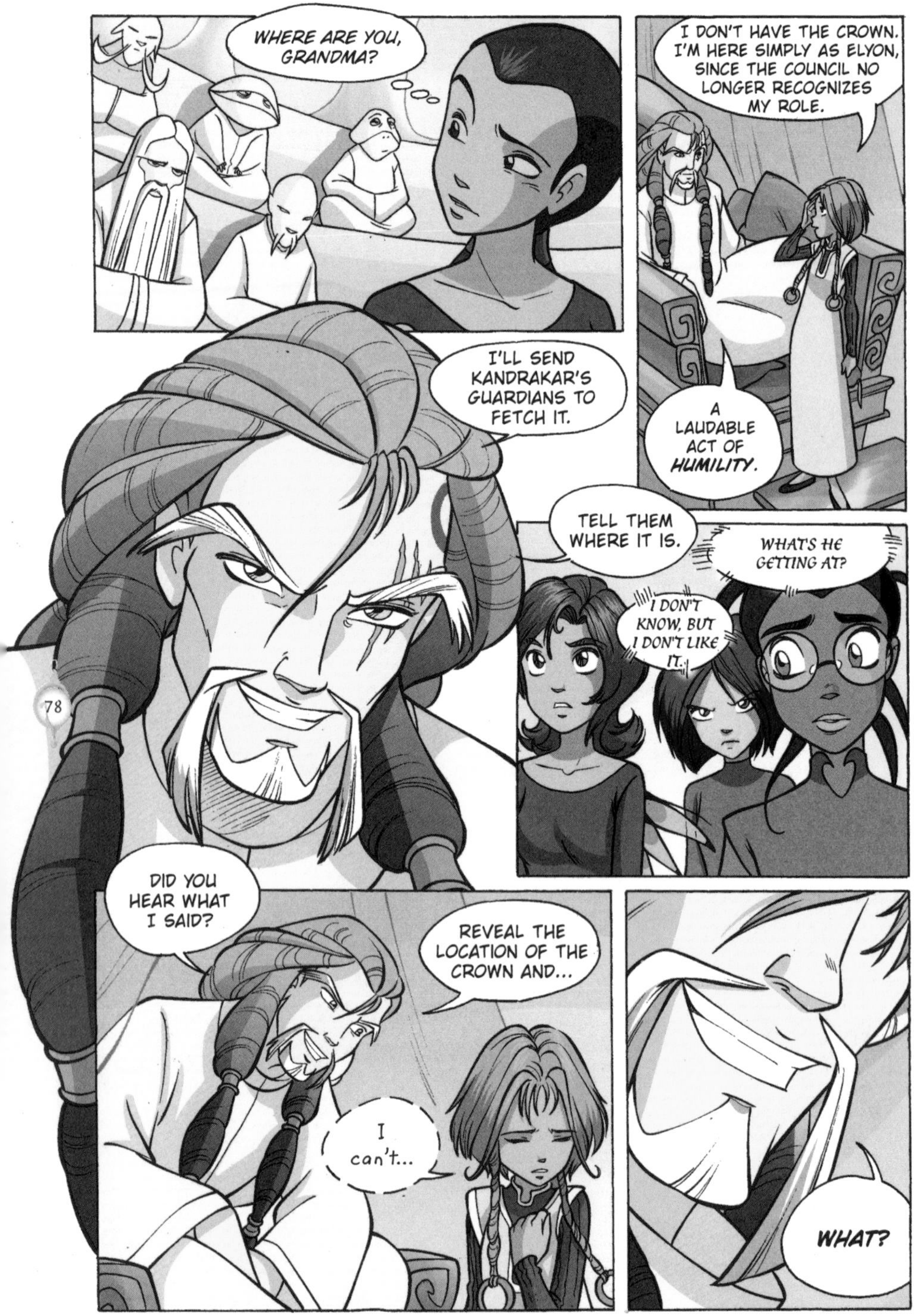
WHERE ARE YOU, GRANDMA?
I DON'T HAVE THE CROWN. I'M HERE SIMPLY AS ELYON, SINCE THE COUNCIL NO LONGER RECOGNIZES MY ROLE.
A LAUDABLE ACT OF HUMILITY.
I'LL SEND KANDRAKAR'S GUARDIANS TO FETCH IT.
TELL THEM WHERE IT IS.
WHAT'S HE GETTING AT?
I DON'T KNOW, BUT I DON'T LIKE IT.
DID YOU HEAR WHAT I SAID?
REVEAL THE LOCATION OF THE CROWN AND...
I can't...
WHAT?

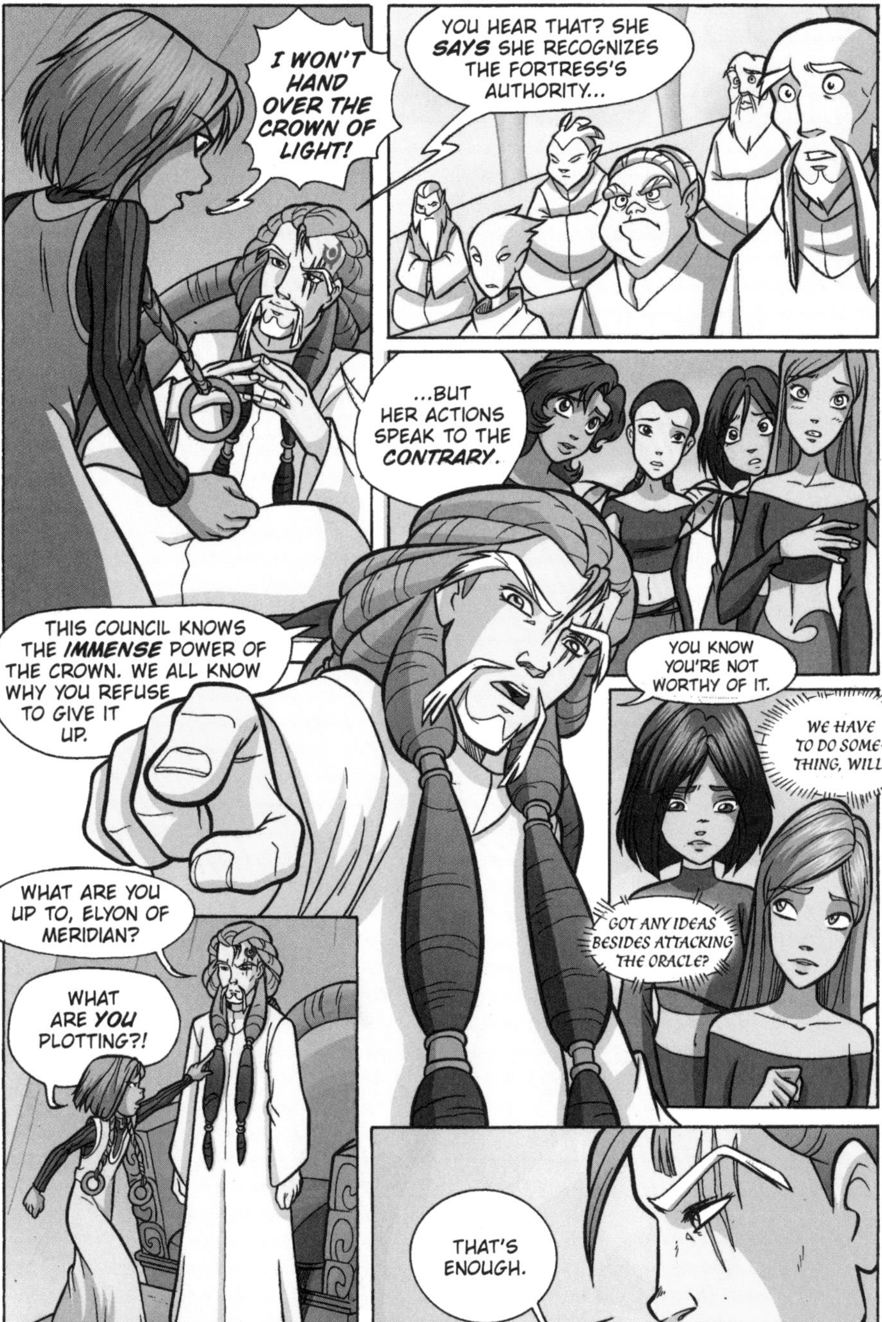

I WON'T HAND OVER THE CROWN OF LIGHT!
YOU HEAR THAT? SHE SAYS SHE RECOGNIZES THE FORTRESS'S AUTHORITY...
...BUT HER ACTIONS SPEAK TO THE CONTRARY.
THIS COUNCIL KNOWS THE IMMENSE POWER OF THE CROWN. WE ALL KNOW WHY YOU REFUSE TO GIVE IT UP.
YOU KNOW YOU'RE NOT WORTHY OF IT.
WE HAVE TO DO SOMETHING, WILL.
GOT ANY IDEAS BESIDES ATTACKING THE ORACLE?
WHAT ARE YOU UP TO, ELYON OF MERIDIAN?
WHAT ARE YOU PLOTTING?!
THAT'S ENOUGH.

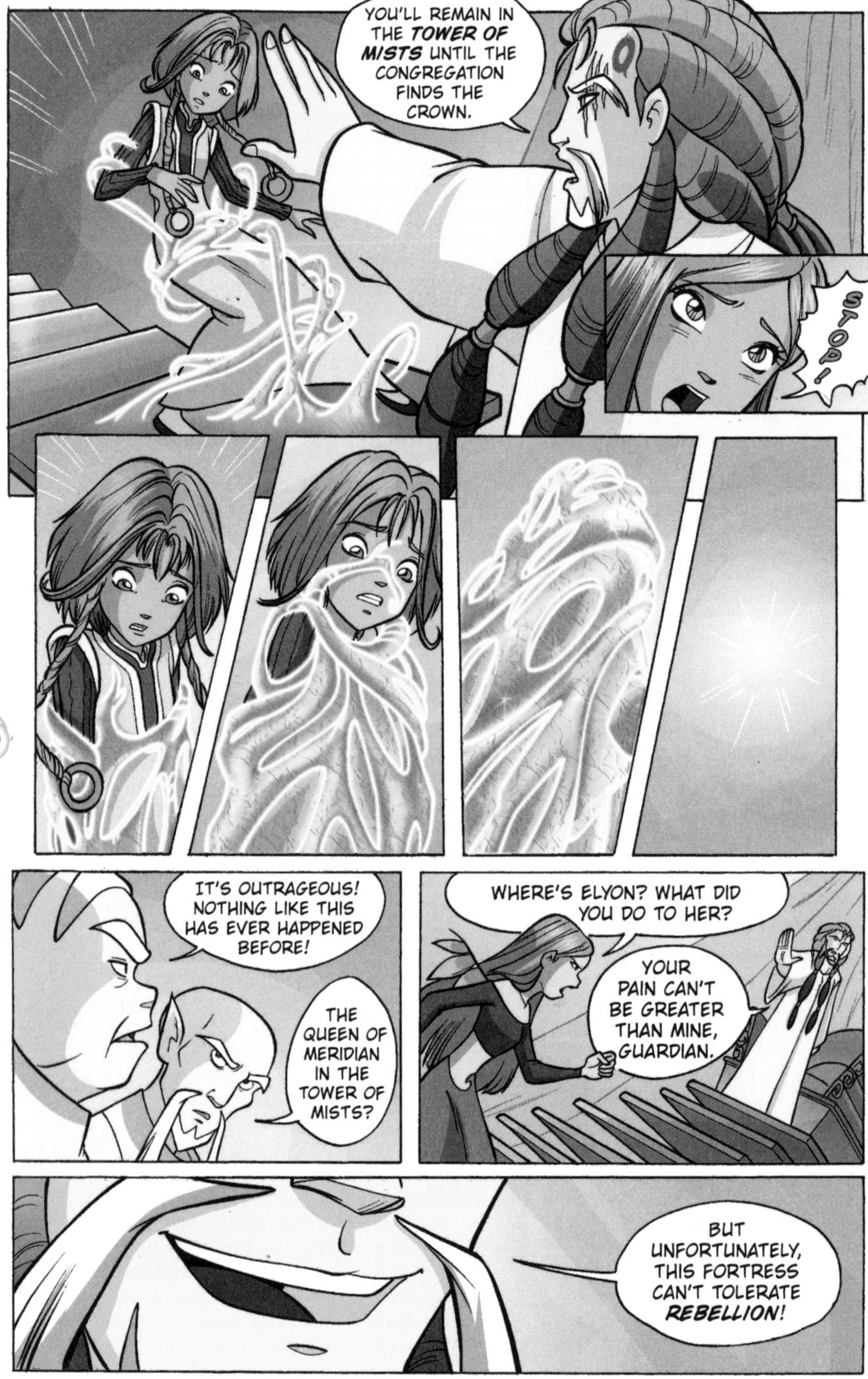
YOU'LL REMAIN IN THE TOWER OF MISTS UNTIL THE CONGREGATION FINDS THE CROWN.
STOP!
IT'S OUTRAGEOUS! NOTHING LIKE THIS HAS EVER HAPPENED BEFORE!
THE QUEEN OF MERIDIAN IN THE TOWER OF MISTS?
WHERE'S ELYON? WHAT DID YOU DO TO HER?
YOUR PAIN CAN'T BE GREATER THAN MINE, GUARDIAN.
BUT UNFORTUNATELY, THIS FORTRESS CAN'T TOLERATE REBELLION!

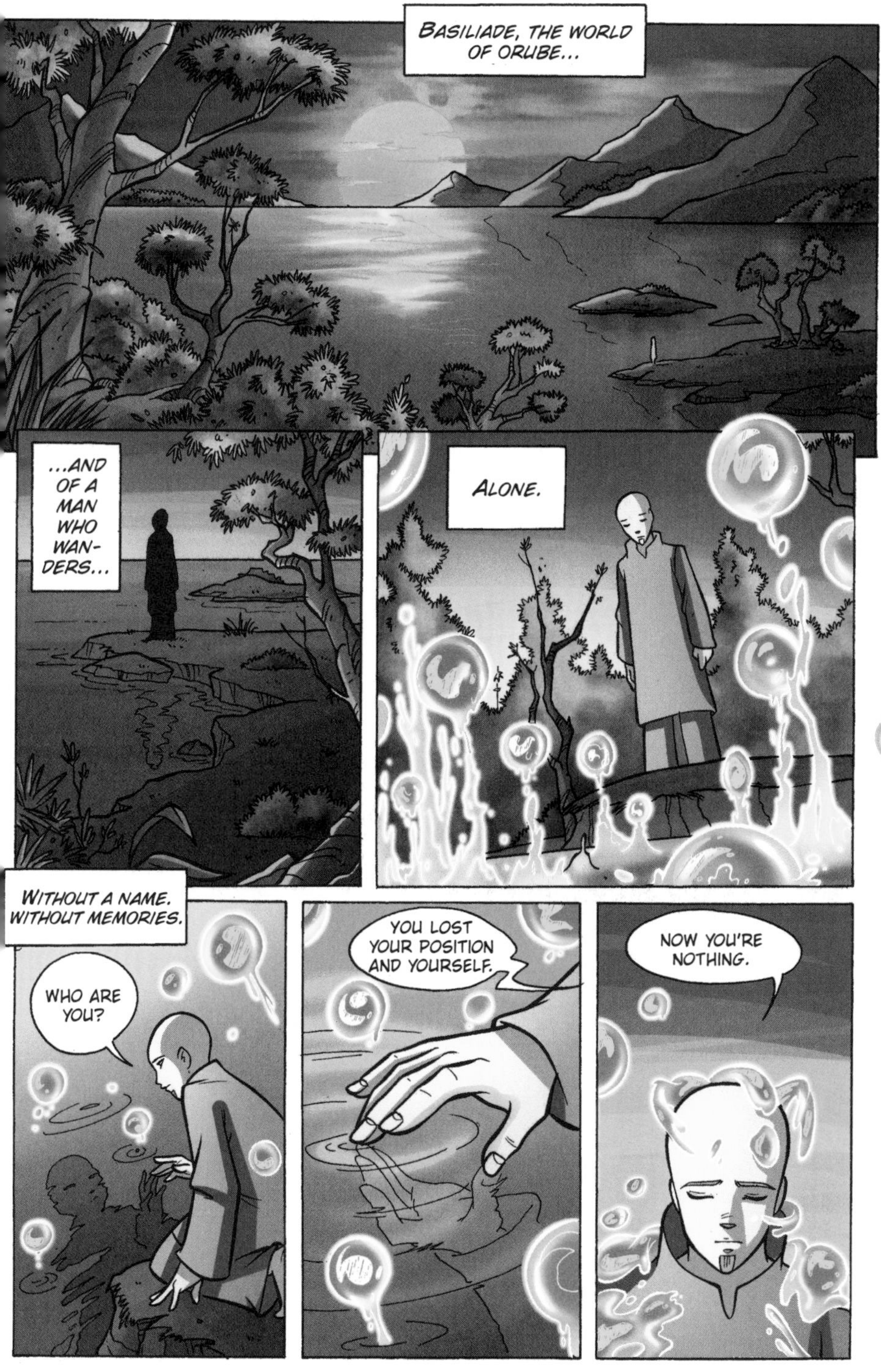
BASILIADE, THE WORLD OF ORUBE...
...AND OF A MAN WHO WAN-DERS...
ALONE.
WITHOUT A NAME. WITHOUT MEMORIES.
WHO ARE YOU?
YOU LOST YOUR POSITION AND YOURSELF.
NOW YOU'RE NOTHING.

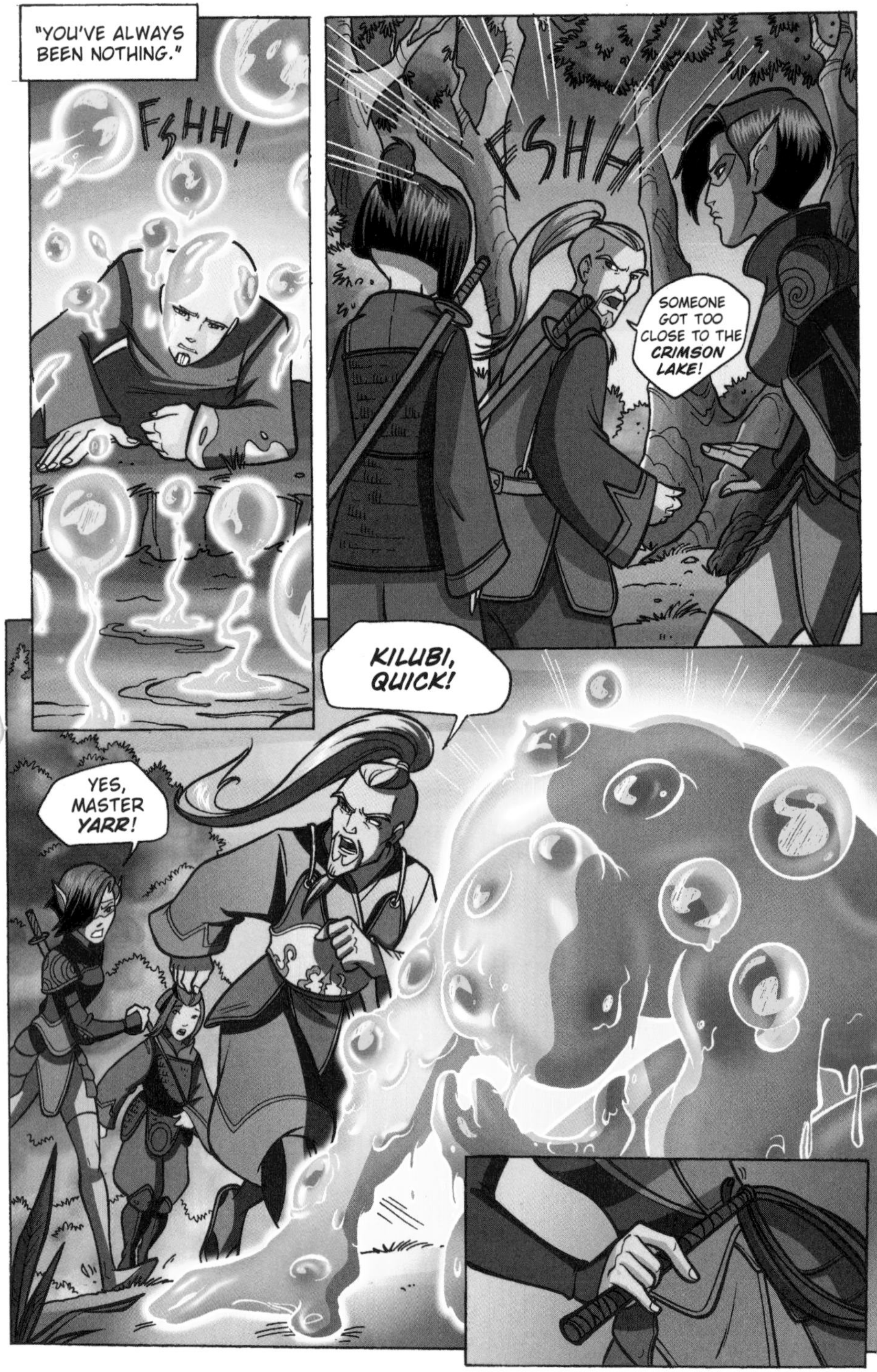
"YOU'VE ALWAYS BEEN NOTHING."
FSHH!
FSHH
SOMEONE GOT TOO CLOSE TO THE CRIMSON LAKE!
KILUBI, QUICK!
YES, MASTER YARR!

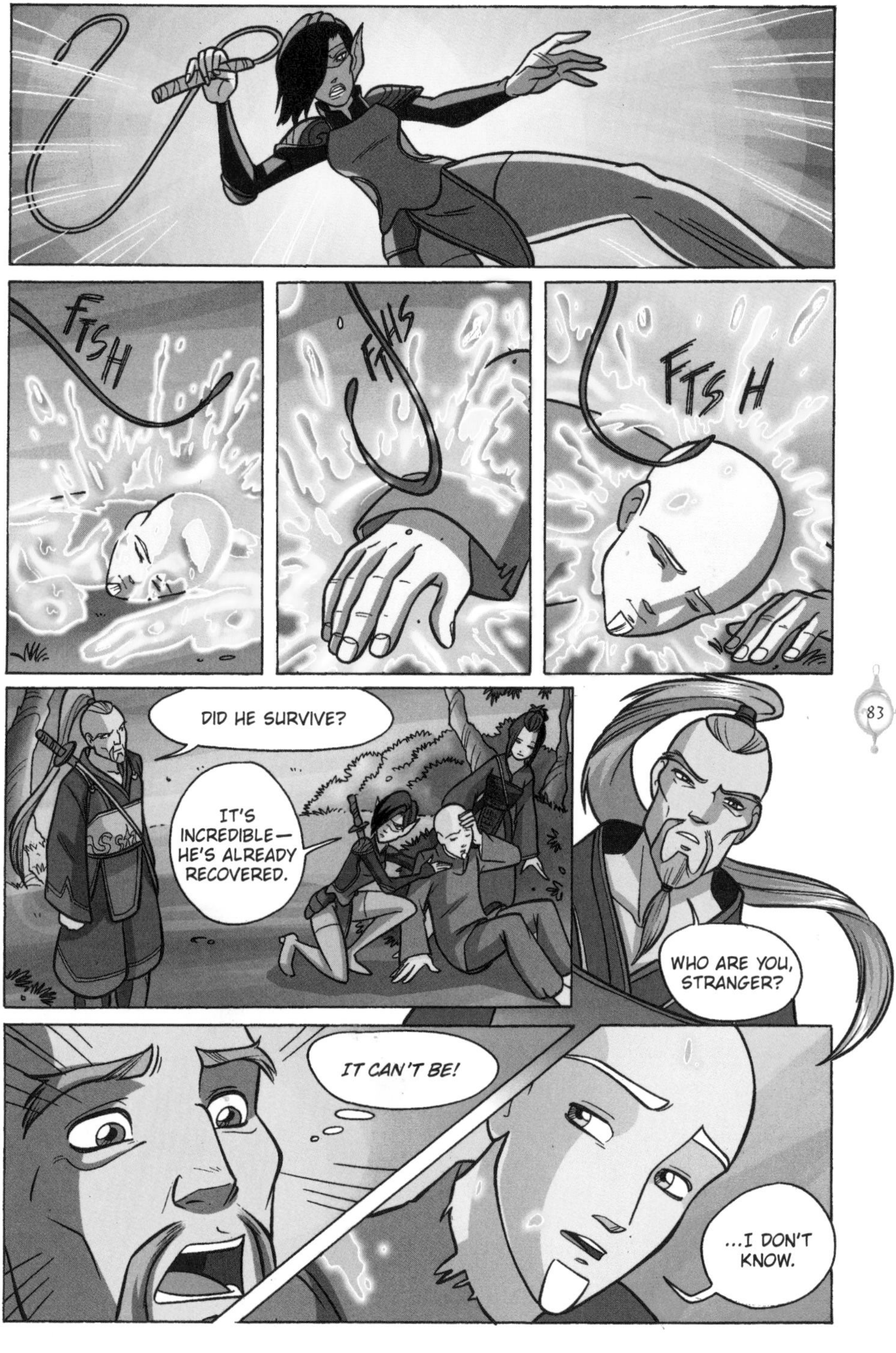
FTSH
FTHS
FTSH
DID HE SURVIVE?
IT'S INCREDIBLE—HE'S ALREADY RECOVERED.
WHO ARE YOU, STRANGER?
IT CAN'T BE!
...I DON'T KNOW.

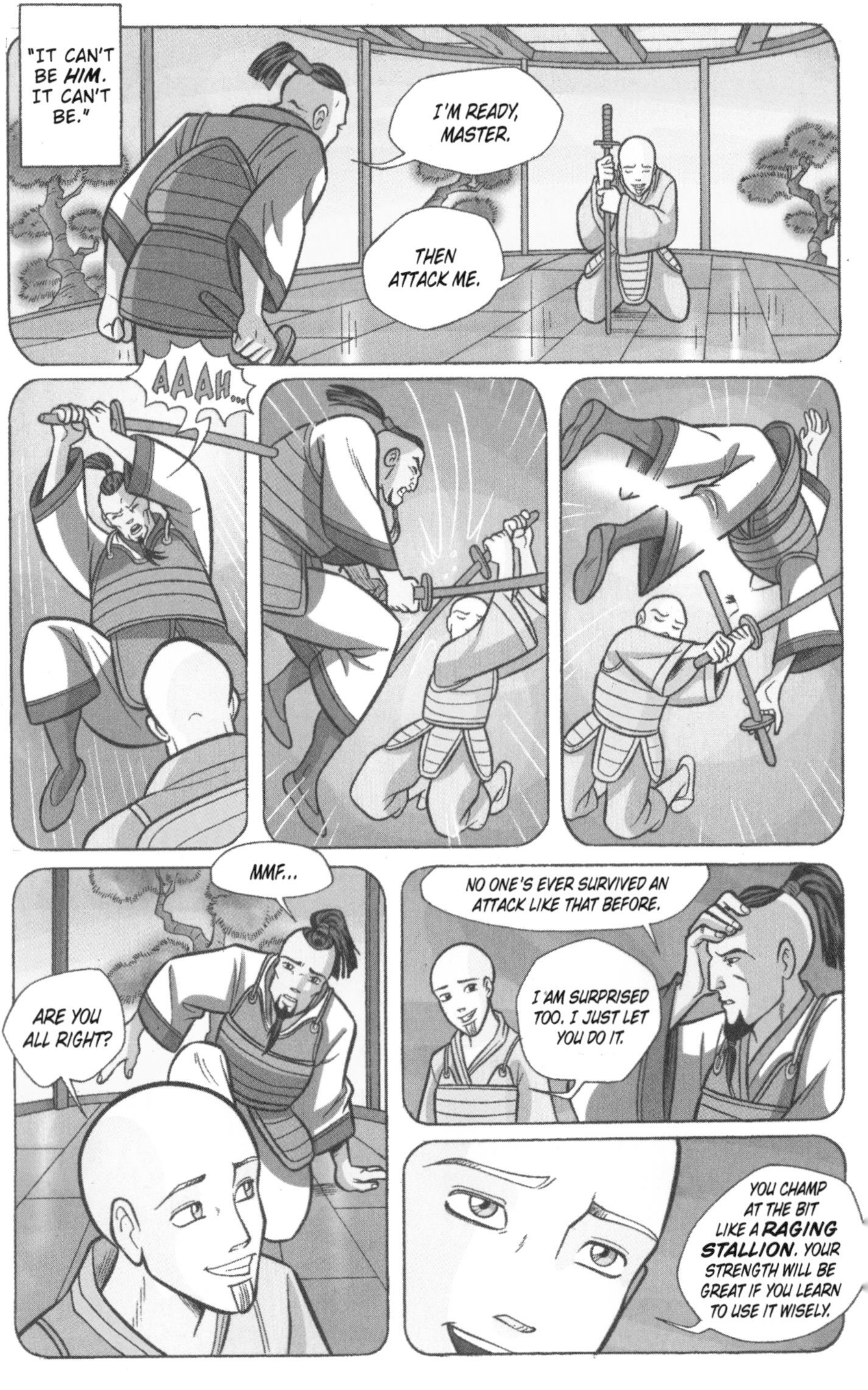
"IT CAN'T BE **HIM**. IT CAN'T BE."
I'M READY, MASTER.
THEN ATTACK ME.
AAAH...
MMF...
ARE YOU ALL RIGHT?
NO ONE'S EVER SURVIVED AN ATTACK LIKE THAT BEFORE.
I AM SURPRISED TOO. I JUST LET YOU DO IT.
YOU CHAMP AT THE BIT LIKE A **RAGING STALLION**. YOUR STRENGTH WILL BE GREAT IF YOU LEARN TO USE IT WISELY.

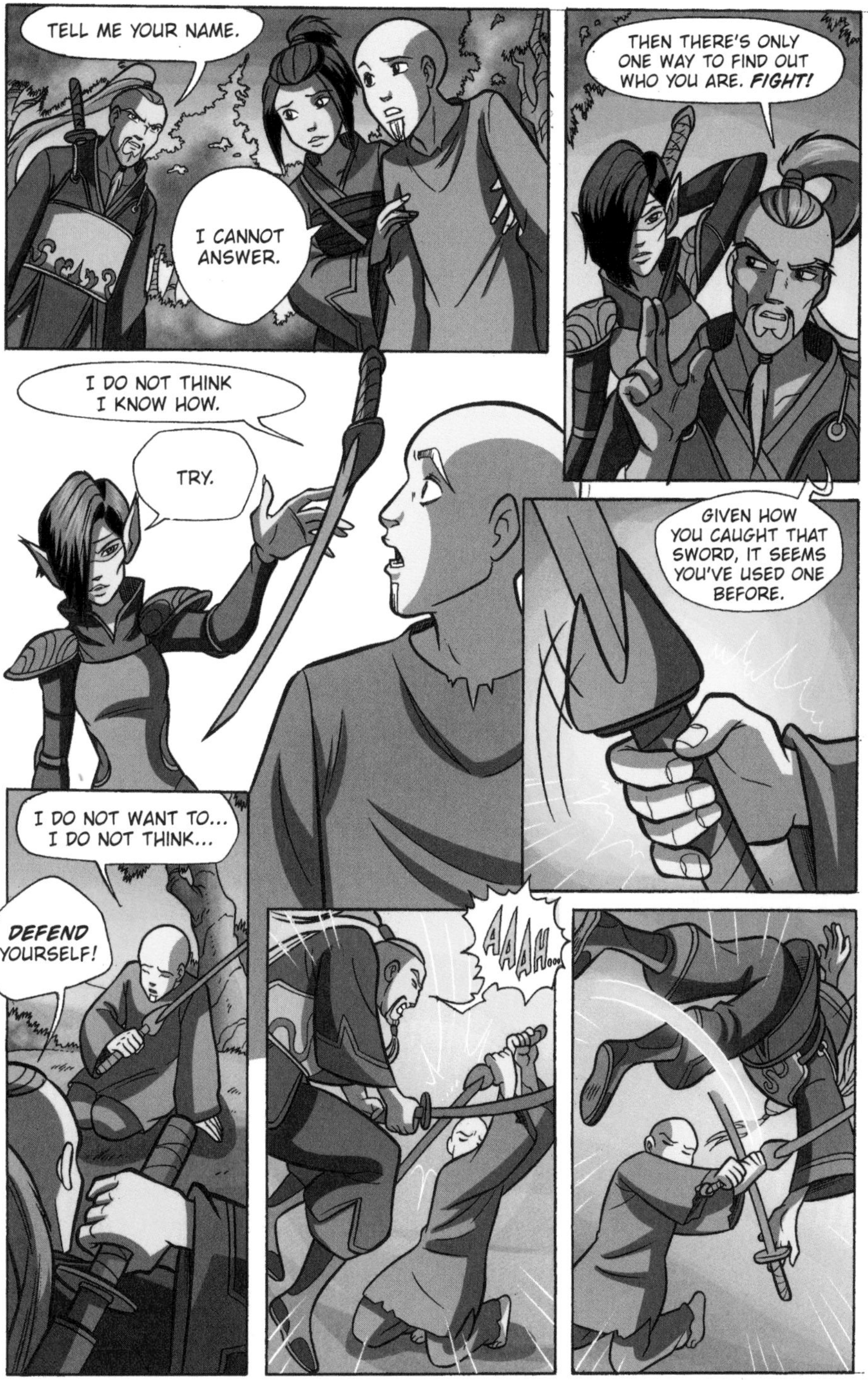
TELL ME YOUR NAME.
I CANNOT ANSWER.
THEN THERE'S ONLY ONE WAY TO FIND OUT WHO YOU ARE. FIGHT!
I DO NOT THINK I KNOW HOW.
TRY.
GIVEN HOW YOU CAUGHT THAT SWORD, IT SEEMS YOU'VE USED ONE BEFORE.
I DO NOT WANT TO... I DO NOT THINK...
DEFEND YOURSELF!
AAAH...

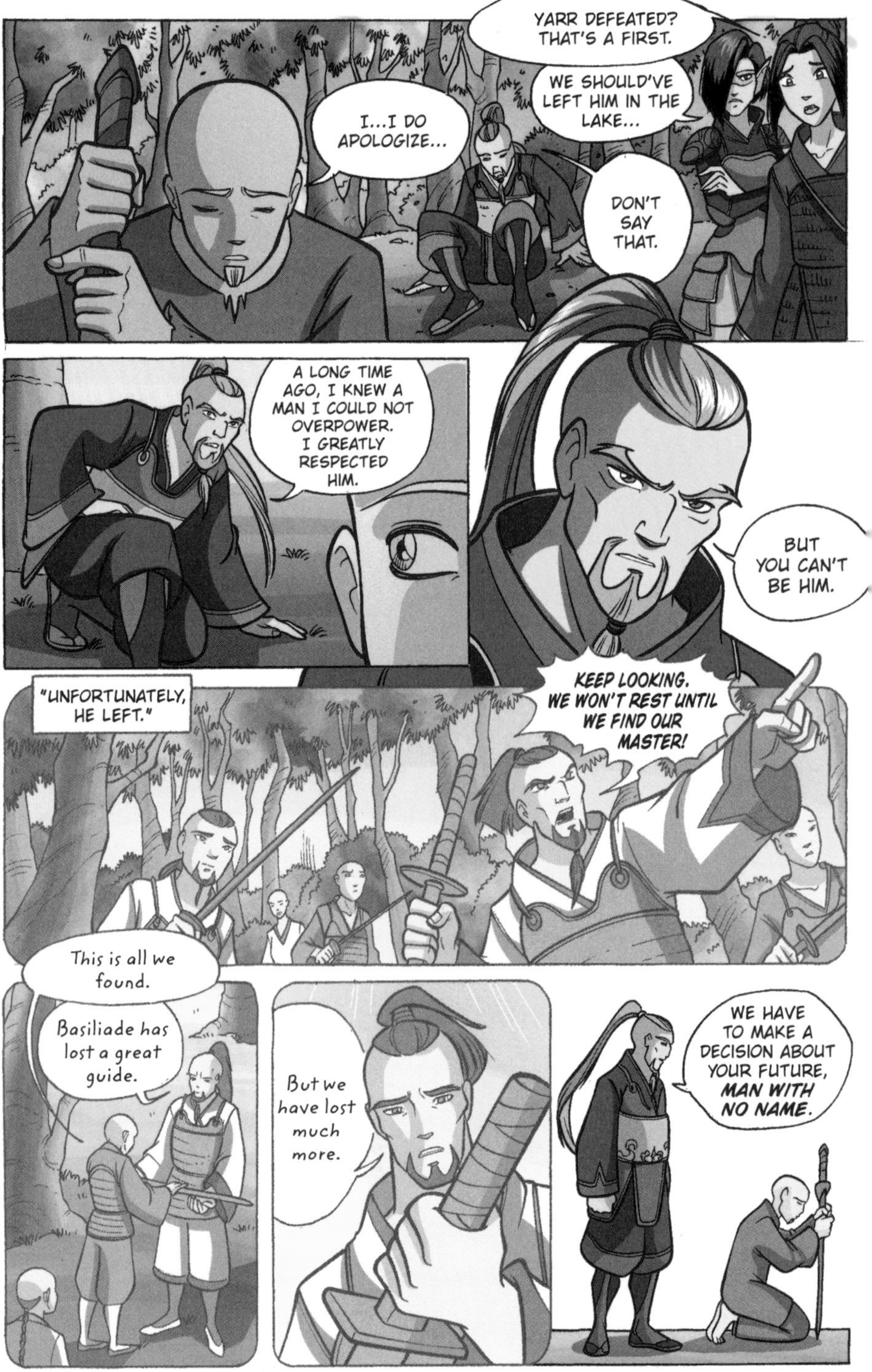

YARR DEFEATED? THAT'S A FIRST.
I...I DO APOLOGIZE...
WE SHOULD'VE LEFT HIM IN THE LAKE...
DON'T SAY THAT.
A LONG TIME AGO, I KNEW A MAN I COULD NOT OVERPOWER. I GREATLY RESPECTED HIM.
BUT YOU CAN'T BE HIM.
"UNFORTUNATELY, HE LEFT."
KEEP LOOKING. WE WON'T REST UNTIL WE FIND OUR MASTER!
This is all we found.
Basiliade has lost a great guide.
But we have lost much more.
WE HAVE TO MAKE A DECISION ABOUT YOUR FUTURE, MAN WITH NO NAME.

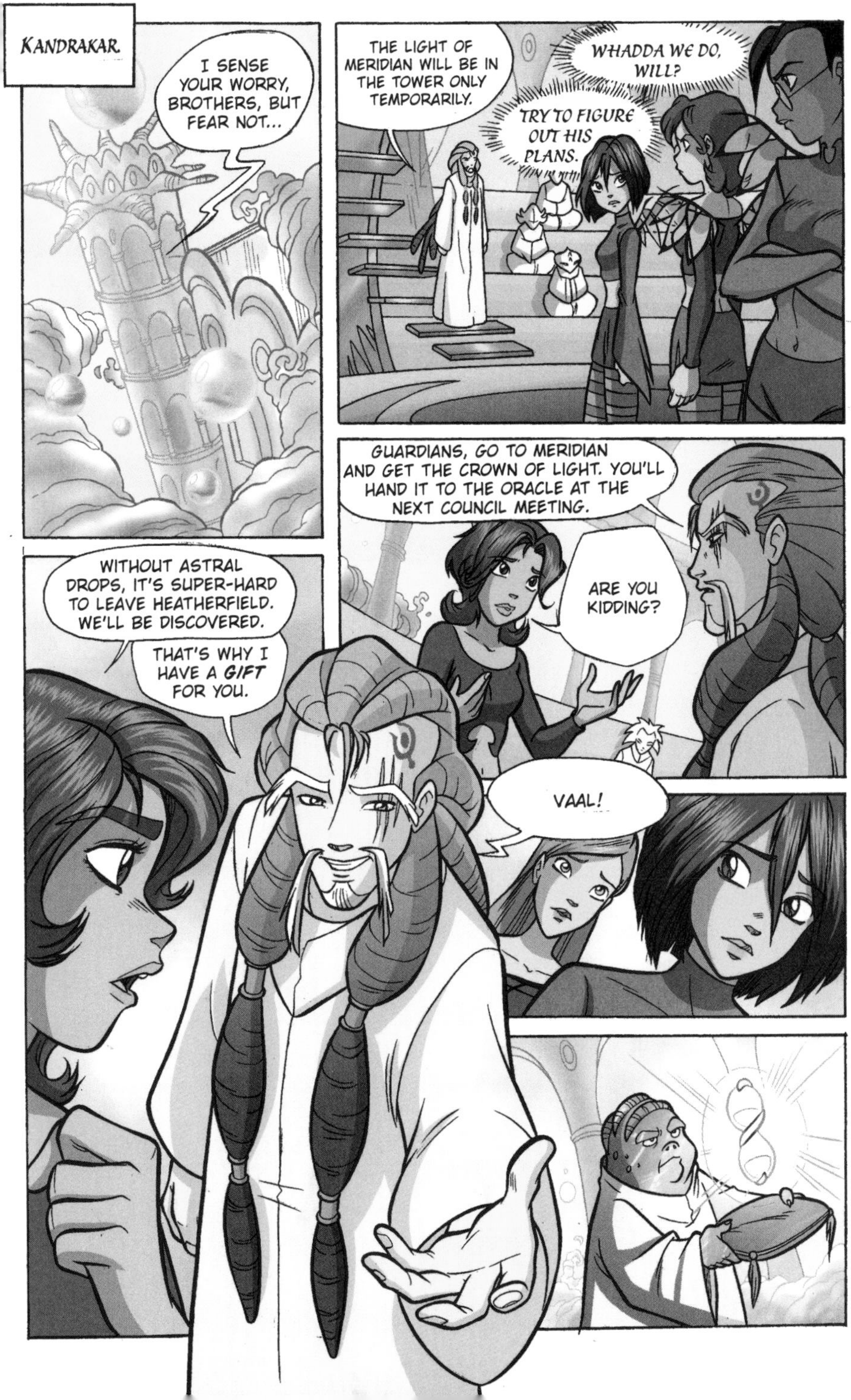
KANDRAKAR
I SENSE YOUR WORRY, BROTHERS, BUT FEAR NOT...
THE LIGHT OF MERIDIAN WILL BE IN THE TOWER ONLY TEMPORARILY.
WHADDA WE DO, WILL?
TRY TO FIGURE OUT HIS PLANS.
GUARDIANS, GO TO MERIDIAN AND GET THE CROWN OF LIGHT. YOU'LL HAND IT TO THE ORACLE AT THE NEXT COUNCIL MEETING.
ARE YOU KIDDING?
WITHOUT ASTRAL DROPS, IT'S SUPER-HARD TO LEAVE HEATHERFIELD. WE'LL BE DISCOVERED.
THAT'S WHY I HAVE A GIFT FOR YOU.
VAAL!

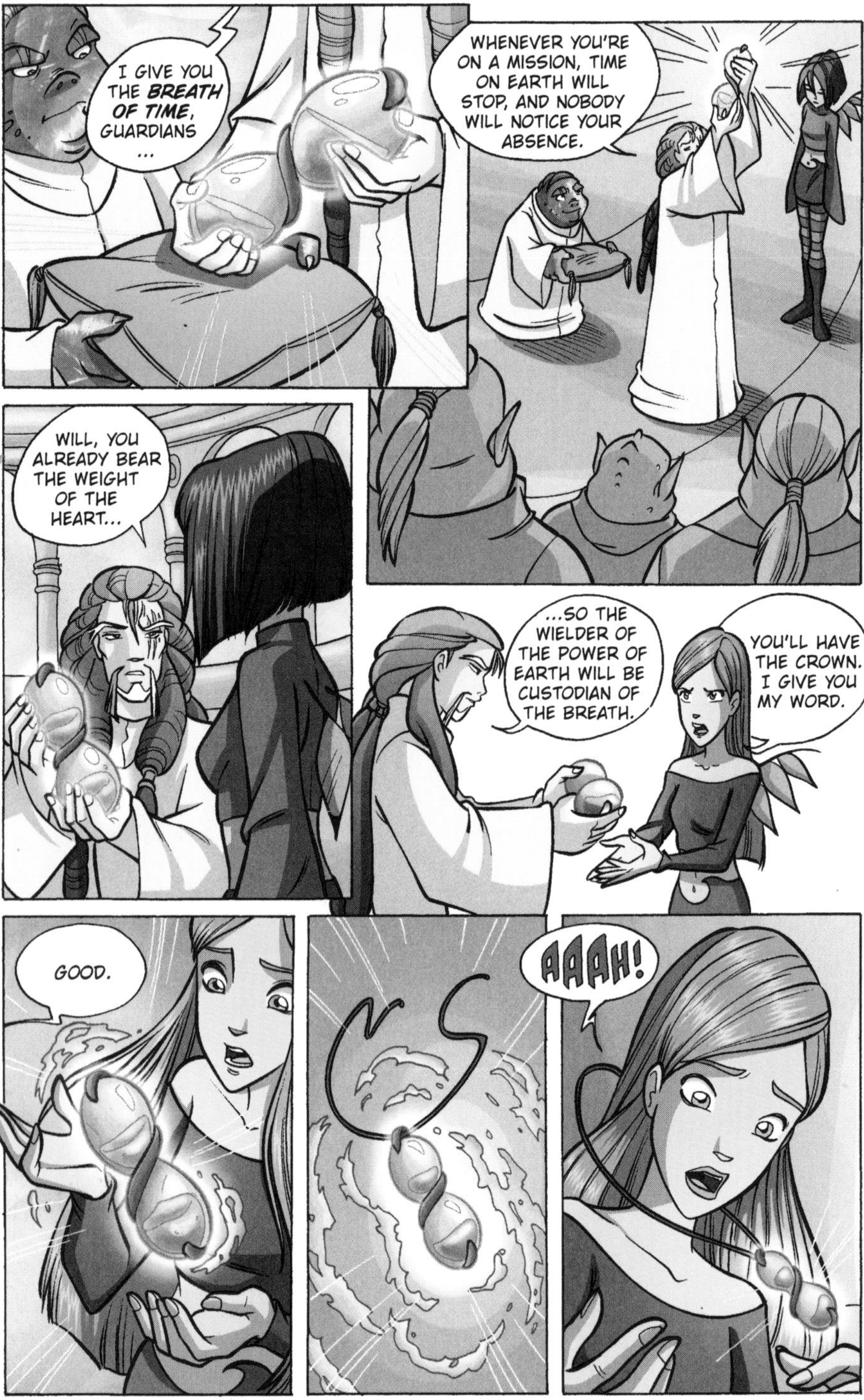
I GIVE YOU THE ***BREATH OF TIME***, GUARDIANS ...
WHENEVER YOU'RE ON A MISSION, TIME ON EARTH WILL STOP, AND NOBODY WILL NOTICE YOUR ABSENCE.
WILL, YOU ALREADY BEAR THE WEIGHT OF THE HEART...
...SO THE WIELDER OF THE POWER OF EARTH WILL BE CUSTODIAN OF THE BREATH.
YOU'LL HAVE THE CROWN. I GIVE YOU MY WORD.
GOOD.
AAAH!

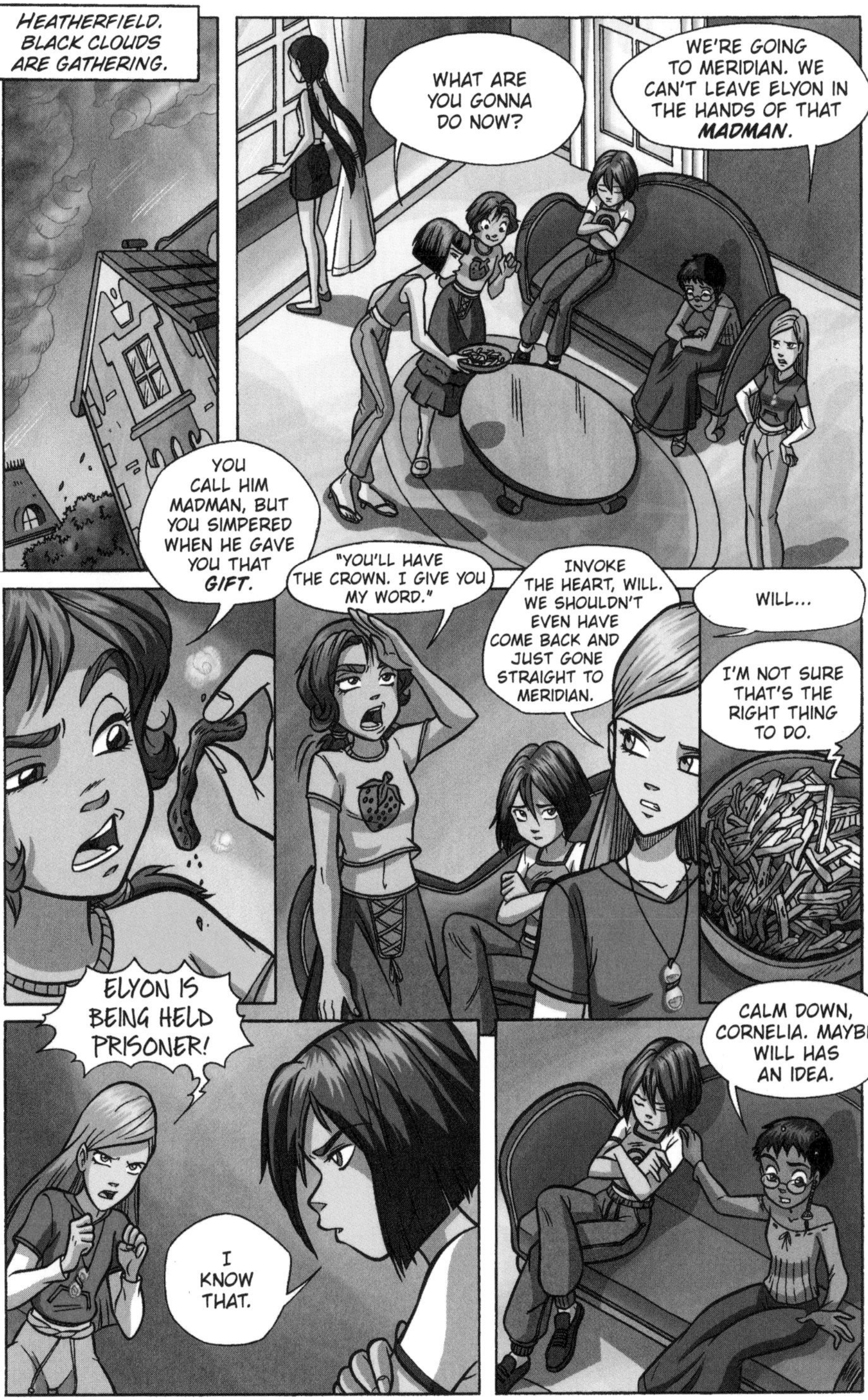
HEATHERFIELD. BLACK CLOUDS ARE GATHERING.
WHAT ARE YOU GONNA DO NOW?
WE'RE GOING TO MERIDIAN. WE CAN'T LEAVE ELYON IN THE HANDS OF THAT MADMAN.
YOU CALL HIM MADMAN, BUT YOU SIMPERED WHEN HE GAVE YOU THAT GIFT.
"YOU'LL HAVE THE CROWN. I GIVE YOU MY WORD."
INVOKE THE HEART, WILL. WE SHOULDN'T EVEN HAVE COME BACK AND JUST GONE STRAIGHT TO MERIDIAN.
WILL...
I'M NOT SURE THAT'S THE RIGHT THING TO DO.
ELYON IS BEING HELD PRISONER!
I KNOW THAT.
CALM DOWN, CORNELIA. MAYBE WILL HAS AN IDEA.

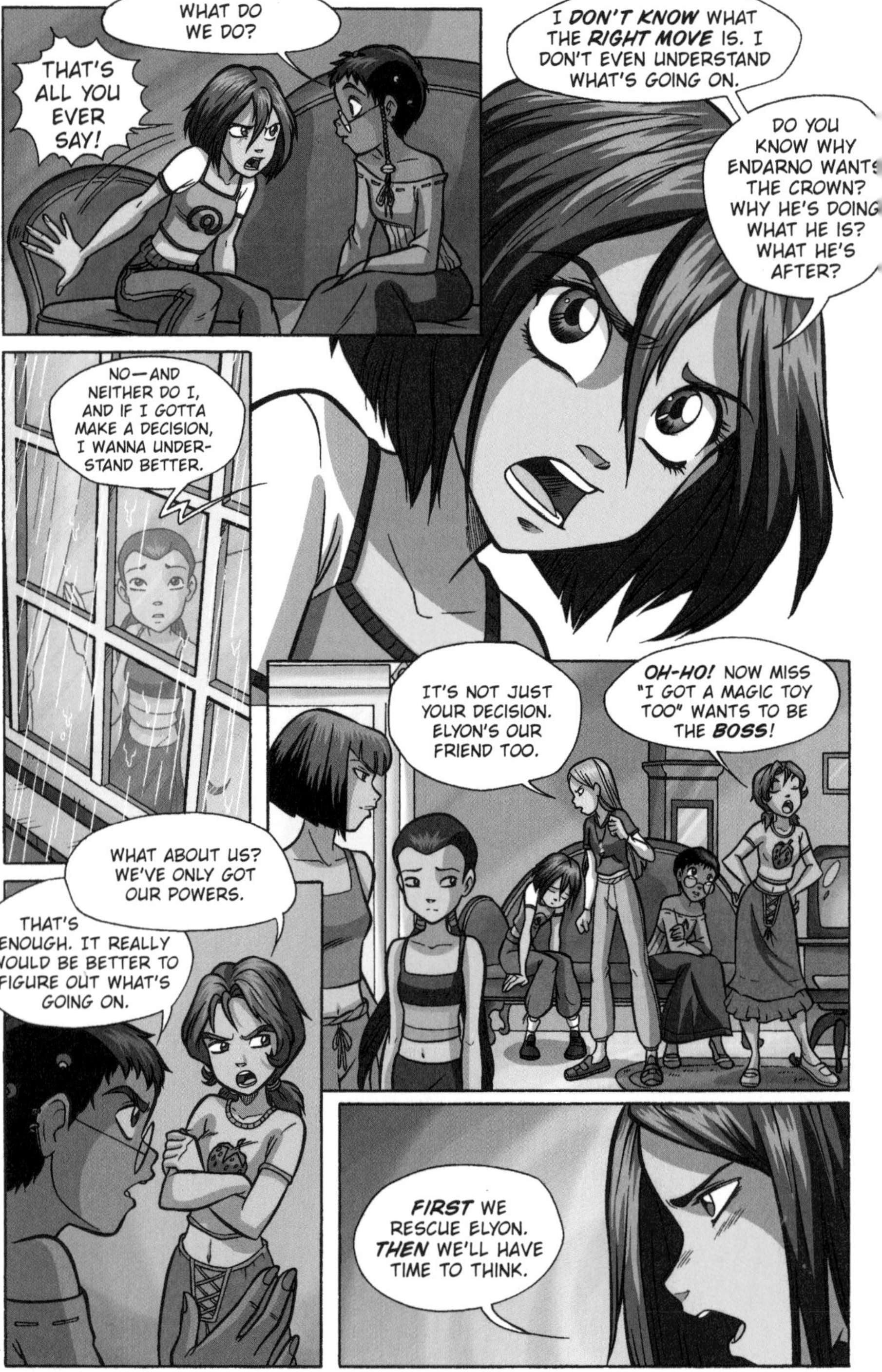
WHAT DO WE DO?
THAT'S ALL YOU EVER SAY!
I DON'T KNOW WHAT THE RIGHT MOVE IS. I DON'T EVEN UNDERSTAND WHAT'S GOING ON.
DO YOU KNOW WHY ENDARNO WANTS THE CROWN? WHY HE'S DOING WHAT HE IS? WHAT HE'S AFTER?
NO—AND NEITHER DO I, AND IF I GOTTA MAKE A DECISION, I WANNA UNDERSTAND BETTER.
IT'S NOT JUST YOUR DECISION. ELYON'S OUR FRIEND TOO.
OH-HO! NOW MISS "I GOT A MAGIC TOY TOO" WANTS TO BE THE BOSS!
WHAT ABOUT US? WE'VE ONLY GOT OUR POWERS.
THAT'S ENOUGH. IT REALLY WOULD BE BETTER TO FIGURE OUT WHAT'S GOING ON.
FIRST WE RESCUE ELYON. THEN WE'LL HAVE TIME TO THINK.

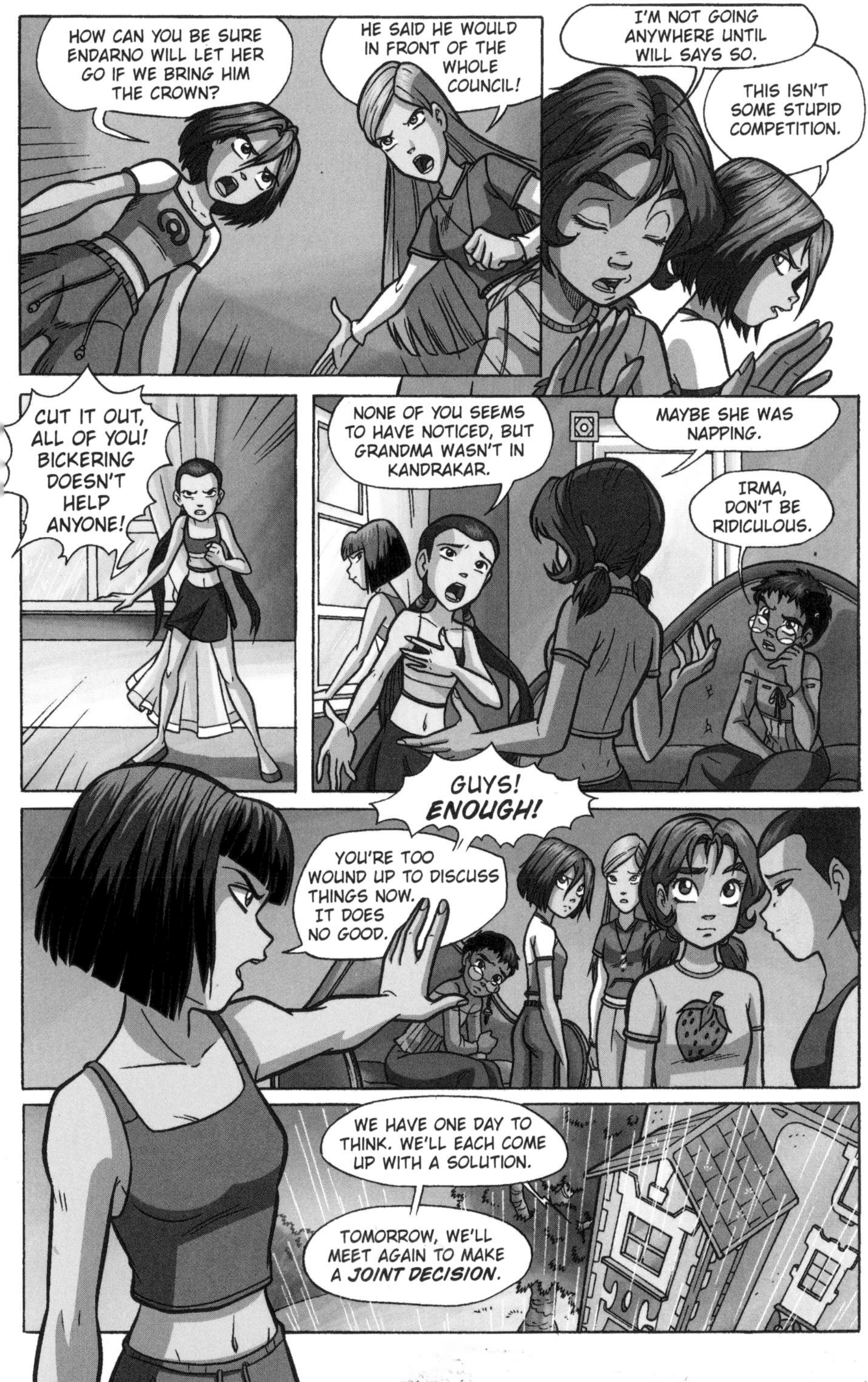
HOW CAN YOU BE SURE ENDARNO WILL LET HER GO IF WE BRING HIM THE CROWN?
HE SAID HE WOULD IN FRONT OF THE WHOLE COUNCIL!
I'M NOT GOING ANYWHERE UNTIL WILL SAYS SO.
THIS ISN'T SOME STUPID COMPETITION.
CUT IT OUT, ALL OF YOU! BICKERING DOESN'T HELP ANYONE!
NONE OF YOU SEEMS TO HAVE NOTICED, BUT GRANDMA WASN'T IN KANDRAKAR.
MAYBE SHE WAS NAPPING.
IRMA, DON'T BE RIDICULOUS.
GUYS! ENOUGH!
YOU'RE TOO WOUND UP TO DISCUSS THINGS NOW. IT DOES NO GOOD.
WE HAVE ONE DAY TO THINK. WE'LL EACH COME UP WITH A SOLUTION.
TOMORROW, WE'LL MEET AGAIN TO MAKE A JOINT DECISION.

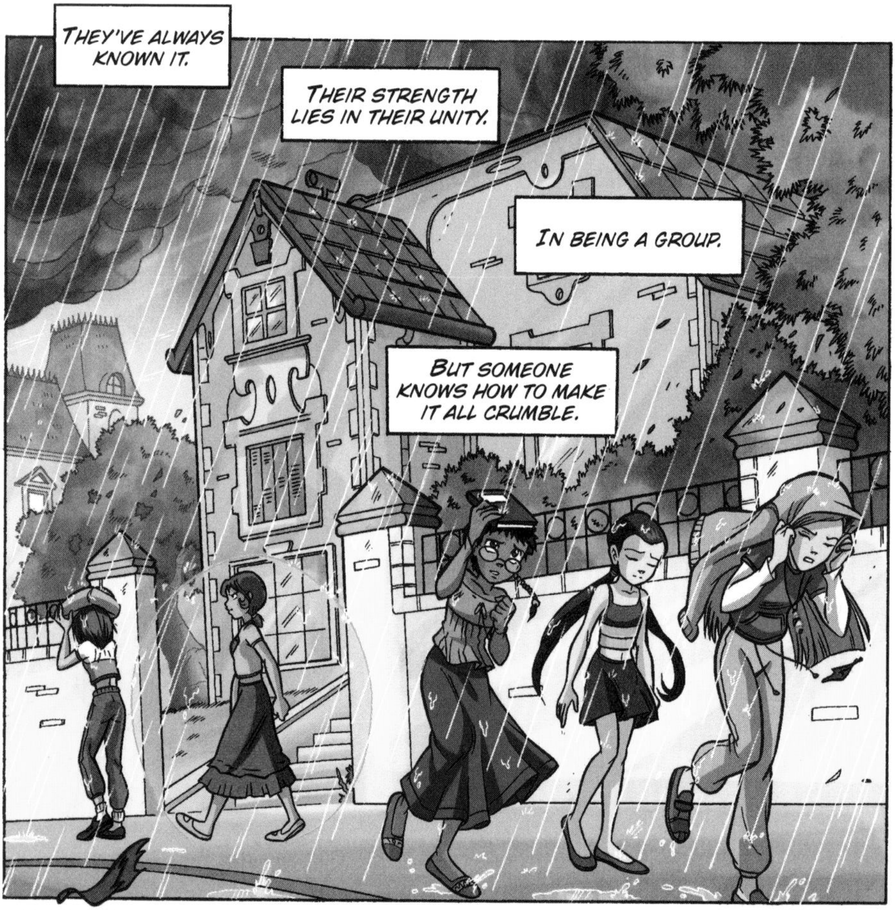
THEY'VE ALWAYS KNOWN IT.
THEIR STRENGTH LIES IN THEIR UNITY.
IN BEING A GROUP.
BUT SOMEONE KNOWS HOW TO MAKE IT ALL CRUMBLE.

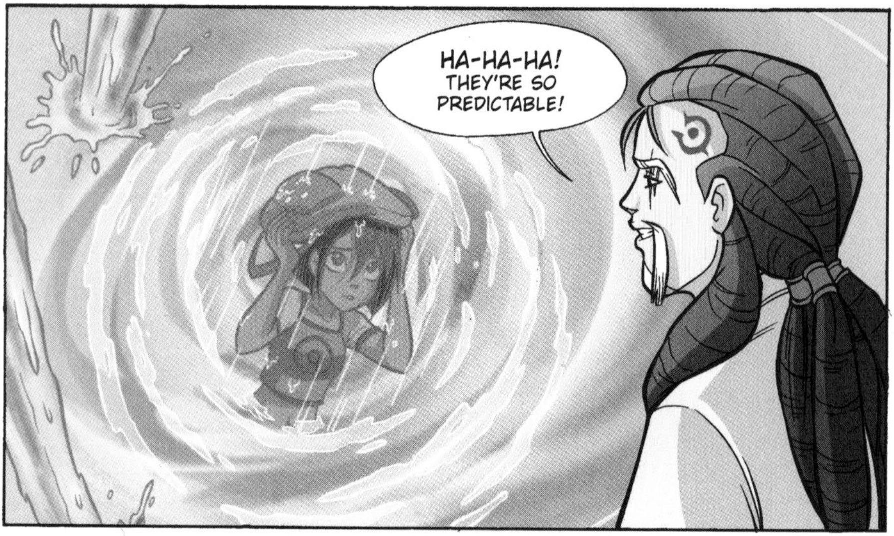
HA-HA-HA! THEY'RE SO PREDICTABLE!

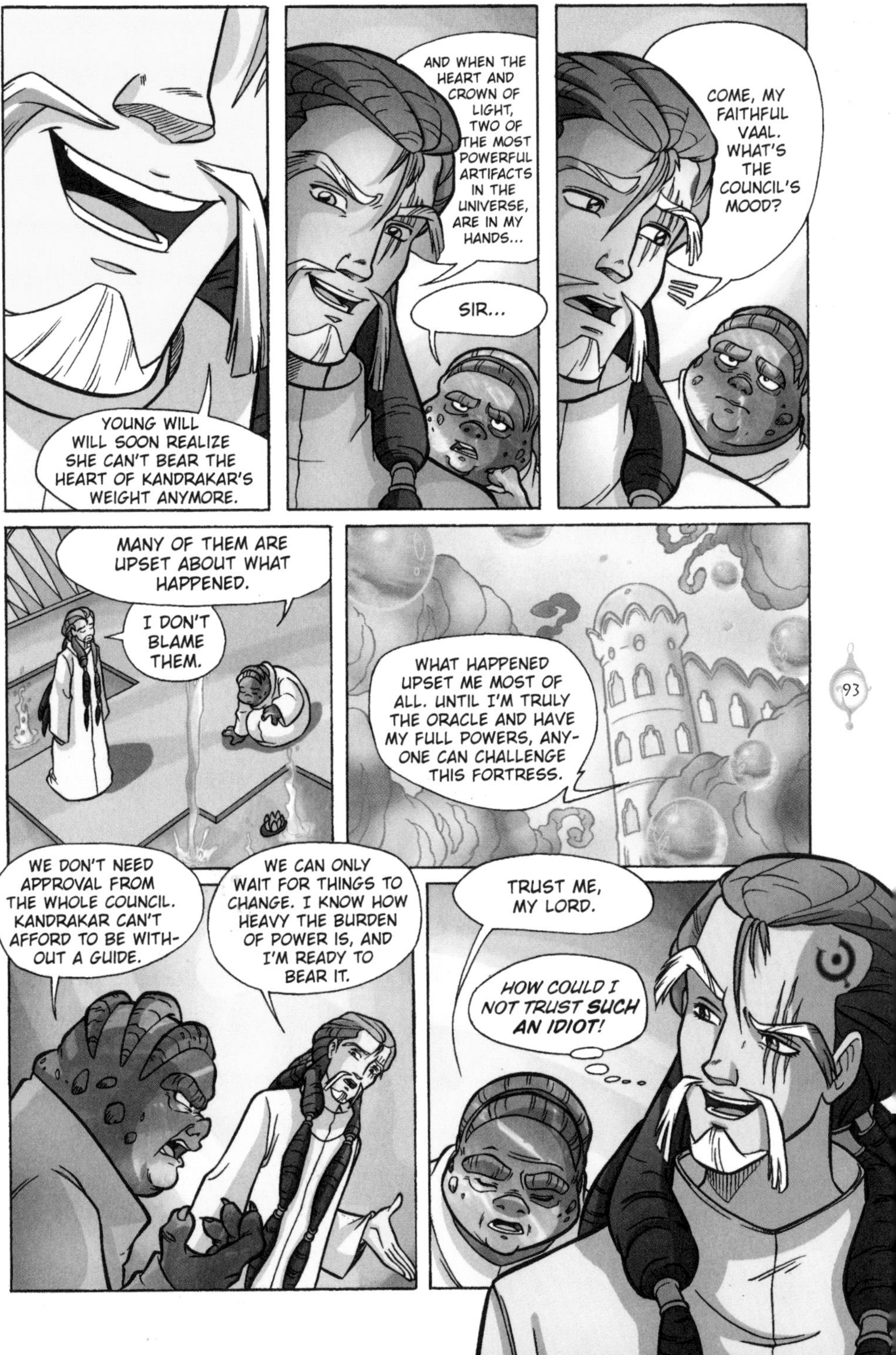
YOUNG WILL WILL SOON REALIZE SHE CAN'T BEAR THE HEART OF KANDRAKAR'S WEIGHT ANYMORE.
AND WHEN THE HEART AND CROWN OF LIGHT, TWO OF THE MOST POWERFUL ARTIFACTS IN THE UNIVERSE, ARE IN MY HANDS...
SIR...
COME, MY FAITHFUL VAAL. WHAT'S THE COUNCIL'S MOOD?
MANY OF THEM ARE UPSET ABOUT WHAT HAPPENED.
I DON'T BLAME THEM.
WHAT HAPPENED UPSET ME MOST OF ALL. UNTIL I'M TRULY THE ORACLE AND HAVE MY FULL POWERS, ANY-ONE CAN CHALLENGE THIS FORTRESS.
WE DON'T NEED APPROVAL FROM THE WHOLE COUNCIL. KANDRAKAR CAN'T AFFORD TO BE WITH-OUT A GUIDE.
WE CAN ONLY WAIT FOR THINGS TO CHANGE. I KNOW HOW HEAVY THE BURDEN OF POWER IS, AND I'M READY TO BEAR IT.
TRUST ME, MY LORD.
HOW COULD I NOT TRUST ***SUCH AN IDIOT!***

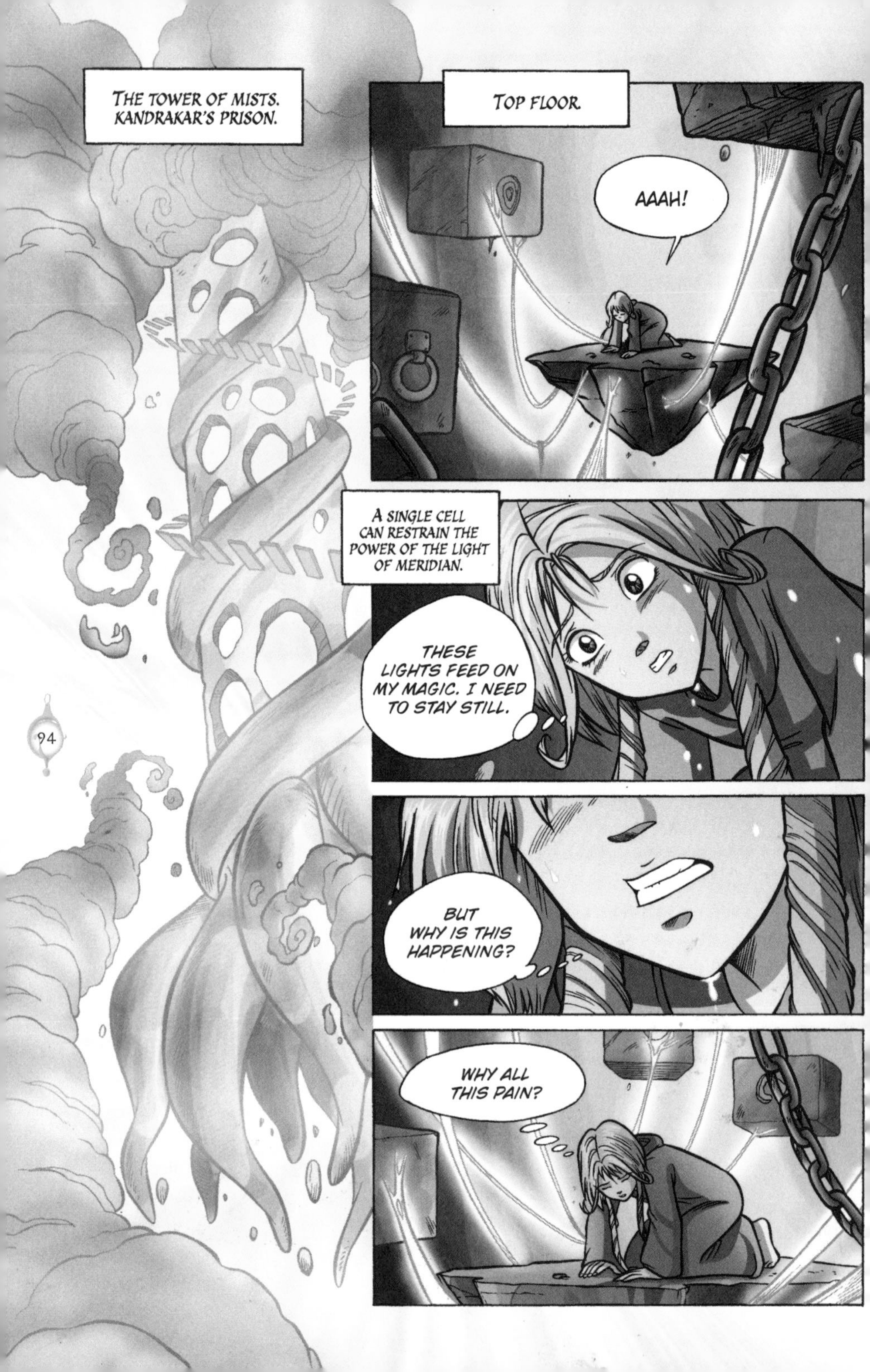
THE TOWER OF MISTS. KANDRAKAR'S PRISON.
TOP FLOOR.
AAAH!
A SINGLE CELL CAN RESTRAIN THE POWER OF THE LIGHT OF MERIDIAN.
THESE LIGHTS FEED ON MY MAGIC. I NEED TO STAY STILL.
BUT WHY IS THIS HAPPENING?
WHY ALL THIS PAIN?

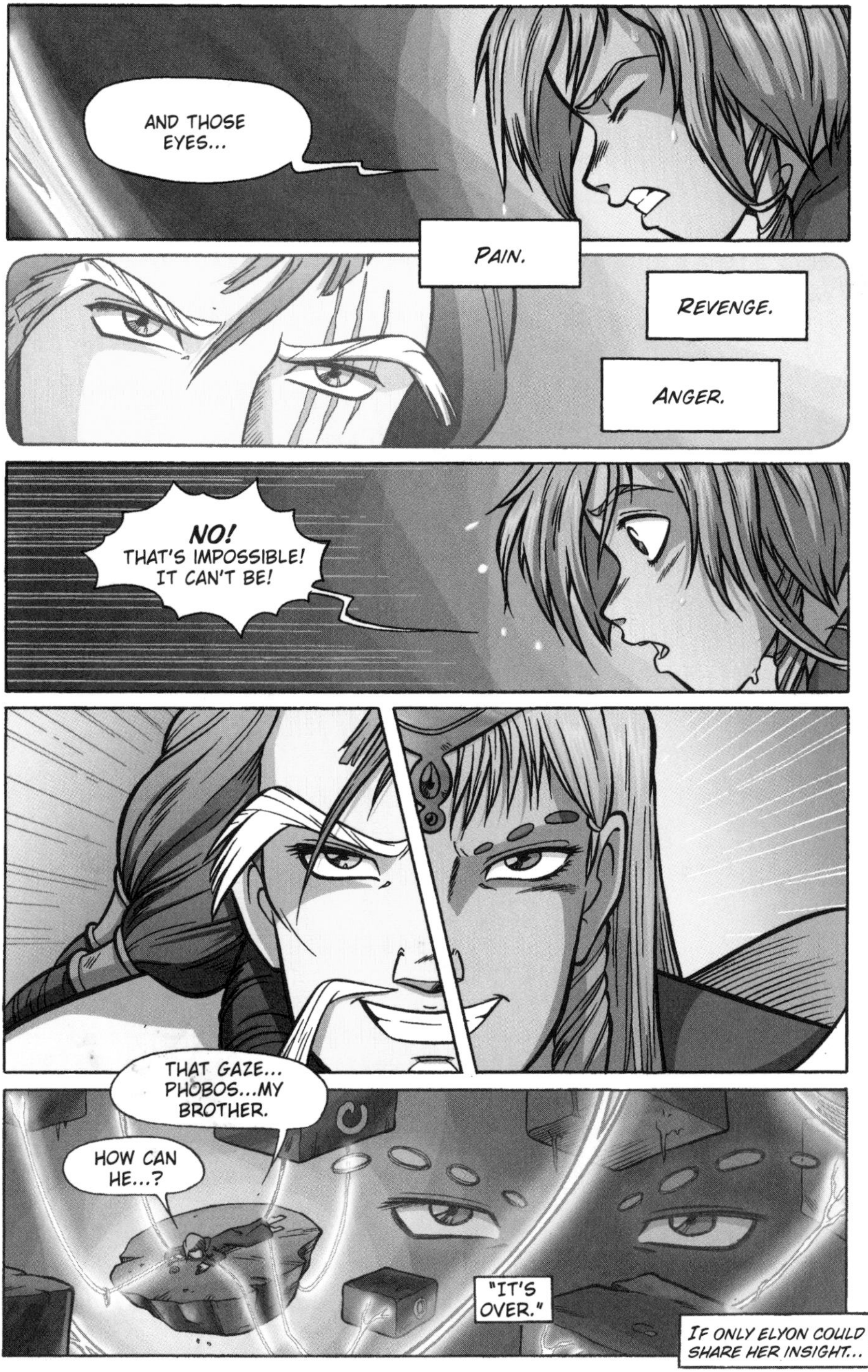
AND THOSE EYES...
PAIN.
REVENGE.
ANGER.
NO! THAT'S IMPOSSIBLE! IT CAN'T BE!
THAT GAZE... PHOBOS...MY BROTHER.
HOW CAN HE...?
"IT'S OVER."
IF ONLY ELYON COULD SHARE HER INSIGHT...

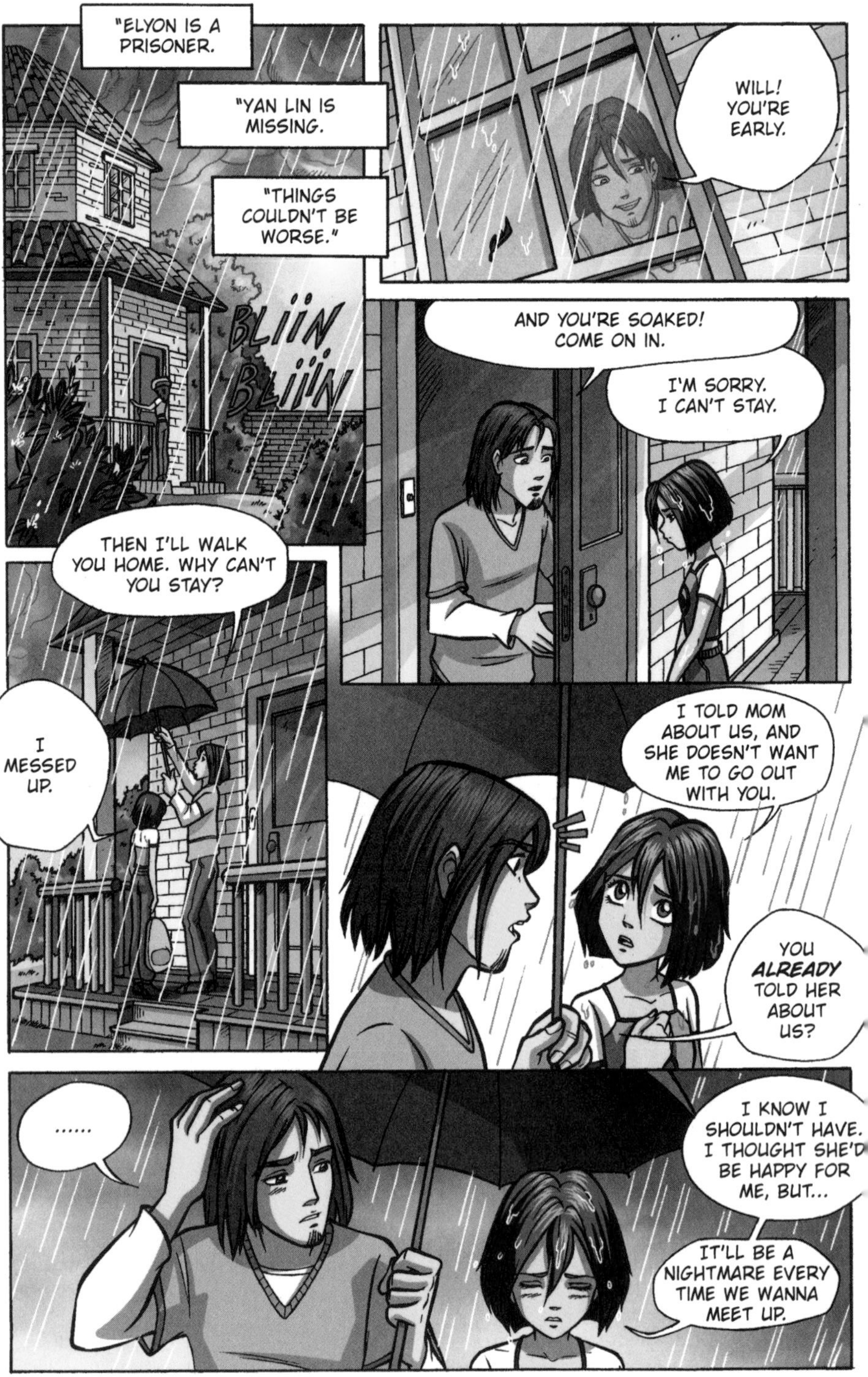
"ELYON IS A PRISONER.
"YAN LIN IS MISSING.
"THINGS COULDN'T BE WORSE."
BLIIN BLIIN
WILL! YOU'RE EARLY.
AND YOU'RE SOAKED! COME ON IN.
I'M SORRY. I CAN'T STAY.
THEN I'LL WALK YOU HOME. WHY CAN'T YOU STAY?
I MESSED UP.
I TOLD MOM ABOUT US, AND SHE DOESN'T WANT ME TO GO OUT WITH YOU.
YOU ALREADY TOLD HER ABOUT US?
......
I KNOW I SHOULDN'T HAVE. I THOUGHT SHE'D BE HAPPY FOR ME, BUT...
IT'LL BE A NIGHTMARE EVERY TIME WE WANNA MEET UP.

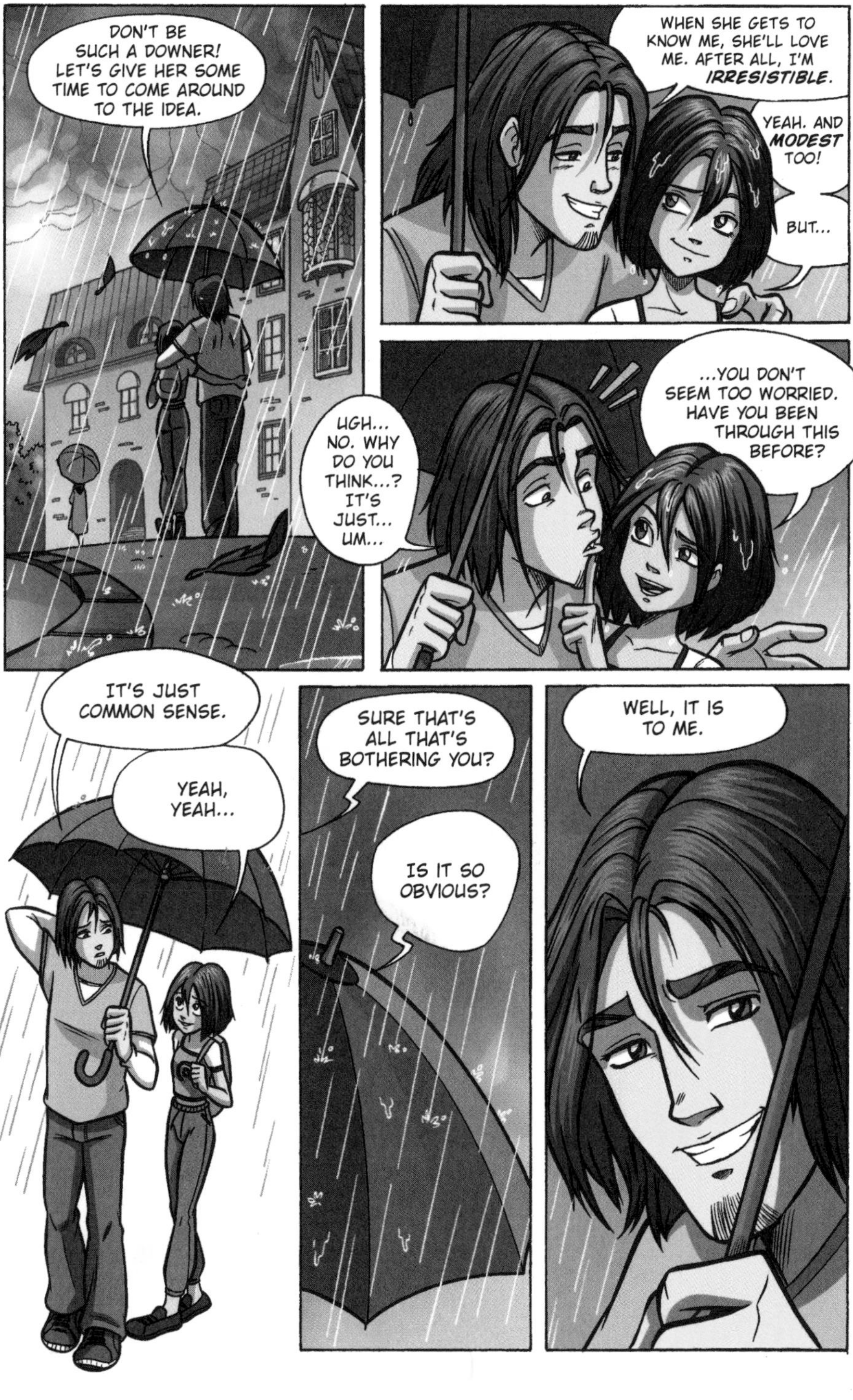
DON'T BE SUCH A DOWNER! LET'S GIVE HER SOME TIME TO COME AROUND TO THE IDEA.
WHEN SHE GETS TO KNOW ME, SHE'LL LOVE ME. AFTER ALL, I'M IRRESISTIBLE.
YEAH. AND MODEST TOO!
BUT...
...YOU DON'T SEEM TOO WORRIED. HAVE YOU BEEN THROUGH THIS BEFORE?
UGH... NO. WHY DO YOU THINK...? IT'S JUST... UM...
IT'S JUST COMMON SENSE.
YEAH, YEAH...
SURE THAT'S ALL THAT'S BOTHERING YOU?
IS IT SO OBVIOUS?
WELL, IT IS TO ME.

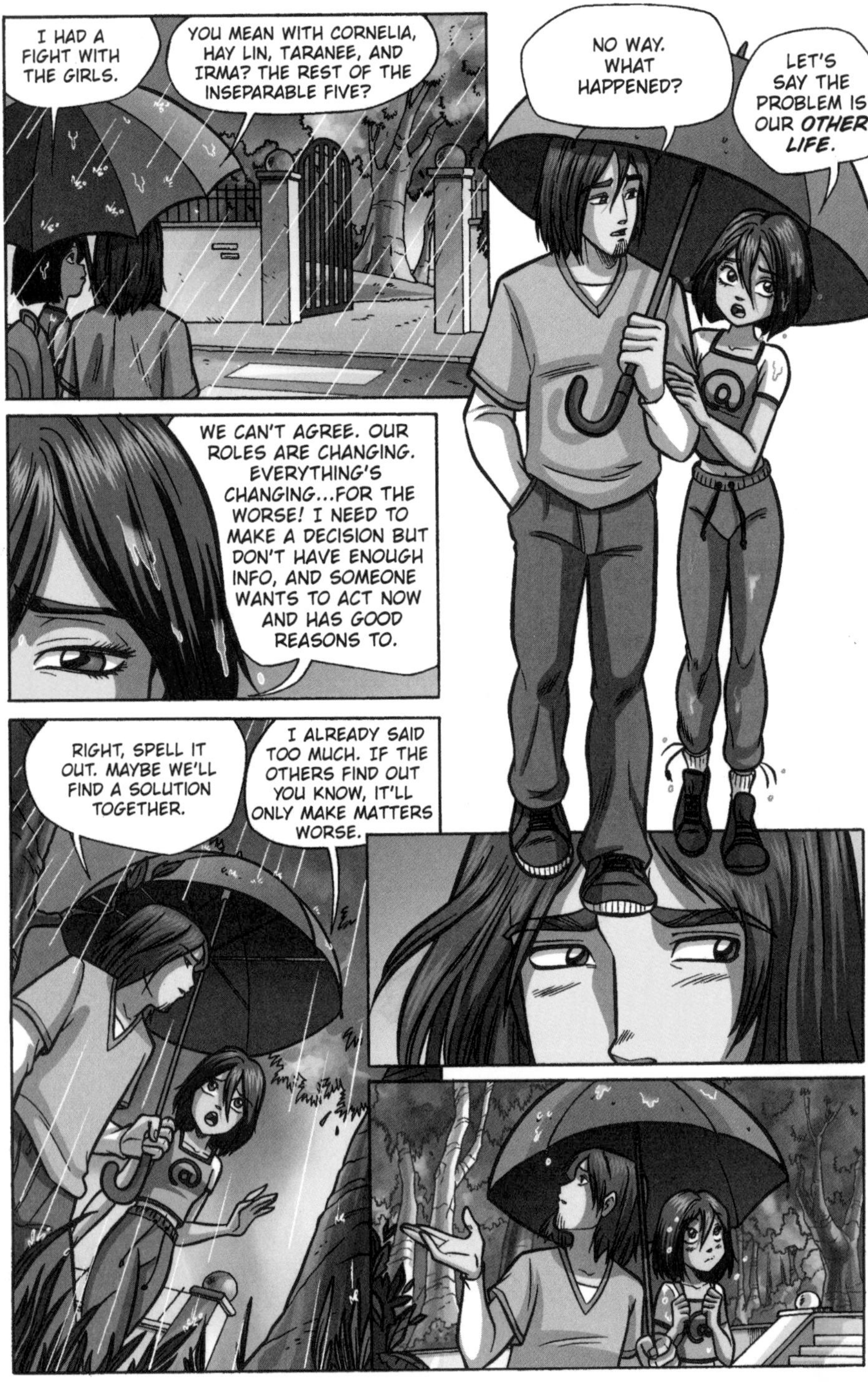

I HAD A FIGHT WITH THE GIRLS.
YOU MEAN WITH CORNELIA, HAY LIN, TARANEE, AND IRMA? THE REST OF THE INSEPARABLE FIVE?
NO WAY. WHAT HAPPENED?
LET'S SAY THE PROBLEM IS OUR *OTHER LIFE*.
WE CAN'T AGREE. OUR ROLES ARE CHANGING. EVERYTHING'S CHANGING...FOR THE WORSE! I NEED TO MAKE A DECISION BUT DON'T HAVE ENOUGH INFO, AND SOMEONE WANTS TO ACT NOW AND HAS GOOD REASONS TO.
RIGHT, SPELL IT OUT. MAYBE WE'LL FIND A SOLUTION TOGETHER.
I ALREADY SAID TOO MUCH. IF THE OTHERS FIND OUT YOU KNOW, IT'LL ONLY MAKE MATTERS WORSE.

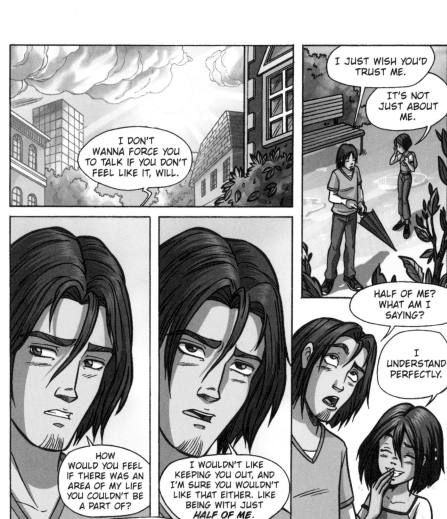

I JUST WISH YOU'D TRUST ME.

IT'S NOT JUST ABOUT ME.

I DON'T WANNA FORCE YOU TO TALK IF YOU DON'T FEEL LIKE IT, WILL.

HALF OF ME? WHAT AM I SAYING?

I UNDERSTAND PERFECTLY.

HOW WOULD YOU FEEL IF THERE WAS AN AREA OF MY LIFE YOU COULDN'T BE A PART OF?

I WOULDN'T LIKE KEEPING YOU OUT, AND I'M SURE YOU WOULDN'T LIKE THAT EITHER. LIKE BEING WITH JUST *HALF OF ME.*

JUST GIVE ME SOME TIME.

ALL THE TIME YOU NEED.

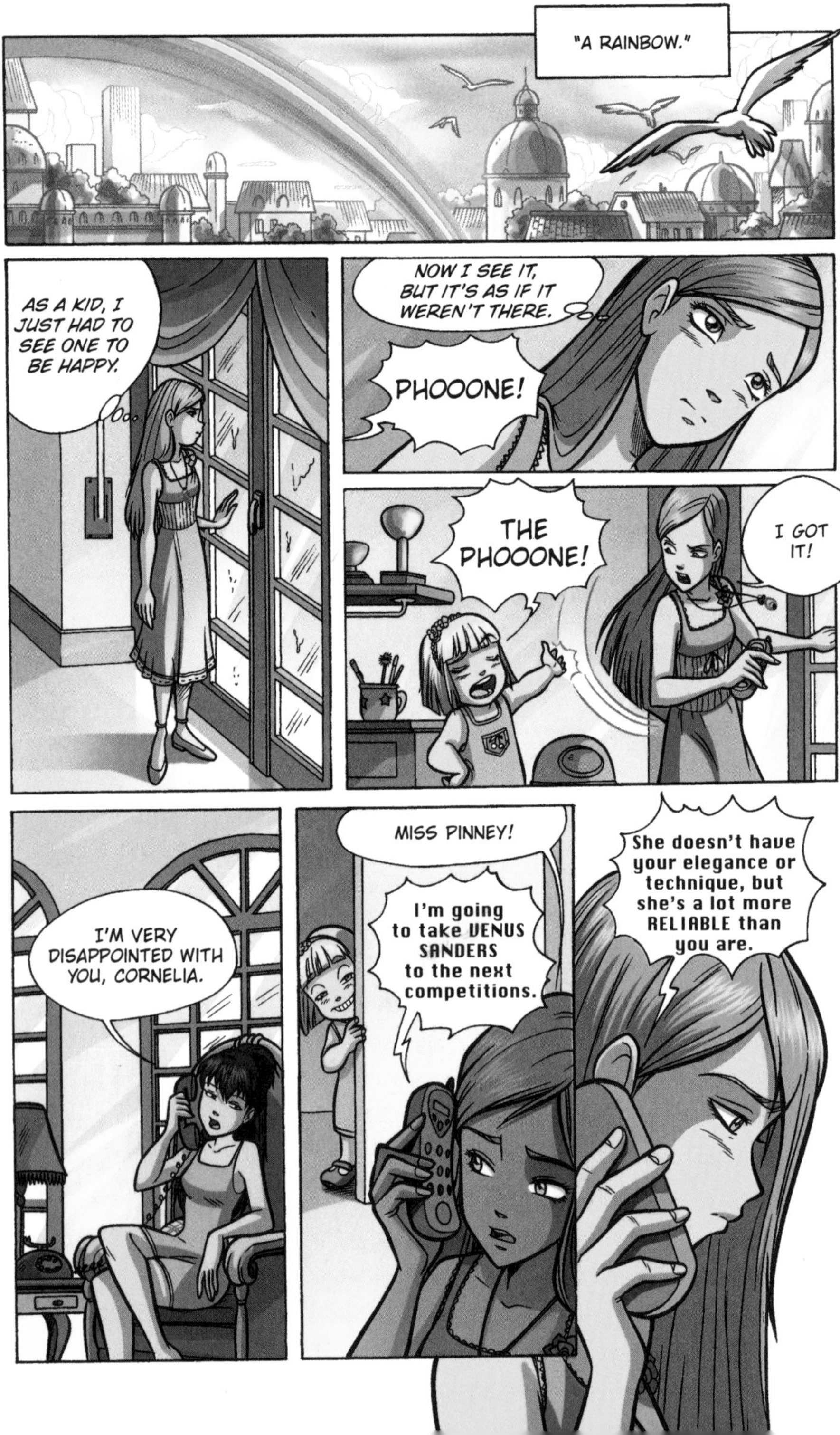
"A RAINBOW."
AS A KID, I JUST HAD TO SEE ONE TO BE HAPPY.
NOW I SEE IT, BUT IT'S AS IF IT WEREN'T THERE.
PHOOONE!
THE PHOOONE!
I GOT IT!
I'M VERY DISAPPOINTED WITH YOU, CORNELIA.
MISS PINNEY!
I'm going to take VENUS SANDERS to the next competitions.
She doesn't have your elegance or technique, but she's a lot more RELIABLE than you are.

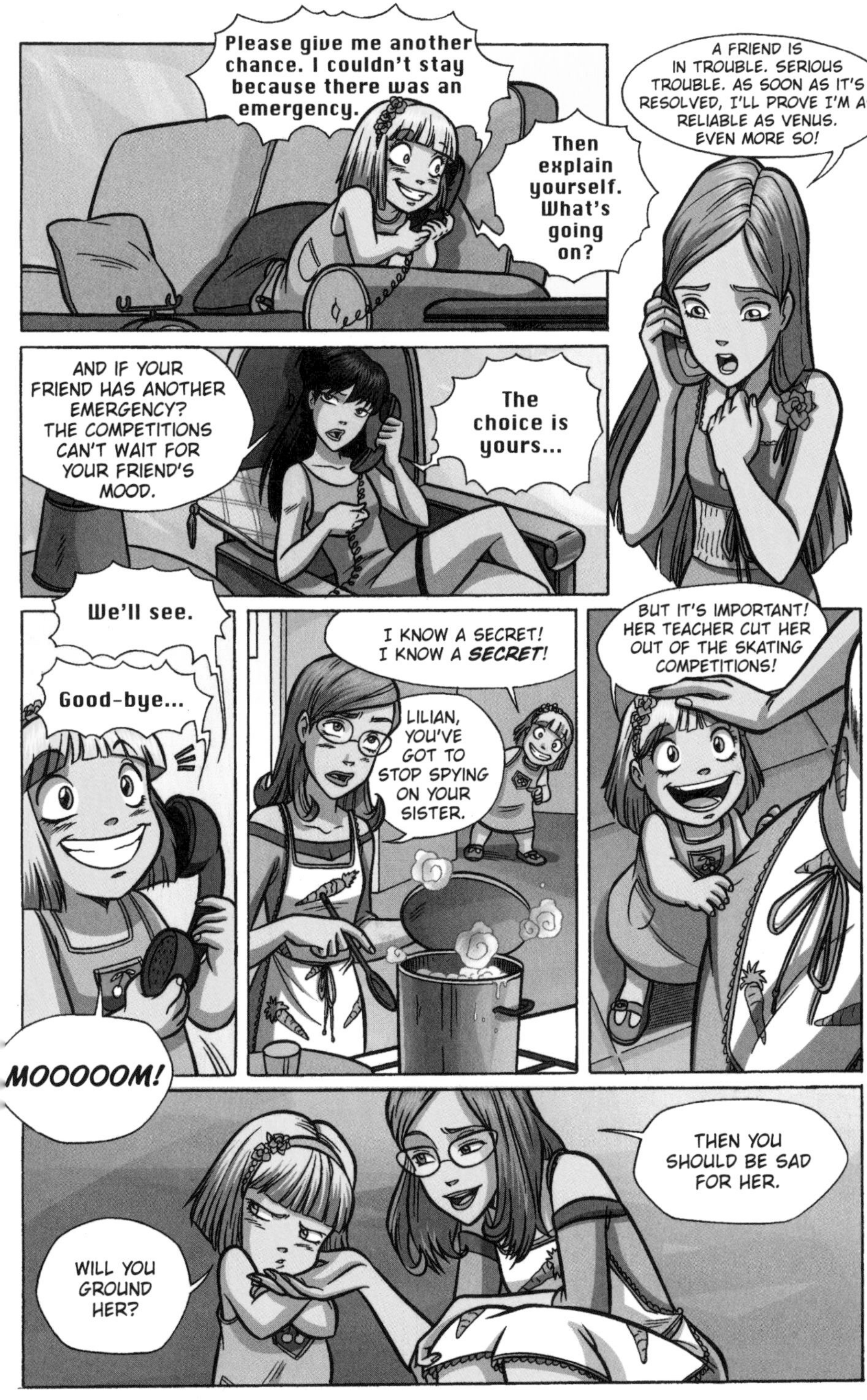

Please give me another chance. I couldn't stay because there was an emergency.
Then explain yourself. What's going on?
A FRIEND IS IN TROUBLE. SERIOUS TROUBLE. AS SOON AS IT'S RESOLVED, I'LL PROVE I'M AS RELIABLE AS VENUS. EVEN MORE SO!
AND IF YOUR FRIEND HAS ANOTHER EMERGENCY? THE COMPETITIONS CAN'T WAIT FOR YOUR FRIEND'S MOOD.
The choice is yours...
We'll see.
Good-bye...
MOOOOOM!
I KNOW A SECRET! I KNOW A *SECRET*!
LILIAN, YOU'VE GOT TO STOP SPYING ON YOUR SISTER.
BUT IT'S IMPORTANT! HER TEACHER CUT HER OUT OF THE SKATING COMPETITIONS!
THEN YOU SHOULD BE SAD FOR HER.
WILL YOU GROUND HER?

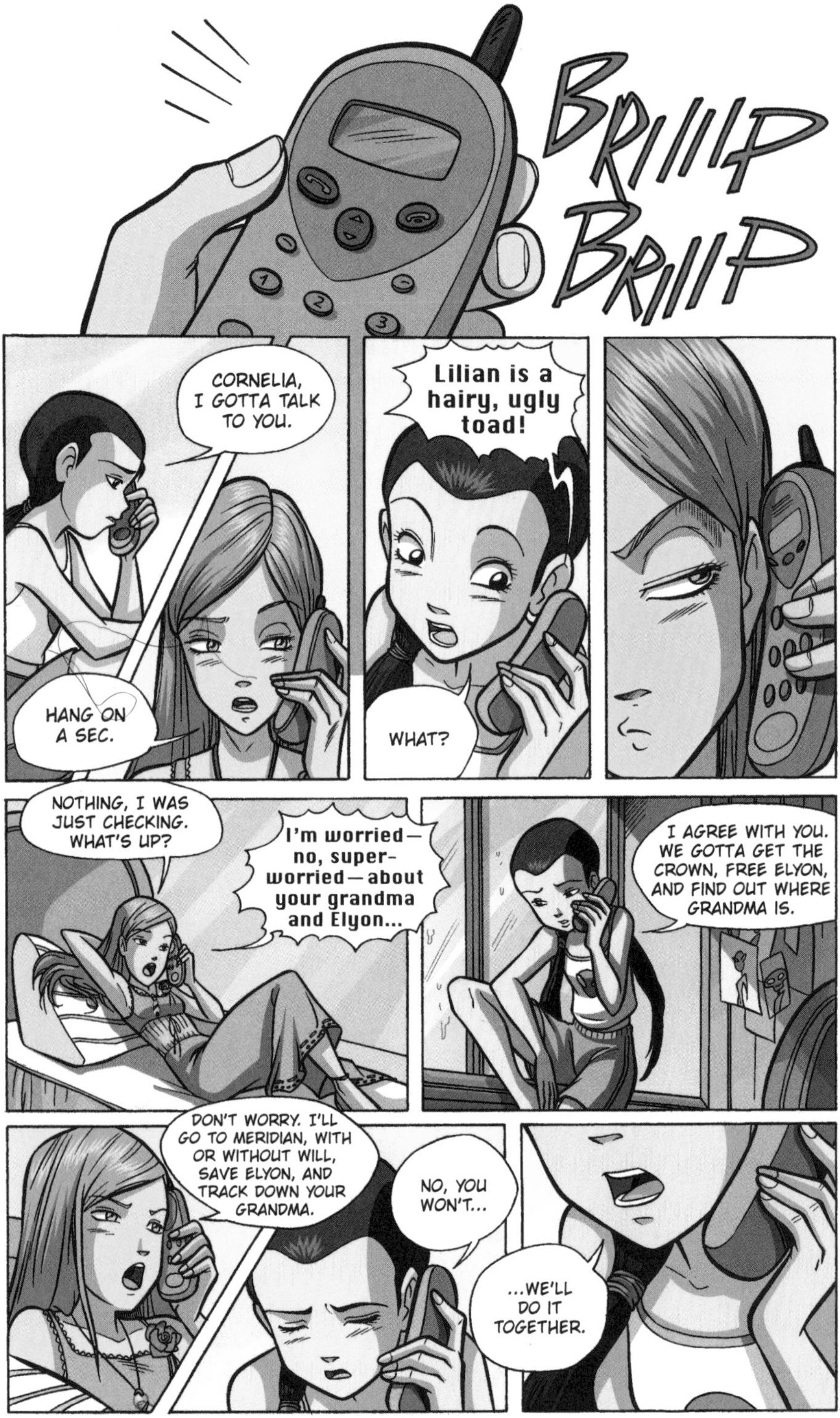
BRIIIP
BRIIIP
CORNELIA, I GOTTA TALK TO YOU.
HANG ON A SEC.
Lilian is a hairy, ugly toad!
WHAT?
NOTHING, I WAS JUST CHECKING. WHAT'S UP?
I'm worried—no, super-worried—about your grandma and Elyon...
I AGREE WITH YOU. WE GOTTA GET THE CROWN, FREE ELYON, AND FIND OUT WHERE GRANDMA IS.
DON'T WORRY. I'LL GO TO MERIDIAN, WITH OR WITHOUT WILL, SAVE ELYON, AND TRACK DOWN YOUR GRANDMA.
NO, YOU WON'T...
...WE'LL DO IT TOGETHER.

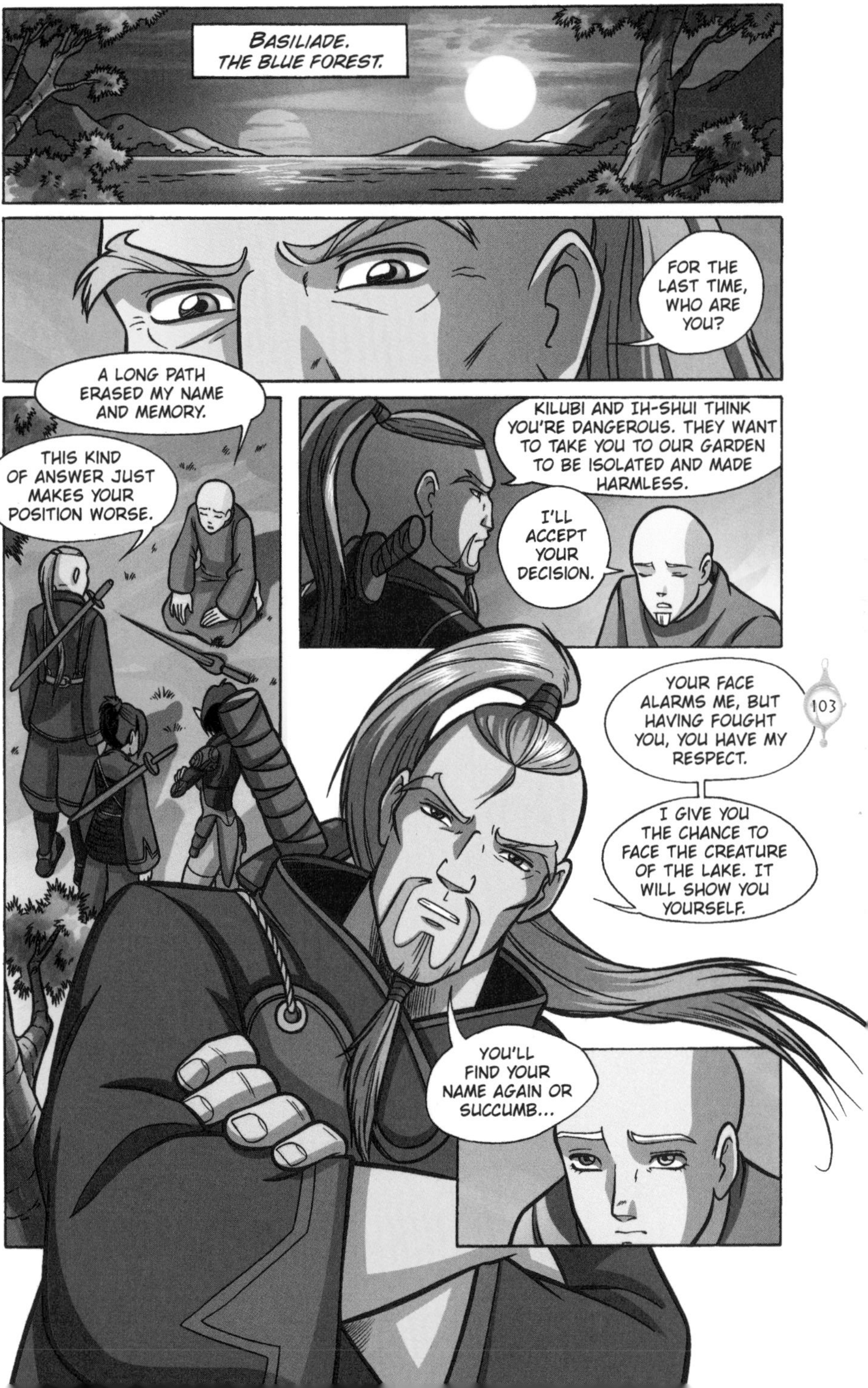
BASILIADE.
THE BLUE FOREST.
FOR THE LAST TIME, WHO ARE YOU?
A LONG PATH ERASED MY NAME AND MEMORY.
THIS KIND OF ANSWER JUST MAKES YOUR POSITION WORSE.
KILUBI AND IH-SHUI THINK YOU'RE DANGEROUS. THEY WANT TO TAKE YOU TO OUR GARDEN TO BE ISOLATED AND MADE HARMLESS.
I'LL ACCEPT YOUR DECISION.
YOUR FACE ALARMS ME, BUT HAVING FOUGHT YOU, YOU HAVE MY RESPECT.
I GIVE YOU THE CHANCE TO FACE THE CREATURE OF THE LAKE. IT WILL SHOW YOU YOURSELF.
YOU'LL FIND YOUR NAME AGAIN OR SUCCUMB...

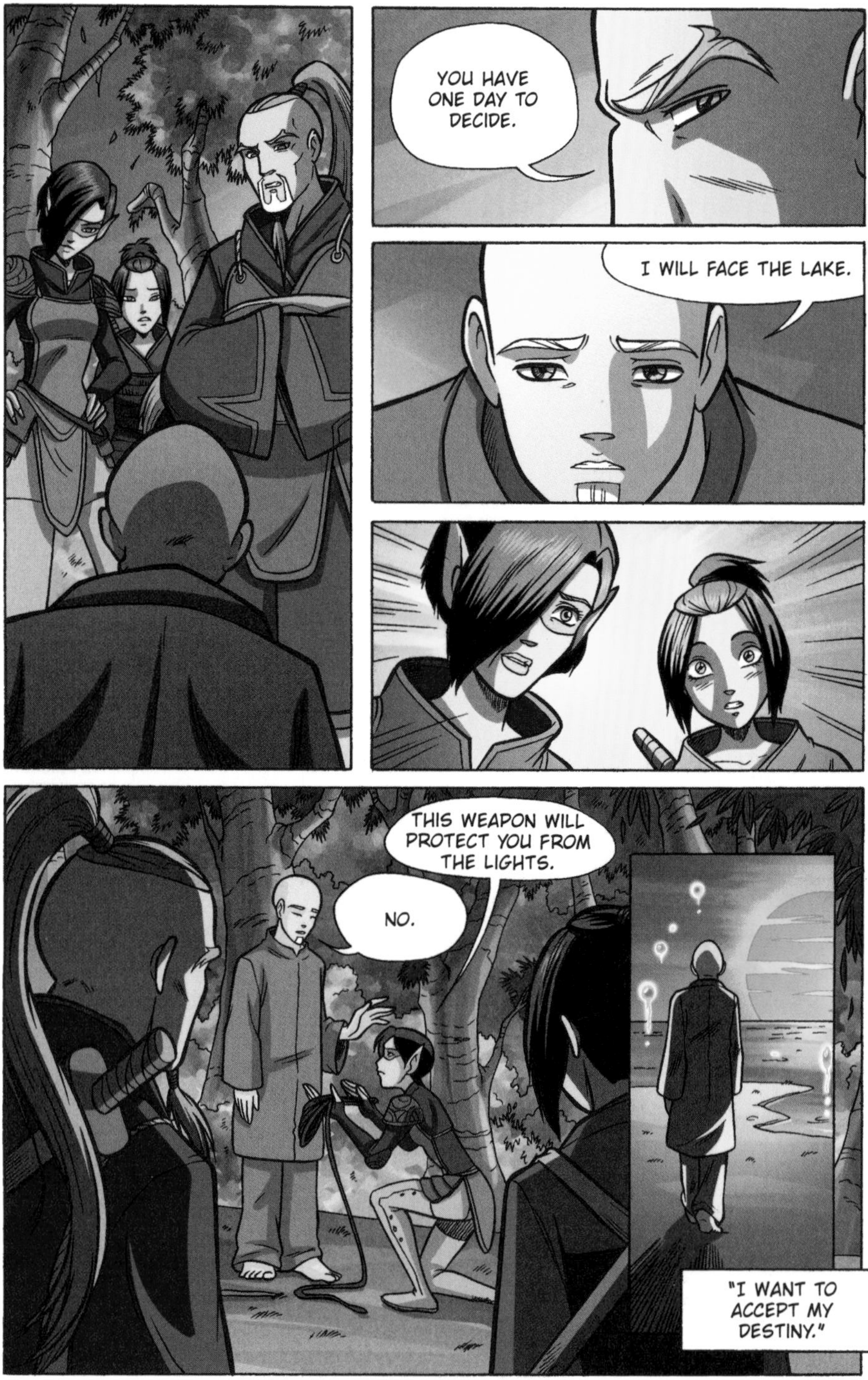
YOU HAVE ONE DAY TO DECIDE.
I WILL FACE THE LAKE.
THIS WEAPON WILL PROTECT YOU FROM THE LIGHTS.
NO.
"I WANT TO ACCEPT MY DESTINY."

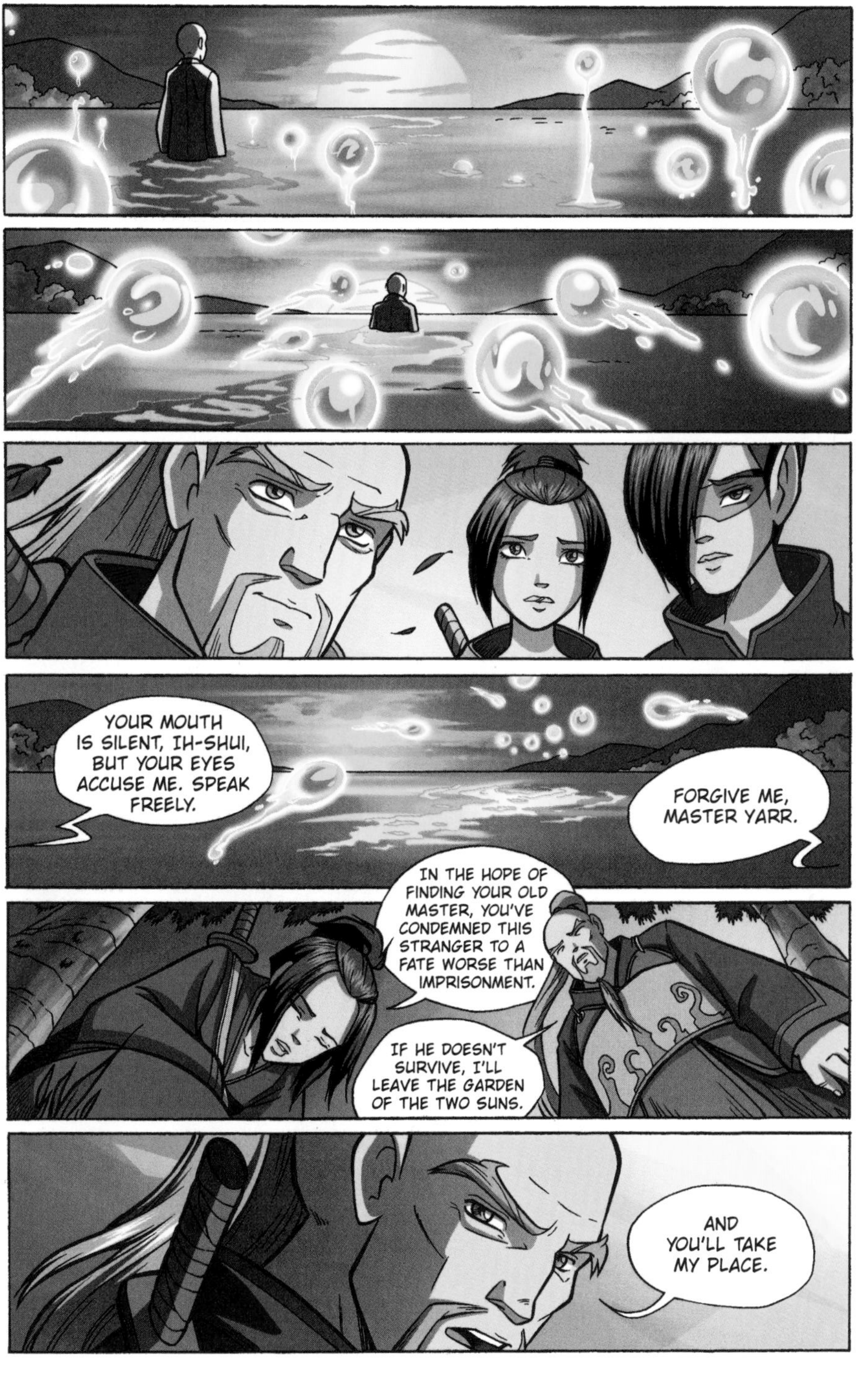
YOUR MOUTH IS SILENT, IH-SHUI, BUT YOUR EYES ACCUSE ME. SPEAK FREELY.
FORGIVE ME, MASTER YARR.
IN THE HOPE OF FINDING YOUR OLD MASTER, YOU'VE CONDEMNED THIS STRANGER TO A FATE WORSE THAN IMPRISONMENT.
IF HE DOESN'T SURVIVE, I'LL LEAVE THE GARDEN OF THE TWO SUNS.
AND YOU'LL TAKE MY PLACE.

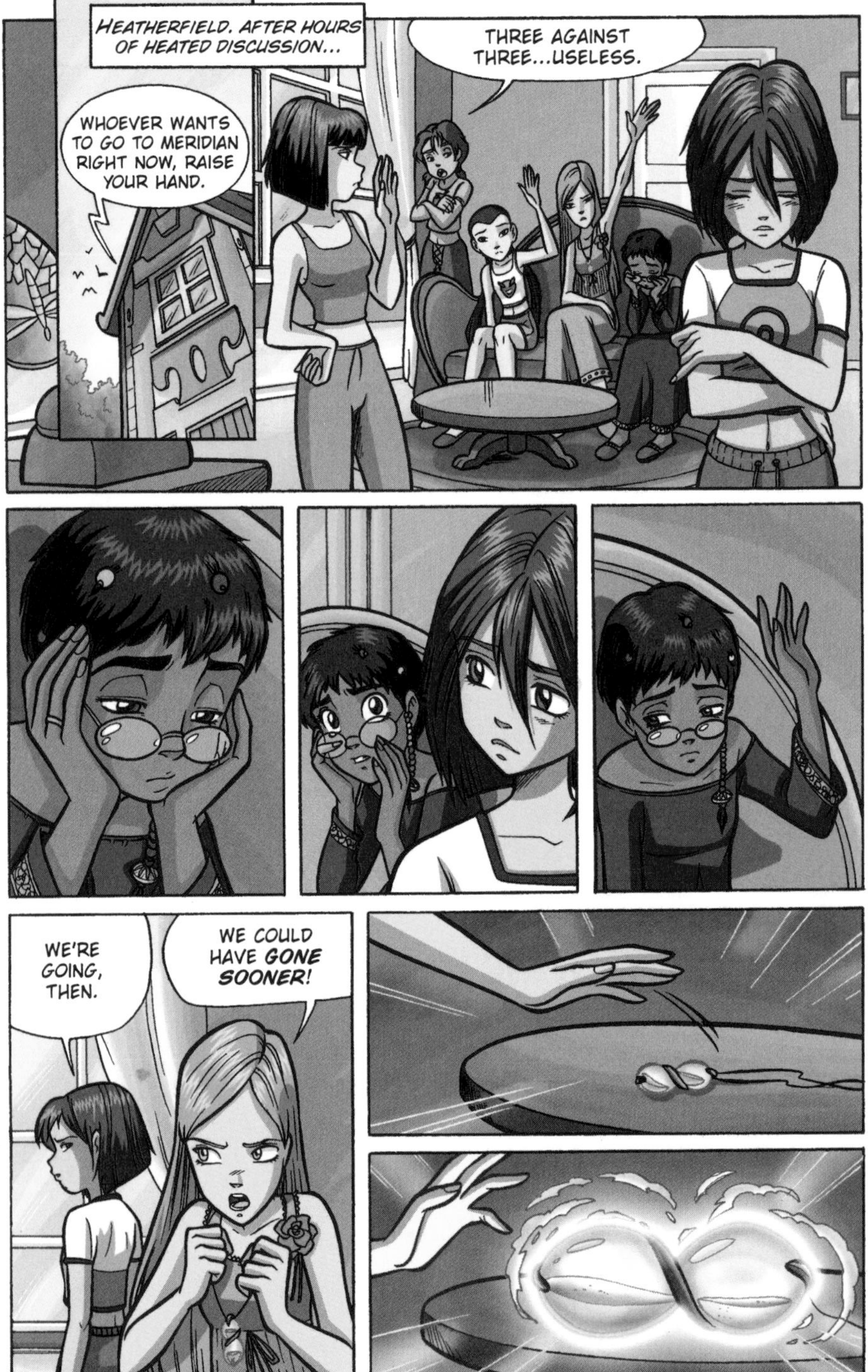
HEATHERFIELD. AFTER HOURS OF HEATED DISCUSSION...
WHOEVER WANTS TO GO TO MERIDIAN RIGHT NOW, RAISE YOUR HAND.
THREE AGAINST THREE...USELESS.
WE'RE GOING, THEN.
WE COULD HAVE GONE SOONER!

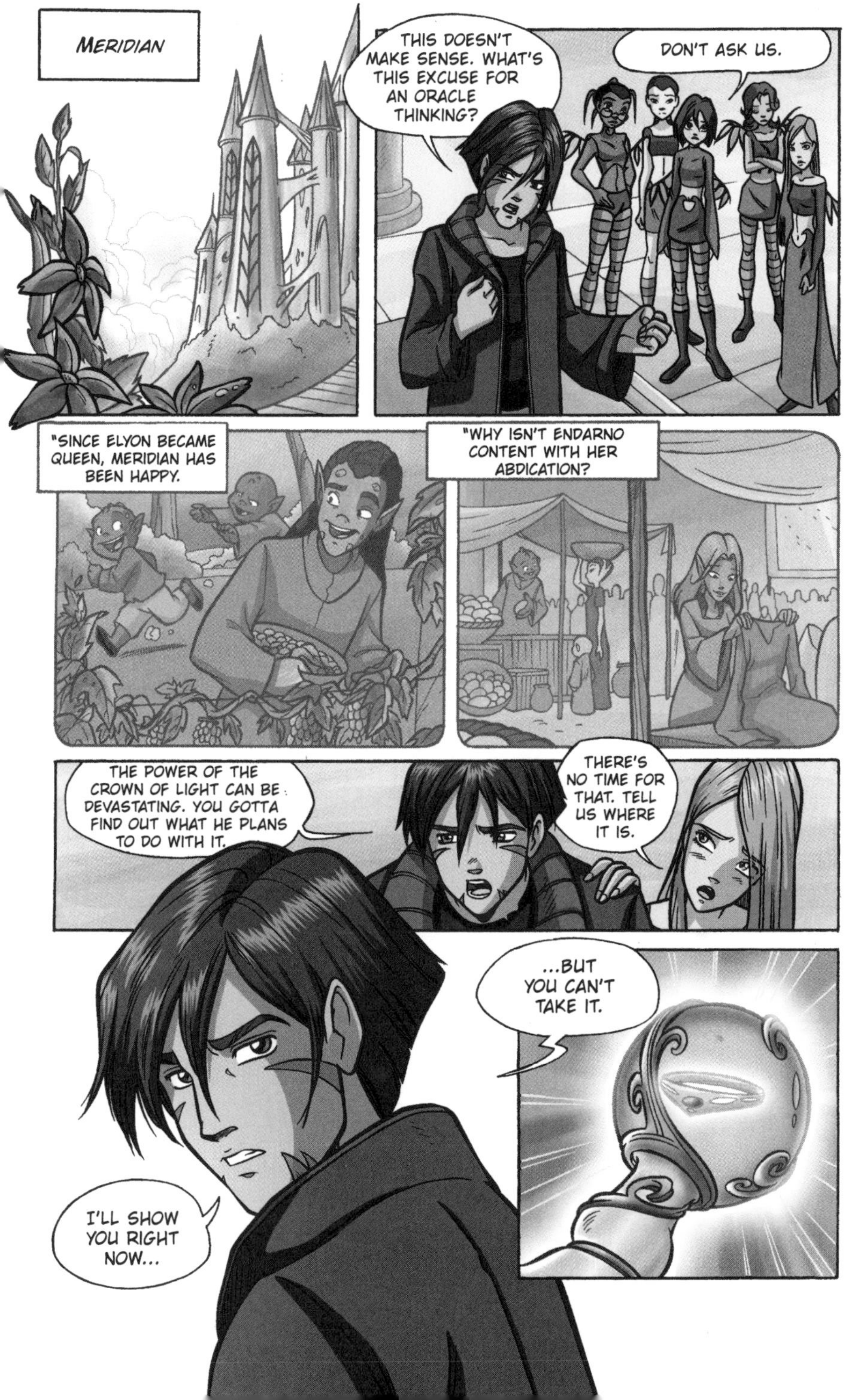
MERIDIAN
THIS DOESN'T MAKE SENSE. WHAT'S THIS EXCUSE FOR AN ORACLE THINKING?
DON'T ASK US.
"SINCE ELYON BECAME QUEEN, MERIDIAN HAS BEEN HAPPY.
"WHY ISN'T ENDARNO CONTENT WITH HER ABDICATION?
THE POWER OF THE CROWN OF LIGHT CAN BE DEVASTATING. YOU GOTTA FIND OUT WHAT HE PLANS TO DO WITH IT.
THERE'S NO TIME FOR THAT. TELL US WHERE IT IS.
I'LL SHOW YOU RIGHT NOW...
...BUT YOU CAN'T TAKE IT.

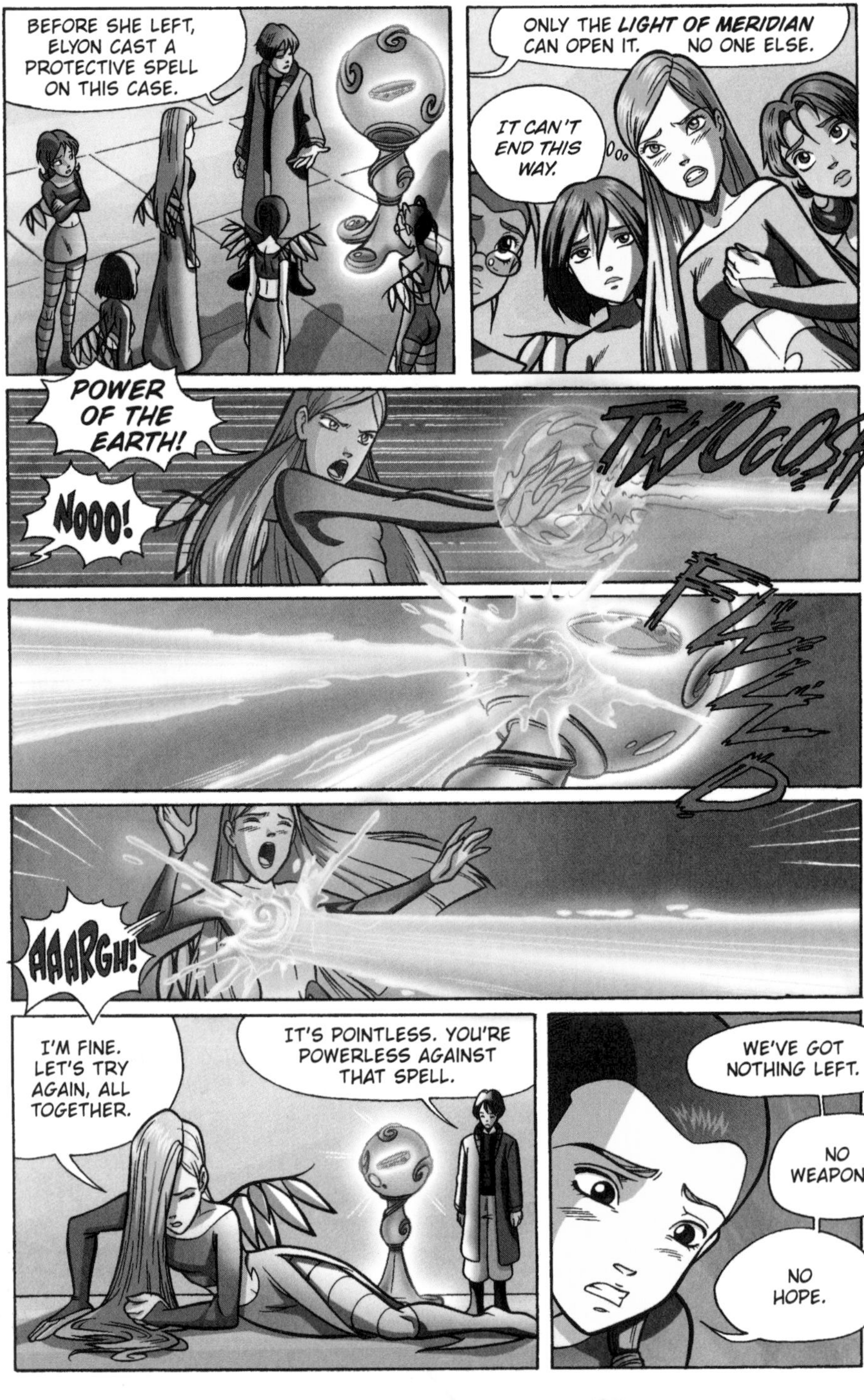
BEFORE SHE LEFT, ELYON CAST A PROTECTIVE SPELL ON THIS CASE.
ONLY THE *LIGHT OF MERIDIAN* CAN OPEN IT. NO ONE ELSE.
IT CAN'T END THIS WAY.
POWER OF THE EARTH!
NOOO!
TWOOOSH
FWWD
AAARGH!
I'M FINE. LET'S TRY AGAIN, ALL TOGETHER.
IT'S POINTLESS. YOU'RE POWERLESS AGAINST THAT SPELL.
WE'VE GOT NOTHING LEFT.
NO WEAPONS.
NO HOPE.

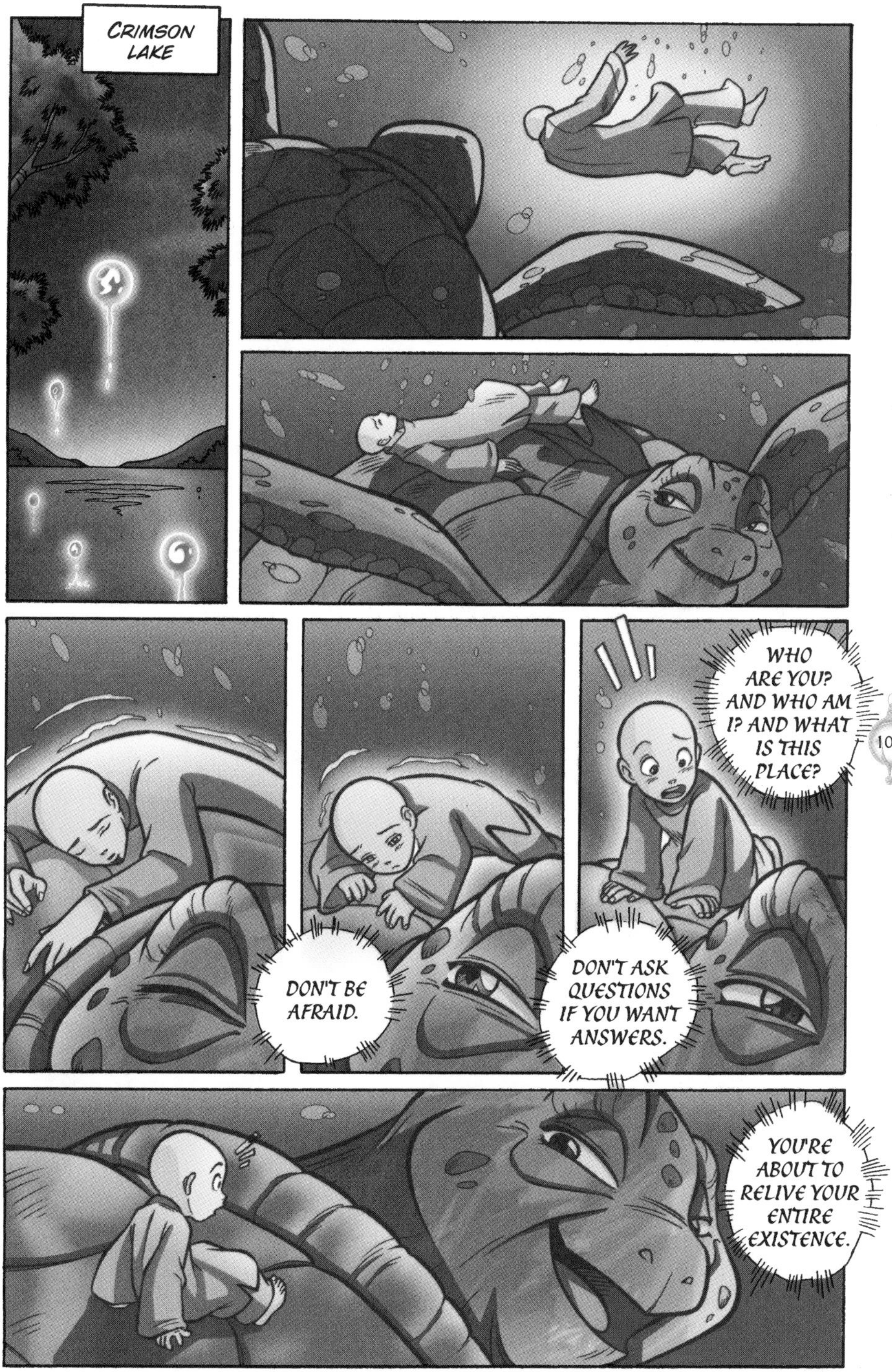
CRIMSON LAKE
WHO ARE YOU? AND WHO AM I? AND WHAT IS THIS PLACE?
DON'T BE AFRAID.
DON'T ASK QUESTIONS IF YOU WANT ANSWERS.
YOU'RE ABOUT TO RELIVE YOUR ENTIRE EXISTENCE.

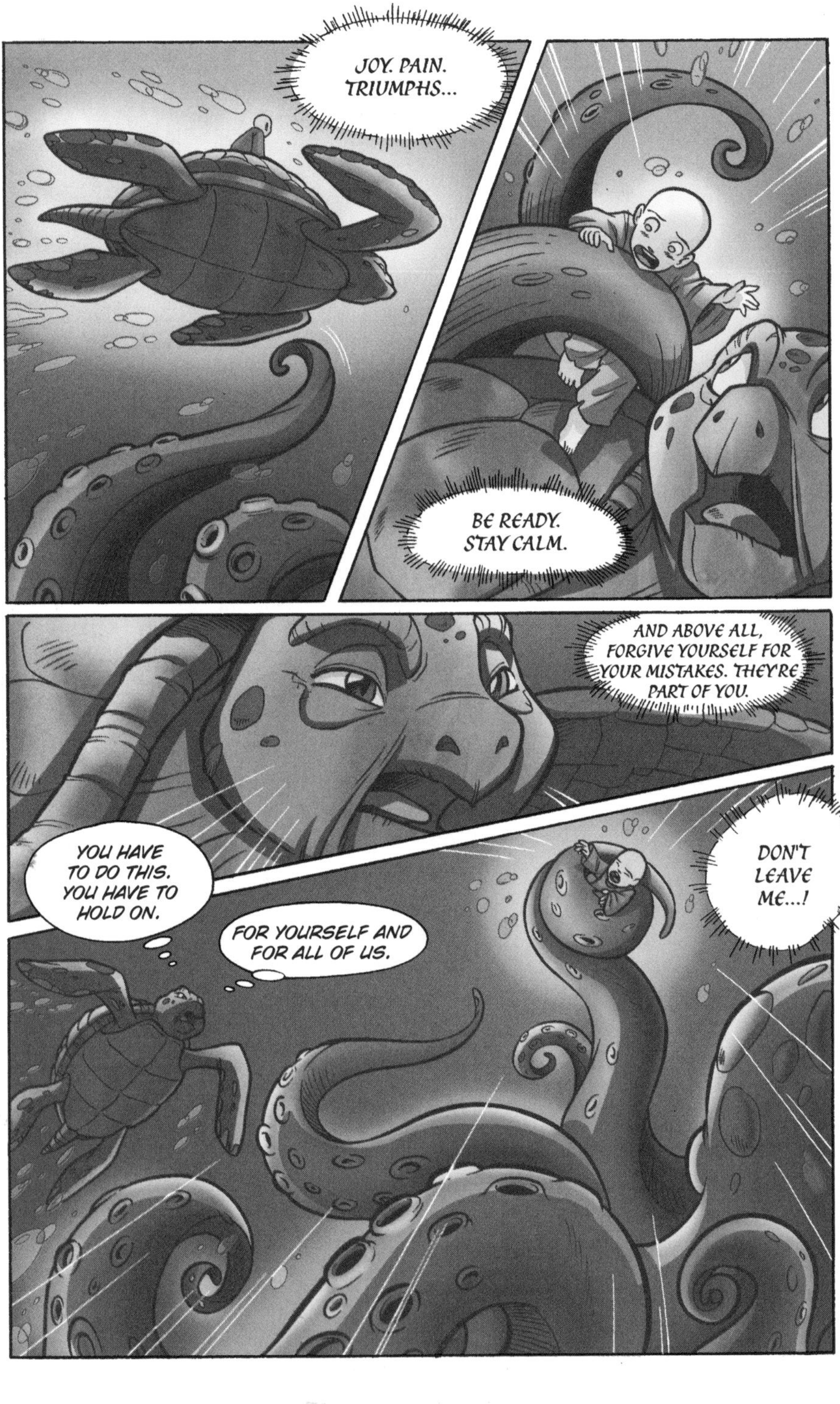

JOY. PAIN. TRIUMPHS...
BE READY. STAY CALM.
AND ABOVE ALL, FORGIVE YOURSELF FOR YOUR MISTAKES. THEY'RE PART OF YOU.
YOU HAVE TO DO THIS. YOU HAVE TO HOLD ON.
FOR YOURSELF AND FOR ALL OF US.
DON'T LEAVE ME...!

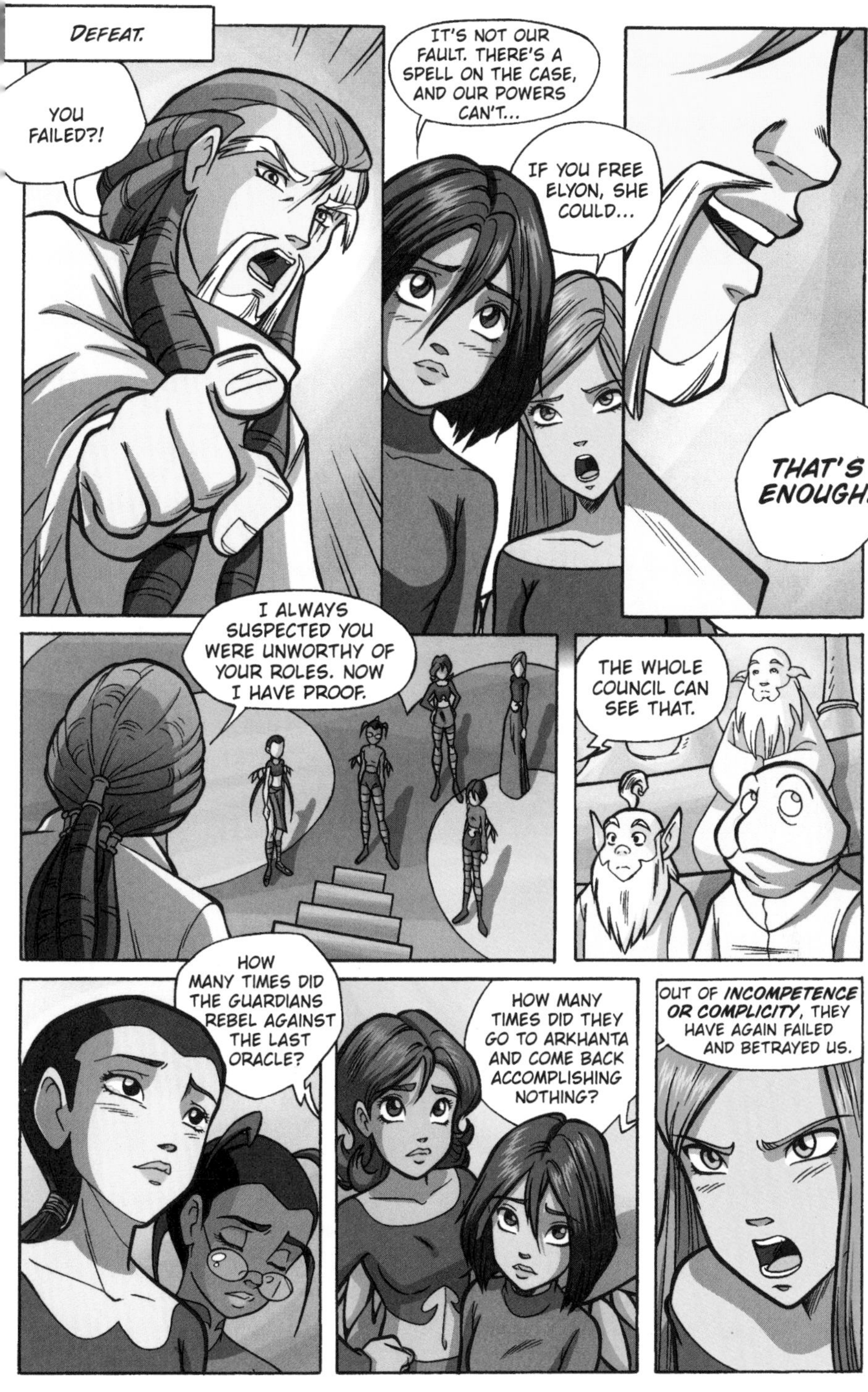
DEFEAT.
YOU FAILED?!
IT'S NOT OUR FAULT. THERE'S A SPELL ON THE CASE, AND OUR POWERS CAN'T...
IF YOU FREE ELYON, SHE COULD...
THAT'S ENOUGH.
I ALWAYS SUSPECTED YOU WERE UNWORTHY OF YOUR ROLES. NOW I HAVE PROOF.
THE WHOLE COUNCIL CAN SEE THAT.
HOW MANY TIMES DID THE GUARDIANS REBEL AGAINST THE LAST ORACLE?
HOW MANY TIMES DID THEY GO TO ARKHANTA AND COME BACK ACCOMPLISHING NOTHING?
OUT OF INCOMPETENCE OR COMPLICITY, THEY HAVE AGAIN FAILED AND BETRAYED US.

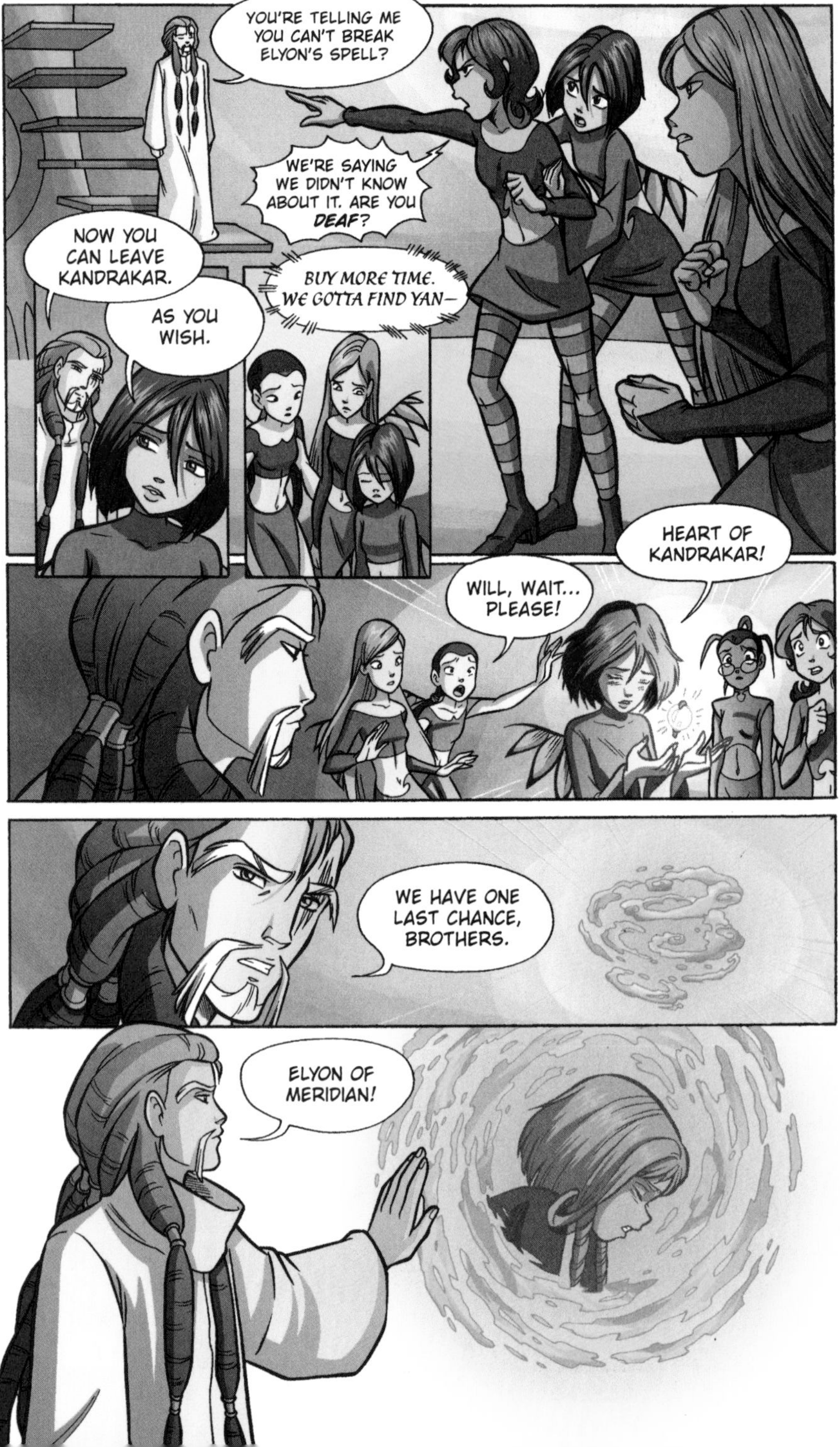
YOU'RE TELLING ME YOU CAN'T BREAK ELYON'S SPELL?
WE'RE SAYING WE DIDN'T KNOW ABOUT IT. ARE YOU DEAF?
NOW YOU CAN LEAVE KANDRAKAR.
AS YOU WISH.
BUY MORE TIME. WE GOTTA FIND YAN—
WILL, WAIT... PLEASE!
HEART OF KANDRAKAR!
WE HAVE ONE LAST CHANCE, BROTHERS.
ELYON OF MERIDIAN!

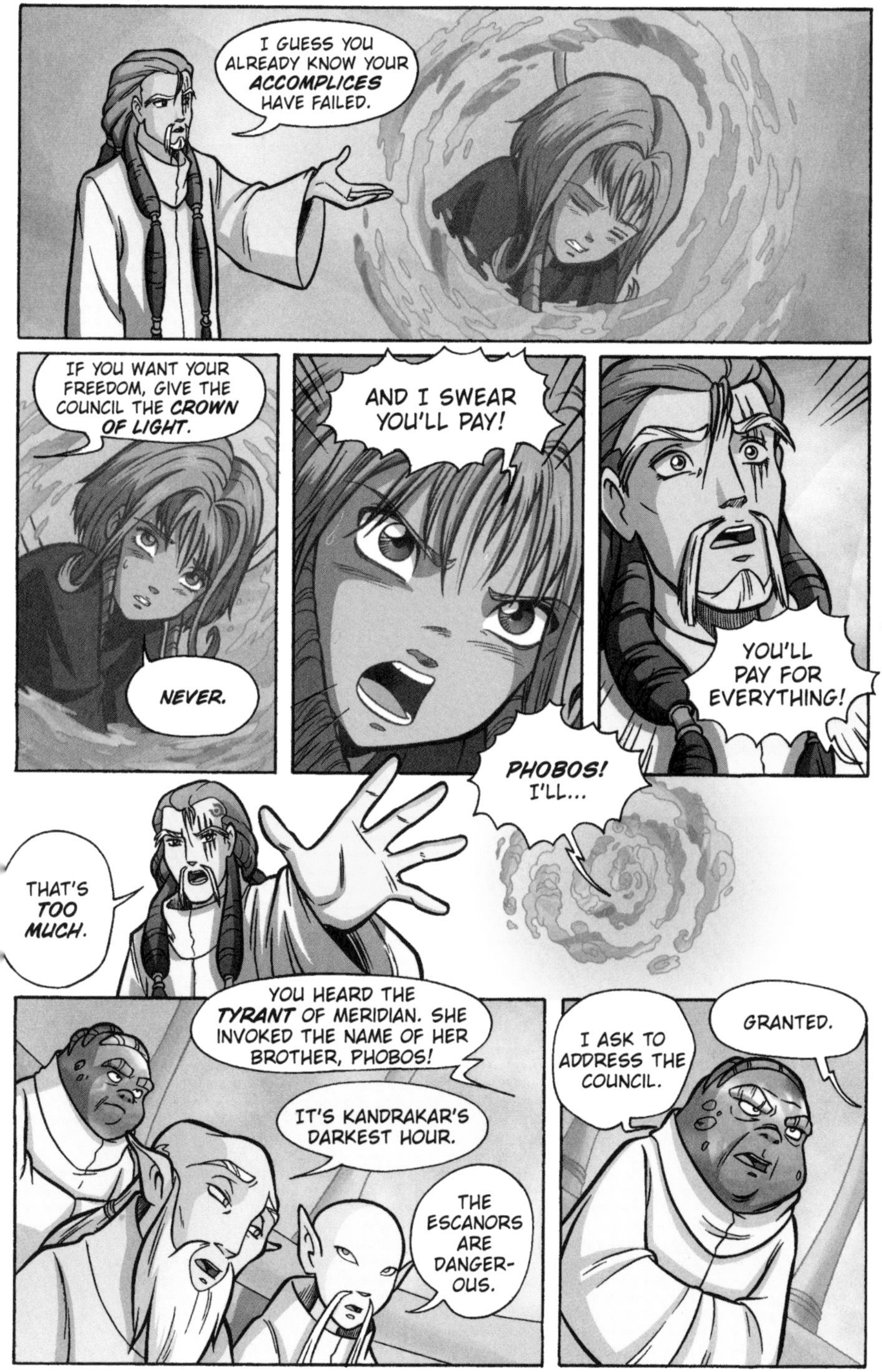
I GUESS YOU ALREADY KNOW YOUR ACCOMPLICES HAVE FAILED.
IF YOU WANT YOUR FREEDOM, GIVE THE COUNCIL THE CROWN OF LIGHT.
NEVER.
AND I SWEAR YOU'LL PAY!
YOU'LL PAY FOR EVERYTHING!
PHOBOS! I'LL...
THAT'S TOO MUCH.
YOU HEARD THE TYRANT OF MERIDIAN. SHE INVOKED THE NAME OF HER BROTHER, PHOBOS!
IT'S KANDRAKAR'S DARKEST HOUR.
THE ESCANORS ARE DANGER-OUS.
I ASK TO ADDRESS THE COUNCIL.
GRANTED.

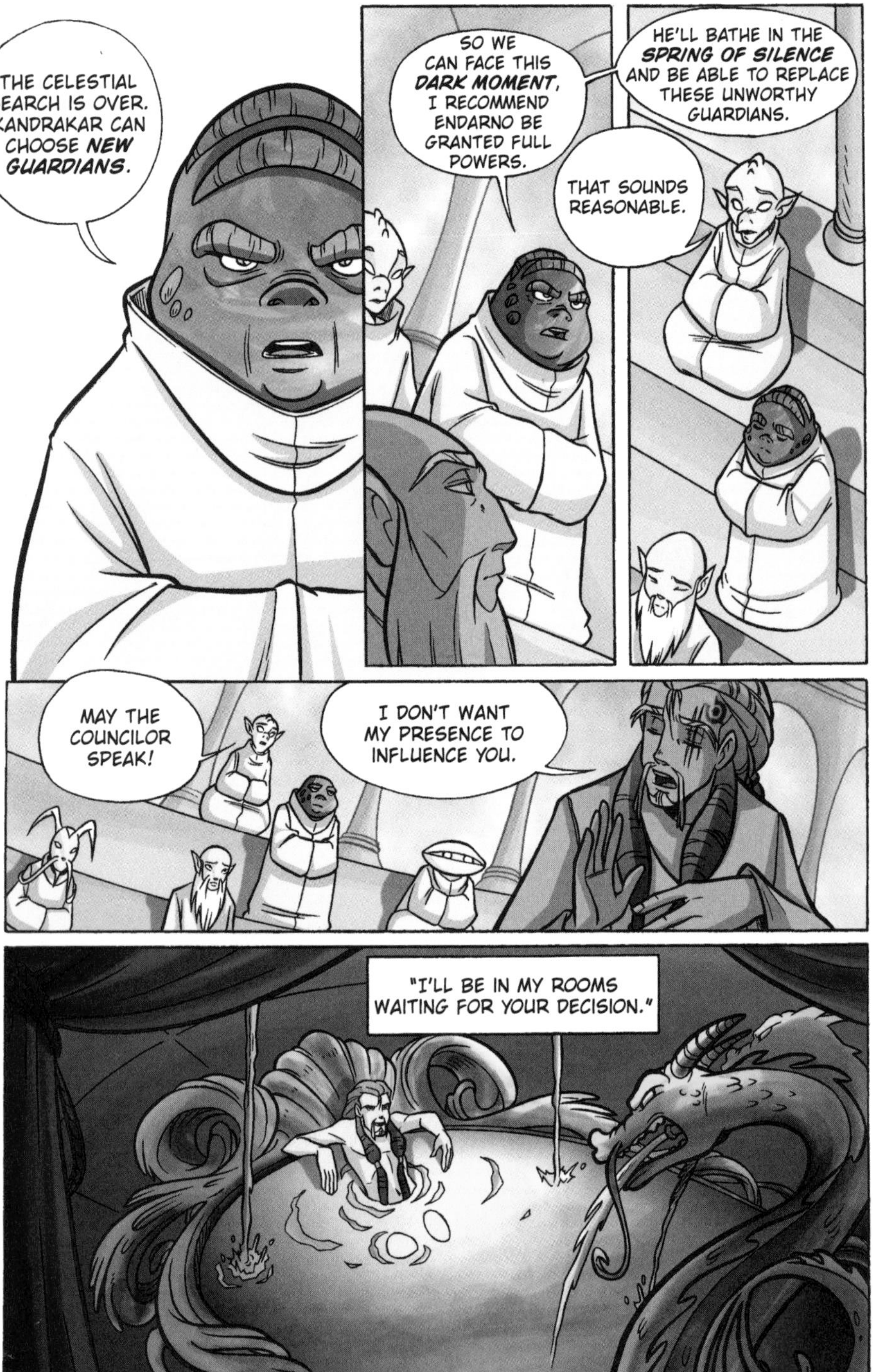
THE CELESTIAL SEARCH IS OVER. KANDRAKAR CAN CHOOSE **NEW GUARDIANS**.
SO WE CAN FACE THIS **DARK MOMENT**, I RECOMMEND ENDARNO BE GRANTED FULL POWERS.
HE'LL BATHE IN THE **SPRING OF SILENCE** AND BE ABLE TO REPLACE THESE UNWORTHY GUARDIANS.
THAT SOUNDS REASONABLE.
MAY THE COUNCILOR SPEAK!
I DON'T WANT MY PRESENCE TO INFLUENCE YOU.
"I'LL BE IN MY ROOMS WAITING FOR YOUR DECISION."

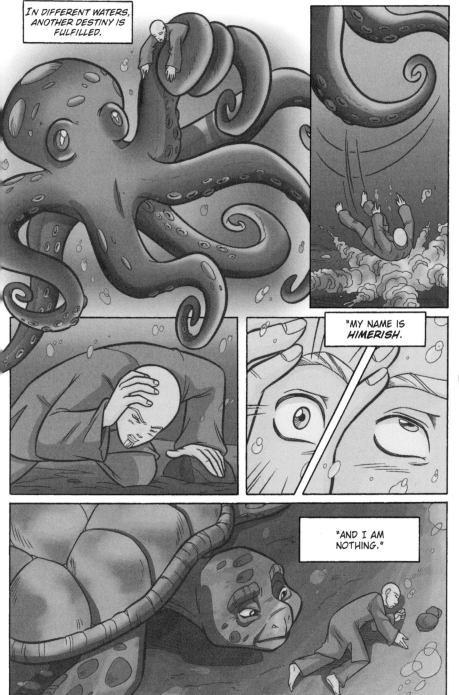

IN DIFFERENT WATERS, ANOTHER DESTINY IS FULFILLED.

"MY NAME IS *HIMERISH*.

"AND I AM NOTHING."

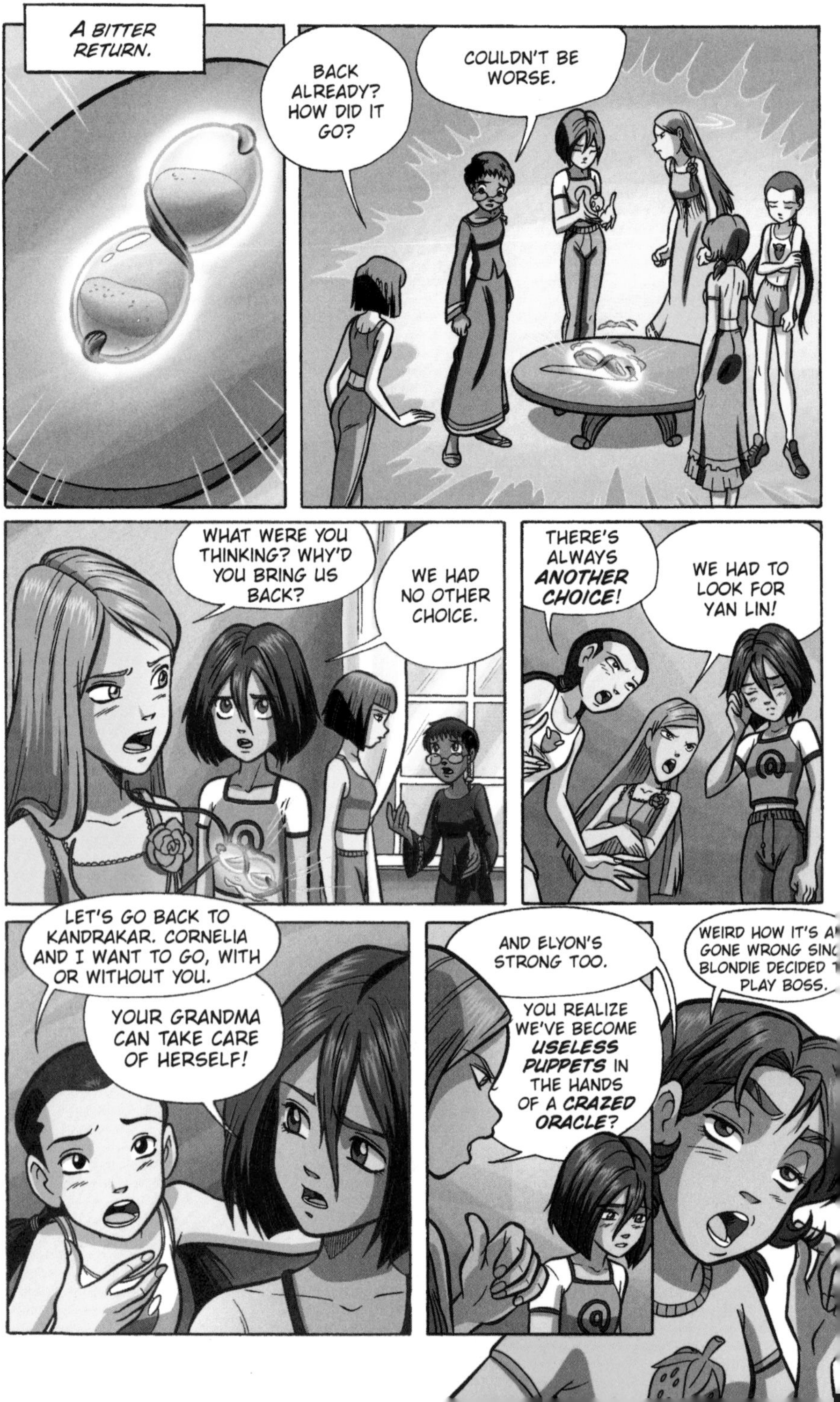
A BITTER RETURN.
BACK ALREADY? HOW DID IT GO?
COULDN'T BE WORSE.
WHAT WERE YOU THINKING? WHY'D YOU BRING US BACK?
WE HAD NO OTHER CHOICE.
THERE'S ALWAYS ANOTHER CHOICE!
WE HAD TO LOOK FOR YAN LIN!
LET'S GO BACK TO KANDRAKAR. CORNELIA AND I WANT TO GO, WITH OR WITHOUT YOU.
YOUR GRANDMA CAN TAKE CARE OF HERSELF!
AND ELYON'S STRONG TOO.
YOU REALIZE WE'VE BECOME USELESS PUPPETS IN THE HANDS OF A CRAZED ORACLE?
WEIRD HOW IT'S A
GONE WRONG SINC
BLONDIE DECIDED T
PLAY BOSS.

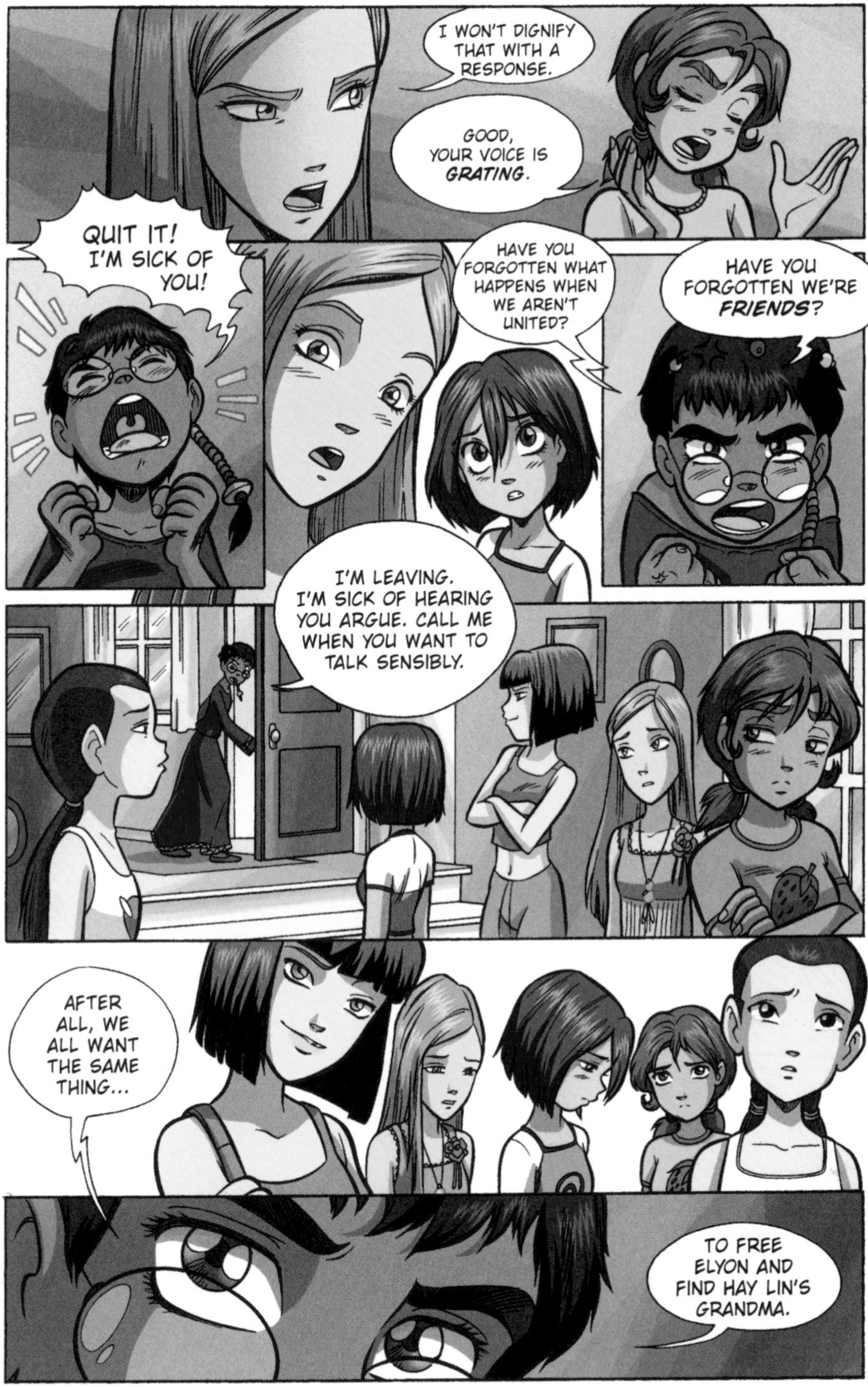
I WON'T DIGNIFY THAT WITH A RESPONSE.
GOOD, YOUR VOICE IS GRATING.
QUIT IT! I'M SICK OF YOU!
HAVE YOU FORGOTTEN WHAT HAPPENS WHEN WE AREN'T UNITED?
HAVE YOU FORGOTTEN WE'RE FRIENDS?
I'M LEAVING. I'M SICK OF HEARING YOU ARGUE. CALL ME WHEN YOU WANT TO TALK SENSIBLY.
AFTER ALL, WE ALL WANT THE SAME THING...
TO FREE ELYON AND FIND HAY LIN'S GRANDMA.

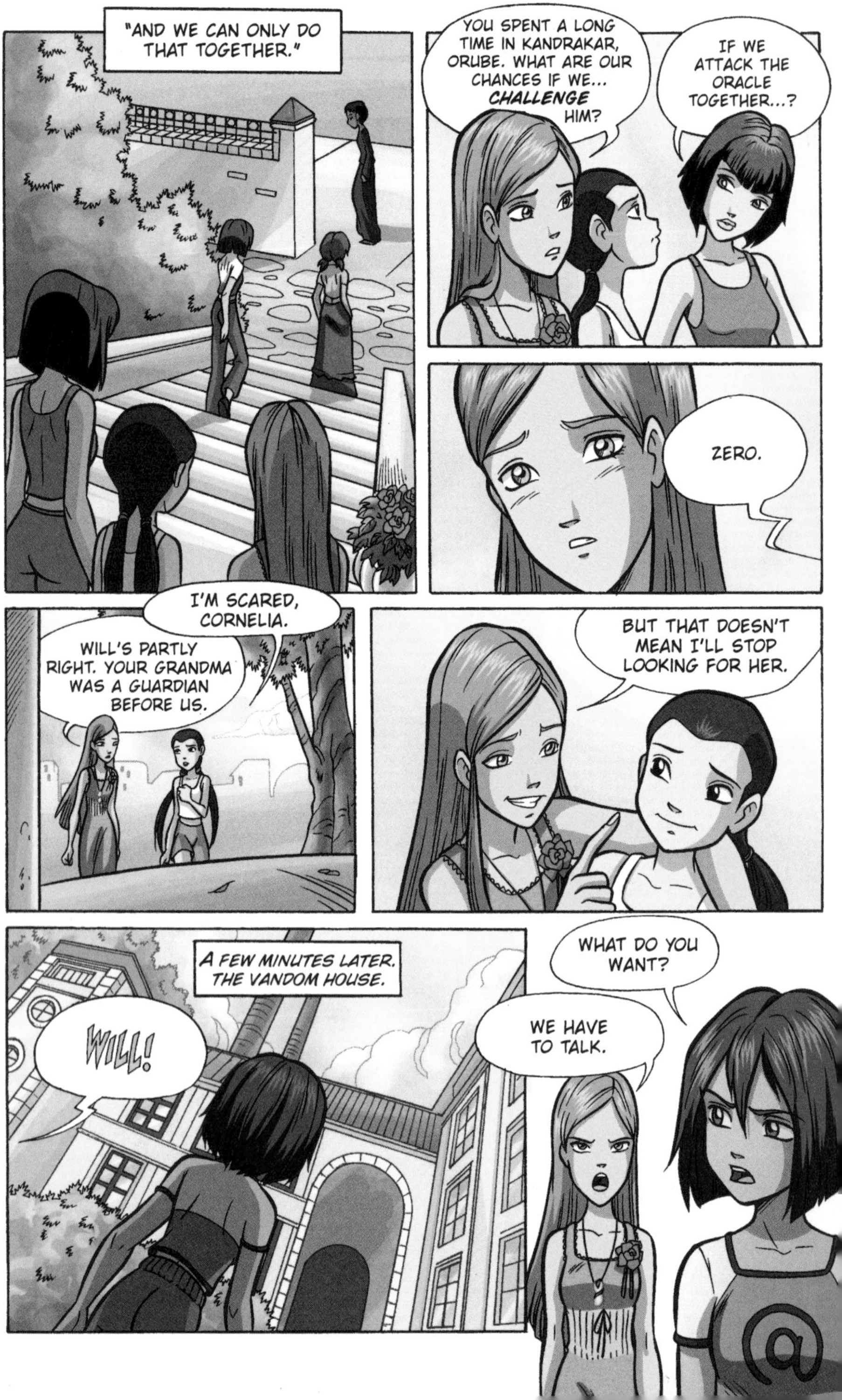

"AND WE CAN ONLY DO THAT TOGETHER."
YOU SPENT A LONG TIME IN KANDRAKAR, ORUBE. WHAT ARE OUR CHANCES IF WE... CHALLENGE HIM?
IF WE ATTACK THE ORACLE TOGETHER...?
ZERO.
WILL'S PARTLY RIGHT. YOUR GRANDMA WAS A GUARDIAN BEFORE US.
I'M SCARED, CORNELIA.
BUT THAT DOESN'T MEAN I'LL STOP LOOKING FOR HER.
A FEW MINUTES LATER. THE VANDOM HOUSE.
WILL!
WE HAVE TO TALK.
WHAT DO YOU WANT?

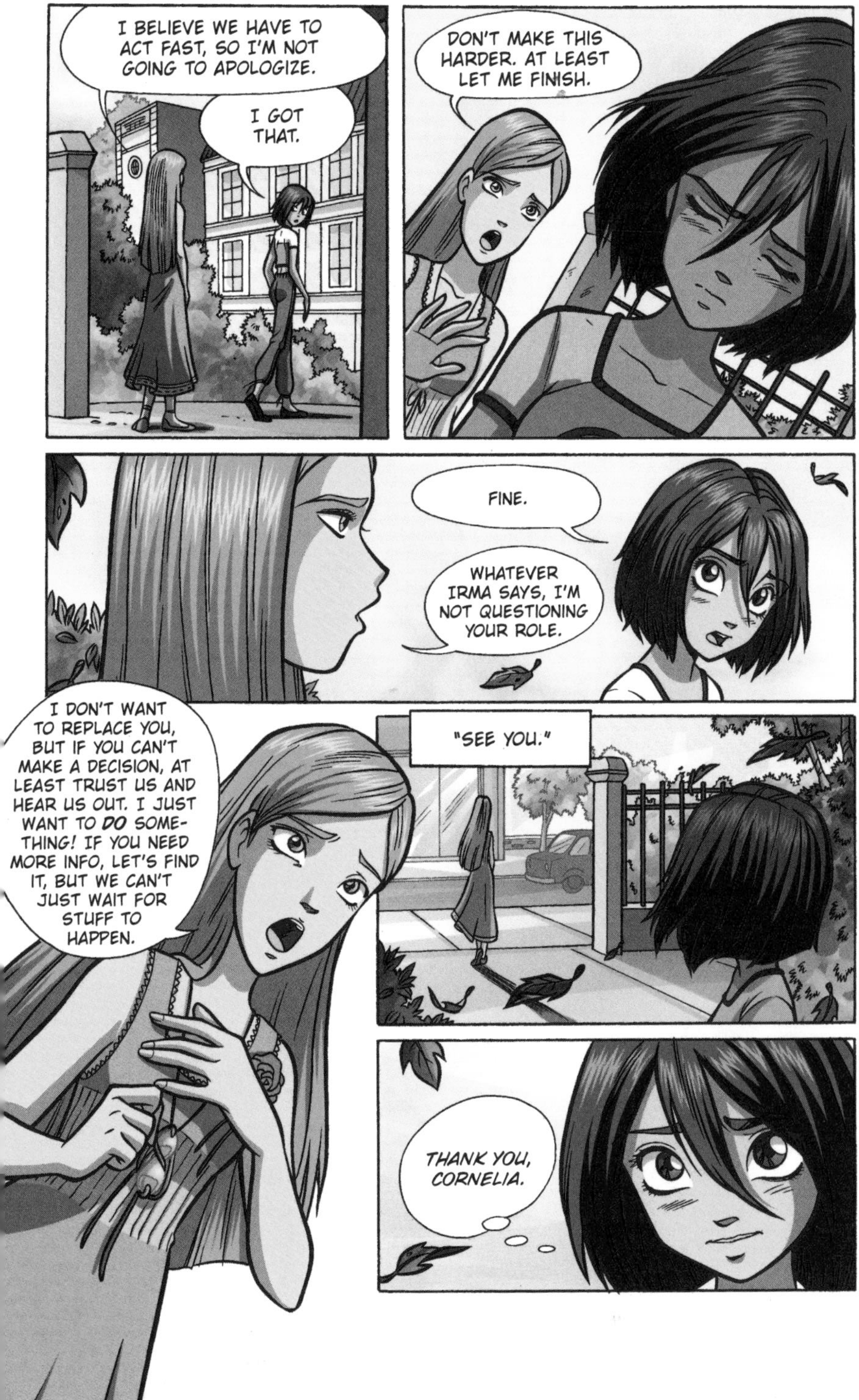
I BELIEVE WE HAVE TO ACT FAST, SO I'M NOT GOING TO APOLOGIZE.
I GOT THAT.
DON'T MAKE THIS HARDER. AT LEAST LET ME FINISH.
FINE.
WHATEVER IRMA SAYS, I'M NOT QUESTIONING YOUR ROLE.
I DON'T WANT TO REPLACE YOU, BUT IF YOU CAN'T MAKE A DECISION, AT LEAST TRUST US AND HEAR US OUT. I JUST WANT TO *DO* SOMETHING! IF YOU NEED MORE INFO, LET'S FIND IT, BUT WE CAN'T JUST WAIT FOR STUFF TO HAPPEN.
"SEE YOU."
THANK YOU, CORNELIA.

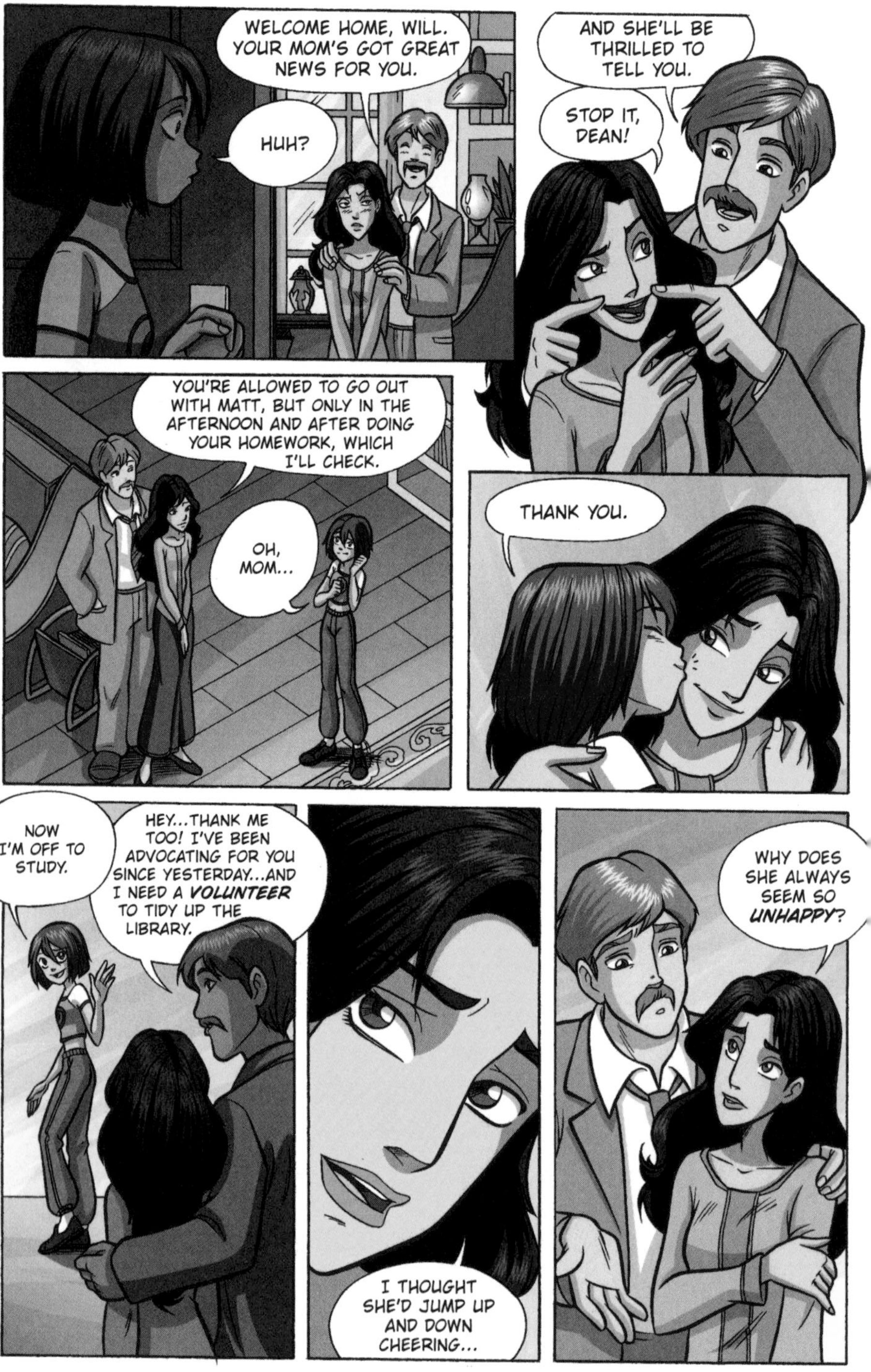
WELCOME HOME, WILL. YOUR MOM'S GOT GREAT NEWS FOR YOU.
HUH?
AND SHE'LL BE THRILLED TO TELL YOU.
STOP IT, DEAN!
YOU'RE ALLOWED TO GO OUT WITH MATT, BUT ONLY IN THE AFTERNOON AND AFTER DOING YOUR HOMEWORK, WHICH I'LL CHECK.
OH, MOM...
THANK YOU.
NOW I'M OFF TO STUDY.
HEY...THANK ME TOO! I'VE BEEN ADVOCATING FOR YOU SINCE YESTERDAY...AND I NEED A VOLUNTEER TO TIDY UP THE LIBRARY.
I THOUGHT SHE'D JUMP UP AND DOWN CHEERING...
WHY DOES SHE ALWAYS SEEM SO UNHAPPY?

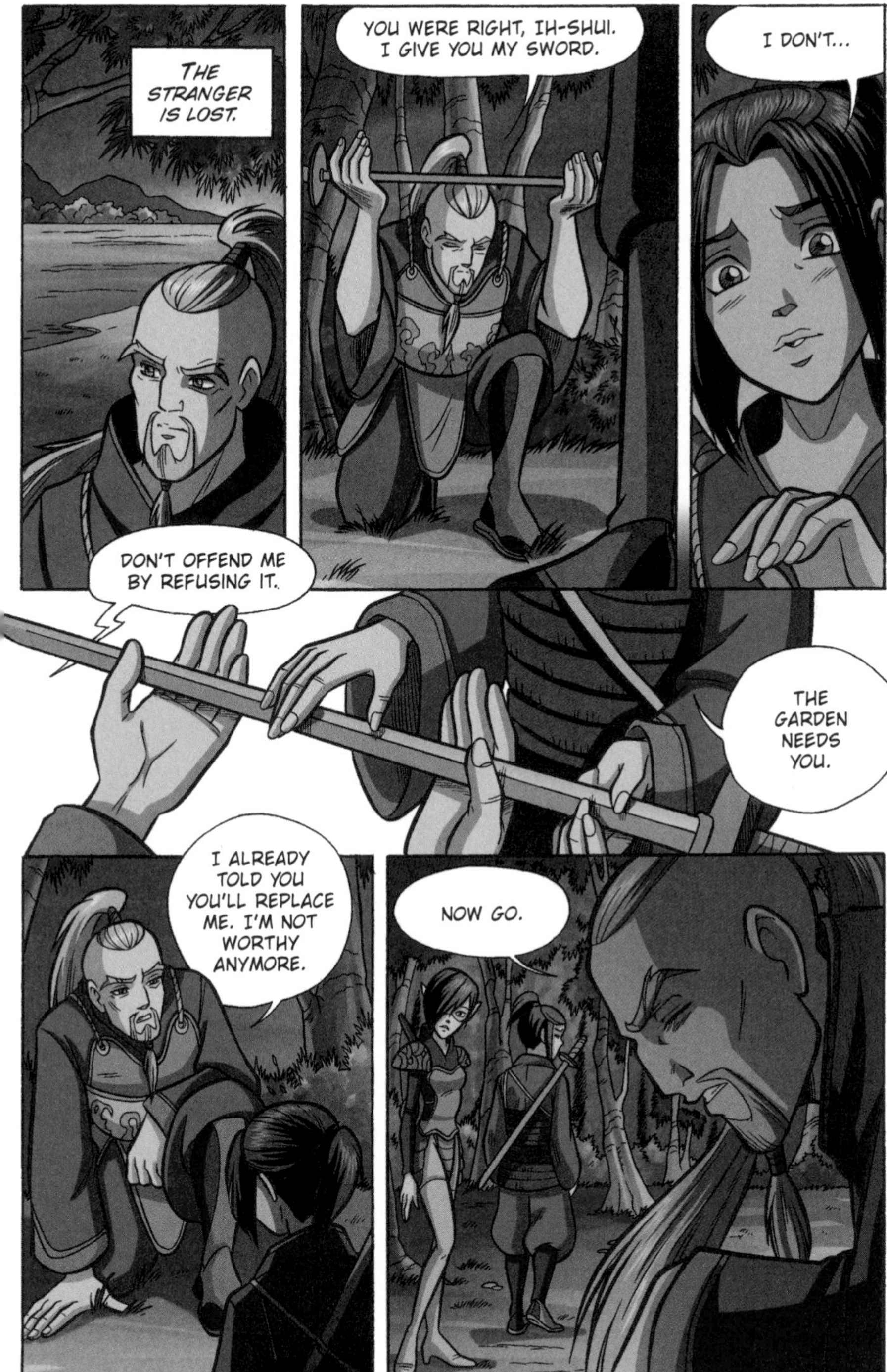
THE STRANGER IS LOST.
YOU WERE RIGHT, IH-SHUI. I GIVE YOU MY SWORD.
I DON'T...
DON'T OFFEND ME BY REFUSING IT.
THE GARDEN NEEDS YOU.
I ALREADY TOLD YOU YOU'LL REPLACE ME. I'M NOT WORTHY ANYMORE.
NOW GO.

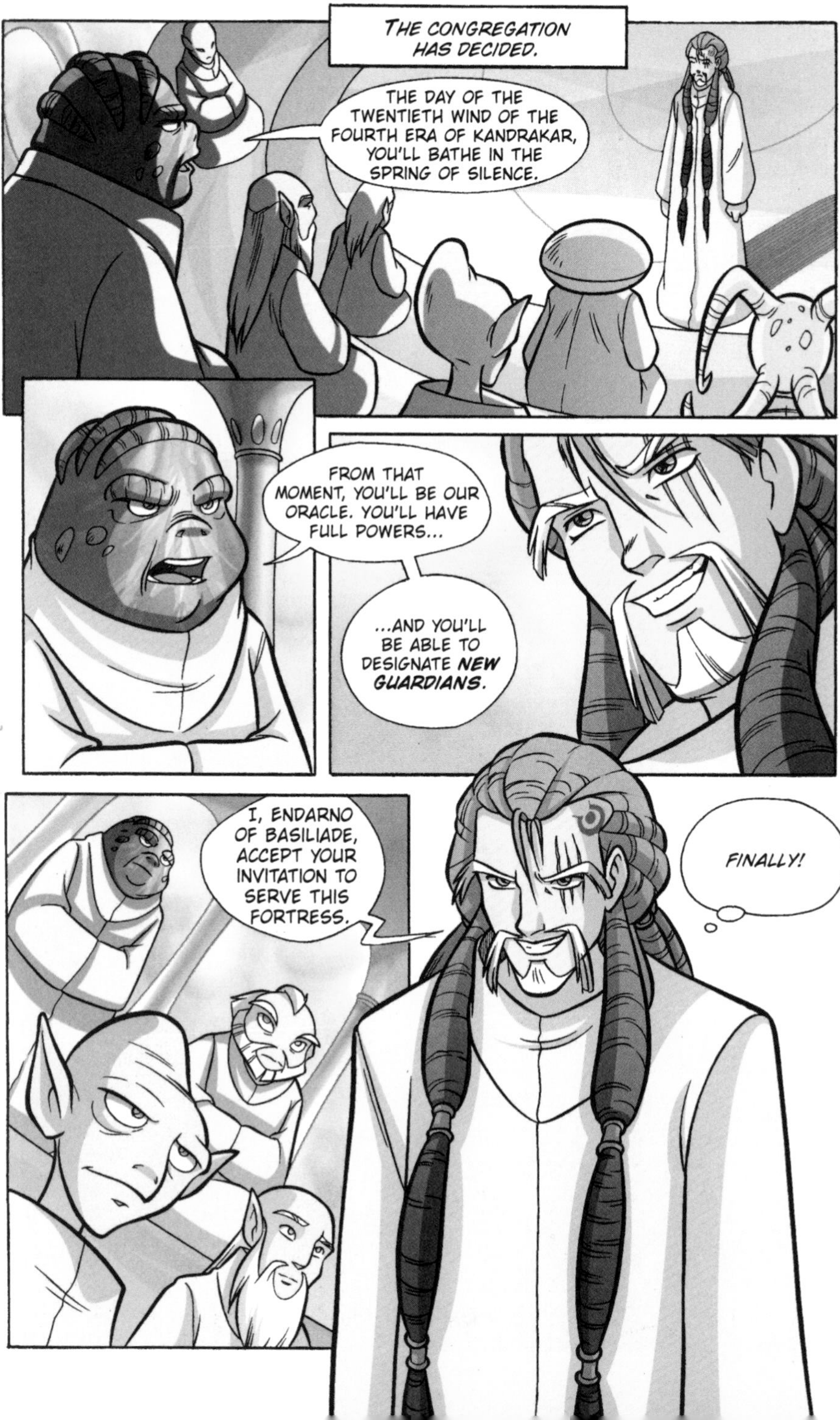
THE CONGREGATION HAS DECIDED.
THE DAY OF THE TWENTIETH WIND OF THE FOURTH ERA OF KANDRAKAR, YOU'LL BATHE IN THE SPRING OF SILENCE.
FROM THAT MOMENT, YOU'LL BE OUR ORACLE. YOU'LL HAVE FULL POWERS...
...AND YOU'LL BE ABLE TO DESIGNATE NEW GUARDIANS.
I, ENDARNO OF BASILIADE, ACCEPT YOUR INVITATION TO SERVE THIS FORTRESS.
FINALLY!

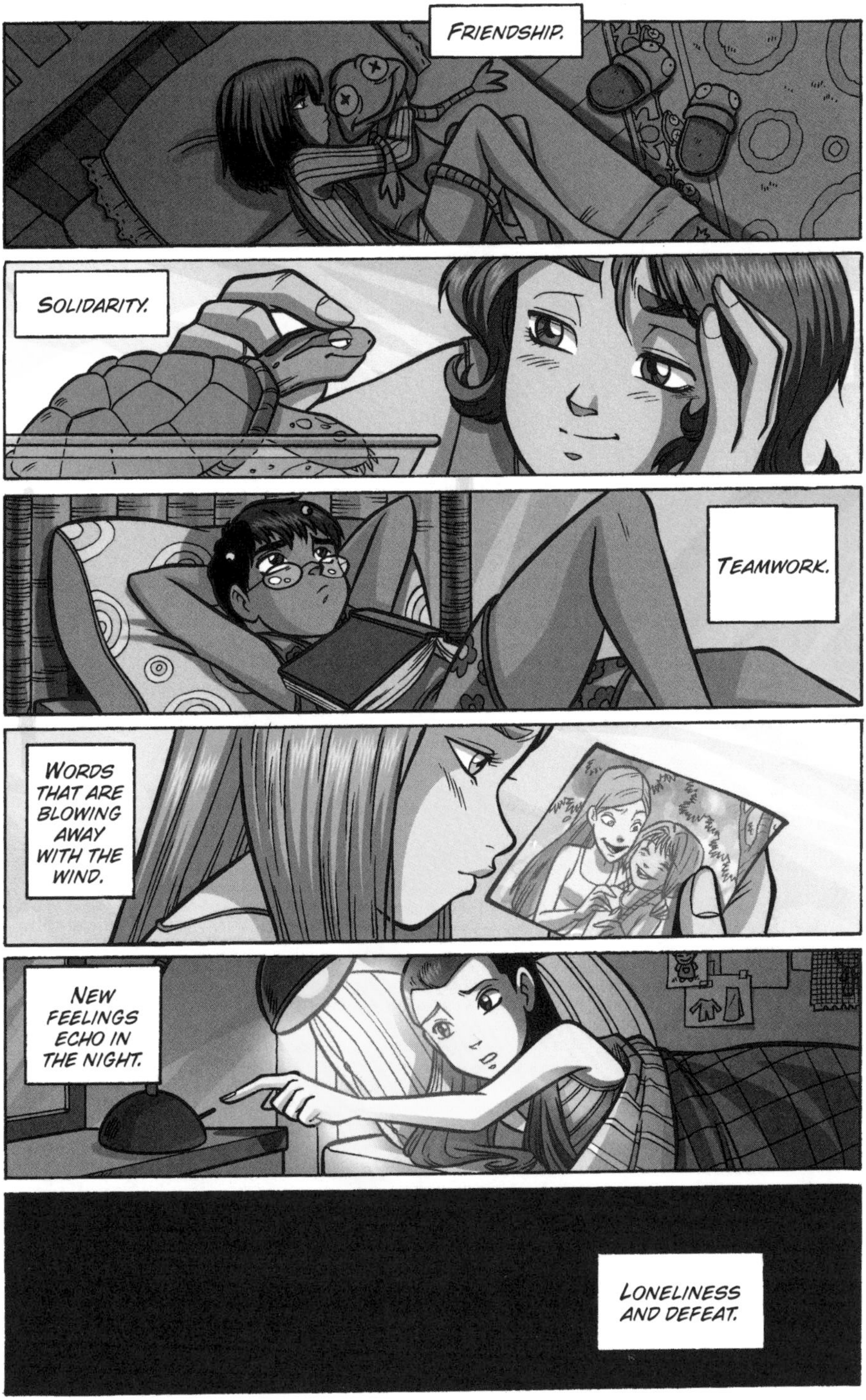
FRIENDSHIP.
SOLIDARITY.
TEAMWORK.
WORDS THAT ARE BLOWING AWAY WITH THE WIND.
NEW FEELINGS ECHO IN THE NIGHT.
LONELINESS AND DEFEAT.

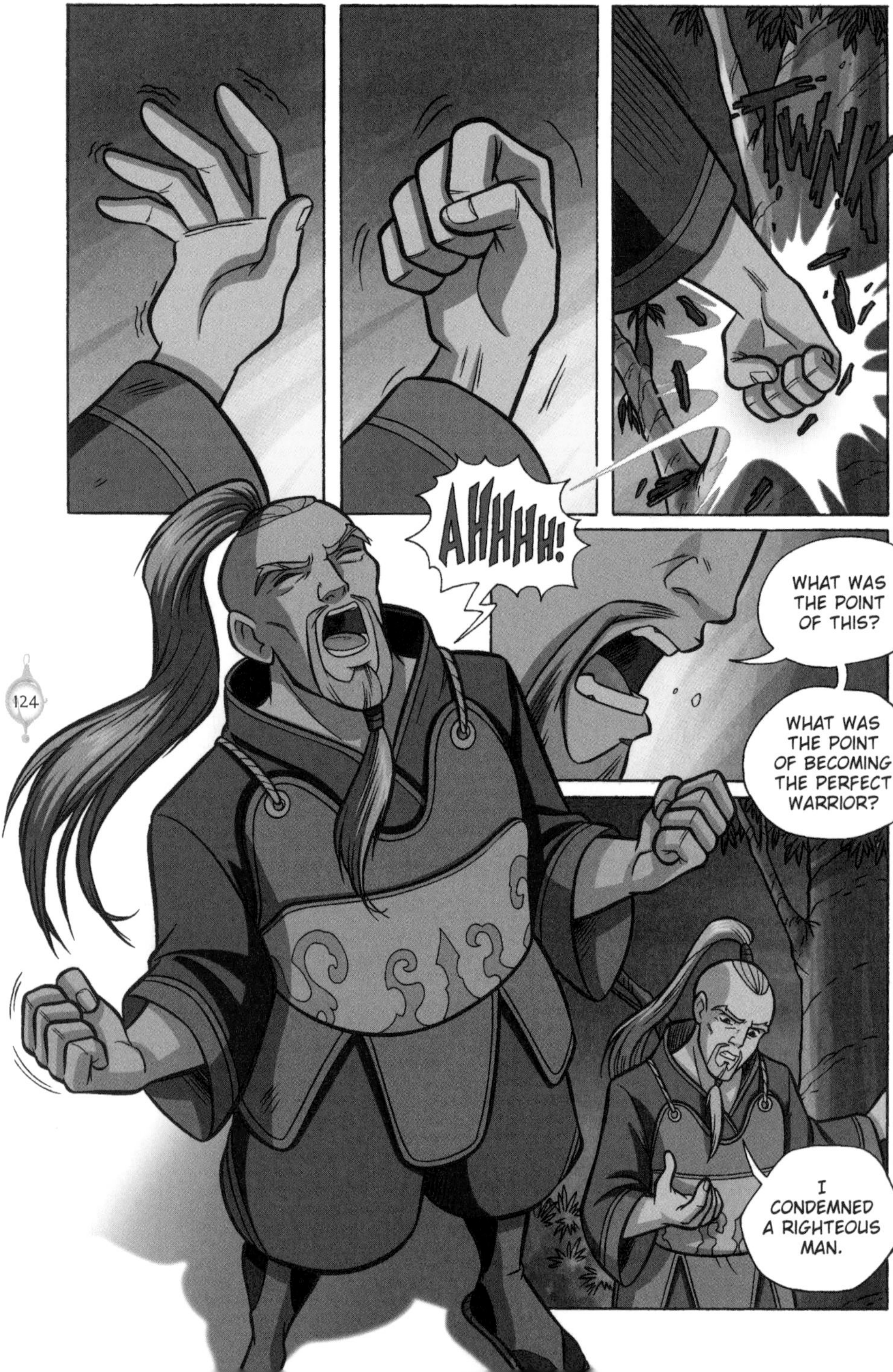
TWNK
AHHHH!
WHAT WAS THE POINT OF THIS?
WHAT WAS THE POINT OF BECOMING THE PERFECT WARRIOR?
I CONDEMNED A RIGHTEOUS MAN.

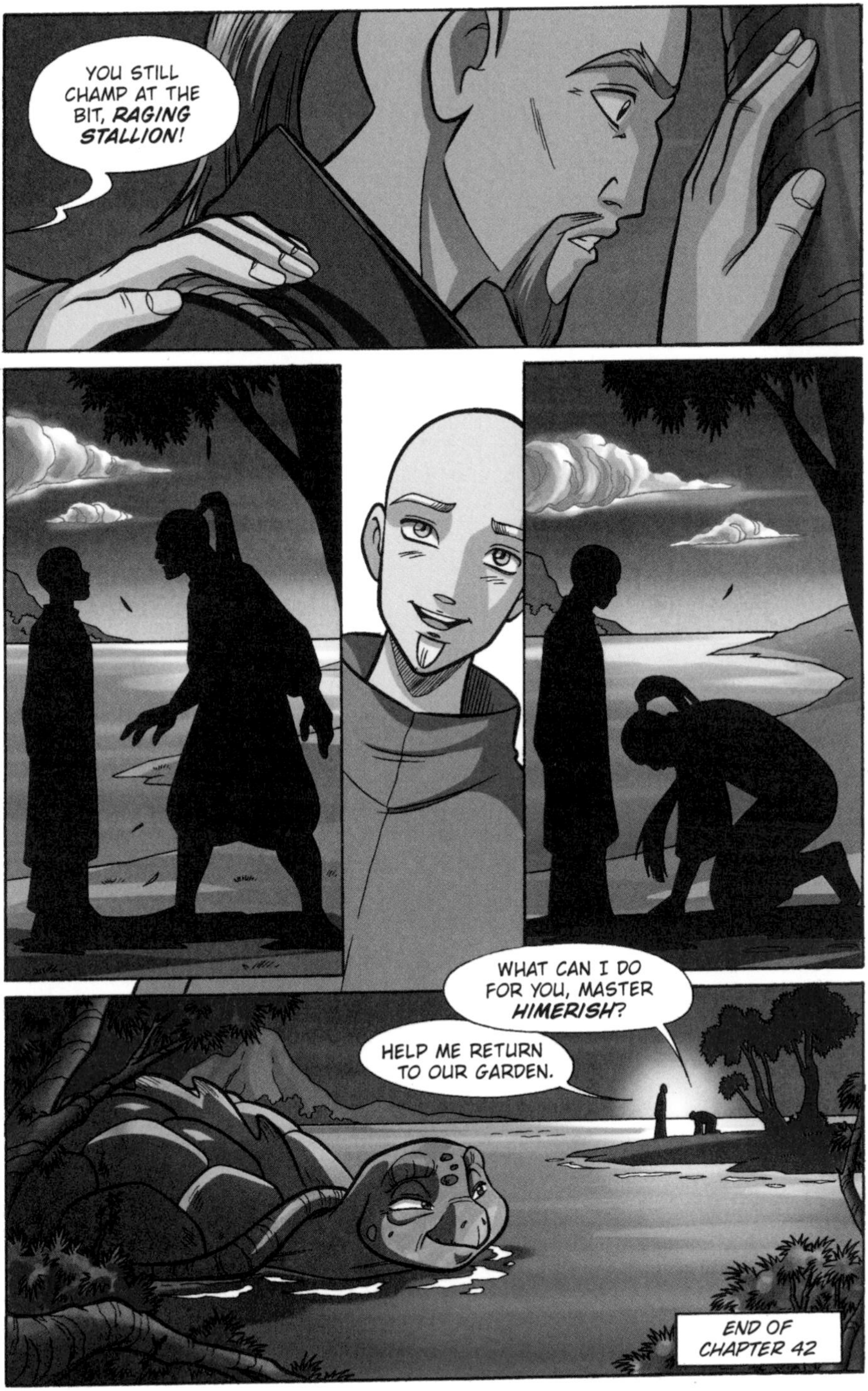
YOU STILL CHAMP AT THE BIT, ***RAGING STALLION***!
WHAT CAN I DO FOR YOU, MASTER ***HIMERISH***?
HELP ME RETURN TO OUR GARDEN.
END OF CHAPTER 42

W.i.t.c.h.

Will Irma Taranee Cornelia Hay Lin

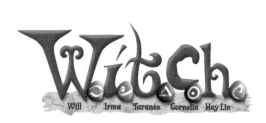

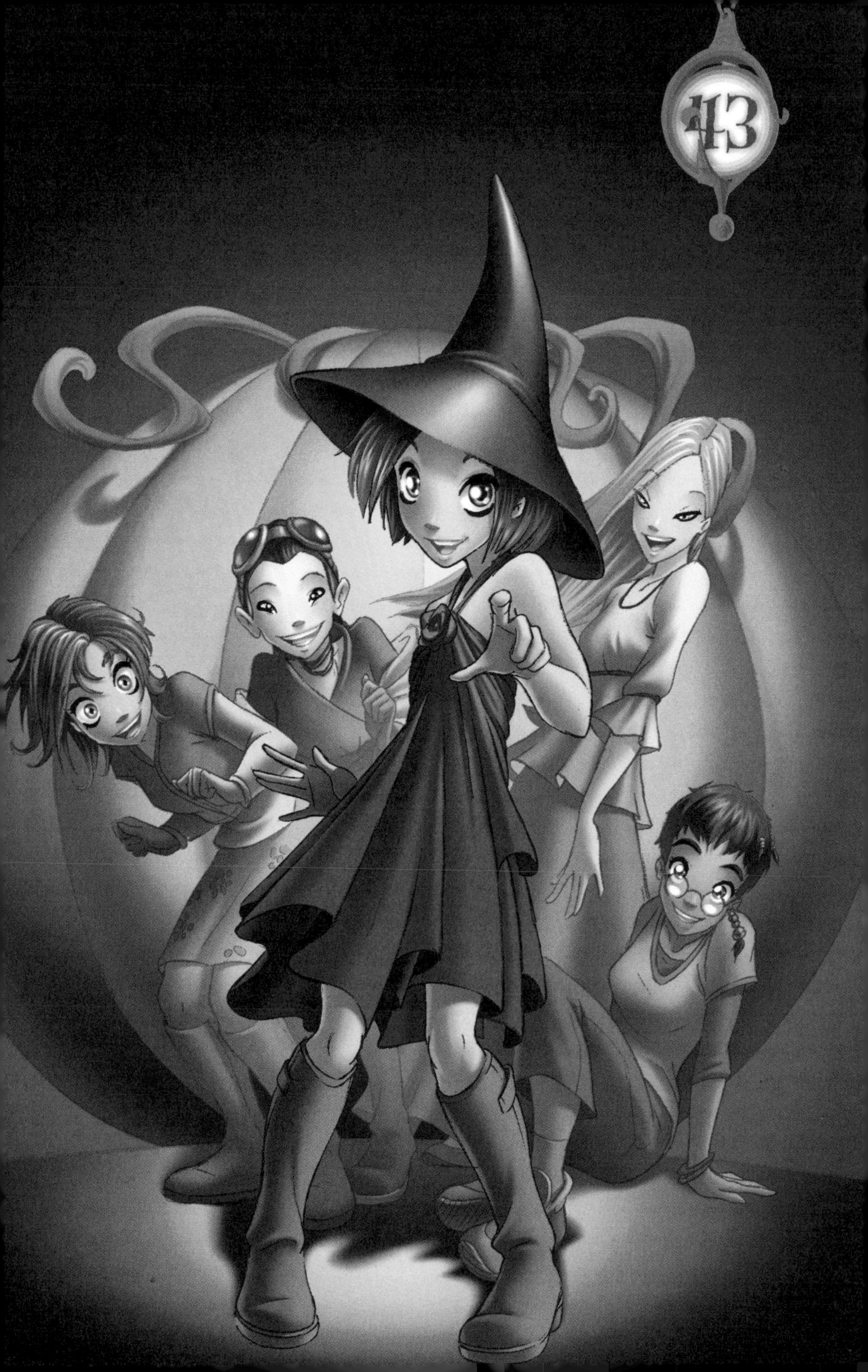
43

The Magic of Light

"The courage to stick together—that's the answer you're looking for."

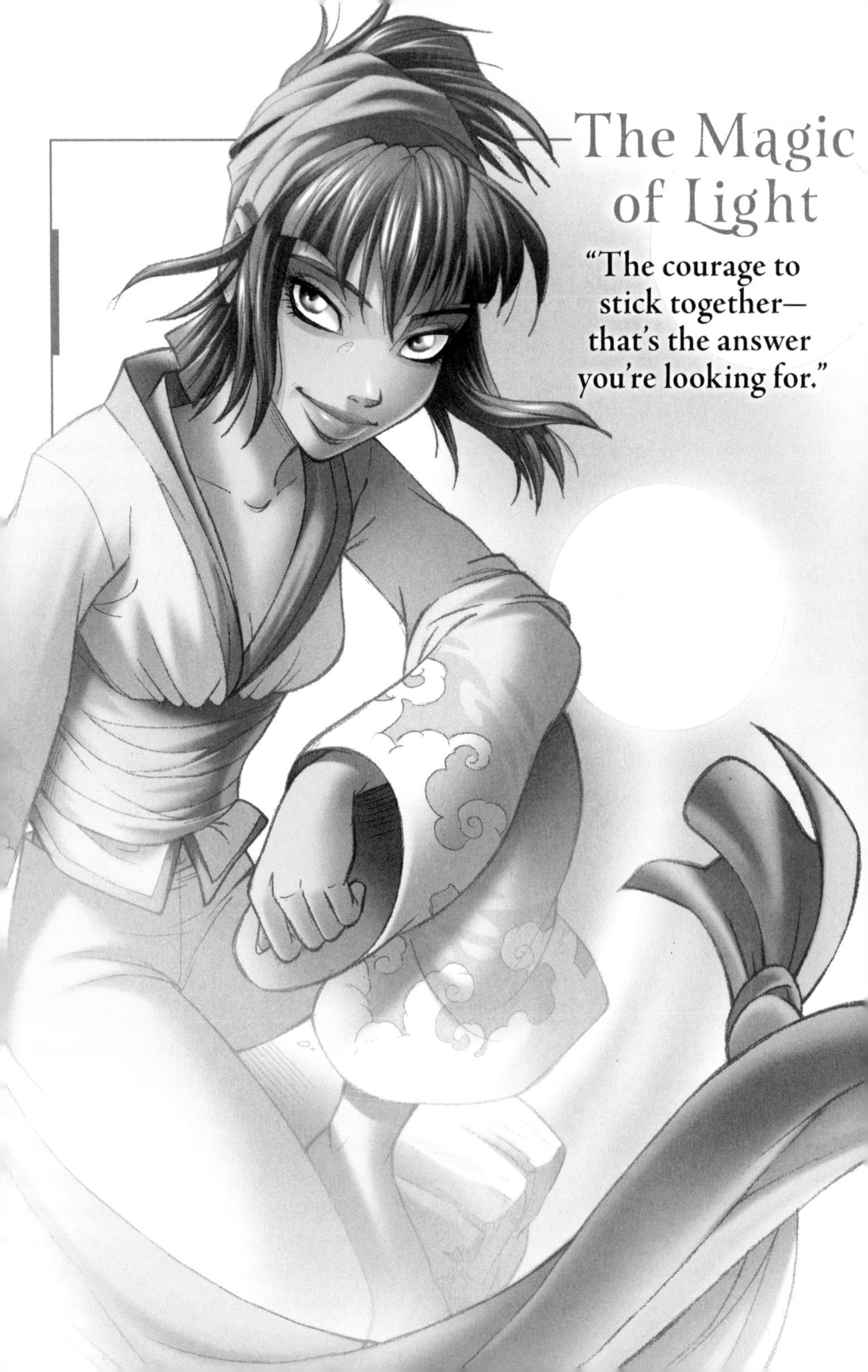

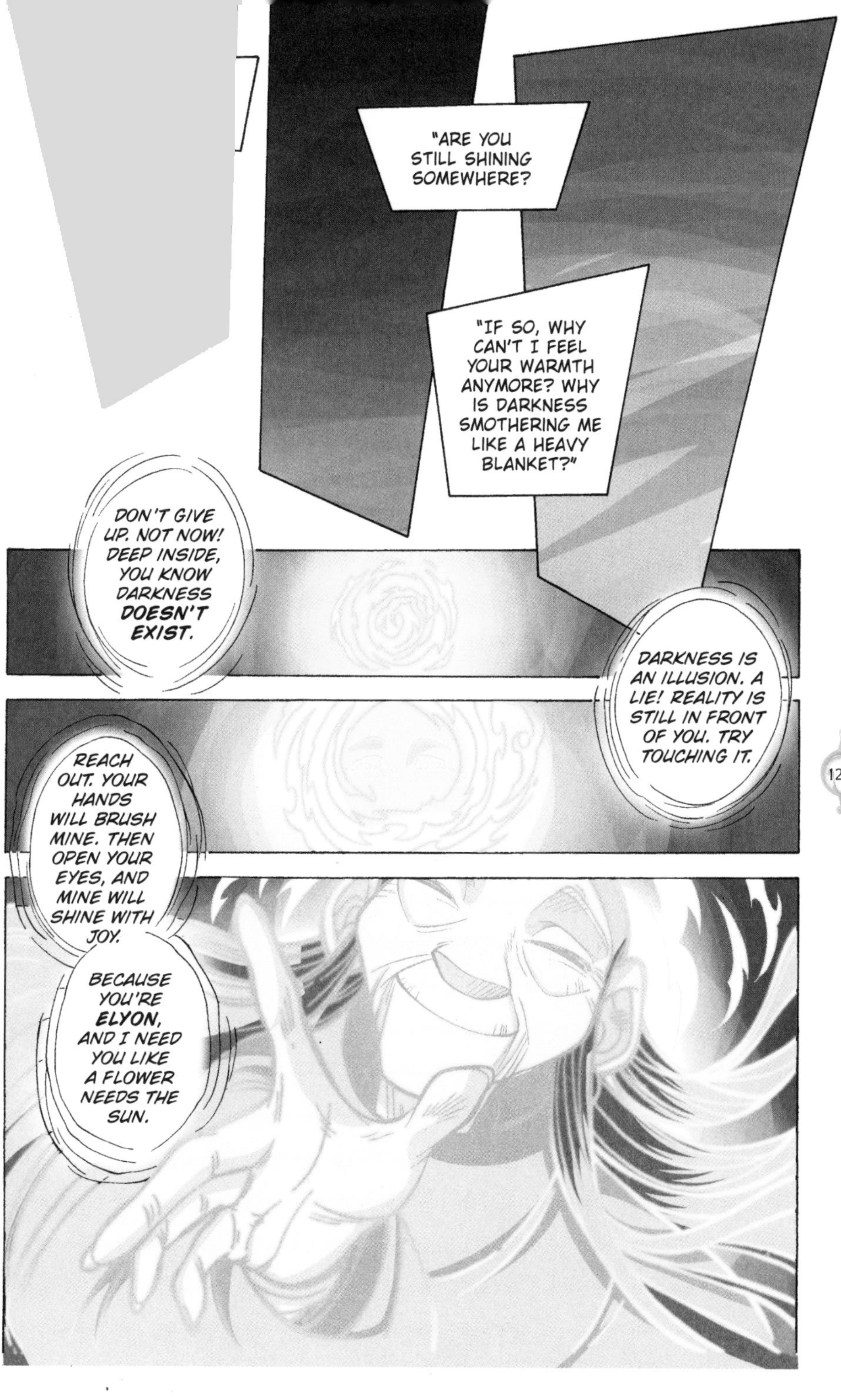
"ARE YOU STILL SHINING SOMEWHERE?
"IF SO, WHY CAN'T I FEEL YOUR WARMTH ANYMORE? WHY IS DARKNESS SMOTHERING ME LIKE A HEAVY BLANKET?"
DON'T GIVE UP. NOT NOW! DEEP INSIDE, YOU KNOW DARKNESS DOESN'T EXIST.
DARKNESS IS AN ILLUSION. A LIE! REALITY IS STILL IN FRONT OF YOU. TRY TOUCHING IT.
REACH OUT. YOUR HANDS WILL BRUSH MINE. THEN OPEN YOUR EYES, AND MINE WILL SHINE WITH JOY.
BECAUSE YOU'RE ELYON, AND I NEED YOU LIKE A FLOWER NEEDS THE SUN.

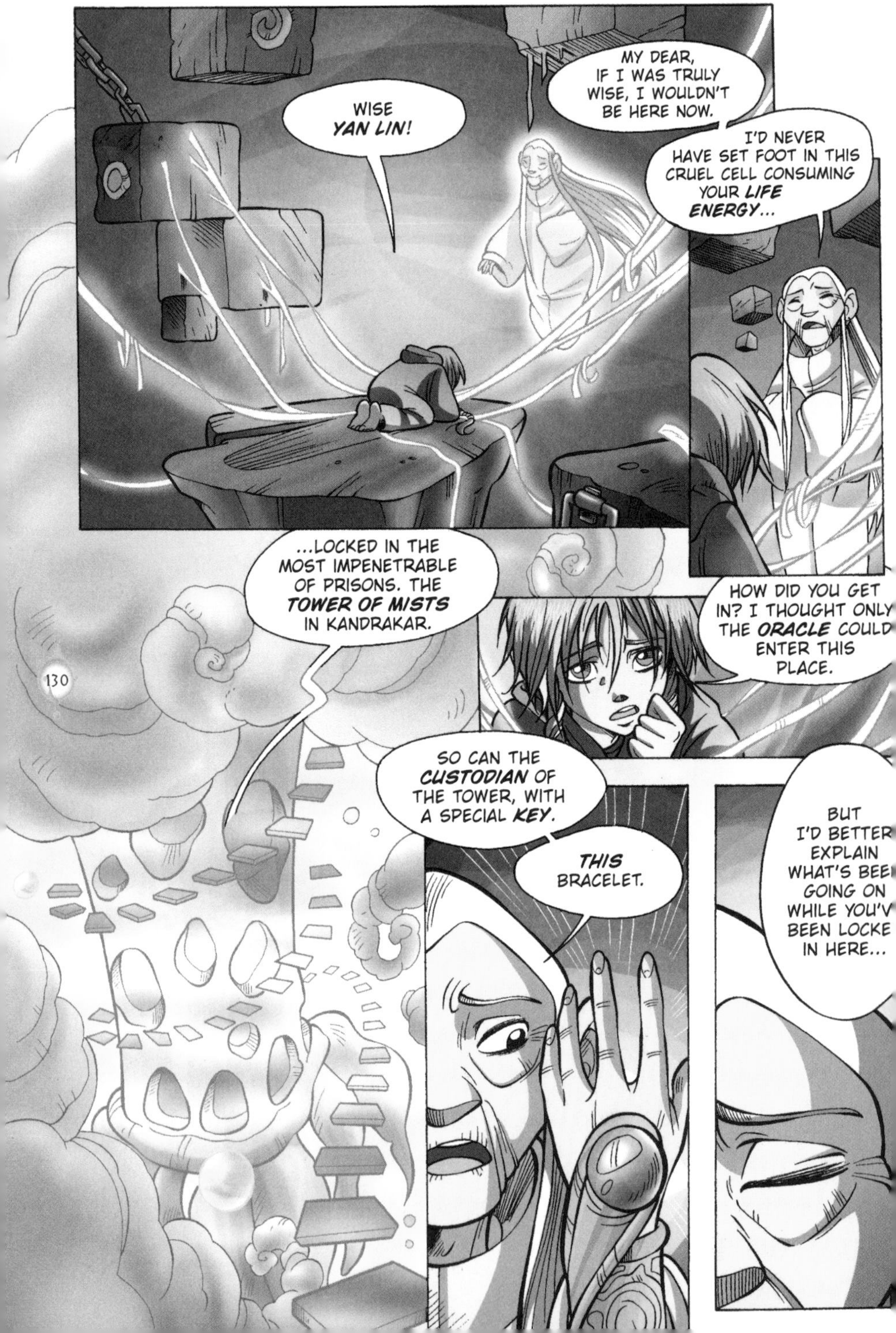
WISE YAN LIN!
MY DEAR, IF I WAS TRULY WISE, I WOULDN'T BE HERE NOW.
I'D NEVER HAVE SET FOOT IN THIS CRUEL CELL CONSUMING YOUR LIFE ENERGY...
...LOCKED IN THE MOST IMPENETRABLE OF PRISONS. THE TOWER OF MISTS IN KANDRAKAR.
HOW DID YOU GET IN? I THOUGHT ONLY THE ORACLE COULD ENTER THIS PLACE.
SO CAN THE CUSTODIAN OF THE TOWER, WITH A SPECIAL KEY.
THIS BRACELET.
BUT I'D BETTER EXPLAIN WHAT'S BEE GOING ON WHILE YOU'V BEEN LOCKE IN HERE...

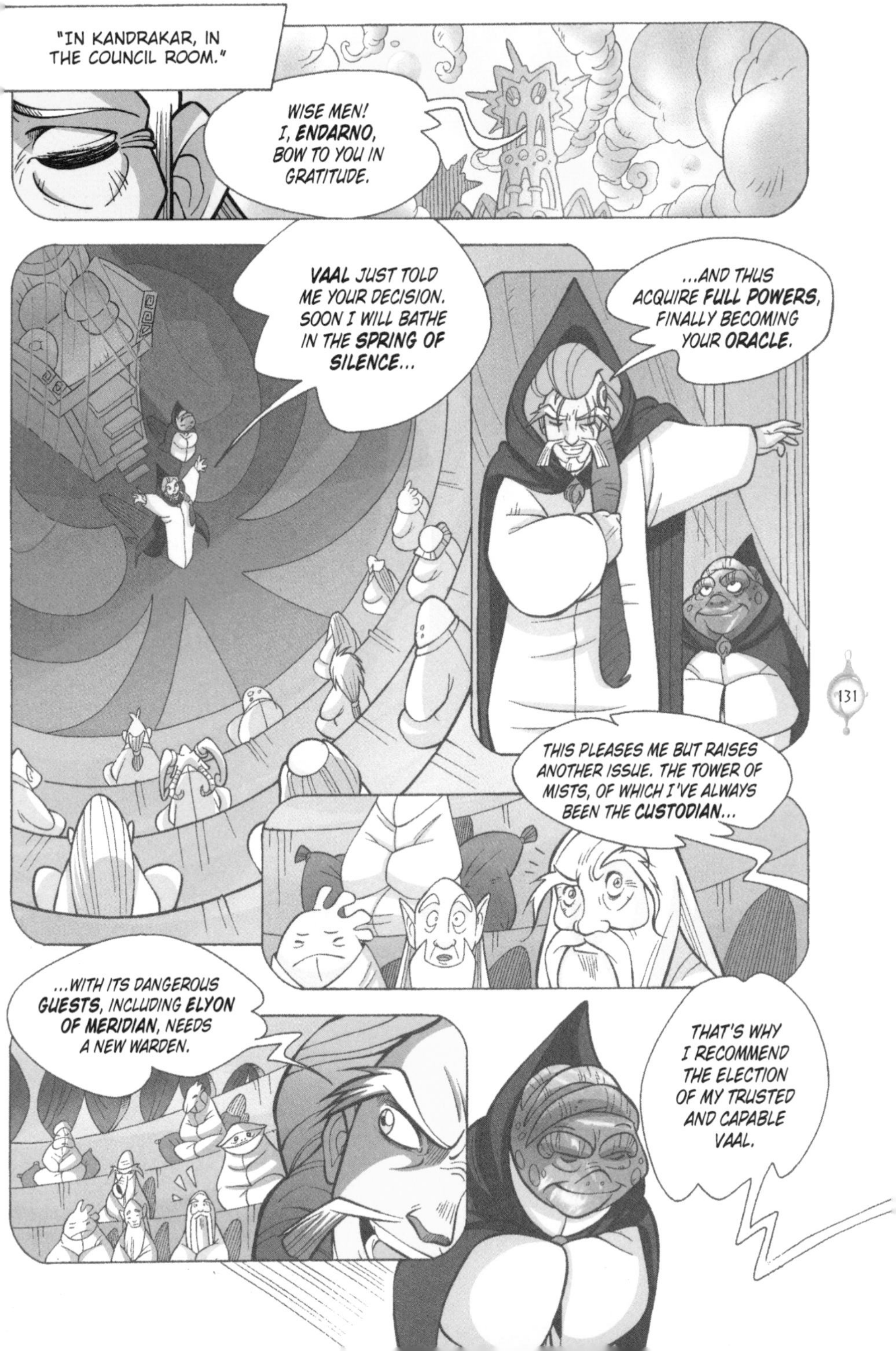
"IN KANDRAKAR, IN THE COUNCIL ROOM."
WISE MEN! I, ENDARNO, BOW TO YOU IN GRATITUDE.
VAAL JUST TOLD ME YOUR DECISION. SOON I WILL BATHE IN THE SPRING OF SILENCE...
...AND THUS ACQUIRE FULL POWERS, FINALLY BECOMING YOUR ORACLE.
THIS PLEASES ME BUT RAISES ANOTHER ISSUE. THE TOWER OF MISTS, OF WHICH I'VE ALWAYS BEEN THE CUSTODIAN...
...WITH ITS DANGEROUS GUESTS, INCLUDING ELYON OF MERIDIAN, NEEDS A NEW WARDEN.
THAT'S WHY I RECOMMEND THE ELECTION OF MY TRUSTED AND CAPABLE VAAL.

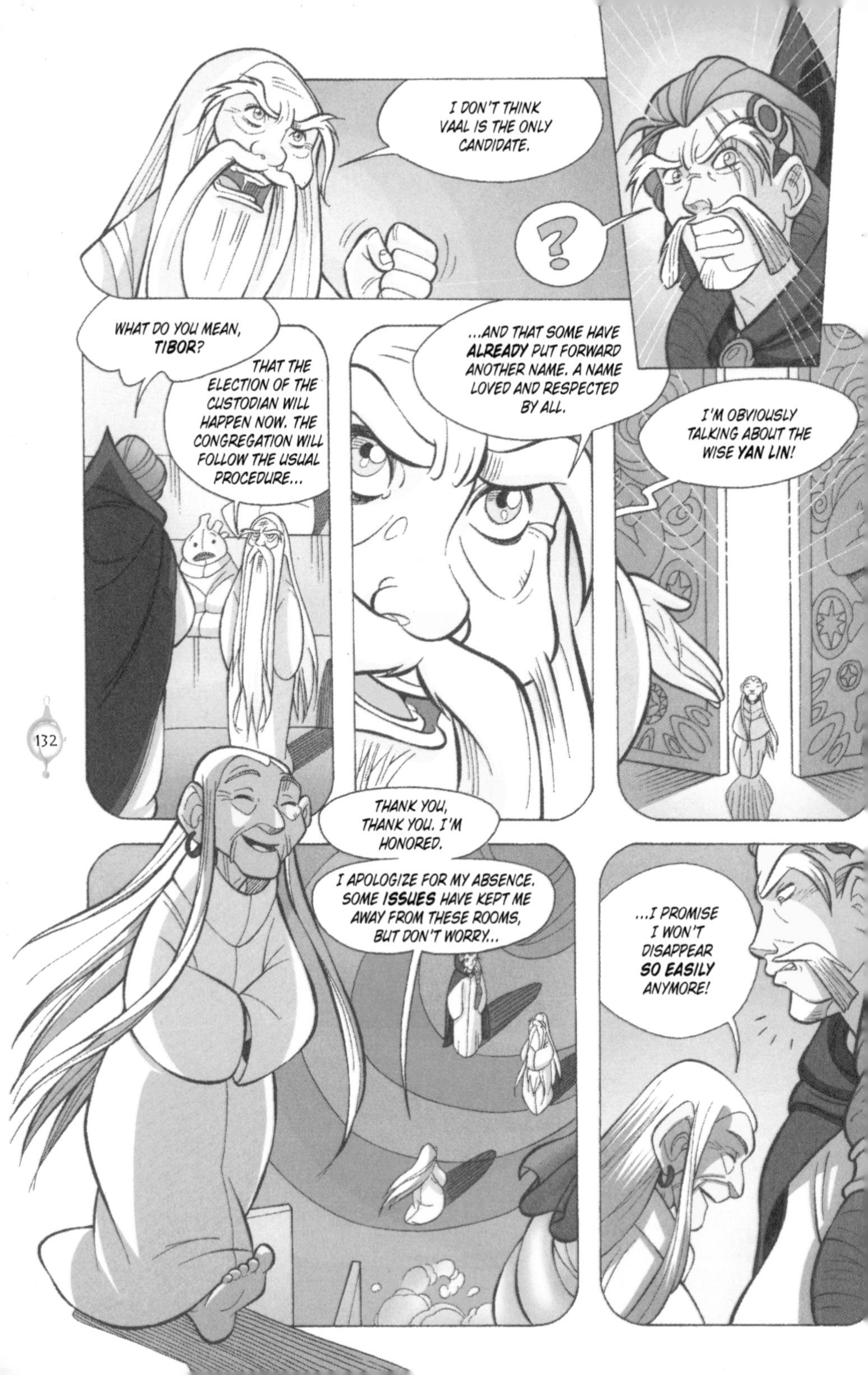
I DON'T THINK VAAL IS THE ONLY CANDIDATE.
?
WHAT DO YOU MEAN, TIBOR?
THAT THE ELECTION OF THE CUSTODIAN WILL HAPPEN NOW. THE CONGREGATION WILL FOLLOW THE USUAL PROCEDURE...
...AND THAT SOME HAVE ALREADY PUT FORWARD ANOTHER NAME. A NAME LOVED AND RESPECTED BY ALL.
I'M OBVIOUSLY TALKING ABOUT THE WISE YAN LIN!
THANK YOU, THANK YOU. I'M HONORED.
I APOLOGIZE FOR MY ABSENCE. SOME ISSUES HAVE KEPT ME AWAY FROM THESE ROOMS, BUT DON'T WORRY...
...I PROMISE I WON'T DISAPPEAR SO EASILY ANYMORE!

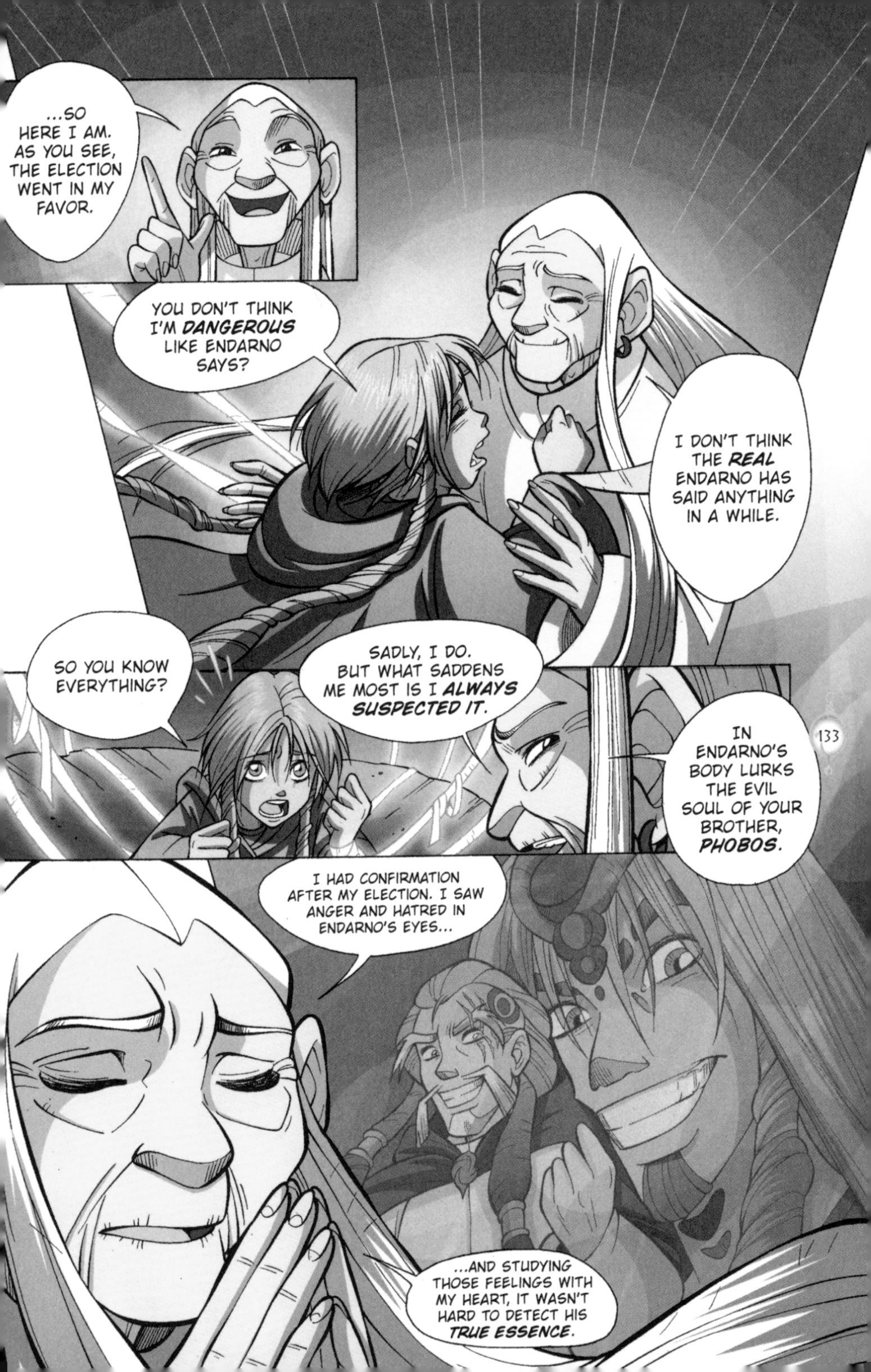
...SO HERE I AM. AS YOU SEE, THE ELECTION WENT IN MY FAVOR.
YOU DON'T THINK I'M DANGEROUS LIKE ENDARNO SAYS?
I DON'T THINK THE REAL ENDARNO HAS SAID ANYTHING IN A WHILE.
SO YOU KNOW EVERYTHING?
SADLY, I DO. BUT WHAT SADDENS ME MOST IS I ALWAYS SUSPECTED IT.
IN ENDARNO'S BODY LURKS THE EVIL SOUL OF YOUR BROTHER, PHOBOS.
I HAD CONFIRMATION AFTER MY ELECTION. I SAW ANGER AND HATRED IN ENDARNO'S EYES...
...AND STUDYING THOSE FEELINGS WITH MY HEART, IT WASN'T HARD TO DETECT HIS TRUE ESSENCE.

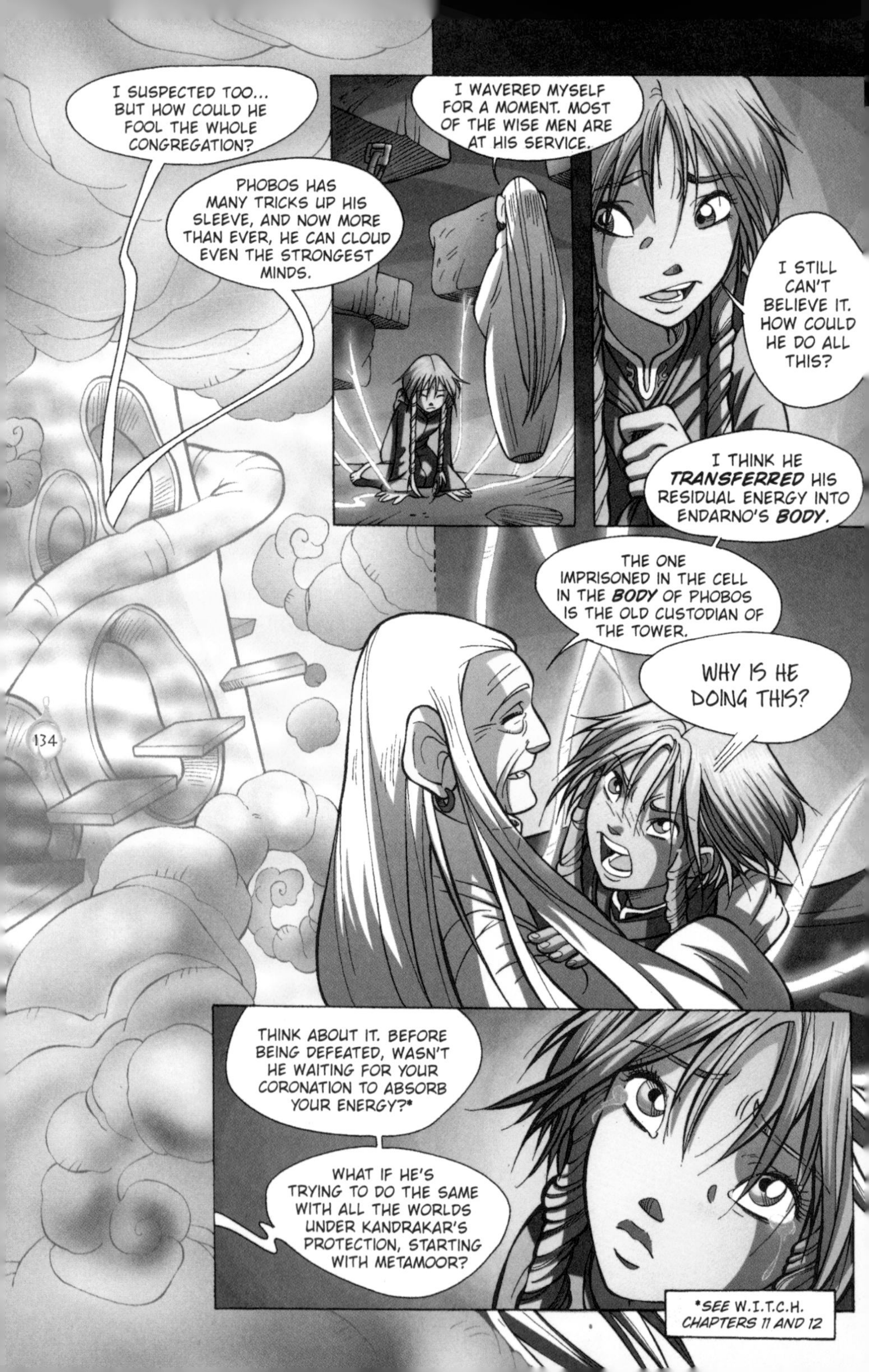
I SUSPECTED TOO... BUT HOW COULD HE FOOL THE WHOLE CONGREGATION?
PHOBOS HAS MANY TRICKS UP HIS SLEEVE, AND NOW MORE THAN EVER, HE CAN CLOUD EVEN THE STRONGEST MINDS.
I WAVERED MYSELF FOR A MOMENT. MOST OF THE WISE MEN ARE AT HIS SERVICE.
I STILL CAN'T BELIEVE IT. HOW COULD HE DO ALL THIS?
I THINK HE TRANSFERRED HIS RESIDUAL ENERGY INTO ENDARNO'S BODY.
THE ONE IMPRISONED IN THE CELL IN THE BODY OF PHOBOS IS THE OLD CUSTODIAN OF THE TOWER.
WHY IS HE DOING THIS?
THINK ABOUT IT. BEFORE BEING DEFEATED, WASN'T HE WAITING FOR YOUR CORONATION TO ABSORB YOUR ENERGY?*
WHAT IF HE'S TRYING TO DO THE SAME WITH ALL THE WORLDS UNDER KANDRAKAR'S PROTECTION, STARTING WITH METAMOOR?
*SEE W.I.T.C.H. CHAPTERS 11 AND 12

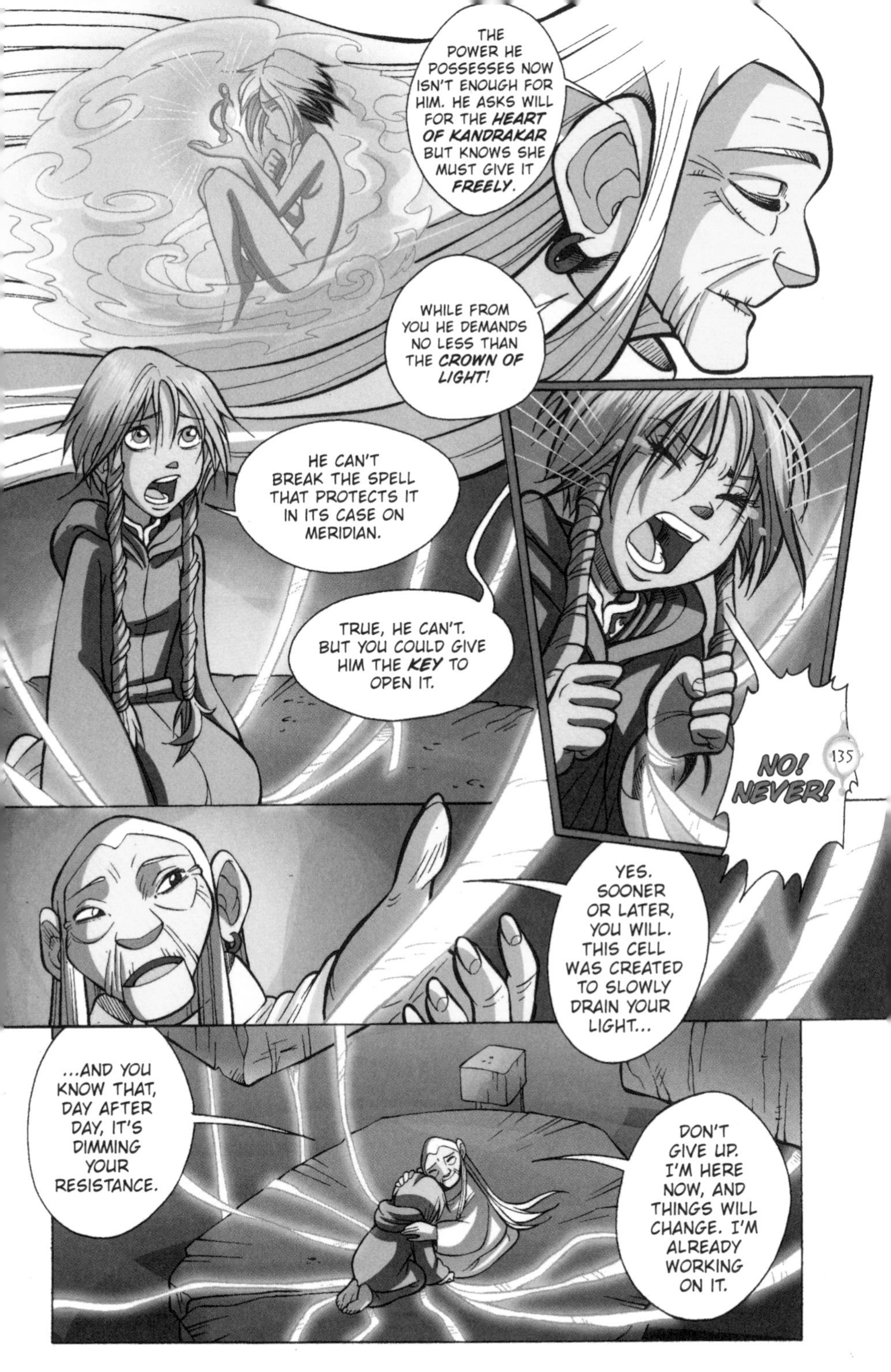
THE POWER HE POSSESSES NOW ISN'T ENOUGH FOR HIM. HE ASKS WILL FOR THE HEART OF KANDRAKAR BUT KNOWS SHE MUST GIVE IT FREELY.
WHILE FROM YOU HE DEMANDS NO LESS THAN THE CROWN OF LIGHT!
HE CAN'T BREAK THE SPELL THAT PROTECTS IT IN ITS CASE ON MERIDIAN.
TRUE, HE CAN'T. BUT YOU COULD GIVE HIM THE KEY TO OPEN IT.
NO! NEVER!
YES. SOONER OR LATER, YOU WILL. THIS CELL WAS CREATED TO SLOWLY DRAIN YOUR LIGHT...
...AND YOU KNOW THAT, DAY AFTER DAY, IT'S DIMMING YOUR RESISTANCE.
DON'T GIVE UP. I'M HERE NOW, AND THINGS WILL CHANGE. I'M ALREADY WORKING ON IT.

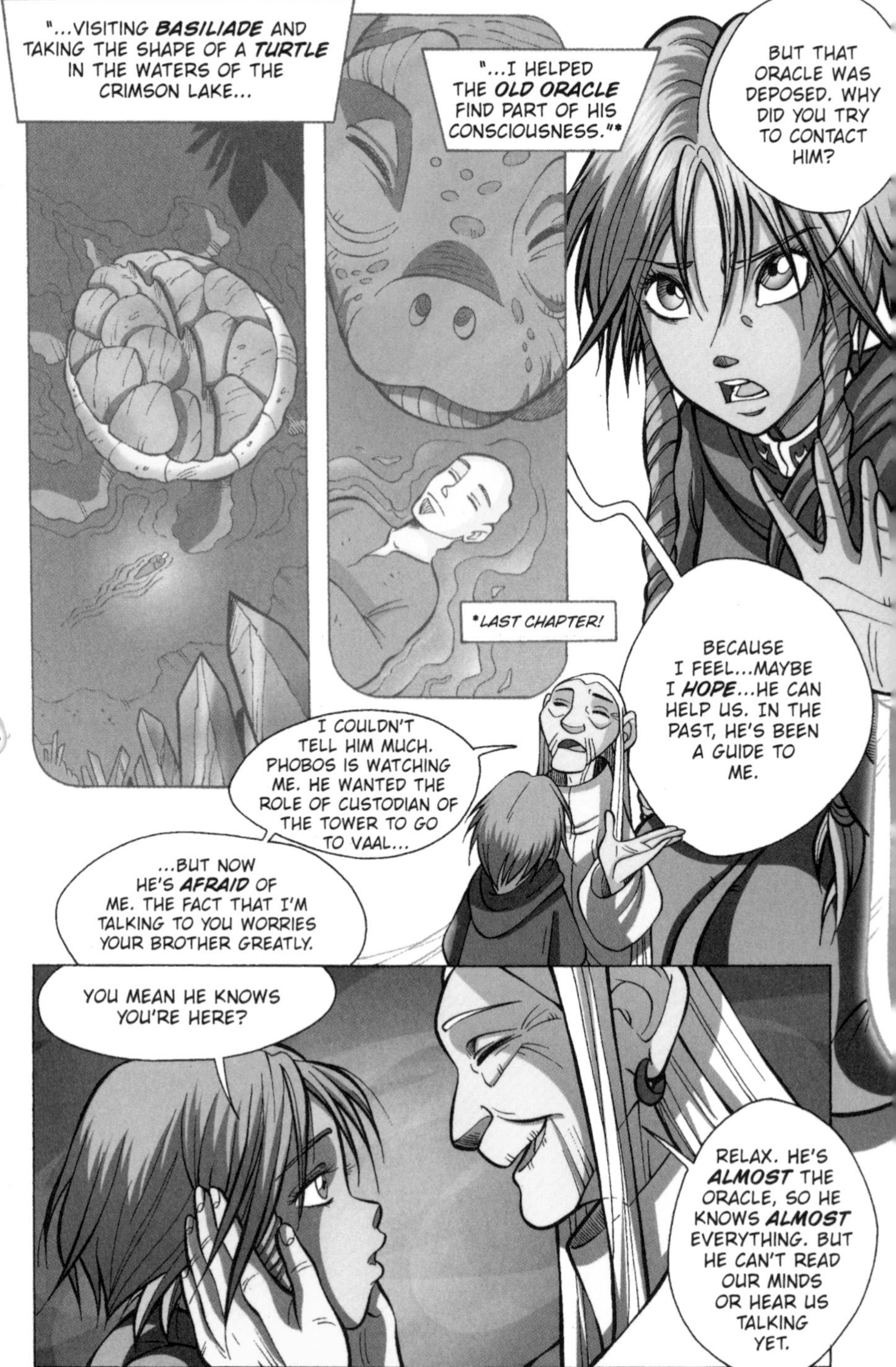
"...VISITING BASILIADE AND TAKING THE SHAPE OF A TURTLE IN THE WATERS OF THE CRIMSON LAKE...
"...I HELPED THE OLD ORACLE FIND PART OF HIS CONSCIOUSNESS."*
BUT THAT ORACLE WAS DEPOSED. WHY DID YOU TRY TO CONTACT HIM?
*LAST CHAPTER!
BECAUSE I FEEL...MAYBE I HOPE...HE CAN HELP US. IN THE PAST, HE'S BEEN A GUIDE TO ME.
I COULDN'T TELL HIM MUCH. PHOBOS IS WATCHING ME. HE WANTED THE ROLE OF CUSTODIAN OF THE TOWER TO GO TO VAAL...
...BUT NOW HE'S AFRAID OF ME. THE FACT THAT I'M TALKING TO YOU WORRIES YOUR BROTHER GREATLY.
YOU MEAN HE KNOWS YOU'RE HERE?
RELAX. HE'S ALMOST THE ORACLE, SO HE KNOWS ALMOST EVERYTHING. BUT HE CAN'T READ OUR MINDS OR HEAR US TALKING YET.

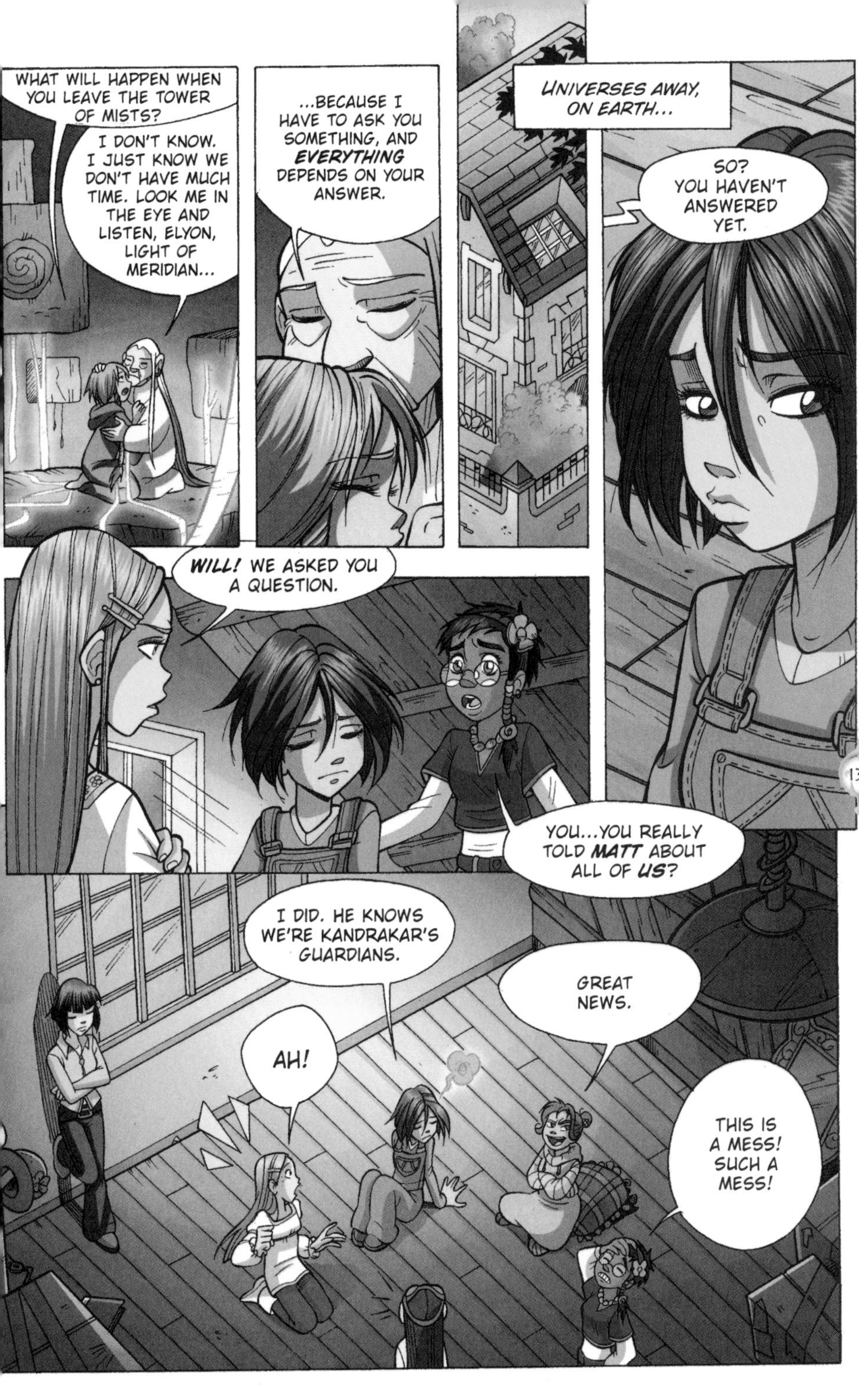
WHAT WILL HAPPEN WHEN YOU LEAVE THE TOWER OF MISTS?
I DON'T KNOW. I JUST KNOW WE DON'T HAVE MUCH TIME. LOOK ME IN THE EYE AND LISTEN, ELYON, LIGHT OF MERIDIAN...
...BECAUSE I HAVE TO ASK YOU SOMETHING, AND EVERYTHING DEPENDS ON YOUR ANSWER.
UNIVERSES AWAY, ON EARTH...
SO? YOU HAVEN'T ANSWERED YET.
WILL! WE ASKED YOU A QUESTION.
YOU...YOU REALLY TOLD MATT ABOUT ALL OF US?
I DID. HE KNOWS WE'RE KANDRAKAR'S GUARDIANS.
AH!
GREAT NEWS.
THIS IS A MESS! SUCH A MESS!

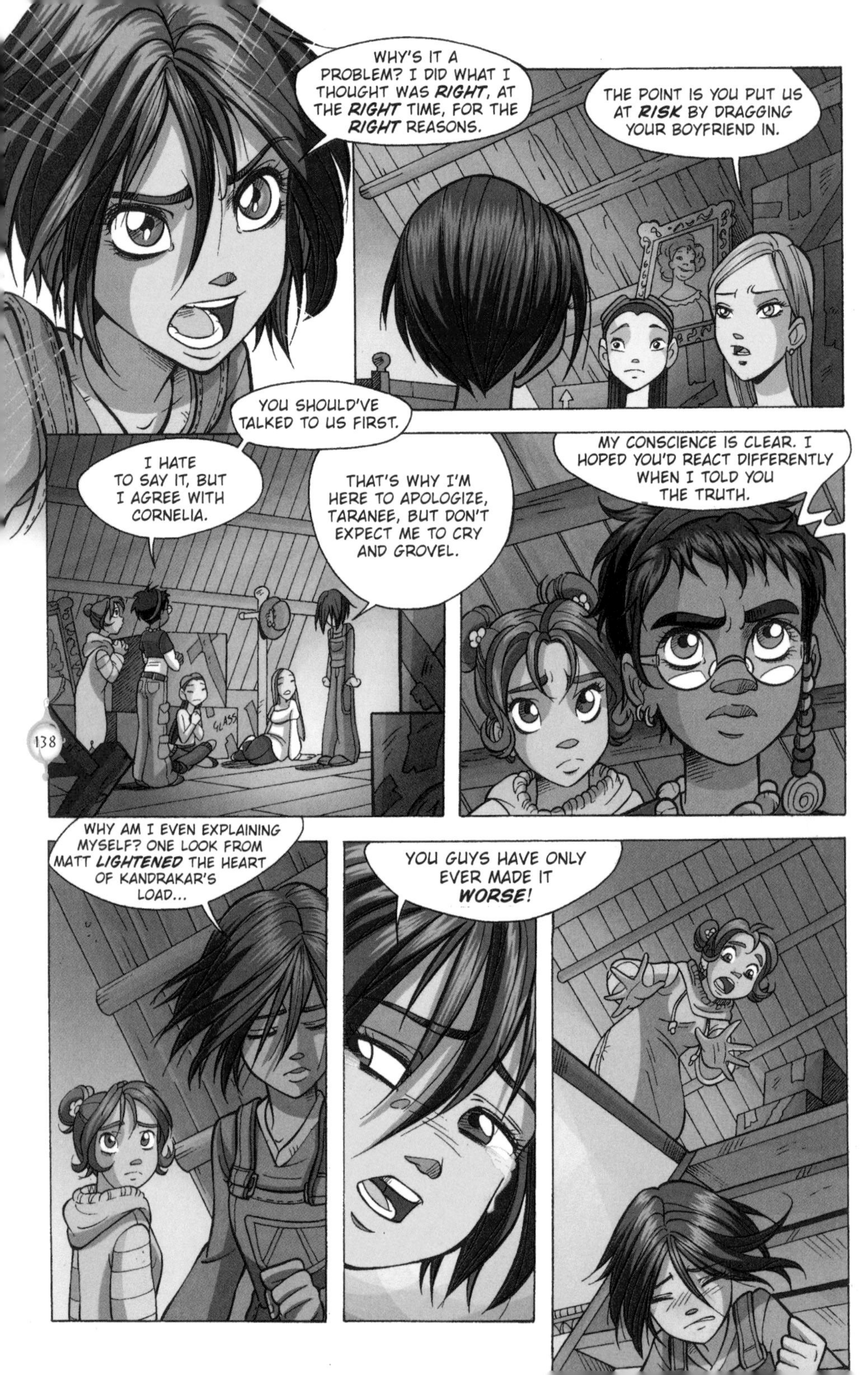
WHY'S IT A PROBLEM? I DID WHAT I THOUGHT WAS RIGHT, AT THE RIGHT TIME, FOR THE RIGHT REASONS.
THE POINT IS YOU PUT US AT RISK BY DRAGGING YOUR BOYFRIEND IN.
YOU SHOULD'VE TALKED TO US FIRST.
I HATE TO SAY IT, BUT I AGREE WITH CORNELIA.
THAT'S WHY I'M HERE TO APOLOGIZE, TARANEE, BUT DON'T EXPECT ME TO CRY AND GROVEL.
MY CONSCIENCE IS CLEAR. I HOPED YOU'D REACT DIFFERENTLY WHEN I TOLD YOU THE TRUTH.
GLASS
WHY AM I EVEN EXPLAINING MYSELF? ONE LOOK FROM MATT LIGHTENED THE HEART OF KANDRAKAR'S LOAD...
YOU GUYS HAVE ONLY EVER MADE IT WORSE!

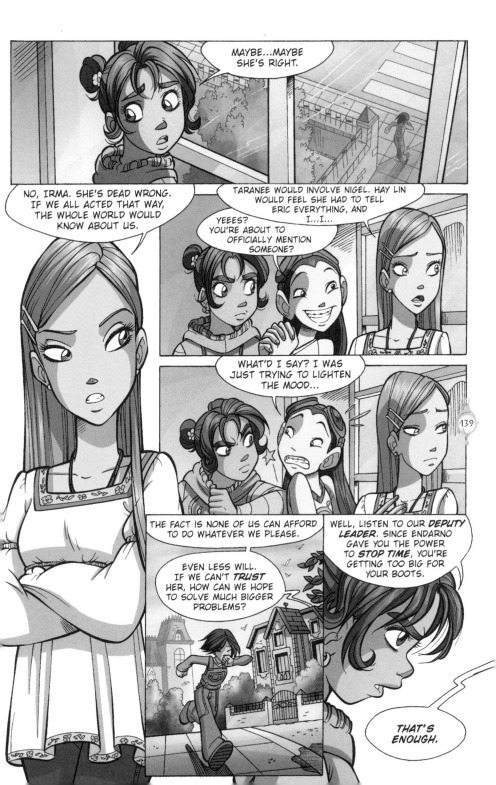

MAYBE...MAYBE SHE'S RIGHT.

NO, IRMA. SHE'S DEAD WRONG. IF WE ALL ACTED THAT WAY, THE WHOLE WORLD WOULD KNOW ABOUT US.

TARANEE WOULD INVOLVE NIGEL. HAY LIN WOULD FEEL SHE HAD TO TELL ERIC EVERYTHING, AND I...I...

YEEES? YOU'RE ABOUT TO OFFICIALLY MENTION SOMEONE?

WHAT'D I SAY? I WAS JUST TRYING TO LIGHTEN THE MOOD...

THE FACT IS NONE OF US CAN AFFORD TO DO WHATEVER WE PLEASE.

EVEN LESS WILL. IF WE CAN'T *TRUST* HER, HOW CAN WE HOPE TO SOLVE MUCH BIGGER PROBLEMS?

WELL, LISTEN TO OUR *DEPUTY LEADER*. SINCE ENDARNO GAVE YOU THE POWER TO *STOP TIME*, YOU'RE GETTING TOO BIG FOR YOUR BOOTS.

THAT'S ENOUGH.

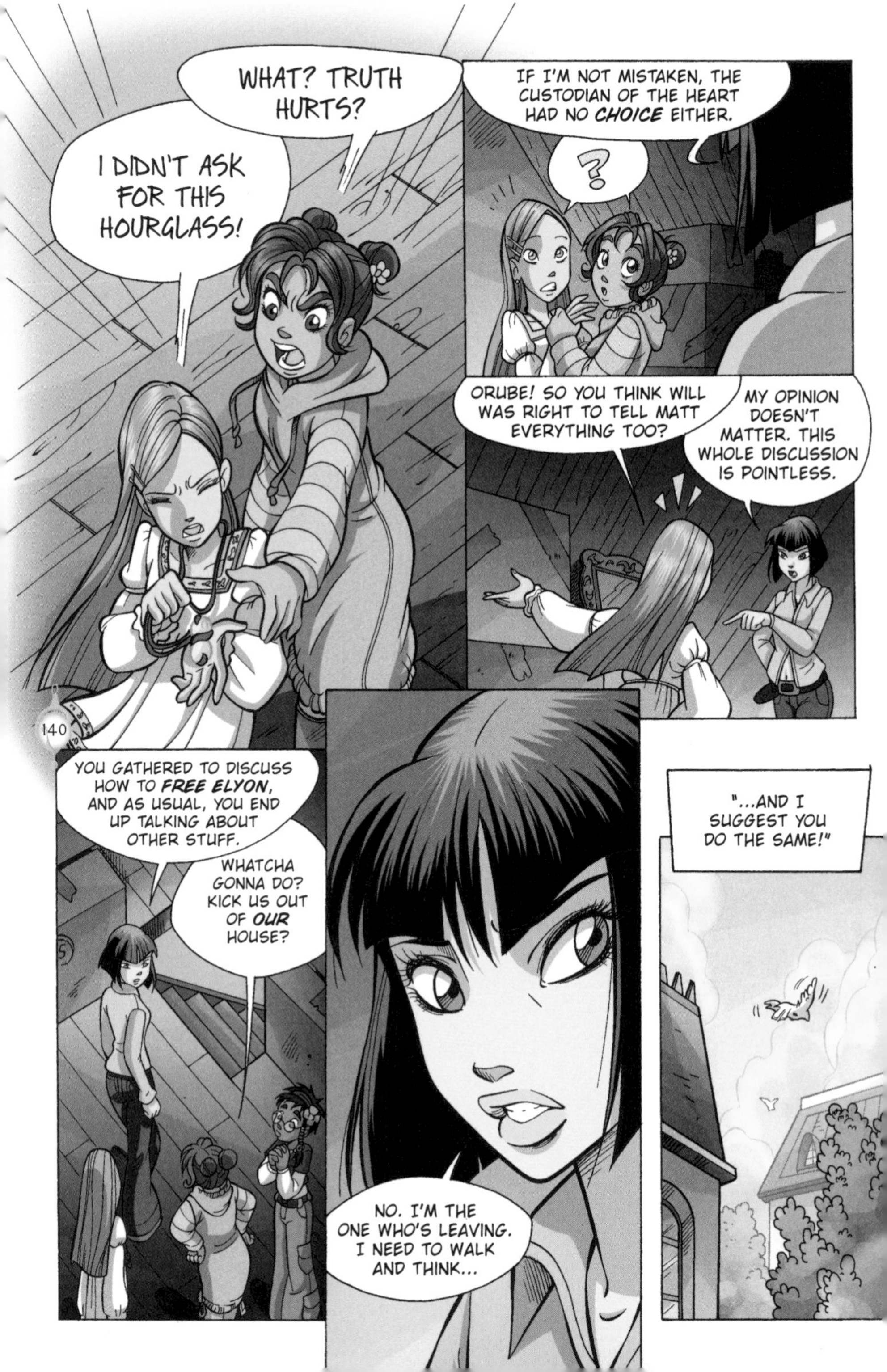

WHAT? TRUTH HURTS?
I DIDN'T ASK FOR THIS HOURGLASS!
IF I'M NOT MISTAKEN, THE CUSTODIAN OF THE HEART HAD NO CHOICE EITHER.
?
ORUBE! SO YOU THINK WILL WAS RIGHT TO TELL MATT EVERYTHING TOO?
MY OPINION DOESN'T MATTER. THIS WHOLE DISCUSSION IS POINTLESS.
YOU GATHERED TO DISCUSS HOW TO FREE ELYON, AND AS USUAL, YOU END UP TALKING ABOUT OTHER STUFF.
WHATCHA GONNA DO? KICK US OUT OF OUR HOUSE?
NO. I'M THE ONE WHO'S LEAVING. I NEED TO WALK AND THINK...
"...AND I SUGGEST YOU DO THE SAME!"

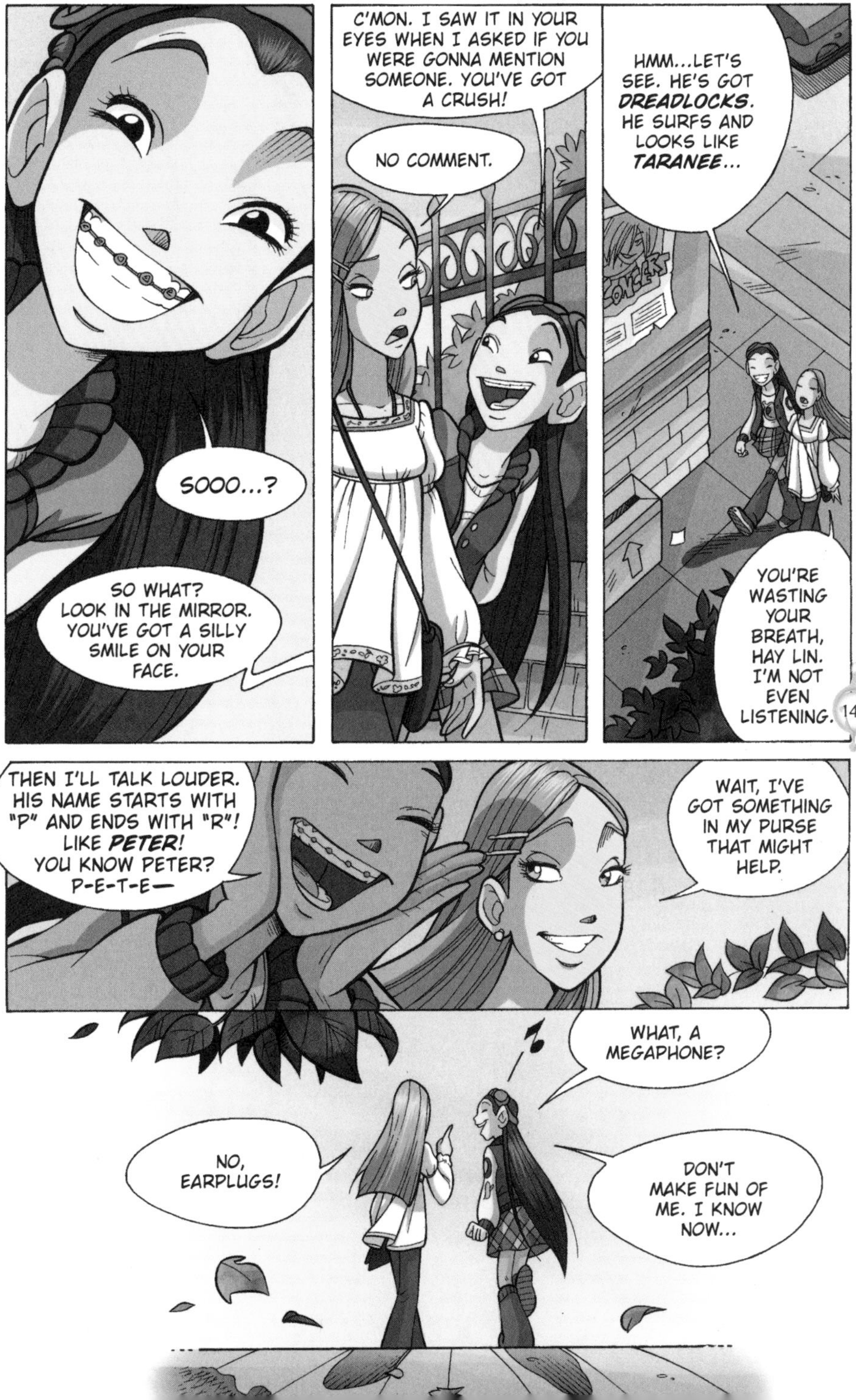
SOOO...?
SO WHAT? LOOK IN THE MIRROR. YOU'VE GOT A SILLY SMILE ON YOUR FACE.
C'MON. I SAW IT IN YOUR EYES WHEN I ASKED IF YOU WERE GONNA MENTION SOMEONE. YOU'VE GOT A CRUSH!
NO COMMENT.
HMM...LET'S SEE. HE'S GOT DREADLOCKS. HE SURFS AND LOOKS LIKE TARANEE...
YOU'RE WASTING YOUR BREATH, HAY LIN. I'M NOT EVEN LISTENING.
THEN I'LL TALK LOUDER. HIS NAME STARTS WITH "P" AND ENDS WITH "R"! LIKE PETER! YOU KNOW PETER? P-E-T-E—
WAIT, I'VE GOT SOMETHING IN MY PURSE THAT MIGHT HELP.
WHAT, A MEGAPHONE?
NO, EARPLUGS!
DON'T MAKE FUN OF ME. I KNOW NOW...

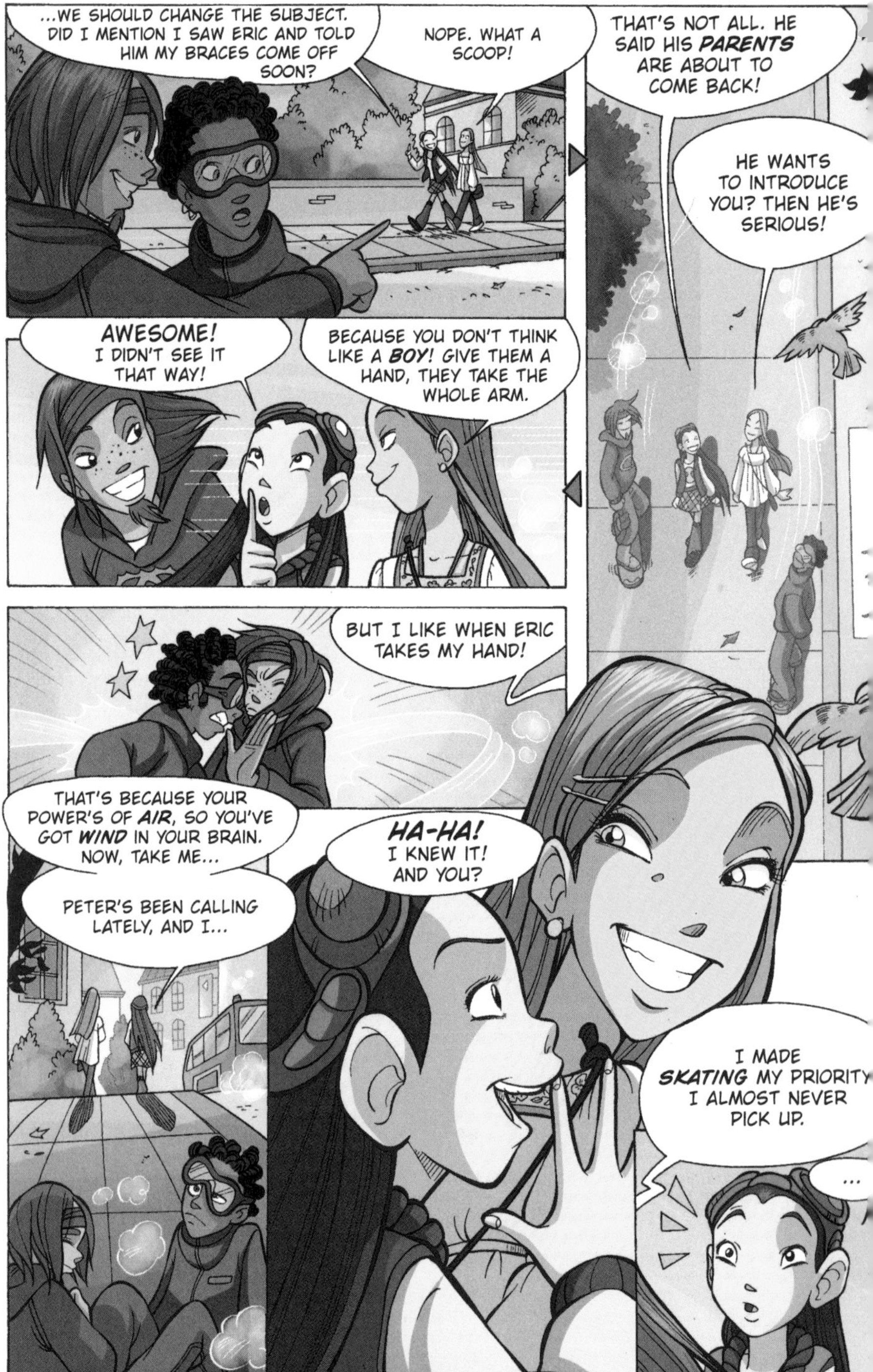
...WE SHOULD CHANGE THE SUBJECT. DID I MENTION I SAW ERIC AND TOLD HIM MY BRACES COME OFF SOON?
NOPE. WHAT A SCOOP!
THAT'S NOT ALL. HE SAID HIS PARENTS ARE ABOUT TO COME BACK!
HE WANTS TO INTRODUCE YOU? THEN HE'S SERIOUS!
AWESOME! I DIDN'T SEE IT THAT WAY!
BECAUSE YOU DON'T THINK LIKE A BOY! GIVE THEM A HAND, THEY TAKE THE WHOLE ARM.
BUT I LIKE WHEN ERIC TAKES MY HAND!
THAT'S BECAUSE YOUR POWER'S OF AIR, SO YOU'VE GOT WIND IN YOUR BRAIN. NOW, TAKE ME...
PETER'S BEEN CALLING LATELY, AND I...
HA-HA! I KNEW IT! AND YOU?
I MADE SKATING MY PRIORITY I ALMOST NEVER PICK UP.
...

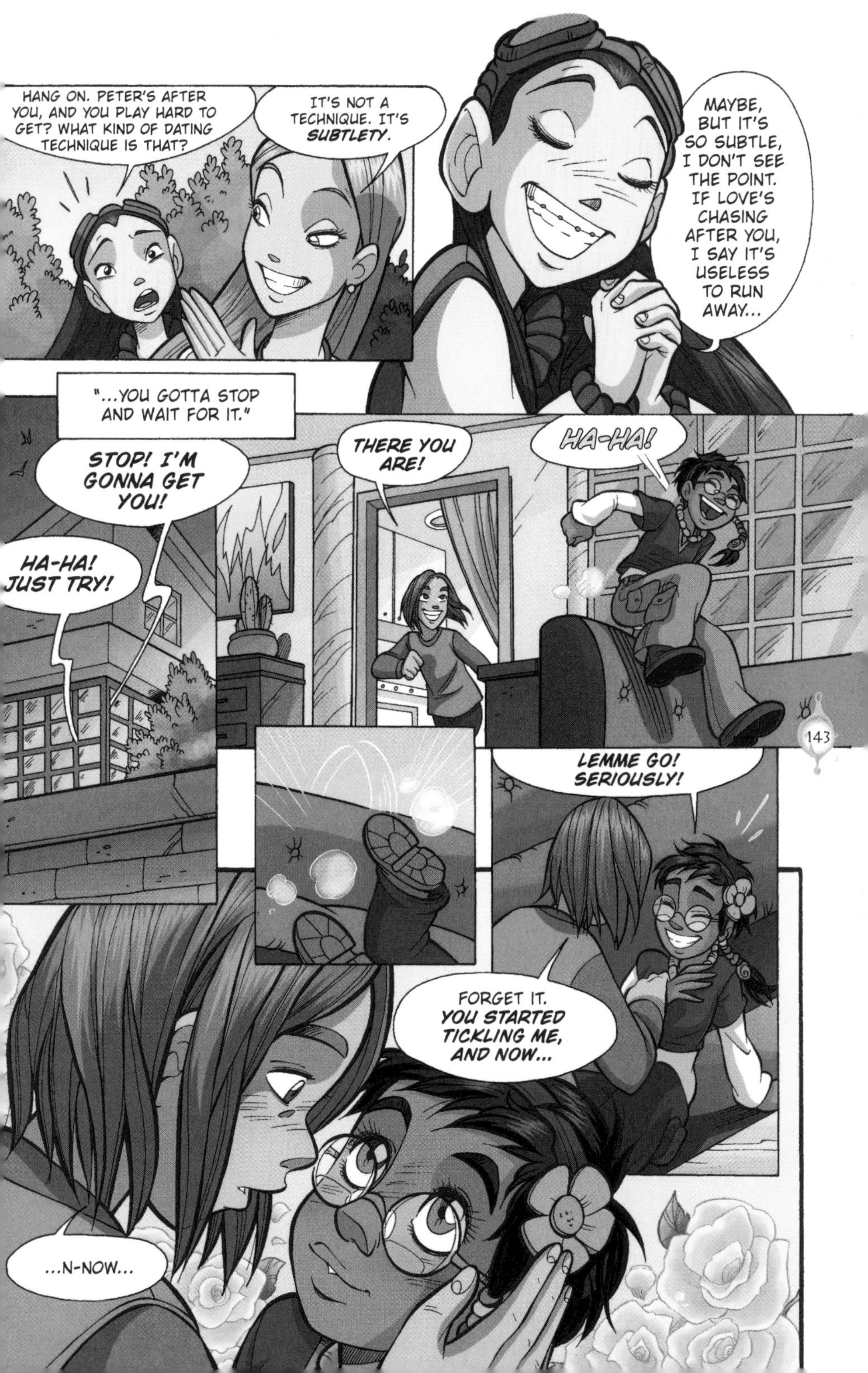
HANG ON. PETER'S AFTER YOU, AND YOU PLAY HARD TO GET? WHAT KIND OF DATING TECHNIQUE IS THAT?
IT'S NOT A TECHNIQUE. IT'S SUBTLETY.
MAYBE, BUT IT'S SO SUBTLE, I DON'T SEE THE POINT. IF LOVE'S CHASING AFTER YOU, I SAY IT'S USELESS TO RUN AWAY...
"...YOU GOTTA STOP AND WAIT FOR IT."
STOP! I'M GONNA GET YOU!
HA-HA! JUST TRY!
THERE YOU ARE!
HA-HA!
LEMME GO! SERIOUSLY!
FORGET IT. YOU STARTED TICKLING ME, AND NOW...
...N-NOW...

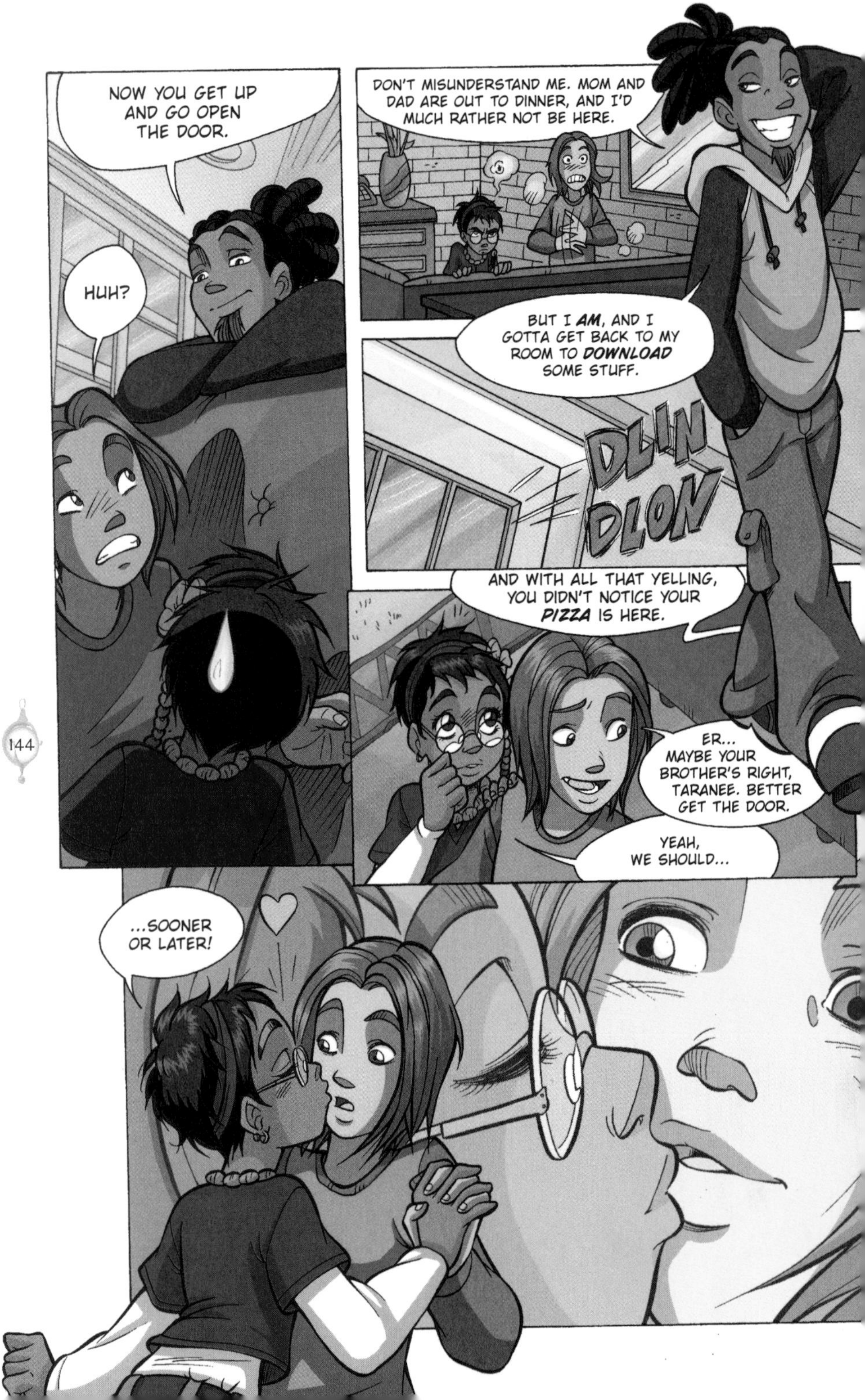
NOW YOU GET UP AND GO OPEN THE DOOR.
HUH?
DON'T MISUNDERSTAND ME. MOM AND DAD ARE OUT TO DINNER, AND I'D MUCH RATHER NOT BE HERE.
BUT I **AM**, AND I GOTTA GET BACK TO MY ROOM TO ***DOWNLOAD*** SOME STUFF.
DLIN DLON
AND WITH ALL THAT YELLING, YOU DIDN'T NOTICE YOUR ***PIZZA*** IS HERE.
ER... MAYBE YOUR BROTHER'S RIGHT, TARANEE. BETTER GET THE DOOR.
YEAH, WE SHOULD...
...SOONER OR LATER!

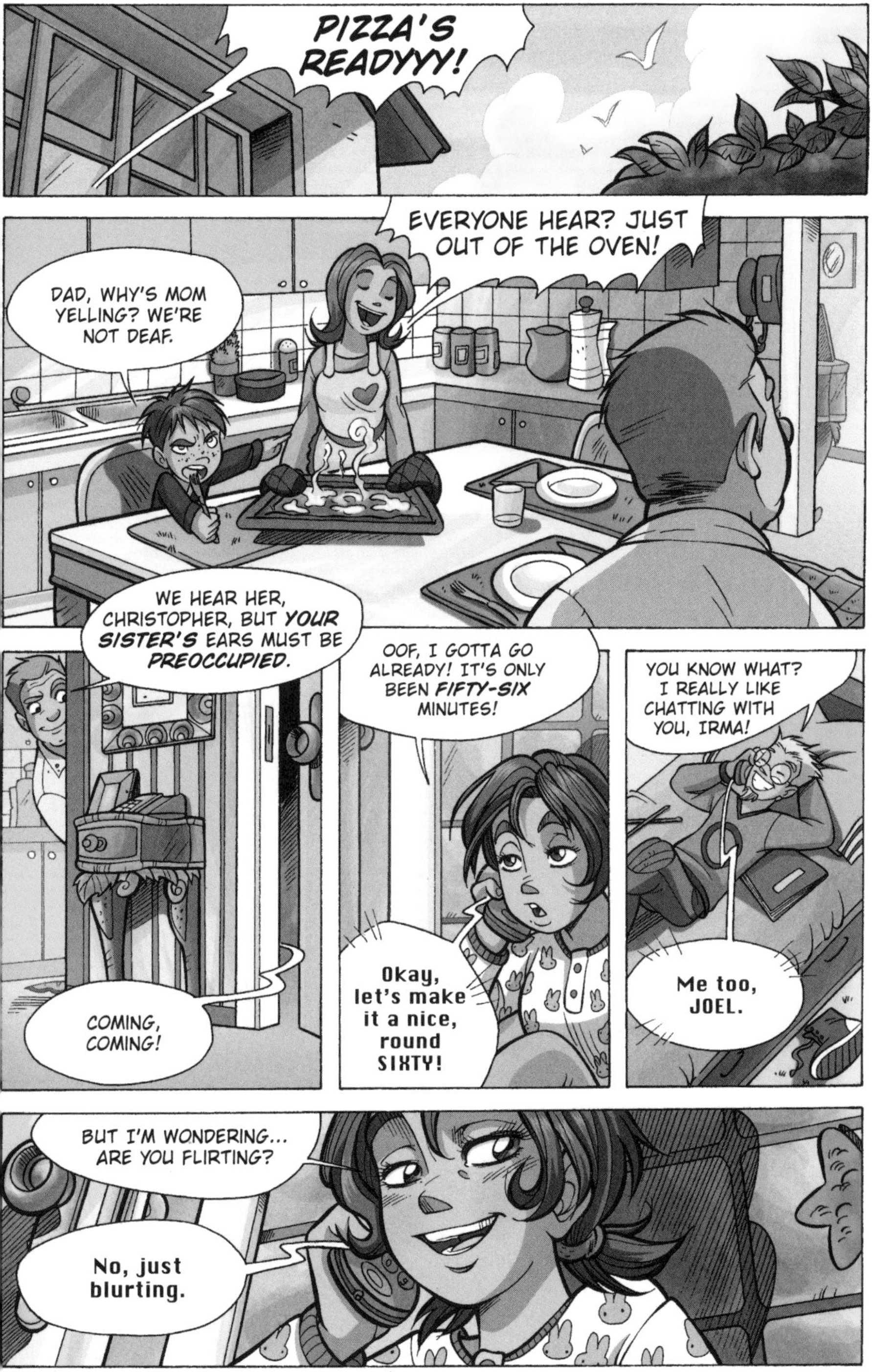
PIZZA'S READYYY!
EVERYONE HEAR? JUST OUT OF THE OVEN!
DAD, WHY'S MOM YELLING? WE'RE NOT DEAF.
WE HEAR HER, CHRISTOPHER, BUT YOUR SISTER'S EARS MUST BE PREOCCUPIED.
COMING, COMING!
OOF, I GOTTA GO ALREADY! IT'S ONLY BEEN FIFTY-SIX MINUTES!
Okay, let's make it a nice, round SIXTY!
YOU KNOW WHAT? I REALLY LIKE CHATTING WITH YOU, IRMA!
Me too, JOEL.
BUT I'M WONDERING... ARE YOU FLIRTING?
No, just blurting.

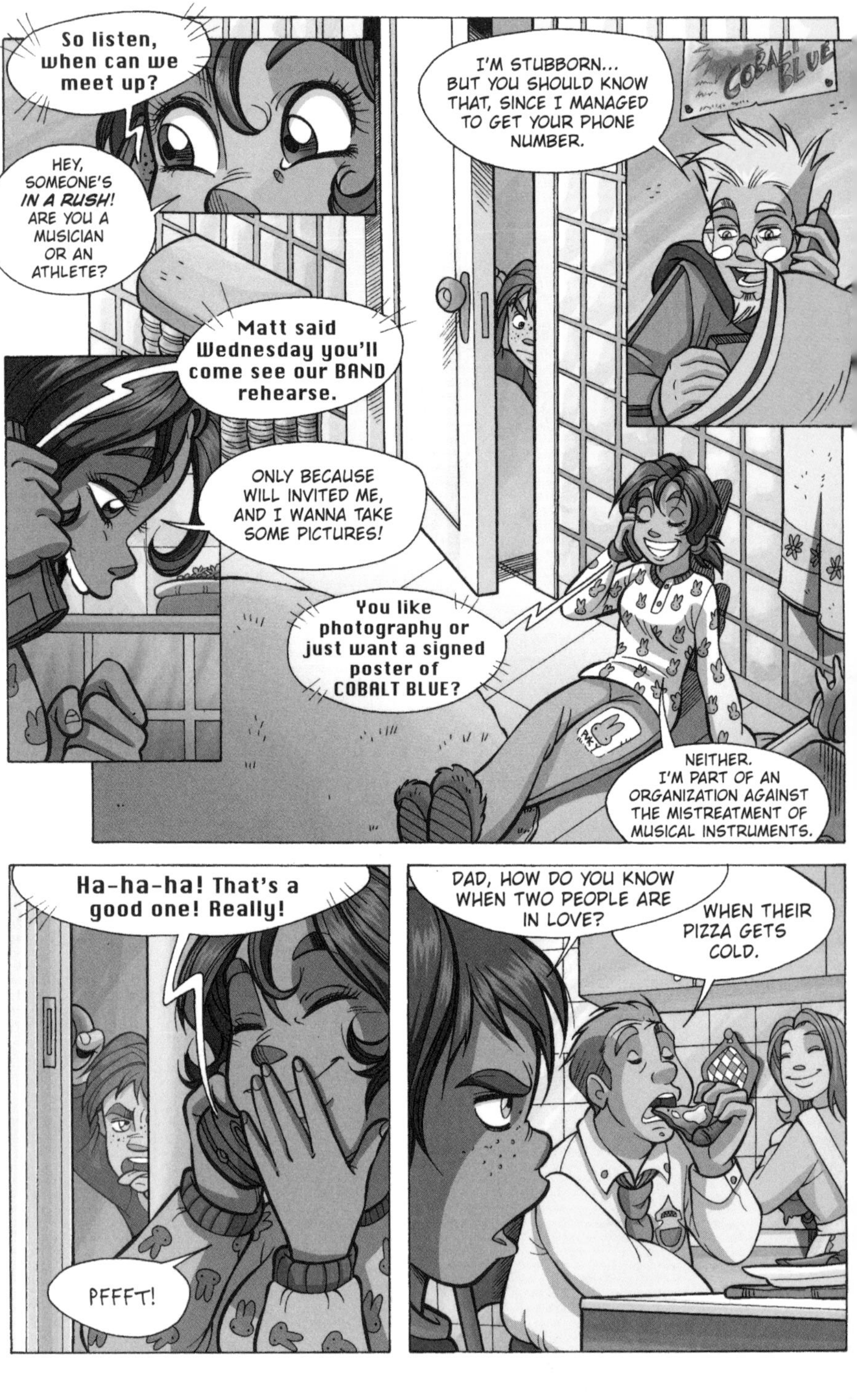
So listen, when can we meet up?
HEY, SOMEONE'S *IN A RUSH*! ARE YOU A MUSICIAN OR AN ATHLETE?
I'M STUBBORN... BUT YOU SHOULD KNOW THAT, SINCE I MANAGED TO GET YOUR PHONE NUMBER.
COBALT BLUE
Matt said Wednesday you'll come see our BAND rehearse.
ONLY BECAUSE WILL INVITED ME, AND I WANNA TAKE SOME PICTURES!
You like photography or just want a signed poster of COBALT BLUE?
NEITHER. I'M PART OF AN ORGANIZATION AGAINST THE MISTREATMENT OF MUSICAL INSTRUMENTS.
Ha-ha-ha! That's a good one! Really!
PFFFT!
DAD, HOW DO YOU KNOW WHEN TWO PEOPLE ARE IN LOVE?
WHEN THEIR PIZZA GETS COLD.

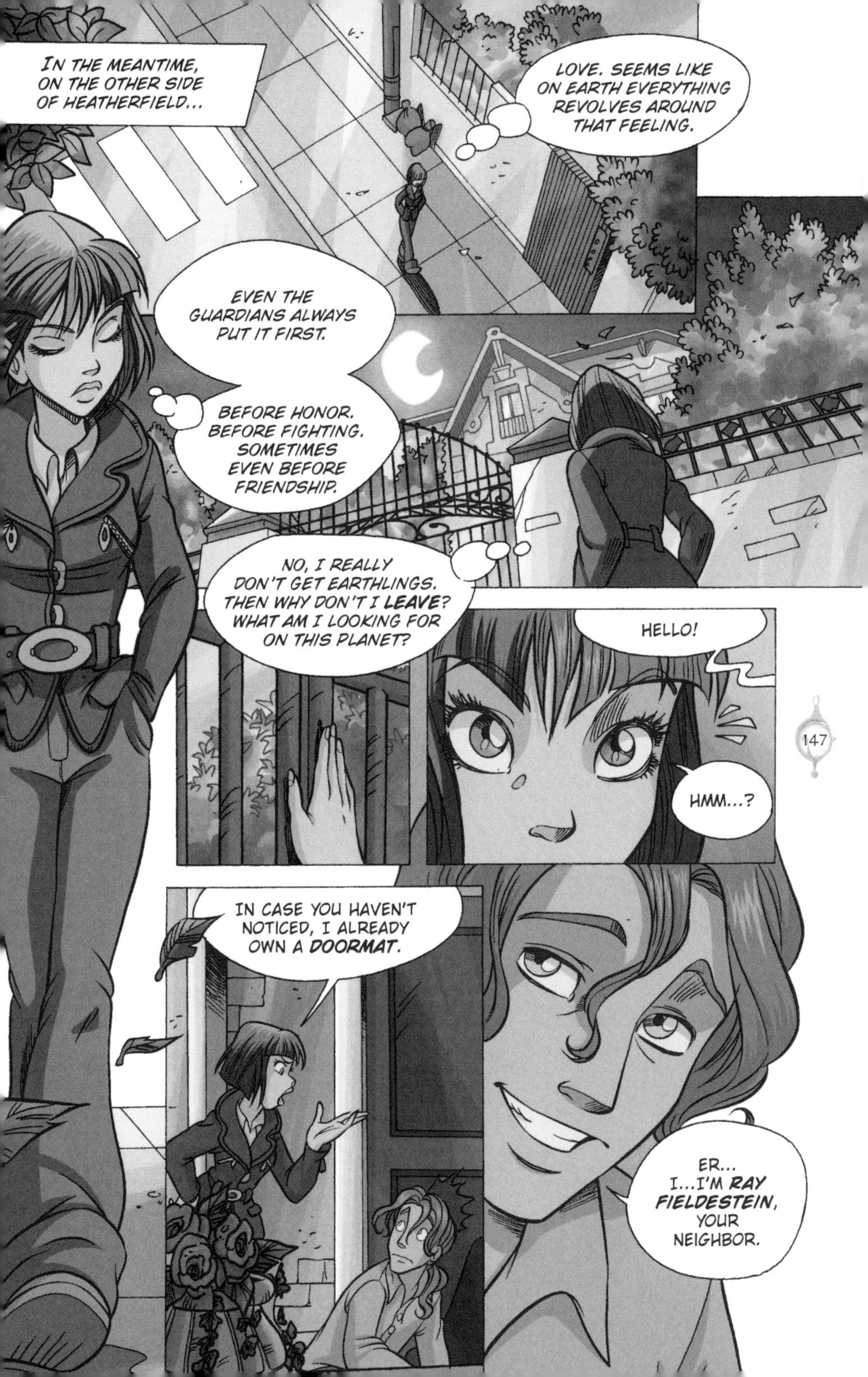
IN THE MEANTIME, ON THE OTHER SIDE OF HEATHERFIELD...
LOVE. SEEMS LIKE ON EARTH EVERYTHING REVOLVES AROUND THAT FEELING.
EVEN THE GUARDIANS ALWAYS PUT IT FIRST.
BEFORE HONOR. BEFORE FIGHTING. SOMETIMES EVEN BEFORE FRIENDSHIP.
NO, I REALLY DON'T GET EARTHLINGS. THEN WHY DON'T I **LEAVE**? WHAT AM I LOOKING FOR ON THIS PLANET?
HELLO!
HMM...?
IN CASE YOU HAVEN'T NOTICED, I ALREADY OWN A **DOORMAT**.
ER... I...I'M **RAY FIELDESTEIN**, YOUR NEIGHBOR.

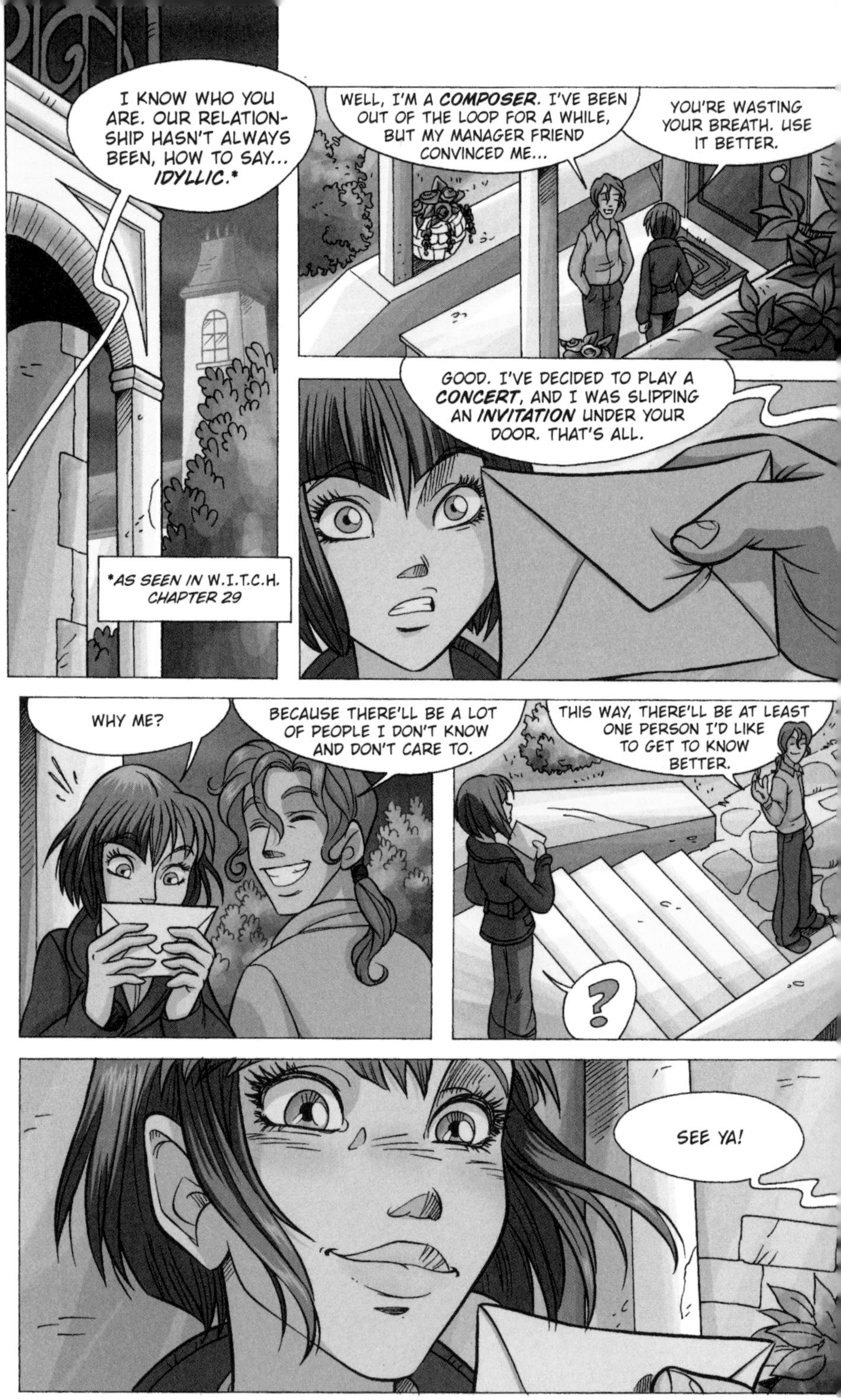
I KNOW WHO YOU ARE. OUR RELATIONSHIP HASN'T ALWAYS BEEN, HOW TO SAY... IDYLLIC.*
*AS SEEN IN W.I.T.C.H. CHAPTER 29
WELL, I'M A COMPOSER. I'VE BEEN OUT OF THE LOOP FOR A WHILE, BUT MY MANAGER FRIEND CONVINCED ME...
YOU'RE WASTING YOUR BREATH. USE IT BETTER.
GOOD. I'VE DECIDED TO PLAY A CONCERT, AND I WAS SLIPPING AN INVITATION UNDER YOUR DOOR. THAT'S ALL.
WHY ME?
BECAUSE THERE'LL BE A LOT OF PEOPLE I DON'T KNOW AND DON'T CARE TO.
THIS WAY, THERE'LL BE AT LEAST ONE PERSON I'D LIKE TO GET TO KNOW BETTER.
?
SEE YA!

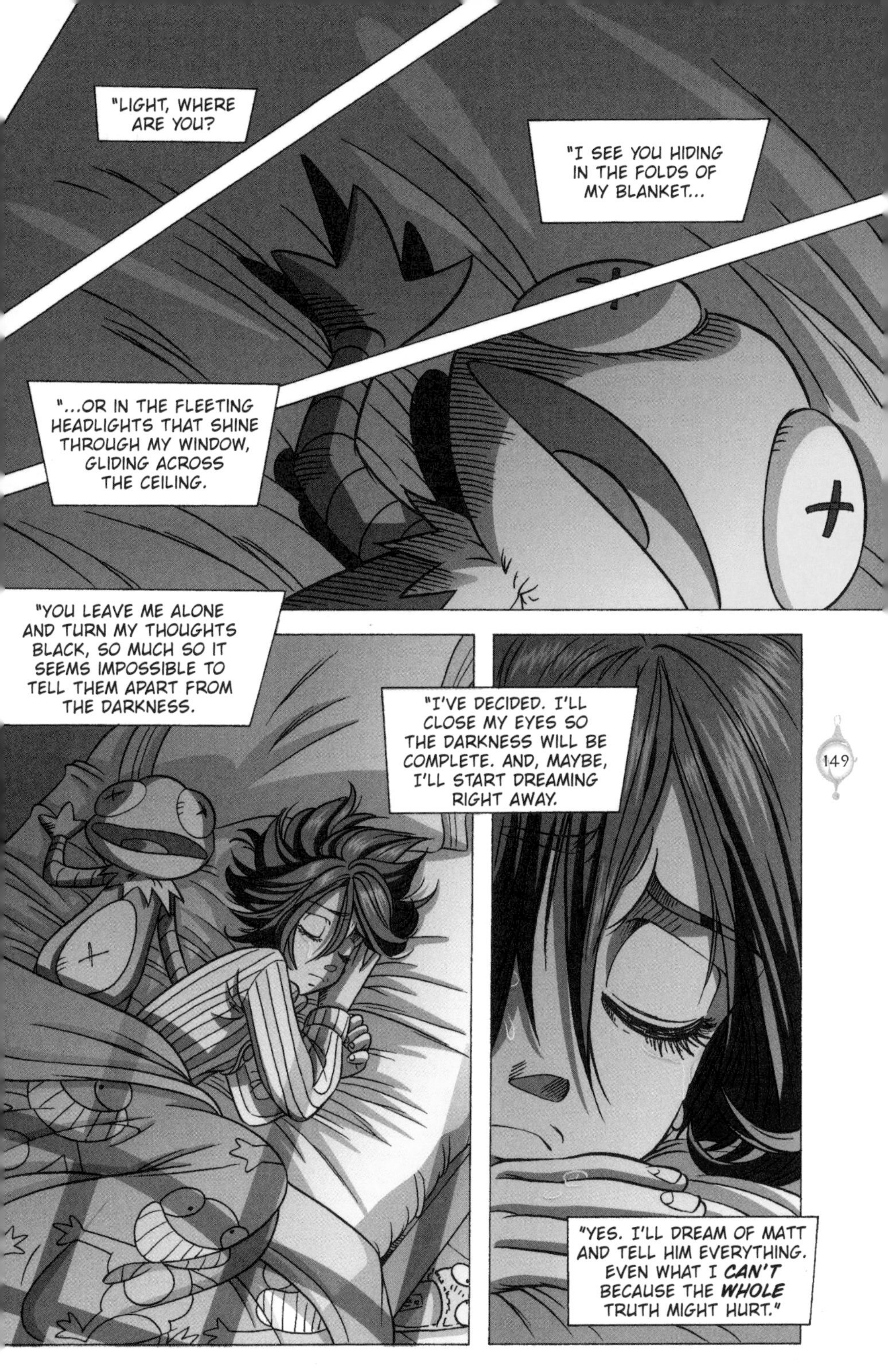
"LIGHT, WHERE ARE YOU?
"I SEE YOU HIDING IN THE FOLDS OF MY BLANKET...
"...OR IN THE FLEETING HEADLIGHTS THAT SHINE THROUGH MY WINDOW, GLIDING ACROSS THE CEILING.
"YOU LEAVE ME ALONE AND TURN MY THOUGHTS BLACK, SO MUCH SO IT SEEMS IMPOSSIBLE TO TELL THEM APART FROM THE DARKNESS.
"I'VE DECIDED. I'LL CLOSE MY EYES SO THE DARKNESS WILL BE COMPLETE. AND, MAYBE, I'LL START DREAMING RIGHT AWAY.
"YES. I'LL DREAM OF MATT AND TELL HIM EVERYTHING. EVEN WHAT I ***CAN'T*** BECAUSE THE ***WHOLE*** TRUTH MIGHT HURT."

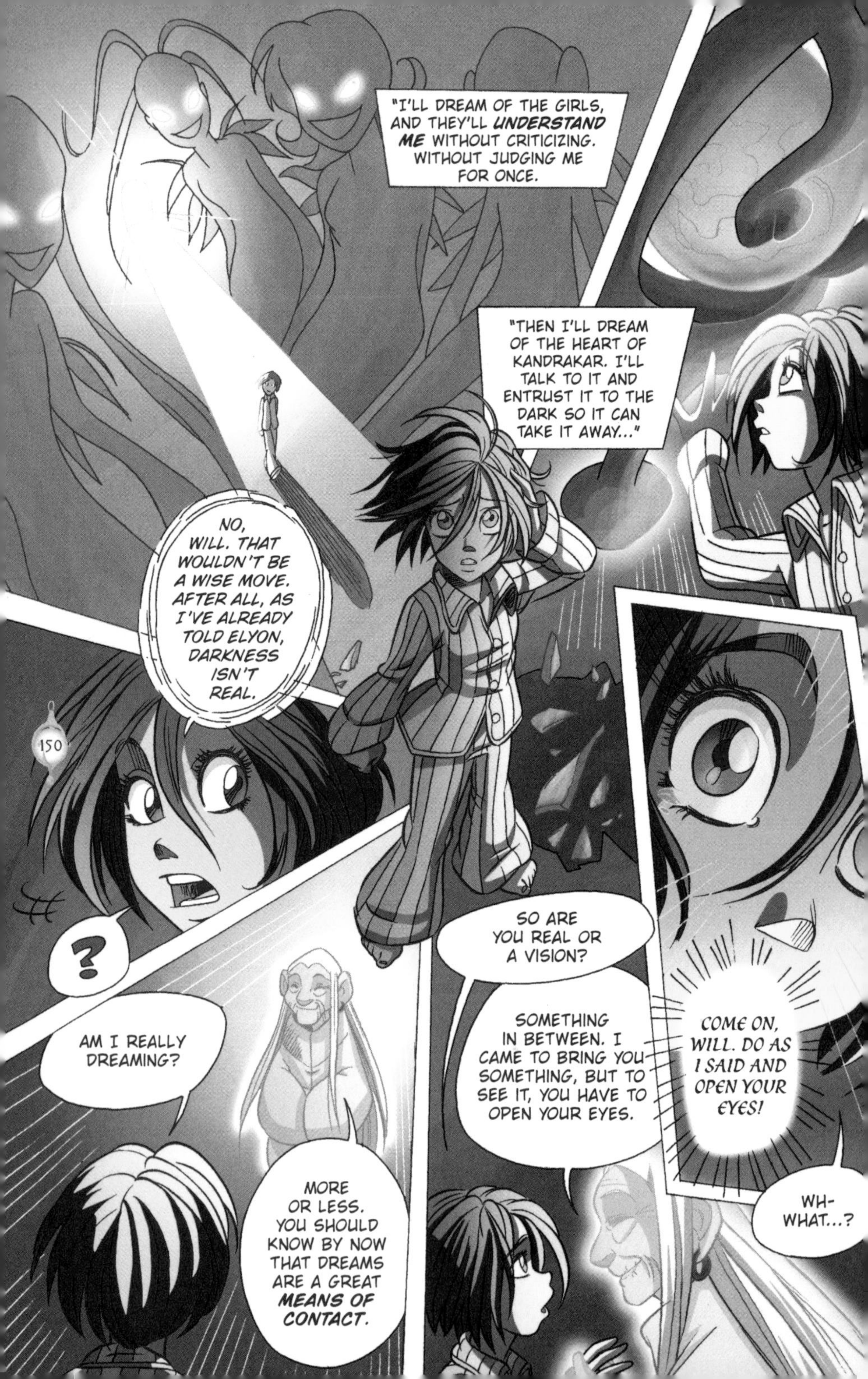
"I'LL DREAM OF THE GIRLS, AND THEY'LL UNDERSTAND ME WITHOUT CRITICIZING. WITHOUT JUDGING ME FOR ONCE.
"THEN I'LL DREAM OF THE HEART OF KANDRAKAR. I'LL TALK TO IT AND ENTRUST IT TO THE DARK SO IT CAN TAKE IT AWAY..."
NO, WILL. THAT WOULDN'T BE A WISE MOVE. AFTER ALL, AS I'VE ALREADY TOLD ELYON, DARKNESS ISN'T REAL.
?
AM I REALLY DREAMING?
MORE OR LESS. YOU SHOULD KNOW BY NOW THAT DREAMS ARE A GREAT MEANS OF CONTACT.
SO ARE YOU REAL OR A VISION?
SOMETHING IN BETWEEN. I CAME TO BRING YOU SOMETHING, BUT TO SEE IT, YOU HAVE TO OPEN YOUR EYES.
COME ON, WILL. DO AS I SAID AND OPEN YOUR EYES!
WH- WHAT...?
150

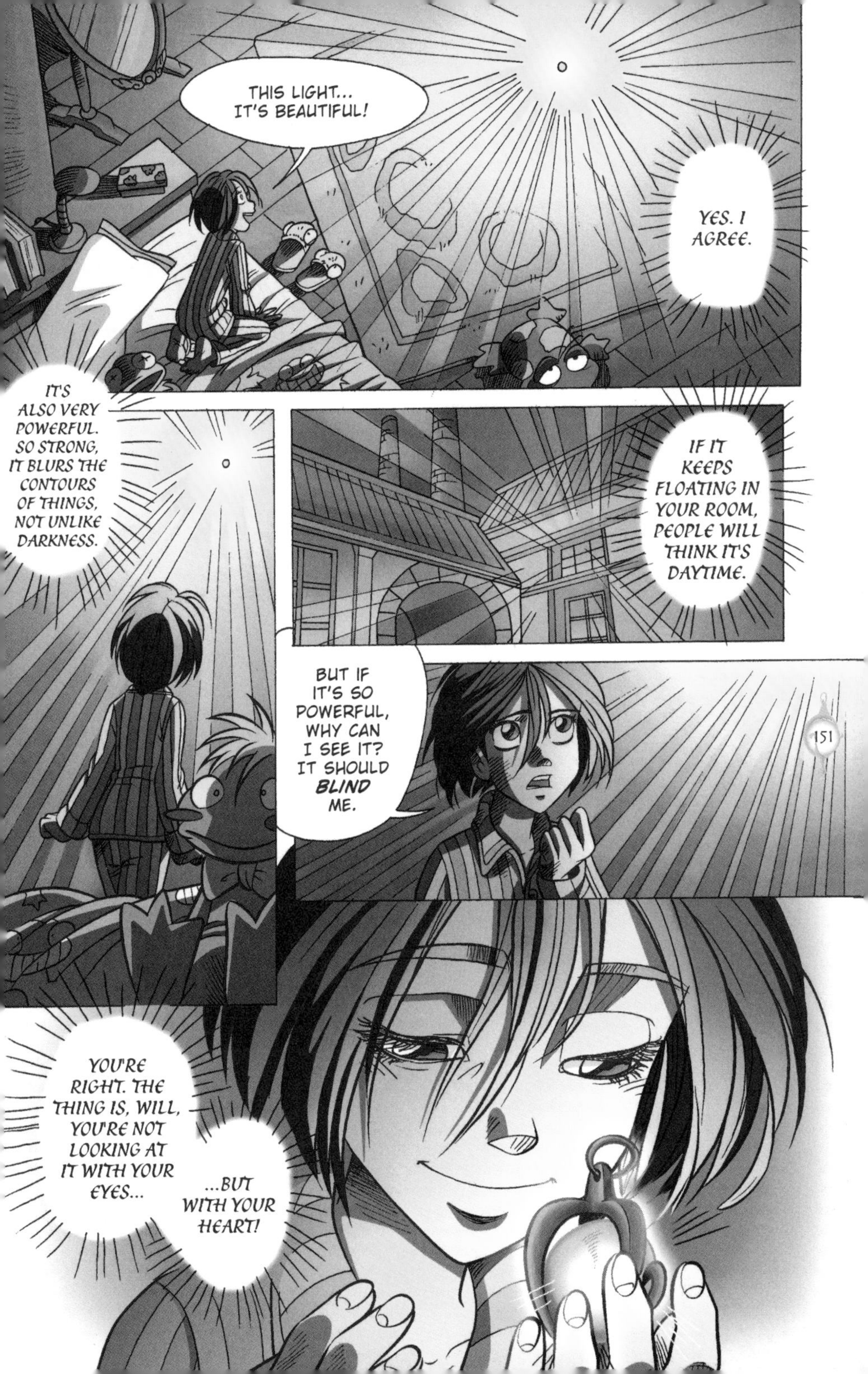
THIS LIGHT... IT'S BEAUTIFUL!
YES. I AGREE.
IT'S ALSO VERY POWERFUL. SO STRONG, IT BLURS THE CONTOURS OF THINGS, NOT UNLIKE DARKNESS.
IF IT KEEPS FLOATING IN YOUR ROOM, PEOPLE WILL THINK IT'S DAYTIME.
BUT IF IT'S SO POWERFUL, WHY CAN I SEE IT? IT SHOULD BLIND ME.
YOU'RE RIGHT. THE THING IS, WILL, YOU'RE NOT LOOKING AT IT WITH YOUR EYES...
...BUT WITH YOUR HEART!

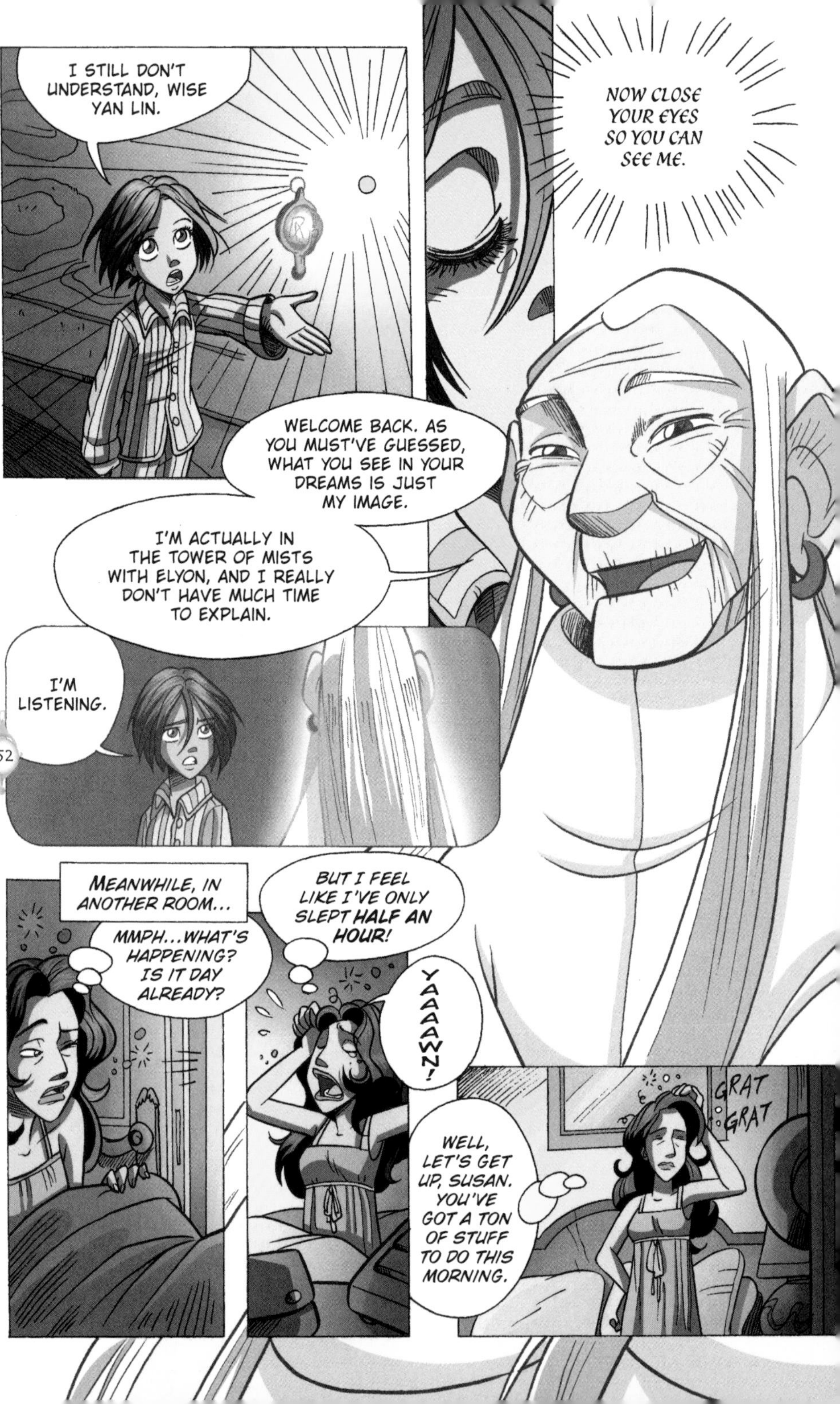
I STILL DON'T UNDERSTAND, WISE YAN LIN.
NOW CLOSE YOUR EYES SO YOU CAN SEE ME.
WELCOME BACK. AS YOU MUST'VE GUESSED, WHAT YOU SEE IN YOUR DREAMS IS JUST MY IMAGE.
I'M ACTUALLY IN THE TOWER OF MISTS WITH ELYON, AND I REALLY DON'T HAVE MUCH TIME TO EXPLAIN.
I'M LISTENING.
MEANWHILE, IN ANOTHER ROOM...
MMPH...WHAT'S HAPPENING? IS IT DAY ALREADY?
BUT I FEEL LIKE I'VE ONLY SLEPT **HALF AN HOUR!**
YAAAAWN!
WELL, LET'S GET UP, SUSAN. YOU'VE GOT A TON OF STUFF TO DO THIS MORNING.
GRAT GRAT

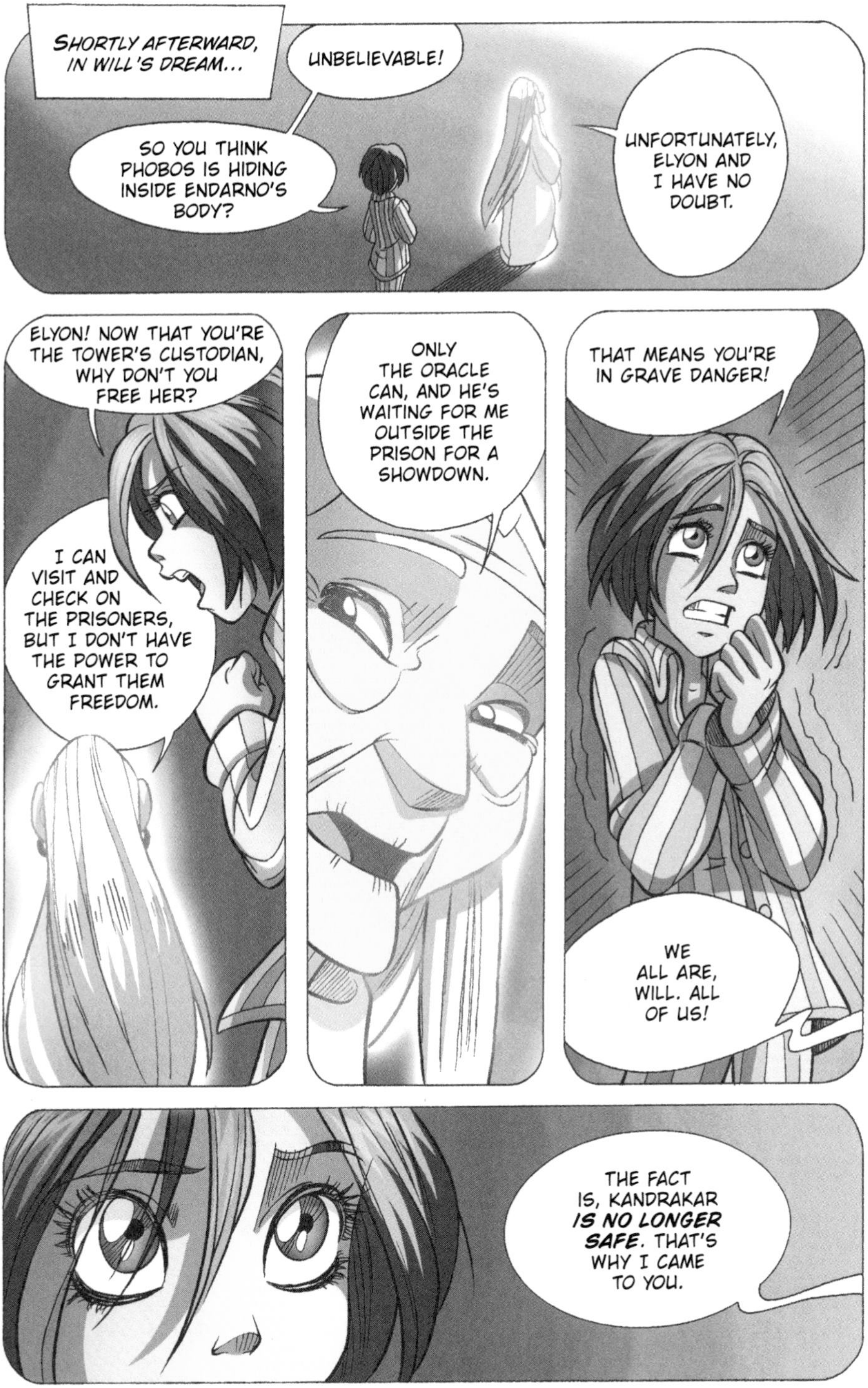
SHORTLY AFTERWARD, IN WILL'S DREAM...
UNBELIEVABLE!
SO YOU THINK PHOBOS IS HIDING INSIDE ENDARNO'S BODY?
UNFORTUNATELY, ELYON AND I HAVE NO DOUBT.
ELYON! NOW THAT YOU'RE THE TOWER'S CUSTODIAN, WHY DON'T YOU FREE HER?
I CAN VISIT AND CHECK ON THE PRISONERS, BUT I DON'T HAVE THE POWER TO GRANT THEM FREEDOM.
ONLY THE ORACLE CAN, AND HE'S WAITING FOR ME OUTSIDE THE PRISON FOR A SHOWDOWN.
THAT MEANS YOU'RE IN GRAVE DANGER!
WE ALL ARE, WILL. ALL OF US!
THE FACT IS, KANDRAKAR ***IS NO LONGER SAFE***. THAT'S WHY I CAME TO YOU.

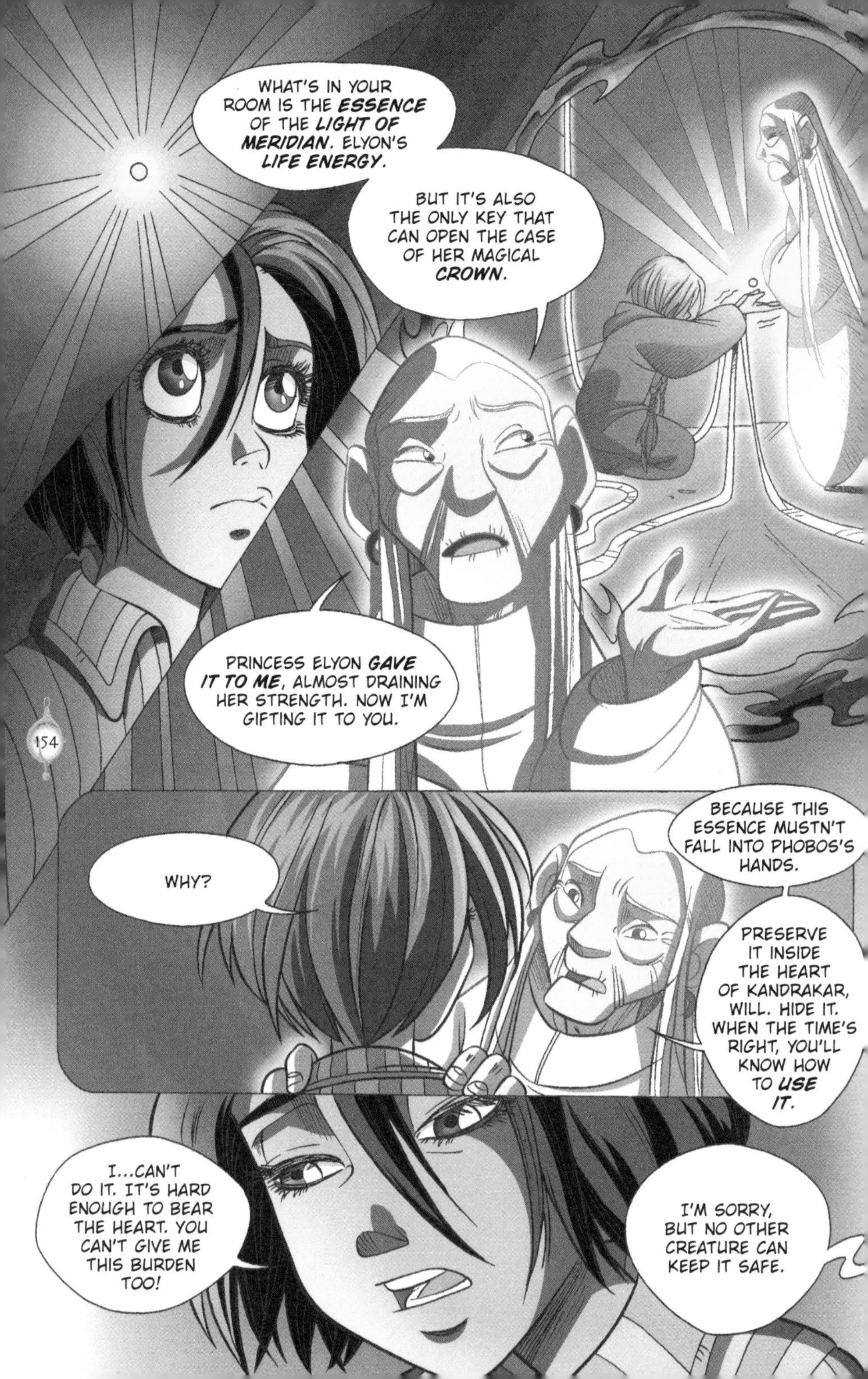
WHAT'S IN YOUR ROOM IS THE ESSENCE OF THE LIGHT OF MERIDIAN. ELYON'S LIFE ENERGY.
BUT IT'S ALSO THE ONLY KEY THAT CAN OPEN THE CASE OF HER MAGICAL CROWN.
PRINCESS ELYON GAVE IT TO ME, ALMOST DRAINING HER STRENGTH. NOW I'M GIFTING IT TO YOU.
WHY?
BECAUSE THIS ESSENCE MUSTN'T FALL INTO PHOBOS'S HANDS.
PRESERVE IT INSIDE THE HEART OF KANDRAKAR, WILL. HIDE IT. WHEN THE TIME'S RIGHT, YOU'LL KNOW HOW TO USE IT.
I...CAN'T DO IT. IT'S HARD ENOUGH TO BEAR THE HEART. YOU CAN'T GIVE ME THIS BURDEN TOO!
I'M SORRY, BUT NO OTHER CREATURE CAN KEEP IT SAFE.

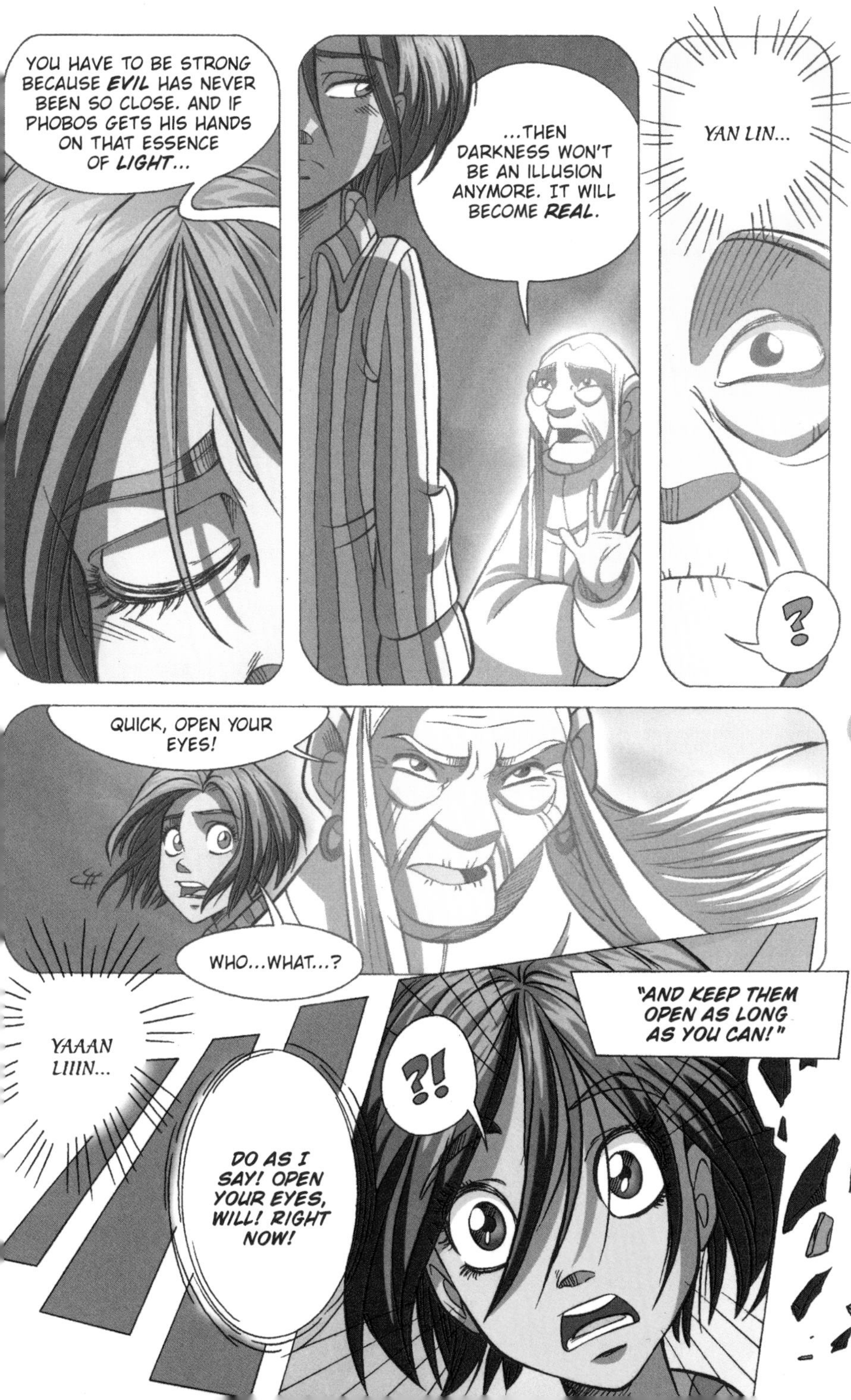
YOU HAVE TO BE STRONG BECAUSE EVIL HAS NEVER BEEN SO CLOSE. AND IF PHOBOS GETS HIS HANDS ON THAT ESSENCE OF LIGHT...
...THEN DARKNESS WON'T BE AN ILLUSION ANYMORE. IT WILL BECOME REAL.
YAN LIN...
?
QUICK, OPEN YOUR EYES!
WHO...WHAT...?
YAAAN LIIIN...
"AND KEEP THEM OPEN AS LONG AS YOU CAN!"
?!
DO AS I SAY! OPEN YOUR EYES, WILL! RIGHT NOW!

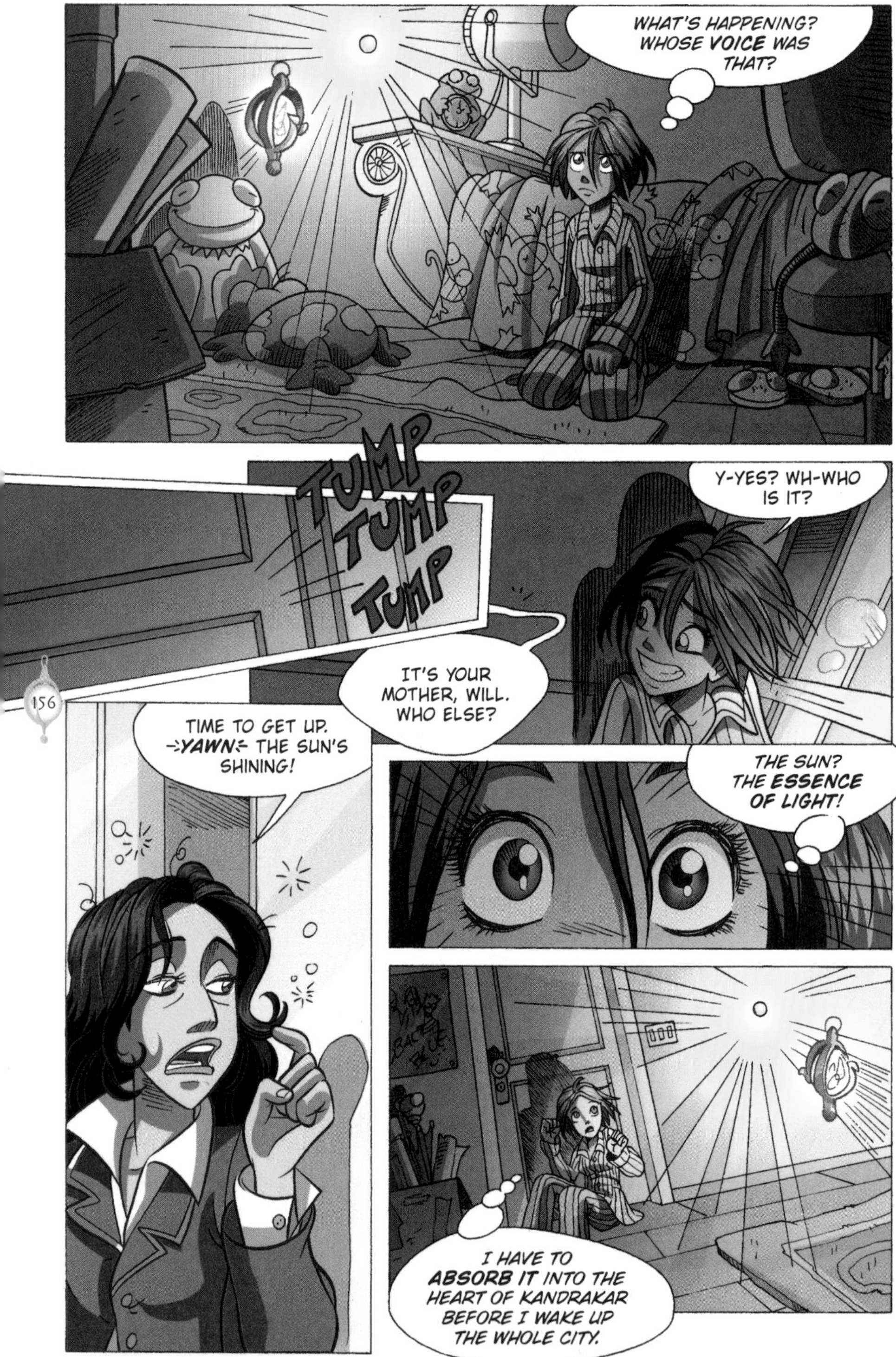
WHAT'S HAPPENING? WHOSE VOICE WAS THAT?
TUMP TUMP TUMP
Y-YES? WH-WHO IS IT?
IT'S YOUR MOTHER, WILL. WHO ELSE?
TIME TO GET UP. -YAWN- THE SUN'S SHINING!
THE SUN? THE ESSENCE OF LIGHT!
I HAVE TO ABSORB IT INTO THE HEART OF KANDRAKAR BEFORE I WAKE UP THE WHOLE CITY.

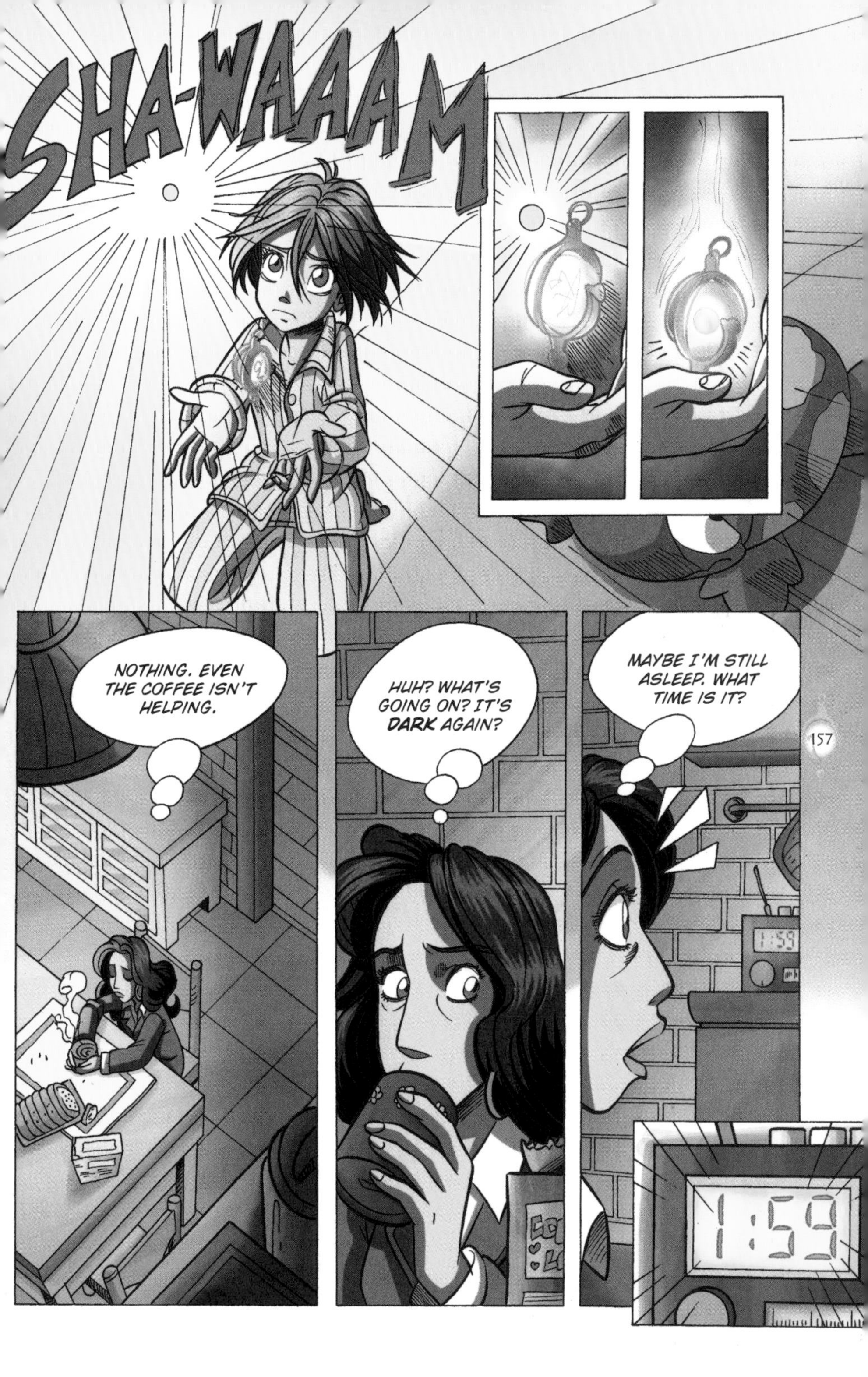
SHA-WAAAM
NOTHING. EVEN THE COFFEE ISN'T HELPING.
HUH? WHAT'S GOING ON? IT'S **DARK** AGAIN?
MAYBE I'M STILL ASLEEP. WHAT TIME IS IT?
1:59
1:59

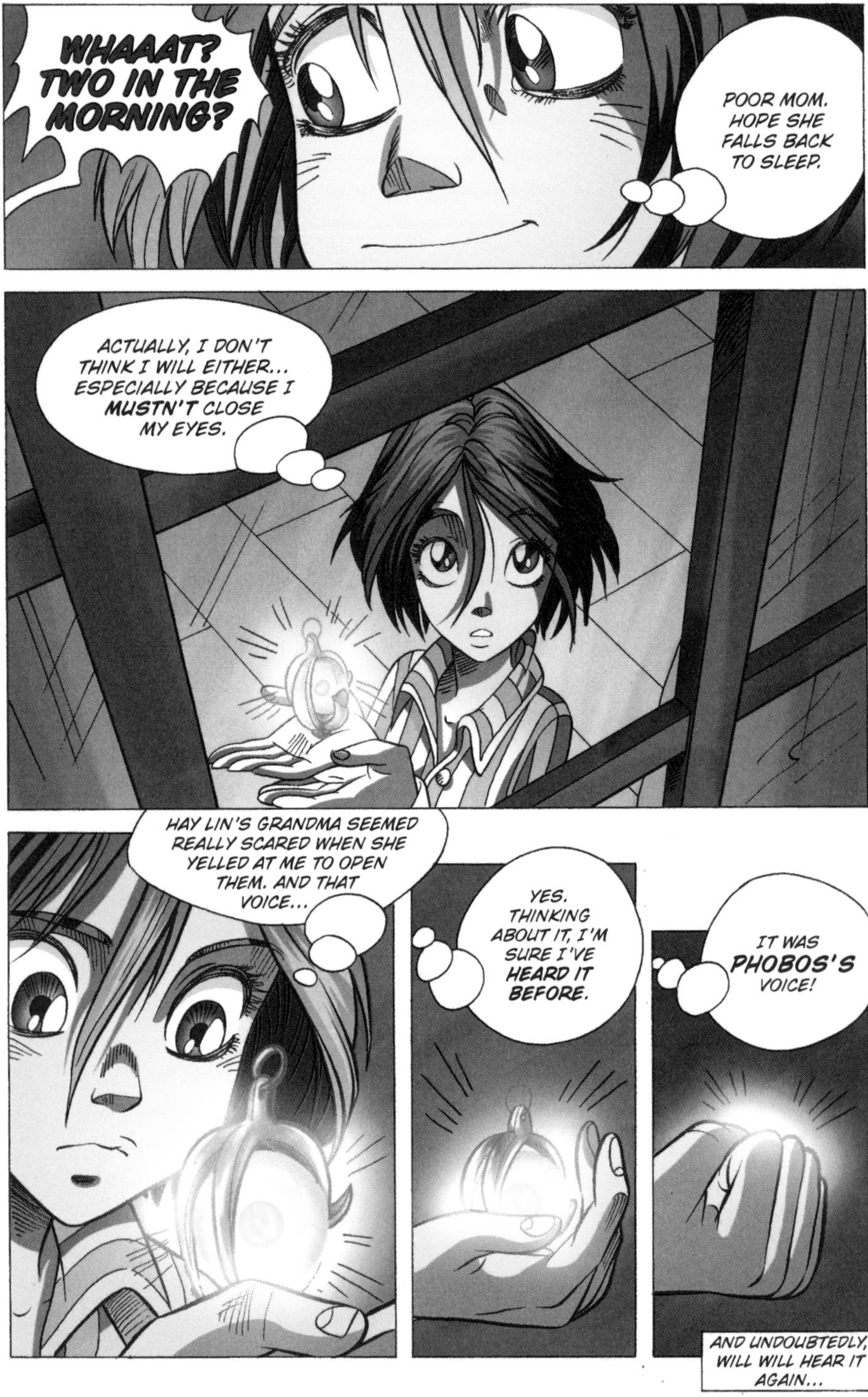
WHAAAT? TWO IN THE MORNING?
POOR MOM. HOPE SHE FALLS BACK TO SLEEP.
ACTUALLY, I DON'T THINK I WILL EITHER... ESPECIALLY BECAUSE I MUSTN'T CLOSE MY EYES.
HAY LIN'S GRANDMA SEEMED REALLY SCARED WHEN SHE YELLED AT ME TO OPEN THEM. AND THAT VOICE...
YES. THINKING ABOUT IT, I'M SURE I'VE HEARD IT BEFORE.
IT WAS PHOBOS'S VOICE!
AND UNDOUBTEDLY, WILL WILL HEAR IT AGAIN...

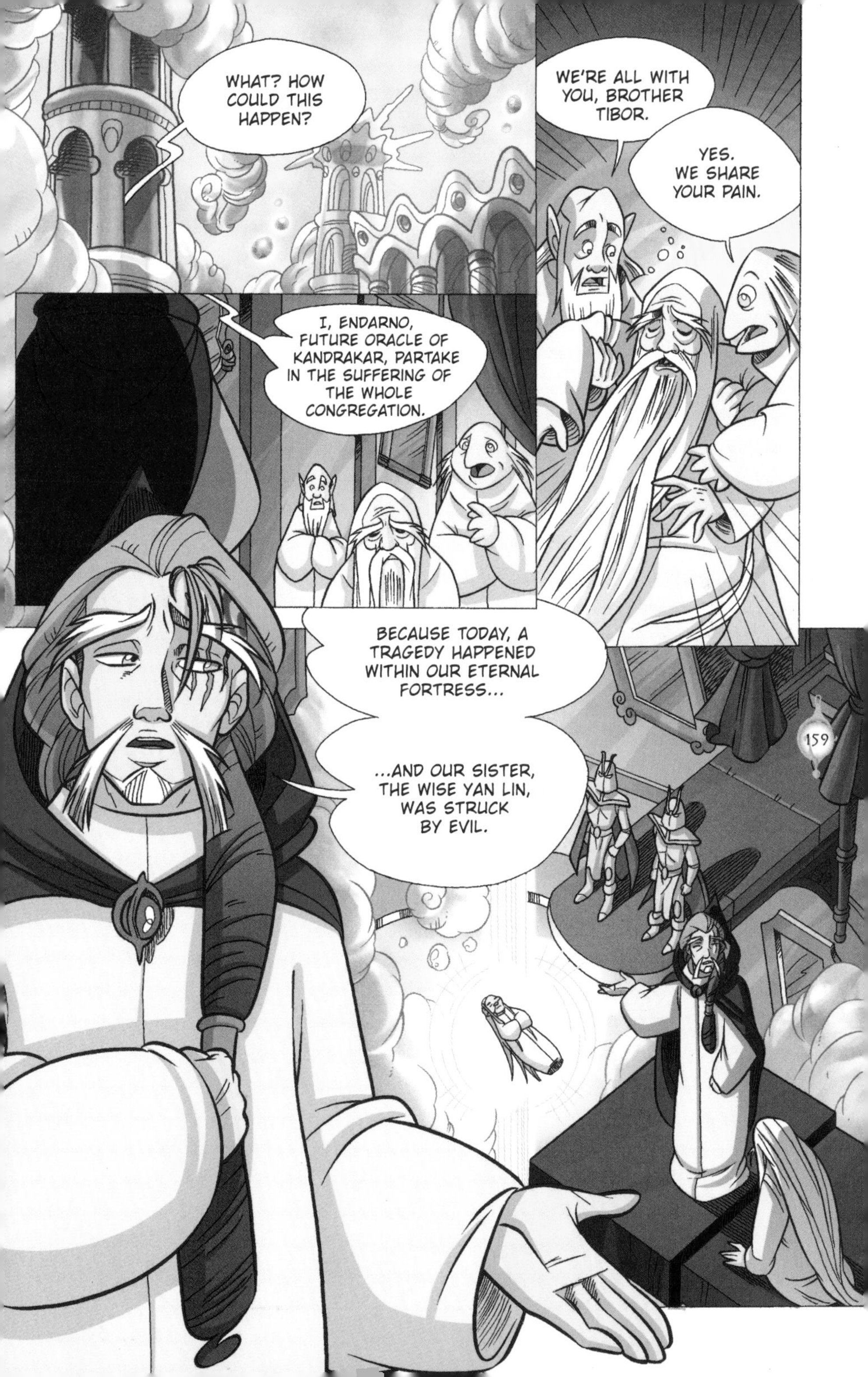
WHAT? HOW COULD THIS HAPPEN?
WE'RE ALL WITH YOU, BROTHER TIBOR.
YES. WE SHARE YOUR PAIN.
I, ENDARNO, FUTURE ORACLE OF KANDRAKAR, PARTAKE IN THE SUFFERING OF THE WHOLE CONGREGATION.
BECAUSE TODAY, A TRAGEDY HAPPENED WITHIN OUR ETERNAL FORTRESS...
...AND OUR SISTER, THE WISE YAN LIN, WAS STRUCK BY EVIL.

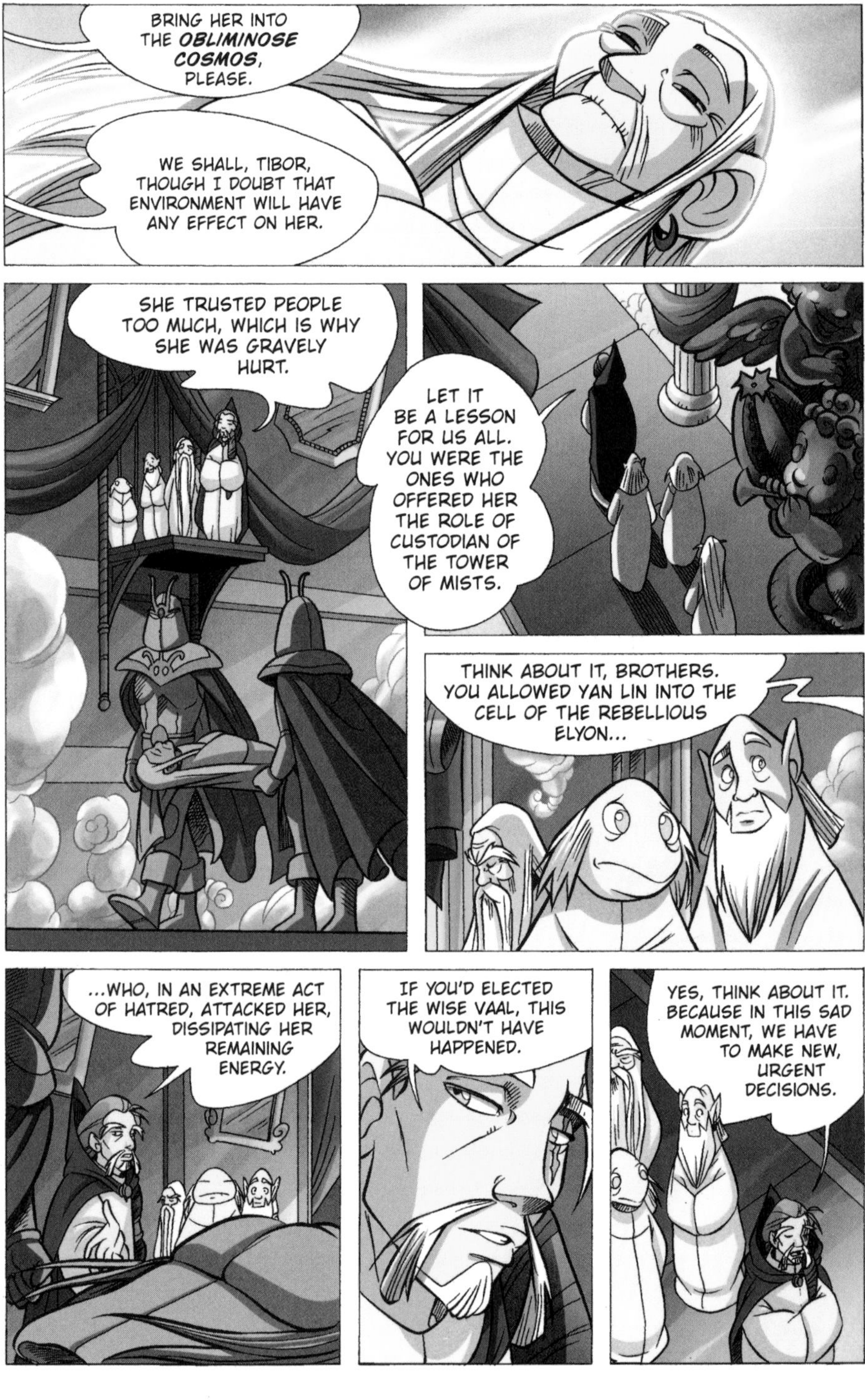
BRING HER INTO THE *OBLIMINOSE COSMOS*, PLEASE.
WE SHALL, TIBOR, THOUGH I DOUBT THAT ENVIRONMENT WILL HAVE ANY EFFECT ON HER.
SHE TRUSTED PEOPLE TOO MUCH, WHICH IS WHY SHE WAS GRAVELY HURT.
LET IT BE A LESSON FOR US ALL. YOU WERE THE ONES WHO OFFERED HER THE ROLE OF CUSTODIAN OF THE TOWER OF MISTS.
THINK ABOUT IT, BROTHERS. YOU ALLOWED YAN LIN INTO THE CELL OF THE REBELLIOUS ELYON...
...WHO, IN AN EXTREME ACT OF HATRED, ATTACKED HER, DISSIPATING HER REMAINING ENERGY.
IF YOU'D ELECTED THE WISE VAAL, THIS WOULDN'T HAVE HAPPENED.
YES, THINK ABOUT IT. BECAUSE IN THIS SAD MOMENT, WE HAVE TO MAKE NEW, URGENT DECISIONS.

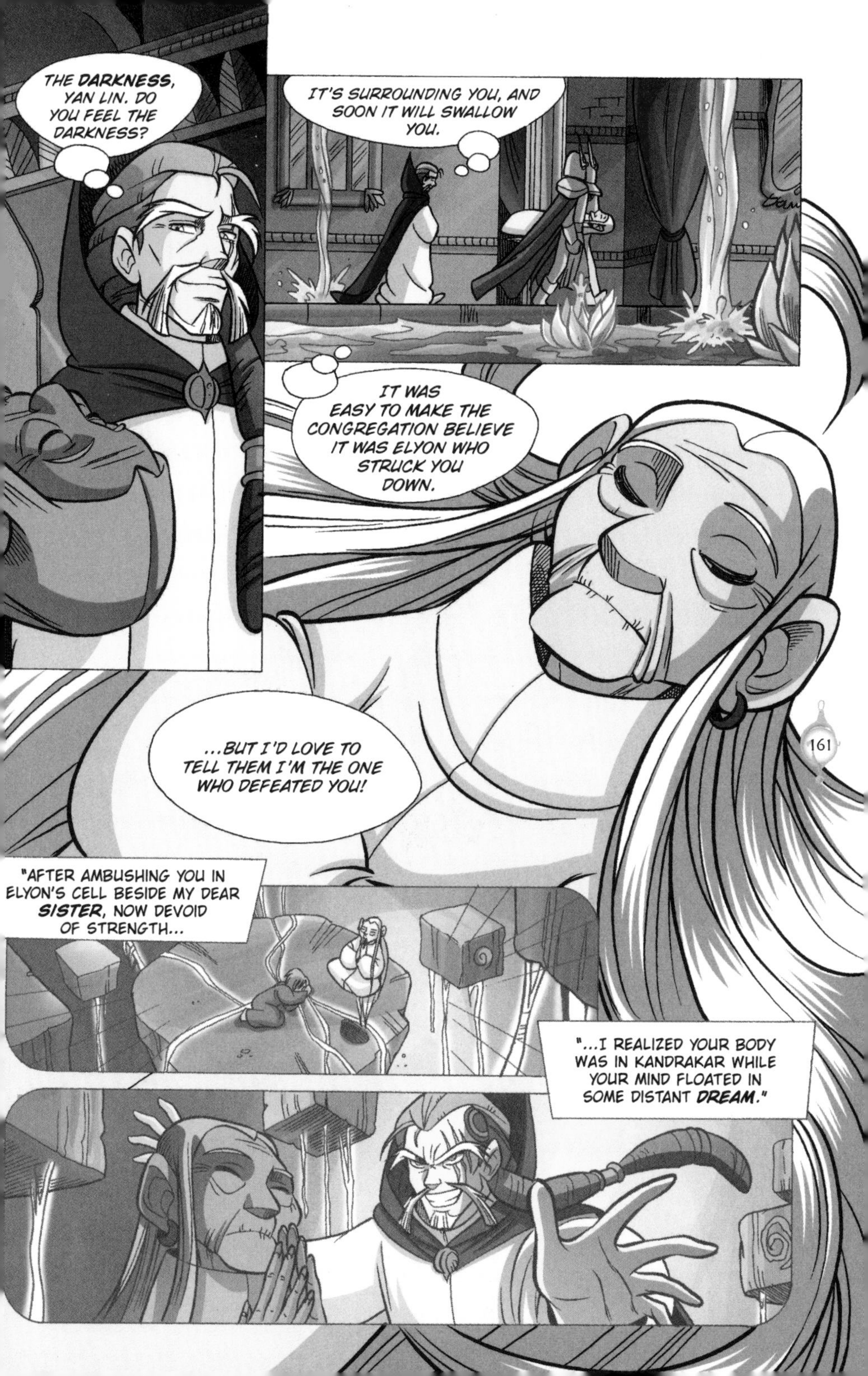
THE DARKNESS, YAN LIN. DO YOU FEEL THE DARKNESS?
IT'S SURROUNDING YOU, AND SOON IT WILL SWALLOW YOU.
IT WAS EASY TO MAKE THE CONGREGATION BELIEVE IT WAS ELYON WHO STRUCK YOU DOWN.
...BUT I'D LOVE TO TELL THEM I'M THE ONE WHO DEFEATED YOU!
"AFTER AMBUSHING YOU IN ELYON'S CELL BESIDE MY DEAR SISTER, NOW DEVOID OF STRENGTH...
"...I REALIZED YOUR BODY WAS IN KANDRAKAR WHILE YOUR MIND FLOATED IN SOME DISTANT DREAM."

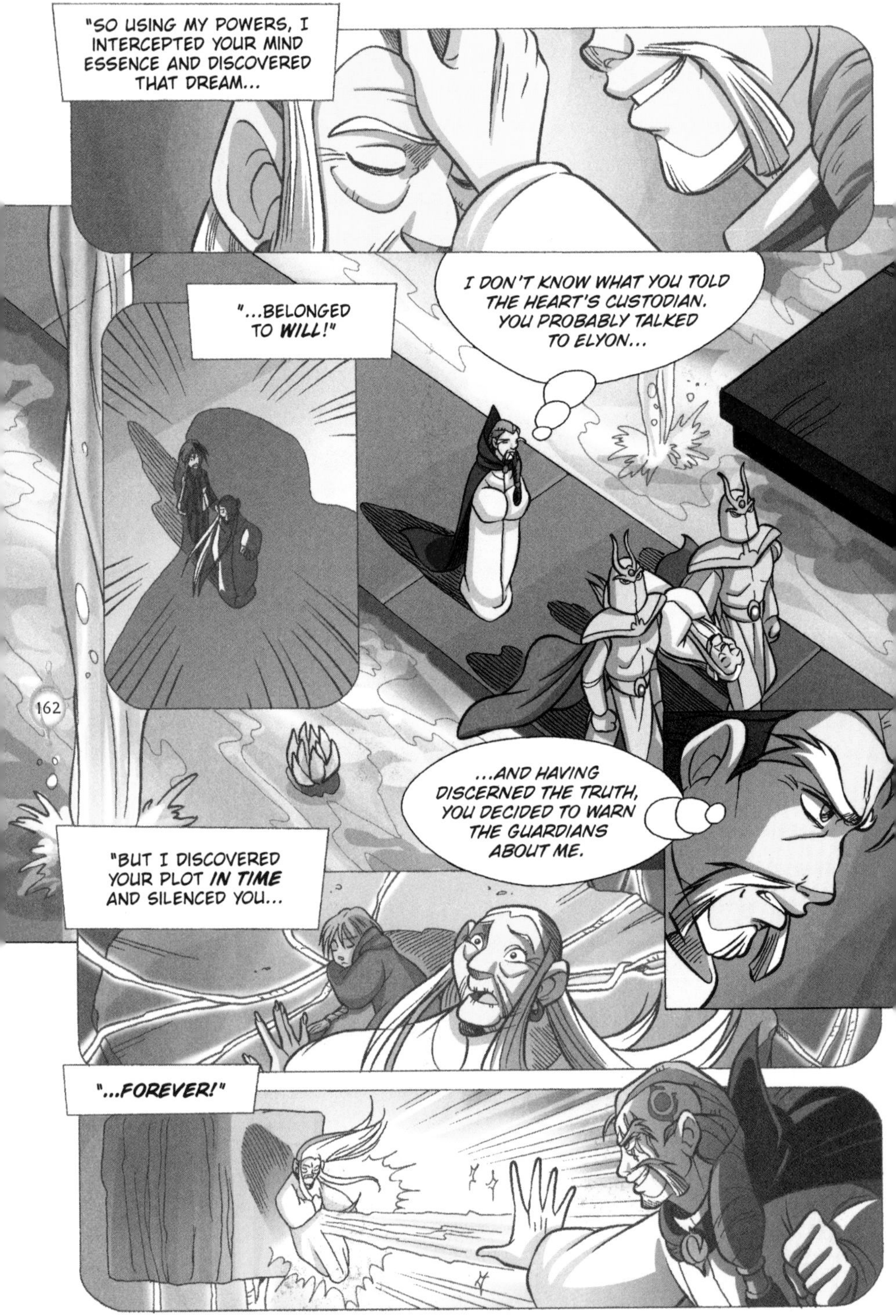
"SO USING MY POWERS, I INTERCEPTED YOUR MIND ESSENCE AND DISCOVERED THAT DREAM...
"...BELONGED TO WILL!"
I DON'T KNOW WHAT YOU TOLD THE HEART'S CUSTODIAN. YOU PROBABLY TALKED TO ELYON...
...AND HAVING DISCERNED THE TRUTH, YOU DECIDED TO WARN THE GUARDIANS ABOUT ME.
"BUT I DISCOVERED YOUR PLOT IN TIME AND SILENCED YOU...
"...FOREVER!"

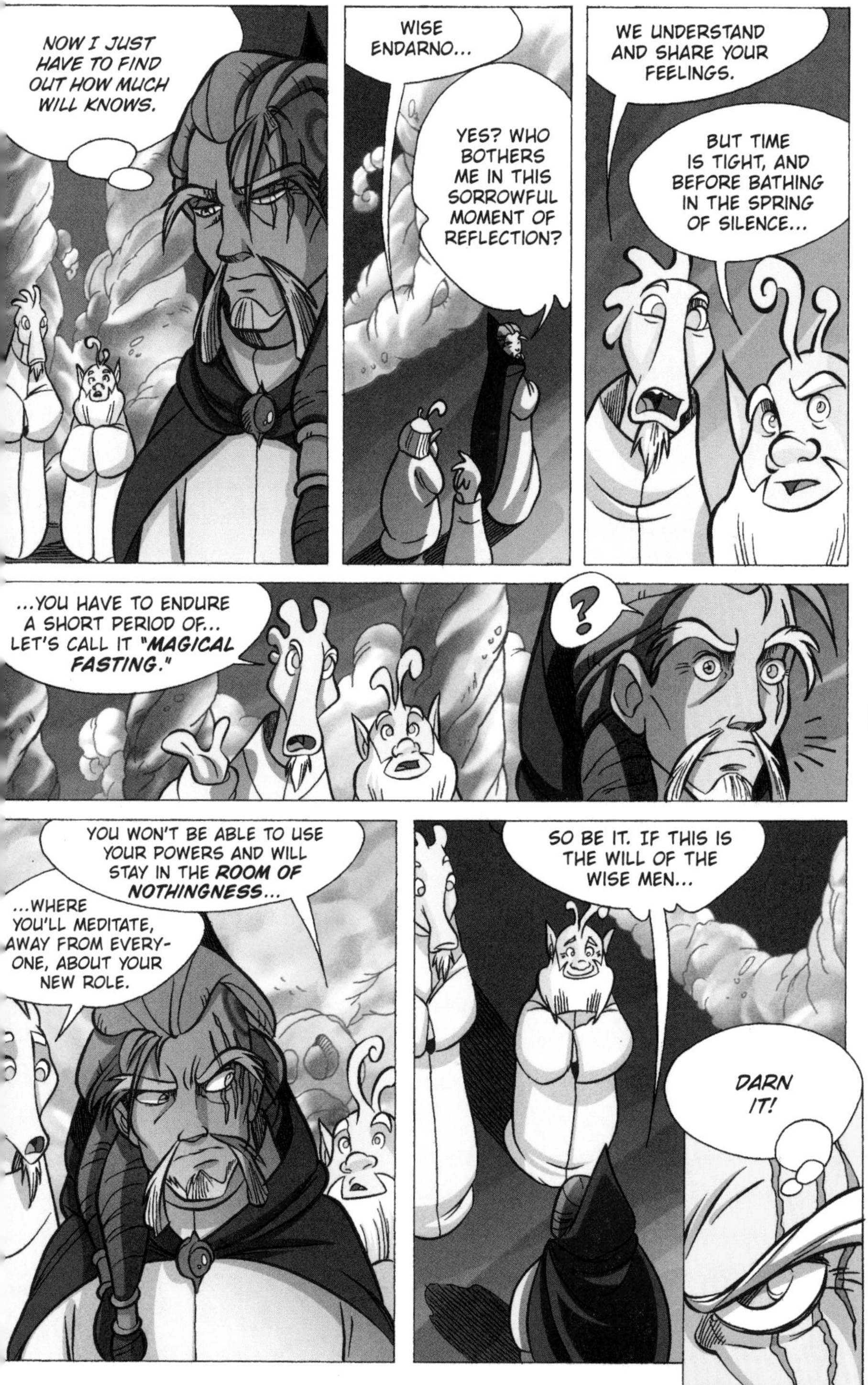
NOW I JUST HAVE TO FIND OUT HOW MUCH WILL KNOWS.
WISE ENDARNO...
YES? WHO BOTHERS ME IN THIS SORROWFUL MOMENT OF REFLECTION?
WE UNDERSTAND AND SHARE YOUR FEELINGS.
BUT TIME IS TIGHT, AND BEFORE BATHING IN THE SPRING OF SILENCE...
...YOU HAVE TO ENDURE A SHORT PERIOD OF... LET'S CALL IT "MAGICAL FASTING."
?
YOU WON'T BE ABLE TO USE YOUR POWERS AND WILL STAY IN THE ROOM OF NOTHINGNESS...
...WHERE YOU'LL MEDITATE, AWAY FROM EVERY-ONE, ABOUT YOUR NEW ROLE.
SO BE IT. IF THIS IS THE WILL OF THE WISE MEN...
DARN IT!

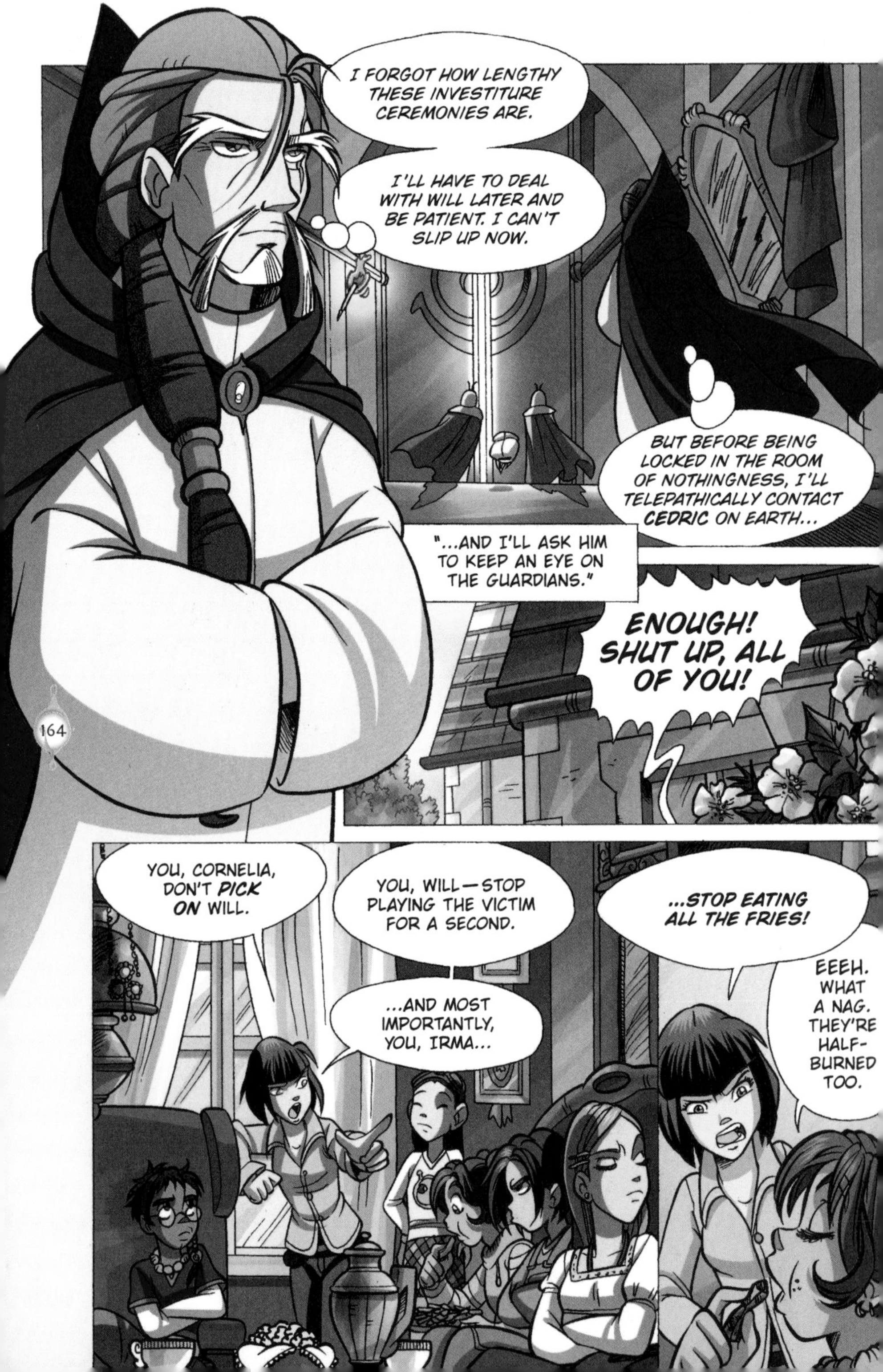
I FORGOT HOW LENGTHY THESE INVESTITURE CEREMONIES ARE.
I'LL HAVE TO DEAL WITH WILL LATER AND BE PATIENT. I CAN'T SLIP UP NOW.
BUT BEFORE BEING LOCKED IN THE ROOM OF NOTHINGNESS, I'LL TELEPATHICALLY CONTACT CEDRIC ON EARTH...
"...AND I'LL ASK HIM TO KEEP AN EYE ON THE GUARDIANS."
ENOUGH! SHUT UP, ALL OF YOU!
YOU, CORNELIA, DON'T PICK ON WILL.
YOU, WILL—STOP PLAYING THE VICTIM FOR A SECOND.
...AND MOST IMPORTANTLY, YOU, IRMA...
...STOP EATING ALL THE FRIES!
EEEH. WHAT A NAG. THEY'RE HALF-BURNED TOO.

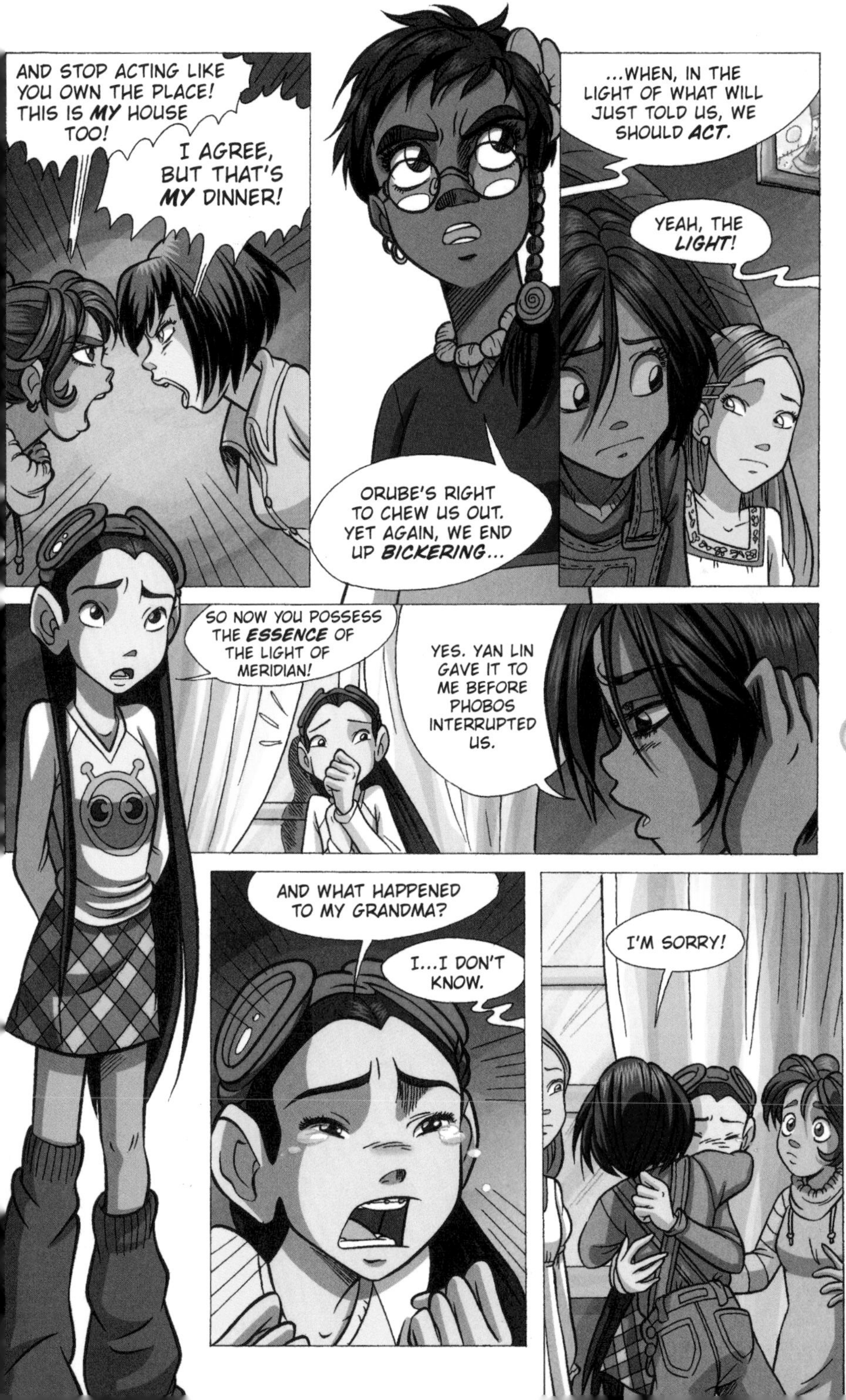
AND STOP ACTING LIKE YOU OWN THE PLACE! THIS IS MY HOUSE TOO!
I AGREE, BUT THAT'S MY DINNER!
ORUBE'S RIGHT TO CHEW US OUT. YET AGAIN, WE END UP BICKERING...
...WHEN, IN THE LIGHT OF WHAT WILL JUST TOLD US, WE SHOULD ACT.
YEAH, THE LIGHT!
SO NOW YOU POSSESS THE ESSENCE OF THE LIGHT OF MERIDIAN!
YES. YAN LIN GAVE IT TO ME BEFORE PHOBOS INTERRUPTED US.
AND WHAT HAPPENED TO MY GRANDMA?
I...I DON'T KNOW.
I'M SORRY!

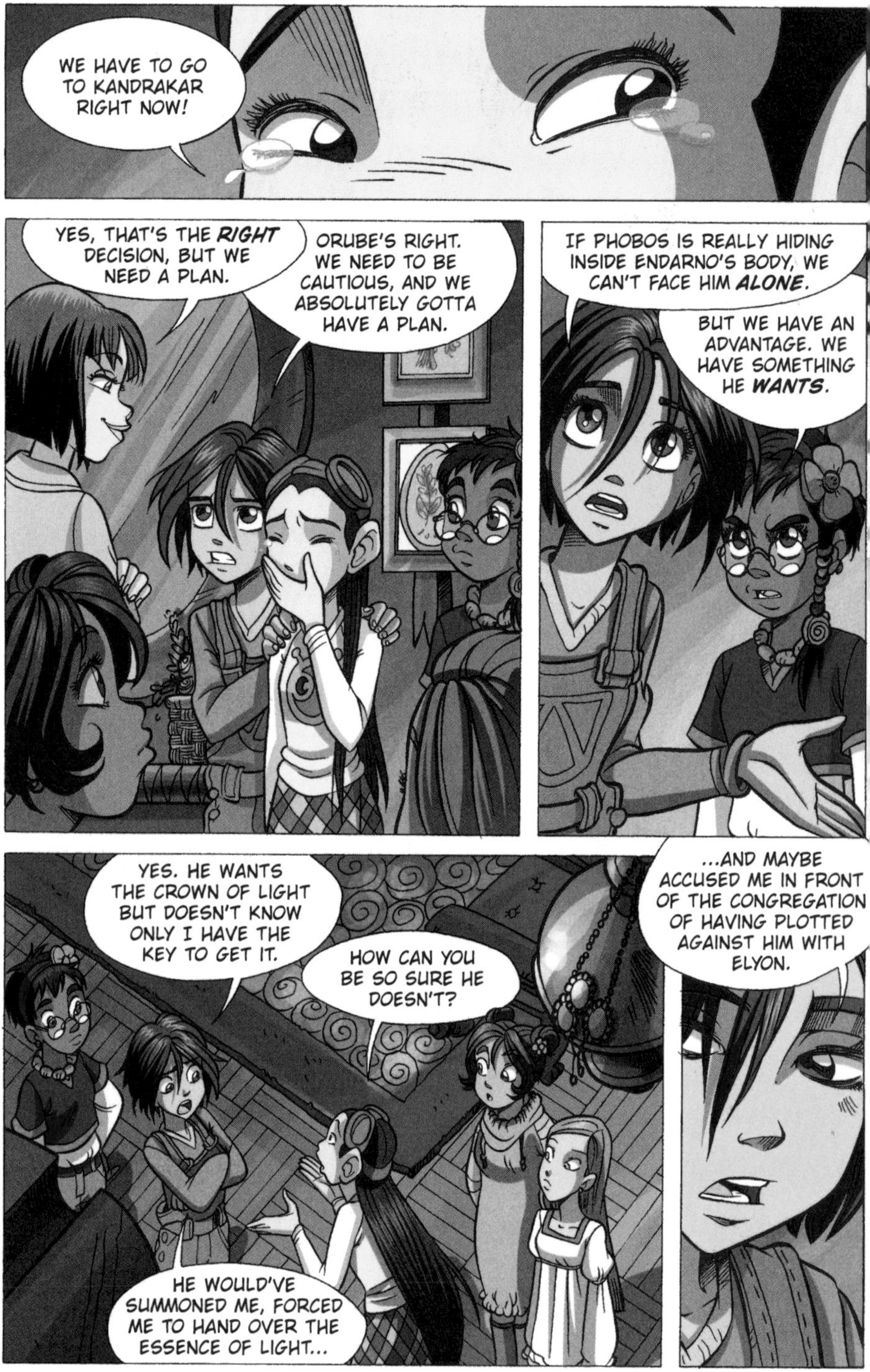
WE HAVE TO GO TO KANDRAKAR RIGHT NOW!
YES, THAT'S THE RIGHT DECISION, BUT WE NEED A PLAN.
ORUBE'S RIGHT. WE NEED TO BE CAUTIOUS, AND WE ABSOLUTELY GOTTA HAVE A PLAN.
IF PHOBOS IS REALLY HIDING INSIDE ENDARNO'S BODY, WE CAN'T FACE HIM ALONE.
BUT WE HAVE AN ADVANTAGE. WE HAVE SOMETHING HE WANTS.
YES. HE WANTS THE CROWN OF LIGHT BUT DOESN'T KNOW ONLY I HAVE THE KEY TO GET IT.
HOW CAN YOU BE SO SURE HE DOESN'T?
HE WOULD'VE SUMMONED ME, FORCED ME TO HAND OVER THE ESSENCE OF LIGHT...
...AND MAYBE ACCUSED ME IN FRONT OF THE CONGREGATION OF HAVING PLOTTED AGAINST HIM WITH ELYON.

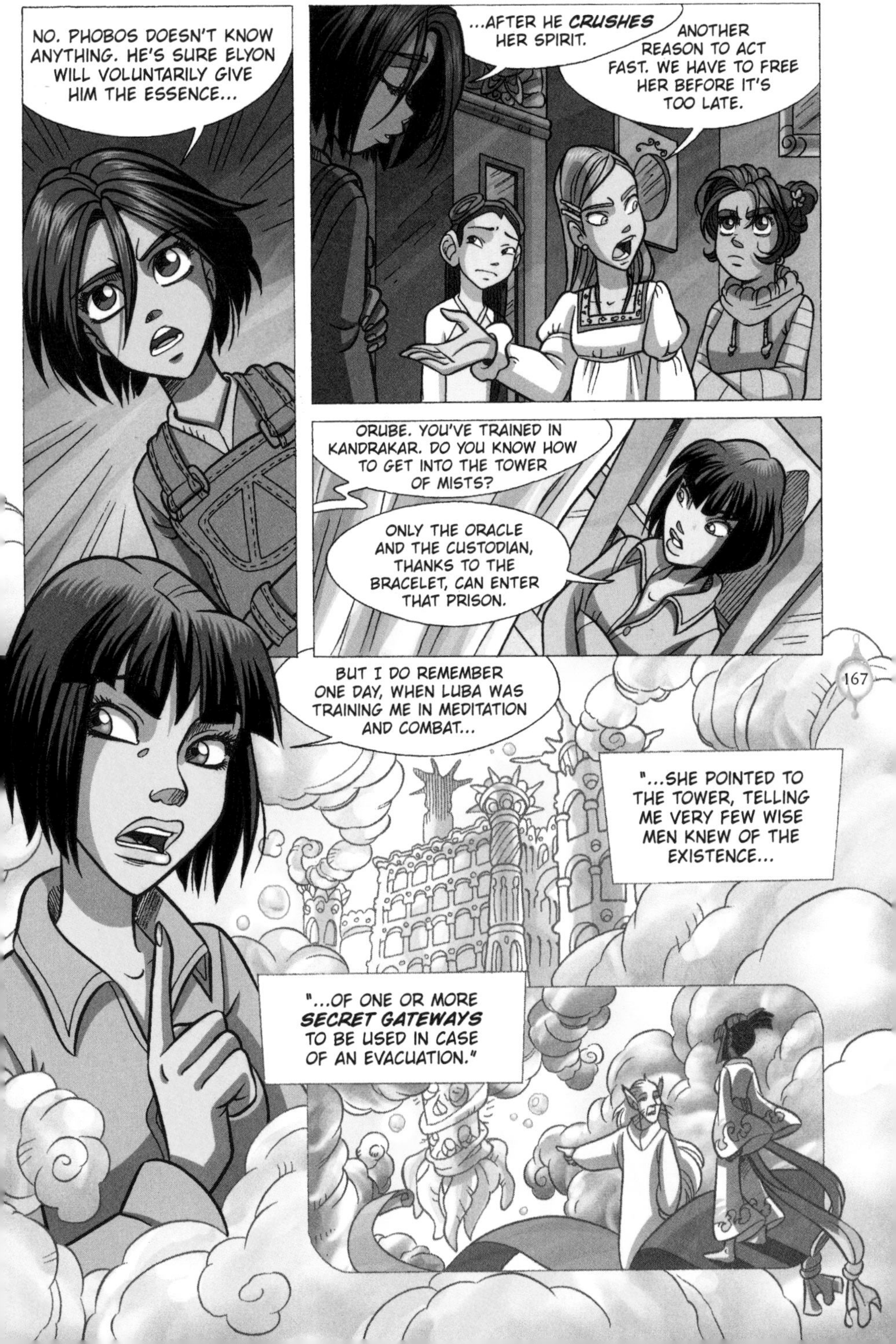

NO. PHOBOS DOESN'T KNOW ANYTHING. HE'S SURE ELYON WILL VOLUNTARILY GIVE HIM THE ESSENCE...
...AFTER HE CRUSHES HER SPIRIT.
ANOTHER REASON TO ACT FAST. WE HAVE TO FREE HER BEFORE IT'S TOO LATE.
ORUBE. YOU'VE TRAINED IN KANDRAKAR. DO YOU KNOW HOW TO GET INTO THE TOWER OF MISTS?
ONLY THE ORACLE AND THE CUSTODIAN, THANKS TO THE BRACELET, CAN ENTER THAT PRISON.
BUT I DO REMEMBER ONE DAY, WHEN LUBA WAS TRAINING ME IN MEDITATION AND COMBAT...
"...SHE POINTED TO THE TOWER, TELLING ME VERY FEW WISE MEN KNEW OF THE EXISTENCE...
"...OF ONE OR MORE SECRET GATEWAYS TO BE USED IN CASE OF AN EVACUATION."

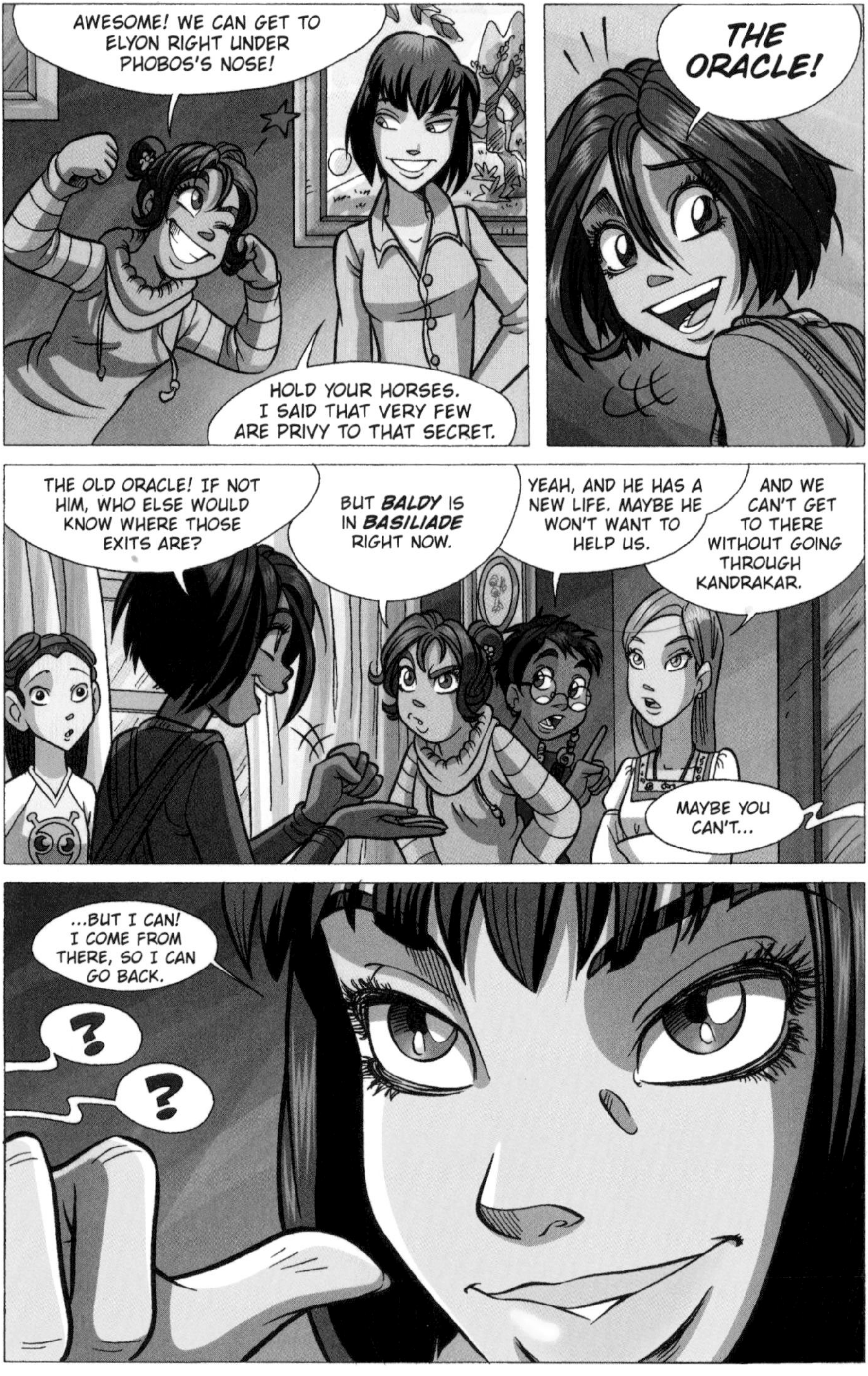
AWESOME! WE CAN GET TO ELYON RIGHT UNDER PHOBOS'S NOSE!
HOLD YOUR HORSES. I SAID THAT VERY FEW ARE PRIVY TO THAT SECRET.
THE ORACLE!
THE OLD ORACLE! IF NOT HIM, WHO ELSE WOULD KNOW WHERE THOSE EXITS ARE?
BUT BALDY IS IN BASILIADE RIGHT NOW.
YEAH, AND HE HAS A NEW LIFE. MAYBE HE WON'T WANT TO HELP US.
AND WE CAN'T GET TO THERE WITHOUT GOING THROUGH KANDRAKAR.
MAYBE YOU CAN'T...
...BUT I CAN! I COME FROM THERE, SO I CAN GO BACK.
?
?

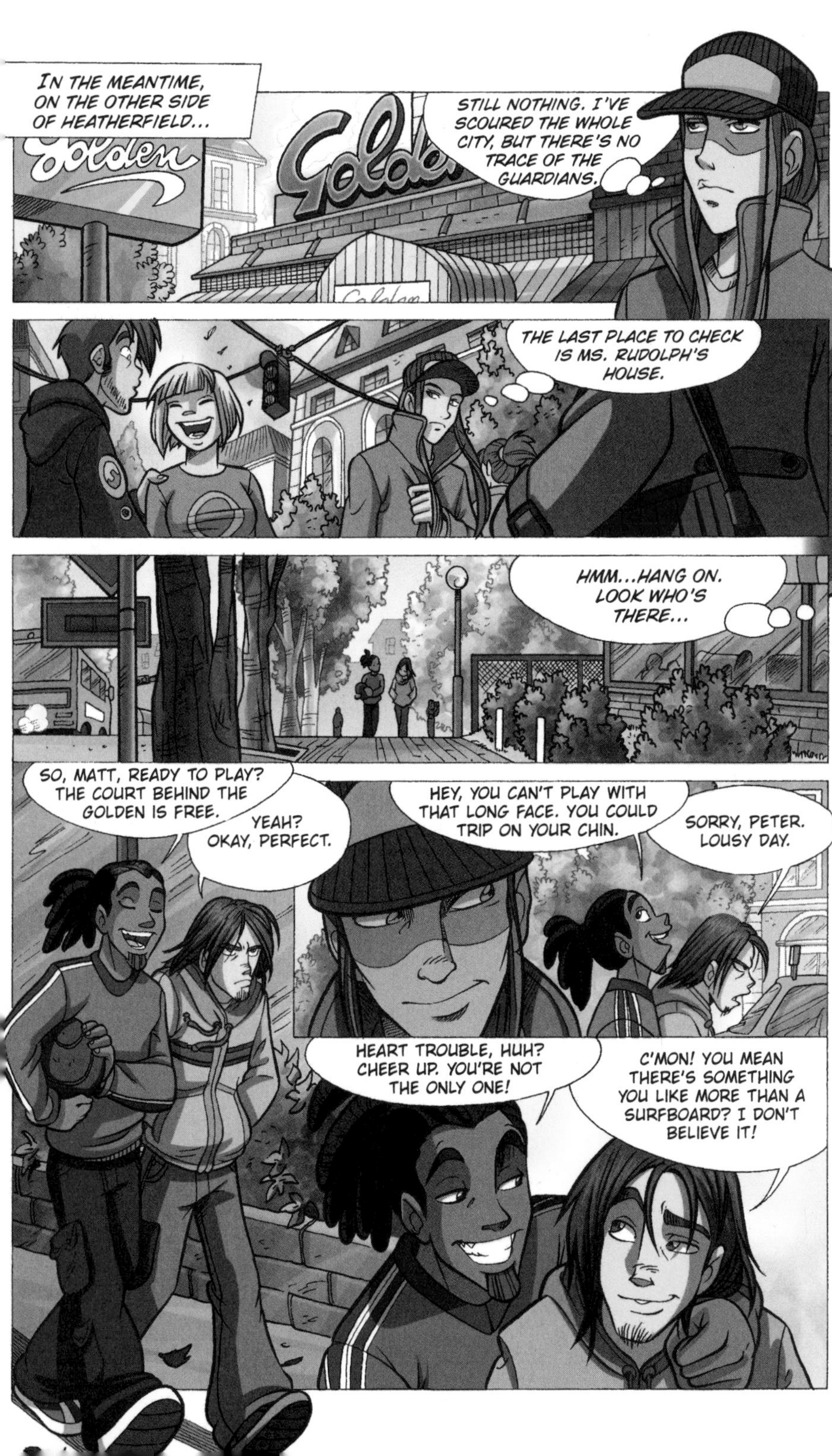

IN THE MEANTIME, ON THE OTHER SIDE OF HEATHERFIELD...
Golden
STILL NOTHING. I'VE SCOURED THE WHOLE CITY, BUT THERE'S NO TRACE OF THE GUARDIANS.
THE LAST PLACE TO CHECK IS MS. RUDOLPH'S HOUSE.
HMM...HANG ON. LOOK WHO'S THERE...
SO, MATT, READY TO PLAY? THE COURT BEHIND THE GOLDEN IS FREE.
YEAH? OKAY, PERFECT.
HEY, YOU CAN'T PLAY WITH THAT LONG FACE. YOU COULD TRIP ON YOUR CHIN.
SORRY, PETER. LOUSY DAY.
HEART TROUBLE, HUH? CHEER UP. YOU'RE NOT THE ONLY ONE!
C'MON! YOU MEAN THERE'S SOMETHING YOU LIKE MORE THAN A SURFBOARD? I DON'T BELIEVE IT!

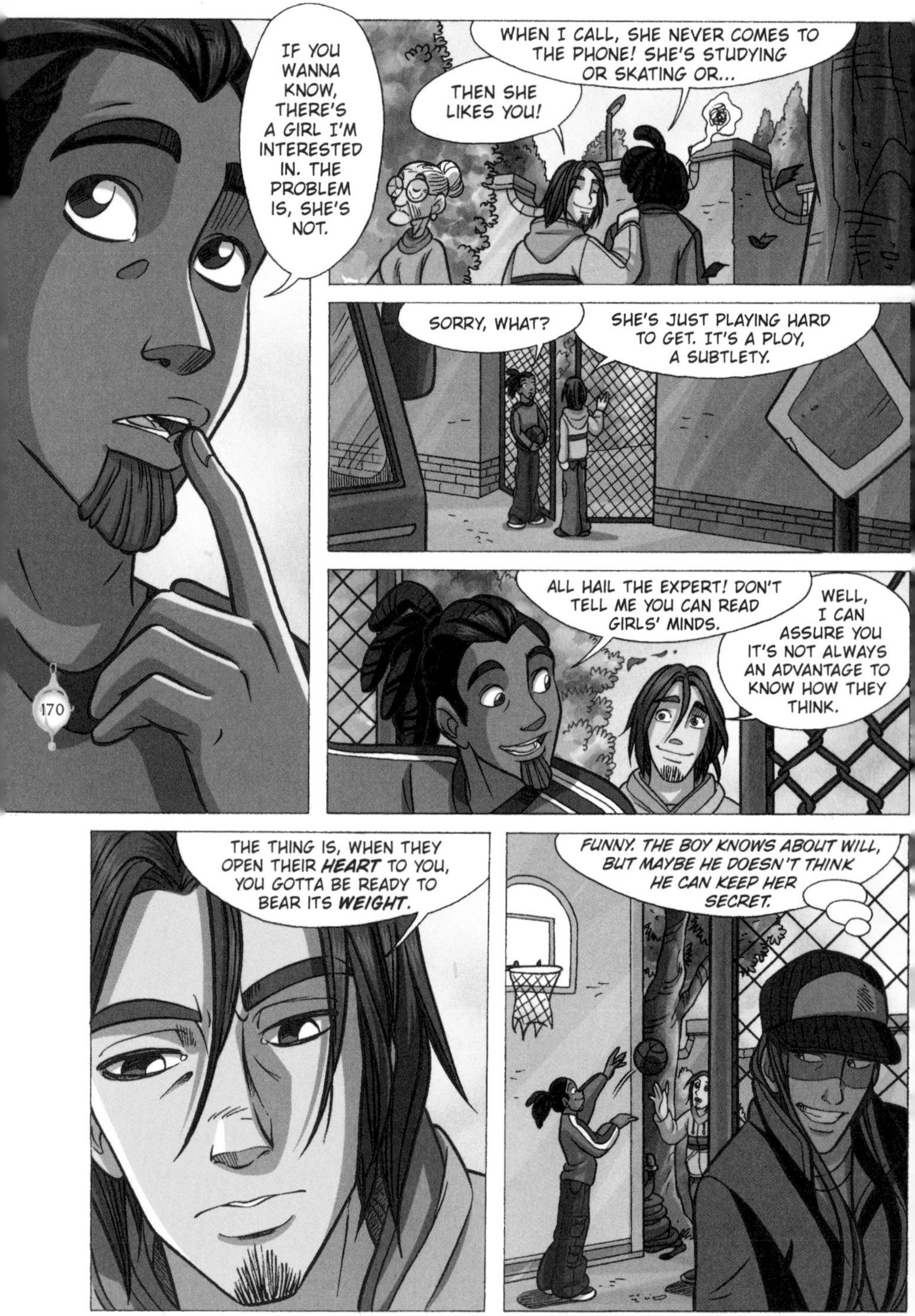
IF YOU WANNA KNOW, THERE'S A GIRL I'M INTERESTED IN. THE PROBLEM IS, SHE'S NOT.
WHEN I CALL, SHE NEVER COMES TO THE PHONE! SHE'S STUDYING OR SKATING OR...
THEN SHE LIKES YOU!
SORRY, WHAT?
SHE'S JUST PLAYING HARD TO GET. IT'S A PLOY, A SUBTLETY.
ALL HAIL THE EXPERT! DON'T TELL ME YOU CAN READ GIRLS' MINDS.
WELL, I CAN ASSURE YOU IT'S NOT ALWAYS AN ADVANTAGE TO KNOW HOW THEY THINK.
THE THING IS, WHEN THEY OPEN THEIR *HEART* TO YOU, YOU GOTTA BE READY TO BEAR ITS *WEIGHT*.
FUNNY. THE BOY KNOWS ABOUT WILL, BUT MAYBE HE DOESN'T THINK HE CAN KEEP HER SECRET.

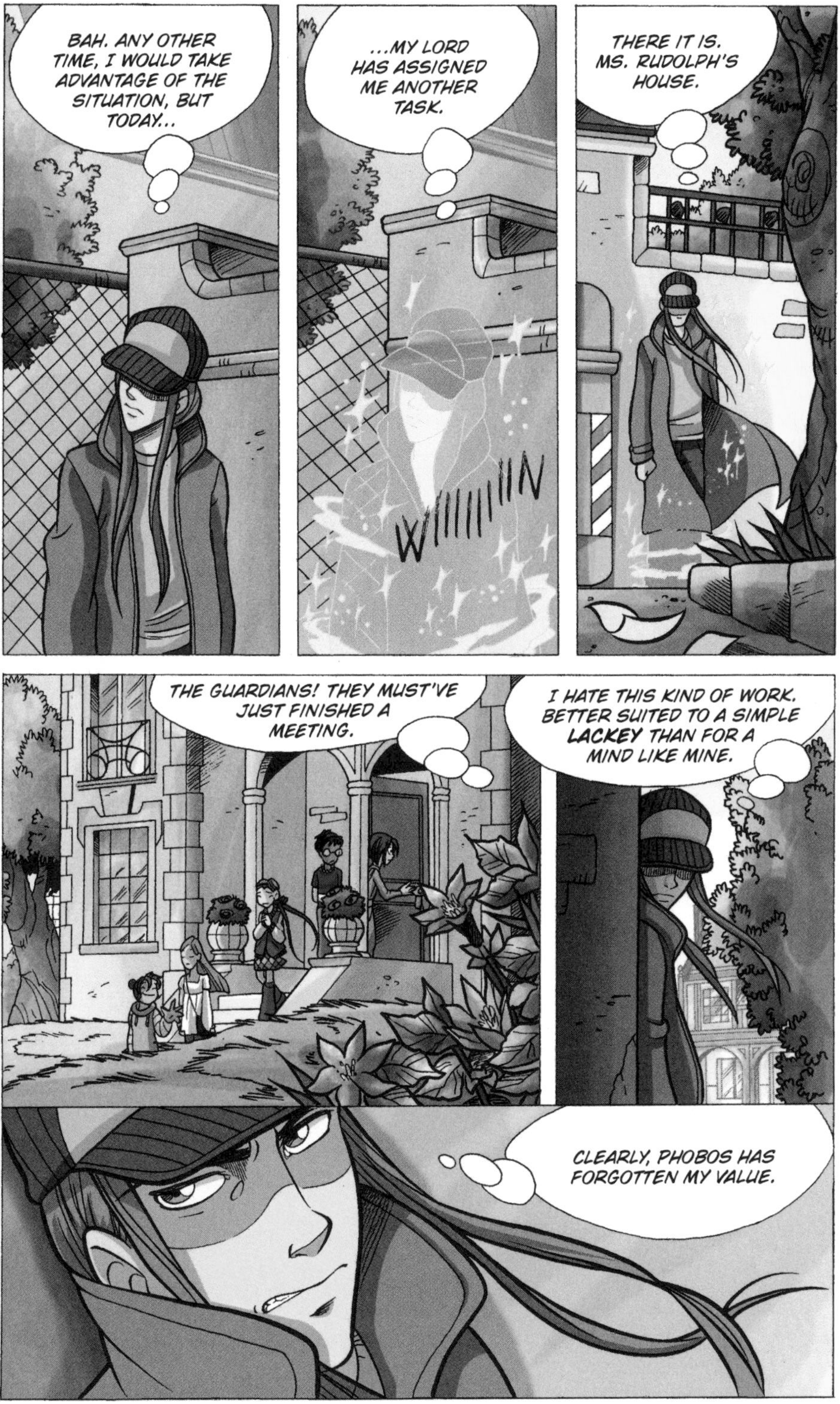

BAH. ANY OTHER TIME, I WOULD TAKE ADVANTAGE OF THE SITUATION, BUT TODAY...
...MY LORD HAS ASSIGNED ME ANOTHER TASK.
WIIIIIIIN
THERE IT IS. MS. RUDOLPH'S HOUSE.
THE GUARDIANS! THEY MUST'VE JUST FINISHED A MEETING.
I HATE THIS KIND OF WORK. BETTER SUITED TO A SIMPLE LACKEY THAN FOR A MIND LIKE MINE.
CLEARLY, PHOBOS HAS FORGOTTEN MY VALUE.

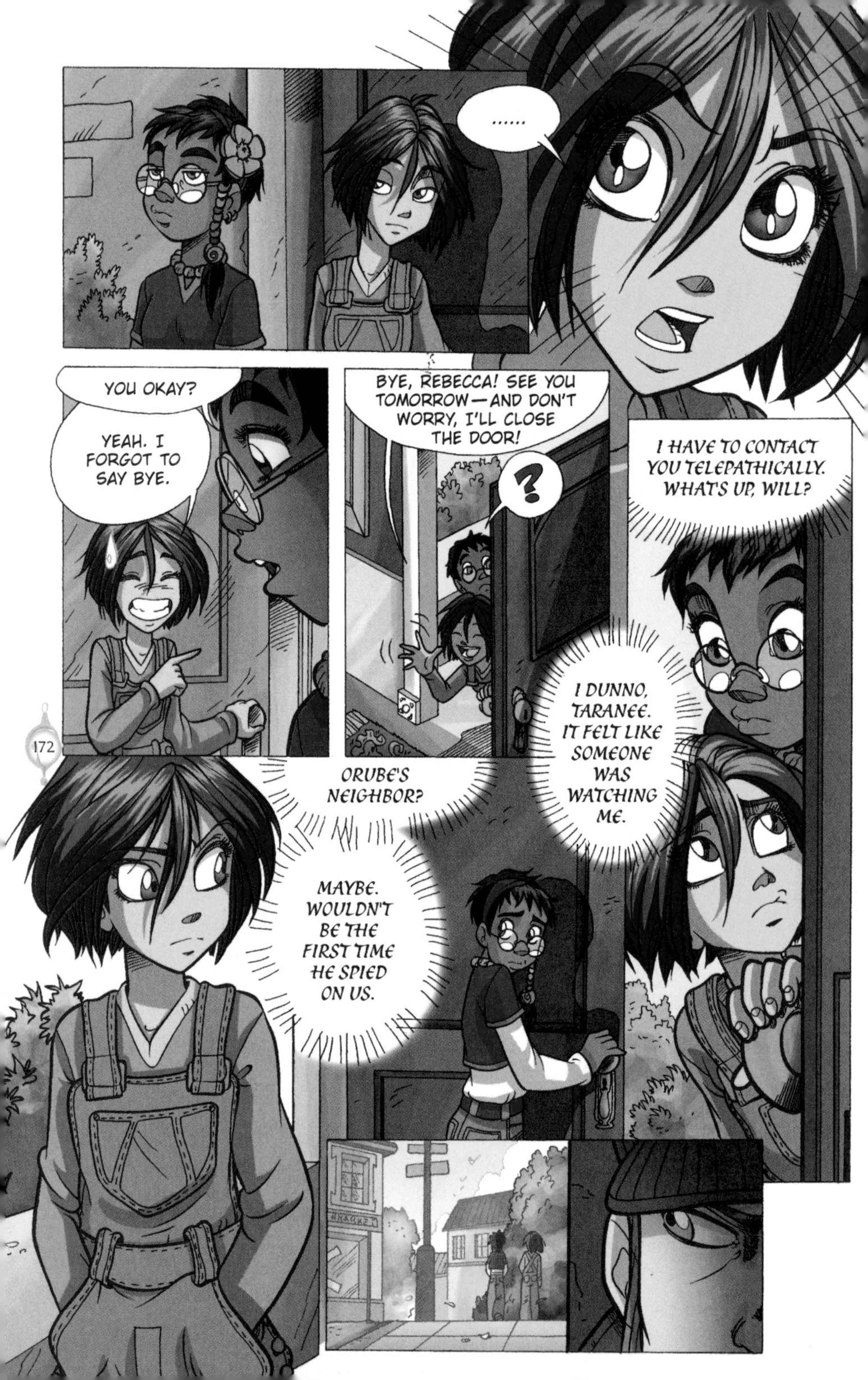
......
YOU OKAY?
YEAH. I FORGOT TO SAY BYE.
BYE, REBECCA! SEE YOU TOMORROW—AND DON'T WORRY, I'LL CLOSE THE DOOR!
?
I HAVE TO CONTACT YOU TELEPATHICALLY. WHAT'S UP, WILL?
I DUNNO, TARANEE. IT FELT LIKE SOMEONE WAS WATCHING ME.
ORUBE'S NEIGHBOR?
MAYBE. WOULDN'T BE THE FIRST TIME HE SPIED ON US.

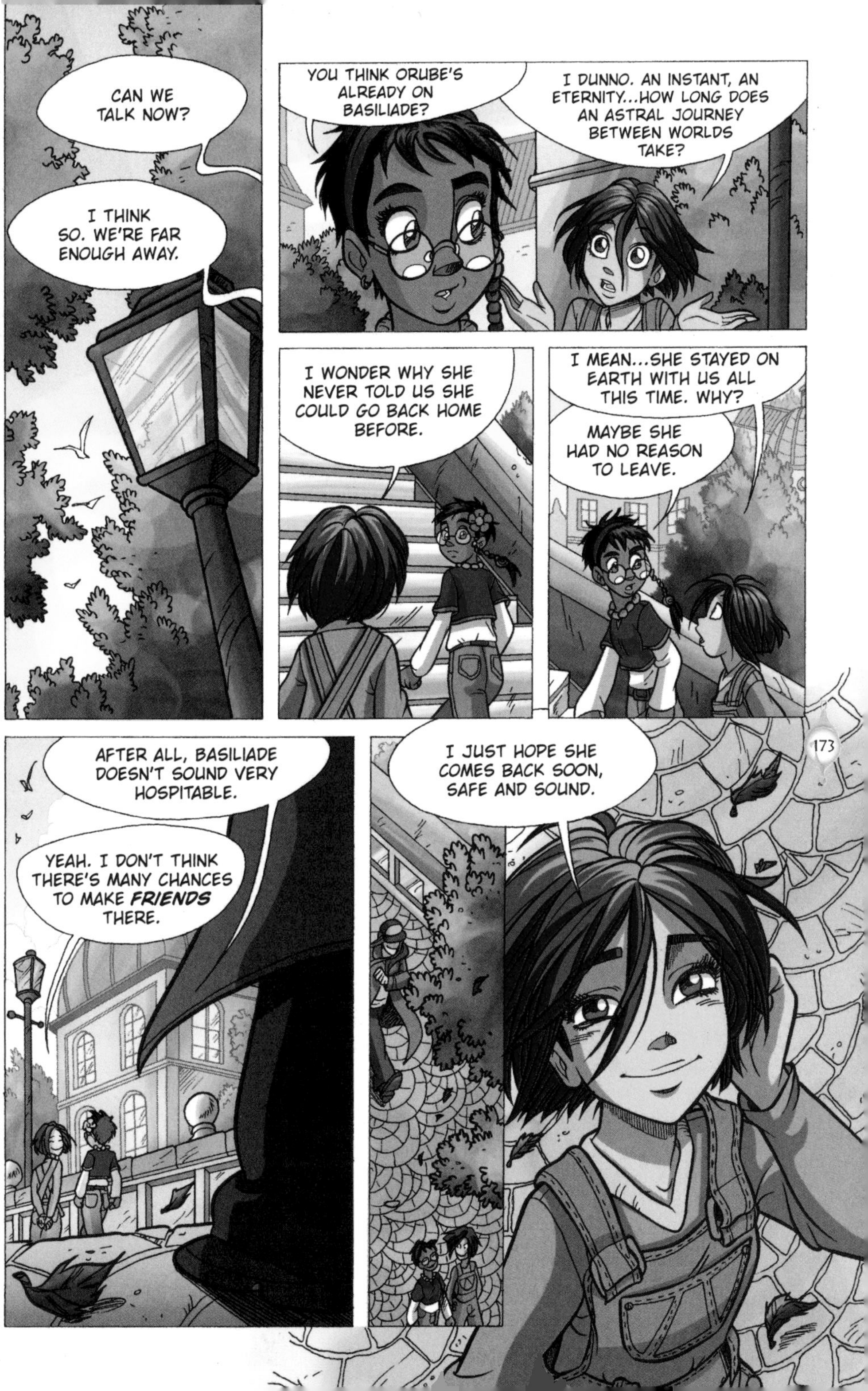

CAN WE TALK NOW?
I THINK SO. WE'RE FAR ENOUGH AWAY.
YOU THINK ORUBE'S ALREADY ON BASILIADE?
I DUNNO. AN INSTANT, AN ETERNITY...HOW LONG DOES AN ASTRAL JOURNEY BETWEEN WORLDS TAKE?
I WONDER WHY SHE NEVER TOLD US SHE COULD GO BACK HOME BEFORE.
I MEAN...SHE STAYED ON EARTH WITH US ALL THIS TIME. WHY?
MAYBE SHE HAD NO REASON TO LEAVE.
AFTER ALL, BASILIADE DOESN'T SOUND VERY HOSPITABLE.
YEAH. I DON'T THINK THERE'S MANY CHANCES TO MAKE *FRIENDS* THERE.
I JUST HOPE SHE COMES BACK SOON, SAFE AND SOUND.

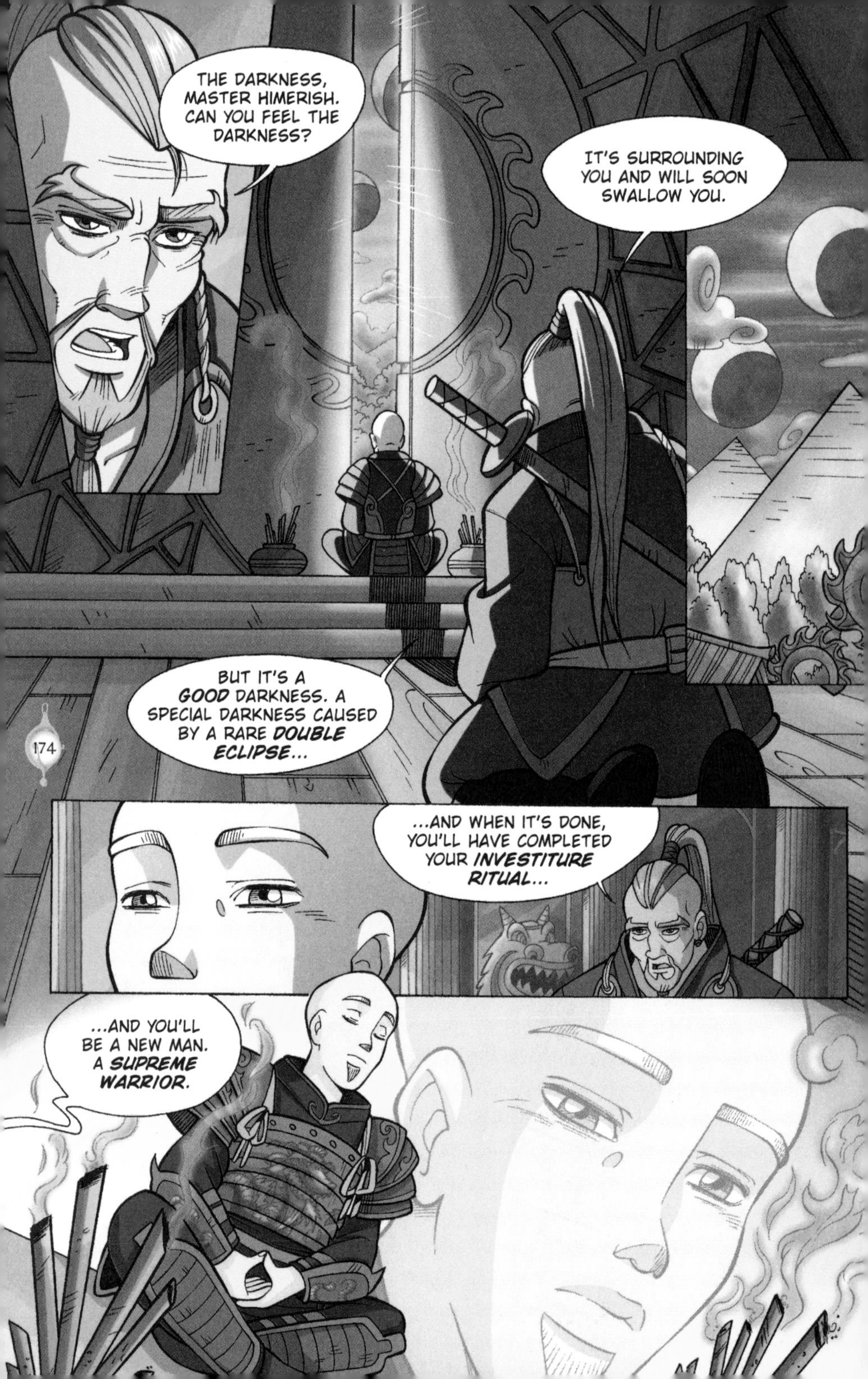
THE DARKNESS, MASTER HIMERISH. CAN YOU FEEL THE DARKNESS?
IT'S SURROUNDING YOU AND WILL SOON SWALLOW YOU.
BUT IT'S A **GOOD** DARKNESS. A SPECIAL DARKNESS CAUSED BY A RARE **DOUBLE ECLIPSE**...
...AND WHEN IT'S DONE, YOU'LL HAVE COMPLETED YOUR **INVESTITURE RITUAL**...
...AND YOU'LL BE A NEW MAN. A **SUPREME WARRIOR**.

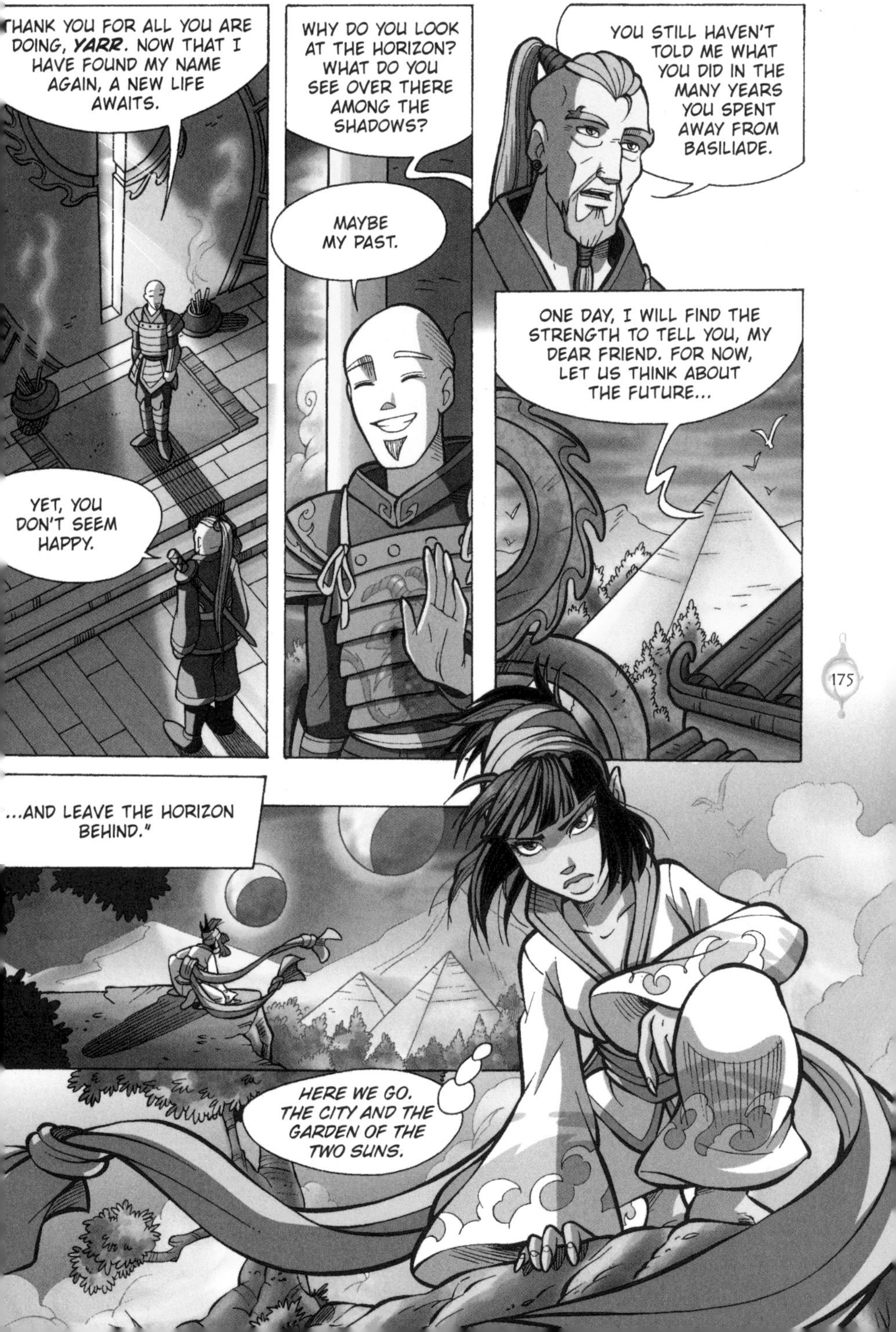
THANK YOU FOR ALL YOU ARE DOING, YARR. NOW THAT I HAVE FOUND MY NAME AGAIN, A NEW LIFE AWAITS.
YET, YOU DON'T SEEM HAPPY.
WHY DO YOU LOOK AT THE HORIZON? WHAT DO YOU SEE OVER THERE AMONG THE SHADOWS?
MAYBE MY PAST.
YOU STILL HAVEN'T TOLD ME WHAT YOU DID IN THE MANY YEARS YOU SPENT AWAY FROM BASILIADE.
ONE DAY, I WILL FIND THE STRENGTH TO TELL YOU, MY DEAR FRIEND. FOR NOW, LET US THINK ABOUT THE FUTURE...
...AND LEAVE THE HORIZON BEHIND."
HERE WE GO. THE CITY AND THE GARDEN OF THE TWO SUNS.

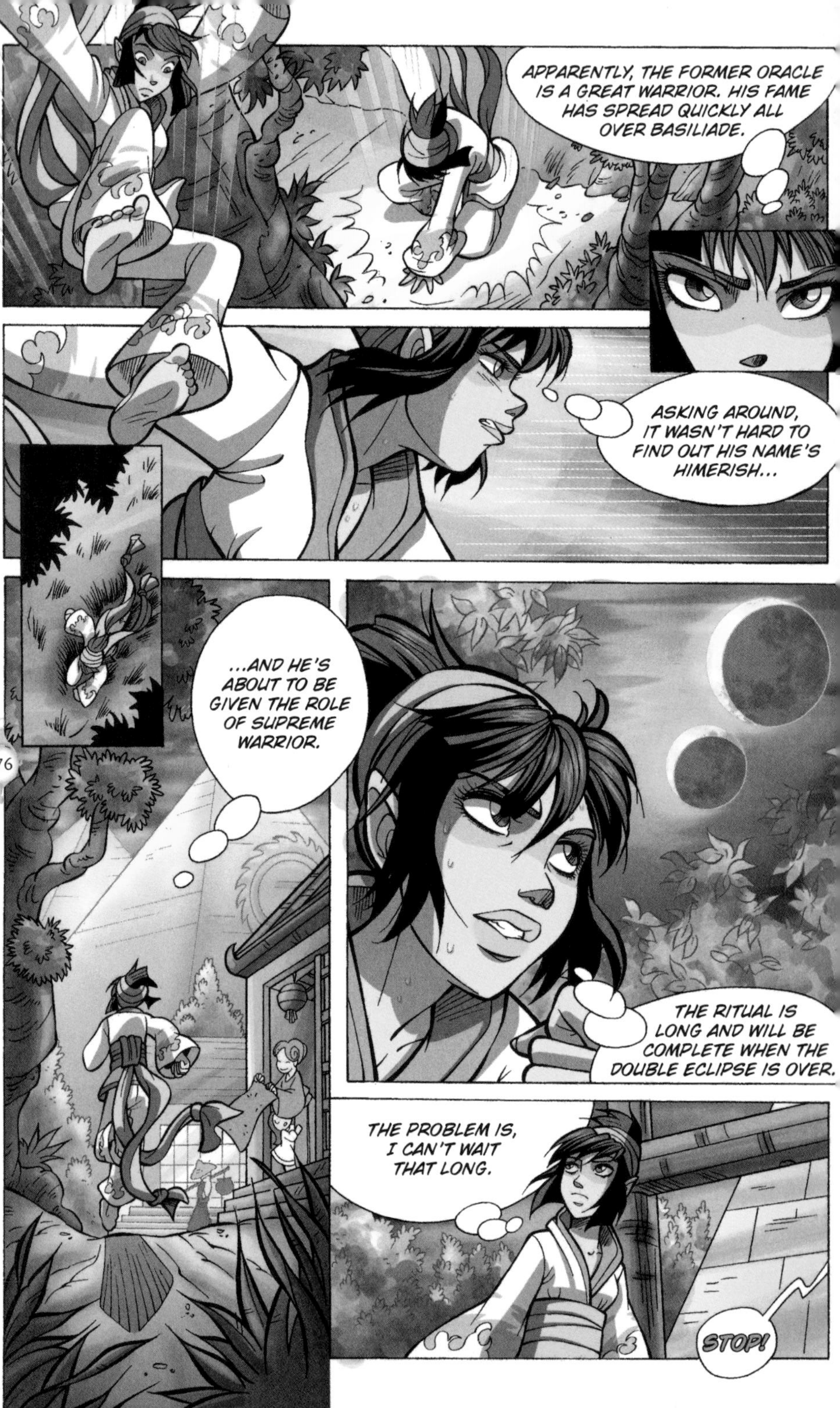
APPARENTLY, THE FORMER ORACLE IS A GREAT WARRIOR. HIS FAME HAS SPREAD QUICKLY ALL OVER BASILIADE.
ASKING AROUND, IT WASN'T HARD TO FIND OUT HIS NAME'S HIMERISH...
...AND HE'S ABOUT TO BE GIVEN THE ROLE OF SUPREME WARRIOR.
THE RITUAL IS LONG AND WILL BE COMPLETE WHEN THE DOUBLE ECLIPSE IS OVER.
THE PROBLEM IS, I CAN'T WAIT THAT LONG.
STOP!

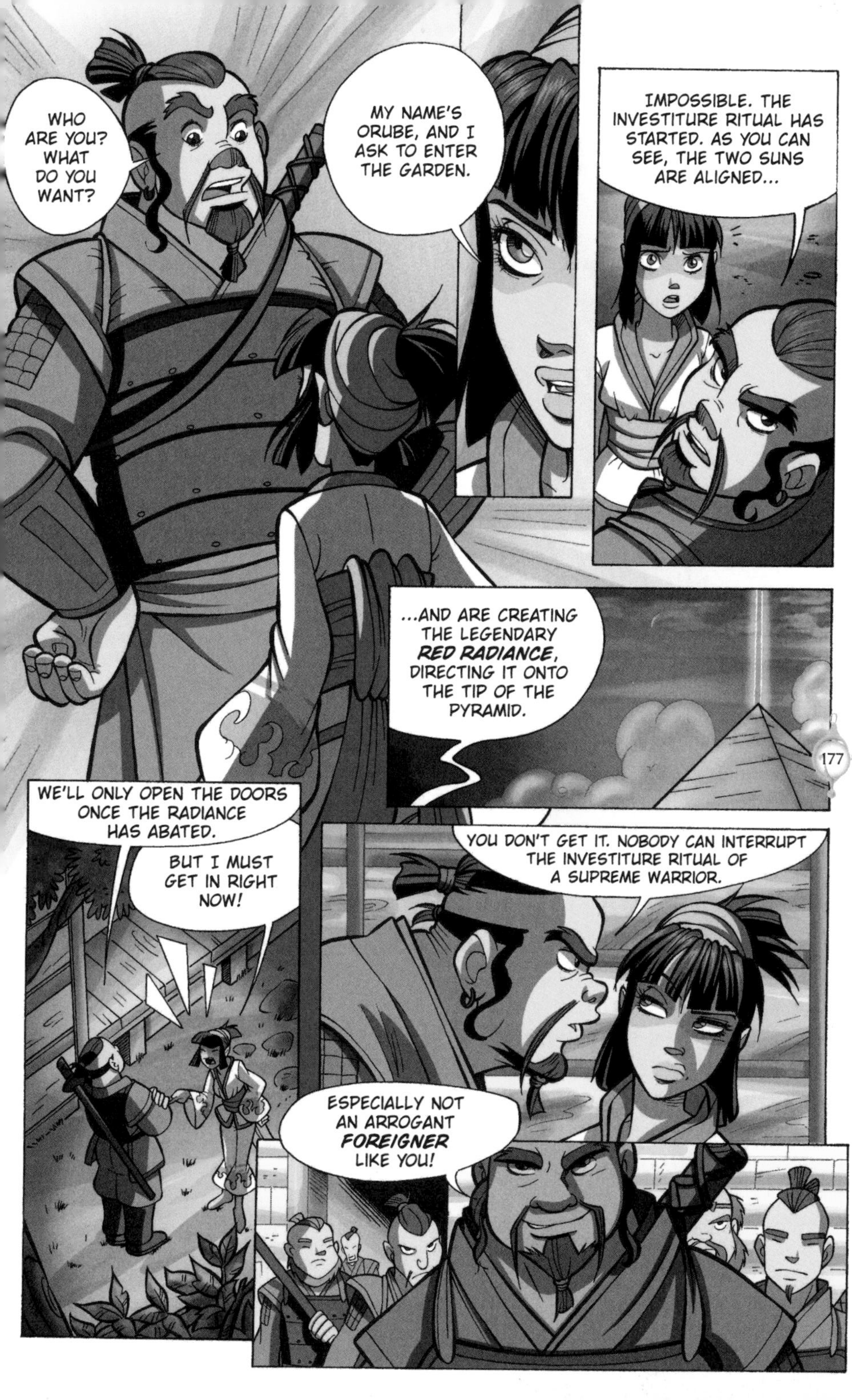
WHO ARE YOU? WHAT DO YOU WANT?
MY NAME'S ORUBE, AND I ASK TO ENTER THE GARDEN.
IMPOSSIBLE. THE INVESTITURE RITUAL HAS STARTED. AS YOU CAN SEE, THE TWO SUNS ARE ALIGNED...
...AND ARE CREATING THE LEGENDARY **RED RADIANCE**, DIRECTING IT ONTO THE TIP OF THE PYRAMID.
WE'LL ONLY OPEN THE DOORS ONCE THE RADIANCE HAS ABATED.
BUT I MUST GET IN RIGHT NOW!
YOU DON'T GET IT. NOBODY CAN INTERRUPT THE INVESTITURE RITUAL OF A SUPREME WARRIOR.
ESPECIALLY NOT AN ARROGANT **FOREIGNER** LIKE YOU!

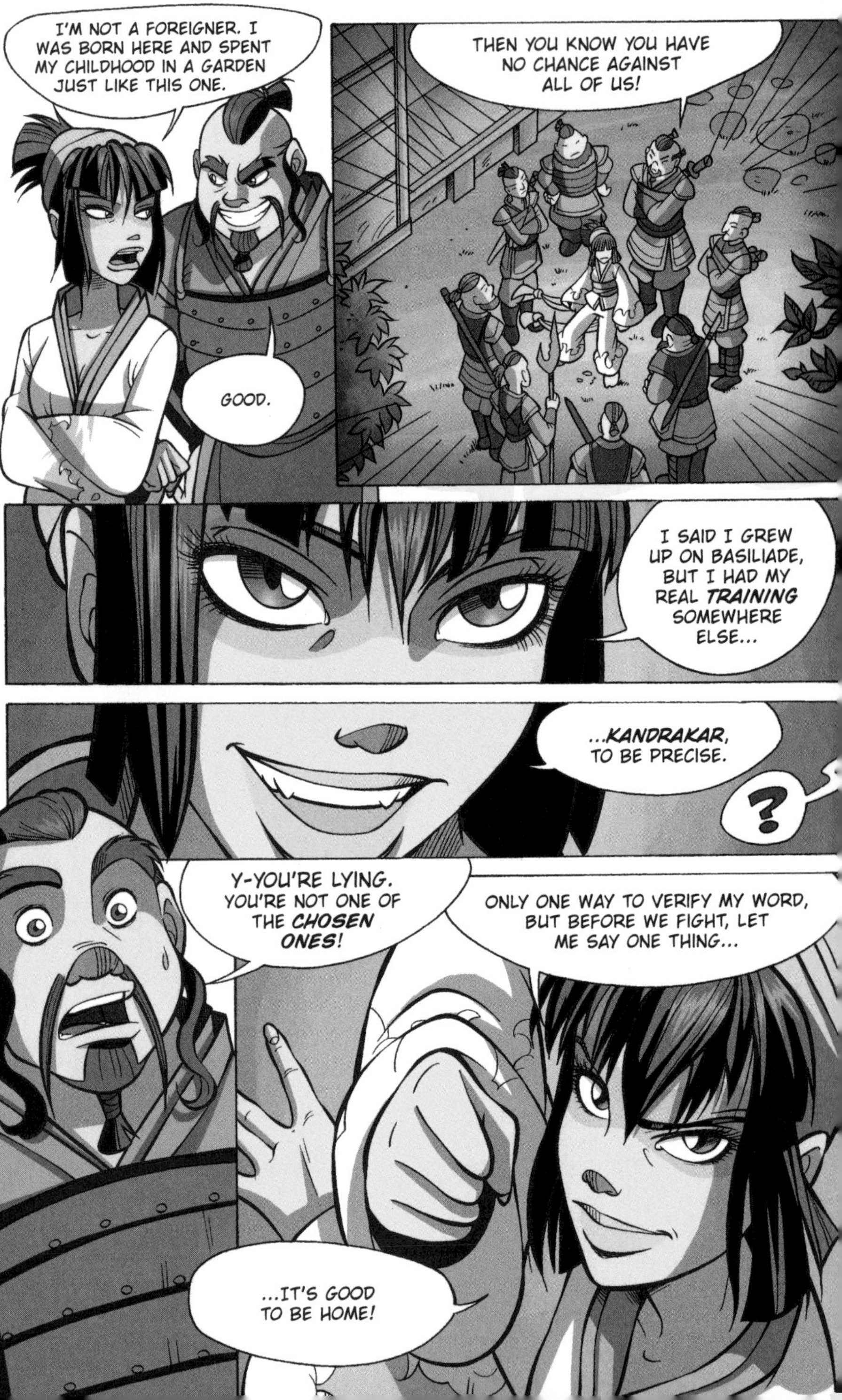
I'M NOT A FOREIGNER. I WAS BORN HERE AND SPENT MY CHILDHOOD IN A GARDEN JUST LIKE THIS ONE.
GOOD.
THEN YOU KNOW YOU HAVE NO CHANCE AGAINST ALL OF US!
I SAID I GREW UP ON BASILIADE, BUT I HAD MY REAL *TRAINING* SOMEWHERE ELSE...
...*KANDRAKAR*, TO BE PRECISE.
?
Y-YOU'RE LYING. YOU'RE NOT ONE OF THE *CHOSEN ONES*!
ONLY ONE WAY TO VERIFY MY WORD, BUT BEFORE WE FIGHT, LET ME SAY ONE THING...
...IT'S GOOD TO BE HOME!

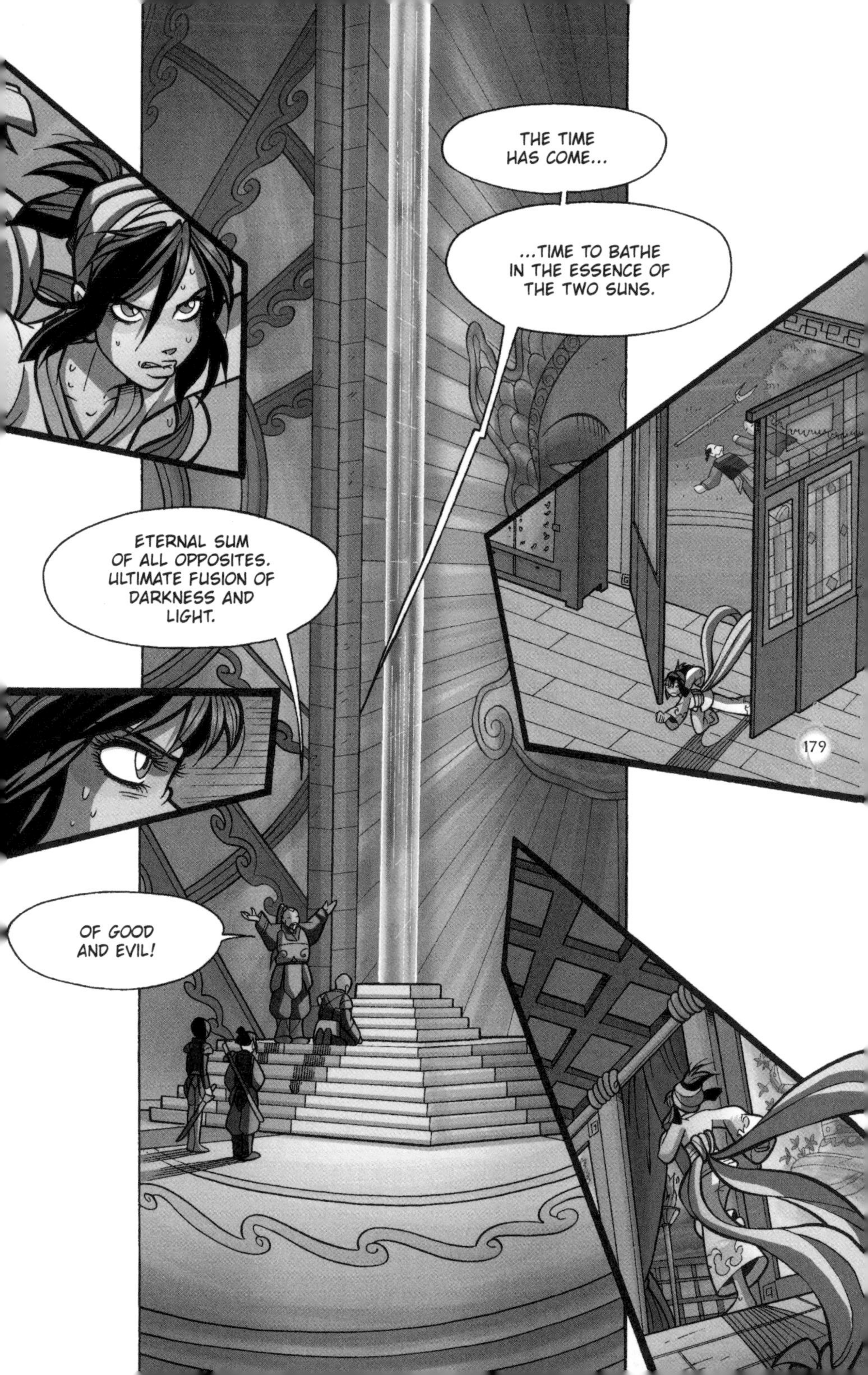
THE TIME HAS COME...
...TIME TO BATHE IN THE ESSENCE OF THE TWO SUNS.
ETERNAL SUM OF ALL OPPOSITES. ULTIMATE FUSION OF DARKNESS AND LIGHT.
OF GOOD AND EVIL!

BUT IT IS ALSO TIME TO UNDERSTAND THAT LIGHT IS NOT ALWAYS GOOD...

...AND DARKNESS IS NOT ALWAYS EVIL.

WE ARE ALL PART OF THE WHOLE, OF EVERYTHING AND NOTHING.

OF ONE UNIQUE...

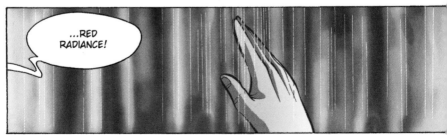

...RED RADIANCE!

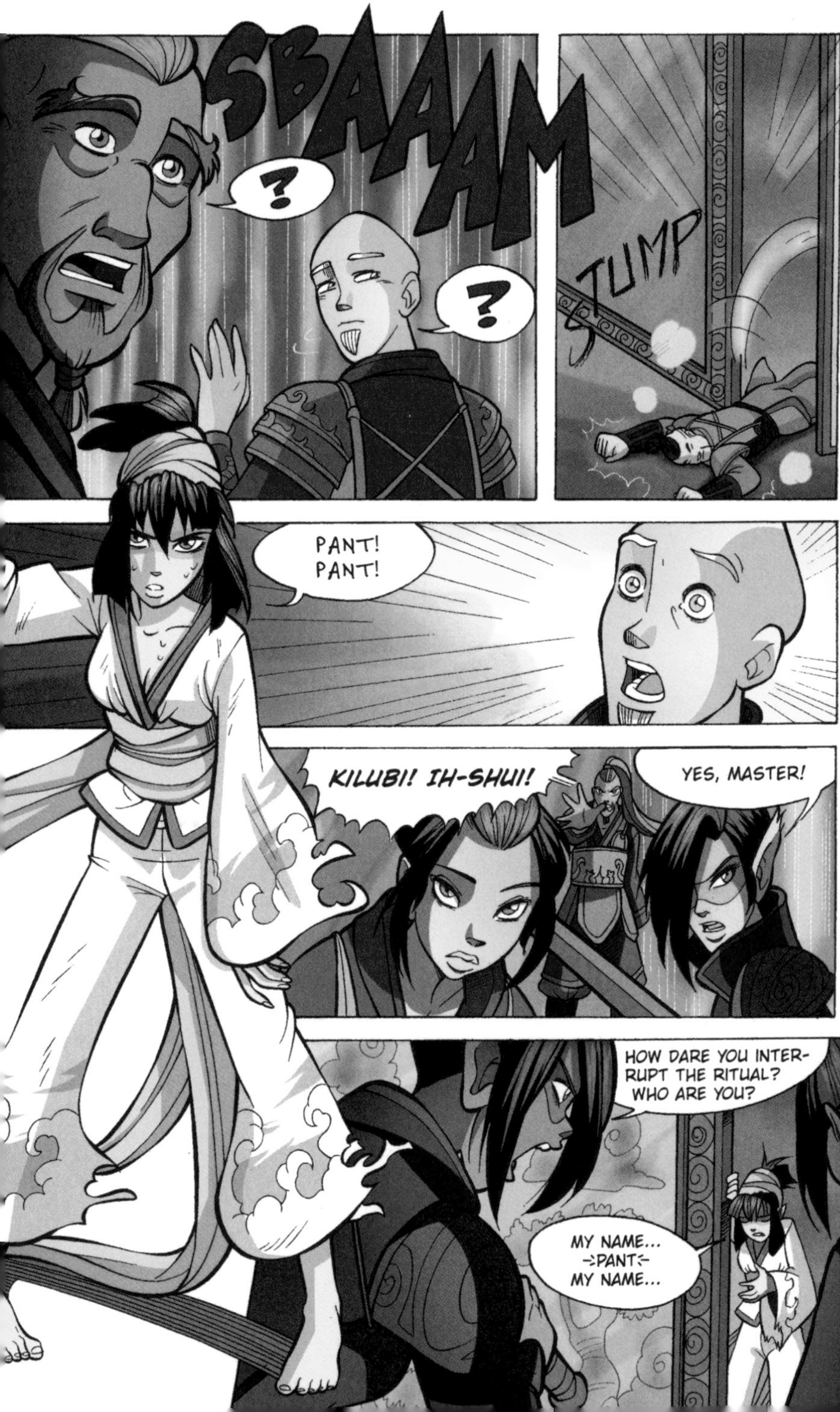

SBAAAM
?
?
STUMP
PANT!
PANT!
KILUBI! IH-SHUI!
YES, MASTER!
HOW DARE YOU INTER-
RUPT THE RITUAL?
WHO ARE YOU?
MY NAME...
-PANT-
MY NAME...

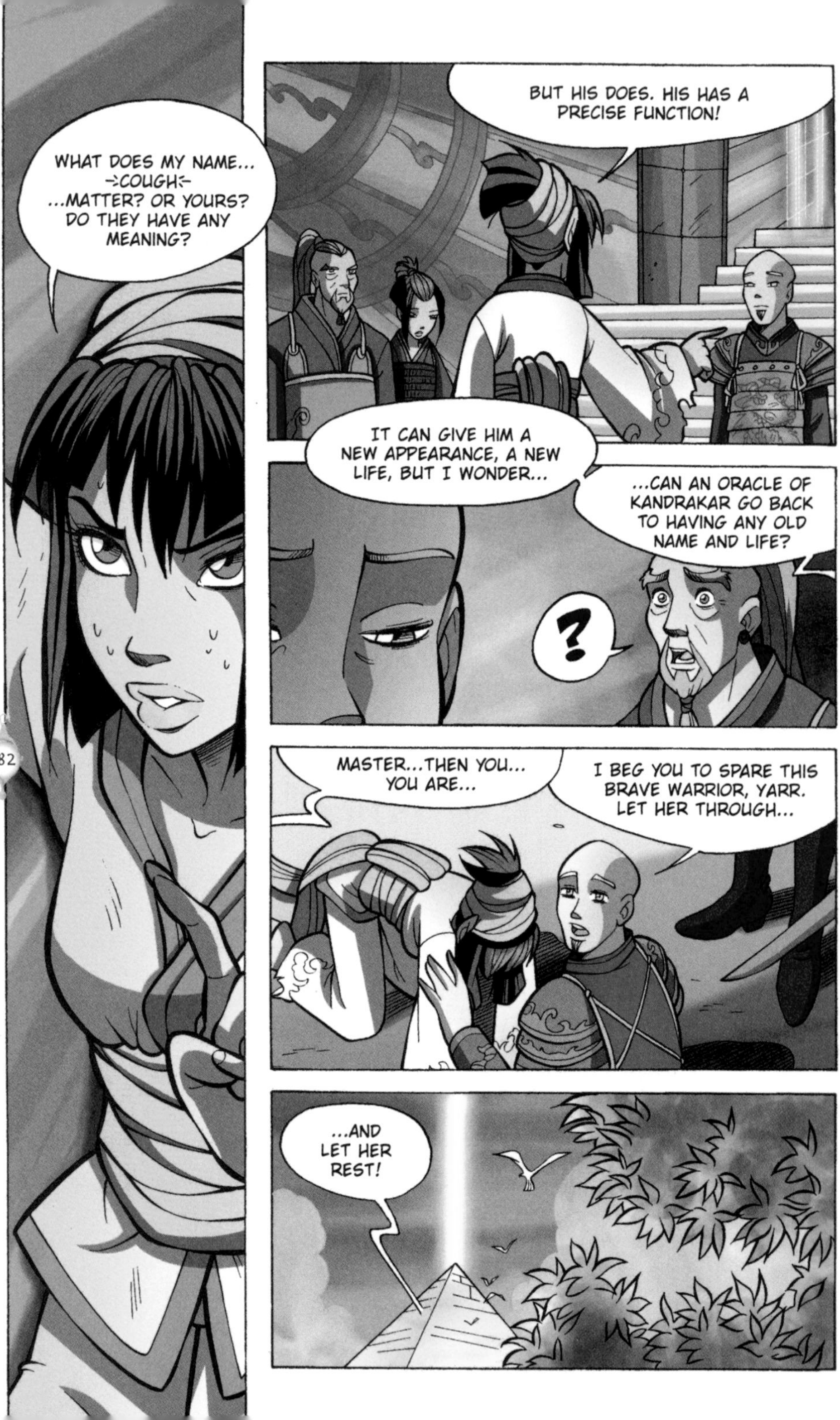
WHAT DOES MY NAME... ⇾COUGH⇽ ...MATTER? OR YOURS? DO THEY HAVE ANY MEANING?
BUT HIS DOES. HIS HAS A PRECISE FUNCTION!
IT CAN GIVE HIM A NEW APPEARANCE, A NEW LIFE, BUT I WONDER...
...CAN AN ORACLE OF KANDRAKAR GO BACK TO HAVING ANY OLD NAME AND LIFE?
?
MASTER...THEN YOU... YOU ARE...
I BEG YOU TO SPARE THIS BRAVE WARRIOR, YARR. LET HER THROUGH...
...AND LET HER REST!

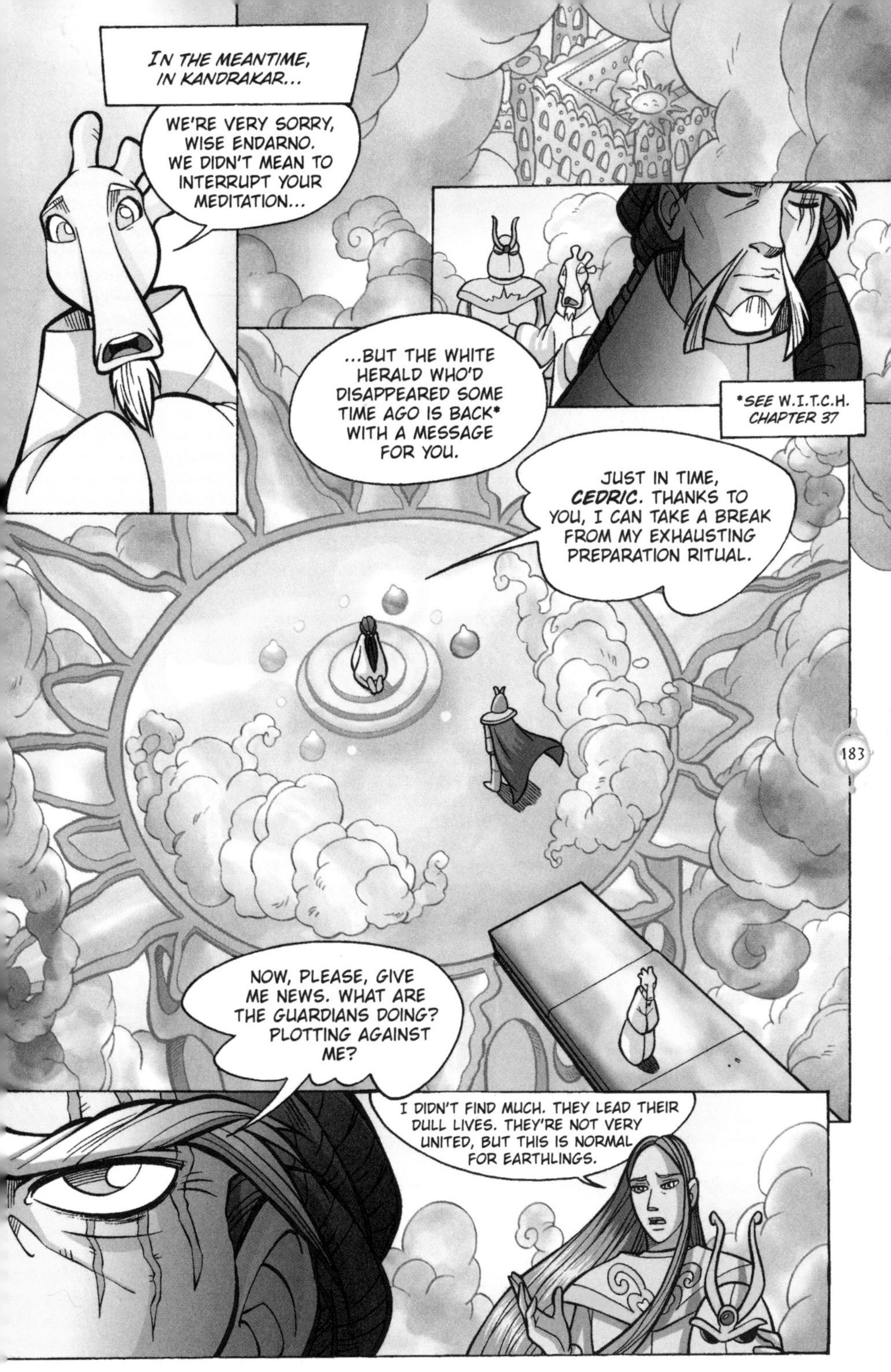
IN THE MEANTIME, IN KANDRAKAR...
WE'RE VERY SORRY, WISE ENDARNO. WE DIDN'T MEAN TO INTERRUPT YOUR MEDITATION...
...BUT THE WHITE HERALD WHO'D DISAPPEARED SOME TIME AGO IS BACK* WITH A MESSAGE FOR YOU.
*SEE W.I.T.C.H. CHAPTER 37
JUST IN TIME, CEDRIC. THANKS TO YOU, I CAN TAKE A BREAK FROM MY EXHAUSTING PREPARATION RITUAL.
NOW, PLEASE, GIVE ME NEWS. WHAT ARE THE GUARDIANS DOING? PLOTTING AGAINST ME?
I DIDN'T FIND MUCH. THEY LEAD THEIR DULL LIVES. THEY'RE NOT VERY UNITED, BUT THIS IS NORMAL FOR EARTHLINGS.

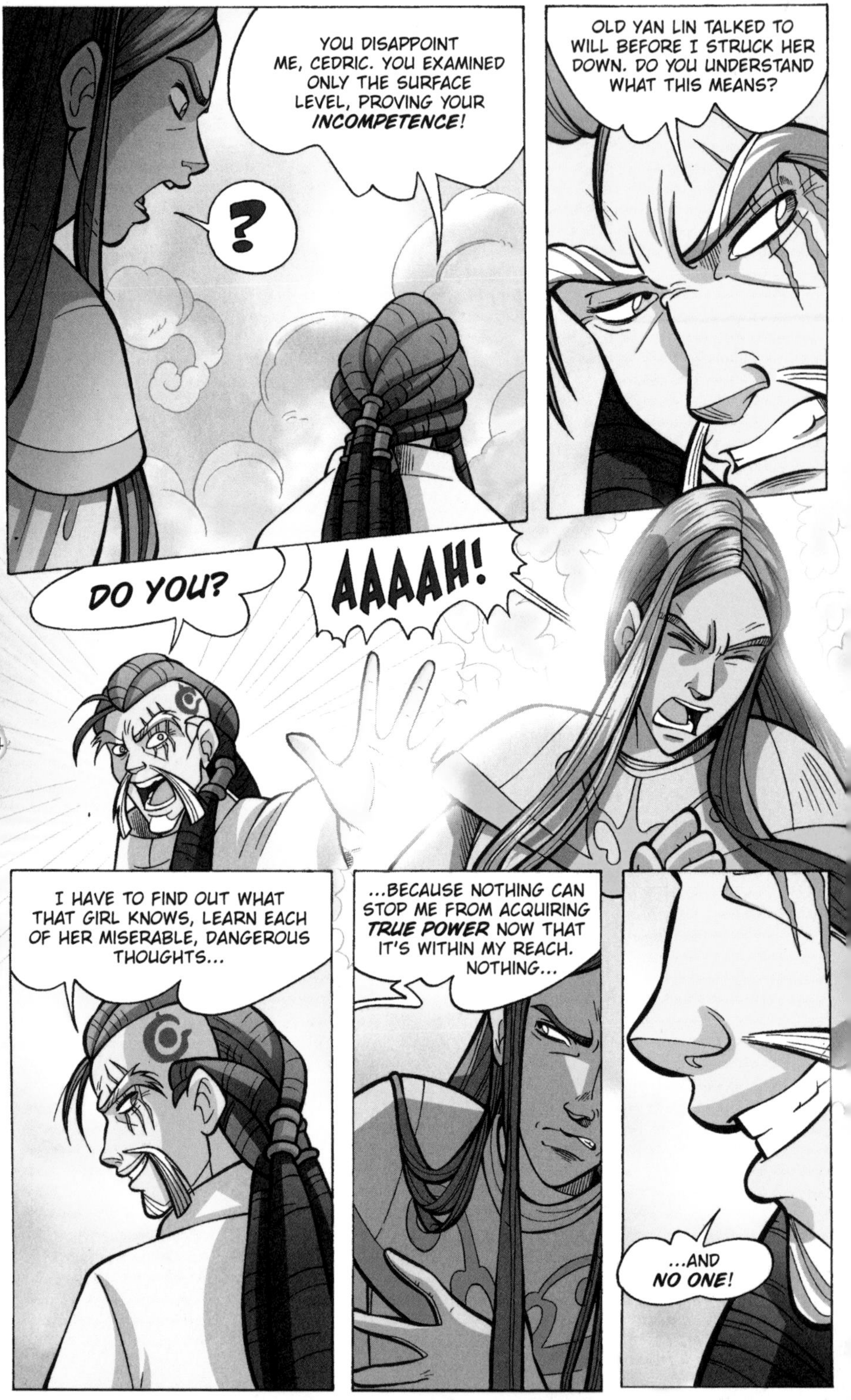
YOU DISAPPOINT ME, CEDRIC. YOU EXAMINED ONLY THE SURFACE LEVEL, PROVING YOUR INCOMPETENCE!
?
OLD YAN LIN TALKED TO WILL BEFORE I STRUCK HER DOWN. DO YOU UNDERSTAND WHAT THIS MEANS?
DO YOU?
AAAAH!
I HAVE TO FIND OUT WHAT THAT GIRL KNOWS, LEARN EACH OF HER MISERABLE, DANGEROUS THOUGHTS...
...BECAUSE NOTHING CAN STOP ME FROM ACQUIRING TRUE POWER NOW THAT IT'S WITHIN MY REACH. NOTHING...
...AND NO ONE!

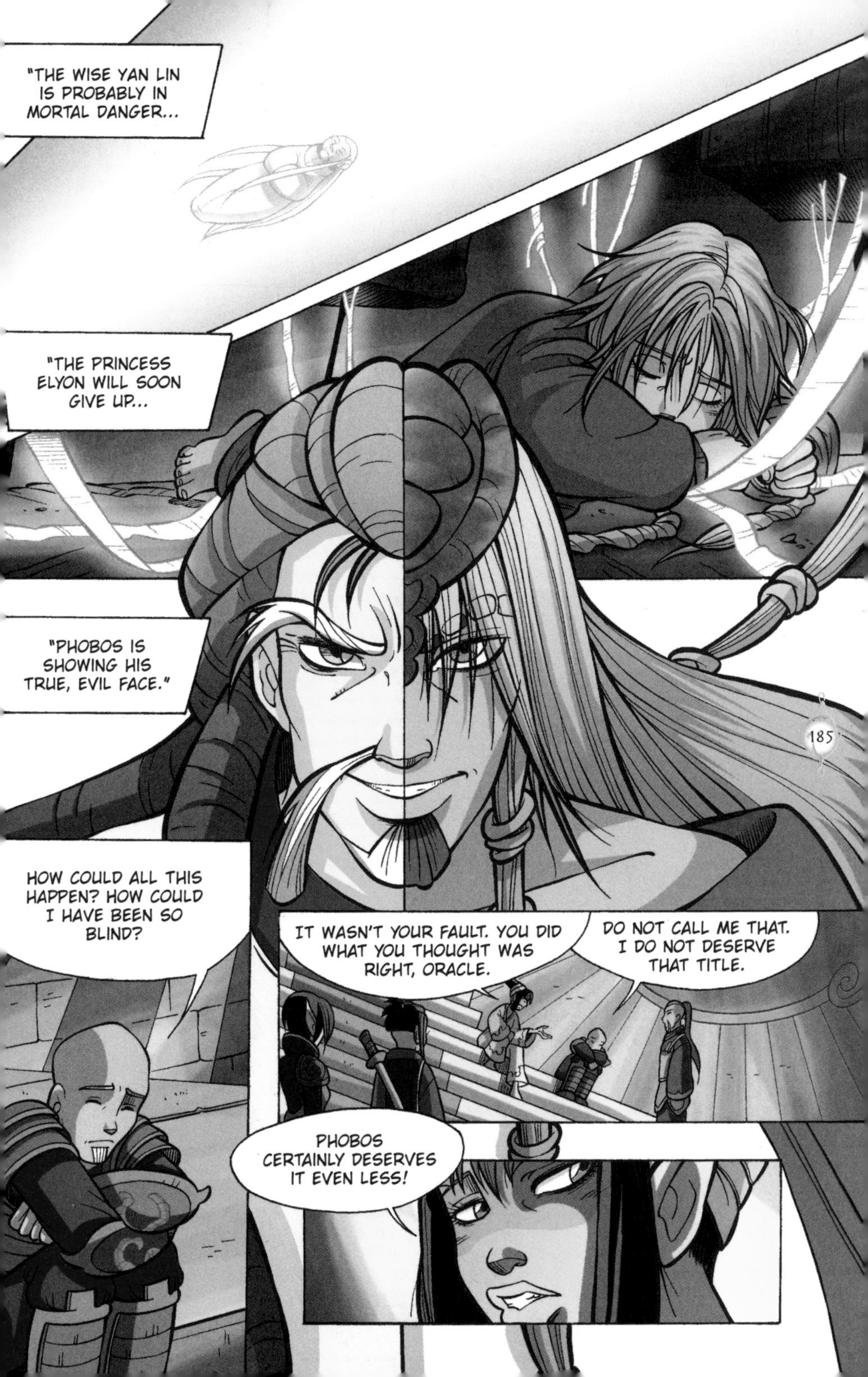
"THE WISE YAN LIN IS PROBABLY IN MORTAL DANGER...
"THE PRINCESS ELYON WILL SOON GIVE UP...
"PHOBOS IS SHOWING HIS TRUE, EVIL FACE."
HOW COULD ALL THIS HAPPEN? HOW COULD I HAVE BEEN SO BLIND?
IT WASN'T YOUR FAULT. YOU DID WHAT YOU THOUGHT WAS RIGHT, ORACLE.
DO NOT CALL ME THAT. I DO NOT DESERVE THAT TITLE.
PHOBOS CERTAINLY DESERVES IT EVEN LESS!

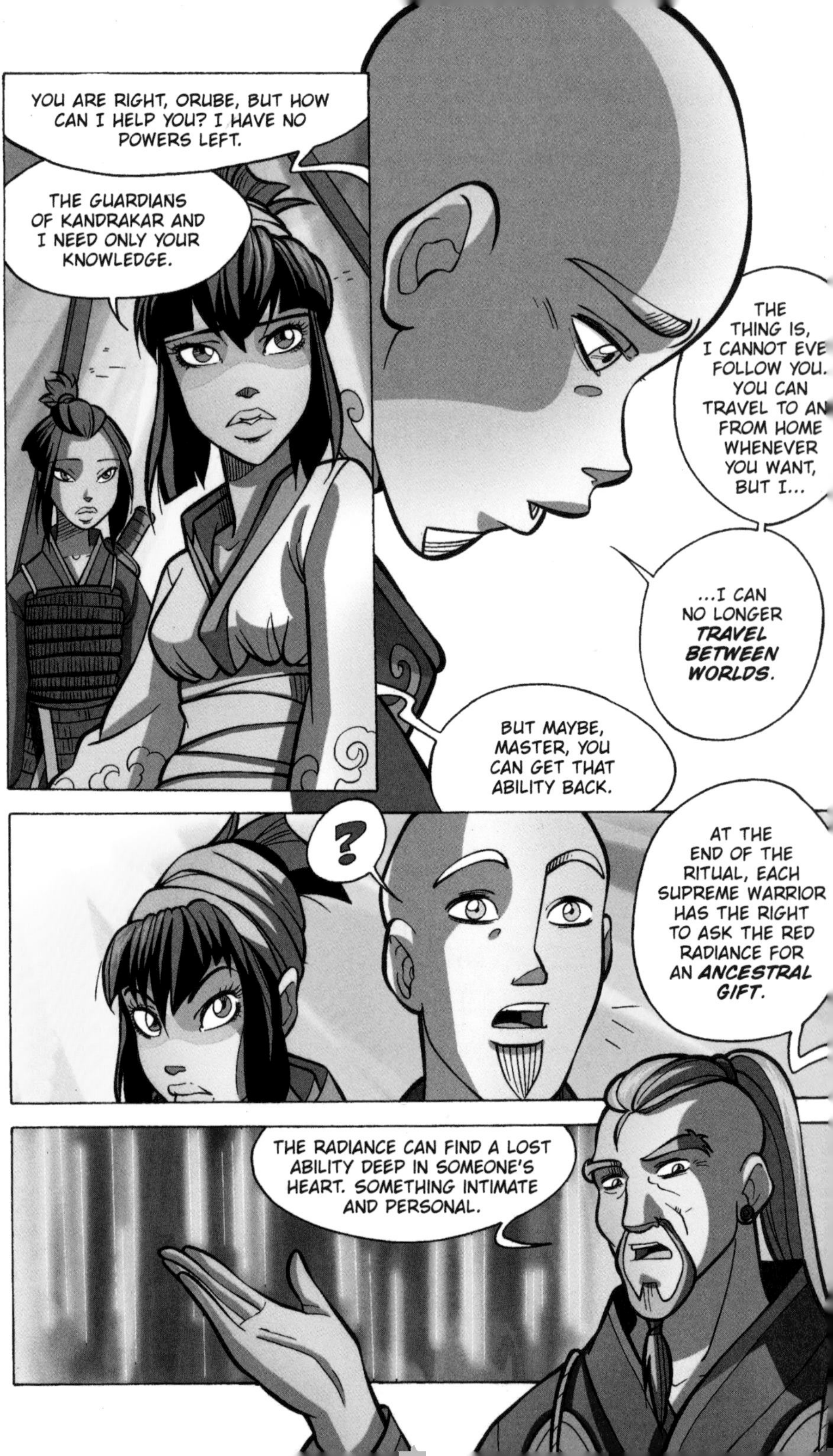
YOU ARE RIGHT, ORUBE, BUT HOW CAN I HELP YOU? I HAVE NO POWERS LEFT.
THE GUARDIANS OF KANDRAKAR AND I NEED ONLY YOUR KNOWLEDGE.
THE THING IS, I CANNOT EVE FOLLOW YOU. YOU CAN TRAVEL TO AN FROM HOME WHENEVER YOU WANT, BUT I...
...I CAN NO LONGER **TRAVEL BETWEEN WORLDS**.
BUT MAYBE, MASTER, YOU CAN GET THAT ABILITY BACK.
?
AT THE END OF THE RITUAL, EACH SUPREME WARRIOR HAS THE RIGHT TO ASK THE RED RADIANCE FOR AN **ANCESTRAL GIFT**.
THE RADIANCE CAN FIND A LOST ABILITY DEEP IN SOMEONE'S HEART. SOMETHING INTIMATE AND PERSONAL.

YES, YOU ARE RIGHT. NOW I UNDERSTAND. I CAN *SENSE* IT.

COME WITH ME, ORUBE. RIGHT NOW, TIME IS MORE VALUABLE THAN WORDS.

MASTER...

YARR?

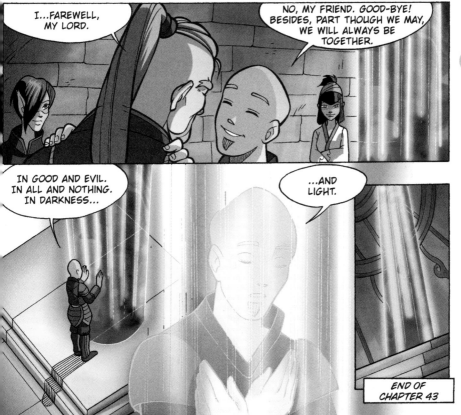

I...FAREWELL, MY LORD.

NO, MY FRIEND. GOOD-BYE! BESIDES, PART THOUGH WE MAY, WE WILL ALWAYS BE TOGETHER.

IN GOOD AND EVIL. IN ALL AND NOTHING. IN DARKNESS...

...AND LIGHT.

END OF CHAPTER 43

W.i.t.c.h.

Will Irma Taranee Cornelia Hay Lin

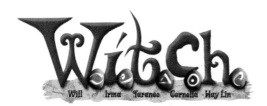

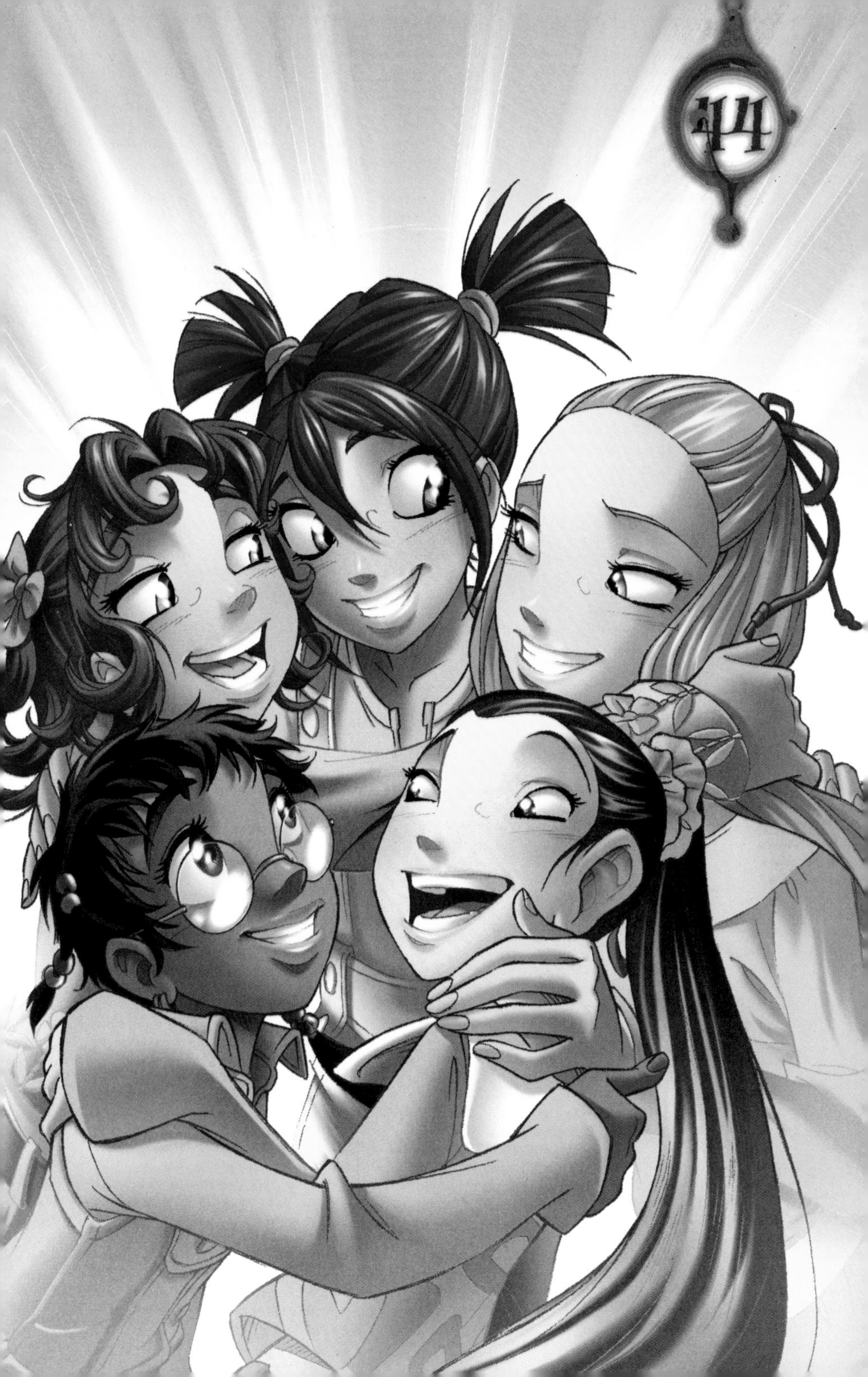
44

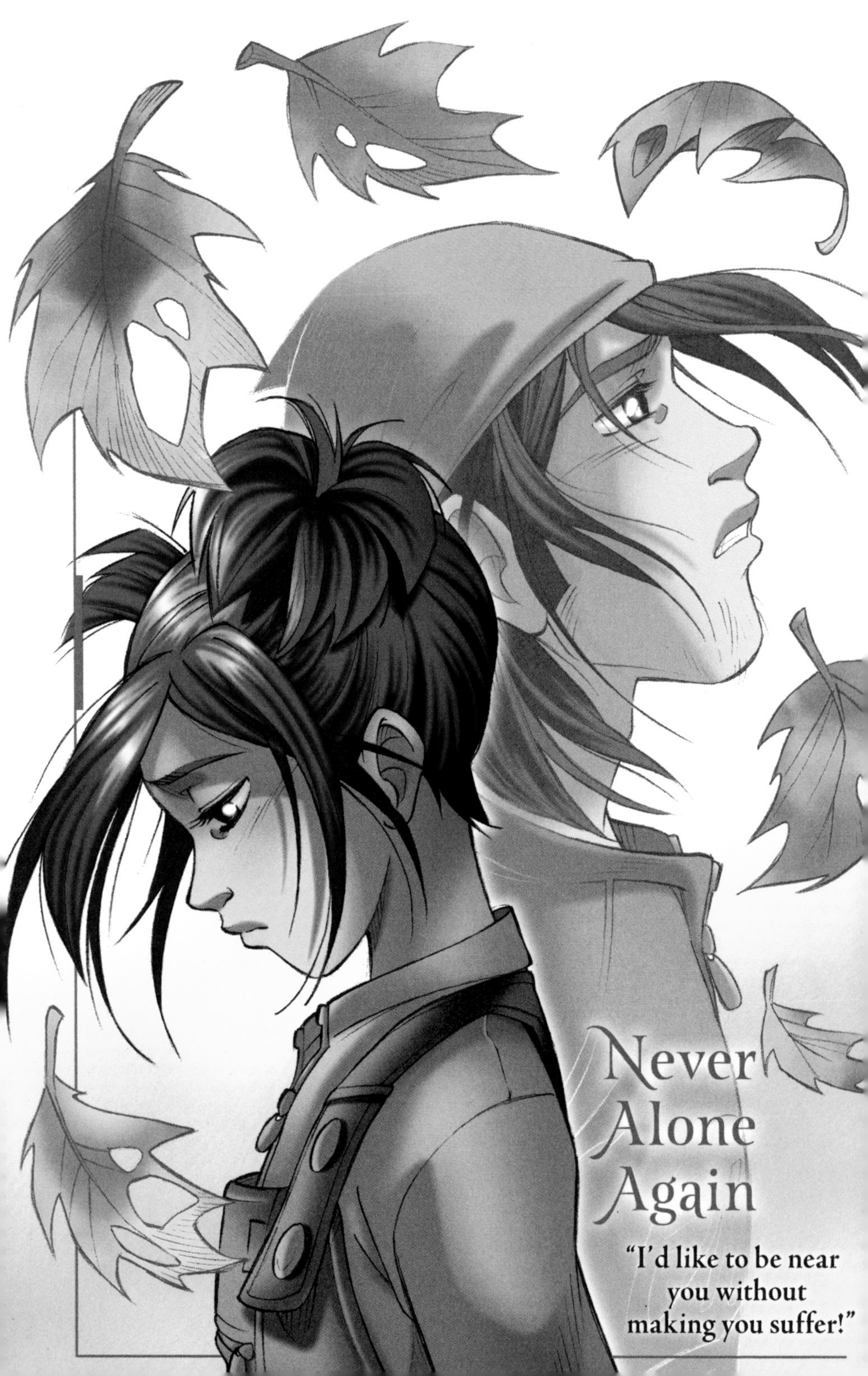
Never
Alone
Again
"I'd like to be near
you without
making you suffer!"

W.i.t.c.h.

Will Irma Taranee Cornelia Hay Lin

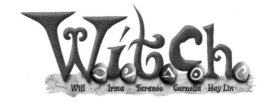

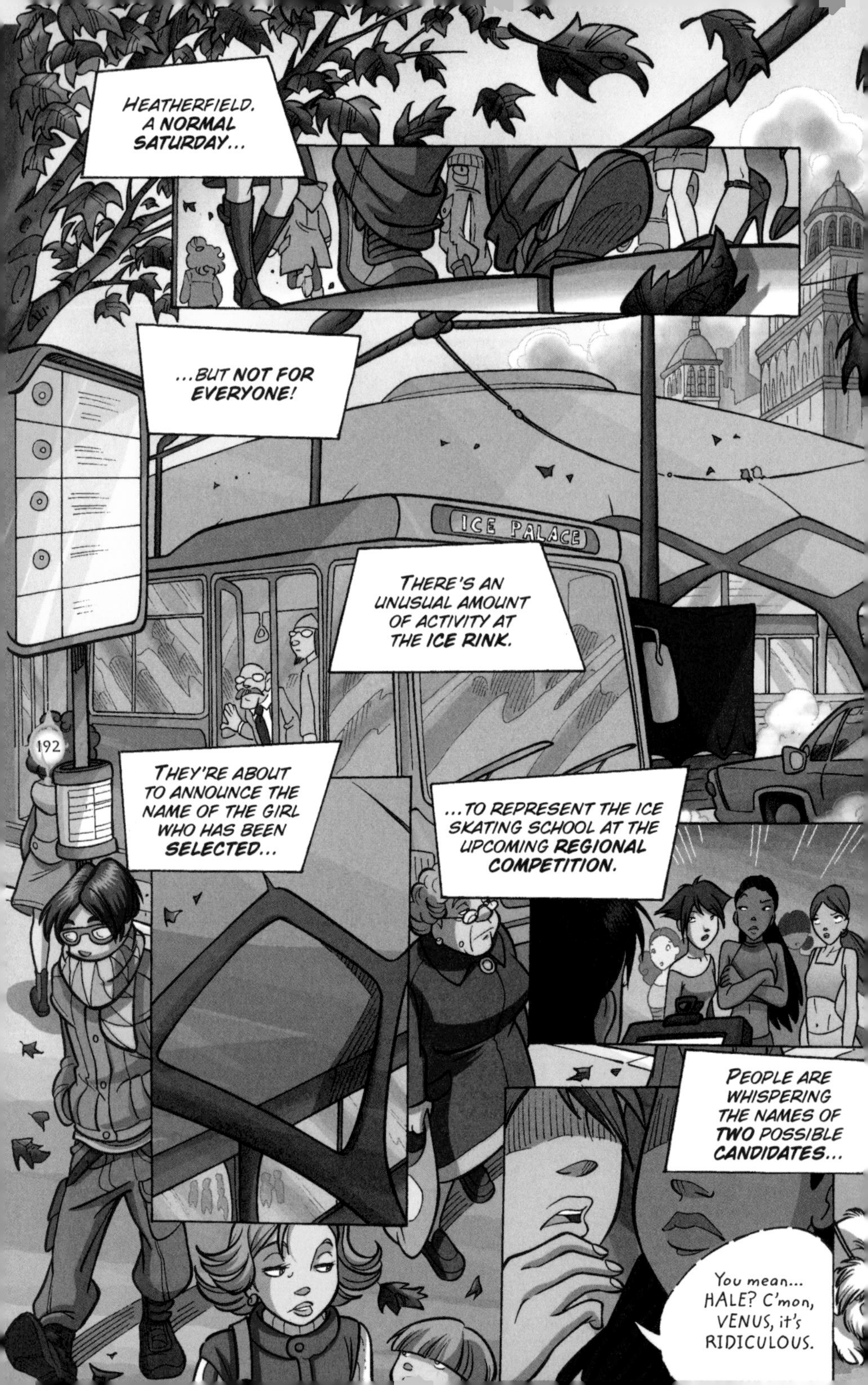

HEATHERFIELD. A NORMAL SATURDAY...
...BUT NOT FOR EVERYONE!
ICE PALACE
THERE'S AN UNUSUAL AMOUNT OF ACTIVITY AT THE ICE RINK.
THEY'RE ABOUT TO ANNOUNCE THE NAME OF THE GIRL WHO HAS BEEN SELECTED...
...TO REPRESENT THE ICE SKATING SCHOOL AT THE UPCOMING REGIONAL COMPETITION.
PEOPLE ARE WHISPERING THE NAMES OF TWO POSSIBLE CANDIDATES...
You mean... HALE? C'mon, VENUS, it's RIDICULOUS.

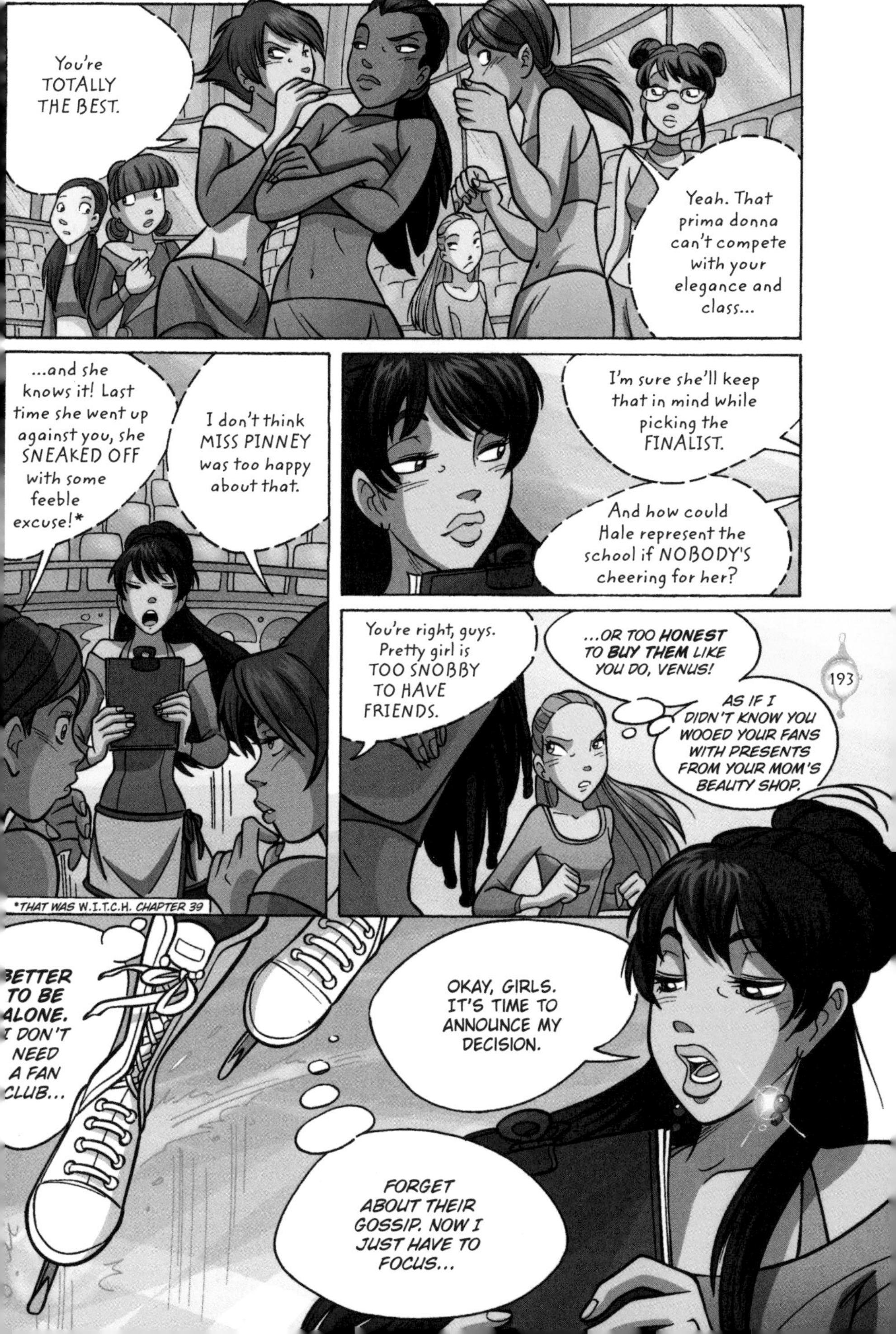

You're TOTALLY THE BEST.
Yeah. That prima donna can't compete with your elegance and class...
...and she knows it! Last time she went up against you, she SNEAKED OFF with some feeble excuse!*
I don't think MISS PINNEY was too happy about that.
I'm sure she'll keep that in mind while picking the FINALIST.
And how could Hale represent the school if NOBODY'S cheering for her?
*THAT WAS W.I.T.C.H. CHAPTER 39
You're right, guys. Pretty girl is TOO SNOBBY TO HAVE FRIENDS.
...OR TOO HONEST TO BUY THEM LIKE YOU DO, VENUS!
AS IF I DIDN'T KNOW YOU WOOED YOUR FANS WITH PRESENTS FROM YOUR MOM'S BEAUTY SHOP.
BETTER TO BE ALONE. I DON'T NEED A FAN CLUB...
OKAY, GIRLS. IT'S TIME TO ANNOUNCE MY DECISION.
FORGET ABOUT THEIR GOSSIP. NOW I JUST HAVE TO FOCUS...

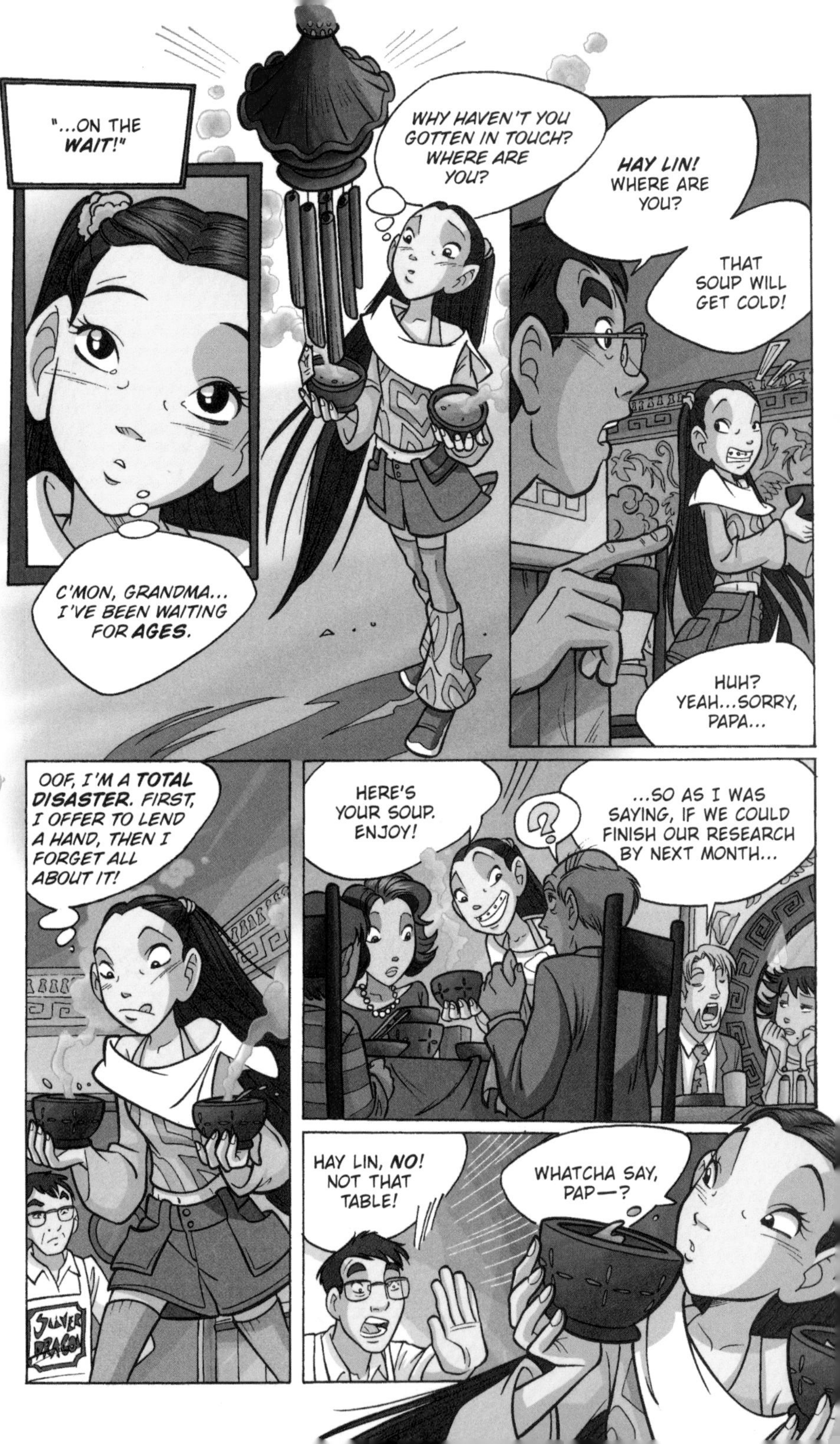
"...ON THE WAIT!"
WHY HAVEN'T YOU GOTTEN IN TOUCH? WHERE ARE YOU?
HAY LIN! WHERE ARE YOU?
THAT SOUP WILL GET COLD!
C'MON, GRANDMA... I'VE BEEN WAITING FOR AGES.
HUH? YEAH...SORRY, PAPA...
OOF, I'M A TOTAL DISASTER. FIRST, I OFFER TO LEND A HAND, THEN I FORGET ALL ABOUT IT!
HERE'S YOUR SOUP. ENJOY!
...SO AS I WAS SAYING, IF WE COULD FINISH OUR RESEARCH BY NEXT MONTH...
SILVER DRAGON
HAY LIN, NO! NOT THAT TABLE!
WHATCHA SAY, PAP—?

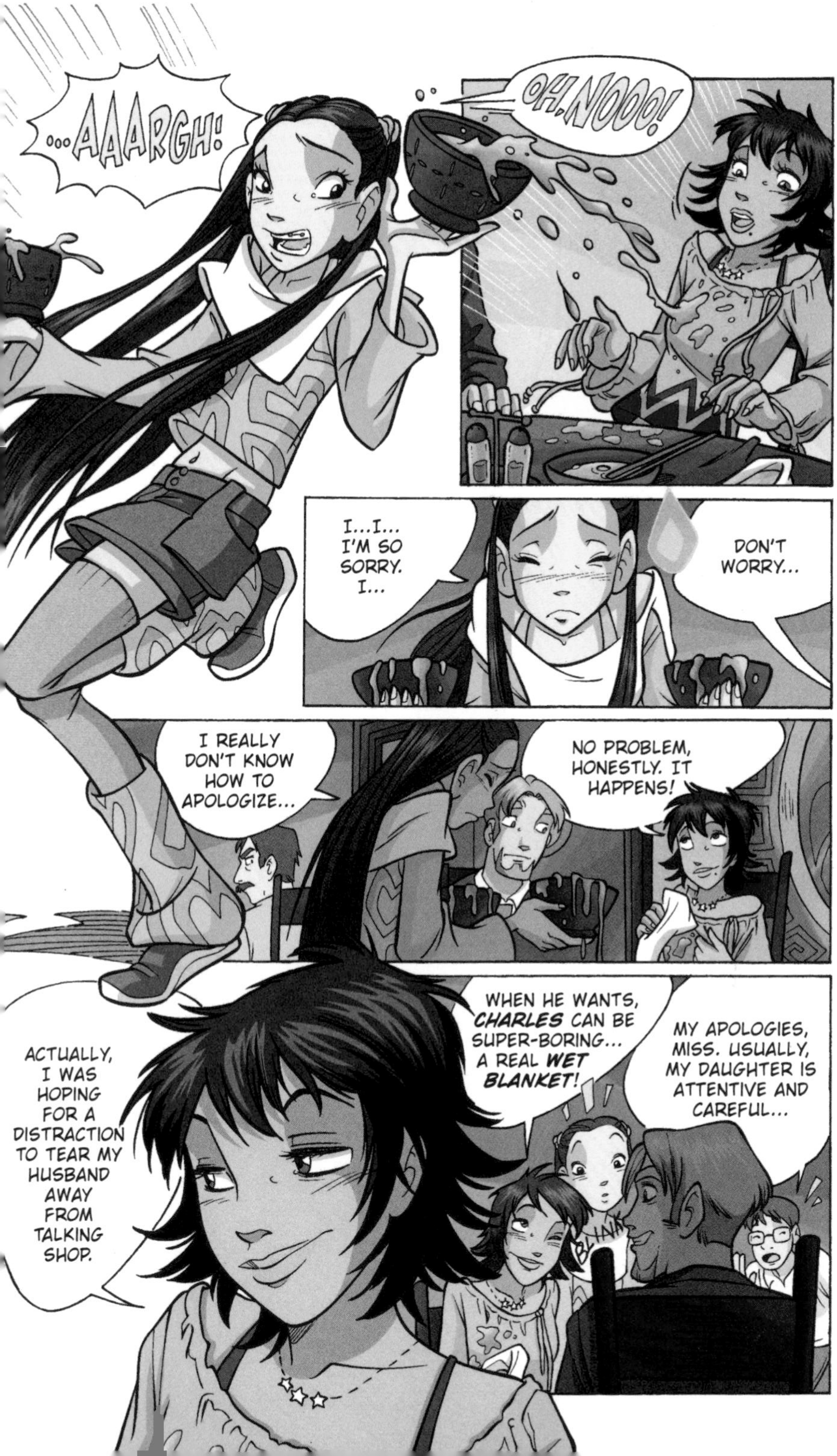

...AAARGH!
OH, NOOO!
I...I... I'M SO SORRY. I...
DON'T WORRY...
I REALLY DON'T KNOW HOW TO APOLOGIZE...
NO PROBLEM, HONESTLY. IT HAPPENS!
ACTUALLY, I WAS HOPING FOR A DISTRACTION TO TEAR MY HUSBAND AWAY FROM TALKING SHOP.
WHEN HE WANTS, CHARLES CAN BE SUPER-BORING... A REAL WET BLANKET!
MY APOLOGIES, MISS. USUALLY, MY DAUGHTER IS ATTENTIVE AND CAREFUL...
BLINK

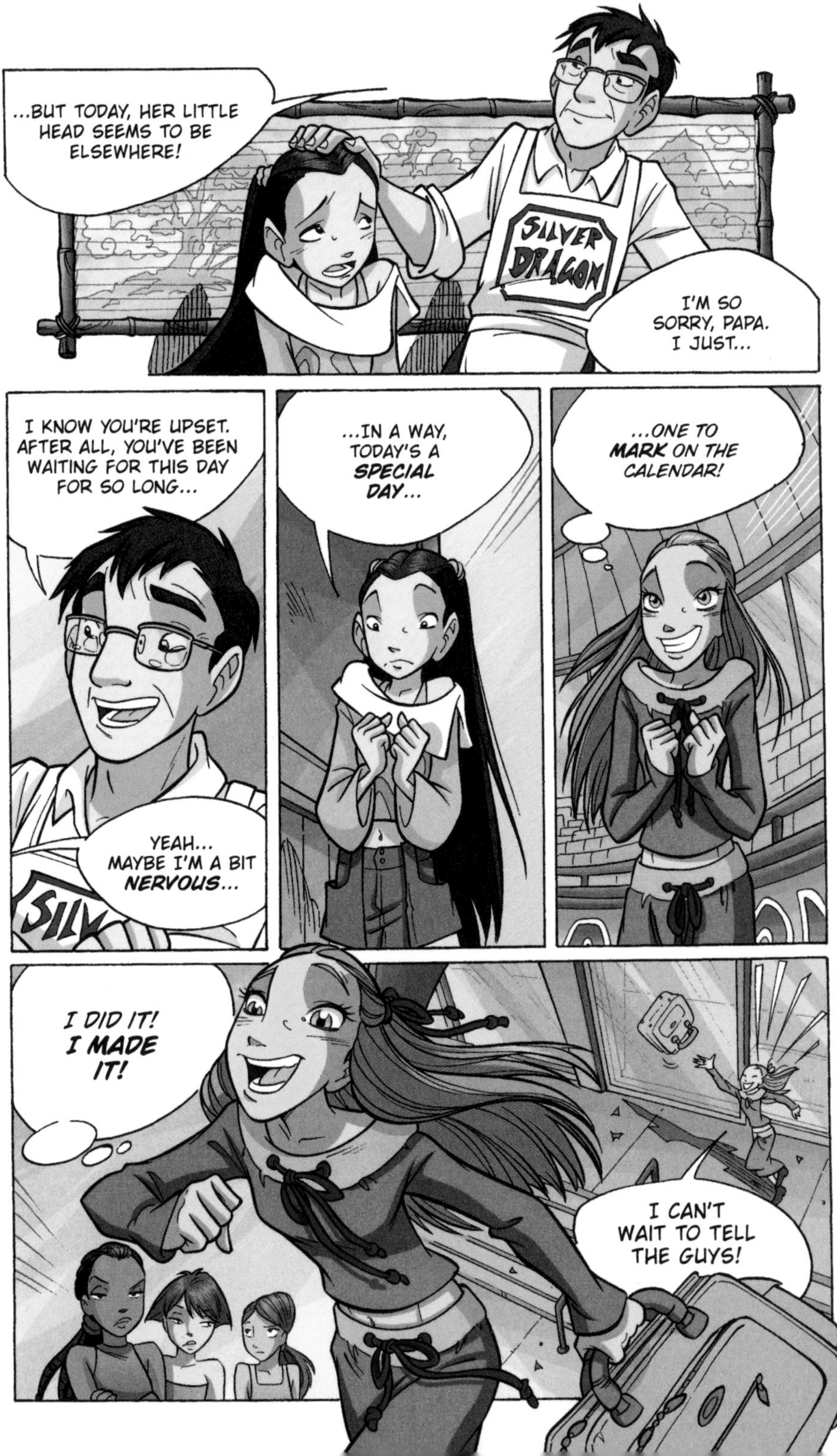
...BUT TODAY, HER LITTLE HEAD SEEMS TO BE ELSEWHERE!
SILVER DRAGON
I'M SO SORRY, PAPA. I JUST...
I KNOW YOU'RE UPSET. AFTER ALL, YOU'VE BEEN WAITING FOR THIS DAY FOR SO LONG...
YEAH... MAYBE I'M A BIT NERVOUS...
...IN A WAY, TODAY'S A SPECIAL DAY...
...ONE TO MARK ON THE CALENDAR!
I DID IT! I MADE IT!
I CAN'T WAIT TO TELL THE GUYS!

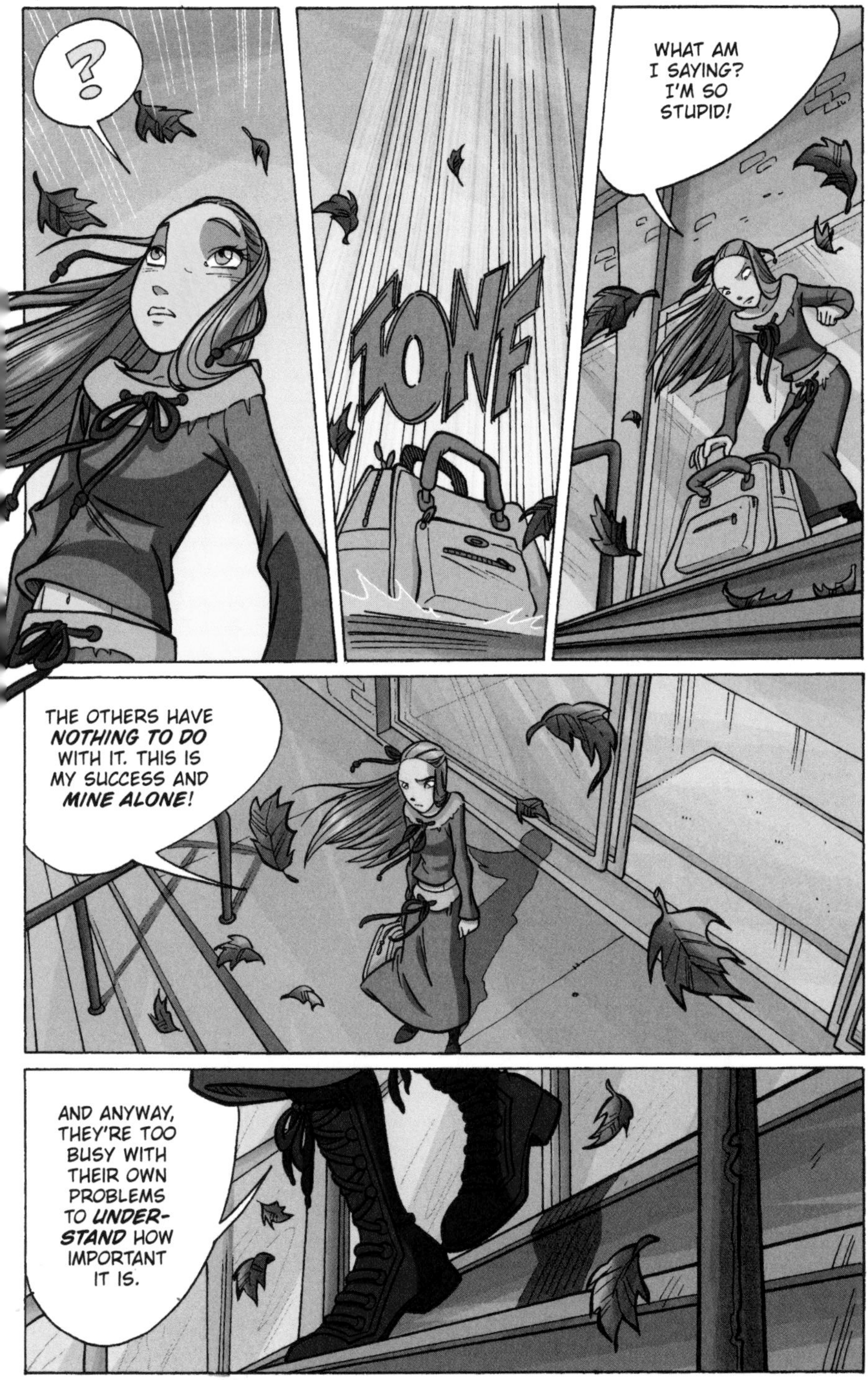
?
TONF
WHAT AM I SAYING? I'M SO STUPID!
THE OTHERS HAVE NOTHING TO DO WITH IT. THIS IS MY SUCCESS AND MINE ALONE!
AND ANYWAY, THEY'RE TOO BUSY WITH THEIR OWN PROBLEMS TO UNDERSTAND HOW IMPORTANT IT IS.

YEAH...**PROBLEMS.** ONCE, I WOULDN'T HAVE THOUGHT ABOUT IT...I'D HAVE RUSHED OFF TO **SHARE THIS MOMENT** WITH THE GUYS...

"...BUT TODAY IS DIFFERENT. **SOMETHING'S BLOCKING ME...**"

"...SOME KIND OF **INVISIBLE BARRIER...** I CAN'T OPEN UP TO THEM ANYMORE."

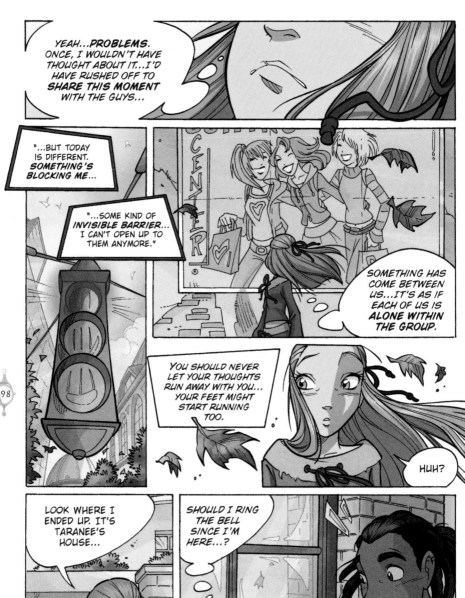

SOMETHING HAS COME BETWEEN US...IT'S AS IF EACH OF US IS **ALONE WITHIN THE GROUP.**

YOU SHOULD NEVER LET YOUR THOUGHTS RUN AWAY WITH YOU... YOUR FEET MIGHT START RUNNING TOO.

HUH?

LOOK WHERE I ENDED UP. IT'S TARANEE'S HOUSE...

SHOULD I RING THE BELL SINCE I'M HERE...?

HEY... THAT'S CORNELIA!

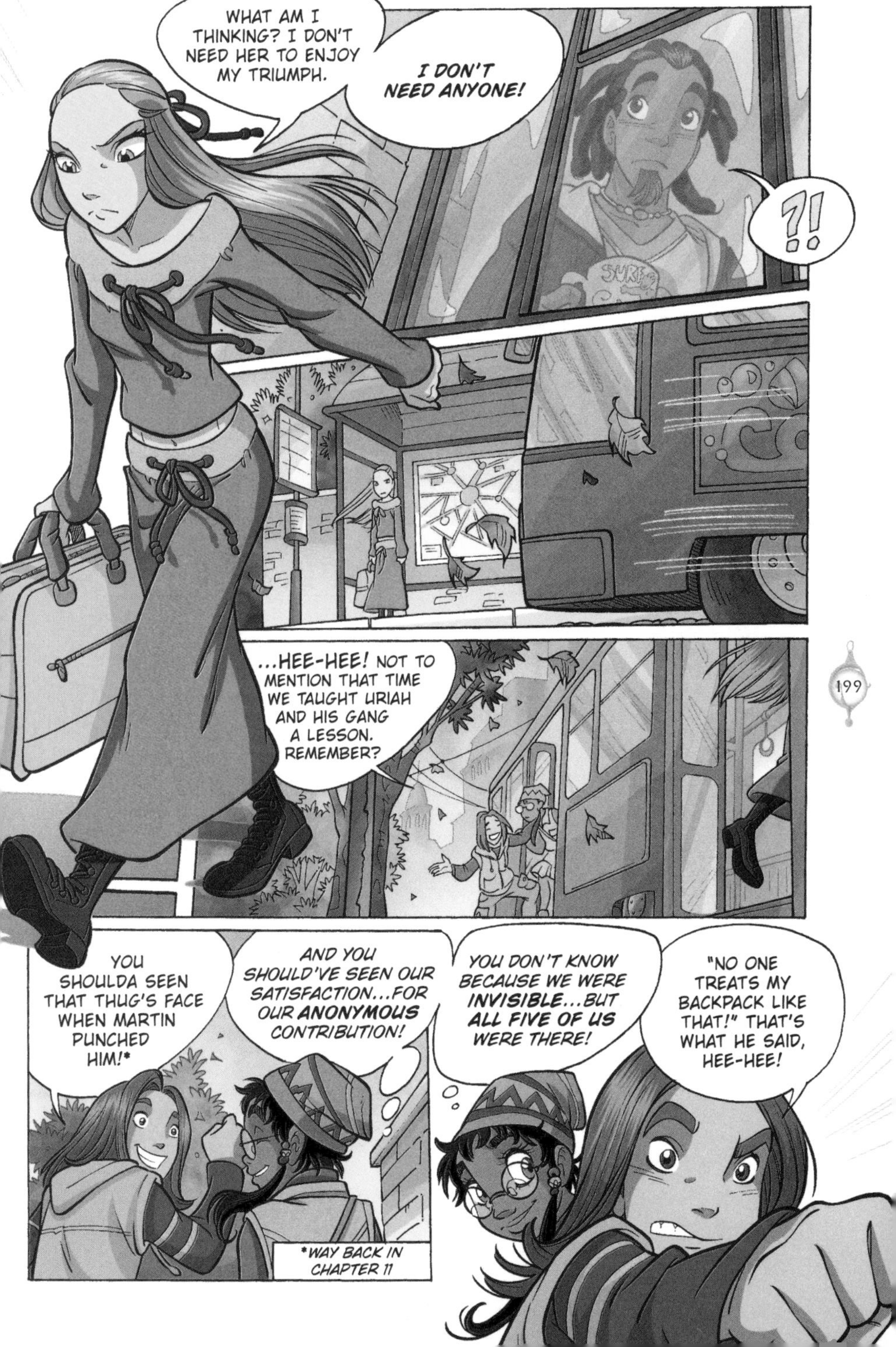
WHAT AM I THINKING? I DON'T NEED HER TO ENJOY MY TRIUMPH.
I DON'T NEED ANYONE!
?!
...HEE-HEE! NOT TO MENTION THAT TIME WE TAUGHT URIAH AND HIS GANG A LESSON. REMEMBER?
YOU SHOULDA SEEN THAT THUG'S FACE WHEN MARTIN PUNCHED HIM!*
AND YOU SHOULD'VE SEEN OUR SATISFACTION...FOR OUR ANONYMOUS CONTRIBUTION!
*WAY BACK IN CHAPTER 11
YOU DON'T KNOW BECAUSE WE WERE INVISIBLE...BUT ALL FIVE OF US WERE THERE!
"NO ONE TREATS MY BACKPACK LIKE THAT!" THAT'S WHAT HE SAID, HEE-HEE!

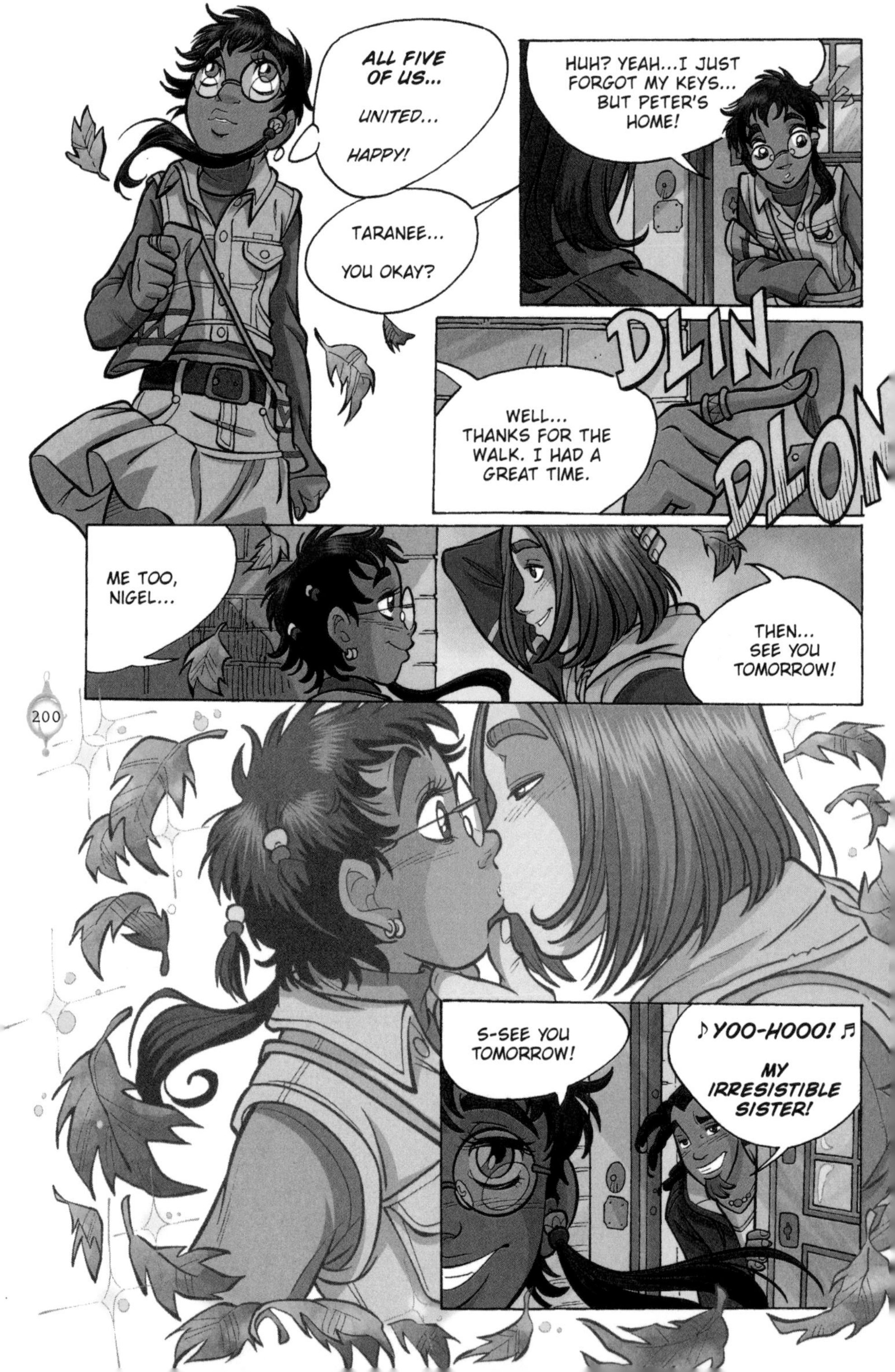
ALL FIVE OF US...
UNITED...
HAPPY!
TARANEE...
YOU OKAY?
HUH? YEAH...I JUST FORGOT MY KEYS... BUT PETER'S HOME!
DLIN
WELL... THANKS FOR THE WALK. I HAD A GREAT TIME.
DLON
ME TOO, NIGEL...
THEN... SEE YOU TOMORROW!
S-SEE YOU TOMORROW!
♪ YOO-HOOO! ♫
MY IRRESISTIBLE SISTER!

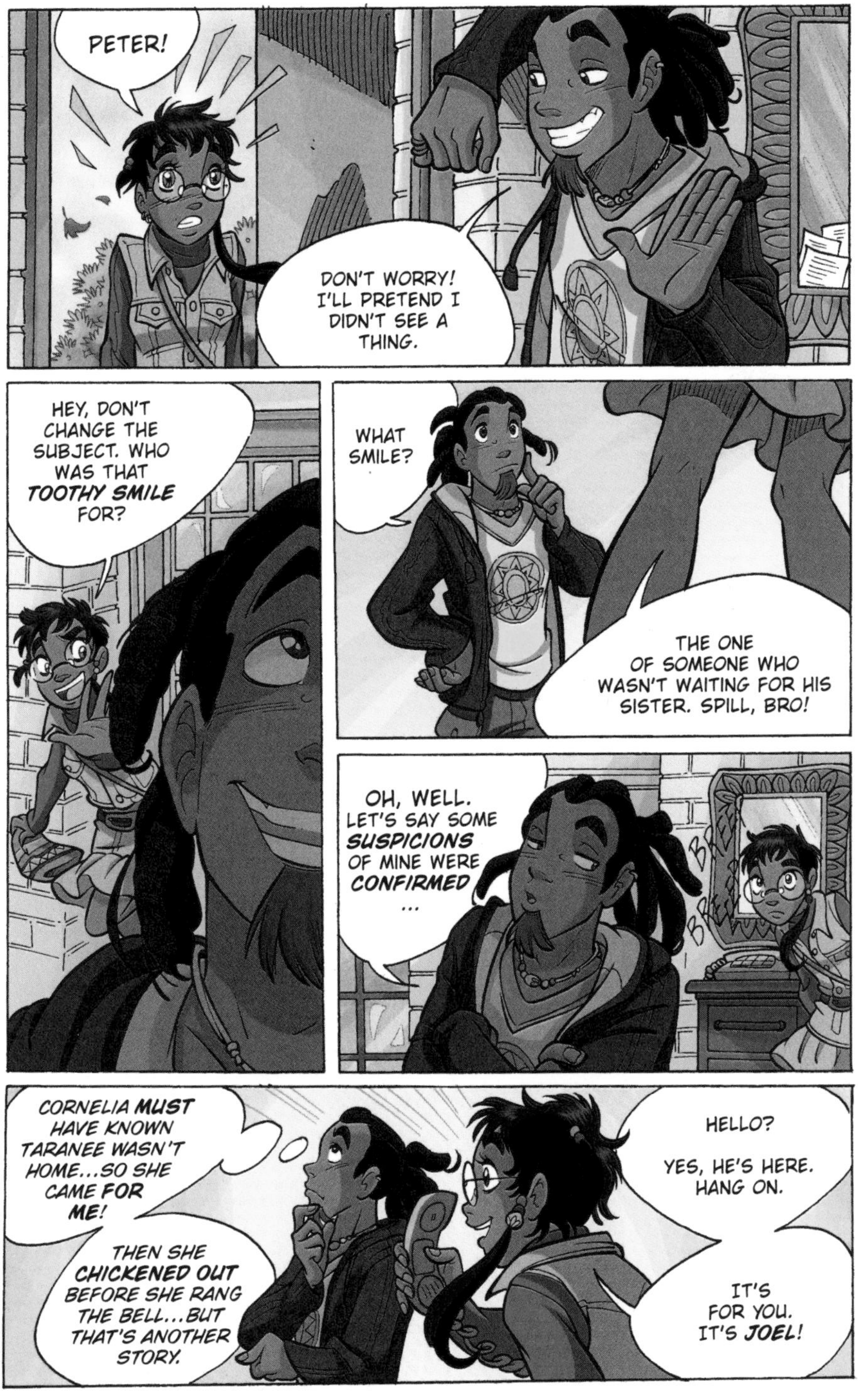
PETER!
DON'T WORRY! I'LL PRETEND I DIDN'T SEE A THING.
HEY, DON'T CHANGE THE SUBJECT. WHO WAS THAT TOOTHY SMILE FOR?
WHAT SMILE?
THE ONE OF SOMEONE WHO WASN'T WAITING FOR HIS SISTER. SPILL, BRO!
OH, WELL. LET'S SAY SOME SUSPICIONS OF MINE WERE CONFIRMED ...
BREEE
CORNELIA MUST HAVE KNOWN TARANEE WASN'T HOME...SO SHE CAME FOR ME!
THEN SHE CHICKENED OUT BEFORE SHE RANG THE BELL...BUT THAT'S ANOTHER STORY.
HELLO?
YES, HE'S HERE. HANG ON.
IT'S FOR YOU. IT'S JOEL!

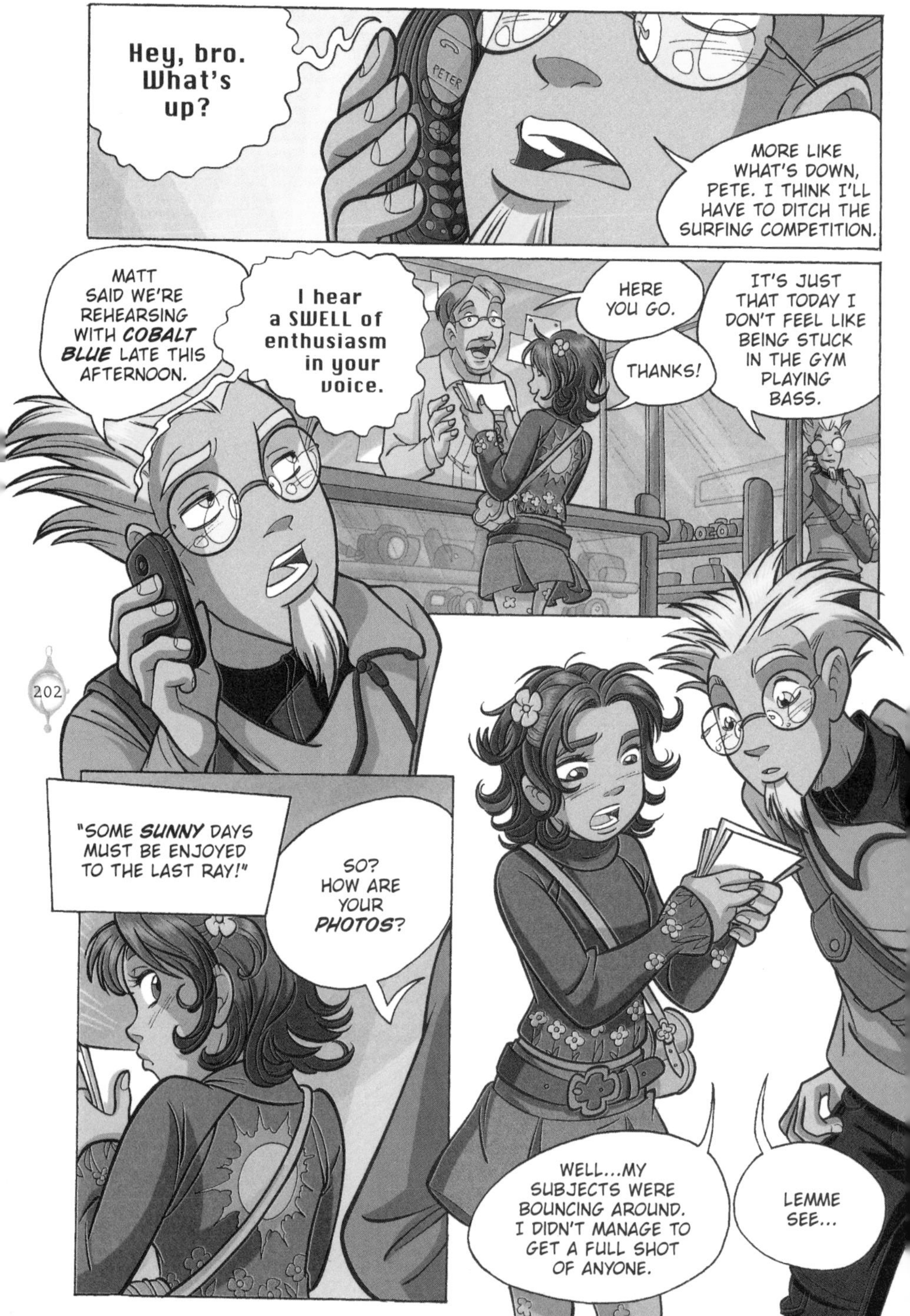

Hey, bro. What's up?
MORE LIKE WHAT'S DOWN, PETE. I THINK I'LL HAVE TO DITCH THE SURFING COMPETITION.
PETER
MATT SAID WE'RE REHEARSING WITH COBALT BLUE LATE THIS AFTERNOON.
I hear a SWELL of enthusiasm in your voice.
HERE YOU GO.
THANKS!
IT'S JUST THAT TODAY I DON'T FEEL LIKE BEING STUCK IN THE GYM PLAYING BASS.
"SOME SUNNY DAYS MUST BE ENJOYED TO THE LAST RAY!"
SO? HOW ARE YOUR PHOTOS?
WELL...MY SUBJECTS WERE BOUNCING AROUND. I DIDN'T MANAGE TO GET A FULL SHOT OF ANYONE.
LEMME SEE...

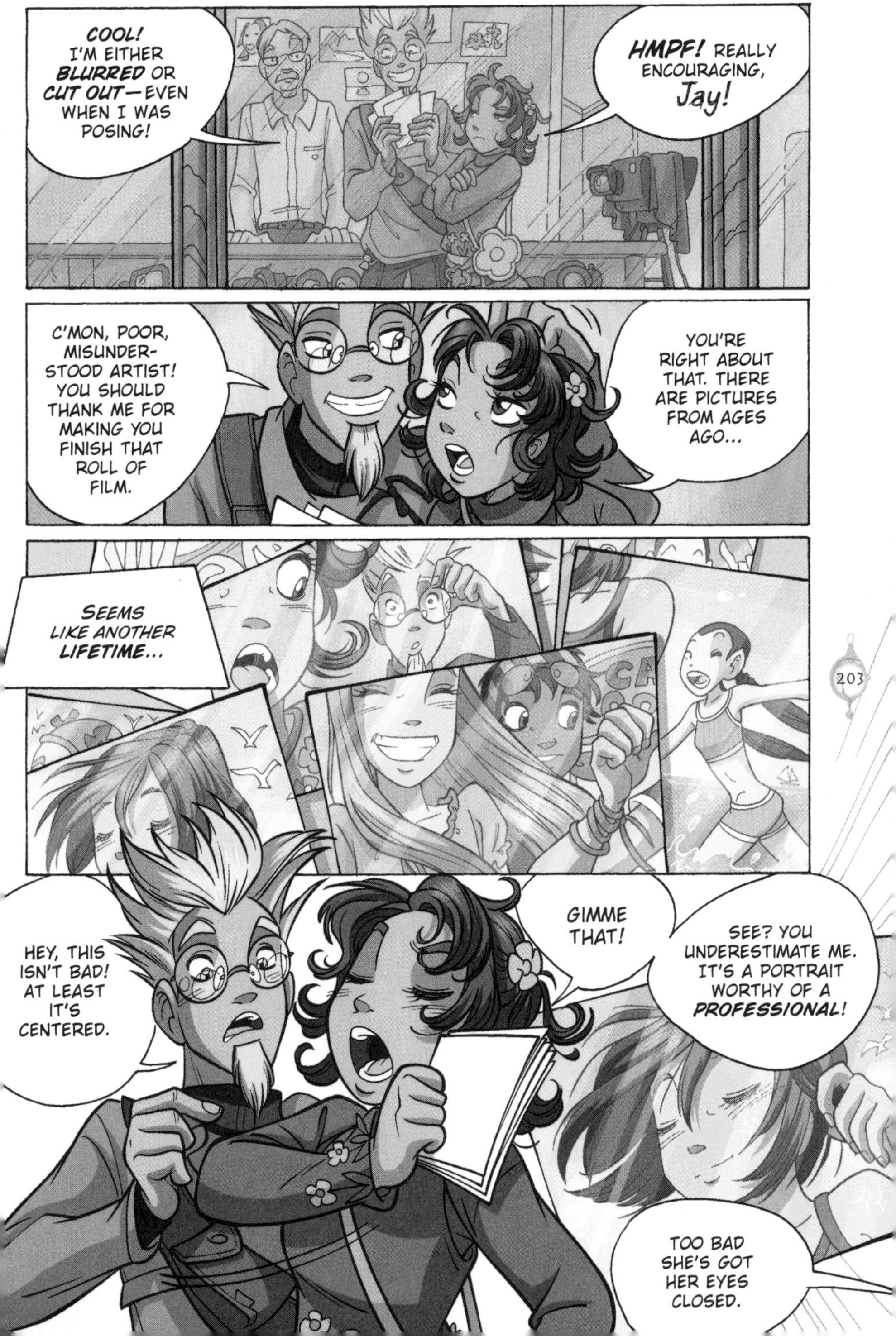
COOL! I'M EITHER BLURRED OR CUT OUT—EVEN WHEN I WAS POSING!
HMPF! REALLY ENCOURAGING, Jay!
C'MON, POOR, MISUNDER-STOOD ARTIST! YOU SHOULD THANK ME FOR MAKING YOU FINISH THAT ROLL OF FILM.
YOU'RE RIGHT ABOUT THAT. THERE ARE PICTURES FROM AGES AGO...
SEEMS LIKE ANOTHER LIFETIME...
HEY, THIS ISN'T BAD! AT LEAST IT'S CENTERED.
GIMME THAT!
SEE? YOU UNDERESTIMATE ME. IT'S A PORTRAIT WORTHY OF A PROFESSIONAL!
TOO BAD SHE'S GOT HER EYES CLOSED.

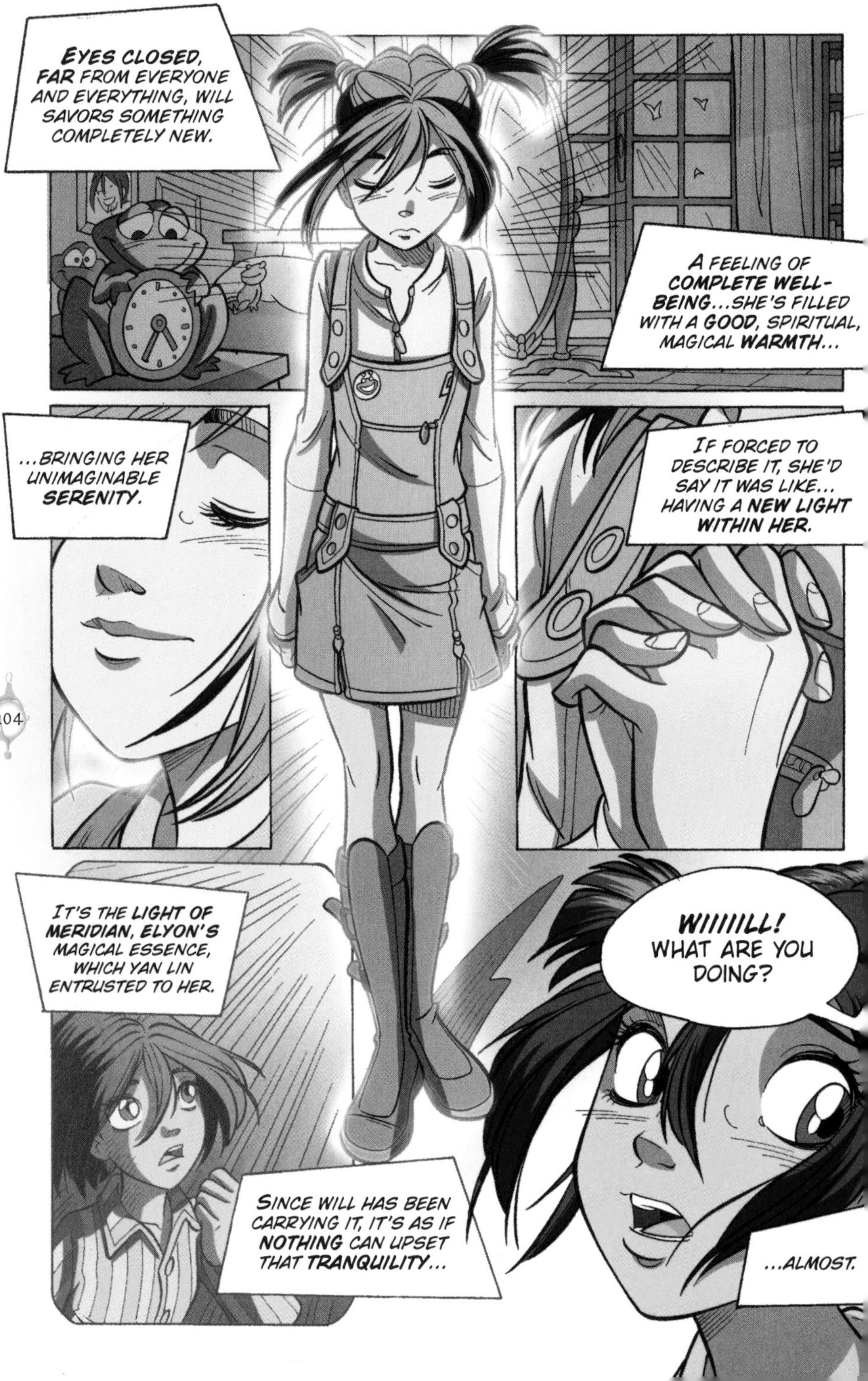
EYES CLOSED, FAR FROM EVERYONE AND EVERYTHING, WILL SAVORS SOMETHING COMPLETELY NEW.
A FEELING OF COMPLETE WELL-BEING...SHE'S FILLED WITH A GOOD, SPIRITUAL, MAGICAL WARMTH...
...BRINGING HER UNIMAGINABLE SERENITY.
IF FORCED TO DESCRIBE IT, SHE'D SAY IT WAS LIKE... HAVING A NEW LIGHT WITHIN HER.
IT'S THE LIGHT OF MERIDIAN, ELYON'S MAGICAL ESSENCE, WHICH YAN LIN ENTRUSTED TO HER.
WIIIIILL! WHAT ARE YOU DOING?
SINCE WILL HAS BEEN CARRYING IT, IT'S AS IF NOTHING CAN UPSET THAT TRANQUILITY...
...ALMOST.

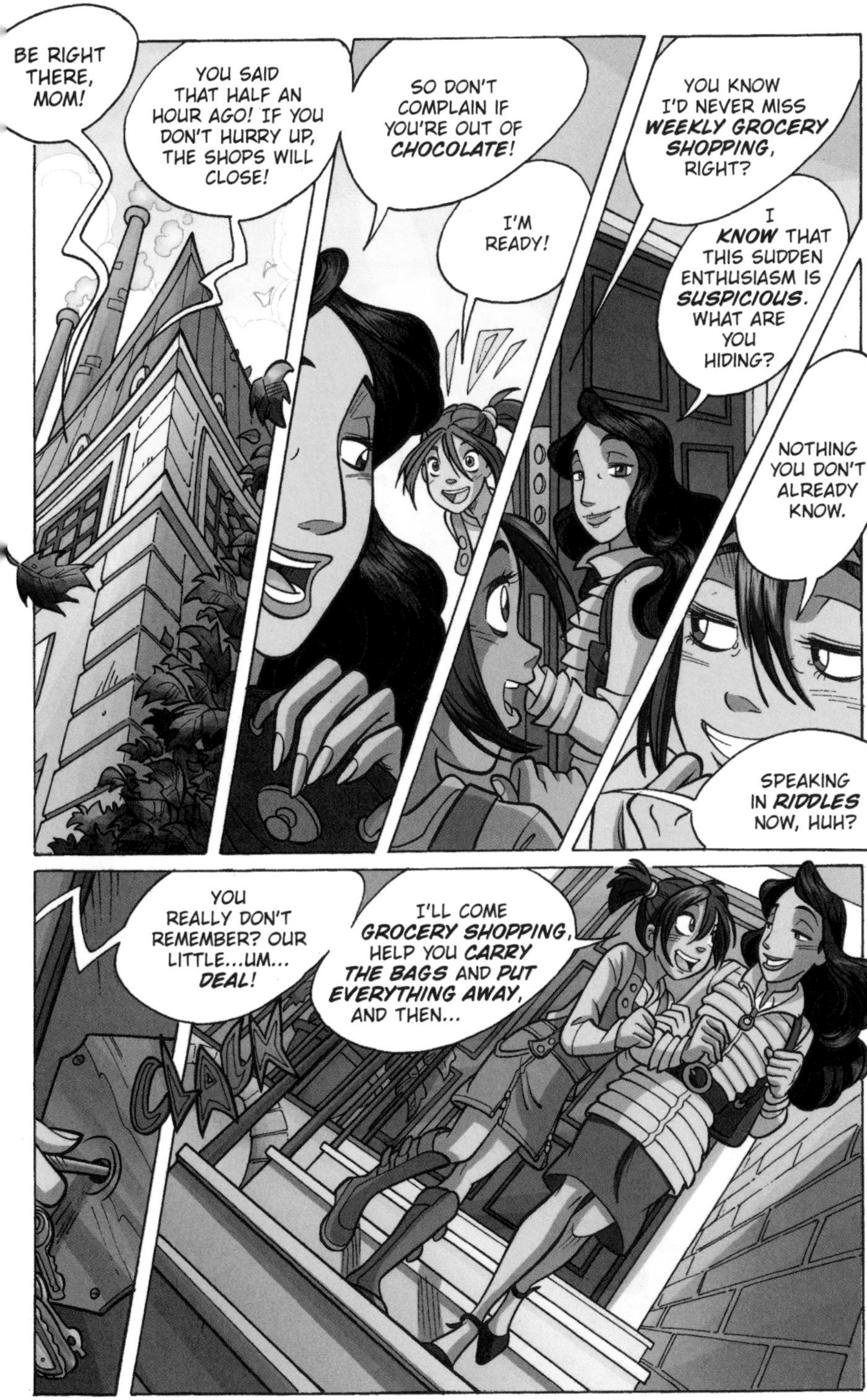

BE RIGHT THERE, MOM!
YOU SAID THAT HALF AN HOUR AGO! IF YOU DON'T HURRY UP, THE SHOPS WILL CLOSE!
SO DON'T COMPLAIN IF YOU'RE OUT OF CHOCOLATE!
I'M READY!
YOU KNOW I'D NEVER MISS WEEKLY GROCERY SHOPPING, RIGHT?
I KNOW THAT THIS SUDDEN ENTHUSIASM IS SUSPICIOUS. WHAT ARE YOU HIDING?
NOTHING YOU DON'T ALREADY KNOW.
SPEAKING IN RIDDLES NOW, HUH?
YOU REALLY DON'T REMEMBER? OUR LITTLE...UM... DEAL!
I'LL COME GROCERY SHOPPING, HELP YOU CARRY THE BAGS AND PUT EVERYTHING AWAY, AND THEN...

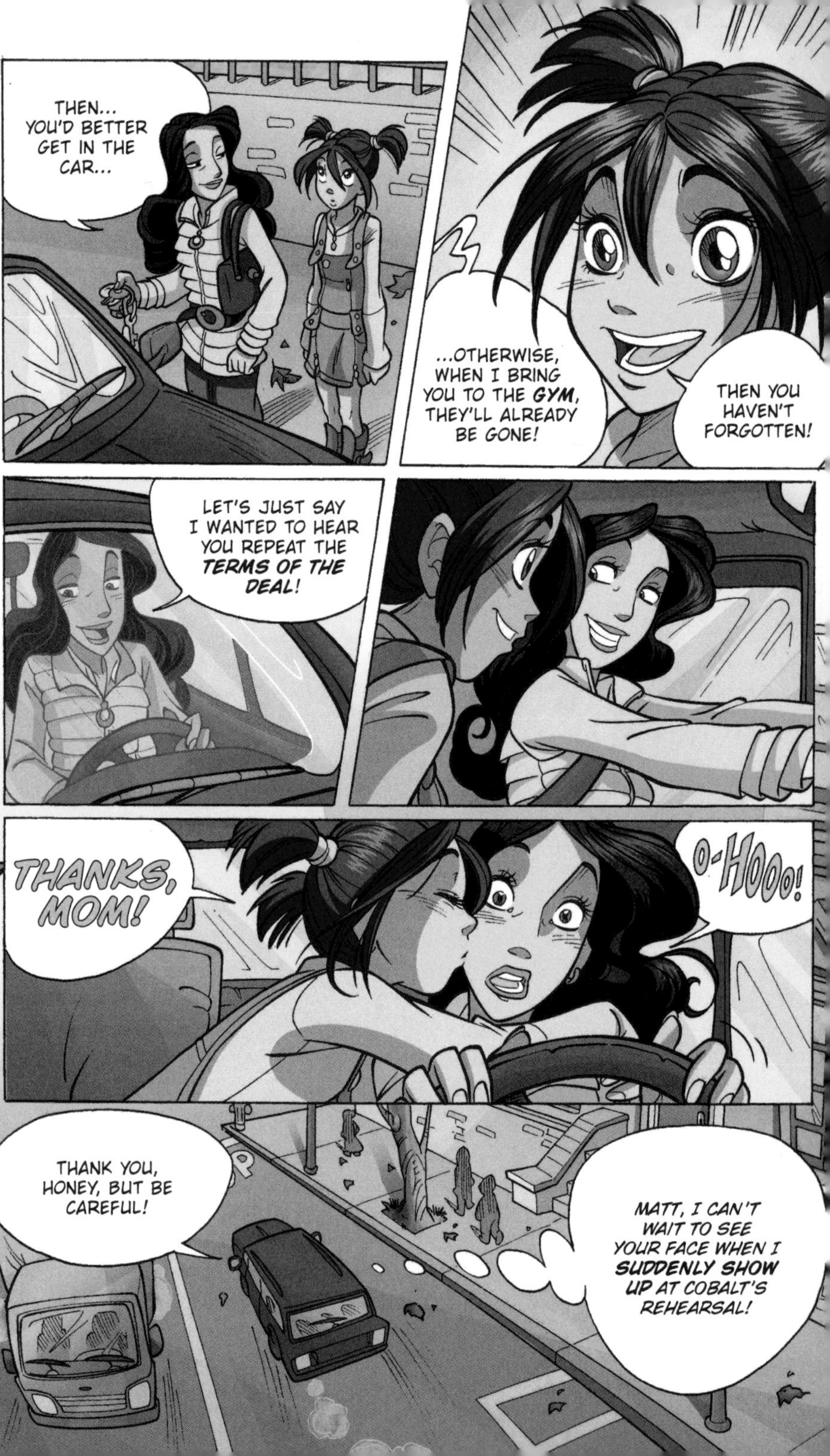

THEN... YOU'D BETTER GET IN THE CAR...
...OTHERWISE, WHEN I BRING YOU TO THE **GYM**, THEY'LL ALREADY BE GONE!
THEN YOU HAVEN'T FORGOTTEN!
LET'S JUST SAY I WANTED TO HEAR YOU REPEAT THE ***TERMS OF THE DEAL***!
THANKS, MOM!
O-HOOo!
THANK YOU, HONEY, BUT BE CAREFUL!
*MATT, I CAN'T WAIT TO SEE YOUR FACE WHEN I **SUDDENLY SHOW UP** AT COBALT'S REHEARSAL!*

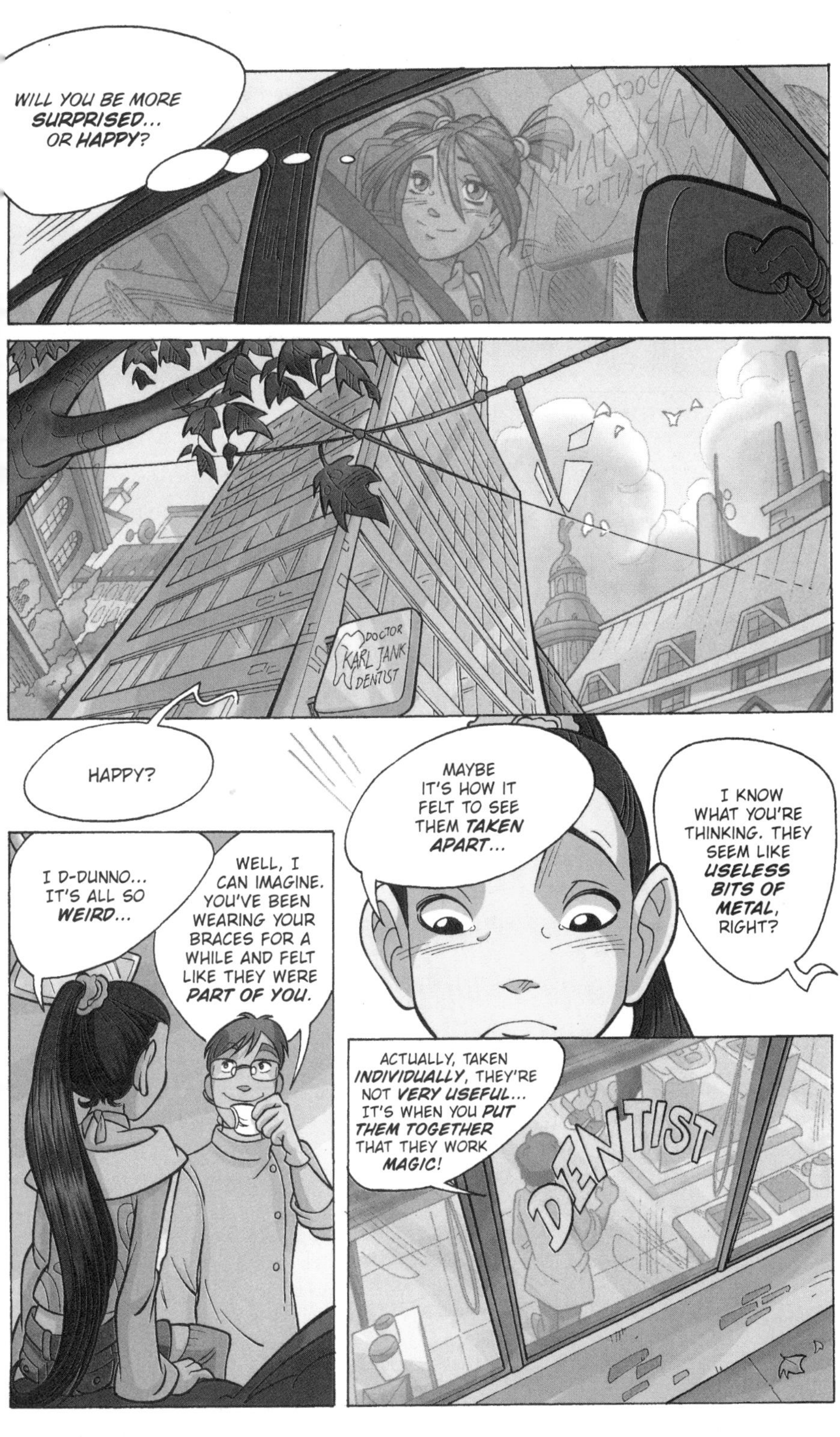
WILL YOU BE MORE SURPRISED... OR HAPPY?
DOCTOR KARL JANK DENTIST
HAPPY?
MAYBE IT'S HOW IT FELT TO SEE THEM TAKEN APART...
I KNOW WHAT YOU'RE THINKING. THEY SEEM LIKE USELESS BITS OF METAL, RIGHT?
I D-DUNNO... IT'S ALL SO WEIRD...
WELL, I CAN IMAGINE. YOU'VE BEEN WEARING YOUR BRACES FOR A WHILE AND FELT LIKE THEY WERE PART OF YOU.
ACTUALLY, TAKEN INDIVIDUALLY, THEY'RE NOT VERY USEFUL... IT'S WHEN YOU PUT THEM TOGETHER THAT THEY WORK MAGIC!
DENTIST

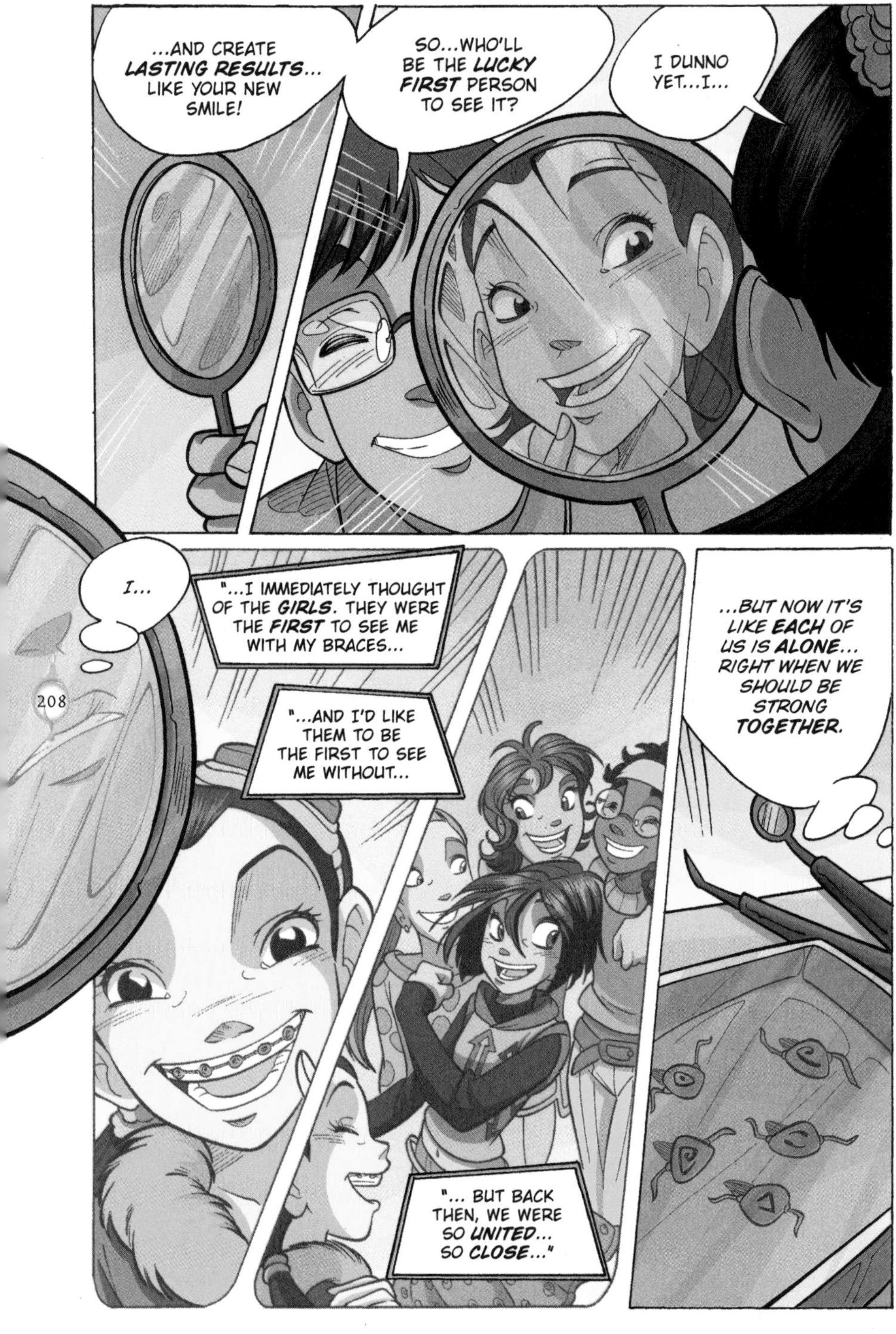

...AND CREATE LASTING RESULTS... LIKE YOUR NEW SMILE!
SO...WHO'LL BE THE LUCKY FIRST PERSON TO SEE IT?
I DUNNO YET...I...
I...
"...I IMMEDIATELY THOUGHT OF THE GIRLS. THEY WERE THE FIRST TO SEE ME WITH MY BRACES...
"...AND I'D LIKE THEM TO BE THE FIRST TO SEE ME WITHOUT...
"... BUT BACK THEN, WE WERE SO UNITED... SO CLOSE..."
...BUT NOW IT'S LIKE EACH OF US IS ALONE... RIGHT WHEN WE SHOULD BE STRONG TOGETHER.

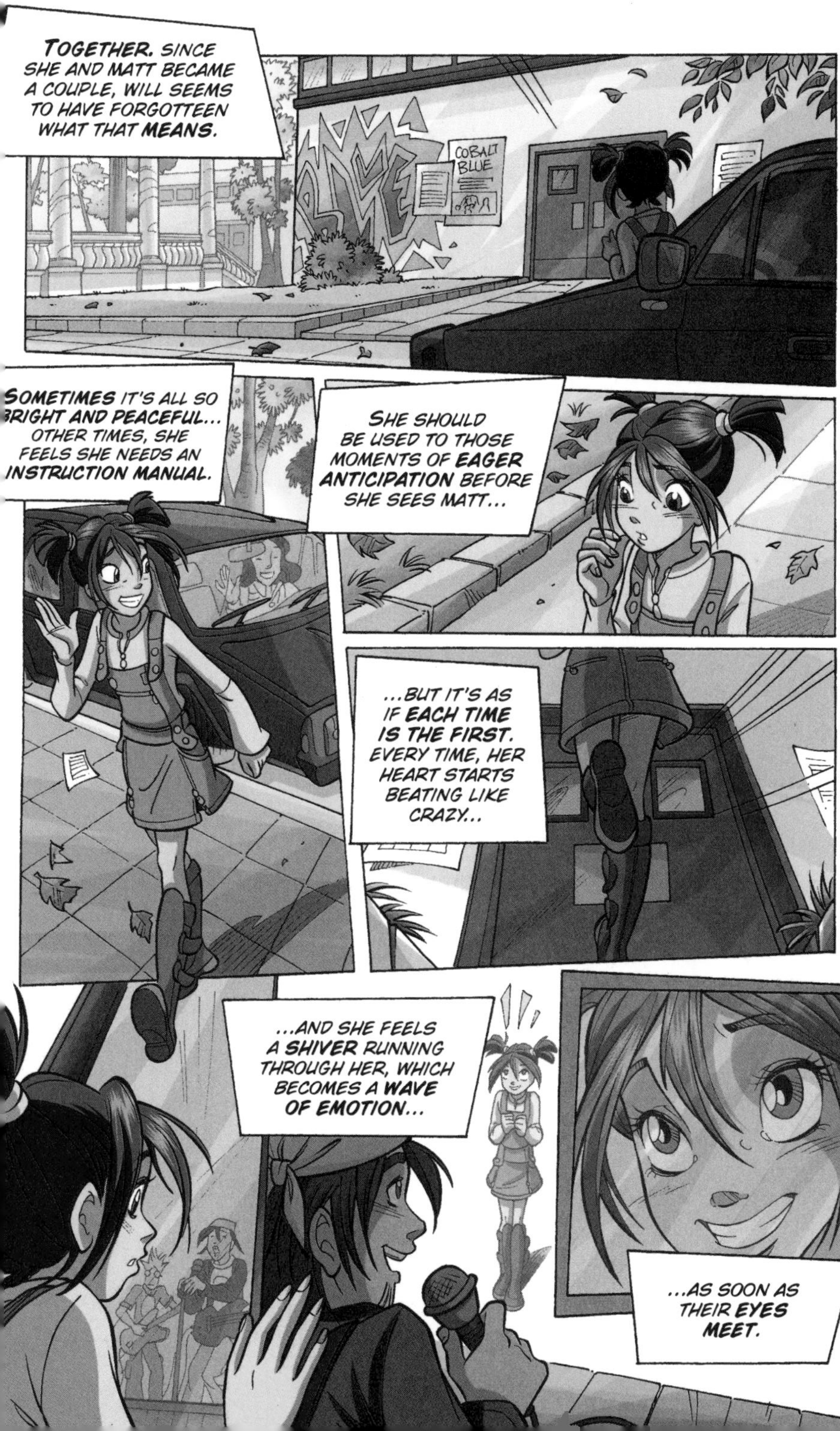
TOGETHER. SINCE SHE AND MATT BECAME A COUPLE, WILL SEEMS TO HAVE FORGOTTEEN WHAT THAT MEANS.
COBALT BLUE
SOMETIMES IT'S ALL SO BRIGHT AND PEACEFUL... OTHER TIMES, SHE FEELS SHE NEEDS AN INSTRUCTION MANUAL.
SHE SHOULD BE USED TO THOSE MOMENTS OF EAGER ANTICIPATION BEFORE SHE SEES MATT...
...BUT IT'S AS IF EACH TIME IS THE FIRST. EVERY TIME, HER HEART STARTS BEATING LIKE CRAZY...
...AND SHE FEELS A SHIVER RUNNING THROUGH HER, WHICH BECOMES A WAVE OF EMOTION...
...AS SOON AS THEIR EYES MEET.

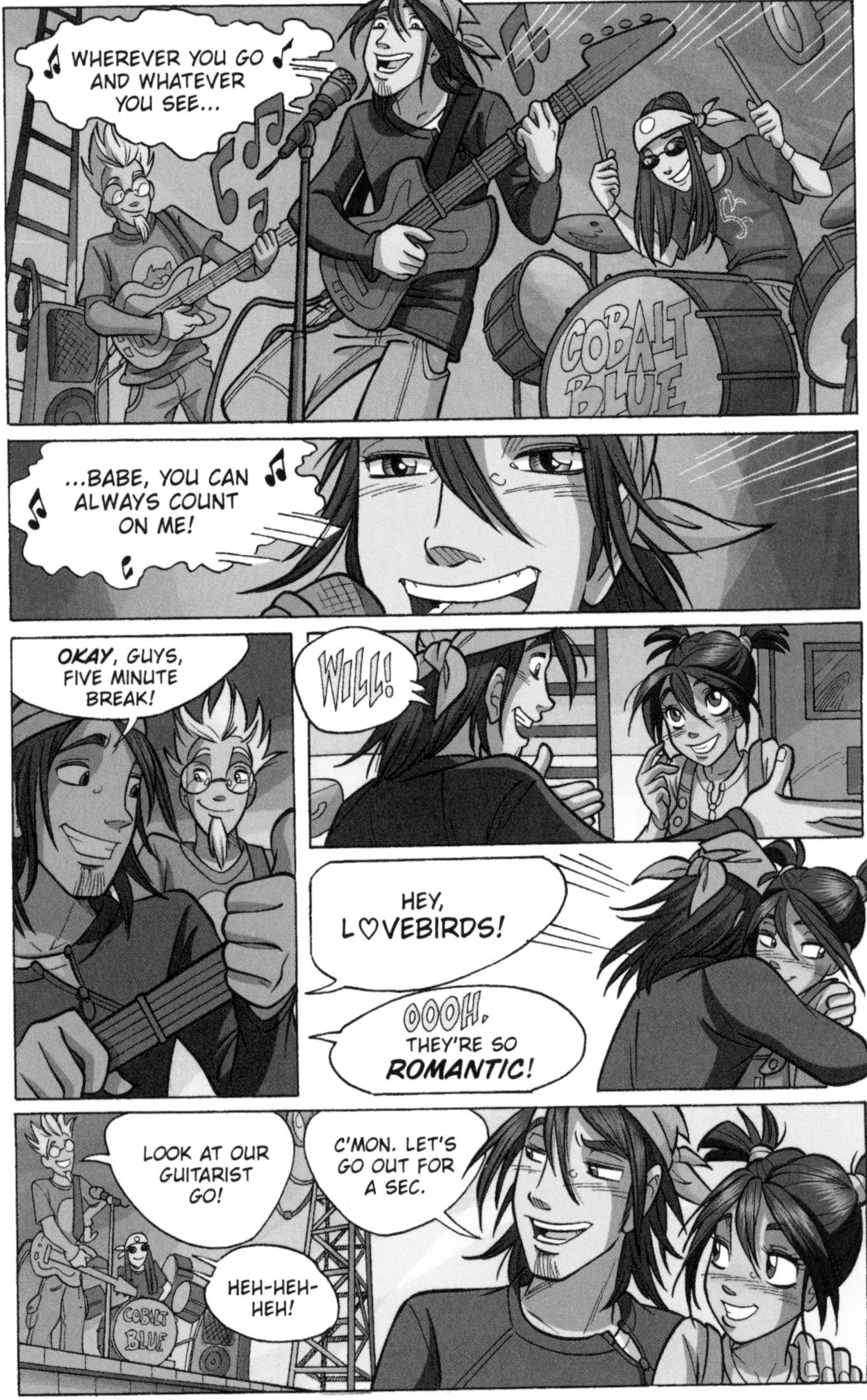
WHEREVER YOU GO AND WHATEVER YOU SEE...
...BABE, YOU CAN ALWAYS COUNT ON ME!
OKAY, GUYS, FIVE MINUTE BREAK!
WILL!
HEY, LOVEBIRDS!
OOOH, THEY'RE SO ROMANTIC!
LOOK AT OUR GUITARIST GO!
C'MON. LET'S GO OUT FOR A SEC.
HEH-HEH-HEH!
COBALT BLUE

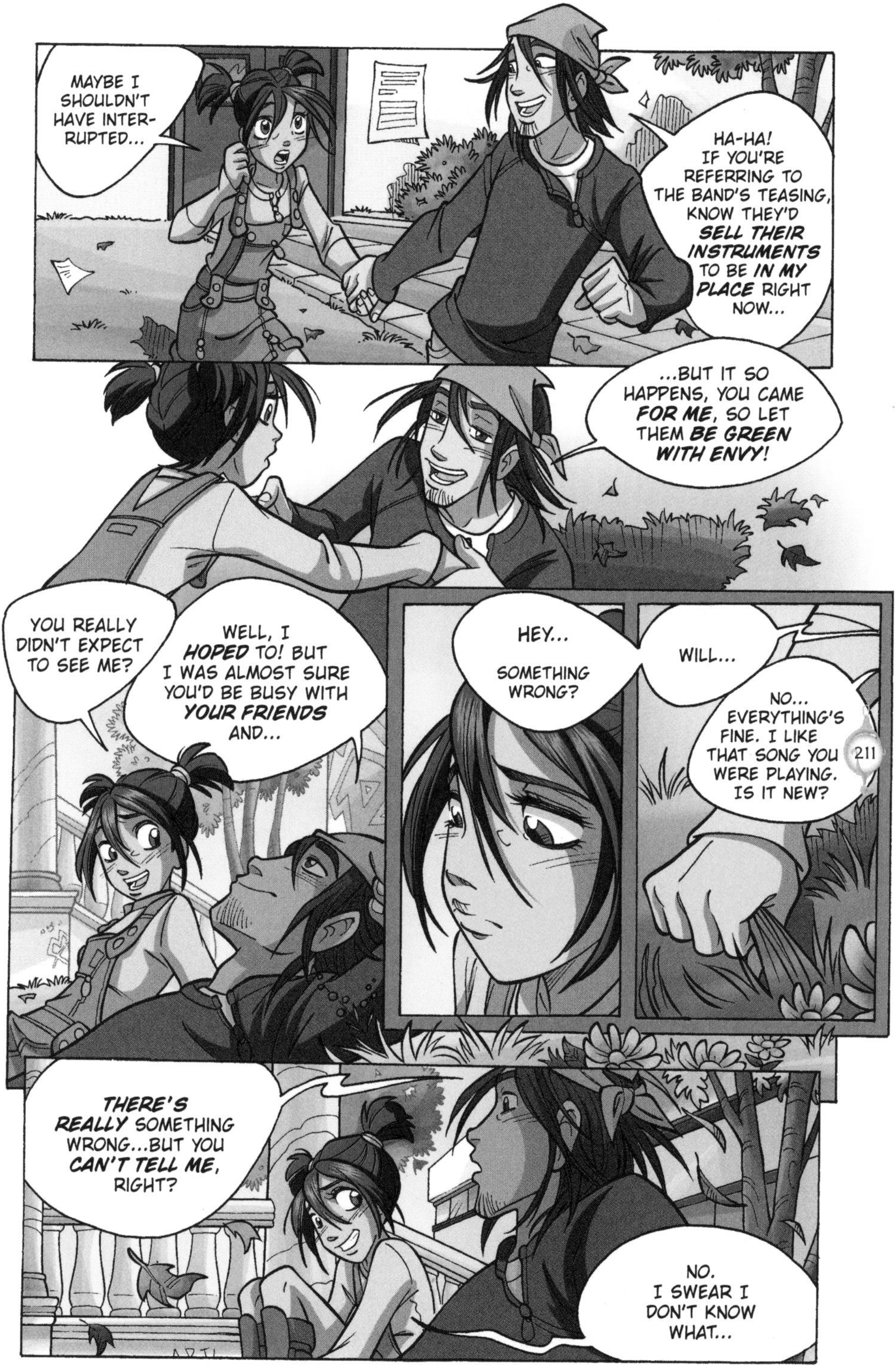
MAYBE I SHOULDN'T HAVE INTER-RUPTED...
HA-HA! IF YOU'RE REFERRING TO THE BAND'S TEASING, KNOW THEY'D SELL THEIR INSTRUMENTS TO BE IN MY PLACE RIGHT NOW...
...BUT IT SO HAPPENS, YOU CAME FOR ME, SO LET THEM BE GREEN WITH ENVY!
YOU REALLY DIDN'T EXPECT TO SEE ME?
WELL, I HOPED TO! BUT I WAS ALMOST SURE YOU'D BE BUSY WITH YOUR FRIENDS AND...
HEY... SOMETHING WRONG?
WILL...
NO... EVERYTHING'S FINE. I LIKE THAT SONG YOU WERE PLAYING. IS IT NEW?
THERE'S REALLY SOMETHING WRONG...BUT YOU CAN'T TELL ME, RIGHT?
NO. I SWEAR I DON'T KNOW WHAT...

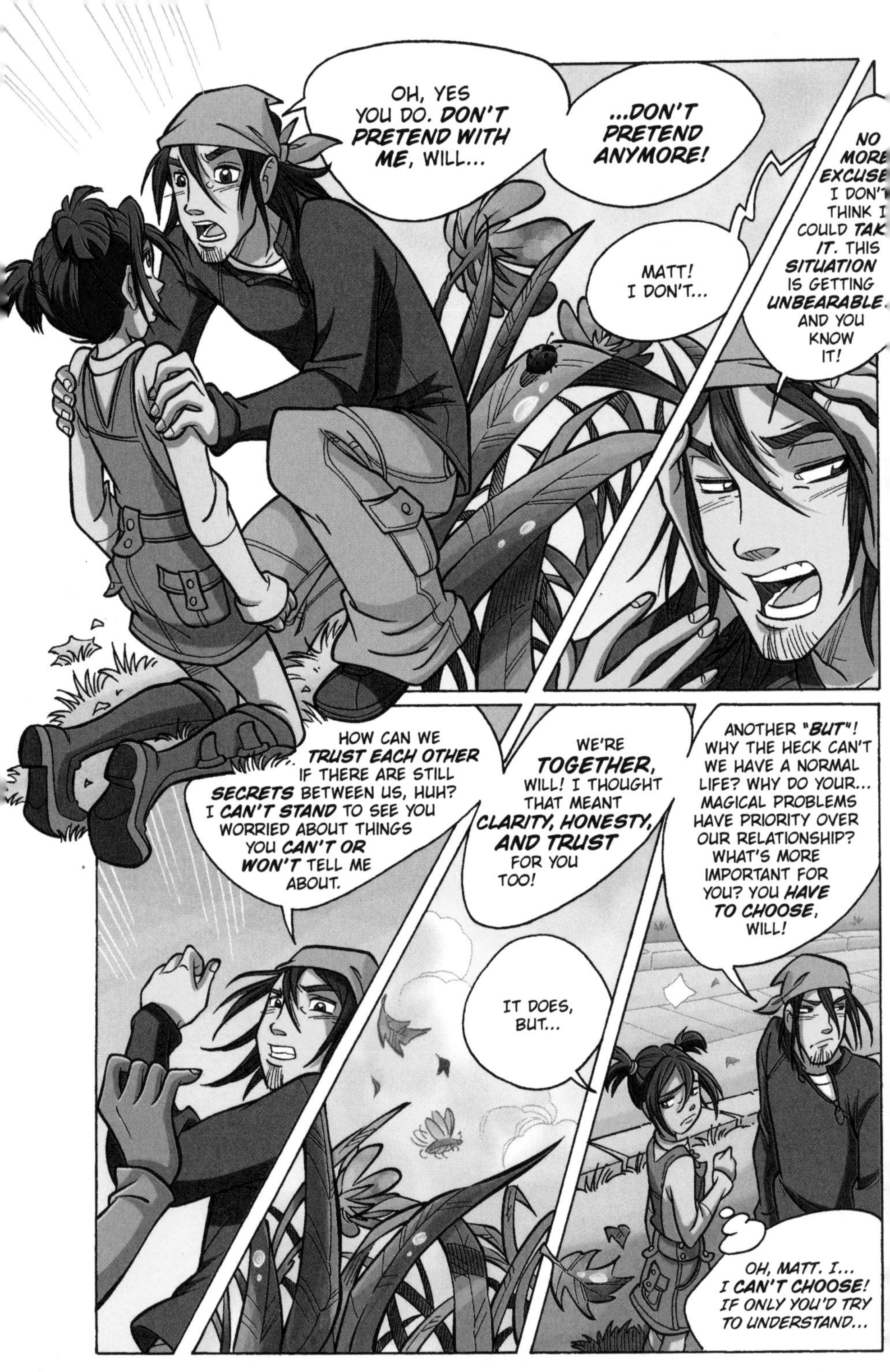
OH, YES YOU DO. DON'T PRETEND WITH ME, WILL...
...DON'T PRETEND ANYMORE!
MATT! I DON'T...
NO MORE EXCUSE I DON'T THINK I COULD TAK IT. THIS SITUATION IS GETTING UNBEARABLE. AND YOU KNOW IT!
HOW CAN WE TRUST EACH OTHER IF THERE ARE STILL SECRETS BETWEEN US, HUH? I CAN'T STAND TO SEE YOU WORRIED ABOUT THINGS YOU CAN'T OR WON'T TELL ME ABOUT.
WE'RE TOGETHER, WILL! I THOUGHT THAT MEANT CLARITY, HONESTY, AND TRUST FOR YOU TOO!
IT DOES, BUT...
ANOTHER "BUT"! WHY THE HECK CAN'T WE HAVE A NORMAL LIFE? WHY DO YOUR... MAGICAL PROBLEMS HAVE PRIORITY OVER OUR RELATIONSHIP? WHAT'S MORE IMPORTANT FOR YOU? YOU HAVE TO CHOOSE, WILL!
OH, MATT. I... I CAN'T CHOOSE! IF ONLY YOU'D TRY TO UNDERSTAND...

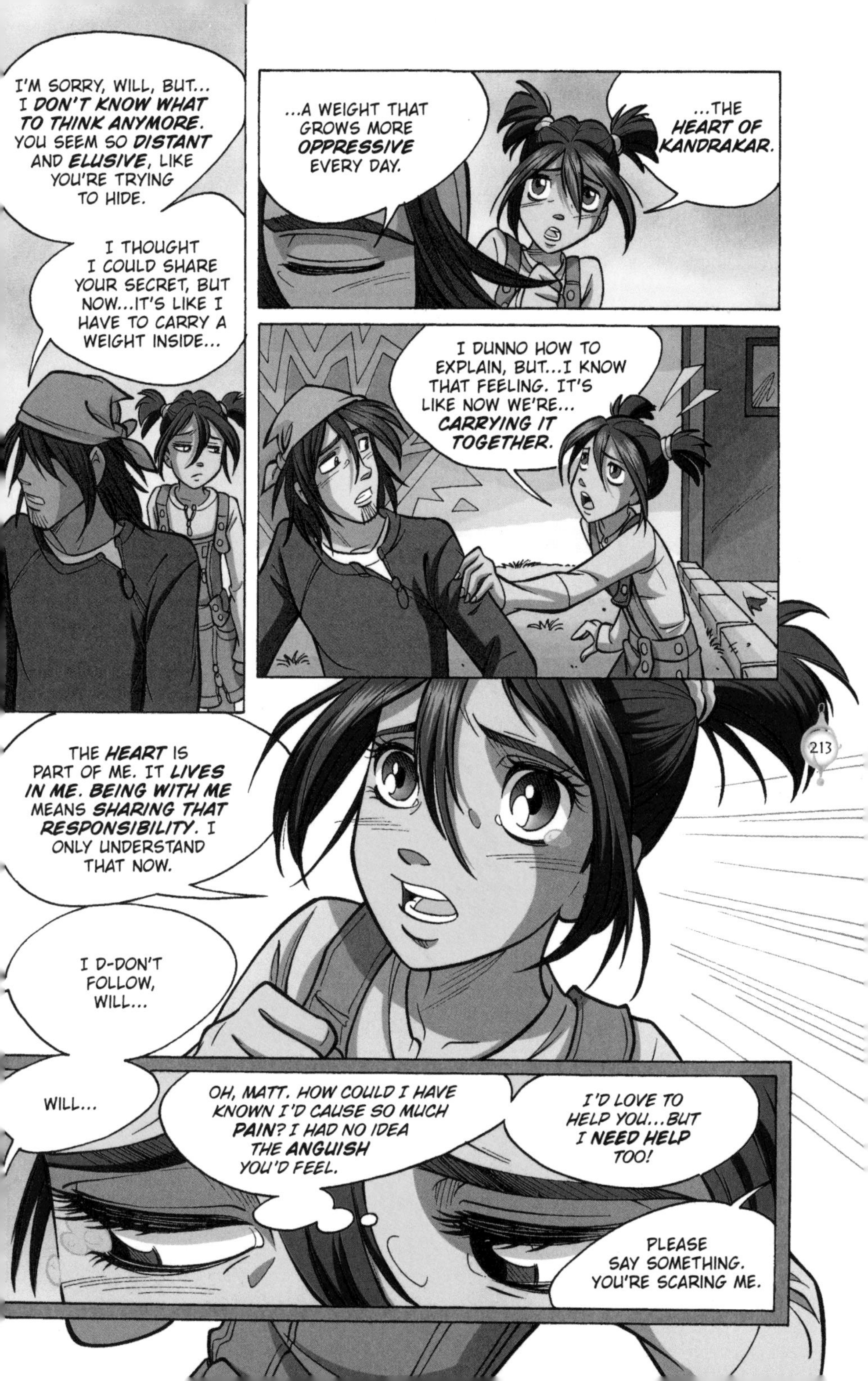
I'M SORRY, WILL, BUT... I DON'T KNOW WHAT TO THINK ANYMORE. YOU SEEM SO DISTANT AND ELUSIVE, LIKE YOU'RE TRYING TO HIDE.
I THOUGHT I COULD SHARE YOUR SECRET, BUT NOW...IT'S LIKE I HAVE TO CARRY A WEIGHT INSIDE...
...A WEIGHT THAT GROWS MORE OPPRESSIVE EVERY DAY.
...THE HEART OF KANDRAKAR.
I DUNNO HOW TO EXPLAIN, BUT...I KNOW THAT FEELING. IT'S LIKE NOW WE'RE... CARRYING IT TOGETHER.
THE HEART IS PART OF ME. IT LIVES IN ME. BEING WITH ME MEANS SHARING THAT RESPONSIBILITY. I ONLY UNDERSTAND THAT NOW.
I D-DON'T FOLLOW, WILL...
WILL...
OH, MATT. HOW COULD I HAVE KNOWN I'D CAUSE SO MUCH PAIN? I HAD NO IDEA THE ANGUISH YOU'D FEEL.
I'D LOVE TO HELP YOU...BUT I NEED HELP TOO!
PLEASE SAY SOMETHING. YOU'RE SCARING ME.

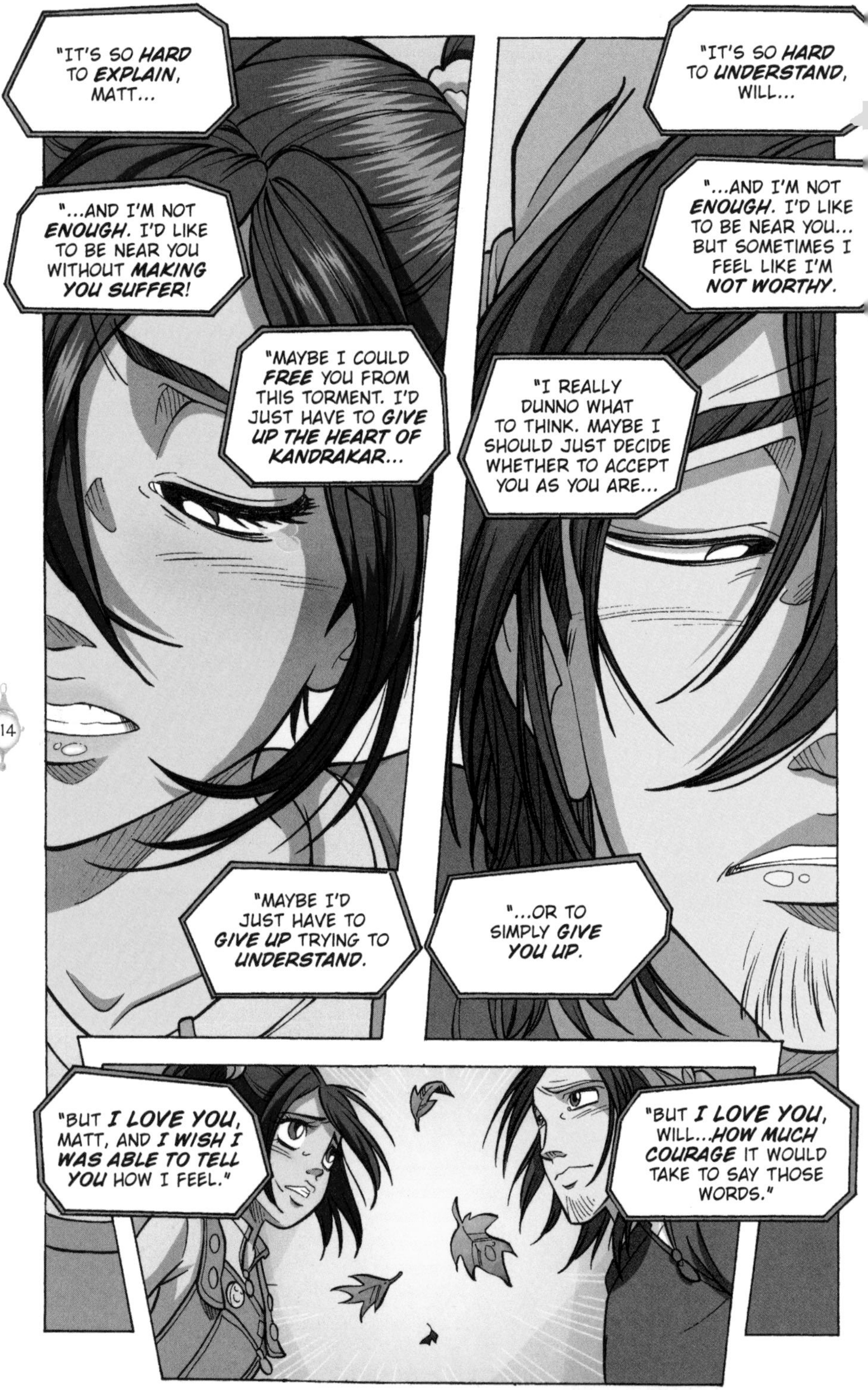
"IT'S SO HARD TO EXPLAIN, MATT...
"IT'S SO HARD TO UNDERSTAND, WILL...
"...AND I'M NOT ENOUGH. I'D LIKE TO BE NEAR YOU WITHOUT MAKING YOU SUFFER!
"...AND I'M NOT ENOUGH. I'D LIKE TO BE NEAR YOU... BUT SOMETIMES I FEEL LIKE I'M NOT WORTHY.
"MAYBE I COULD FREE YOU FROM THIS TORMENT. I'D JUST HAVE TO GIVE UP THE HEART OF KANDRAKAR...
"I REALLY DUNNO WHAT TO THINK. MAYBE I SHOULD JUST DECIDE WHETHER TO ACCEPT YOU AS YOU ARE...
"MAYBE I'D JUST HAVE TO GIVE UP TRYING TO UNDERSTAND.
"...OR TO SIMPLY GIVE YOU UP.
"BUT I LOVE YOU, MATT, AND I WISH I WAS ABLE TO TELL YOU HOW I FEEL."
"BUT I LOVE YOU, WILL...HOW MUCH COURAGE IT WOULD TAKE TO SAY THOSE WORDS."

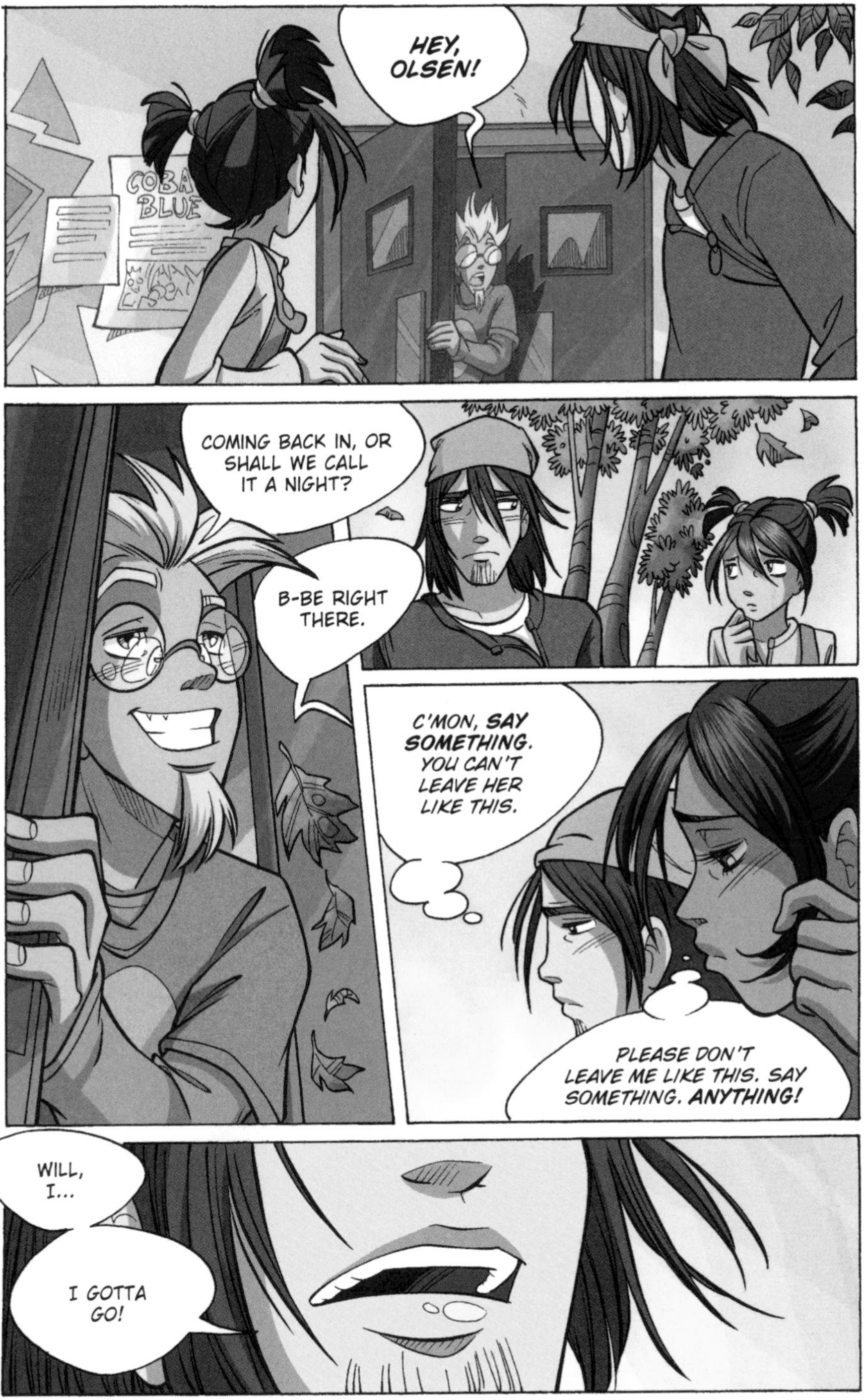
HEY, OLSEN!
COBA BLUE
COMING BACK IN, OR SHALL WE CALL IT A NIGHT?
B-BE RIGHT THERE.
C'MON, SAY SOMETHING. YOU CAN'T LEAVE HER LIKE THIS.
PLEASE DON'T LEAVE ME LIKE THIS. SAY SOMETHING. ANYTHING!
WILL, I...
I GOTTA GO!

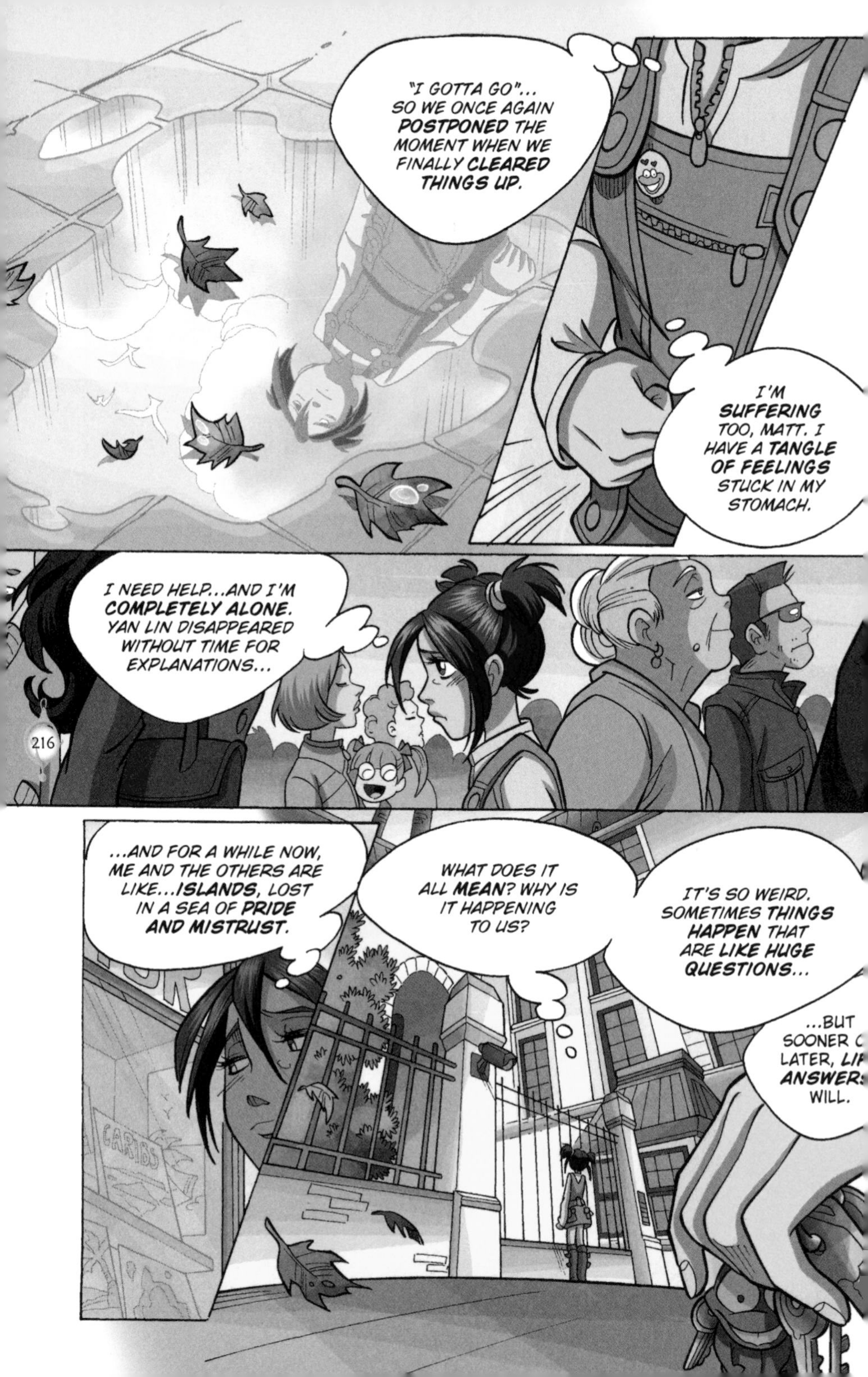
"I GOTTA GO"... SO WE ONCE AGAIN POSTPONED THE MOMENT WHEN WE FINALLY CLEARED THINGS UP.
I'M SUFFERING TOO, MATT. I HAVE A TANGLE OF FEELINGS STUCK IN MY STOMACH.
I NEED HELP...AND I'M COMPLETELY ALONE. YAN LIN DISAPPEARED WITHOUT TIME FOR EXPLANATIONS...
...AND FOR A WHILE NOW, ME AND THE OTHERS ARE LIKE...ISLANDS, LOST IN A SEA OF PRIDE AND MISTRUST.
WHAT DOES IT ALL MEAN? WHY IS IT HAPPENING TO US?
IT'S SO WEIRD. SOMETIMES THINGS HAPPEN THAT ARE LIKE HUGE QUESTIONS...
...BUT SOONER LATER, ANSWERS WILL.
CARIBS

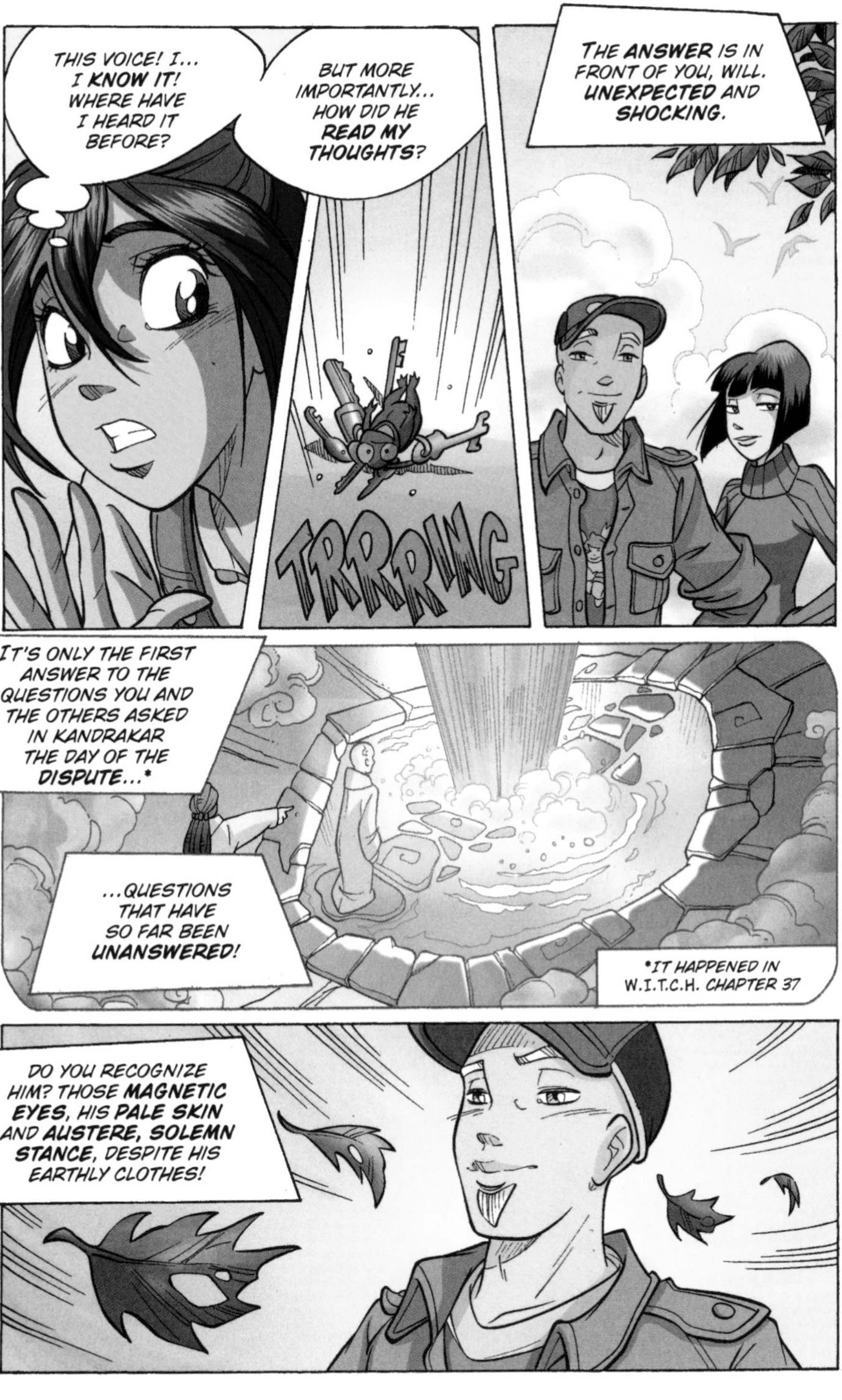
THIS VOICE! I... I KNOW IT! WHERE HAVE I HEARD IT BEFORE?
BUT MORE IMPORTANTLY... HOW DID HE READ MY THOUGHTS?
TRRRING
THE ANSWER IS IN FRONT OF YOU, WILL. UNEXPECTED AND SHOCKING.
IT'S ONLY THE FIRST ANSWER TO THE QUESTIONS YOU AND THE OTHERS ASKED IN KANDRAKAR THE DAY OF THE DISPUTE...*
...QUESTIONS THAT HAVE SO FAR BEEN UNANSWERED!
*IT HAPPENED IN W.I.T.C.H. CHAPTER 37
DO YOU RECOGNIZE HIM? THOSE MAGNETIC EYES, HIS PALE SKIN AND AUSTERE, SOLEMN STANCE, DESPITE HIS EARTHLY CLOTHES!

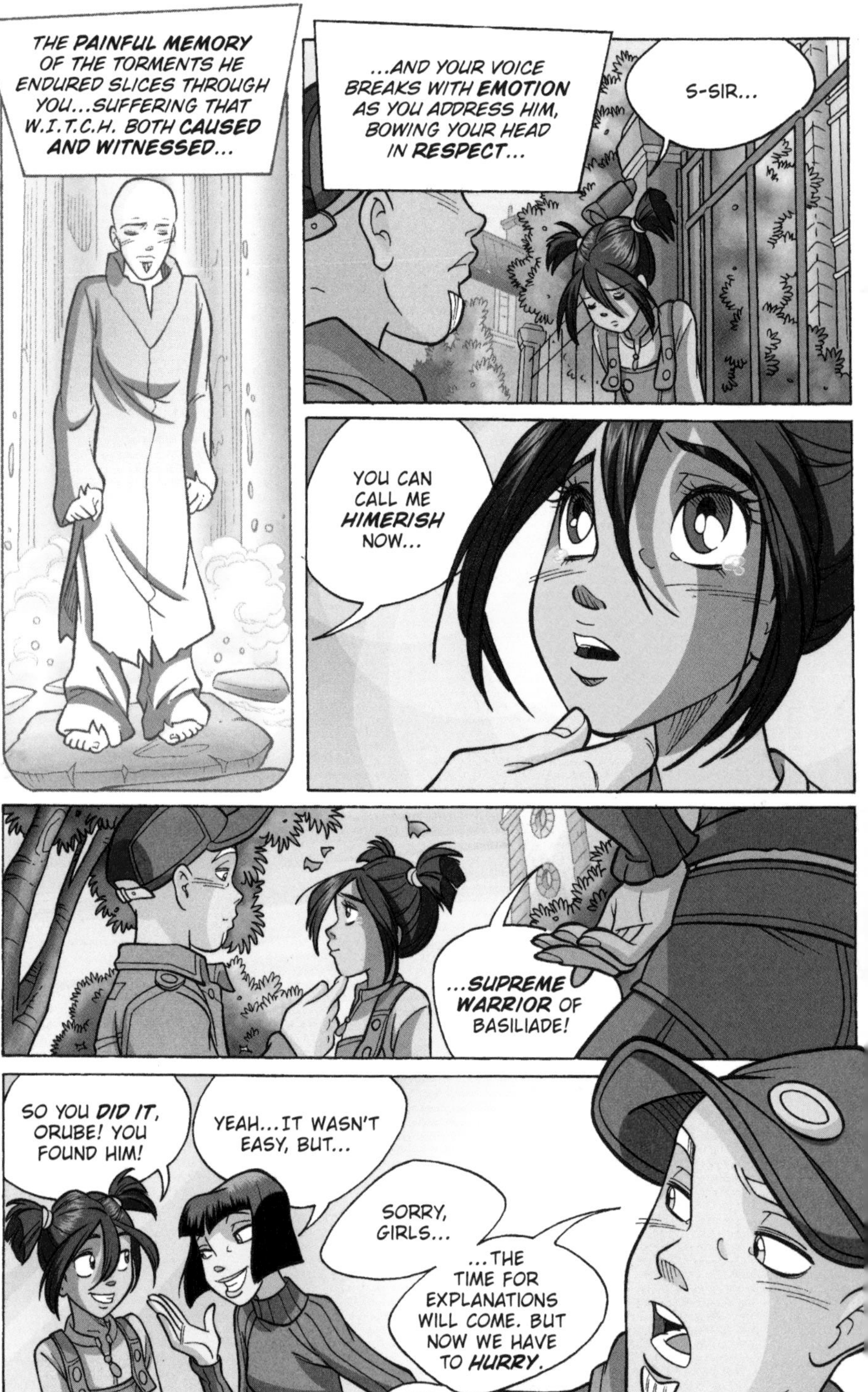
THE PAINFUL MEMORY OF THE TORMENTS HE ENDURED SLICES THROUGH YOU...SUFFERING THAT W.I.T.C.H. BOTH CAUSED AND WITNESSED...
...AND YOUR VOICE BREAKS WITH EMOTION AS YOU ADDRESS HIM, BOWING YOUR HEAD IN RESPECT...
S-SIR...
YOU CAN CALL ME HIMERISH NOW...
...SUPREME WARRIOR OF BASILIADE!
SO YOU DID IT, ORUBE! YOU FOUND HIM!
YEAH...IT WASN'T EASY, BUT...
SORRY, GIRLS...
...THE TIME FOR EXPLANATIONS WILL COME. BUT NOW WE HAVE TO HURRY.
?

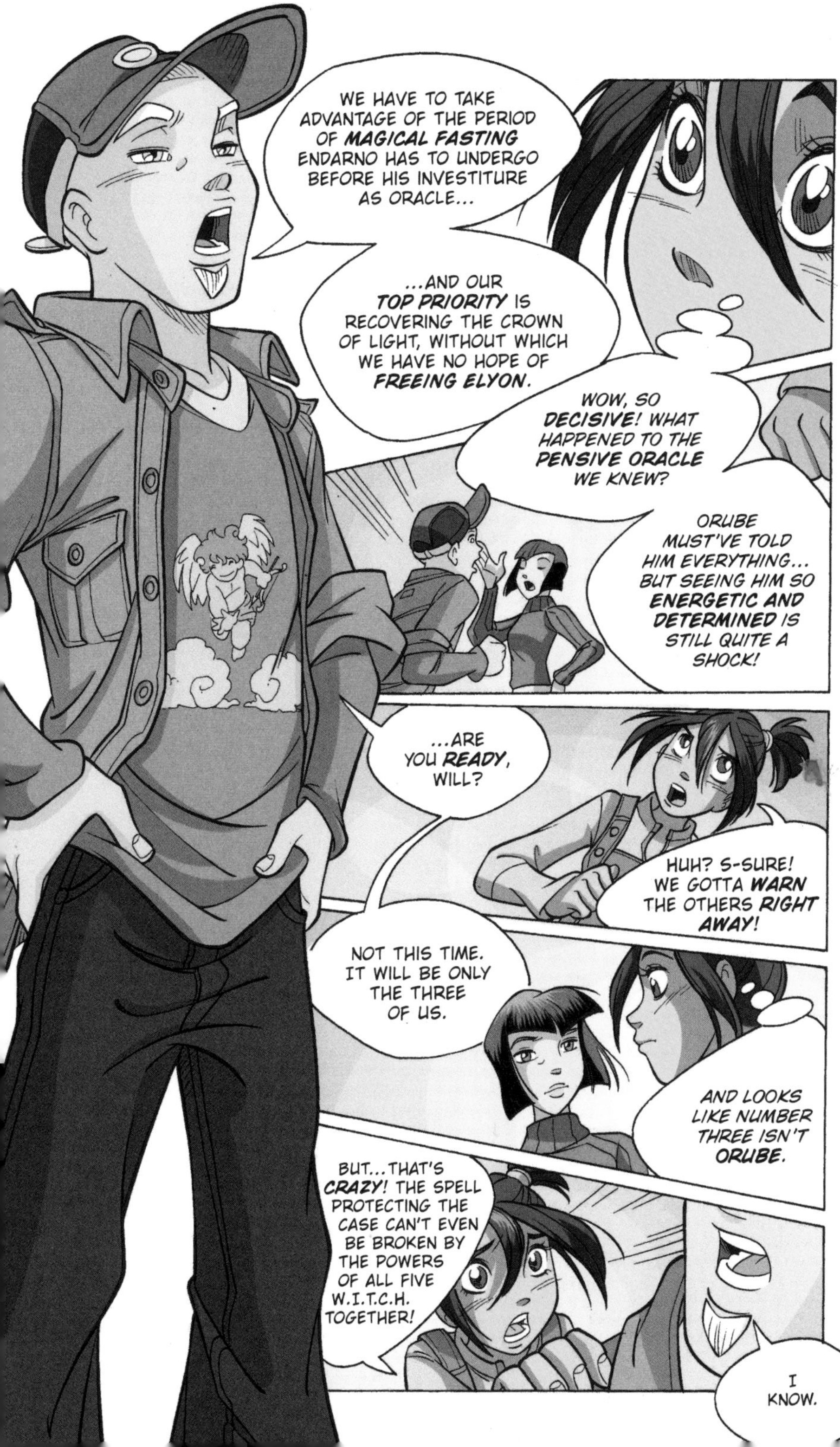
WE HAVE TO TAKE ADVANTAGE OF THE PERIOD OF MAGICAL FASTING ENDARNO HAS TO UNDERGO BEFORE HIS INVESTITURE AS ORACLE...
...AND OUR TOP PRIORITY IS RECOVERING THE CROWN OF LIGHT, WITHOUT WHICH WE HAVE NO HOPE OF FREEING ELYON.
WOW, SO DECISIVE! WHAT HAPPENED TO THE PENSIVE ORACLE WE KNEW?
ORUBE MUST'VE TOLD HIM EVERYTHING... BUT SEEING HIM SO ENERGETIC AND DETERMINED IS STILL QUITE A SHOCK!
...ARE YOU READY, WILL?
HUH? S-SURE! WE GOTTA WARN THE OTHERS RIGHT AWAY!
NOT THIS TIME. IT WILL BE ONLY THE THREE OF US.
AND LOOKS LIKE NUMBER THREE ISN'T ORUBE.
BUT...THAT'S CRAZY! THE SPELL PROTECTING THE CASE CAN'T EVEN BE BROKEN BY THE POWERS OF ALL FIVE W.I.T.C.H. TOGETHER!
I KNOW.

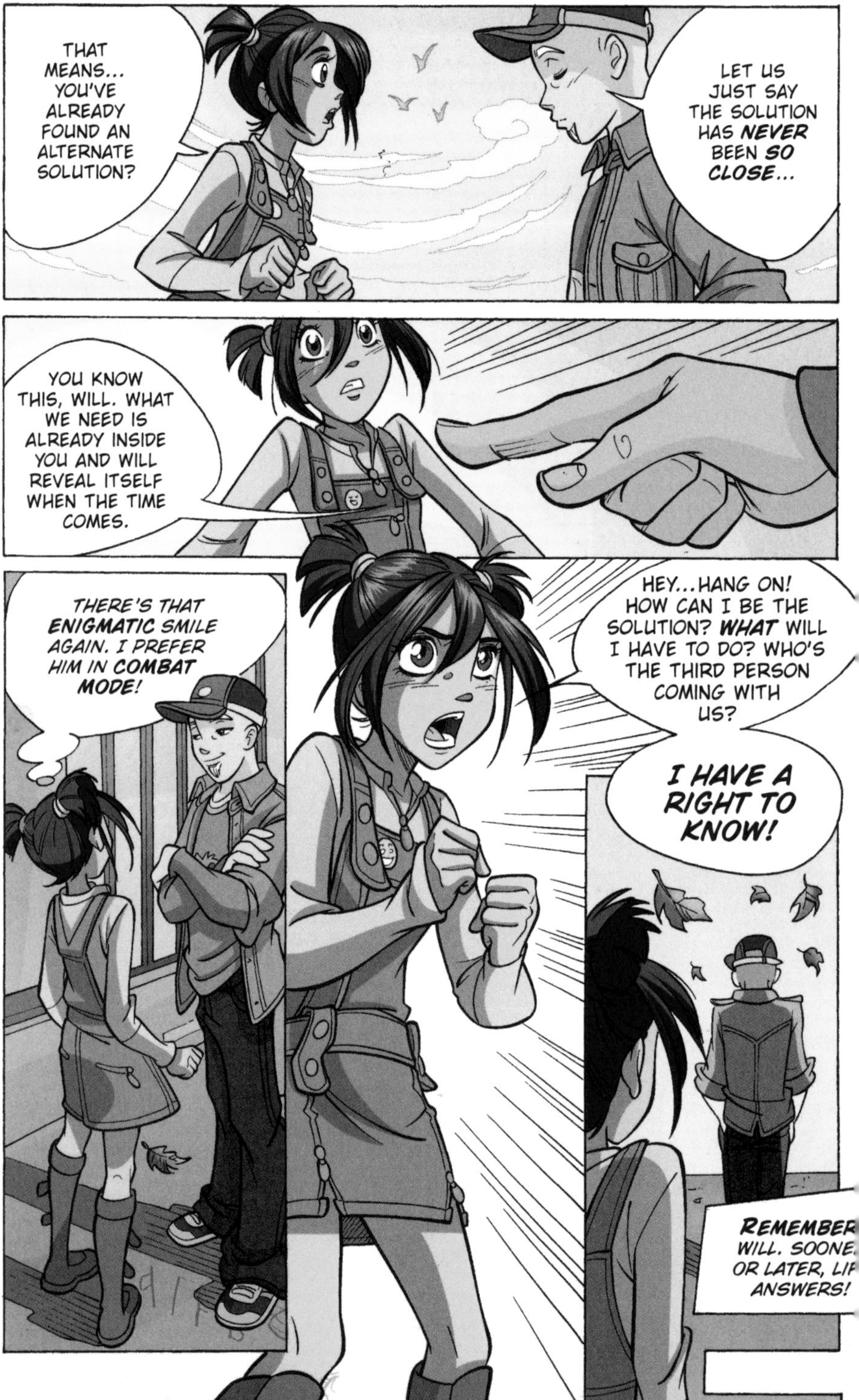
THAT MEANS... YOU'VE ALREADY FOUND AN ALTERNATE SOLUTION?
LET US JUST SAY THE SOLUTION HAS NEVER BEEN SO CLOSE...
YOU KNOW THIS, WILL. WHAT WE NEED IS ALREADY INSIDE YOU AND WILL REVEAL ITSELF WHEN THE TIME COMES.
THERE'S THAT ENIGMATIC SMILE AGAIN. I PREFER HIM IN COMBAT MODE!
HEY...HANG ON! HOW CAN I BE THE SOLUTION? WHAT WILL I HAVE TO DO? WHO'S THE THIRD PERSON COMING WITH US?
I HAVE A RIGHT TO KNOW!
REMEMBER WILL. SOONE OR LATER, LI ANSWERS!

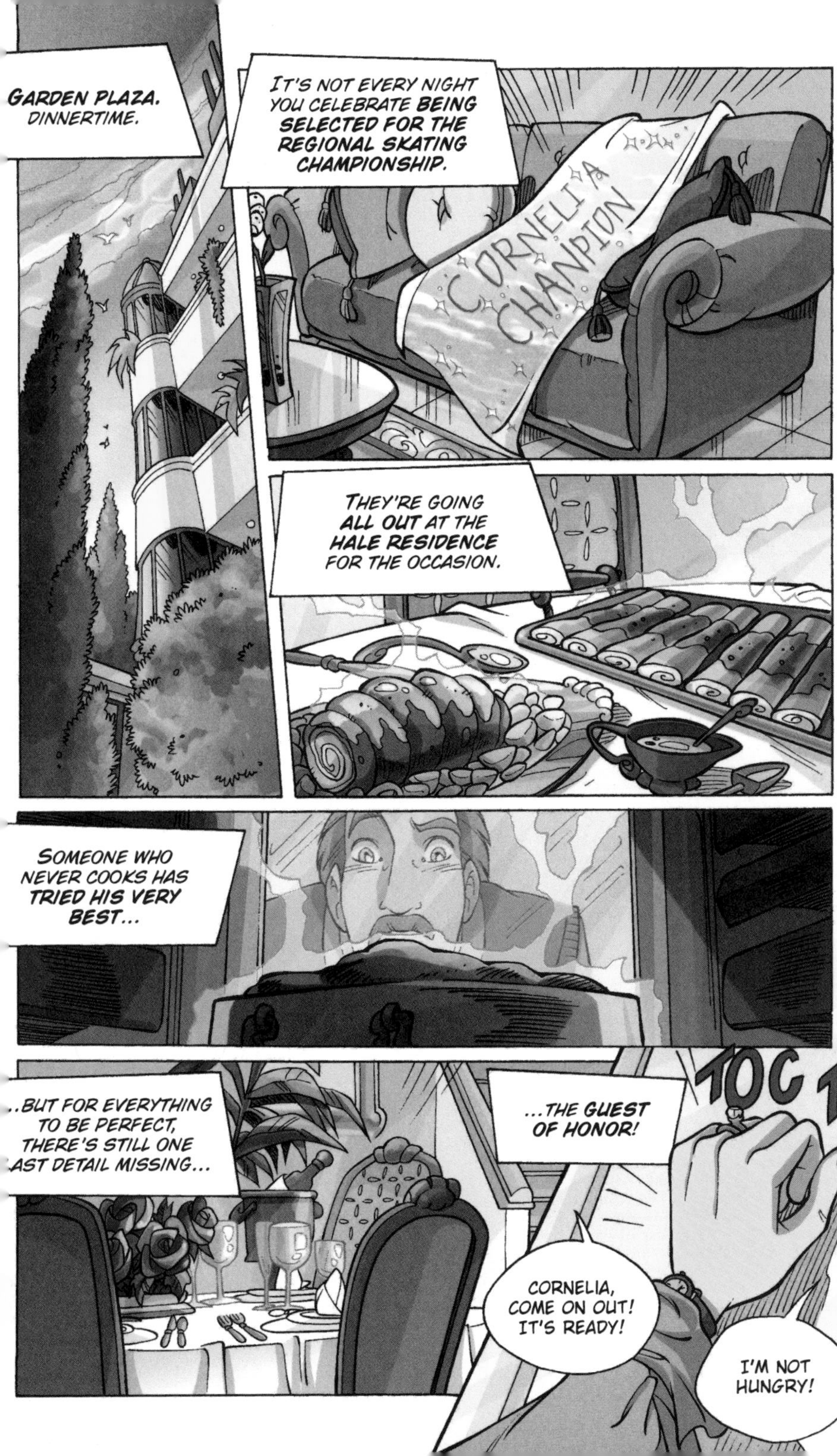
GARDEN PLAZA.
DINNERTIME.
IT'S NOT EVERY NIGHT YOU CELEBRATE BEING SELECTED FOR THE REGIONAL SKATING CHAMPIONSHIP.
CORNELIA CHAMPION
THEY'RE GOING ALL OUT AT THE HALE RESIDENCE FOR THE OCCASION.
SOMEONE WHO NEVER COOKS HAS TRIED HIS VERY BEST...
..BUT FOR EVERYTHING TO BE PERFECT, THERE'S STILL ONE AST DETAIL MISSING...
...THE GUEST OF HONOR!
TOC TOC
CORNELIA, COME ON OUT! IT'S READY!
I'M NOT HUNGRY!

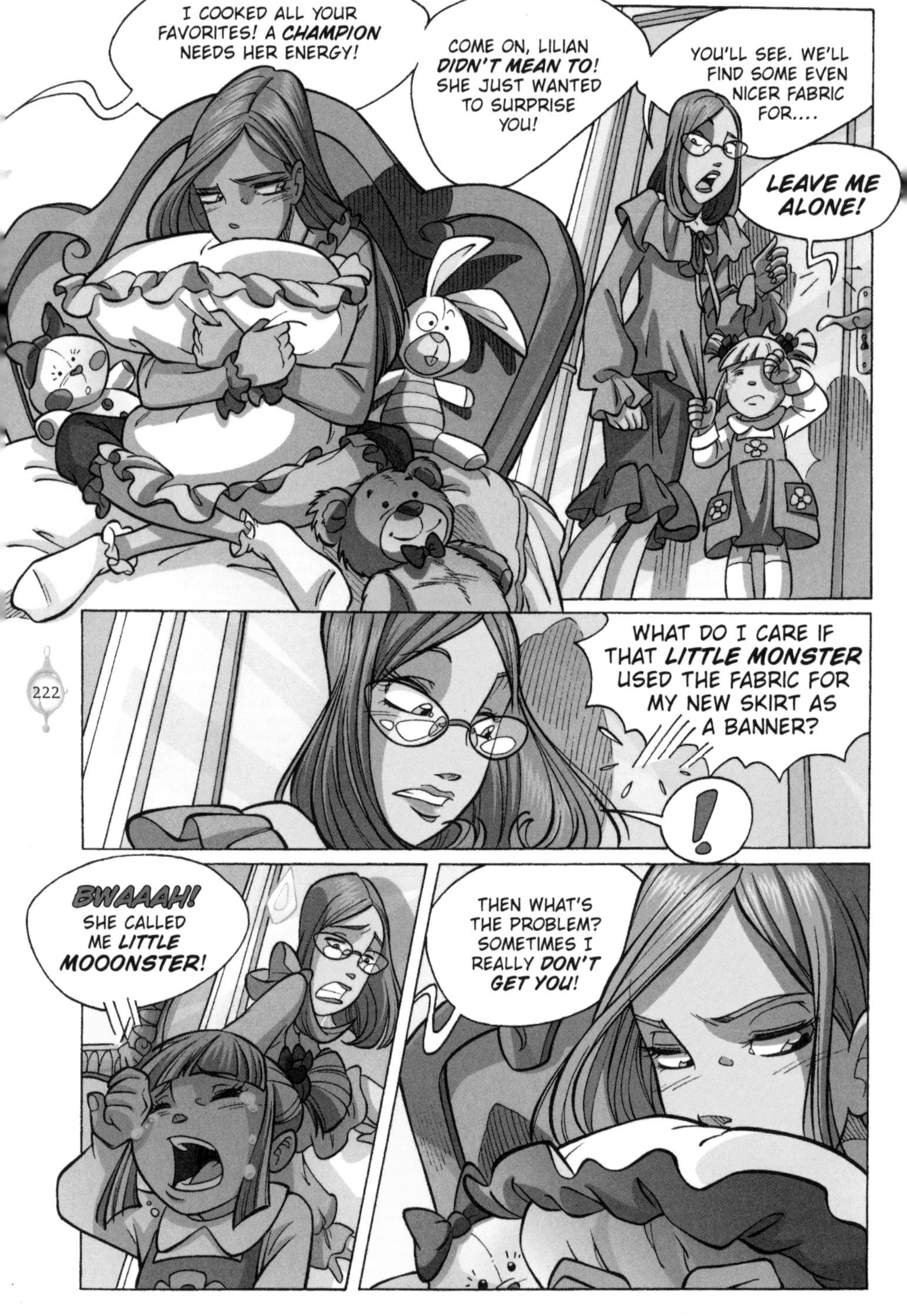
I COOKED ALL YOUR FAVORITES! A CHAMPION NEEDS HER ENERGY!
COME ON, LILIAN DIDN'T MEAN TO! SHE JUST WANTED TO SURPRISE YOU!
YOU'LL SEE. WE'LL FIND SOME EVEN NICER FABRIC FOR....
LEAVE ME ALONE!
WHAT DO I CARE IF THAT LITTLE MONSTER USED THE FABRIC FOR MY NEW SKIRT AS A BANNER?
!
BWAAAH! SHE CALLED ME LITTLE MOOONSTER!
THEN WHAT'S THE PROBLEM? SOMETIMES I REALLY DON'T GET YOU!

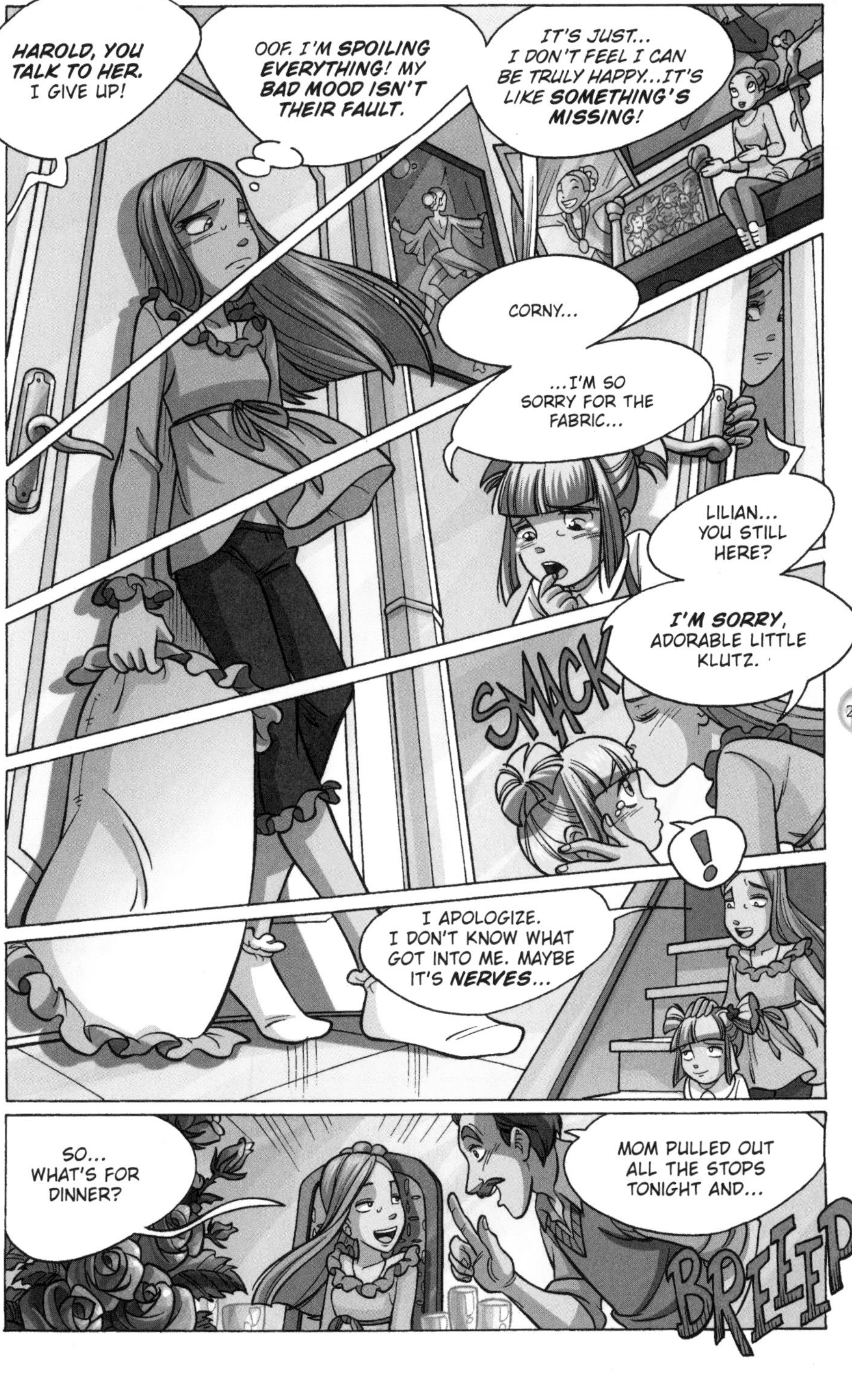
HAROLD, YOU TALK TO HER. I GIVE UP!
OOF. I'M SPOILING EVERYTHING! MY BAD MOOD ISN'T THEIR FAULT.
IT'S JUST... I DON'T FEEL I CAN BE TRULY HAPPY...IT'S LIKE SOMETHING'S MISSING!
CORNY...
...I'M SO SORRY FOR THE FABRIC...
LILIAN... YOU STILL HERE?
I'M SORRY, ADORABLE LITTLE KLUTZ.
SMACK
!
I APOLOGIZE. I DON'T KNOW WHAT GOT INTO ME. MAYBE IT'S NERVES...
SO... WHAT'S FOR DINNER?
MOM PULLED OUT ALL THE STOPS TONIGHT AND...
BREEEP

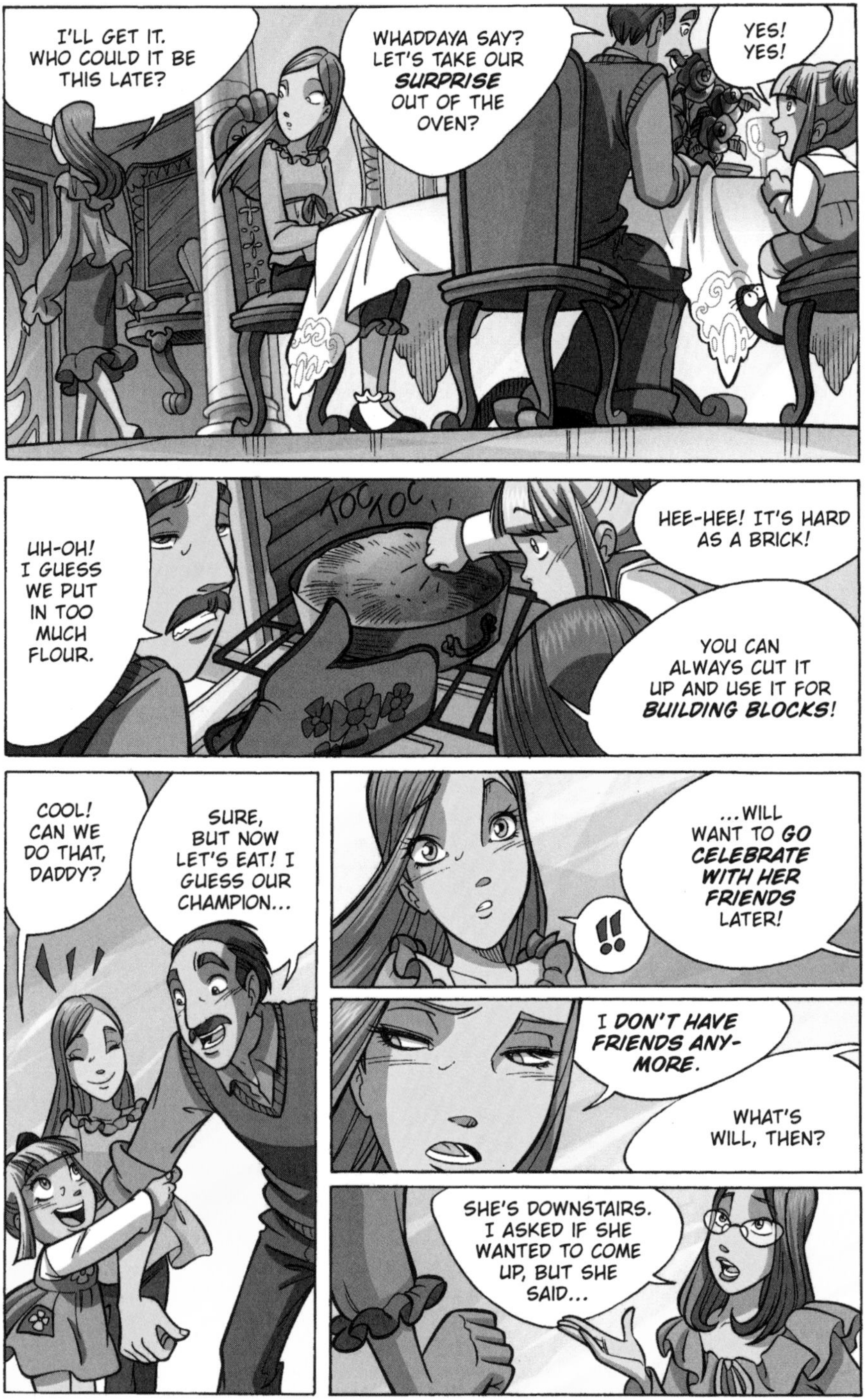
I'LL GET IT. WHO COULD IT BE THIS LATE?
WHADDAYA SAY? LET'S TAKE OUR SURPRISE OUT OF THE OVEN?
YES! YES!
TOC TOC
UH-OH! I GUESS WE PUT IN TOO MUCH FLOUR.
HEE-HEE! IT'S HARD AS A BRICK!
YOU CAN ALWAYS CUT IT UP AND USE IT FOR BUILDING BLOCKS!
COOL! CAN WE DO THAT, DADDY?
SURE, BUT NOW LET'S EAT! I GUESS OUR CHAMPION...
...WILL WANT TO GO CELEBRATE WITH HER FRIENDS LATER!
!!
I DON'T HAVE FRIENDS ANYMORE.
WHAT'S WILL, THEN?
SHE'S DOWNSTAIRS. I ASKED IF SHE WANTED TO COME UP, BUT SHE SAID...

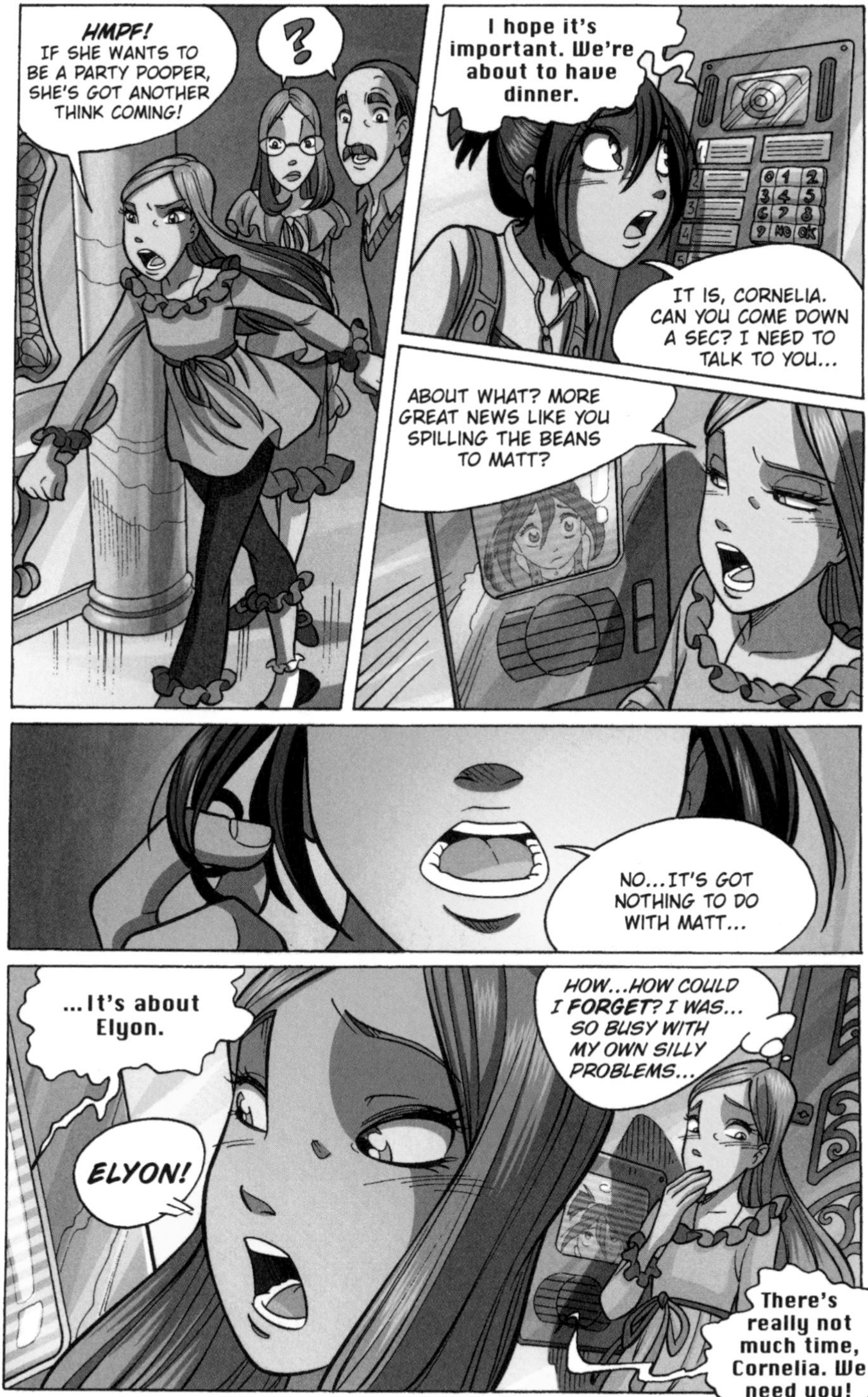
HMPF!
IF SHE WANTS TO BE A PARTY POOPER, SHE'S GOT ANOTHER THINK COMING!
?
I hope it's important. We're about to have dinner.
IT IS, CORNELIA. CAN YOU COME DOWN A SEC? I NEED TO TALK TO YOU...
1
2
3
4
5
0 1 2
3 4 5
6 7 8
9 NO OK
ABOUT WHAT? MORE GREAT NEWS LIKE YOU SPILLING THE BEANS TO MATT?
NO...IT'S GOT NOTHING TO DO WITH MATT...
...It's about Elyon.
ELYON!
HOW...HOW COULD I **FORGET**? I WAS... SO BUSY WITH MY OWN SILLY PROBLEMS...
There's really not much time, Cornelia. We need you!

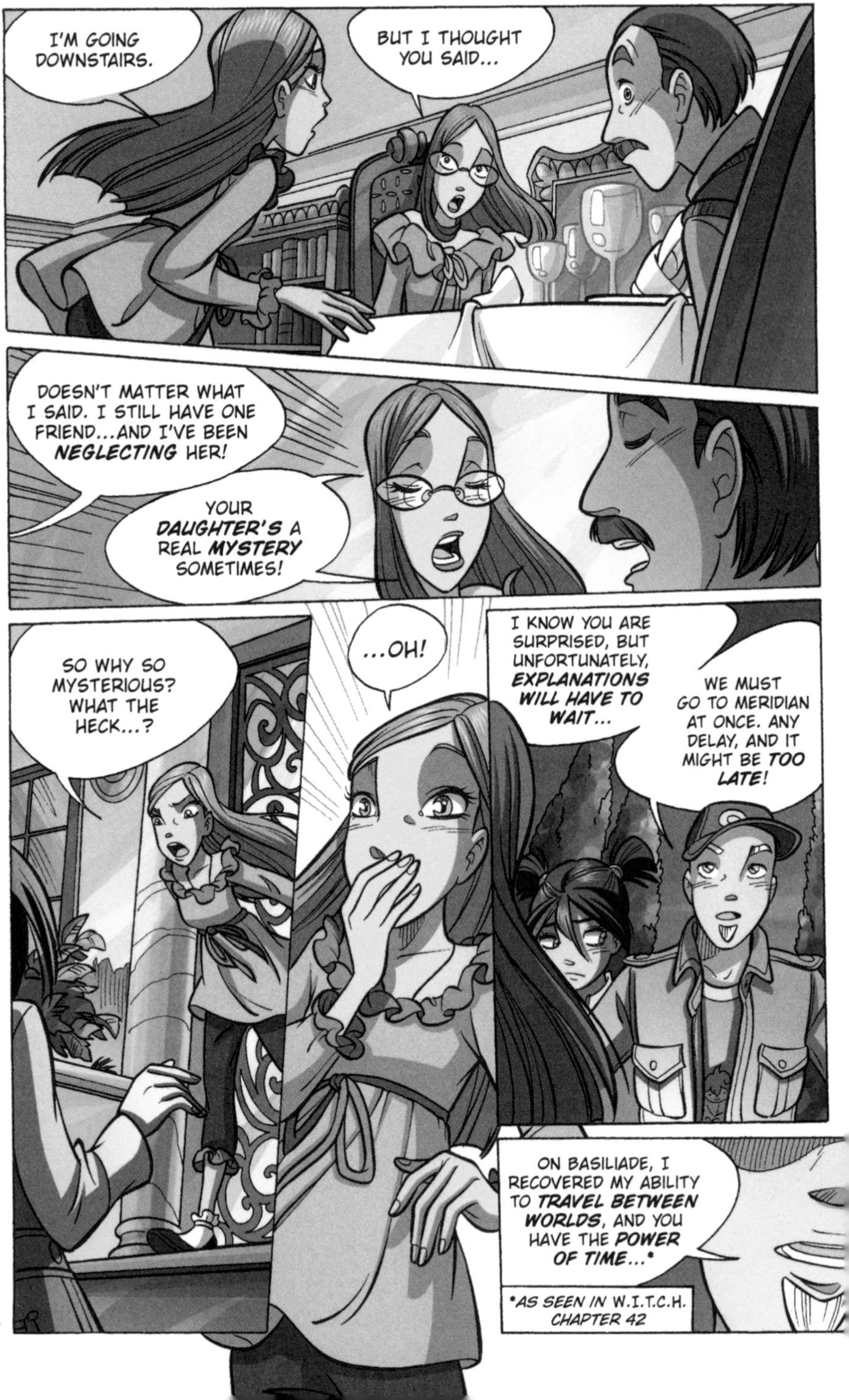
I'M GOING DOWNSTAIRS.
BUT I THOUGHT YOU SAID...
DOESN'T MATTER WHAT I SAID. I STILL HAVE ONE FRIEND...AND I'VE BEEN NEGLECTING HER!
YOUR DAUGHTER'S A REAL MYSTERY SOMETIMES!
SO WHY SO MYSTERIOUS? WHAT THE HECK...?
...OH!
I KNOW YOU ARE SURPRISED, BUT UNFORTUNATELY, EXPLANATIONS WILL HAVE TO WAIT...
WE MUST GO TO MERIDIAN AT ONCE. ANY DELAY, AND IT MIGHT BE TOO LATE!
ON BASILIADE, I RECOVERED MY ABILITY TO TRAVEL BETWEEN WORLDS, AND YOU HAVE THE POWER OF TIME...*
*AS SEEN IN W.I.T.C.H. CHAPTER 42

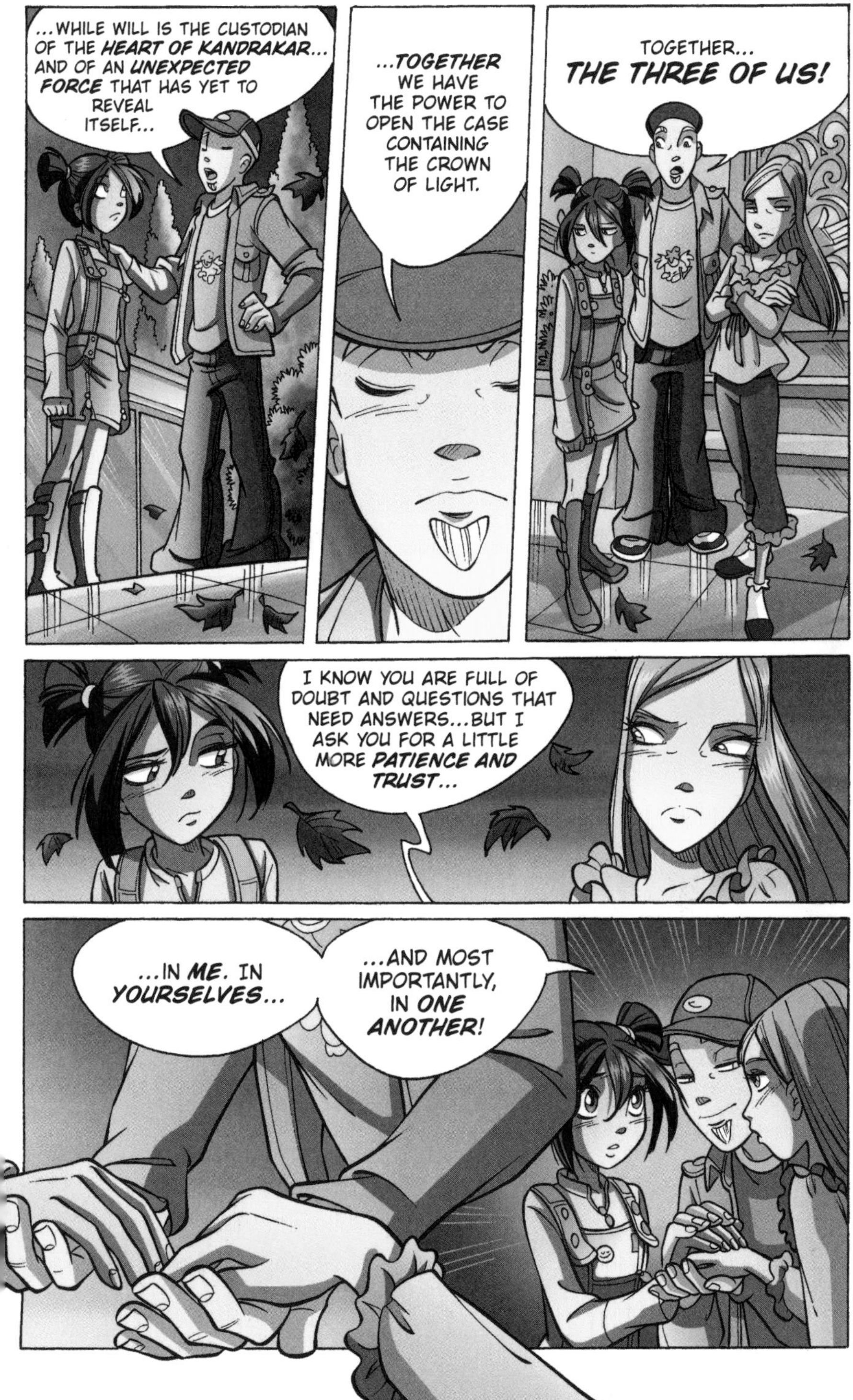
...WHILE WILL IS THE CUSTODIAN OF THE HEART OF KANDRAKAR... AND OF AN UNEXPECTED FORCE THAT HAS YET TO REVEAL ITSELF...
...TOGETHER WE HAVE THE POWER TO OPEN THE CASE CONTAINING THE CROWN OF LIGHT.
TOGETHER... THE THREE OF US!
I KNOW YOU ARE FULL OF DOUBT AND QUESTIONS THAT NEED ANSWERS...BUT I ASK YOU FOR A LITTLE MORE PATIENCE AND TRUST...
...IN ME. IN YOURSELVES...
...AND MOST IMPORTANTLY, IN ONE ANOTHER!

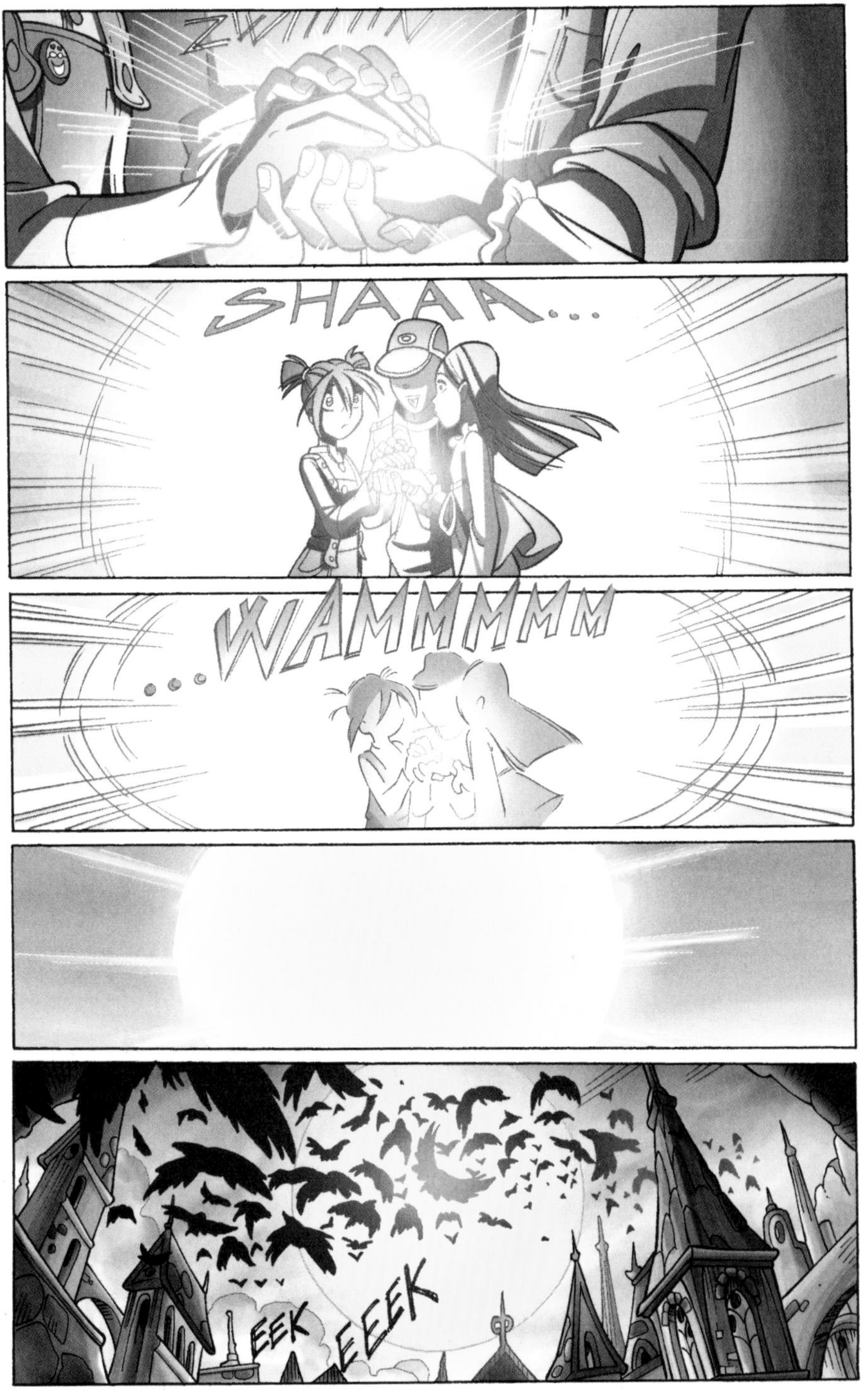
ZWIIIIIN
SHAAA...
...WAMMMMM
EEK
EEEK

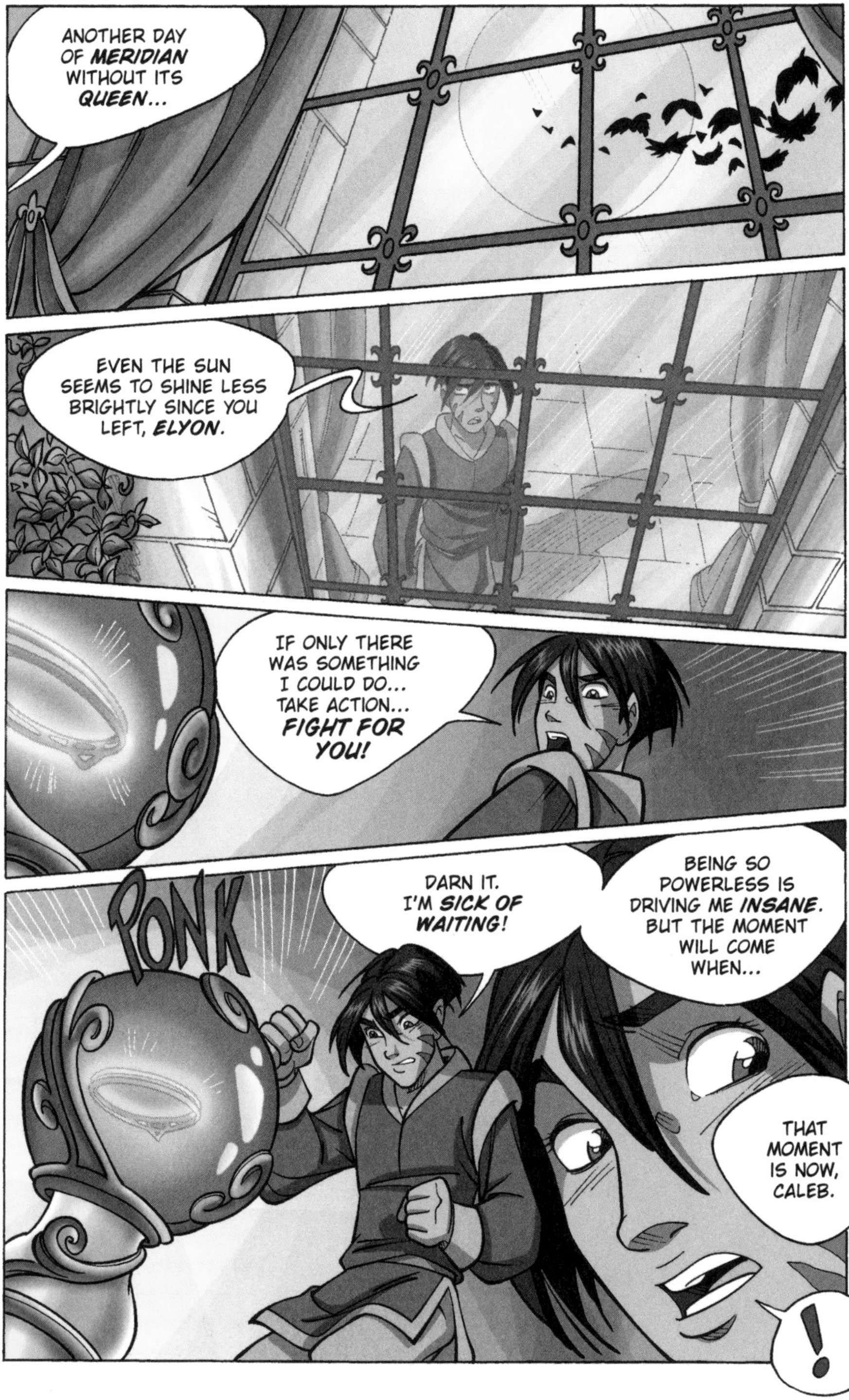
ANOTHER DAY OF MERIDIAN WITHOUT ITS QUEEN...
EVEN THE SUN SEEMS TO SHINE LESS BRIGHTLY SINCE YOU LEFT, ELYON.
IF ONLY THERE WAS SOMETHING I COULD DO... TAKE ACTION... FIGHT FOR YOU!
PONK
DARN IT. I'M SICK OF WAITING!
BEING SO POWERLESS IS DRIVING ME INSANE. BUT THE MOMENT WILL COME WHEN...
THAT MOMENT IS NOW, CALEB.
!

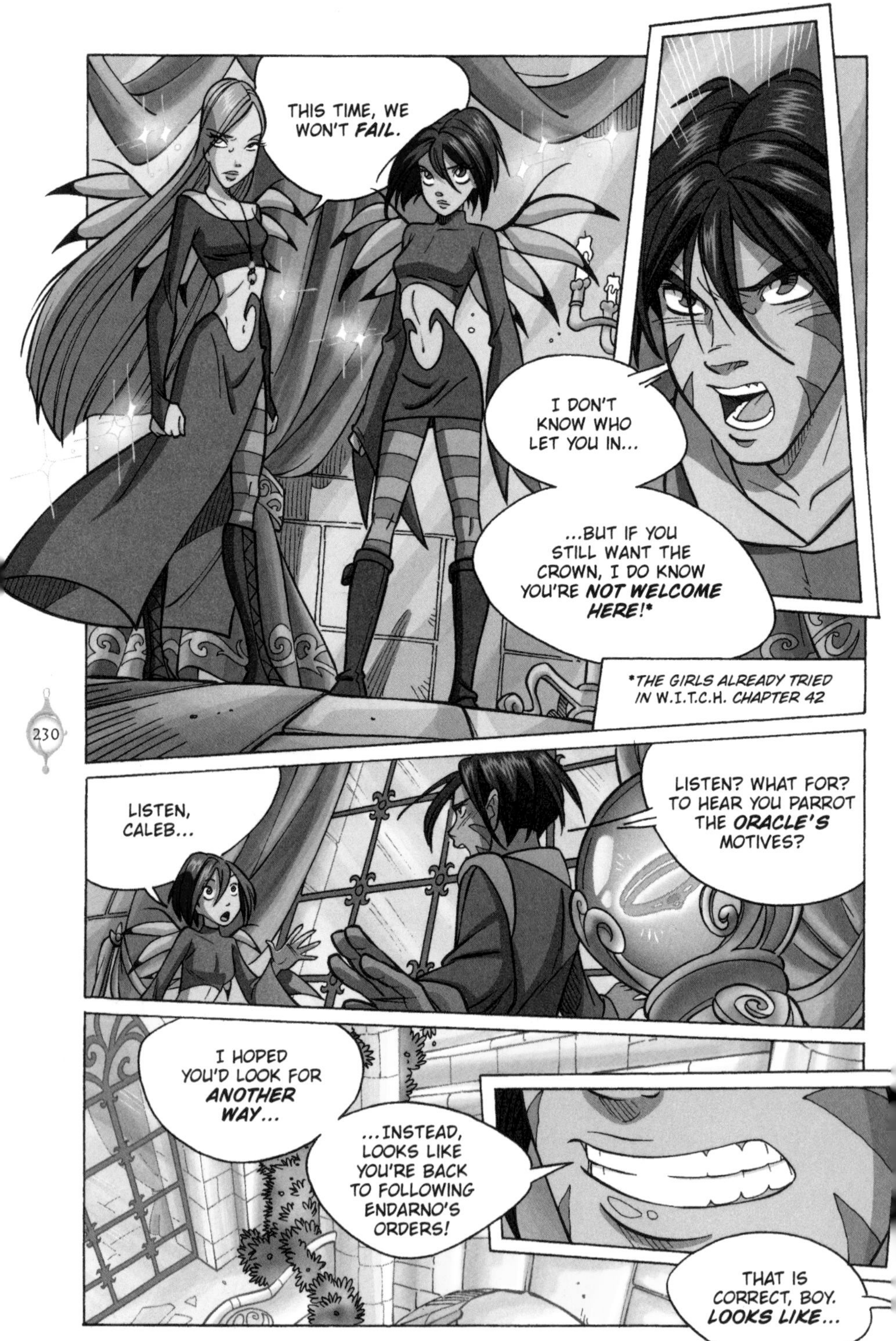

THIS TIME, WE WON'T **FAIL**.
I DON'T KNOW WHO LET YOU IN...
...BUT IF YOU STILL WANT THE CROWN, I DO KNOW YOU'RE **NOT WELCOME HERE!***
*THE GIRLS ALREADY TRIED IN W.I.T.C.H. CHAPTER 42
LISTEN, CALEB...
LISTEN? WHAT FOR? TO HEAR YOU PARROT THE **ORACLE'S** MOTIVES?
I HOPED YOU'D LOOK FOR **ANOTHER WAY...**
...INSTEAD, LOOKS LIKE YOU'RE BACK TO FOLLOWING ENDARNO'S ORDERS!
THAT IS CORRECT, BOY. **LOOKS LIKE...**

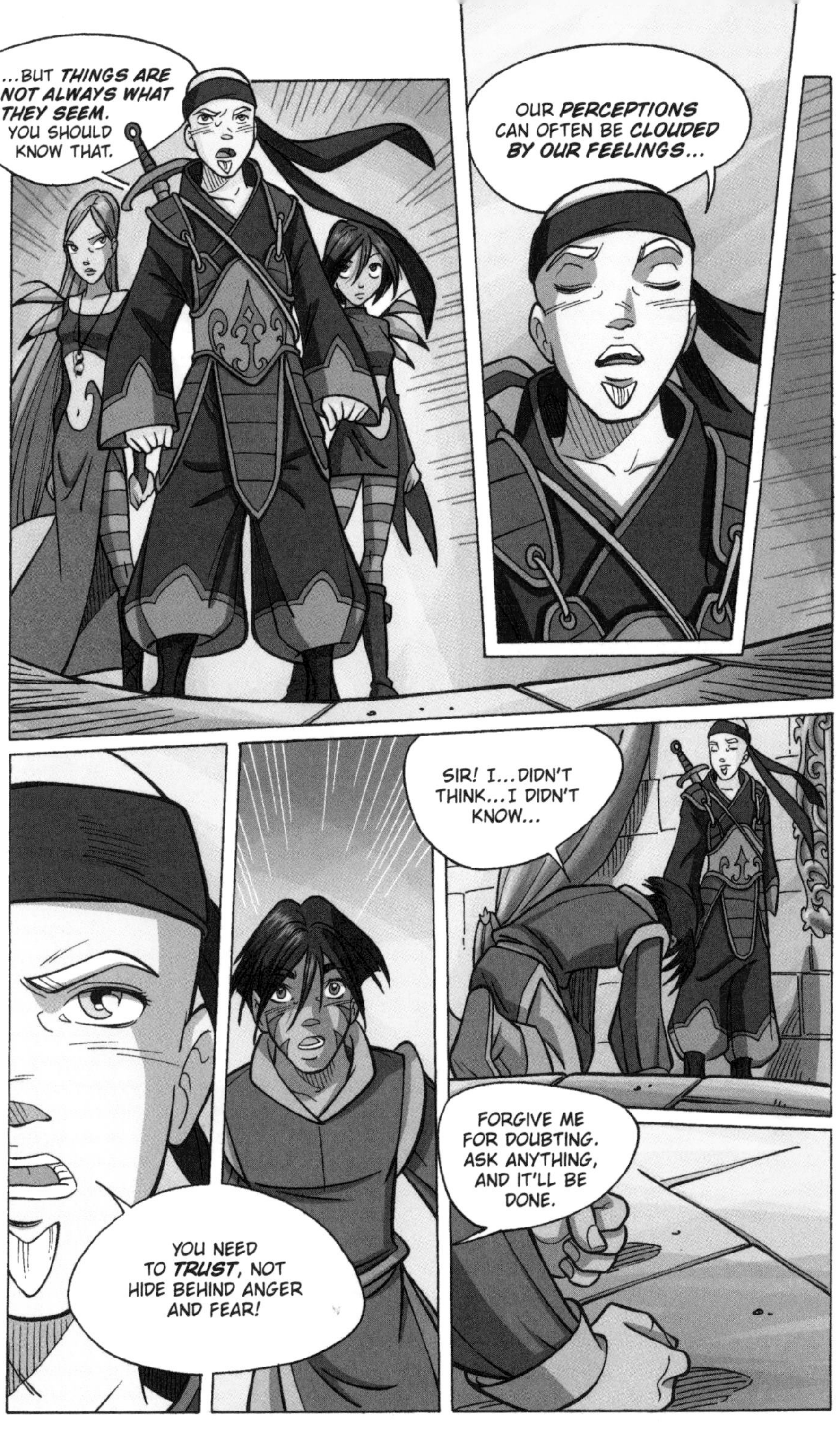

...BUT THINGS ARE NOT ALWAYS WHAT THEY SEEM. YOU SHOULD KNOW THAT.
OUR PERCEPTIONS CAN OFTEN BE CLOUDED BY OUR FEELINGS...
YOU NEED TO TRUST, NOT HIDE BEHIND ANGER AND FEAR!
SIR! I...DIDN'T THINK...I DIDN'T KNOW...
FORGIVE ME FOR DOUBTING. ASK ANYTHING, AND IT'LL BE DONE.

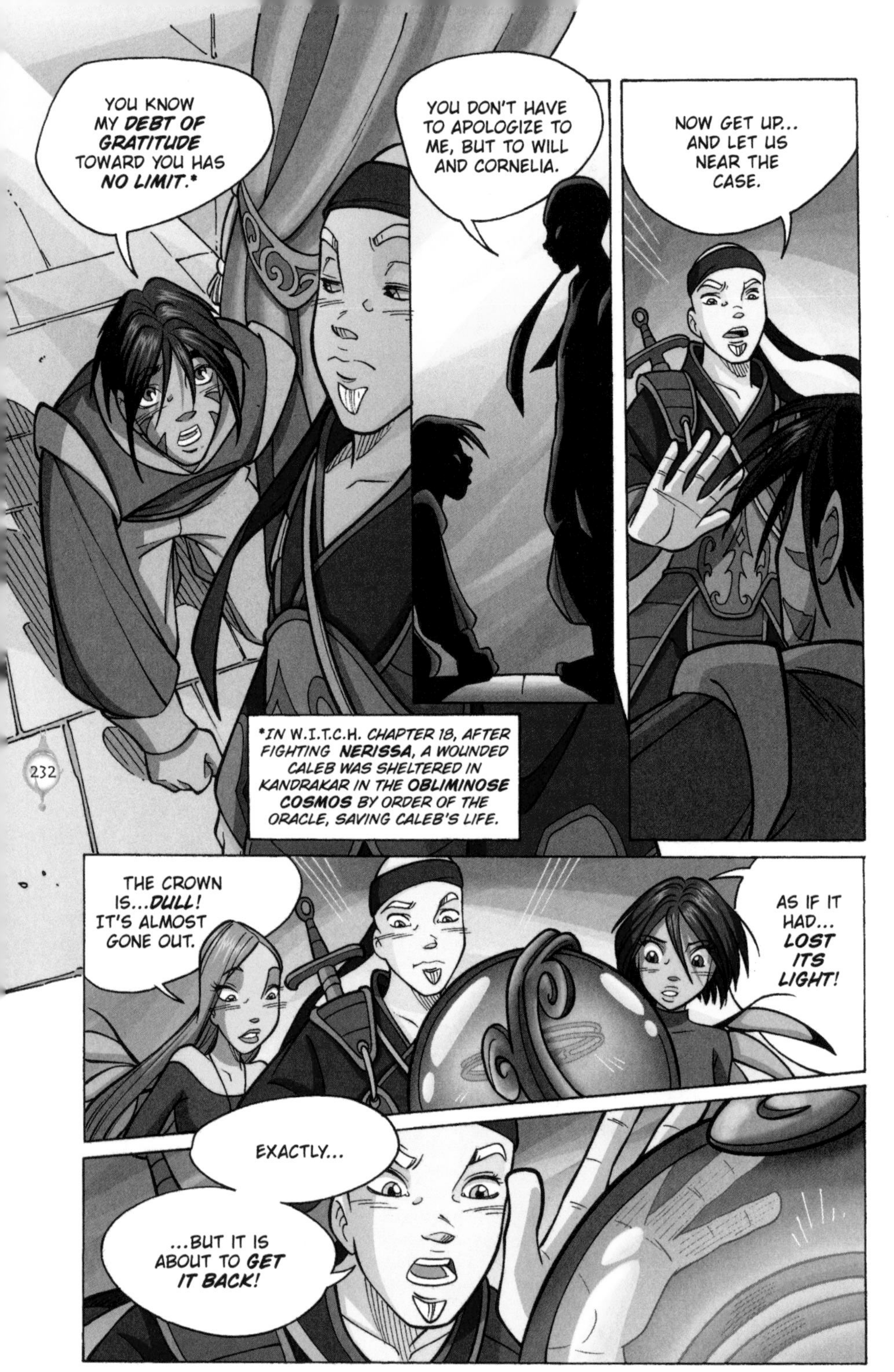
YOU KNOW MY DEBT OF GRATITUDE TOWARD YOU HAS NO LIMIT.*
YOU DON'T HAVE TO APOLOGIZE TO ME, BUT TO WILL AND CORNELIA.
NOW GET UP... AND LET US NEAR THE CASE.
*IN W.I.T.C.H. CHAPTER 18, AFTER FIGHTING NERISSA, A WOUNDED CALEB WAS SHELTERED IN KANDRAKAR IN THE OBLIMINOSE COSMOS BY ORDER OF THE ORACLE, SAVING CALEB'S LIFE.
THE CROWN IS...DULL! IT'S ALMOST GONE OUT.
AS IF IT HAD... LOST ITS LIGHT!
EXACTLY...
...BUT IT IS ABOUT TO GET IT BACK!

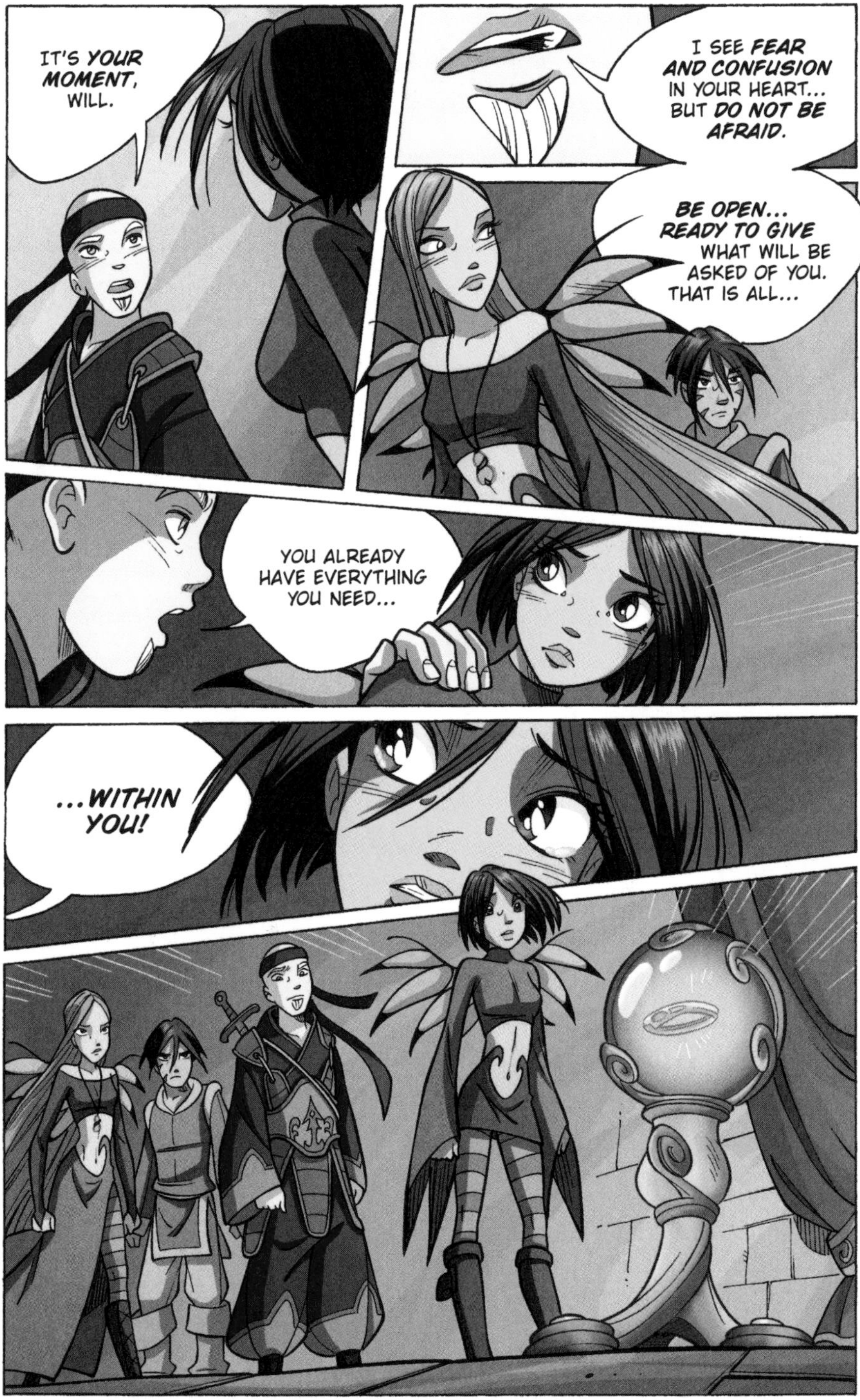
IT'S YOUR MOMENT, WILL.
I SEE FEAR AND CONFUSION IN YOUR HEART... BUT DO NOT BE AFRAID.
BE OPEN... READY TO GIVE WHAT WILL BE ASKED OF YOU. THAT IS ALL...
YOU ALREADY HAVE EVERYTHING YOU NEED...
...WITHIN YOU!

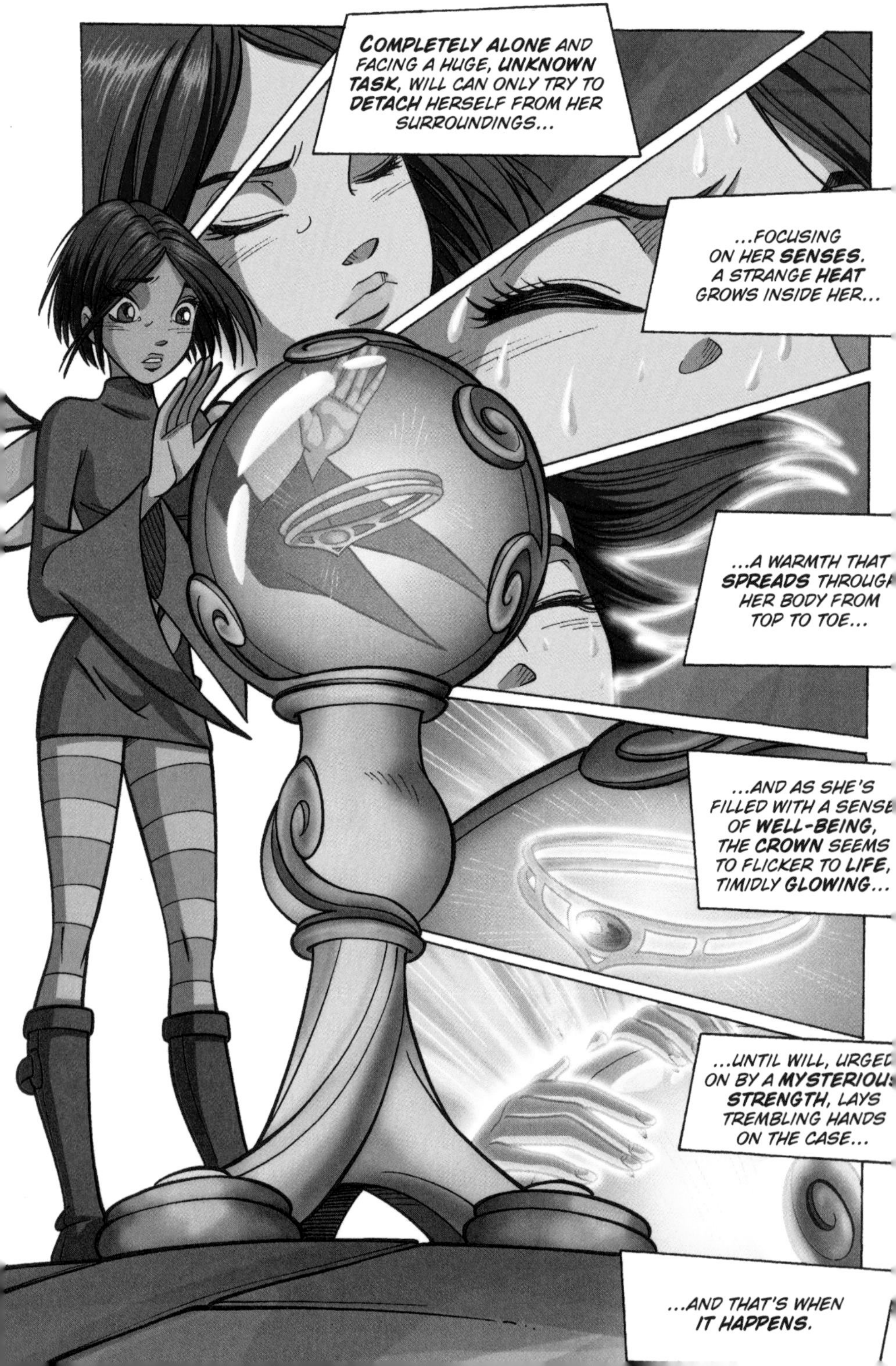
COMPLETELY ALONE AND FACING A HUGE, UNKNOWN TASK, WILL CAN ONLY TRY TO DETACH HERSELF FROM HER SURROUNDINGS...
...FOCUSING ON HER SENSES. A STRANGE HEAT GROWS INSIDE HER...
...A WARMTH THAT SPREADS THROUGH HER BODY FROM TOP TO TOE...
...AND AS SHE'S FILLED WITH A SENSE OF WELL-BEING, THE CROWN SEEMS TO FLICKER TO LIFE, TIMIDLY GLOWING...
...UNTIL WILL, URGED ON BY A MYSTERIOUS STRENGTH, LAYS TREMBLING HANDS ON THE CASE...
...AND THAT'S WHEN IT HAPPENS.

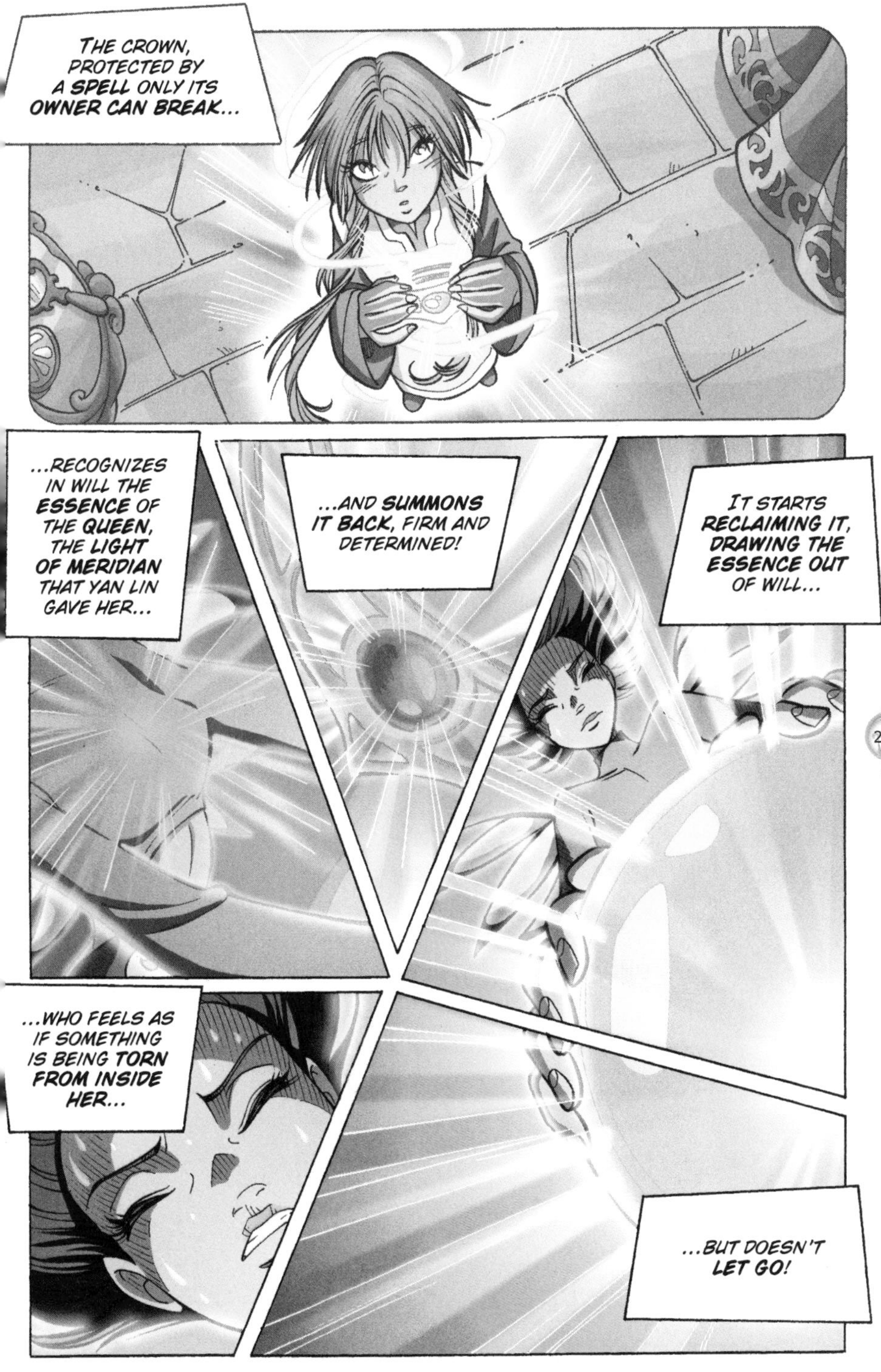
THE CROWN, PROTECTED BY A SPELL ONLY ITS OWNER CAN BREAK...
...RECOGNIZES IN WILL THE ESSENCE OF THE QUEEN, THE LIGHT OF MERIDIAN THAT YAN LIN GAVE HER...
...AND SUMMONS IT BACK, FIRM AND DETERMINED!
IT STARTS RECLAIMING IT, DRAWING THE ESSENCE OUT OF WILL...
...WHO FEELS AS IF SOMETHING IS BEING TORN FROM INSIDE HER...
...BUT DOESN'T LET GO!

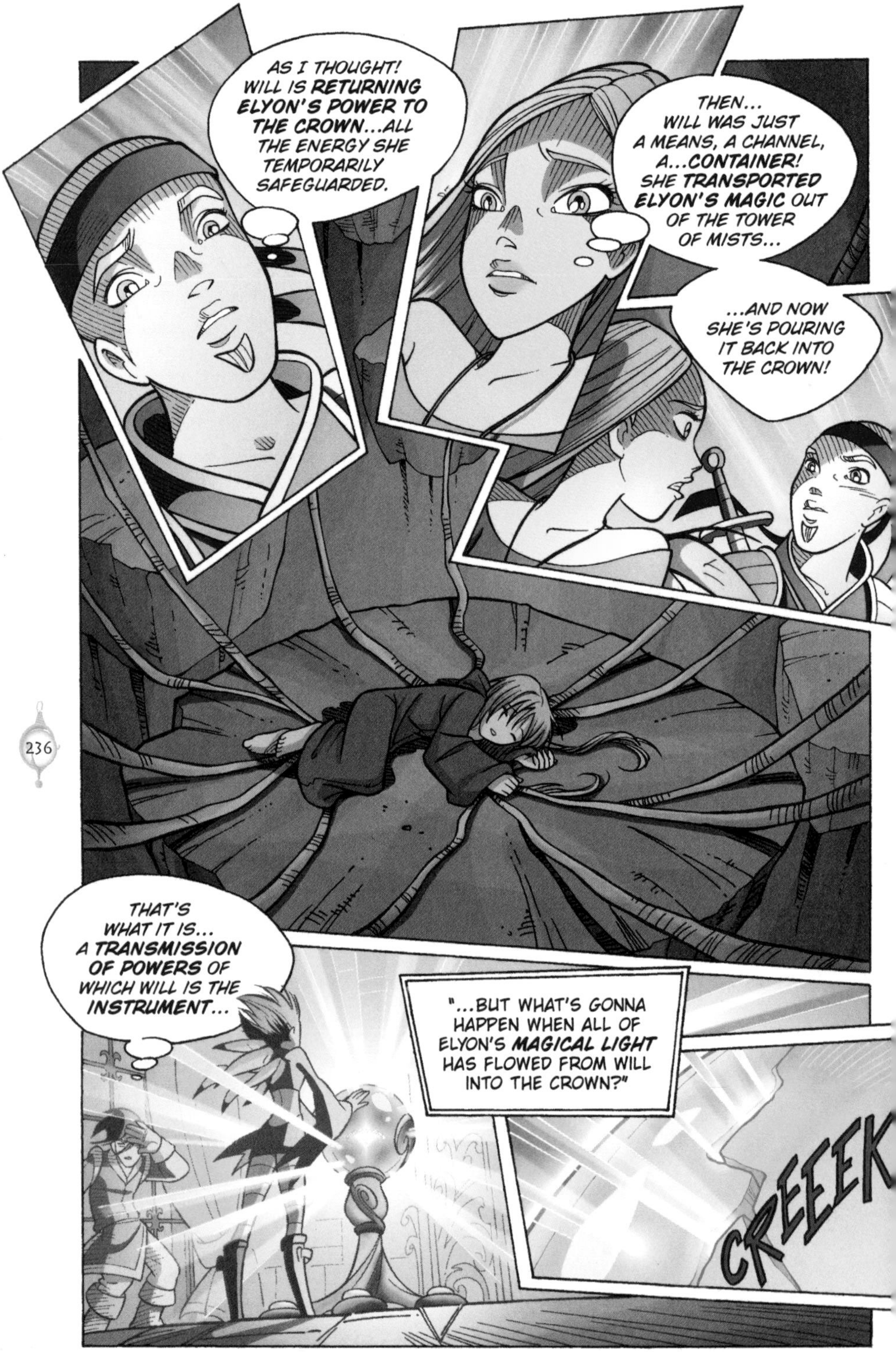
AS I THOUGHT! WILL IS RETURNING ELYON'S POWER TO THE CROWN...ALL THE ENERGY SHE TEMPORARILY SAFEGUARDED.
THEN... WILL WAS JUST A MEANS, A CHANNEL, A...CONTAINER! SHE TRANSPORTED ELYON'S MAGIC OUT OF THE TOWER OF MISTS...
...AND NOW SHE'S POURING IT BACK INTO THE CROWN!
THAT'S WHAT IT IS... A TRANSMISSION OF POWERS OF WHICH WILL IS THE INSTRUMENT...
"...BUT WHAT'S GONNA HAPPEN WHEN ALL OF ELYON'S MAGICAL LIGHT HAS FLOWED FROM WILL INTO THE CROWN?"
CREEEK

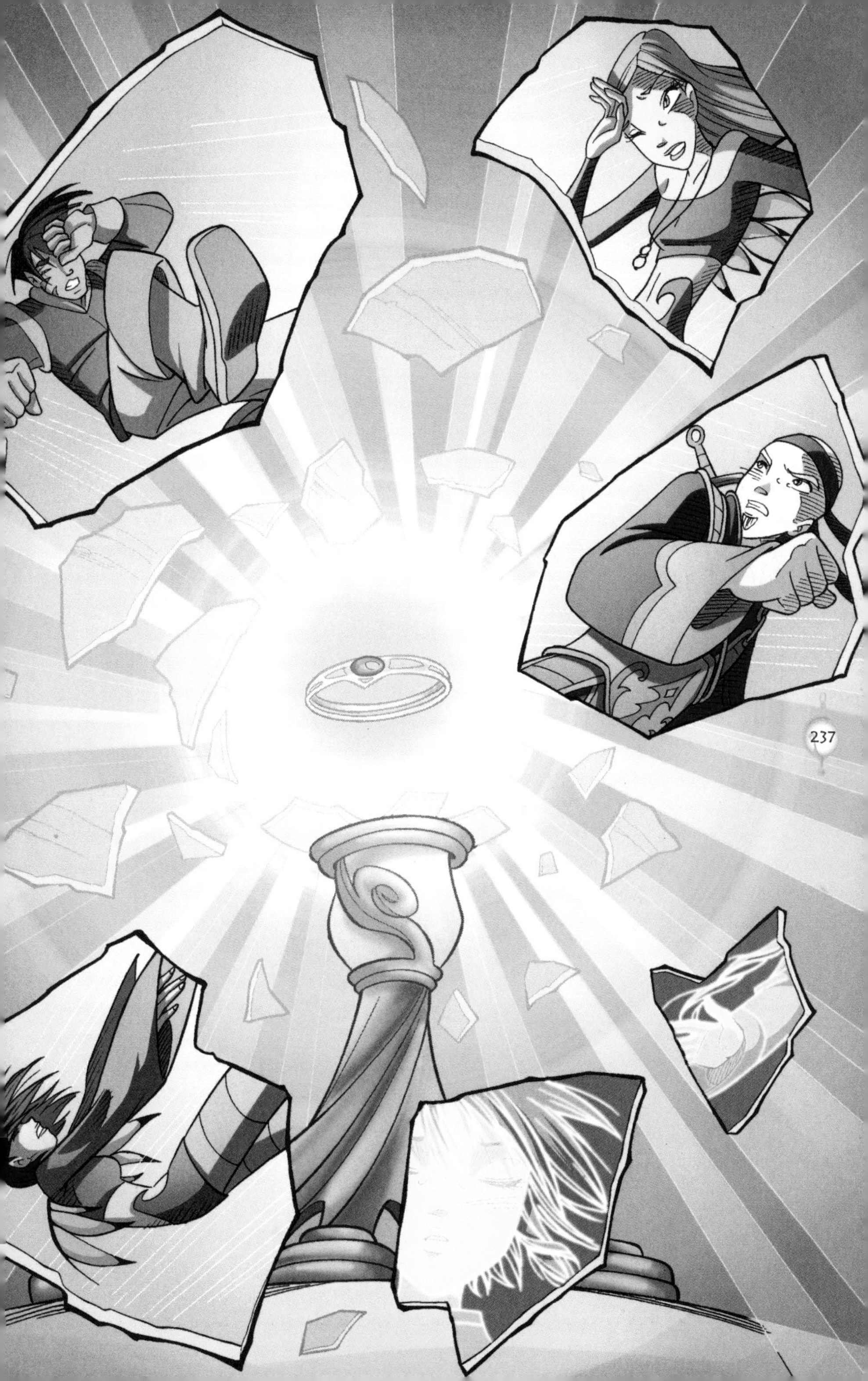

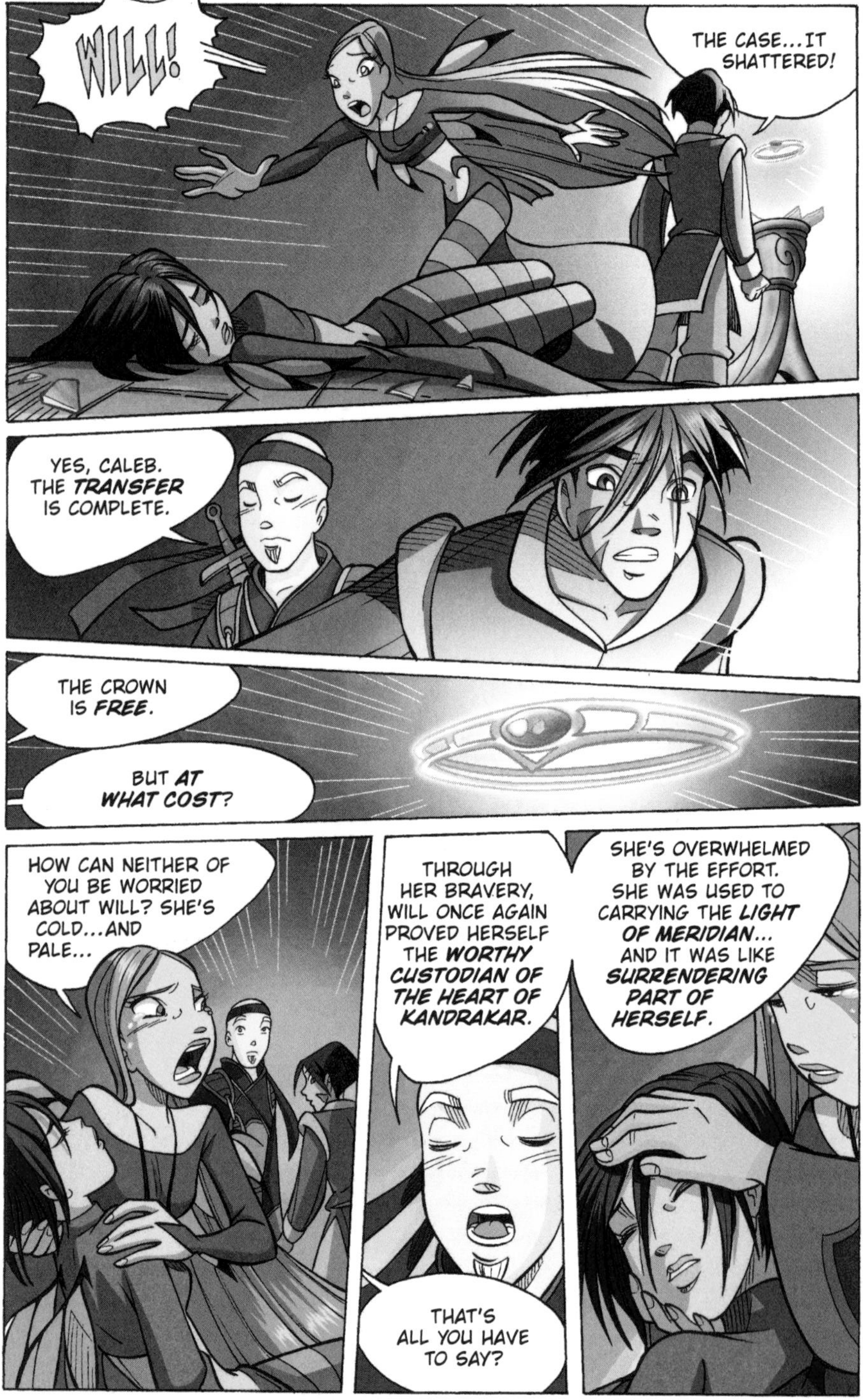

WILL!
THE CASE...IT SHATTERED!
YES, CALEB. THE TRANSFER IS COMPLETE.
THE CROWN IS FREE.
BUT AT WHAT COST?
HOW CAN NEITHER OF YOU BE WORRIED ABOUT WILL? SHE'S COLD...AND PALE...
THROUGH HER BRAVERY, WILL ONCE AGAIN PROVED HERSELF THE WORTHY CUSTODIAN OF THE HEART OF KANDRAKAR.
THAT'S ALL YOU HAVE TO SAY?
SHE'S OVERWHELMED BY THE EFFORT. SHE WAS USED TO CARRYING THE LIGHT OF MERIDIAN... AND IT WAS LIKE SURRENDERING PART OF HERSELF.

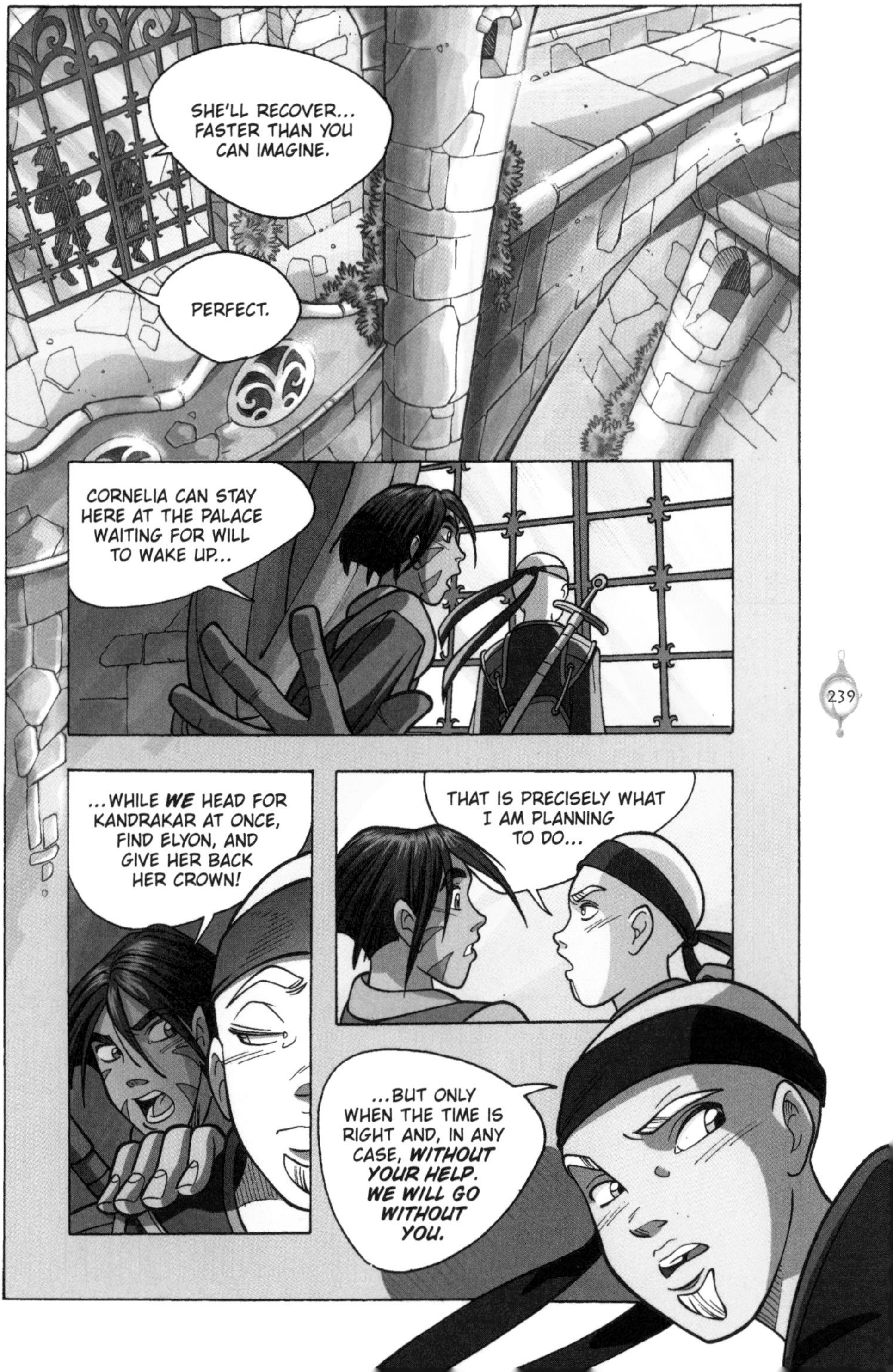
SHE'LL RECOVER... FASTER THAN YOU CAN IMAGINE.
PERFECT.
CORNELIA CAN STAY HERE AT THE PALACE WAITING FOR WILL TO WAKE UP...
...WHILE ***WE*** HEAD FOR KANDRAKAR AT ONCE, FIND ELYON, AND GIVE HER BACK HER CROWN!
THAT IS PRECISELY WHAT I AM PLANNING TO DO...
...BUT ONLY WHEN THE TIME IS RIGHT AND, IN ANY CASE, ***WITHOUT YOUR HELP. WE WILL GO WITHOUT YOU.***

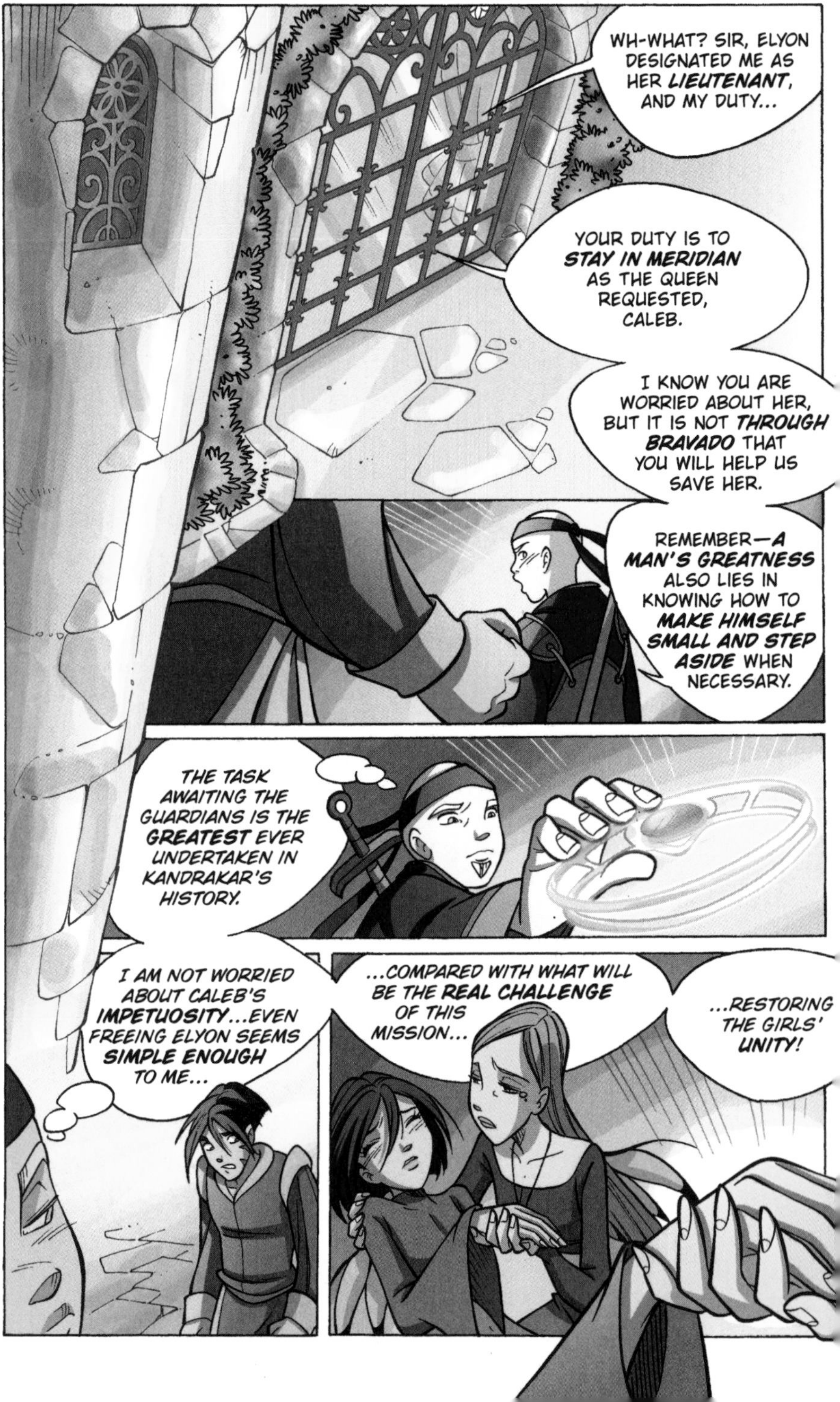
WH-WHAT? SIR, ELYON DESIGNATED ME AS HER LIEUTENANT, AND MY DUTY...
YOUR DUTY IS TO STAY IN MERIDIAN AS THE QUEEN REQUESTED, CALEB.
I KNOW YOU ARE WORRIED ABOUT HER, BUT IT IS NOT THROUGH BRAVADO THAT YOU WILL HELP US SAVE HER.
REMEMBER—A MAN'S GREATNESS ALSO LIES IN KNOWING HOW TO MAKE HIMSELF SMALL AND STEP ASIDE WHEN NECESSARY.
THE TASK AWAITING THE GUARDIANS IS THE GREATEST EVER UNDERTAKEN IN KANDRAKAR'S HISTORY.
I AM NOT WORRIED ABOUT CALEB'S IMPETUOSITY...EVEN FREEING ELYON SEEMS SIMPLE ENOUGH TO ME...
...COMPARED WITH WHAT WILL BE THE REAL CHALLENGE OF THIS MISSION...
...RESTORING THE GIRLS' UNITY!

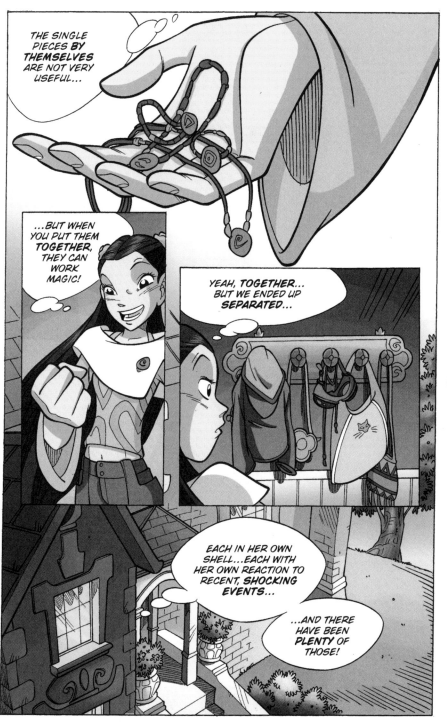

THE SINGLE PIECES **BY THEMSELVES** ARE NOT VERY USEFUL...

...BUT WHEN YOU PUT THEM **TOGETHER,** THEY CAN WORK **MAGIC!**

YEAH, TOGETHER... BUT WE ENDED UP **SEPARATED**...

EACH IN HER OWN SHELL...EACH WITH HER OWN REACTION TO RECENT, **SHOCKING** EVENTS...

...AND THERE HAVE BEEN **PLENTY** OF THOSE!

241

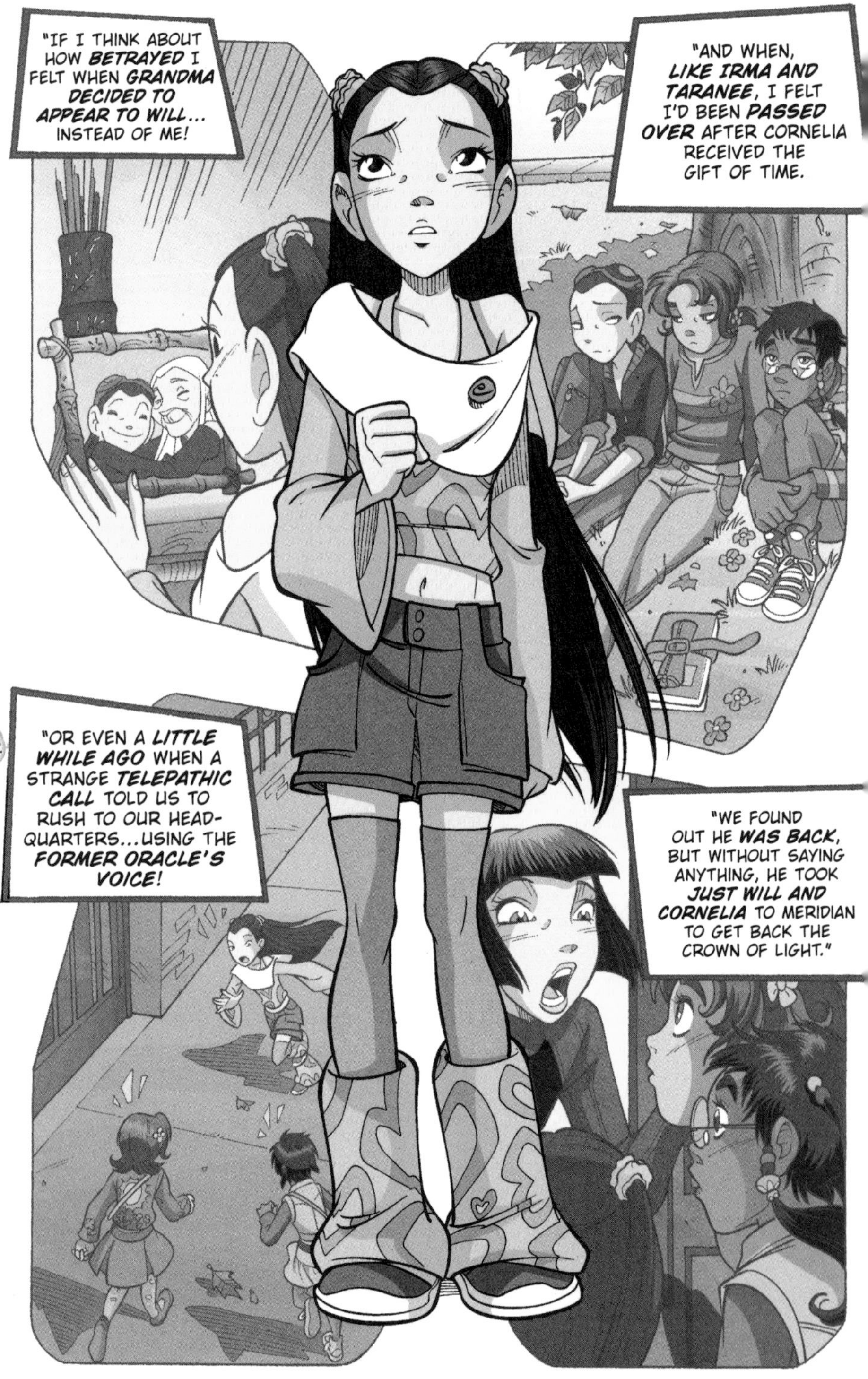
"IF I THINK ABOUT HOW **BETRAYED** I FELT WHEN **GRANDMA DECIDED TO APPEAR TO WILL**... INSTEAD OF ME!
"AND WHEN, **LIKE IRMA AND TARANEE**, I FELT I'D BEEN **PASSED OVER** AFTER CORNELIA RECEIVED THE GIFT OF TIME.
"OR EVEN A **LITTLE WHILE AGO** WHEN A STRANGE **TELEPATHIC CALL** TOLD US TO RUSH TO OUR HEADQUARTERS...USING THE **FORMER ORACLE'S VOICE**!
"WE FOUND OUT HE **WAS BACK**, BUT WITHOUT SAYING ANYTHING, HE TOOK **JUST WILL AND CORNELIA** TO MERIDIAN TO GET BACK THE CROWN OF LIGHT."

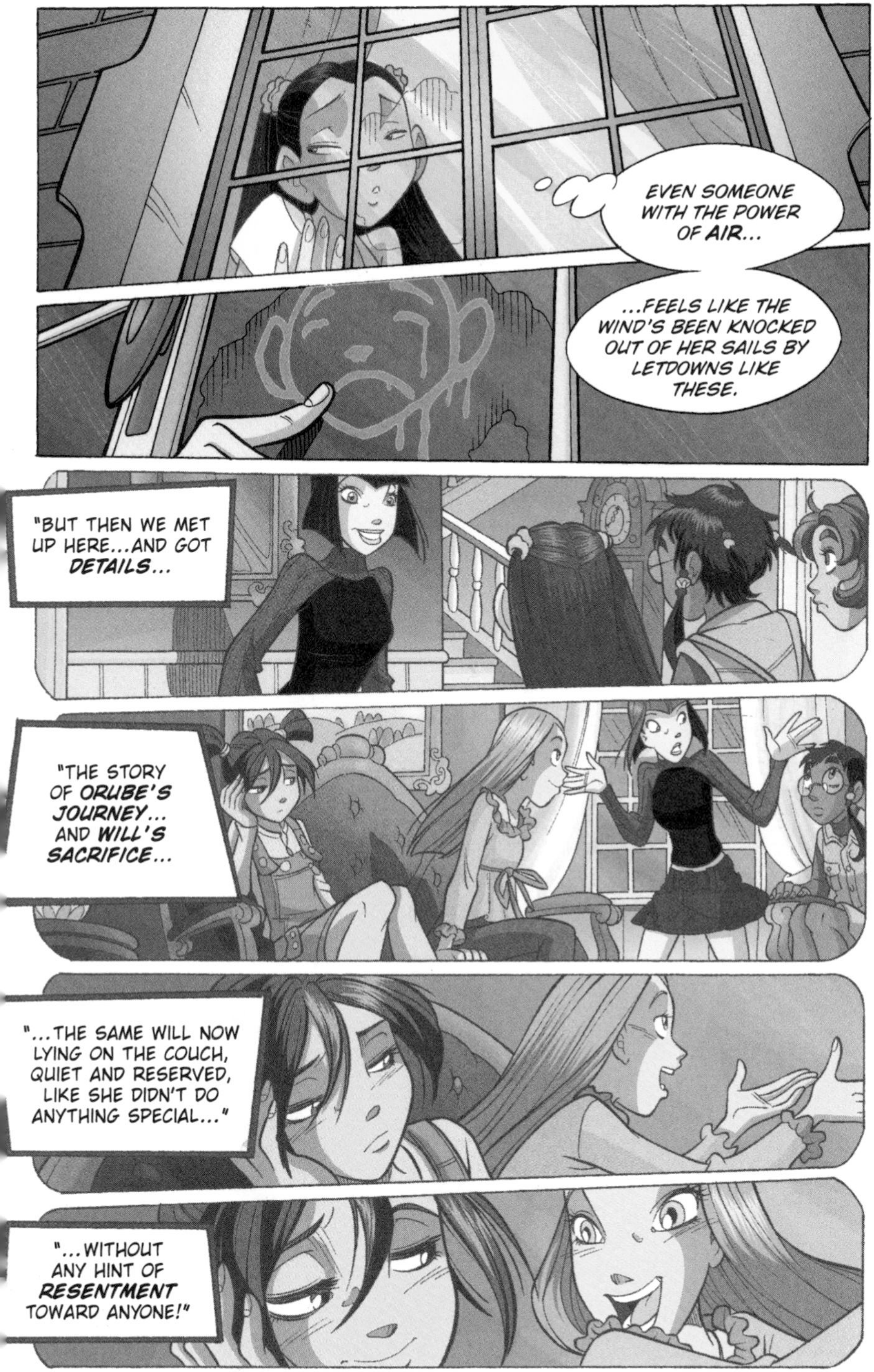
EVEN SOMEONE WITH THE POWER OF AIR...
...FEELS LIKE THE WIND'S BEEN KNOCKED OUT OF HER SAILS BY LETDOWNS LIKE THESE.
"BUT THEN WE MET UP HERE...AND GOT DETAILS...
"THE STORY OF ORUBE'S JOURNEY... AND WILL'S SACRIFICE...
"...THE SAME WILL NOW LYING ON THE COUCH, QUIET AND RESERVED, LIKE SHE DIDN'T DO ANYTHING SPECIAL..."
"...WITHOUT ANY HINT OF RESENTMENT TOWARD ANYONE!"

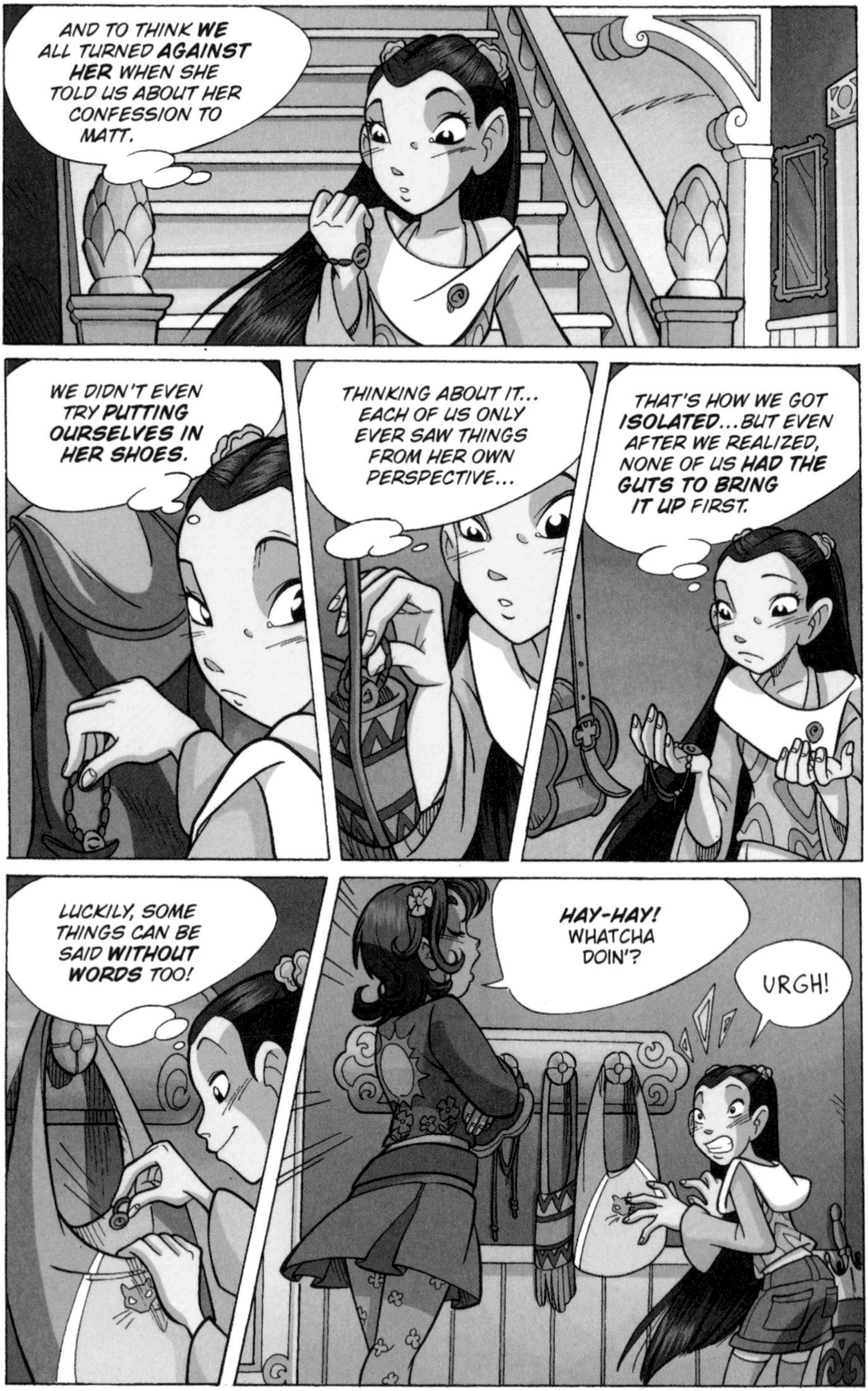
AND TO THINK WE ALL TURNED AGAINST HER WHEN SHE TOLD US ABOUT HER CONFESSION TO MATT.
WE DIDN'T EVEN TRY PUTTING OURSELVES IN HER SHOES.
THINKING ABOUT IT... EACH OF US ONLY EVER SAW THINGS FROM HER OWN PERSPECTIVE...
THAT'S HOW WE GOT ISOLATED...BUT EVEN AFTER WE REALIZED, NONE OF US HAD THE GUTS TO BRING IT UP FIRST.
LUCKILY, SOME THINGS CAN BE SAID WITHOUT WORDS TOO!
HAY-HAY! WHATCHA DOIN'?
URGH!

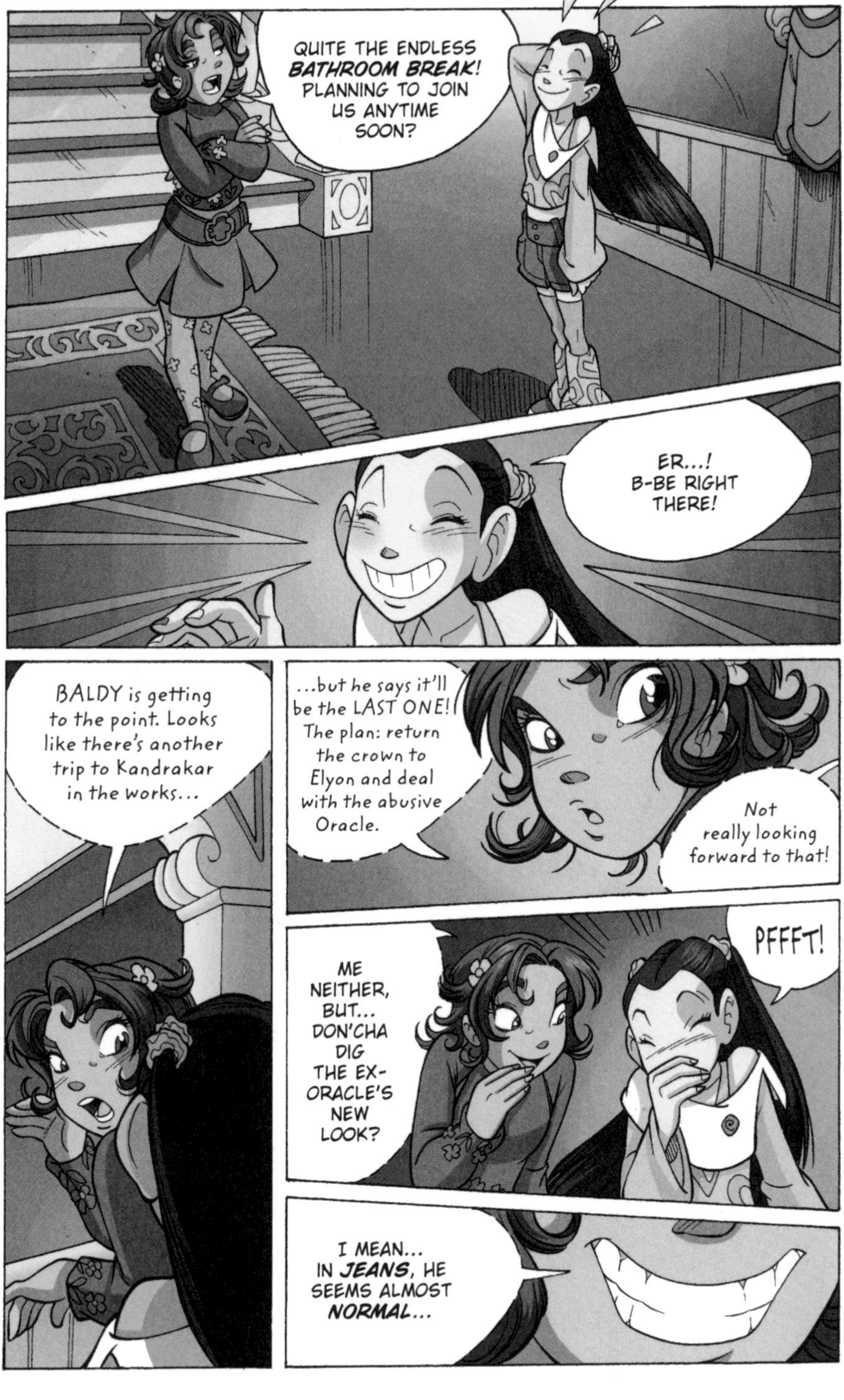
QUITE THE ENDLESS **BATHROOM BREAK**! PLANNING TO JOIN US ANYTIME SOON?
ER...! B-BE RIGHT THERE!
BALDY is getting to the point. Looks like there's another trip to Kandrakar in the works...
...but he says it'll be the LAST ONE! The plan: return the crown to Elyon and deal with the abusive Oracle.
Not really looking forward to that!
ME NEITHER, BUT... DON'CHA DIG THE EX-ORACLE'S NEW LOOK?
PFFFT!
I MEAN... IN **JEANS**, HE SEEMS ALMOST **NORMAL**...

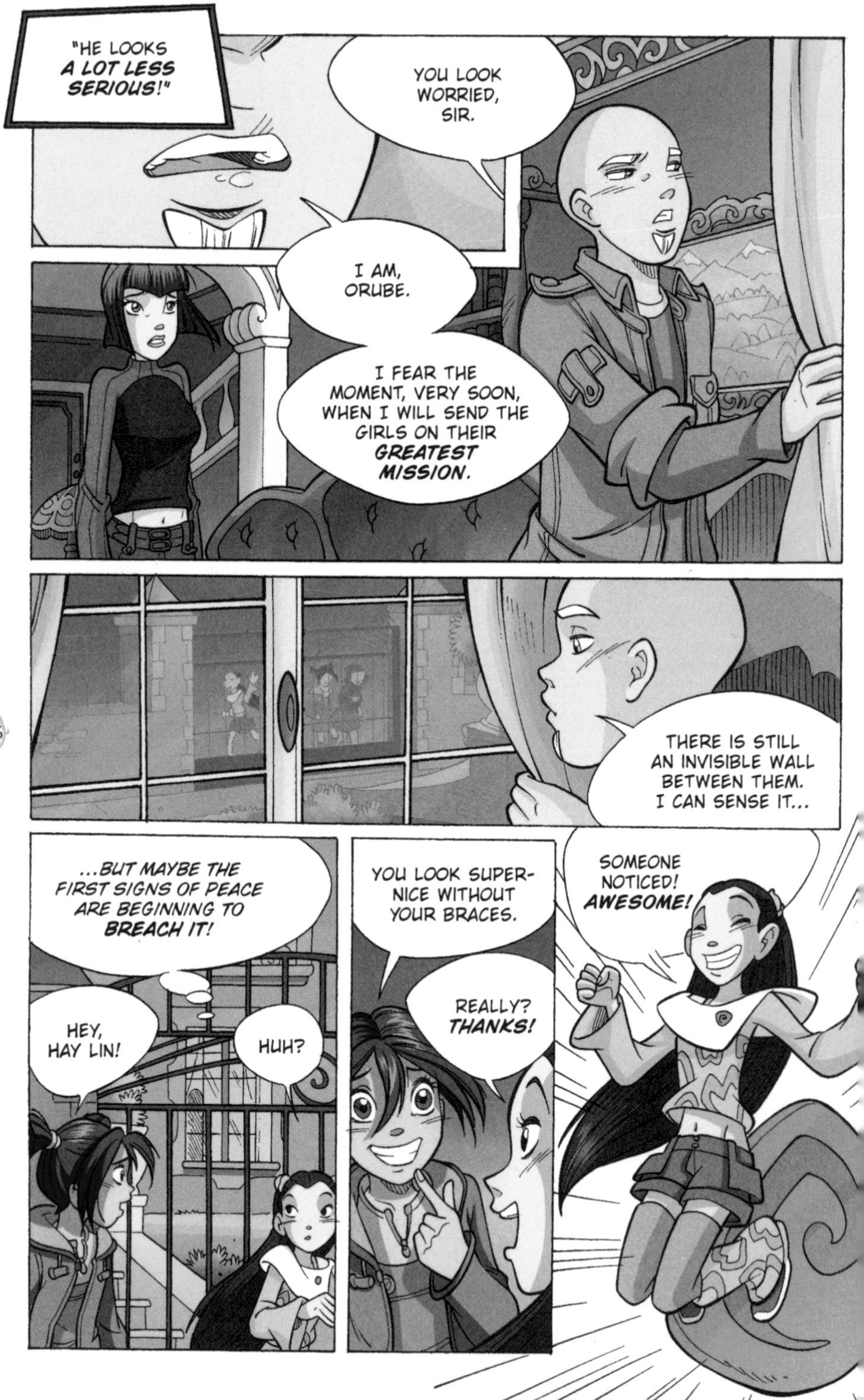
"HE LOOKS A LOT LESS SERIOUS!"
YOU LOOK WORRIED, SIR.
I AM, ORUBE.
I FEAR THE MOMENT, VERY SOON, WHEN I WILL SEND THE GIRLS ON THEIR GREATEST MISSION.
THERE IS STILL AN INVISIBLE WALL BETWEEN THEM. I CAN SENSE IT...
...BUT MAYBE THE FIRST SIGNS OF PEACE ARE BEGINNING TO BREACH IT!
HEY, HAY LIN!
HUH?
YOU LOOK SUPER-NICE WITHOUT YOUR BRACES.
REALLY? THANKS!
SOMEONE NOTICED! AWESOME!

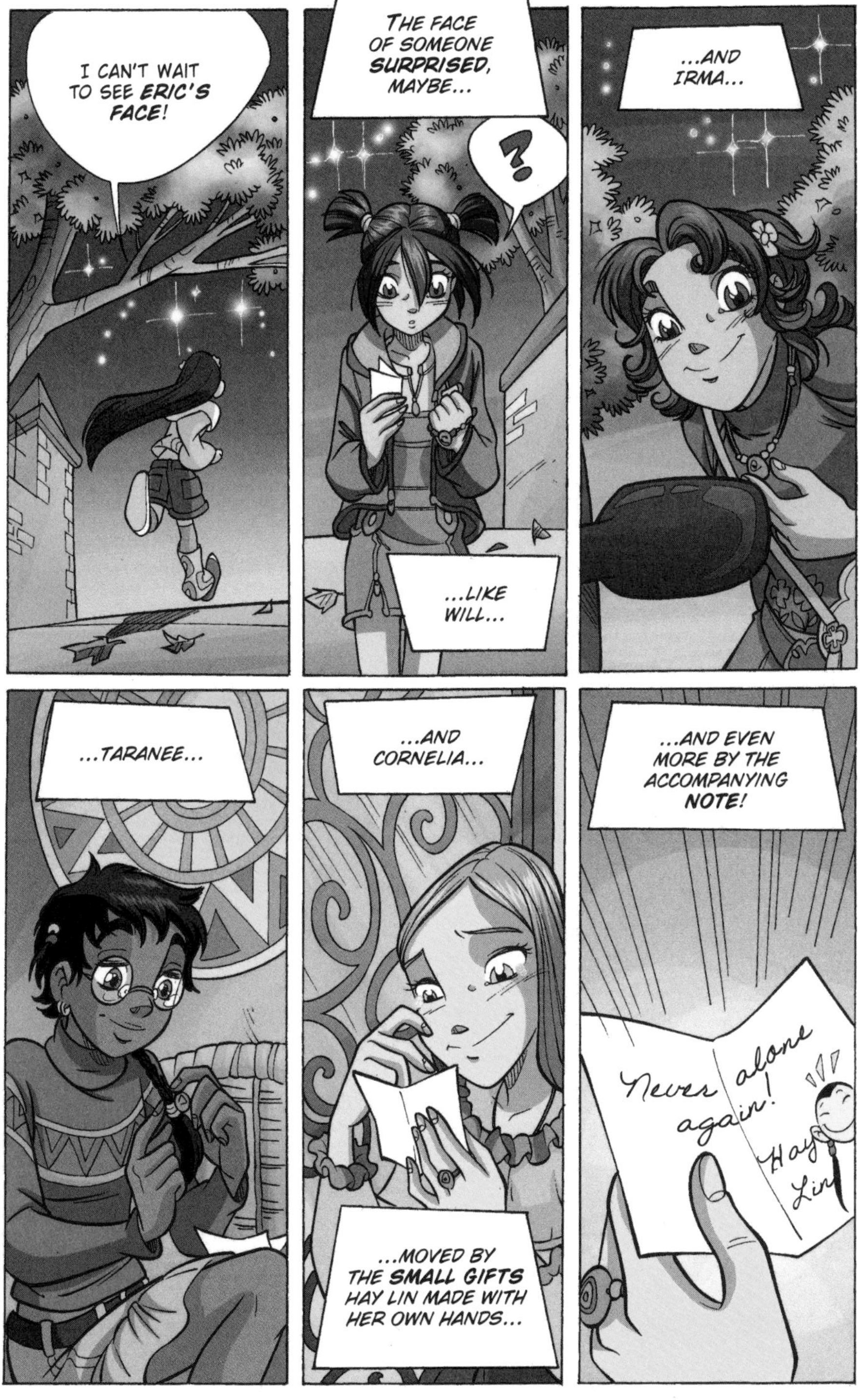
I CAN'T WAIT TO SEE ERIC'S FACE!
THE FACE OF SOMEONE SURPRISED, MAYBE...
?
...LIKE WILL...
...AND IRMA...
...TARANEE...
...AND CORNELIA...
...MOVED BY THE SMALL GIFTS HAY LIN MADE WITH HER OWN HANDS...
...AND EVEN MORE BY THE ACCOMPANYING NOTE!
Never alone again!
Hay Lin

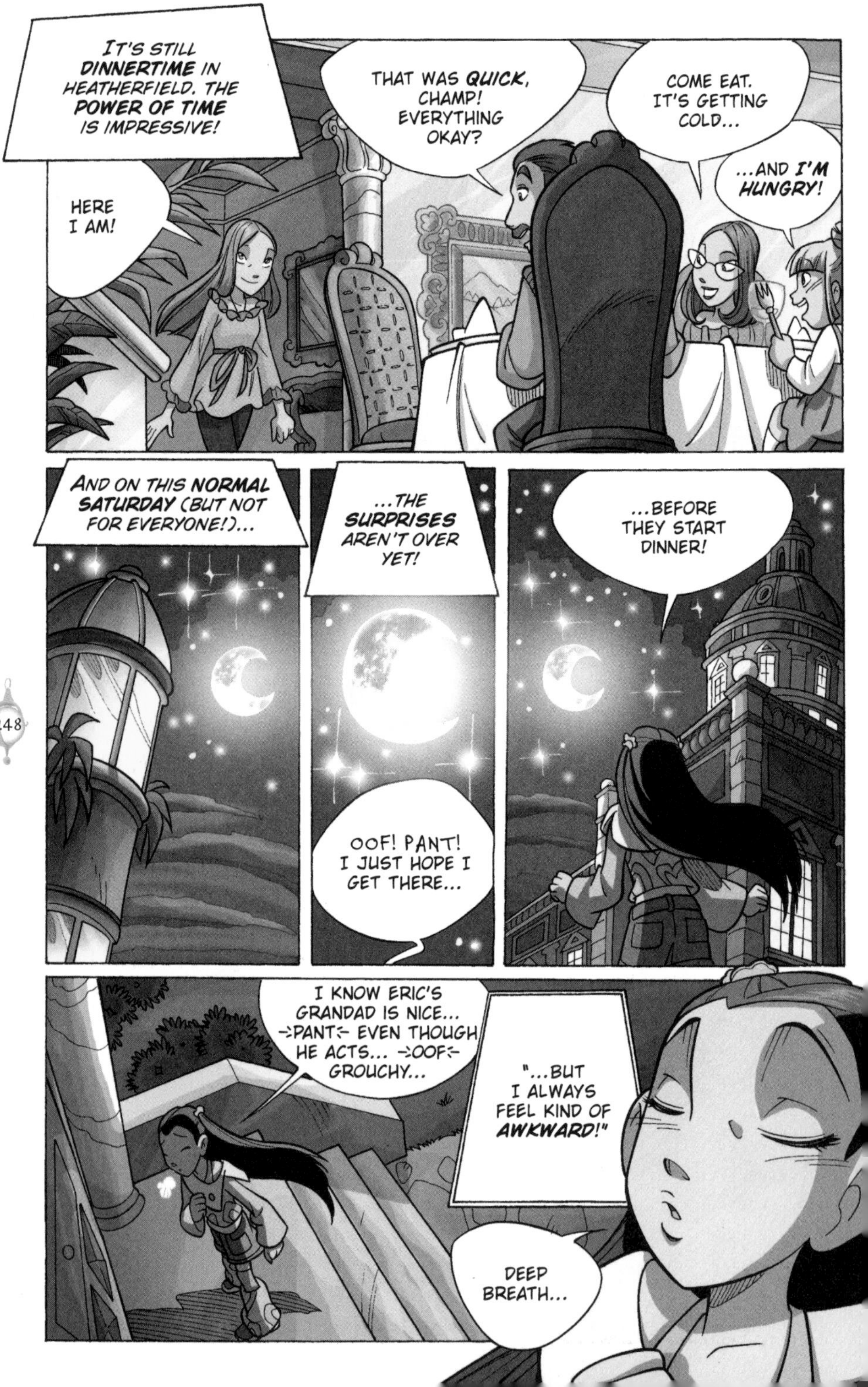
IT'S STILL DINNERTIME IN HEATHERFIELD. THE POWER OF TIME IS IMPRESSIVE!
THAT WAS QUICK, CHAMP! EVERYTHING OKAY?
COME EAT. IT'S GETTING COLD...
...AND I'M HUNGRY!
HERE I AM!
AND ON THIS NORMAL SATURDAY (BUT NOT FOR EVERYONE!)...
...THE SURPRISES AREN'T OVER YET!
OOF! PANT! I JUST HOPE I GET THERE...
...BEFORE THEY START DINNER!
I KNOW ERIC'S GRANDAD IS NICE... ⇾PANT⇽ EVEN THOUGH HE ACTS... ⇾OOF⇽ GROUCHY...
"...BUT I ALWAYS FEEL KIND OF AWKWARD!"
DEEP BREATH...

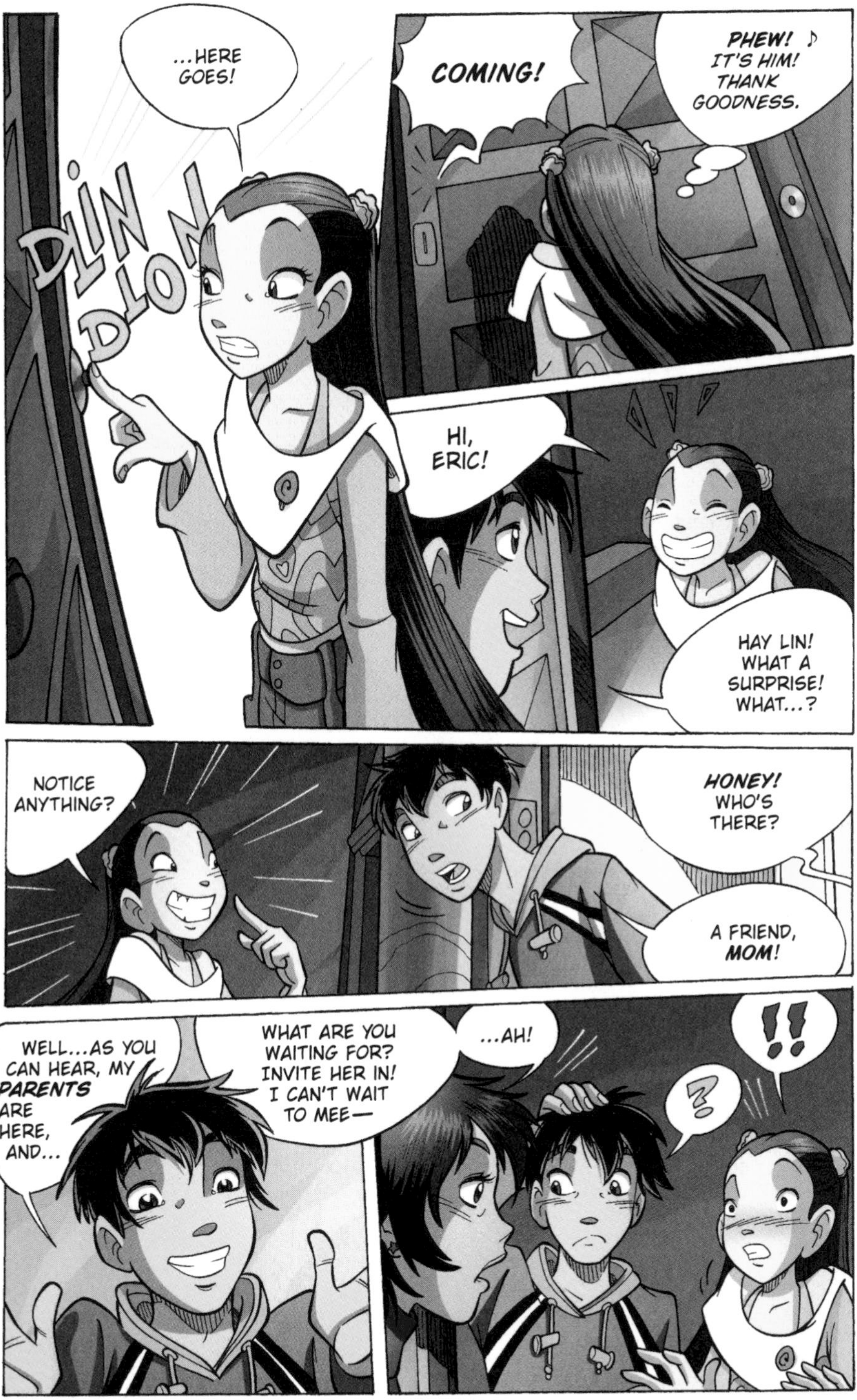

...HERE GOES!
DLIN DLON
COMING!
PHEW! ♪ IT'S HIM! THANK GOODNESS.
HI, ERIC!
HAY LIN! WHAT A SURPRISE! WHAT...?
NOTICE ANYTHING?
HONEY! WHO'S THERE?
A FRIEND, MOM!
WELL...AS YOU CAN HEAR, MY PARENTS ARE HERE, AND...
WHAT ARE YOU WAITING FOR? INVITE HER IN! I CAN'T WAIT TO MEE—
...AH!
!!
?

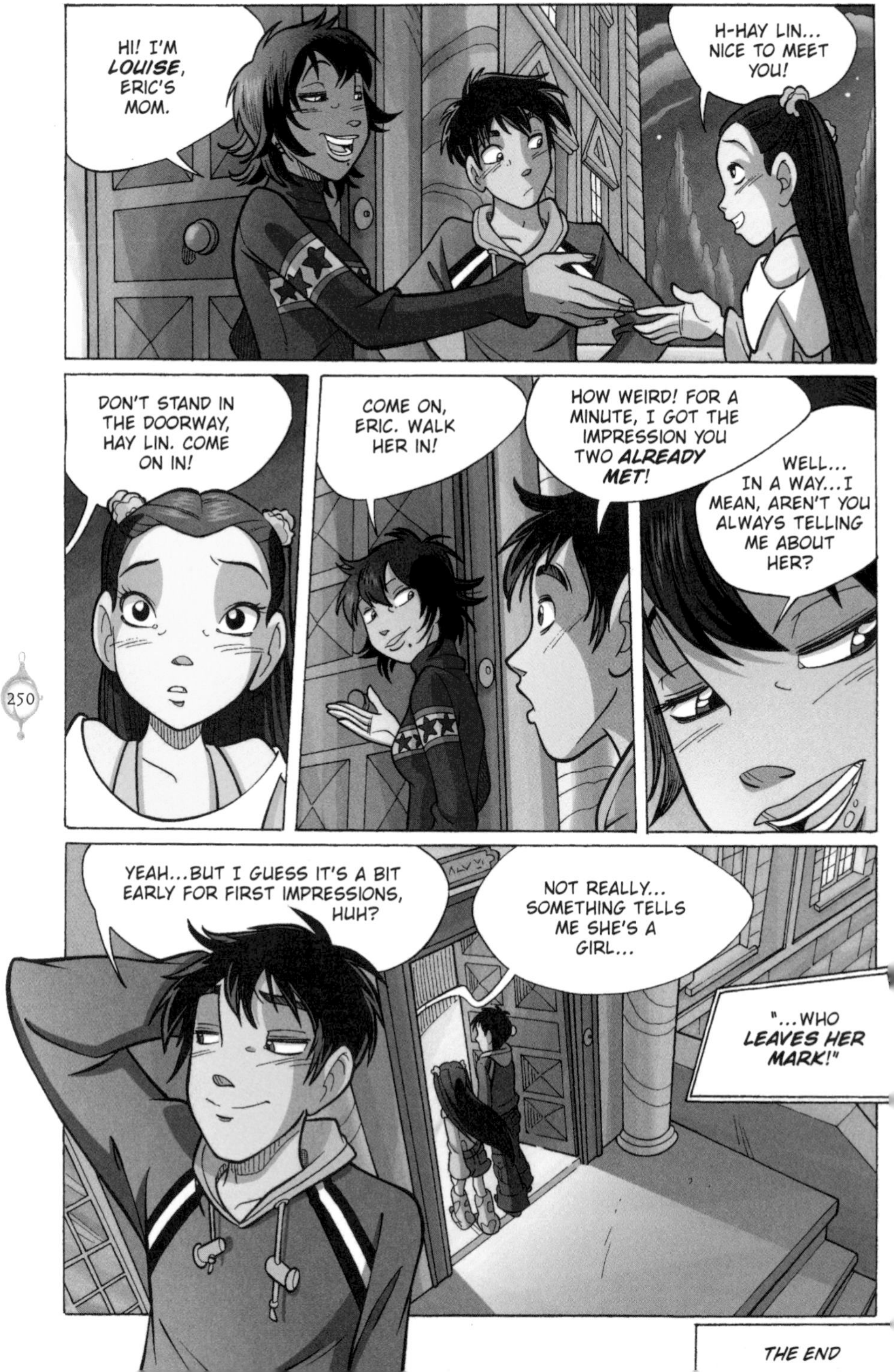
HI! I'M *LOUISE*, ERIC'S MOM.
H-HAY LIN... NICE TO MEET YOU!
DON'T STAND IN THE DOORWAY, HAY LIN. COME ON IN!
COME ON, ERIC. WALK HER IN!
HOW WEIRD! FOR A MINUTE, I GOT THE IMPRESSION YOU TWO *ALREADY MET*!
WELL... IN A WAY... I MEAN, AREN'T YOU ALWAYS TELLING ME ABOUT HER?
YEAH...BUT I GUESS IT'S A BIT EARLY FOR FIRST IMPRESSIONS, HUH?
NOT REALLY... SOMETHING TELLS ME SHE'S A GIRL...
"...WHO *LEAVES HER MARK!*"
THE END

Read on in Volume 12!

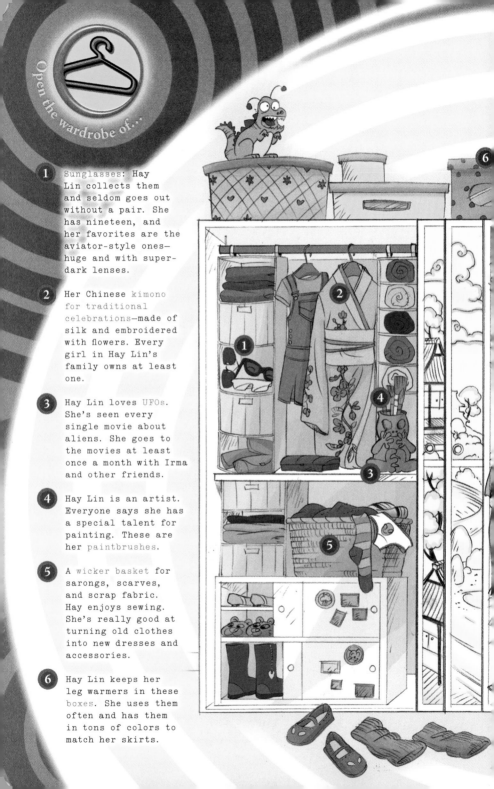

1 Sunglasses: Hay Lin collects them and seldom goes out without a pair. She has nineteen, and her favorites are the aviator-style ones—huge and with super-dark lenses.

2 Her Chinese kimono for traditional celebrations—made of silk and embroidered with flowers. Every girl in Hay Lin's family owns at least one.

3 Hay Lin loves UFOs. She's seen every single movie about aliens. She goes to the movies at least once a month with Irma and other friends.

4 Hay Lin is an artist. Everyone says she has a special talent for painting. These are her paintbrushes.

5 A wicker basket for sarongs, scarves, and scrap fabric. Hay enjoys sewing. She's really good at turning old clothes into new dresses and accessories.

6 Hay Lin keeps her leg warmers in these boxes. She uses them often and has them in tons of colors to match her skirts.

Fashion and Creativity with Hay Lin

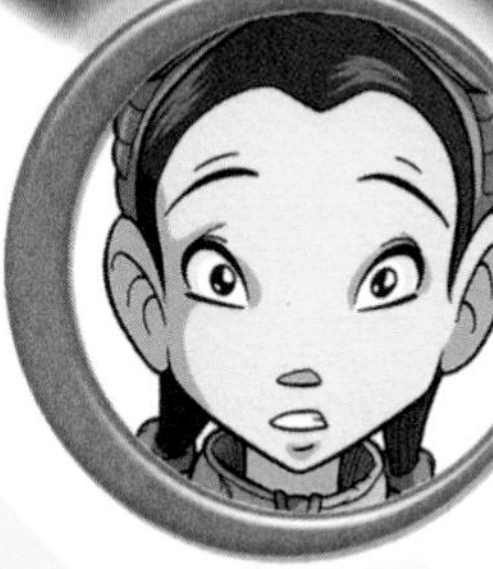

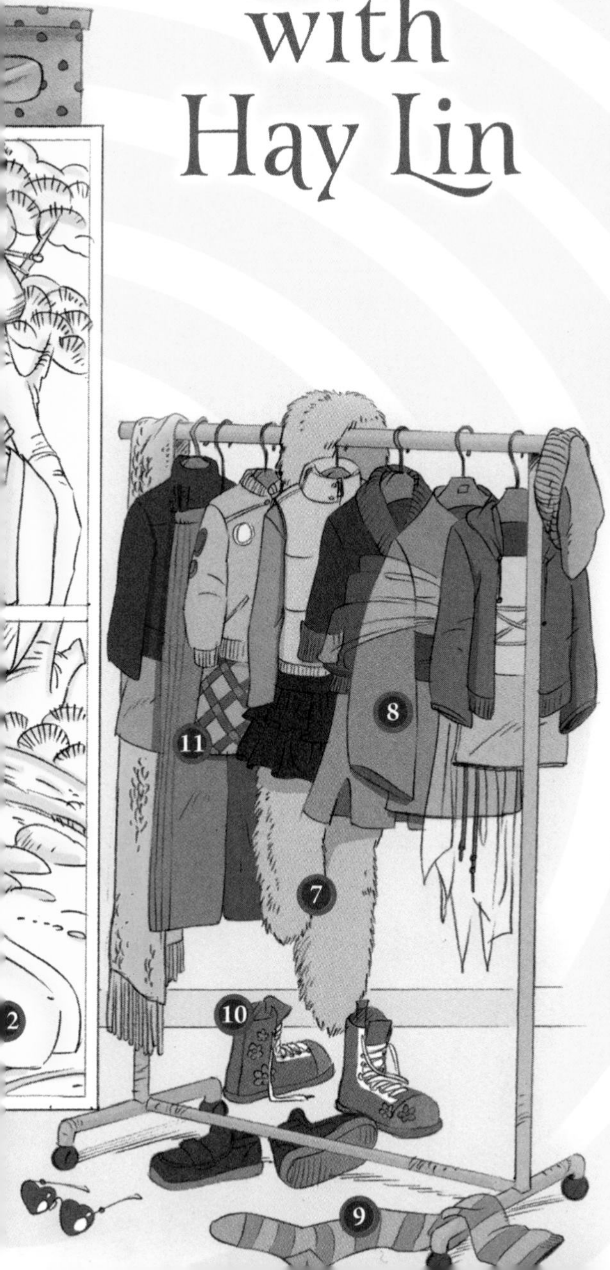
11
8
7
10
9
2

7 Fake fur maxi-scarf: Hay Lin used it for a school play. Way too flashy to wear offstage!

8 Hay is proud of this dress. She drew the model, and her grandma sewed it. It was her costume for the Halloween party.

9 She is crazy about striped socks. Her mom complains because she has too many, but Hay keeps finding new color combinations.

10 These were a pair of plain winter boots. Colorful fabric paint and glitter turned them into a one-of-a-kind design!

11 The tartan skirt she wore the first time she went to the movies with Eric.

12 Her wardrobe doors were white, but Hay Lin thought it would be nice to spice them up!

Witch Planet

Yan Lin

Former Guardian

When she was young, Yan Lin was a Guardian of Kandrakar along with Nerissa, Kadma, Halinor, and Cassidy. She's the one who gave Will the Heart of Kandrakar, telling W.I.T.C.H. about the fortress and revealing the secrets of their powers. After she fulfilled her duty on Earth, Yan Lin was called back to Kandrakar, where she now sits among the Wise Ones of the Congregation.

A Special Grandma

In Heatherfield as in Kandrakar, Yan Lin is a guide and trusted friend for Hay Lin. The grandma and granddaughter love each other deeply. She's very wise and peaceful. When necessary, Yan Lin can talk to W.I.T.C.H. through their dreams.

A WITCH? HA-HA-HA! I KNOW THAT'S WHAT YOU CALL THEM THESE DAYS...
HELLO, HAY LIN.
GRAMMY!

Yan Lin

Phobos's Prisoner

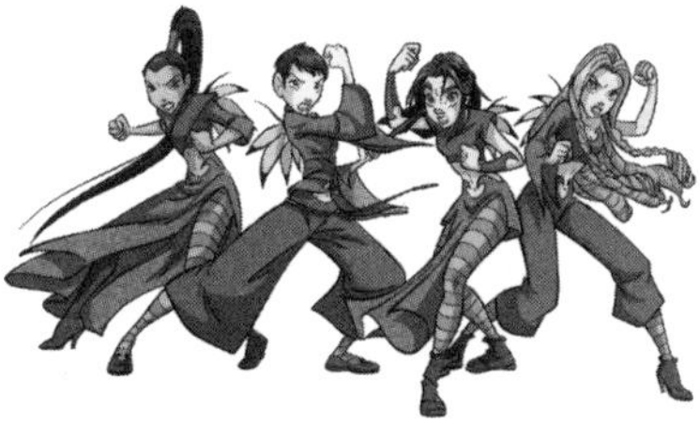

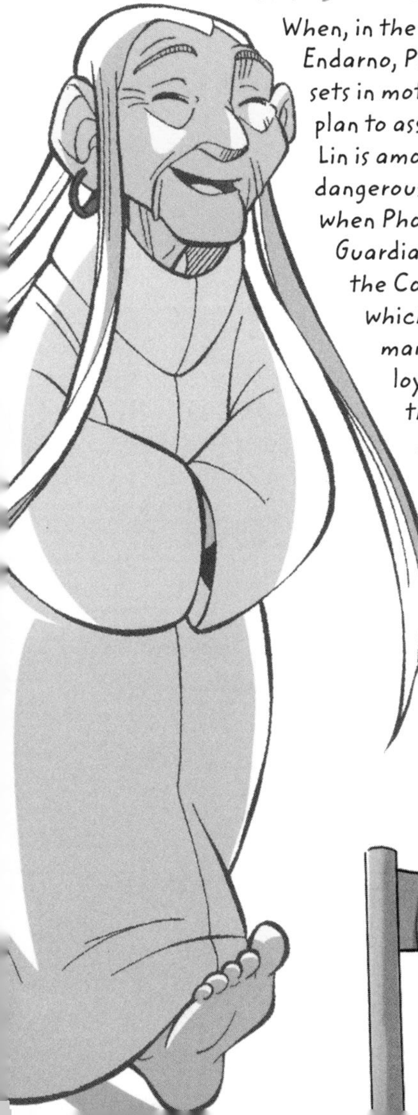

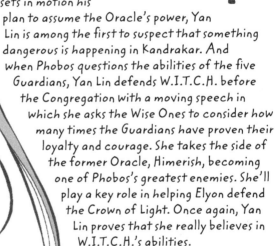

When, in the guise of Endarno, Phobos sets in motion his plan to assume the Oracle's power, Yan Lin is among the first to suspect that something dangerous is happening in Kandrakar. And when Phobos questions the abilities of the five Guardians, Yan Lin defends W.I.T.C.H. before the Congregation with a moving speech in which she asks the Wise Ones to consider how many times the Guardians have proven their loyalty and courage. She takes the side of the former Oracle, Himerish, becoming one of Phobos's greatest enemies. She'll play a key role in helping Elyon defend the Crown of Light. Once again, Yan Lin proves that she really believes in W.I.T.C.H.'s abilities.

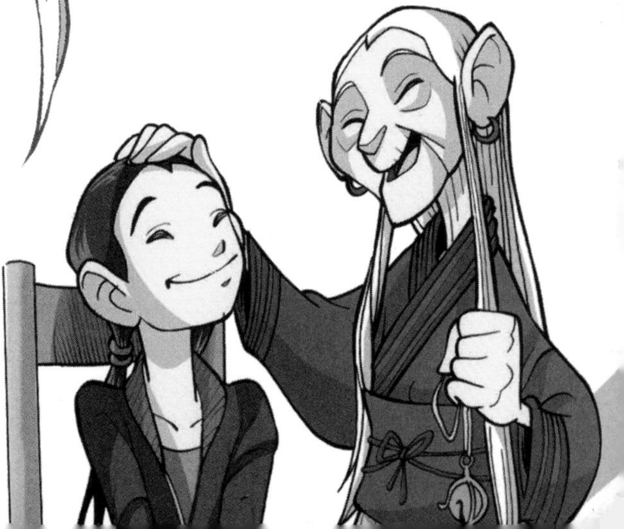

Part IV. Trial of the Oracle • Volume 2

Series Created by Elisabetta Gnone
Comic Art Direction: Alessandro Barbucci, Barbara Canepa

W.I.T.C.H.: The Graphic Novel, Part IV: Trial of the Oracle © Disney Enterprises, Inc.

English translation © 2018 by Disney Enterprises, Inc.

JY
1290 Avenue of the Americas
New York, NY 10104

Visit us at yenpress.com
facebook.com/yenpress
twitter.com/yenpress
yenpress.tumblr.com
instagram.com/yenpress

First JY Edition: September 2018

JY is an imprint of Yen Press, LLC.
The JY name and logo are trademarks of Yen Press, LLC.

The publisher is not responsible for websites (or their content) that are not owned by the publisher.

Library of Congress Control Number: 2017950917

ISBNs:
978-0-316-47712-3 (paperback)
978-1-9753-0185-9 (ebook)

10 9 8 7 6 5 4 3 2

LSC-C

Printed in the United States of America

Cover Art by Elisabetta Melaranci
Colors by Andrea Cagol

Translation by Linda Ghio and Stephanie Dagg at Editing Zone
Lettering by Katie Blakeslee

THE WHOLE TRUTH

Concept by Teresa Radice
Script by Giulia Conti
Layout and Pencils by Manuela Razzi
Inks by Roberta Baggio and Marina Zanotta
Color and Light Direction by Francesco Legramandi
Title Page Art by Manuela Razzi
with Colors by Andrea Cagol

NO HOPE

Concept and Script by Paola Mulazzi
Layout by Gianluca Panniello
Pencils by Elisabetta Melaranci
Inks by Roberta Baggio and Marina Zanotta
Color and Light Direction by Francesco Legramandi
Title Page Art by Gianluca Panniello
with Colors by Francesco Legramandi

THE MAGIC OF LIGHT

Concept and Script by Bruno Enna
Layout and Pencils by Giada Perissinotto
Inks by Riccardo Sisti and Santa Zangari
Color and Light Direction by Francesco Legramandi
Title Page Art by Alberto Zanon
with Colors by Andrea Cagol

NEVER ALONE AGAIN

Concept and Script by Teresa Radice
Layout and Pencils by Alessia Martusciello
Inks by Roberta Zanotta
Color and Light Direction by Francesco Legramandi
Title Page Art by Alessia Martusciello with Colors by Francesco Legramandi